SHADOW
AND
FLAME

Just then, one of the guards opened the door to the great hall and leaned in. "M'lord," he said to Tormod. "There's a *talishte* here who claims to have been invited by Lord McFadden."

"Is this your doing?" Tormod asked, looking sharply at Blaine.

"Yes. And if you want the slaughter to end, you'll hear what he has to say," Blaine replied.

It was clear that doing so went against Tormod's grain, but he gave a stiff nod. "Send him in."

A moment later, a well-dressed, dark-haired man entered the great room. His clothing was simple but expensive, and he carried himself like someone accustomed to power. Shoulder-length black hair fell loose around his face, framing dark eyes and a dusky complexion. He looked like an aristocratic cousin to Borya and Desya—or to the raiders themselves. His walk and stance made it clear that he had been a man of war.

"Peace to you all," the stranger said in a voice that still carried a trace of a Lesser Kingdoms accent. "I am Bayard, and I've come to save my people."

By Gail Z. Martin

SHADOW
AND
FLAME

BOOK FOUR OF THE ASCENDANT KINGDOMS SAGA

GAIL Z. MARTIN

www.orbitbooks.net

ORBIT

First published in Great Britain in 2016 by Orbit

13 5 7 9 10 8 6 4 2

Copyright © 2016 by Gail Z. Martin

Excerpt from *Black Wolves* by Kate Elliott
Copyright © 2015 by Katrina Elliott

A CIP catalogue record for this book
is available from the British Library.

ISBN 978-0-356-50495-7

Printed and bound by CPI Group (UK) Ltd, Croydon, CR0 4YY

Papers used by Orbit are from well-managed forests
and other responsible sources.

MIX
Paper from
responsible sources
FSC® C104740

Orbit
An imprint of
Little, Brown Book Group
Carmelite House
50 Victoria Embankment
London EC4Y 0DZ

An Hachette UK Company
www.hachette.co.uk

www.orbitbooks.net

To my very patient and supportive family: my husband,
Larry, and my children, Kyrie, Chandler, and Cody.
You make these books possible.

CHAPTER ONE

"I THOUGHT THAT WINNING THE BATTLE MEANT we could stop fighting for a while," Blaine McFadden grumbled as he swung his sword.

"Kill the cat and the rats multiply," Piran Rowse muttered, landing a strike that took off his opponent's right arm. The second swing sent the man's head rolling.

Blaine had scant time for conversation as one of the nomads came at him in a fury. A flicker of his magic let him know where his opponent would be an instant before the man struck, just enough time for Blaine to be where the man didn't expect. Another spark of magic made Blaine just fast enough to evade a killing strike as he roared in response and brought his own sword down in a lethal blow.

The Battle of the Northern Plains was supposed to have brought an end to fighting in Donderath, at least for a while. Four powerful warlords and an insane mage had been destroyed along with most of their armies. That left two enemy warlords and some vicious undead *talishte*, temporarily routed and pushed back to their strongholds to lick their wounds.

It should have brought a respite from the constant skirmishing and open battles. But here they were, just a few months later, on campaign again.

Not far away, two dark-haired men on horseback rode their galloping steeds while standing in their saddles, firing their bows again and again with lethal accuracy. Borya and Desya had grown up on the plains, and fighting the nomads was familiar work to them. The two brothers cut a swath right through the battle, and looked to be enjoying themselves far more than seemed sane. Just behind the combat line, Kestel Falke slipped among the wounded, slitting the throats of the fallen enemy soldiers.

Blaine and Piran were bloodied to the elbows, their cuirasses and tunics spattered with gore. The day was warm, and the sun made the pooled blood and corpses stink. Flies swarmed the fallen, buzzing around the living as if to anticipate their deaths. Blaine was soaked with sweat, aching and hungry, and he channeled all of his foul mood into the force he used to meet the next attack with a series of uncompromising blows.

Blaine swung and parried, hacking his way through a stand of three raiders. Off to the north, smoke rose from the wreckage of a town. Sondermoor had been a collection of sod and thatch houses, a blacksmith's shop, and a gristmill, along with an inn that had long ago seen better days. Now, Sondermoor was a ghost town, and its residents lay where they had been slaughtered. The raiders had made off with anything of value: coins, food, whiskey, horses, and women. Sondermoor was the third outpost to fall to the nomads, and each incursion brought the raiders closer to the lands held by Blaine and his allies, the Solveig twins and Birgen Verner.

"They fight like Cursed Ones," Blaine said as he and Piran finished off four more of the raiders.

"Yeah, well, they'll have plenty of time to cool off once they're across the Sea of Souls," Piran remarked, cleaning his blade on the shirt of a dead nomad.

"Makes me wonder how many of them are still out there," Blaine said, looking out toward the horizon.

"More than we want to admit," Piran replied. "The Great Fire and the Cataclysm pretty much passed them by, so they didn't have to rebuild and regroup, like the rest of us."

Blaine nodded. "And before that, King Merrill didn't want to deal with them, so his garrisons pushed them back toward the Lesser Kingdoms. Out of sight, out of mind."

"That's not going to work anymore," Piran muttered. "Looks like they've decided to get a share of what's left."

The last few days had shown Blaine just how big a problem the raiders had become. In good times, the raiders spread out in small bands linked by blood and marriage. They were fierce warriors, and a tribe with twenty or thirty warriors was something even a seasoned troop of soldiers dismissed at their own peril. But now, united by hardship over the last year since the Cataclysm, the bands had gathered into larger tribes, thousands strong, fighting with desperation that came from scarce food and scant resources.

Waves of attacks had worn down the soldiers commanded by sibling warlords Rinka and Tormod Solveig. With more raiders massing for another assault, the Solveigs had called on the alliance Blaine had pieced together months before, requesting help from Blaine's army and from that of Birgen Verner, the third warlord ally.

"They've retreated," Piran observed, shading his eyes and looking toward the horizon. The raiders had withdrawn, and the warlords' armies were under orders to pursue only so far, to keep the raiders from drawing them into an ambush.

"They'll be back," Blaine replied. "You heard what Borya

said. The raiders actually don't have a word for retreat. Their honor won't let them leave until they're victorious—or dead."

Piran shrugged. "We can take care of that for them."

Despite Piran's bravado, they both knew it would not be that easy. Still, when Blaine had rallied a third of his army and come to the Solveigs' aid, he had a plan in mind. Now that blood had been shed and they were in the thick of things, he hoped his plan worked.

"How sure are you about what Borya and Desya told us about the raiders?" Piran asked, giving Blaine a questioning glance.

"They're our best source, since they've traveled all over the Western Plains," Blaine replied. "If they're right, and it's possible to strike an accord, we'll all be better off. We've got better things to do than fight."

"You saw how the nomads came at us," Piran protested. "And they've been attacking the Solveigs' forces for a month. Do you really think they'll even entertain the idea of an accord? And how would we believe them if they did?"

Blaine shrugged. "I guess we're going to find out."

The battle was done except for the looting. Kestel picked her way among the enemy dead, finding few items worth taking except for their well-forged swords. She and some of the other soldiers scavenged what they could find, making a pile at the edge of the battlefield. The Cataclysm had brought Donderath's mining to a halt, and until more peaceful and prosperous times made it likely to restart, metal was at a premium. The nomads were known for their metalwork, and their sword blades were true, sharp, and strong. They were prized spoils of war.

"I saved the nicest two for us," Kestel said, sauntering up to Blaine and Piran with a couple of still-bloody swords.

"Very considerate of you," Blaine replied.

Kestel shrugged, with the hint of a tired, mischievous smile. "One of the perks of being on the victorious side," she said.

"Begging your pardon, sir. What do you want us to do with the bodies, m'lord?" Captain Waren, one of Blaine's commanders, gave a nod in acknowledgment to Piran and Kestel and waited for orders.

Blaine sighed. "If our intelligence is correct, those bodies are a bargaining chip," he said. "Make sure they're treated with respect, and covered to keep the birds away. Bring our own men back behind our lines and bury them the best you can." He paused. "As for the villagers, gather them up and burn a house down over them."

"Aye, sir." Captain Waren turned and began shouting orders to his men as he walked away.

"I hate this part of it," Blaine said after Waren was out of earshot.

"You thought being a warlord was all fun and games, did you?" Piran replied, raising one eyebrow.

"I wouldn't have put it that way," Blaine said. "But then again, I never actually bargained on being a warlord."

"That's what you get for not telling your closest mates that you were a lord of any kind," Piran retorted. Even now, he was not about to stop tweaking Blaine for not mentioning the title he had forfeited with his exile and conviction for murder. Piran, Blaine, and Kestel had been convicts together in the Velant prison camp, and their friendship ran deep.

"Like you told us everything," Kestel replied with a snort. "I bet there are stories we still haven't heard. We need to get you drunk again."

Piran grinned. "Anytime, anywhere! Bring it on!"

Blaine gave an exaggerated sigh. "Maintain some level of decorum, please? We're meeting with our allies."

"Nothing like a fancy dinner after a good slaughter on the battlefield," Piran said, sheathing his sword. "Kind of works up an appetite."

"Not all of the barbarians were with the nomads," Kestel muttered.

"Excuse me?" Piran said, looking up sharply. "Did you say something?"

"Me? Never." Kestel's grin showed how much she enjoyed the long-running friendly banter.

Blaine McFadden, the disgraced lord of Glenreith, the last of the original Lords of the Blood, had returned from exile in Edgeland at the top of the world with a handful of convict friends to set the magic right and restore the rule of law in a devastated land. Before the Cataclysm, Kestel had been the most sought-after courtesan in Donderath, but it was her work as a spy and assassin that earned her a ticket to Velant. Piran had been a promising young officer in the king's army before his court-martial and exile. Piran had sworn his loyalty to Blaine, and Kestel had become Lady McFadden just a few months ago. Now, in the aftermath of restoring magic, Blaine was discovering how difficult it was to govern what they had fought so hard to win.

Blaine watched the cleanup until he was assured that Waren had matters well in hand. Borya and Desya emerged out of the smoke from the pyres and the dust clouds raised by the horses' hooves. "Glad to see that everyone survived," Borya noted as he swung down from his horse. Desya joined him, flushed from the fight. The twins had the same dark hair and dusky coloring of the Lesser Kingdoms and plains, with one notable exception. Both young men's eyes had yellow, catlike irises with vertical black pupils, a change inflicted on them when they had been trapped in a wild-magic storm.

"You were right about how they'd engage," Blaine said, greeting the twins with a hearty handshake and a slap on the shoulder.

"Classic plains warfare," Desya replied. "Strike hard and refuse to go away. Retreat, and wait for negotiation. Repeat until someone comes out to talk."

"Glad you were here to translate," Piran replied. "In the rest of Donderath and Meroven, that's a recipe for annihilation."

Borya shrugged. "The nomads have lived on the wastelands and plains for a long, long time, largely left to themselves by the kingdoms on both sides of us. They have their own ways of doing things, and an approach to war that's less wasteful. Make a show of strength, allow the other side to test their strength against yours, then hash out an agreement rather than slaughtering each other."

"I'm willing to give their way a shot," Blaine replied. "Since we all know how the win-at-any-cost version plays out." The war between Donderath and neighboring Meroven had escalated over the years until a doomsday strike by battle mages devastated both sides and left magic dangerous and uncontrollable.

"You think the Solveigs and Verner will go for it?" Piran asked. "It's going to take a lot for them to trust that their enemies make an agreement and all of a sudden become allies."

"If things go the way we've planned, I think an agreement could solve a lot of problems," Blaine answered, though part of him echoed Piran's doubts. *Nothing has gone easily so far. Maybe it's time for our luck to change.* "Let's hope our allies see things our way."

"Not a bad showing today, eh?" Birgen Verner rode up to join them, accompanied by two of his officers. Birgen was stocky and powerfully built, a career soldier.

"It's never a bad day when you live through it," Blaine commented. He was still taking the measure of his new allies. He and Verner's father and the Solveigs had barely shaken hands on their alliance when an attack inked their agreement in blood.

"True enough," Verner replied. He was a little older than Blaine, in his early thirties. A new scar creased one cheek, and his left thigh was tied up with a bandage, but he sat his horse as if nothing bothered him.

Some men thrive on battle, Blaine thought, *while others regard it as a necessary evil. Piran is in the first group. Verner and I are weary of it already.*

"Any idea how the Solveigs' forces held up today?" Verner asked as he brought his horse up to ride alongside Blaine's. "I couldn't see their part of the battle from where my men were." Kestel rode beside Blaine, on guard for trouble, while Piran dropped back to ride behind with Verner's bodyguard.

"From what we could see, they did well," Blaine replied. "At a cost, to be sure." The Solveigs had been battling the Plainsmen the longest, and while their soldiers were brave and well trained, the toll of victory had been high.

"No end of it in sight, either," Verner said. "Those nomads aren't going to go away until they win, and we can't let them do that. But wiping them out is going to be expensive."

"I may have an alternative," Blaine said, pleased to hear Verner make such a strong case against a purely military solution. "I was planning to put it out for discussion at dinner."

Verner gave him an appraising look. "If you've got a better idea, I'm all for hearing it. Too many good men died today, and I don't fancy having this go on indefinitely."

"Neither do I," Blaine assured him. "We might be able to turn this around—but it will take all of us to do it."

It was a relatively short ride back to the Solveig twins' fortress at Bleak Hollow. The name suited it. High stone walls rose from the flat land like bleached bones of an ancient, fell predator. Bleak Hollow was as stark as its surroundings, an outpost on the edge of civilization, a sentinel against the wilds.

"You're really planning to go in there?" Piran questioned under his breath as they rode toward the massive wooden front gates.

"We were invited for dinner," Kestel said in a reproving voice. "It would be rude to refuse."

Blaine thanked the gods for Kestel's social skill. Long accustomed to the vicious politics of King Merrill's court, astute as a spy and with the sharpened instincts of a top assassin, Kestel could navigate any situation with ease. Knowing that she had his back made Blaine cautiously optimistic that the situation could end well.

The huge oaken doors swung open, revealing an ascetic bailey and keep. None of the buildings had the gracious extras of Quillarth Castle, King Merrill's stronghold, or Blaine's own manor, Glenreith. Bleak Hollow was meant to be a toehold of civilization against the lawless plains.

Rinka and Tormod Solveig were the masters of Bleak Hollow, a brother-and-sister warlord duo who were as mysterious as they were intriguing. Blaine had heard plenty of stories about them when they, too, had been exiled to Velant. He had seen both in battle, and acknowledged their formidable skills. But his alliance had been forged more from necessity than from longstanding knowledge, and he was curious to get a glimpse of his new allies in their own domain.

"Honored guests." A gray-templed man in his middle years greeted them with hands clasped at chest level. "Lord and Lady Solveig are honored by your presence. Please, allow our grooms to care for your horses, and leave your swords with me while you dine. I assure you that all will be restored to you when the time comes for you to go."

Piran glanced at Blaine, who nodded in the affirmative.

Blaine surrendered his sword, secure in the knowledge that both Piran and Kestel had enough small, hidden weapons to wage a two-person war. Kestel had shared some of her secrets with Blaine, and he had his own hold-out dagger hidden where a casual observer was unlikely to find it.

Piran looked unhappy at the prospect, but turned over his sword as requested, and so did his officers. "I thought we were on the same side," he muttered.

Blaine shrugged. "These days, trust is in short supply, and caution in abundance." He gave Piran a look. "And you know you would have demanded the same thing if they came to Glenreith."

Piran scowled. "Yeah, but that's us. It's different when someone else does it."

Escorts showed them to guest rooms where they could wash off the grit and blood of the battlefield. Blaine was thrilled to find a room with three tubs of hot water drawn for their baths, as well as clean outfits for them to change into. A flask of whiskey with glasses on a table near the tubs was an unexpected indulgence.

Kestel crowded ahead of him, sipped the whiskey, and stirred the hot bath with the handle of a broom she grabbed from near the fire.

"What are you doing?" Piran asked, looking at her as if she had lost her mind.

Kestel was unmoved. "Verifying that everything is as it seems."

"I notice she checks *your* tub and *your* whiskey and leaves *me* to fend for myself," Piran groused good-naturedly.

"Just the chance I'll have to take," Kestel said with feigned angst and a wicked grin. "Personally, I can't wait to climb in. I ache *everywhere*."

The tubs grew cold far too quickly, and the flask drained even faster. Bells in the tower rang eight times, the signal that it was time to get ready to join the others for dinner. When they were dressed and ready, the seneschal of Bleak Hollow led them downstairs. Verner and his bodyguard were waiting for them in the foyer, and he looked as if he also had enjoyed the largesse of a hot bath and fresh clothing.

"It's something when a hot bath and the safety to enjoy it is the ultimate luxury, isn't it?" Verner mused when they regrouped. "Funny how the small things we used to take for granted loom so large these days."

Two guards opened tall doors into a long, high-ceiling room. Tapestries on the walls regaled battles long past. Three large fireplaces, each with openings as tall as a man, sat darkened at one end of the room. A large, long table with chairs stretched the length of the room. Battle pennants from wars fought generations ago hung overhead, as well as hunting trophies and one suit of armor that looked as if it had been a spoil of war.

"Welcome." Rinka Solveig met them in the doorway. It was the first time Blaine had seen her without the red leather armor she wore on the battlefield. Tonight, she wore a scarlet gown. Her blond hair was wrapped atop her head in a braid. Rinka Solveig was striking if not conventionally pretty. Her features were angular, not quite regular, but there was such a sense of character, clarity, and self-possession about her that she was memorable.

"My brother and I welcome you to Bleak Hollow," she said, and gestured for them to enter the great hall.

A figure dressed in a black doublet and trews awaited them halfway into the room, and it took Blaine a moment to recognize Tormod Solveig without his armor. Tall, slender, with sharp features, crow-black hair, and dark eyes, Tormod looked younger off the battlefield, although his eyes had a world-weary glint to them. Given his apparent youth, it was hard to remember just how powerful he was as a necromancer.

"Glad everyone is still in one piece," Tormod said, sparing them a perfunctory smile that did not reach his eyes. Blaine got the impression that Tormod did not smile often.

"With a few more scratches and dents," Verner replied.

"I understand Blaine believes he has an alternative to our situation," Rinka said, giving Blaine an appraising look. "We'll be most interested to hear him out."

Bleak Hollow's great room looked more like a place to rally troops than the site for a state dinner. The walls were gray stone, and the room's only embellishments were battle flags draped like tapestries along the sides of the room. A large iron chandelier hung in the middle of the common room. The only furnishings were large tables and benches, as if the room doubled as a mess hall. One of those large tables had been set with pewter chargers and goblets. Roasted venison and pheasant seasoned with onions and apples lay on large serving boards. Baskets of bread, platters of cooked carrots, parsnips, and turnips, along with tankards full of ale looked inviting.

"Come. Eat. We have a lot to talk about," Tormod said, gesturing for them to follow him to the table.

"To our alliance," Tormod said, lifting his tankard when they were seated. "And to a rebirth for Donderath." The others murmured their agreement as they lifted their cups in a toast. Kestel had obtained a charm that would alert her to the presence of poison, and she made sure to sprinkle a few drops of the ale onto the ring charm before they drank. The stone remained dark, signifying that the ale was safe to drink.

"So cautious," Rinka said, noting Kestel's movements. "Even among allies?"

"I know how easy it is to kill," Kestel replied nonchalantly. "There's no truly 'safe' place except the grave." She glanced toward Tormod. "And perhaps, not even there."

For a while, conversation lulled as they ate. The food was well seasoned, tasty, and plentiful. After the last two days of camp rations, and three days of skirmishing, Blaine found the prospect of a good meal and passable ale almost irresistible.

"How long have you had problems with the nomads?" Blaine asked when he had eaten his fill and the others were sliding their empty plates away from them.

Tormod set down his tankard and blotted his lips with his napkin. "There have been raids as long as there have been nomads," he replied. "Merrill paid them little attention, and most of the trading caravans that crossed to the Lesser Kingdoms hired mercenaries to make sure they got where they were going."

"So you've had raids all along, or have they gotten worse of late?" Piran asked. It would be a mistake to count the tankards of ale Piran had consumed and guess about his sobriety. Piran could drink more than any man Blaine had ever met and still keep his wits about him and his aim true.

"The plains weren't hit as hard by the Great Fire and the Cataclysm because there were no noble houses there," Rinka replied. "But they paid dearly with the storms and the beasts. And for a while, the beasts were the equals of the nomads. The trade caravans stopped traveling the routes south. Most of the local traders paid tribute for protection. And after the Cataclysm, they had no goods to sell."

"So now that the storms are gone and the beasts have been mostly destroyed, the nomads are back in business," Verner summarized.

Rinka shrugged. "After a fashion. Their raids often leave behind gold and silver. They want tools, food, livestock, and weapons. And if they can't find those, they'll take hostages to barter for what they can't steal." She paused. "If it's true that the Lesser Kingdoms were hit as badly as Donderath, then the nomads are probably fighting for their survival."

"The raiders haven't launched attacks on this level since the days of their greatest warrior, Bayard, centuries ago," Tormod said. "He was the one who united the tribes and made them see themselves as one people. Bayard was a legend—almost a god to the Plainsmen."

"We need a solution to the nomad problem, because we intend to expand our control westward," Rinka said abruptly. "Tormod has spoken with the plains dead. The old spirits know things we've forgotten about plants that can survive drought, that are good for eating or making into cloth, plants that don't grow farther east. If we can learn from them, we'll have wares to trade, maybe even with the plains towns that survived and the Lesser Kingdoms."

"I have no designs on the West," Verner said. "My hands are full with my own lands, and the territory I gained after we destroyed Rostivan and Lysander. That's plenty for me."

Blaine shrugged. "We have enough to do rebuilding Castle Reach and the port, as well as the heartland. And since I doubt we've seen the last of Hennoch and Pollard, I've got no desire to tie up troops where I can't easily bring them back if they're needed."

"So neither of you will oppose us extending our territory westward?" Tormod confirmed.

Blaine frowned. "Not unless it causes you to default on your oath to our alliance," he cautioned. "We lose all that we've fought to gain if we can't keep our core territories should another threat arise—and it will, sooner or later. We're depending on you to do your part, and if you stretch yourself too thin or get tied up in fighting on the western frontier, you're of no use to us."

Tormod nodded. "Agreed. We have every intention of honoring our alliance. And you are correct to be cautious regarding Pollard. The dead do not hold him in high regard," Tormod said.

"And of Pentreath Reese? Have your ghosts brought you any news?" Pollard, though mortal, was liegeman to Reese, an immortal *talishte* vampire. Reese had been judged and sentenced to torture and exile by the Elders among the *talishte*.

"Reese remains in his prison, for now," Tormod replied. "But the ghosts fear Reese may soon be freed."

"Probably by Pollard," Piran said, making the name a curse. "It figures."

Kestel shook her head. "Pollard can't free Reese himself. He's just a mortal, and Reese was imprisoned by the Elders—very powerful *talishte*. Someone would have to help him—which is why having his maker, Thrane, show up now is worrisome."

"Surely Reese had a brood of his own," Verner said. "And they would certainly wish to aid their master."

"Maybe," Blaine said, "and maybe not. From what Lanyon Penhallow has said, the *talishte* tend to be rather competitive. Knock off someone at the top and everyone else moves up. Maybe they don't have the incentive—or the loyalty—to put Reese back on top."

"Then you'd best watch Thrane carefully," Rinka said. "Pack animals must have a leader. Reese's imprisonment leaves a void, and nature always fills the empty places."

"You've heard the news we had to share," Tormod said. "Now I would learn your news." He managed an awkward smile. "We get few visitors out here. News is always welcome."

Verner told of his efforts to rebuild his forces after the Battle of the Northern Plains. "Now we need peace long enough to plant our crops and harvest them," he finished. "Another hungry winter, and our own people are likely to turn on us."

"You never said what you gained from helping to anchor the magic," Kestel said with a disarming smile. Piran, Verner, and Tormod had been among those Blaine had chosen to be the new Lords of the Blood, who stood with him in a powerful ritual to bring the wild magic back under human control. Each of the Lords of the Blood had gained a magical benefit from the ritual, but when they had parted company to return to their respective lands, some had not yet realized what their new gift was or how to use it.

"From what we've been able to tell, magic doesn't 'stick' to me," Verner replied, looking self-conscious. "Magical attacks seem to slide off me."

Blaine nodded. "Not a bad talent to come away with," he said.

Rinka turned to Blaine. "Now, you said you had a way to turn the situation with the raiders around. Let's hear it. I'm tired of burying good soldiers."

Blaine looked from Rinka to Tormod to Verner. "You've noticed my men, Borya and Desya? The ones with the cat-slit eyes? They're from the Western Plains, though they weren't raiders. But they know the people, the way the Plainsmen think. And they're certain that the attack-withdraw-wait-attack pattern is the raiders' way of enabling both sides to size each other up—as potential allies, not enemies."

Rinka gave Blaine a skeptical look. "They've killed a lot of men for nothing if that's true."

"The point is, we may be able to stop the killing—and create a valuable alliance," Blaine said. "If you're open to the idea."

"Ally with the raiders?" Tormod asked sharply. "How could we ever trust them?"

"Solveig is right," Verner said. "And why should they trust us?"

"They might not trust us," Blaine replied, "but I think we've got someone they will trust—implicitly."

The sun had set while they were dining, and Blaine hoped his guest would be punctual. Just then, one of the guards opened the door to the great hall and leaned in. "M'lord," he said to Tormod. "There's a *talishte* here who claims to have been invited by Lord McFadden."

"Is this your doing?" Tormod asked, looking sharply at Blaine.

"Yes. And if you want the slaughter to end, you'll hear what he has to say," Blaine replied.

It was clear that doing so went against Tormod's grain, but he gave a stiff nod. "Send him in."

A moment later, a well-dressed, dark-haired man entered the great room. His clothing was simple but expensive, and he carried himself like someone accustomed to power. Shoulder-length black hair fell loose around his face, framing dark eyes and a dusky complexion. He looked like an aristocratic cousin to Borya and Desya—or to the raiders themselves. His walk and stance made it clear that he had been a man of war.

"Peace to you all," the stranger said in a voice that still carried a trace of a Lesser Kingdoms accent. "I am Bayard, and I've come to save my people."

CHAPTER TWO

R INKA, TORMOD, AND VERNER STARED AT THE
newcomer in stunned silence. Kestel worked to hide a triumphant smile, while Piran gave the *talishte* an appraising glance.

"That's impossible," Rinka said, lifting her chin. "The real Bayard vanished and died centuries ago."

The dark-haired man smiled wryly. "Yes, I did. Five centuries ago, give or take a few years. Not long after my greatest victory, I was turned by a maker who liked to collect 'accomplished' fledglings. I vanished, because my work at that time was complete. My victory gave the Plainsmen control of their lands, repulsed an invasion force, and brought them together as a people. They no longer needed me, and I was weary of war."

Rinka looked from Bayard to Blaine. "How do we know you're really Bayard?"

"I have the word of Lanyon Penhallow and Kierken Vandholt, the Wraith Lord," Blaine replied. "For the last several centuries, Bayard has been one of the Elder Council of the *talishte*."

Tormod had remained silent, staring intently at Bayard. Finally, he nodded. "Yes," Tormod said. "I believe he is who he says he is. His spirit could not lie to me."

Bayard inclined his head in acknowledgment. "It is as you say, lord necromancer."

"When Borya and Desya told me their interpretation of what was going on, I realized that we had two different groups sending signals to each other that were being misunderstood," Blaine said as Bayard found a seat at the table. "Geir, one of Penhallow's top men, told me that one of the Elders was from the plains. I sent him to ask Penhallow and that Elder for assistance and advice."

"And here I am," Bayard finished. His dark eyes had a wary cunning to them, and he possessed the body of a fighter, frozen in immortality at the peak of his prowess. "It has been a very long time since my people stood in real peril. And so I came."

"You've intervened before?" Rinka asked, staring at him with a combination of concern and fascination. "There are legends to that effect."

Bayard gave a self-deprecating half smile. "A useful fiction," he replied. "Only once in all that time did I feel my assistance was truly needed. I discovered that the legend itself became a useful deterrent. Until now."

Tormod's eyes narrowed. "We did not attack the Plainsmen," he said. "But we have defended ourselves when attacked."

"In a warrior culture, the suitability of an ally in battle must be seen before an offer of alliance is extended," Bayard replied. Though he was dressed in the Donderath aristocratic fashion with a waistcoat, shirt, and breeches, it did not take much imagination for Blaine to picture him in the loose-fitting tunic and trews of the plains horsemen.

"I find it difficult to grasp the logic in attacking someone to see if they are suitable as an ally," Rinka said.

"Perhaps difficult for a Donderan to grasp, but intuitive for a Plainsman," Bayard replied. "How better to see whether a potential ally is fierce in a fight?"

"But the deaths—" Rinka protested.

"Would have been avoided if we had understood the customs of the Plainsmen," Tormod replied. He had watched Bayard with a distracted expression, but now he seemed fully focused. "I have verified what he is telling us—and who he is—with the spirits."

"It's the ferocity of the fight, not the number of kills that would have mattered to the Plainsmen," Bayard said.

"The question is, will your kin accept a truce—and perhaps even an alliance—given how much blood has been spilled?" Piran asked.

"Tell me what has happened since the fighting began," Bayard said. He listened, his gaze downcast and intense, as the others told him of the battles that had transpired.

When they finished, Bayard turned to Tormod. "What say the dead?" he asked. "Would the fallen accept an alliance with so worthy an opponent?"

Tormod closed his eyes, concentrating. It seemed to Blaine that he could hear the whisper of distant voices, some raised, some calm, but he could not make out their words. After a time, Tormod came back to himself.

"They acknowledge the worthiness of the warriors," Tormod replied. "And they fear that if an agreement of some kind is not reached, too many of their kinsmen will die young."

Verner had been quiet thus far. Now, he leaned forward earnestly. "We need to make this alliance," he said. "We've all got better things to do than fight an army that doesn't really want to be an enemy. And if we ally with the Plainsmen, that would strengthen the Solveigs' hold on the border, so Blaine and I can go back to taking care of our own lands, or fighting off the real threat."

Blaine knew that Verner spoke from the heart. Although he

was a skillful warrior, Verner had made it clear more than once that his true priority was to rebuild the lands that owed him fealty and see to the safety of his people. He cared nothing for adding territory or gaining power, and Blaine had to talk him into becoming one of the new Lords of the Blood.

"I agree." Piran had listened to Bayard's story without giving much away in his expression. "Verner's right—we've got bigger, badder enemies on the horizon, and we need to give them our full attention. We can't do that if we're fighting off the Plainsmen time and again."

"If there's a chance to end the fighting without slaughter, I'm all for it." Kestel nodded her agreement.

Blaine turned back to Rinka and Tormod. "Well?" He asked. "You two would be most immediately impacted by an alliance. No more raids. Allies in extending your control over the Western Plains, and protection for the trade routes so the caravans will travel again. Additional troops with skilled fighters to fight against Pollard and Hennoch—and whoever else they pull into this." He raised an eyebrow. "All you have to do is be able to trust them."

Rinka hesitated, then nodded. "If Bayard will agree to oversee the alliance to make sure promises are honored, then yes. We've lost enough soldiers already."

Everyone turned to Tormod. "You've heard the testimony of the dead," Blaine said. "What do you say?"

It was difficult to guess when Tormod was merely giving thought to a matter and when he was listening to the whispers of the ghosts. Even at his most decisive, Tormod seemed to be only half paying attention to the real world, and Blaine wondered if controlling his necromancy required that much constant attention. If so, Tormod Solveig was truly a man torn between the world of the living and the realm of the dead.

"If Bayard can broker the alliance, and if he agrees to return to lead his people—at least for a while—then I can accept the bargain," Tormod replied. "Now, how do we go about making an offer to the people we've spent months trying to kill?"

At sundown the next evening, Blaine waited nervously beneath a tent on the plains beyond Bleak Hollow. He wore an outfit more befitting a lord than a warlord, with a somber brocade waistcoat and dark pants. Kestel made sure he had his cuirass on beneath the coat, and his amulet to deflect magic. The Solveigs and Verner had deferred to him as the lead ambassador, and Blaine was still unsure whether he was being flattered or set up to take the fall.

"If you believe we will surrender, you are mistaken." Simon, the leader of the Plainsmen, faced Blaine beneath the large open tent erected in the middle of an open field. They were far enough from the site of the last battle that they were spared the stench of the dead, and the clouds of flies and the circling carrion birds. But Blaine was certain those deaths were as much on Simon's mind as they were on his.

"Not a surrender—but a truce," Blaine countered. "An end to the bloodshed, on both sides. With honor."

Simon's eyes narrowed, and in the delegation of six leaders who stood behind him, Blaine could clearly read expressions of anger and distrust. "Why should we believe you?" Simon demanded.

"We protected the bodies of your dead from scavengers, and bring them to you unmolested," Blaine said, pointing to the canvas-covered wagon far enough away to mask the smell. "A gesture of goodwill."

Simon gave a dismissive snort. "Was killing them also a gesture of goodwill?"

Kestel stepped forward from where she stood beside Blaine. She was dressed in a black tunic and trews beneath her cuirass. Her smile and her beauty were a fascinating contradiction to her garb, as was the warmth in her voice when she spoke.

"We believe that this battle between our people rests in a misunderstanding, Your Lordship," Kestel said, fixing Simon with her gaze. "We did not understand your customs. We have learned more, and wish to begin anew." Kestel's graciousness took some of the steam out of Simon's anger, but the men behind him continued to mutter, and Blaine knew the delegation was far from convinced.

"We cannot raise those who have been lost to either side," Blaine said. "But we can come to an agreement that stops the killing—and stands to the advantage of both our peoples."

"What offer do you make, that we should trust you?" Simon demanded.

Blaine and his allies had spent most of the last few days learning the ways of the Plainsmen from Borya, Desya, and Bayard. The nomadic culture was rich and complex, and its nuances would require a lifetime to fully grasp, but Blaine and the others had learned enough by the time of the meeting to make an effort at diplomacy. Just in case, Borya and Desya, dressed like courtiers rather than warriors, stood nearby should translation be needed.

"If we were to reckon bloodgild, it would pauper both sides," Blaine said. "Instead, we offer trade, supplies, and protection— in return for the same, as well as safe passage."

Simon looked dubious. "Others before you have made such claims," he said, meeting Blaine's gaze defiantly. "Their promises ended once they got what they wanted."

Blaine nodded. "I know that King Merrill and his father did not keep faith with the Plainsmen. They are gone. We rule Donderath now, and it is our word we give to you."

Simon regarded Blaine with suspicion. Two of his advisers crowded forward and spoke to him in low tones. He listened, then dismissed them with a raise of his hand.

"We have heard of you, Blaine McFadden, the Convict Lord," Simon said. "We know the Ghost-Talker," he said with a nod toward Tormod, "the Red Lady, and the Quiet Soldier," he added with a glance in Verner's direction. "You are admirable fighters, as the number of our casualties attest. If your word is good, you would be valuable allies."

Blaine inclined his head in acknowledgment. "Graciously spoken, Lord Simon. Your men are courageous in battle, and fearless against strong magic."

"This protection and trade, passage and supplies, you speak of," Simon replied, "at what cost do they come to my people? We are used to being part of Donderath in name only, ignored when we are not hunted. What claims would you make on us, in exchange for these things?"

Simon was no one's fool, and from the little Blaine recalled of the Plainsmen's history, the nomads had been ill-used by the kings of Donderath when they were not ignored or persecuted.

Simon is right to doubt us. I've got to make some kind of connection, or even Bayard's presence may not be enough.

"We can offer you new breeding stock, to replace the flocks you lost with the wild-magic storms," Blaine said. "Our first crops will be harvested this spring, with seeds to share for the villages to restore their gardens and fields, so your people can trade with them once more. The Lesser Kingdoms were hurt just as badly as Donderath and Meroven in the Cataclysm. Restoring trade will mean the need for guides and guards for the caravans. And if attackers come from the coast or from the southlands, we will pledge our soldiers to help you protect your people."

He met Simon's gaze. "The truth is, Lord Simon, we need your people and your people need us. It is foolishness to pretend otherwise."

"If we're to have peace, it will require intent from both sides," Kestel said, presenting Simon the contradiction of a woman with the manner of a diplomat and the clothing of a warrior. "What do you offer Lord McFadden and the allied lords in exchange for an end to war and death? He has offered you things of great value. What do you present in return?"

Blaine tried not to hold his breath. Bayard and the twins had emphasized that the Plainsmen valued the process of bartering, and would weigh the value of promises carefully. They had also instructed Blaine to be prepared for several rounds of offers and counteroffers. It was difficult to be patient, when Blaine was certain that equally urgent matters required his attention and his troops back east.

I'd rather use Bayard and the ghosts of their dead to validate a decision they've already made rather than push them into a choice, Blaine thought.

Blaine studied the delegation that accompanied Simon. Several of the men wore stern expressions, but whether that was part of the negotiations or because they opposed a truce, he had no way to know. Two of the men appeared to be paying close attention. *Keepers of tribal law?* Blaine wondered. *Or men tasked with remembering what was said?*

Simon's eyes narrowed. *Surely he came prepared to bargain,* Blaine thought. *Then again, just because bargaining is part of their culture, it doesn't mean he's entirely on board with making peace. Some men just like to fight, and he's good at it.*

"We can offer a breeding pair of our fine plains horses, the swiftest on the Continent," Simon replied. "Plus breeding pairs of our best goats, sheep, and chickens, strong and healthy, able to endure harsh weather and thin grazing. We can also offer safe passage to your caravans and traders through our lands, and trustworthy guides across the plains to the Lesser Kingdoms."

Simon regarded Blaine and Kestel levelly. "Perhaps most valuable is a truce, our promise not to attack Bleak Hollow so long as your armies uphold their promises."

"I will take your offer back to my people," Blaine said solemnly. "Will you present our offer to yours?" Simon nodded, and then he and his delegation withdrew to their camp.

"This is taking forever," Piran grumbled.

"That's the beauty of the Western Plains," Borya said. "There's no reason to hurry anywhere, because there's never anything going on."

"I've got to admit, diplomacy has never been my strong point," Verner said. "I'm not very patient."

"I can tolerate their game—up to a point," Rinka replied. "Let's hope their response is reasonable."

"The truth is, both sides have precious little to bargain with, since the Cataclysm," Blaine said with a sigh. "Gold, silver, gems—none of that means much until trade begins again. We can spare only so much food and livestock, and the same is true for them. The most valuable thing both sides have to offer is a truce, safe passage, and protection, but that means the Plainsmen would be putting up with strangers in their lands again, and at least nominal governance from Donderath. They may like it the way they've had it, on their own without having to answer to anyone else."

"That won't last," Borya pointed out. "It never does."

A candlemark later, Simon returned. This time, the delegation with him looked even less happy than before. One of the men, who had been Simon's most frequent consultant during the last round of negotiations, looked red in the face, as if he had been arguing. It was difficult to read Simon's expression.

"The heads of the families have heard your offering," Simon reported. "With our war dead yet unburied and unmourned, they found your offering insufficient." The man standing next to Simon smiled maliciously. Some of the others in the delegation looked uncomfortable, but said nothing.

"What would make an offering 'sufficient' to the heads of the families?" Blaine asked, holding his temper in check.

"To see you and yours lie bleeding in the dirt beside the graves of our sons!" the man next to Simon cried, and threw himself at Blaine, a knife ready in his hand.

There was a blur of motion, a dark shape moving impossibly fast, and the silver streak of a knife. Kestel and Piran were seconds too slow, as was Simon, who dove after his companion with an anguished cry.

"Is this what has become of my sons?" Bayard stood between Blaine and the would-be assassin, holding the attacker's knife hand in a merciless grip. He repeated his comment in a language Blaine did not understand, but the words made Simon and the delegation grow pale.

"Bayard." Simon's eyes widened. "Can it be?"

"I am Bayard," the *talishte* confirmed as the delegation whispered among themselves, staring at him with astonishment. "When I left the plains, I believed that my people had reached the point where they no longer needed me." He gave a disdainful look at the man whose knife hand was crushed in his grip, then tossed the raider aside. The man landed in the dirt and remained kneeling, cradling his mangled hand. "Apparently, I was wrong."

"Bayard!" The name was taken up by the delegation like a prayer, and one by one, the men knelt in fealty. Bayard nodded to Tormod, who stepped forward, closed his eyes, and began to chant, raising his hands slowly, palms up. A cold mist began to rise around them, though the evening had been warm. The mist thickened, shapes became visible, and the members of Simon's delegation gasped as the figures solidified enough to be recognizable.

"Here are your dead," Tormod said. "Ask them yourself whether they wish for more of your kin to die, or whether they would see you accept the chance for peace that has been offered to you." After a moment's pause, the ghosts also knelt. What the Plainsmen saw in the mist was enough to assure them that the ghosts—and Bayard—were real. Over to one side, the man who had attacked Blaine rocked back and forth on his knees, his broken hand pressed against his chest, sobbing his apology.

"Simon." Bayard said the name slowly, drawing out the syllables. Simon trembled, but lifted his head and faced Bayard squarely. "I will return to the Plainsmen, for a time, and lead you once more, until you have rebuilt. One thing I ask: that my people accept this alliance, and support it with full vigor. Will you help me make this happen?"

Conflicting emotions played across Simon's face. Shame at the unexpected attack by someone who had betrayed his trust. Fear of the spirits of the dead and their judgment. Awe at confronting a legend. "Y-yes," Simon stammered. "Yes. I will help you." He gave a stern glance toward his delegation. "*We* will help you," he said, his voice gaining strength. "We accept the offering, and pledge to fulfill what we have offered. So I swear, so *we* swear, on our lives and souls." One by one, the other men pledged themselves to the alliance.

"Then we will rebuild together," Bayard said, walking out to stand among the delegation, bidding them to rise.

"Your dead are satisfied with your decision," Tormod said as the spirits rose and formed a circle around them dozens of ghosts deep. "They will be watching to make sure you keep your word. Know that you have their blessing." With that, Tormod murmured another quiet phrase and lowered his upturned hands. As quickly as they appeared, the ghosts vanished.

"Then it is done," Bayard said, turning to nod to Blaine. "You will have nothing to fear from the Plainsmen. We will be your allies in this struggle, so long as you keep your bargain."

"We'll keep it," Blaine assured him. "Count on it."

With that, Bayard and the Plainsmen departed, heading back to their camp. No one moved until the raiders and their long-dead leader were gone. Finally, Piran spoke. "Think they'll actually keep their word?"

Blaine nodded. "I think Bayard will handle it." He turned to Rinka and Tormod. "If you're not under threat of attack from the Plainsmen, and they're sworn to help defend Bleak Hollow, I need to ask Tormod's help with another threat."

Rinka glared at him. "Just like that, you trust that enemies have become friends?"

"He's correct," Tormod replied. "The ghosts were in full accord. The Plainsmen will follow Bayard. And just to be careful, we'll keep our forces on alert." He turned to Blaine. "Say on."

"Bayard is one of the Elders who once formed the council," Blaine replied. "Those who didn't join Penhallow have gone rogue—and taken sides with Pollard and Thrane." He met Tormod's gaze. "There's going to be a *talishte* civil war. There's precious little mortals can do to help—but you're not the average mortal."

"You want me to use my magic against the rogue *talishte*?" Tormod had gone very still, as if he had focused his entire concentration on Blaine.

"Yes. With that help, we might be able to hold off Thrane, and help Penhallow's forces win their war." Blaine met his gaze levelly.

Once again, it seemed that Tormod was listening to voices Blaine could not hear. After a moment, Tormod nodded. "Very well," he said. "I will go with you."

"Tormod—" Rinka began to object.

Tormod shook his head. "No. Blaine's right. I'm one of the few mortals who can make a difference against Thrane. I have a responsibility to go." A bitter smile twisted his thin lips. "We would not care to exist in a future ruled by Thrane."

"Before Thrane went into exile, he destroyed every necromancer he could find," Rinka said, lifting her chin defiantly. "Or did you forget that piece of history?"

"All the more reason this is my—our—fight," Tormod countered. "If Thrane survives, he'll make sure I don't."

Rinka crossed her arms, clearly unconvinced, but she said nothing more. *Tormod's likely to get an earful once we get back to Bleak Hollow,* Blaine thought.

"Come on," Blaine said. "It's been a long day. Let's go. We got what we came for."

The short ride back to the fortress passed in murmured conversation, though Rinka said nothing and Tormod was quiet. When they returned to Bleak Hollow, Tormod stopped Blaine just inside the great hall. "There's something you've wanted to ask since you arrived."

Blaine felt his cheeks color. Piran looked at him with a puzzled frown, but Kestel nodded. "Go ahead," she urged.

"You're a necromancer. You speak to spirits as well as raise them," Blaine said. "Can you speak to my brother, Carr?"

Tormod stared at him, and for a moment, Blaine did not think the other had heard him. Then he realized that Tormod was concentrating on his magic.

"The young man with dark hair and grievous wounds?"

Blaine swallowed hard and nodded. "Yes."

Tormod frowned, and his gaze was distant. "He wants you to know that he did not betray you."

"I know that," Blaine said. "But why in Raka did he have to go and get his fool self killed?" Grief welled up as anger.

"He said to tell you, 'now you know how it feels,'" Tormod reported with a puzzled tone. Kestel caught her breath. Piran swore softly. Blaine caught the meaning immediately, and swallowed back a sob. For six years, Carr and what remained of Blaine's family had believed him dead in the frozen northland. Since his return, Carr had been angry, going out of his way to provoke Blaine, taking defiant chances that had gotten him captured and killed.

"Can he rest?" Blaine asked in a voice just above a whisper. "Can he cross to the Sea of Souls?"

Tormod's gaze lost its focus once more. "He says he'll go when he's ready."

The comment was so completely like Carr that Blaine let out a strangled laugh. "What does he mean by that?"

"He's not the only ghost near you," Tormod said. "There are other, dark spirits that trouble your dreams and steal your energy." He frowned. "It would appear that your brother is trying to protect you from them."

"What kind of dark spirits?" Blaine pressed. *Gods know, if I'm haunted by the spirits of every man I've killed in battle, I'll have no rest living or dead.*

"Two spirits who in life put their mark on you, and in their death at your hands, cursed you with their last thoughts," Tormod said. "One of them is Commander Prokief."

Prokief, the sadistic commander of Velant Prison and the corrupt governor of the convict colony of Edgeland, had been killed by Blaine in the uprising that freed the outpost. Tormod would recognize Prokief, Blaine knew, since he and Rinka had also been exiled to Velant.

"Sounds like something that stinking sack of shit would do," Piran said. "Can you kill the bastard dead again, and make it stick?"

"And the other?" Blaine asked, although he had a hunch about the answer.

"This spirit is as dark as Prokief's, maybe darker," Tormod replied after a moment consulting his vision. "A stocky, brown-haired man with angular features and a nasty glower. The sense of malice is intense."

Blaine sighed. "That's my father, Torven take his soul."

"That's the problem," Kestel muttered. "Torven didn't."

Tormod stilled, moving back into trance. "The two malicious spirits have clawed at your energy, weakening you. But the third spirit, your brother, forced them back. The damage has begun to heal."

"How did he do that?" Blaine asked.

"He stands between you and them and battles them off," Tormod replied. "Taking the damage himself."

"Can you free them?" Blaine asked, meeting Tormod's gaze intently. "Can you destroy Prokief and my father so that Carr can go to his rest?"

"You ask a great favor," Rinka said.

"Blaine's the one who figured out how to solve your Western raider problem," Piran pointed out. "That ought to be worth something."

Tormod nodded. "Rinka is protective of me," he said with a fond half smile. "But Piran is correct. You've already done us a great service. I will do as you ask," Tormod replied. "Come with me."

Rinka looked decidedly unhappy as they followed Tormod from the great room down a long hallway toward a set of descending steps. She hurried to catch up with her brother, and they exchanged whispered comments. Although Blaine and the others could not hear the content of the conversation, it was clear that Rinka did not like the bargain, but what roused her anger, Blaine could not guess.

"Mick, are you sure about this?" Piran asked, using the nickname Blaine had assumed when he had gone to Velant as a convict.

"I've had nightmares for a long time," Blaine admitted. "First about Father, and later, after we freed Velant, about Prokief. Not just memories, or regular dreams. There have been enough of those as well. These nightmares were much more real," he said.

"In the dreams, I would fight Father or Prokief off, but they would always draw blood, and when I woke, I felt weakened," Blaine continued. "That's why I think Tormod is telling the truth. When anchoring the magic was killing me, I dreamed that Father and Prokief were feeding from my connection to the magic, like *talishte* hungry for blood."

"And Carr?" Kestel asked. "How do you know Tormod's telling the truth about that?"

Blaine took her hand. "Tormod wasn't around for Carr's madness, or his crazy risk taking."

"A spy among our troops could have heard of it easily enough," Kestel argued.

"True," Blaine admitted. "But since his death, I've dreamed of Carr standing between me and darkness, just as Tormod said."

"Can a mage of Tormod's strength send you dreams of his liking?" Piran asked in a voice just above a whisper. "Set you up to be indebted to him, manipulate you into making a bad bargain?"

"I could, but I didn't." Tormod's voice carried back to them from farther down the stone stairs. "Rinka also faults me, says the working will squander my power," he added with a hint of bitter humor. "Such are the concerns of those who care for us."

Although the summer night had been pleasantly warm, it became cooler the deeper they descended, cold enough to raise gooseflesh on Blaine's arms. Tormod opened an iron-bound door and led them into a large room. A wooden worktable sat along one wall, covered with relics and artifacts. Shelves lined one wall, filled with skulls and bones from a variety of creatures, stained and discolored jars, and bits of pelts, feathers, and leathery skin. In the center of the floor was a large circle.

Tormod turned to Kestel. "The magic-dampening amulet you wear is a hindrance," he said with a smile. "As you have seen, it does not stop my magic, but it makes it twice as difficult. So does the deflection amulet Blaine wears," he added, raising an eyebrow. "I must ask you to remove the amulets. I will need to raise a substantial amount of power for this working."

Kestel gave him a murderous glare, but she removed the amulet from beneath her tunic and handed it to Piran. Blaine did likewise. "Here," she said. "I'll stay near Blaine, and you can watch the door." *Kestel knew how much Piran mistrusted mages,* Blaine thought. She was giving him an out, letting him stand sentry away from the main working. She fixed Piran with a pointed look. "I want it back when we're through."

"I'd take it all the way back to camp if I had my way," Piran muttered. But he tucked the amulets inside his tunic and went to stand by the door, sword drawn.

Rinka looked worried, and she moved closer to Tormod's circle. "Do you need to draw from me?"

Kestel and Blaine exchanged a glance. *She's worried about the magic, and Tormod doesn't want to discuss it,* Blaine thought.

"Something's not right. There's a risk you haven't told us about," Kestel said, moving a step closer to where Tormod and Rinka stood.

"It's nothing that should concern you," Tormod said, a little too quickly.

"Nothing to worry *you*," Rinka snapped. "But my brother should think twice."

"Why?" Kestel pressed.

Rinka faced her with a sneer. "Because my brother isn't all-powerful. His magic has dangers. And when he wades into the netherworld to vanquish your ghosts, all kinds of creatures try to drag him under. You have no idea how dangerous it is for a necromancer to step across the threshold."

"Rinka!" Tormod's voice was sharp. "I choose my battles. Allow me this."

Rinka glared at her brother, but gave a nod. *Watching the interplay between brother and sister was fascinating,* Blaine thought. Rinka was a fearsome warrior on the battlefield, like a blood-drenched goddess of retribution. Tormod was a powerful necromancer. Yet it was clear that they were as protective of each other as they were seemingly invincible.

Tormod moved around his workshop, gathering the things he needed to call his magic. Rinka helped him set out candles and light them. Then he took a charred staff of wood and carefully drew a larger circle outside the first circle, with a gap between the two circles.

"Step inside the inner circle," Tormod said to Blaine. "We will face your foes together."

Blaine gave Kestel a reassuring nod and went to stand inside the inner blackened circle, careful not to touch its outline. Tormod positioned Blaine in the center, and then walked the inside of the outer circle as Rinka walked the outside. Tormod chanted, and Rinka scattered a powdered mixture along the circumference of the circle. As they walked, a faint golden light rose from the circle that was drawn on the floor. When they had made the full round, Tormod gestured and Blaine saw the power snap closed. The glow rose in a golden cylinder around them, shimmering in the gloom of the workshop.

Tormod repeated the process by himself, walking widdershins around the inner circle from the inside, until the power closed around him and Blaine, raising a second golden column inside the first.

Tormod's chanting changed. His tone became strident, and his words were guttural and harsh, in a language Blaine did not understand. The golden energy of the warding dimmed, becoming the dark indigo of twilight, shimmering now and again with light like falling stars. The area within the circle grew colder, and the glow of the outside circle darkened to the obsidian of a starless night.

Mist swirled between the circles. Tormod's voice grew more commanding, the intent unmistakable.

Forms began to take shape from the mist, taking form slowly as if the spirits fought the commands and obeyed grudgingly. Carr's ghost was first to appear. Tall and lanky, rawboned and angular, Carr looked as he had on the night of his death, bloodied by a mage's torture, and from his own self-inflicted death wounds.

Carr faced them defiantly, his battle sword grasped in one hand, a short sword in the other. He said nothing, but he met Blaine's gaze unswervingly, as if daring Blaine to fault him for his choices either before or after death. Even now, Blaine could not find the words to respond to the ghost's silent challenge. *I'm sorry* seemed woefully insufficient. *Thank you* stuck in his craw. Carr's expression changed from a defiant glower to a lopsided, bitter grin as if he knew Blaine's struggle. Then he turned his back on Blaine and Tormod and moved into a defensive posture as two more figures appeared in the mist.

Commander Prokief was the first to step from the swirling fog. He was a tall, hulking brawler with a cruel set to his thin-lipped mouth and cold, angry eyes. Prokief had been as much a prisoner as his inmates in the inhospitable, brutal cold of Velant Prison. Too successful on the battlefield to dismiss, too brutal to remain in a peacetime kingdom, Prokief had been named warden of Velant by King Merrill, making him chief among exiles.

Those who were not lucky enough to be hanged were exiled to Velant, on the northernmost continent of Edgeland, an arctic wasteland claimed by Donderath and colonized by the convicts who did not die under Prokief's inhumane rule. Ruby mines and herring fished from the Northern Sea made the colony lucrative for Donderath. Prokief ruled with brutal, ironfisted effectiveness, knowing that those he killed would die unlamented.

Prokief's ghost fixed Blaine with a baleful stare, his fleshy features twisting into a mask of hatred. It was clear in Prokief's mad gaze that the commander desired to finish in death what he had been denied in life. Prokief moved toward Blaine, but

Carr shifted between them, and the indigo light of the inner warding flared, forcing Prokief to keep his distance. Prokief's murderous glare made it easy for Blaine to hear the dead commander's voice in his memory.

Only a matter of time, boy, before I kill you. Only a matter of time.

To the left, the mist coalesced into a second shape, and although Blaine knew that the man he saw striding from the fog was dead, that he himself had struck the deathblow, the sight of Ian McFadden made Blaine's heart constrict with fear out of old, hard-learned habit.

Someone needs to teach this cur a lesson. The memory of that harsh voice echoed in Blaine's mind. Ian McFadden had taken out his foul temper on his family for years. Blaine had taken blows meant for Carr and their sister Mari, and had done his best to rescue servants, pets, and horses from Ian's cruelty. But when Blaine discovered that Ian had dishonored Mari, his temper found its limits.

Ian glowered at Blaine with the vicious intent Blaine remembered well from his youth. Broad-shouldered and stout, Ian McFadden had won renown on the battlefield and the regard of King Merrill. The murderous glint in Ian's ghostly eyes made it clear that he still longed to even the score.

In one accord, Ian and Prokief rushed at the indigo warding. Carr blocked Prokief's advance with his sword, and as Prokief's blade raked Carr's arm, Carr's ghost trembled, losing some of its luster. Ian dodged to one side, throwing himself in a fury at the dark-blue, glimmering warding as if to tear it apart with his bare hands in order to get at Blaine within.

"*Zerak-aggo!*" Tormod cried out, a guttural war cry. The indigo barrier flared like a cold-burning blue flame. Ian fell back, glowering.

"Ian McFadden and Commander Prokief. You have transgressed against the accords between the dead and the living, against the edicts of Esthrane and Torven, masters of the Sea of Souls and the Unseen Realm," Tormod said, proclaiming justice. "For this transgression, I send your souls to their reckoning in Raka, where you can no longer harm the living. So shall it be!"

Tormod raised his hands, and Blaine felt the shift in the air around them and sensed the use of magic. Tormod's presence grew stronger as his magic filled the inner warding, and then a rush of power surged from inside the warded circle. The magic passed right through Carr's spirit without harm, but it immobilized Prokief and Ian McFadden's shades, transfixing them. A black, gaping hole opened along the inside of the outer warding, as if Tormod had split the room open to face an empty, starless night.

The darkness reached out for Ian and Prokief, snagging them like flies on a spider's web. As the two doomed ghosts were pulled into the rift, their mouths formed soundless screams, eyes wide with terror. The shapes grew dimmer as their lingering consciousness unraveled, spooled off into the hungry, endless night of Raka. And then, the rift vanished, leaving the outer warding as if nothing had ever happened.

"Carr McFadden," Tormod said, and Carr's ghost turned to the necromancer as if he had no choice. "You are free of your burden. Would you go now to the Sea of Souls?"

Ian and Prokief had been denied the ability to speak, but now, Carr's familiar voice sounded from the other side of the inner warding.

"Not yet," Carr's ghost said, avoiding Blaine's gaze. "Things aren't settled. I'm a soldier. Leave me my last duty. Let me do this, and when Blaine's place is secure, I'll be glad to go."

Finally, he looked at Blaine with such a mixture of emotions that Blaine could not decide what to read from his brother's expression. "Let me do this right. I mucked it up the last time."

Tormod looked to Blaine. Blaine swallowed hard, trying to find his voice. Before his exile, he had been Carr's protector, and they had been close. Since his return, Carr's resentment had created an angry gap between them, and his death in willful defiance of orders had left Blaine angry as well as grieving. Now words did not seem sufficient.

Blaine nodded to Tormod. "So shall it be," Tormod said. "Carry out your last service with honor, and the gods will favor you when you cross the Sea of Souls."

Carr looked as if he meant to say something sarcastic. Instead, he gave a sardonic smile and a flippant mock salute to Blaine, made a respectful bow to Tormod, then turned his back on them, taking up his position on guard once more.

Tormod gestured with his right hand, palm forward, and Carr's ghostly form vanished. He turned to Blaine. "Ian McFadden and Commander Prokief can't hurt you again," he said. "They've passed beyond the boundaries of return, and they can have no more contact with the mortal world. I read no deception in your brother's intent. It's a geas he has placed upon himself, and his soul won't rest until it's completed." Tormod's expression softened. "In such dangerous times, a protector against unseen threats isn't a bad thing to have."

"You'll see that he rests when the time is right?"

Tormod nodded. "There's nothing to hold him back. But yes, I'll help if needed. You have my word."

"Thank you," Blaine said. Tormod inclined his head in acknowledgment. Once more, Tormod began to chant, walking the circle in the opposite direction to dispel the outer protections first, and then the inner shields.

The wardings vanished, and it felt to Blaine as if the room had stopped holding its breath. Kestel and Rinka moved toward them. "Could you see?" Blaine asked Kestel.

"Not clearly," she replied.

"I'll tell you all about it later," Blaine said quietly, and Kestel nodded in assent. Rinka and Tormod spoke in low tones, paying the others no attention.

Piran joined them, his relief clear in his expression. "Thank the gods that's over with. Now that we've had our fill of ghosts and Plainsmen and *talishte* legends, can we go home? We've got work to do."

CHAPTER THREE

DAYS WERE DIFFICULT, BUT NIGHTS WERE INTOLerable. During the day, Pollard had the thankless task of keeping Solsiden running and managing both Hennoch and the mages. But come nightfall, Thrane and the *talishte* awoke and returned to the manor, making it clear who was really in charge, should anyone have doubted.

"He's just gone back to the troops," Pollard said of Hennoch to Thrane's question. "I gave him his orders today, and planned to update you on his report now that you've risen."

"Not enough," Thrane said, and his gaze lingered on Pollard, a crafty, powerful look that made it clear who was servant and who was master. Thanks to the *kruvgaldur*, Pollard could meet Thrane's gaze, but the raw need for dominance in his eyes made Pollard wish he dared look away.

"I've left Hennoch to your management for too long. It's time I took the reins. Bring him—and his son. I would look on them," Thrane demanded.

Pollard was certain that Thrane knew just how much he detested giving in. "As you wish, m'lord," he said neutrally, and went to make it so.

"Send a rider on a swift horse," Pollard said to the guard at the front door to the manor. "Tell General Hennoch to come as quickly as he can. Emphasize that his son's life depends on it." He made the guard repeat the instructions, then sent him on his way. Kerr was waiting for him at the bottom of the steps with a flask, and Pollard knocked back a mouthful of the raw whiskey to fortify him before he went back in to pacify Thrane and his wastrel brood.

Thrane, the ancient renegade *talishte* better known as Hemlock, sat in Pollard's chair behind the desk in the parlor, the desk that had belonged to Pollard before Thrane and his supporters showed up. Black-eyed and sharp-featured, broadshouldered and powerfully built, Thrane looked more like hired muscle than someone of noble blood. Then again, he had existed for centuries, and in that time, even a street ruffian could amass a fortune, given a little talent and a ruthless streak. Thrane had both.

"I hope Hennoch realizes I don't like to be kept waiting," Thrane said with the hint of a malicious smile. His hangers-on chuckled, a cold sound that reminded Pollard of the growls of hungry wolves.

"He knows," Pollard replied. Long years with Pentreath Reese had trained him to keep his face expressionless, his thoughts distant and bland. Reese was Thrane's get, and Pollard had come to realize that Reese was a pale shadow of his maker's image.

"We dally on trivialities." Vasily Aslanov leaned against the wall, toying with a goblet of dark blood. He shook his long blond hair away from his face. Tall and slender with a long, pointed nose and sharp chin, Aslanov was as mean as he was plain. Aslanov had always been critical of Reese and a thorn in his side. Now, he prodded Thrane to free Reese sooner rather than later, certainly out of concern for his own agenda more so than Reese's well-being. Aslanov was older than Reese, maybe even one of the renegade Elders who had left the *talishte* council.

"Patience." Marat Garin lounged in Pollard's favorite chair near the fireplace. "Such 'trivialities' become important in the grand scheme. Time is on our side." Garin, Pollard knew, was one of the most loyal of Reese's followers, maybe one of the first fledges Reese had made. He did not look like he was of Donderath, with a forehead a bit too high, eyes a little too close-set. Pollard did not doubt that Garin had his sights set on becoming one of Thrane's trusted lieutenants.

Kiril looked out of the window at the darkened grounds, seemingly indifferent to the conversation. He was stocky, with a fighter's build and the look of a man who had seen serious battle before he had been turned. He said nothing, but Pollard had the feeling Kiril was listening intently. That was his role, keeping a low profile but always remaining within earshot so as not to miss out on important information. Elise, yet another of Reese's brood, moved from bookshelf to bookshelf, perusing the titles with a studied air of ennui. Her dark hair was pinned up in a knot. With her thin, finely featured face and slender build, Elise might well have been noble before Reese added her to his 'collection' of followers.

That left Sonders, a dark-haired man who looked like he was probably a pickpocket or worse during his life. He appeared to be in his early thirties, relatively old for the mortal age of the *talishte* Pollard had seen, Sonders had a streetwise look. Other *talishte* had wandered in and out of Solsiden since Thrane made his reappearance, but these were Thrane's inner circle, or at least appeared to be his handpicked minions until someone better came along.

Putting up with all of them was the price Pollard paid for a chance at the throne of Donderath. Nights like this, he reminded himself repeatedly that he was playing a long game, one with a crown at the end if he was savvy and successful.

It took more than a candlemark for Hennoch to present himself. Pollard knew the delay was entirely reasonable, given the distance and Hennoch's desire to make a respectable appearance to the man who held his life and that of his son in the balance. The *talishte*, however, grew bored with the wait, so far removed from the constraints of mortal speed and mobility that they imagined sleights where Pollard was certain none were intended.

"Finally," Thrane said as Hennoch entered the room. From his flushed features, Pollard was certain that Hennoch had ridden at full speed. He wore what nowadays passed for his best uniform, mended and clean of fresh bloodstains. His face and hands were clean, and his boots, while battered, were free of mud. *All in all,* Pollard thought, *it was the best one might hope for, given the realities.*

"My lord," Hennoch said, making a deep bow. "I came as quickly as my horse would carry me." Larska Hennoch was a decade younger than Pollard, but one look made it clear he had spent his years soldiering. Stocky and solid, Hennoch was built like a boxer and carried himself like a man who had seen his share of fights. He wore a patch over his right eye, and a jagged scar marred his face on the same side, running from hairline to chin.

"Then you'd best get a faster horse," Garin remarked, to the mirthless chuckles of the others. Hennoch flushed, but remained silent, mindful that his son, Eljas, stood in the shadows between two *talishte* guards.

"Let me have a look at you," Thrane said, striding forward.

"Older than I expected. Getting fat." He turned to Pollard. "Is this really the best you can do for a commander?"

Hennoch's cheeks burned. Pollard was careful to keep his voice dry. "As you know, m'lord, these days we make do with what we have. All in all, he has been suitable."

Thrane's expression made it clear that he was not entirely satisfied. He walked once around Hennoch, and Pollard knew the inspection was intended to be as menacing as it appeared. "Still," Thrane remarked, eyeing Hennoch as if he were a horse for trade, "there's some muscle beneath the lard. And I imagine he has a trick or two up his tattered sleeves or he wouldn't have lasted this long."

Without warning, Thrane lashed out one hand and grabbed Hennoch's left wrist, twisting so suddenly and with such strength that Hennoch had no choice except to go down on his knees or have his arm broken. He sank his long eyeteeth into Hennoch's forearm and drew several mouthfuls of blood.

"From now on, I am your lord," Thrane said, his voice cold and utterly terrifying. "You are nothing aside from what you achieve for me, and if that ever becomes less valuable, you have no existence at all."

Thrane tore a gash in his own forearm with his teeth and pressed the bloody slit against his prisoner's mouth. "Drink, or I will drain your son dry while you watch me do it."

Hennoch's eyes flashed in anger, then his gaze flickered to the pale young man on the other side of the room. Eljas strained for valor, though he looked as if he might throw up from sheer panic. Hennoch let out a defeated breath and parted his lips, allowing the cold, black blood into his mouth.

"It's not that bad," Thrane said in a voice meant to be triumphant instead of reassuring. "Perhaps eventually, as I bind you further, you'll reap the benefits of a bond. If I choose to bind you tightly enough, you'll heal faster, move quicker, and live longer. Just like Lord Pollard. He's been Pentreath Reese's vassal for years."

Hennoch's expression made his revulsion clear as he struggled not to gag. Eljas turned and retched, shaking and heaving as if he might pass out. Both of the guards looked amused at Eljas's discomfort.

Vedran Pollard watched the spectacle from his place to the right of the ornate wooden chair Thrane used when he held his 'court.' Pollard winced as Thrane made public his closely held shame, and he knew that shaming him was intentional. Until now, only two trusted confidants had known Reese regularly 'read' Pollard's blood, forcibly taking the information he wanted from a feeding meant to be as painful and demeaning as possible, to remind Pollard of his place. *Then again,* Pollard thought, *Thrane relied on such tactics so often and openly that his own secret was unlikely to have remained hidden.*

Thrane released Hennoch's arm, and the large man dropped to the floor like a stone. Two deep, bloody puncture wounds marked Larska Hennoch's left forearm. All his military prowess, his thousands of soldiers, his valor in battle did Hennoch no good now, on his knees before a dark nightmare returned from exile.

"Remember this," Thrane warned, as Hennoch clasped his wounded arm with his other hand to staunch the bleeding. "I can read every memory, every action, and every thought from your blood whenever I please. The *kruvgaldur* bond lies between us now, unbreakable except by your death. We are bound together. Your fears, your victories, your dreams—I will know. And if you show bad faith, I will also know, and I will drain your precious son of every drop and turn him to serve me forever. Are we clear?"

Hennoch nodded, though it was evident from every line of his posture that he fought the servitude. "Clear," he muttered.

"So good to hear it," Thrane replied, walking over to where Eljas stood. Pollard had taken the young man captive months before, as a surety for Hennoch's loyalty. Thrane had raised the stakes.

Eljas was sixteen summers old, no longer a boy and not yet a man. Pollard grudgingly gave the boy credit for having comported himself with dignity during his captivity. For Eljas's compliance, and his father's allegiance, Pollard favored the boy with better treatment, contingent on obedience. Thrane did not believe in leaving anything to chance.

Thrane clapped a hand on Eljas's shoulder, and the young man winced. Eljas tried to be strong, but his fear was evident in his face and manner. Pollard knew that Thrane relished that fear. "I thought you might want to know I've taken your son under my wing, made him my personal servant," Thrane said, watching Hennoch's reaction.

"It's quite an honor," Thrane continued, enjoying the discomfort he was causing both father and son. "I'm never without his presence. He has served me well." He ran his hand down Eljas's arm, turning the pale flesh of his soft forearm upward. "I may extend his service," Thrane said, deliberately baiting Hennoch. "Create the *kruvgaldur* with him, too. Like father, like son."

The room was silent, waiting for Hennoch's reply. "As you wish, m'lord," Hennoch spat out through clenched teeth.

Thrane smiled, having bent the two men to his will. "Very well. We have an understanding." He looked to Hennoch. "Go back to your army. There will be more survivors straggling in from what remains of Rostivan's and Lysander's armies. I've sent messengers to the north to gather additional soldiers.

When the time comes to fight Blaine McFadden's army again, you must be ready to shatter his defenses and annihilate his troops. I do not hold to half measures."

"Yes, m'lord." The words were grudging, but Hennoch knew his duty. He rose to his feet, his hand still pressed against the wound that had been inflicted with intentional, and unnecessary, cruelty. Hennoch glanced to Eljas, and gave a curt nod. The young man gathered what dignity remained and replied in kind. Then Hennoch turned and left the room, followed by the guards.

"Sit," Thrane said to Eljas, and the young man took up his spot on the floor at the left side of Thrane's chair like a favored pet. Much as Pollard hated to admit it to himself, there was not so much distance between his own situation and that of the lad.

"I think that went well, don't you?" Thrane asked, taking his seat once more.

"Quite effective," Pollard agreed tonelessly.

Thrane held court in the room Pollard had previously claimed for his own office and war room. Solsiden was a stronghold occupied because Pollard's family manor home had been destroyed in the Great Fire. Even so, the Cataclysm had not gone easy on Solsiden, badly damaging much of the upper floors. With Thrane claiming the only respectable room as his own, it left Pollard seeing to his tasks out of a small room that had once been a pantry. Thrane made sure everyone around him knew their place.

Thrane chuckled. "Don't fret," he said, tone thick with insincere reassurance. "You remain my favored commander. And if we succeed, you'll be my agent on Donderath's throne. Surely such a prize is worth the aggravation."

He says 'agent,' Pollard thought. *He means 'puppet.'*

"Show in the next guests."

The guards brought in two men Pollard did not know, but he was certain they were *talishte* by one look at them. Both men had the appearance of down-at-the-heels aristocrats, but then again, in post-Cataclysm Donderath, even the nobility could not muster a better showing than that. One of the men carried himself with the unconscious entitlement of someone of noble blood, while the other moved with the furtive grace of a predator.

"You're not of my brood, but you both might be useful to me," Thrane said without preamble. "I intend to raise a puppet mortal government that will never subject our kind to purges again, never drive us into the wilderness, never burn us to quell their own fear. I am assembling an army. This is your opportunity to join me. What say you?"

The aristocrat looked to have been turned in his early thirties, and by his manner, Pollard guessed the man was already well on his way to being a wastrel when his miserable life was cut short. He possessed the bland good looks of a Donderath blue blood, with the horsey face that came from too much noble inbreeding.

"What's in it for me?" he asked, regarding Thrane with an acquisitive look.

Thrane moved more quickly than Pollard's mortal sight could track, and apparently far faster than the much younger *talishte* could respond. In less than the blink of Pollard's eye, Thrane left his chair, swept the young aristocrat's head from his shoulder with a casual jerk of his right hand, and returned to his seat, blood-spattered but unruffled, before the body could crumple to the floor.

Thrane turned his attention to the furtive one with the clothing of a noble and the manner of a pickpocket. "Now,"

Thrane continued calmly, "as I was saying. You have an opportunity to join me. What say you?"

The pickpocket *talishte* licked his lips, an old mortal habit, and the look in his eyes was sly and calculating. "Sure thing, sir. You can count on me. My fledges, too. Just say the word. We're your men."

"Glad to hear it," Thrane said with a flat, cold tone that said he was already thinking about the next action to be taken. "I will let you know when I have need of you."

The pickpocket turned to go.

"Oh, and remember," Thrane said, with a glance toward the body that lay in a pool of its own black ichor on the floor, crumbling to dust. "I take promises very seriously. Don't disappoint me."

The pickpocket swallowed hard, avoiding looking at the dead aristocrat, and gave a nod.

The guards showed him out. Thrane regarded the pile of dust and looked at Pollard. "What do you think? Have it removed, or let him stay for a bit? We hardly got to know each other."

Pollard guarded his thoughts carefully. At close range, Thrane could read him through the *kruvgaldur* Pollard shared with Reese, Thrane's get. But because that link was removed a generation, Pollard had discovered he had a bit more freedom when he was out of Thrane's immediate vicinity.

"You might as well leave him for now," Pollard replied. "Since we'll have trouble getting the stain out of the carpet."

One after another, men came to Thrane. Most had been called to Solsiden to swear allegiance, *talishte* who were either those Thrane himself had turned or, more often, those who were brought across by *talishte* of Thrane's making. The ashes of the dead *talishte* cut the conversations short and ensured compliance. No one else made the same mistake.

After a few candlemarks, Thrane tired of his game. "I have plans to review with you," Thrane said, standing and stretching. He walked around the black stain on the carpet and over to the desk that Pollard had once claimed as his own. Pollard was certain Thrane knew just how annoying it was to confiscate every small trapping of power that had been Pollard's, including Pollard's stock of whiskey, which Thrane could not drink.

"Can I pour you a glass of something?" Thrane asked, watching for a reaction.

Pollard pushed down his irritation. Whiskey was an essential tool in surviving Thrane's occupation. "If it pleases you," Pollard replied diffidently. He had learned that Thrane enjoyed denying objects of desire. Therefore, affecting a manner of complete indifference was key.

Thrane withdrew a bottle of whiskey from the desk, pouring it into a chipped crystal glass and sliding it across the surface. "It's been several hundred years since I could appreciate a good whiskey as it was meant to be enjoyed," Thrane mused, leaning back in Pollard's old chair. "I've found that it doesn't fully infuse into the blood in the same way. Pity."

The implied threat was not lost on Pollard. He ignored it and sipped the whiskey, taking small comfort where he could.

"How may I be of service?" Pollard asked. He could not allow his pride to get in the way of the longer game he played and the ultimate prize at its end. *I wouldn't be the first man to survive humiliation and emerge with a crown,* he thought. *And I'll be damned if I'll let that fall to someone else. Quillarth Castle is worth bending my knee.*

"I've called together the former members of the council, the ones sympathetic to our cause," Thrane said, toying with a small, smooth onyx sphere he kept on the desk, rolling it back and forth between his fingers.

"They have gathered their broods—their extended get—and are sworn to support us," Thrane continued. The now-disbanded Elder Council included some of the oldest *talishte* on the Continent. The number of people they had turned during their long existence would be large, and the extended get would be substantial.

So many, Pollard thought, *and yet not sufficient to overthrow armies without mortal help.*

"Our space here at Solsiden is limited for such a large gathering," Pollard warned. The usable space of the ruined manor house was already fully occupied, and the only thing worse than the present situation, in Pollard's mind, would be being overrun by dozens—perhaps hundreds—of additional *talishte*.

Thrane chuckled, a cold, mirthless sound. "I have no desire to host them on my lands," he said, and his casual declaration of ownership over the holdings Pollard had claimed for himself was a calculated barb. "Calling attention to our numbers at this point would be unwise, and the number of mortals needed to slake our thirst would place too high a strain on the surrounding area. People would notice. That kind of threat would not be ignored. We are still...vulnerable."

For all of Thrane's arrogance, and in spite of his inhuman speed and strength, the *talishte* were still prisoners of their Dark Gift during daylight. Only the oldest could recover from any significant exposure to the sun, and while it was light outside, their strength and other abilities waned. During their enforced rest, they were relatively easy prey should substantial numbers of mortals launch an effort to exterminate them. Such purges had been devastatingly effective in the past. It was wise of Thrane to remember that.

"The army continues to grow," Pollard replied. "Our forces should equal McFadden's soon."

Thrane made a dismissive gesture. "Equal is not sufficient. He still has allies. Traher Voss's mercenaries are a powerful fighting force. The Solveigs remain in control of their lands and their army. And with things as they are, there's little profit tilling the land or working a trade. That leaves men to be recruited—or pressed—into service on both sides. We have work to do."

"Agreed," Pollard said. *Talishte* could not lead armies in daylight, nor could they win the allegiance of those soldiers, and they would never win the acceptance of the mortal population as king. Those realities were why Thrane still needed Pollard and Hennoch. Pollard suspected Thrane's frustration over that truth spurred his more spiteful efforts to humiliate both men. It was the only true power Pollard had, and he intended to use it carefully.

"You've been very useful to me," Thrane said. It was as close to praise as he was likely to come. "And you can make yourself more so in the weeks to come. We will have new allies, and it's important we keep an eye on them to ensure their loyalty and make certain their goals align with ours." Thrane's smile was cold. "I can't think of anyone better at subterfuge than you," he added, a left-handed compliment to be sure, but any acknowledgment from Thrane came dearly. "I'll want you to suss them out, make sure they are keeping to their bargain." He paused for effect. "You've suffered much on Reese's account. Continue as you have been, and when all is settled, you'll have your share of the spoils."

That was Thrane, Pollard thought. Faint praise and damnation in one package. It was so like him to hold out the prize, just beyond reach, to ensure compliance. Pollard hated Thrane for his manipulation as much as he hated himself for being Thrane's willing victim.

"Do you have orders for the mages?" Pollard asked, changing the subject.

Thrane leaned back in his chair as he thought. "How are they progressing?"

Pollard was certain that Thrane had a general idea through the *talishte* guards he had posted on every one of the mage workshops. Still, Pollard gathered that what would be read through the *kruvgaldur*, at least at a distance, was not complete. A small, carefully hidden, part of himself noted that with hope.

Taking blood from someone once or only occasionally makes a very light kruvgaldur, Pollard thought, confirming his suspicions. *It gives Thrane influence, but he doesn't get all the details from their thoughts without more blood. Perhaps it takes multiple, frequent, deeper 'readings' to tie the bond as tightly as Reese has bound me to him. Interesting—and promising.*

"We've seeded the mages throughout our holdings, and secured their workshops with walls and guards," Pollard replied. "McFadden's efforts at Mirdalur have changed the equation once more," he added with distaste. "He found a way to broaden the anchor, spread it among thirteen Lords of the Blood once again. That stabilizes the power, though I'm told it still has differences from what it was before the Cataclysm."

Thrane shrugged. "The details don't concern me. What have you learned about the power of this 'new' magic?"

"It's only been a few weeks," Pollard replied. "The mages are still working with it, adjusting to what they call the 'currents' of the power. But they're confident that the new anchoring makes the magic stable." He paused. "That should save us a few incinerated mages."

"McFadden will hesitate to use the same kind of battle magic that brought the Great Fire," Thrane said. "We can't afford such qualms. Make sure the mages know I place a priority on any magic that can be used as an effective weapon."

"Except for the necromancers you ordered executed," Pollard said, his voice carefully neutral.

Thrane's expression grew shadowed. "I will not permit a necromancer to live. I don't care how skilled they are. That will not, cannot, be allowed."

Again, Pollard felt a flicker of hope deep inside. *Talishte* were not invulnerable. Sunlight, a stake to the heart for those young in the Dark Gift, a severed head for those with more power, all were effective ways to destroy even the most powerful *talishte*. And necromancy, magic that gave the wielder control over the soul and the ability to control the dead, was one of the few things men like Thrane had reason to fear.

"As you wish, m'lord. We've killed two such mages so far. We will be watchful for others," Pollard replied. He paused. "May I ask—what is your next priority?"

Thrane smiled. It was a terrifying expression, absent of mirth, full of malice. "My next priority is to take my blood-son back from the traitors who have imprisoned him. I intend to rescue Reese, and to make Lanyon Penhallow pay dearly for it."

CHAPTER FOUR

NOT FOR THE FIRST TIME, VEDRAN POLLARD found himself wondering if the gods had cursed him by not allowing him to die in battle. Looking at Hennoch's weary expression, Pollard wondered if they both were thinking the same thing.

"If you can't find recruits to replace the dead soldiers, conscript them. We need to be able to field an army against McFadden and his allies," Pollard ordered ill-temperedly.

Larksa Hennoch met Pollard's gaze evenly, unfazed by Pollard's increasingly foul mood after having dealt with Thrane and come out alive. "Conscripts are more trouble than they're worth, m'lord," he replied. "For every conscript, it takes a second soldier watching to ensure they don't hare off as soon as we're not looking. Conscripts desert when we go to battle, and executing them lowers morale."

"Then raise the dead. Hex the living. I don't care so long as we replace the men we've lost and have an army that can fight when the battle comes to us again," Pollard snapped.

"We've taken on the soldiers who survived from Rostivan's and Lysander's troops," Hennoch replied. "All told, a few hundred, though I imagine some of them ran from the rear lines during the worst of the battle and that's how they saved their necks."

Pollard shrugged. "Prudence isn't always cowardice. Rostivan and Lysander were thoroughly routed. Keep looking for survivors. The offer of regular meals and tents to sleep in should be a potent inducement, given the state of the countryside."

Hennoch gave a bitter laugh. "They don't mind the food and the shelter. It's the fighting and the dying that gives them pause."

"Whatever it takes to raise an army," Pollard emphasized. "Lysander was using mercenaries from Meroven. If you can speak their bloody language, I have no qualms about hiring them."

Hennoch gave him a skeptical look. "What can we promise them? We've got precious little gold, and there's nothing to spend it on. There's no food to spare, or whiskey or ale to trade—"

"Find out what they want, and make a deal," Pollard cut him off. "McFadden's allies still have armies. They'll come after us soon enough, and I have no desire to fight a defensive war."

"What of the biters?" Hennoch asked, with a quick glance over his shoulder. It was nearly noon, broad daylight, and the *talishte*, including Thrane, were asleep wherever they had gone to ground.

"Don't worry, he can't sense your thoughts during daylight. Though trust me, if you think of betraying him or going against his wishes, he will know when he wakes," Pollard assured him. "For all their strengths, *talishte* have limits. They can't fight in daylight," Pollard replied. "And while they're powerful, there aren't legions of them, thank the gods."

"They helped make a route of the battle with Lysander, so I

hear from the survivors," Hennoch observed. "Snatching the officers from their horses, lifting them up in the air and twisting off their heads—quite an impressive show."

"They're a strike force, one with a very good 'show,' as you put it," Pollard replied. "But they're no replacement for a proper army. We need to turn that situation around before it's our heads on pikes and our rotting guts in the gibbets."

Hennoch's expression made it clear that he had reasoned out the consequences. "Since you mentioned it, you might be interested that we're hearing rumors about Meroven," he said. "Someone may have beat us to the punch. There's talk that the raiding squads coming across the border aren't foragers: They're spies and mercenaries."

"For whom?" Pollard moved over to stand by the window, looking out from Solsiden's parlor over the once-fine lawns that had been converted to a military campground. The sympathetic wounds from Reese crippled him. Layered on top of his own battle wounds, they were mementos from too many conflicts, reminders that he was not as young as he used to be.

Vedran Pollard was in his early fifties. His hair had gone gray when he was still a young man, but he hoped it added a touch of dignity instead of making him look as old as he felt. Dignity had been in short supply of late. Once, before the Great Fire, he had been one of King Merrill's nobles, a minor noble house to be sure, but still privileged. As a bastard son of his mother's, he had still inherited the manor by dint of being the last heir alive, but when the magic failed, he learned that the interrupted paternal bloodline meant he was not one of the Lords of the Blood.

His own manor house had burned in the Cataclysm, and so he had taken Solsiden, the late Lord Arvo's home, for his headquarters. He and Pentreath Reese had wielded a formidable army in the early days of the Aftermath, with grand designs on claiming a kingdom for themselves from the ruins. Then it had all gone so wrong. McFadden had returned from exile, not only alive but bent on restoring magic and gathering the Lords of the Blood. With his allies, McFadden had beaten Pollard's forces at the Battle of Valshoa, and re-anchored the magic.

Reese had been censured by the Elder Council, the ruling body of the *talishte*, and imprisoned for fifty years with tortures only an immortal undead could endure. Bound to his *talishte* master through a blood bond, the *kruvgaldur*, Reese's wounds had appeared in sympathetic fashion on Pollard's body, growing increasingly debilitating. And to make it all worse, after a second, humiliating defeat at the Battle of the Northern Plains, Reese's maker Thrane had shown up with demands of his own that were both impossible to ignore and equally impossible to fulfill.

"Warlords," Hennoch said. "Is it so difficult to imagine that Meroven has been trying to pick itself up from the ashes just as we have? That they're battling to see whose army is triumphant and who will rule? And when they've sorted that out among themselves, what's not to say they might take a look over the border and decide to grab some land or take whatever they can carry?"

Pollard shifted his position. Whatever had been done to Reese in his imprisonment bore out in the wounds to Pollard's body. A deep, raw sore directly over Pollard's heart resisted even the healer's magic, seeping and festering. Red pinpricks all over Pollard's body itched ceaselessly and maddeningly, and in his dreams, his master's screams kept him from sound rest. Bloody scratches on both wrists marked where Reese was bound with rope soaked in poison. Only whiskey gave Pollard a measure of peace.

"Rumors. Tales. I need facts," Pollard said. "How many warlords? What's their troop strength? And these marauders—are they raiders or can they be hired with some confidence of at least as much loyalty as coin will buy?"

"Good questions all, m'lord," Hennoch replied. "But I don't have answers for you." Hennoch had served King Merrill before the Cataclysm and, in the devastation afterward, gathered a small army to carve out a piece of the ruined countryside for himself. Pollard had worked to secure his loyalty, but now with the bond to Thrane their fates were inextricably bound together, whether Hennoch fully realized it or not.

"Well, get them." Pollard's mood was darker than usual this morning. He had slept little the night before. Reese's screams sounded more frantic of late, not mere nightmares but echoes across distance through the *kruvgaldur* bond of what torment his master endured in his imprisonment.

"Thrane's got plans, and they involve winning," he added. "For that, we need an army and all the intelligence we can get about what's going on out there. We have problems enough without a new force coming in from Meroven."

"There are also rumors about Thrane," Hennoch added, his voice quiet, with another nervous look over his shoulder. "He disappeared from Donderath seventy years ago. Where was he? What was he doing? I've heard it said he was in Meroven, maybe even the one who pushed their mages into the strike that caused the Cataclysm."

Pollard had heard similar rumors, but Thrane had been maddeningly closemouthed, other than to announce his return and his intention to free Reese from his imprisonment. "What's your point?" Pollard grumbled.

Hennoch gave a wily smile. "If it's true that he was in Meroven, then perhaps Thrane's already got the answers about Meroven warlords. Maybe he's been meddling there the way he's meddling here. After all, he's only just returned. We haven't had the extra men to send more than a couple spies into Meroven since the Cataclysm, and not as many came back as went in."

"Maybe," Pollard allowed. "But as you'll soon learn, Thrane shares very little information, and only on his own timing. I prefer to have my own sources."

"I have a couple of men who hail from up near the border," Hennoch replied. "If they can speak the gibberish those Meroven blighters talk, I can send them over the line to see what they see."

Pollard gave a nod of grudging approval. "Do it. I know too damn little about what's going on out there." He paused, and for a moment, looked longingly toward the decanters that held what passed for whiskey and brandy since the kingdom's fall. Thrane had seized the more drinkable bottles for himself, though he could not actually partake, leaving the worst for Pollard. Once, he would have disdained the thought of drinking this early in the day as weakness. Now, anything that dulled the pain and made it possible for him to function seemed a blessing. He sighed, forcing his thoughts away from the bottles, entering a quiet stalemate with the discomfort.

"And the mages? What of them?" Pollard asked, taking his bad temper out on Hennoch.

Hennoch brightened. "That, m'lord, I have some good news about. Most of our mages survived the last battle, and we've gathered in a handful of Vigus Quintrel's mages who had been deployed with Rostivan and Lysander. They're skilled, and fairly powerful."

"Meaning?" Pollard growled. Conversation tired him, and he wanted nothing more than to sink into a chair, drop the facade, and acknowledge the pain. That was something he dared not do in front of Hennoch.

Hennoch drew a deep breath, but when he spoke, his voice was even. Any frustration he felt with Pollard, he was wise enough to mask. For now, they needed each other, and that was enough to overcome even intense dislike. "Meaning that those experienced mages can bring along our younger mages quickly. Now that the magic's stable, we'll lose fewer of them in the Workshop, because the power should be predictable, safer. It's something to factor into the strategy."

Nothing was turning out as Pollard had wanted. But he grudgingly admitted the wisdom in Hennoch's words. Battle capabilities constantly shifted, and a victorious commander made the most of any advantage, however small or inglorious.

"Then figure out how to use the mages to our advantage," Pollard said. "McFadden has mages as well. Tormod Solveig is a necromancer. That creates some risk for our *talishte* allies," he added with the barest hint of sarcasm. "Find out how the necromancy affects them and what we can do about it."

If Hennoch was as smart as Pollard believed him to be, he would hear the dual meaning in that order. First, to discover how to protect Thrane and his *talishte*, and second, to determine just how severe a weakness Thrane's *talishte* had when it came to necromancy, and whether or not that could be exploited to free Pollard—and Hennoch—from a hated master.

"I'll make it the priority," Hennoch replied. He paused, and the flicker of emotion in his eyes gave Pollard to know what Hennoch was going to ask before he spoke.

"And Eljas? How is my son?" Hennoch tried to keep his voice rough, doing his best to hide from Pollard just what a surety his son was for him. But Pollard had been at this game for long enough to read the secrets others hid, and he understood how strong the hold was over Hennoch so long as Eljas remained in good health.

"The boy is well," Pollard replied offhandedly. "He handles his situation with dignity. Thrane treats him well, or as well as he treats any of us."

Hennoch let out a long breath. "He knows his role," he replied, and while his voice strained for indifference, his eyes gave the game away. "If he has books, he will be no trouble at all."

"He earns his privileges by being 'no trouble' at any time," Pollard said sharply. "But so far, he has been the model prisoner." Hennoch cringed, just a bit, at that last word, and Pollard felt satisfied that his point had been made.

"If that's all, m'lord, I'd best get back to the troops," Hennoch said. "I'll have answers for you on your questions, one way or the other."

"Best you do," Pollard replied, making no effort to hide his mood. "Now leave me."

Hennoch left the room, a converted parlor Pollard had taken for his place of business during the daylight when Thrane was in his crypt. Pollard waited until the door shut, and then sank into his favorite chair and permitted himself a low moan.

"M'lord, shall I bring you tea?" Kerr, Pollard's longtime valet, had an uncanny ability to show up at precisely the right moment. Pollard suspected that was due less to magic and more to a habit of listening at the door.

"Tea, with the powders," Pollard groaned. "Make it strong."

Kerr disappeared for a moment, and came back quickly enough that Pollard knew the tea had already been set to boil long before the request was made. Kerr bustled into the room, hiding whatever pity he might feel for Pollard's condition beneath a mask of brusque efficiency.

Kerr had served Pollard before the Cataclysm, back when servants and well-staffed manor houses were the due of those born to noble blood. That world had burned with the Great Fire, and Pollard privately despaired that it would not return again in his lifetime, but Kerr stalwartly did his best to pretend that nothing had changed, at least not the role of servant and lord. It was a pleasant fiction that comforted both of them.

"Shall I fetch more salve, as well?" Kerr asked as he poured the tea.

Pollard shook his head. "No. I don't have time to remove all the damn bandages and put them on again. By Torven's horns, I hate this!"

Kerr's smile was crisply professional. Not for the first time, Pollard wondered if his valet clung to his sanity through the pretense of normalcy his role afforded. "As you wish, m'lord. Then shall I send Commander Jansen in, when he arrives? He had expected to be here by first bells."

Pollard gave a curt nod. "Very well. He'd better get here soon. I'm hungry." He left it unsaid that being hungry or tired made enduring his wounds more difficult.

"Lunch is ready. I trust Commander Jansen will be punctual, as usual." Kerr poured Pollard's tea, and pushed a plate with a few slices of hard cheese toward him. Cheese and meat helped keep up Pollard's strength, and he wondered privately whether it was Reese's thwarted bloodlust finding expression.

"Send him in as soon as he arrives," Pollard ordered. "We have urgent matters to discuss."

Pollard had scarcely finished his tea when Kerr leaned into the parlor. "Commander Jansen to see you, m'lord."

Nilo Jansen strode into the room with a hardiness Pollard envied. Nilo was a small, wiry man with close-shaven dark hair and shrewd eyes that missed nothing. He was the closest thing Pollard had to a confidant and his most loyal ally, at least while their goals were aligned. Pollard had no illusions of friendship, but Nilo came as close to that fiction as anyone could approximate.

"Bad night?" Nilo asked, sizing up Pollard's condition with a glance. Out of necessity, Pollard had been forced to share the truth about his wounds with Nilo, and the pity in his second-in-command's gaze galled Pollard nearly as much as the wounds themselves.

"As most are, these days," Pollard replied. Kerr brought a second, steaming pot of tea and a cup for Nilo, as well as a plate of biscuits and cured meat, and then left them to their discussion.

Nilo sat down in the chair facing Pollard. "You've seen Hennoch?'

Pollard nodded. "And I gave him his orders, as we discussed. Just because I know it's damned near impossible doesn't mean he had to understand that I'm aware of that," he said with a dark half smile. "Who knows? He's desperate enough to keep that son of his alive that he might find a way to build us an army, after all."

"By Charrot, we need one, and soon," Nilo said, taking a sip of his tea and savoring it as if it were the kind of whiskey he and Pollard used to share long ago, before the world burned.

"What do your spies hear, about McFadden and Penhallow?" Pollard asked, leaning back in his chair and sipping his tea. At least with Nilo, he was spared the burden of pretending not to be in pain.

"Probably not too much different from what Hennoch's spies hear. Despite his lumbering appearance, Hennoch is shrewd and good at what he does," Nilo said, finishing one cup of tea and pouring himself another. "Right now, McFadden and his allies have superior numbers. None of their men are conscripts or mercenaries, which means they'll fight with everything they have. Their mages are volunteers, not forcibly brought across as *talishte* and compelled to serve." Nilo shrugged. "If he were focused on attacking us right now, we wouldn't stand a chance."

"And yet, you don't think that's his intent? To follow up on his victory and crush us?" Pollard asked, knowing that Kerr had added some healing potions to his tea to keep him upright and functioning.

"From what our sentries tell us, no," Nilo said. "And before you ask, we've had damn poor luck getting spies into his ranks. People on the edges willing to trade information—yes. But nothing useful from anyone inside his troops or manor."

"Keep trying. No one is that well liked, and that large a group of people can't all be honest," Pollard replied. "But I'm intrigued. He knows he set us back on our heels in the last battle. Hennoch and I are the last warlords standing. How is it that he's not at our gate with an army?"

Nilo shrugged. "It may be that they believe they've already vanquished us," he said. "There's no love lost between you and McFadden, but by all reports, he's not as driven by vengeance as some." *Meaning that he isn't impatient to see my head on a pike,* Pollard inferred.

"Noble, perhaps, but from a military standpoint, a weakness," Pollard replied.

"Maybe. Then again, perhaps not," Nilo answered, his tone academic rather than contradictory. "Many an army has come to grief because its commander couldn't see past his personal vendetta to recognize a larger threat."

"And you think McFadden sees a larger threat?"

Nilo nodded. "Sad to say, but I believe McFadden sees our army as the least of his concerns. He's got more men, and it will take us a while to catch up." He shook his head. "If he's as smart as I think he is, he knows that Thrane—and maybe the unrest on the Meroven border—is the real threat."

To all of us, Pollard thought.

"And how are you expecting him to act on that threat?"

Nilo ran a finger around the chipped rim of his teacup as he thought. "Not sure. Certainly Lanyon Penhallow and the Wraith Lord will figure into his thinking. Penhallow and Traher Voss are close, and I have no doubt that they're keeping a very tight watch on us."

Pollard snorted. "Surely we're better at ferreting out spies than that."

Nilo fixed him with a pointed glare. "The truth? Or what you want to hear?" Pollard grunted in reply, and Nilo continued. "The only ones who are absolutely loyal are the *talishte*, and their loyalty is to Thrane or Reese, not to us. Hennoch serves us only so long as his son lives, and that's as much up to Thrane as to us," Nilo said bluntly.

"And as you've said, conscripts and sellswords are only loyal until the winds turn," Pollard finished, contempt thick in his voice. "By Charrot and Esthrane! How in Raka did you and I end up here?"

"We had the ill fortune to survive," Nilo remarked, and raised his cup of tea in a mock toast.

"There's something you should know," Pollard said. "Thrane bound Hennoch. He's got Eljas at his feet whenever Hennoch's in his presence. You need to do your best to stay clear of him, because any hopes we have are lost if he chooses to bind you as well."

Pollard glowered, thinking. "And Hennoch's right, much as

I hate to admit it. We need to know more about the Meroven raiders. Thrane's let slip that he spent at least part of his time in exile in Meroven. He's only just shown up here. So what has he been doing? It would be just like him to be meddling with the warlords and *talishte* over there, like he is here." He sighed. "We need to know what Thrane's real game is," he said finally. "Particularly if he's able to free Reese."

Nilo set down his cup. "You believe he means to do it?"

Pollard nodded.

"Damn. How does Thrane expect to get around the *talishte* Elder who's guarding Reese?" Nilo asked, his voice equal parts incredulity and grudging respect.

"If my presence is required, I'll no doubt be told," Pollard replied, making no effort to hide his bitterness. Given his *kruvgaldur* bond with both Reese and Thrane, Pollard was ever mindful that his words—even his thoughts—could be betrayed by reading his blood. Yet over the years, he had discovered how to hide through misdirection and ambiguity, and Nilo was quick enough to read between the lines. Perhaps such subterfuge would not survive a thorough reading, but then again, neither would Pollard.

"Bloody bastard," Pollard muttered. "Not enough for Reese to just read my blood—he had to force his blood on me to get more control and ensure my loyalty," he said bitterly. "Now I'm bound so tightly I feel his pain, but there's no leaving him at this point. If his injuries wound me, I'd certainly share his destruction." Pollard sighed. "At least Thrane hasn't thought—yet—to bind me in the same way. Although who knows what hold he has on me through Reese."

"What makes you think Thrane's 'game' is limited to Donderath's throne?" Nilo asked. "Maybe he wants the whole continent. For all we know, he's got a counterpart for each of us so he can have puppet kings on both sides of the border." Pollard tried not to wince at the term, though he did not dispute its accuracy.

"Maybe Thrane's plan to free Reese might work in our favor for adding fighters," Nilo mused aloud. "After all, he never shied away from adding to his brood. Unlike Penhallow."

"Over centuries, I'm sure both have killed their share," Pollard replied. He shifted in his chair to ease his discomfort. Nilo noted the movement, but said nothing.

"Thrane certainly has loyal fledglings at his beck and call," Nilo continued.

"And Reese's fledges as well," Pollard added. "Through the bond."

Nilo nodded. "Then, theoretically, the broods of Reese's fledges, too, and on down the line?"

Pollard shrugged. "*Talishte* are notorious for not explaining themselves to mortals," he replied. "And presumably, they don't have to explain themselves to other *talishte*, because to become one is to understand." Despite himself, he shivered. That was one area of forbidden knowledge he did not want to discover.

"If the call is blood to blood, from the most powerful master to the most junior fledges, then it's entirely possible Thrane has called in his own 'family,'" Nilo mused. "Surely Reese's brood have felt his suffering, perhaps even more keenly than you."

"I have no doubt that they feel it," Pollard said. "Those of his brood who have come 'home' have told me as much."

"Reese is centuries old, and so is Penhallow," Nilo replied. "Thrane is older, and the Wraith Lord is perhaps the eldest of the *talishte*?"

Pollard shrugged. "Perhaps. I don't know the identities of the rest of the Elders."

Nilo nodded. "And the Elders split, some to Thrane and the

rest to Penhallow and the Wraith Lord." He leaned forward. "McFadden hasn't marched his army over here because the deciding battle of this war won't be fought among mortals," he said, meeting Pollard's gaze.

"It will be the *talishte*, fighting for whose vision of the future wins out," Pollard finished the thought, horrified and intrigued. "Creating that future through their mortal vassals." The possibility had occurred to him before, but hearing Nilo make the case so baldly, it seemed irrefutably clear.

"Penhallow, with his ever-so-noble view that the *talishte* should rule—or at least influence—from behind the scenes," Nilo continued.

"And Thrane, with Reese as his right hand, ruling through mortal thralls, presiding over a kingdom of mortals like a land-owner with a million head of cattle," Pollard said. "And here we are, greatest among cattle."

Nilo gave an eloquent shrug. "Death is inevitable," he said. "But I have found that usefulness is one's best bet to forestall the inevitable as much as possible."

CHAPTER FIVE

"WELCOME BACK." EDWARD, GLENREITH'S SEN-
eschal, greeted Blaine, Kestel, and Piran. Glenreith was
Blaine's family manor, damaged in the Cataclysm but still liv-
able, though the misfortune of the years since Blaine's exile had
taken its toll on the once-grand manor.

"Glad to be back," Blaine sighed wearily.

"You have no idea," Piran added.

"Did we miss anything?" Kestel asked, managing an engaging smile despite the long ride back from Bleak Hollow.

"Dawe and Lady Judith have things well in hand," Edward
replied with a smile. Edward had been Glenreith's seneschal
and secret-keeper since before Blaine was born. In the years
since the Cataclysm, he and Judith, Blaine's aunt, had moved
beyond friendship into a relationship built on long affection
and deep trust.

"I never doubted it," Blaine answered with a tired smile.
"Please tell me you've got some food for us in the pantry,
although we're unforgivably late for supper."

"It doesn't have to be warm," Kestel added as her stomach
rumbled audibly. "Just edible!"

Edward chuckled. "I think we can more than meet those requirements. Come with me."

They followed Edward into the kitchen. Long ago, when the McFadden family and the kingdom had known better times, a full staff of servants kept the kitchen bustling throughout the day and evening. Those days were long gone. The family's fortunes had begun their decline under Blaine's late, unlamented father, Ian, and the scandal caused when Blaine killed Ian to protect Mari had led to hard times even before the Great Fire.

Now, only a few servants remained, men and women who had served the family for generations and believed Glenreith to be their home. Most had nowhere else to go, and Judith had made them welcome, though she could offer little other than a roof over their heads, the protection of the manor walls, and a share of whatever food there was to be had. In the chaos after the Cataclysm, that was a generous stipend.

"The cook kept a pot of soup on the coals, in case you turned up," Edward said with a chuckle, leading them to seats around the worn worktable. One of the serving girls ladled soup into bowls for them and then fetched a pitcher of ale and tankards. Edward returned with a loaf of freshly baked bread, along with cheese and honey.

"A pauper's supper, I'm afraid," he said.

Piran had already torn a piece of bread from the loaf and stuffed it hungrily into his mouth. "No complaints from me," he said, his voice muffled by bread.

"It smells delicious," Kestel replied. "I'm hungry enough, my saddle was starting to look good!"

"Your journey was successful?" Edward said to Blaine.

Blaine took a sip of ale and nodded. "More so than I hoped. Tormod Solveig will be joining us very soon."

Edward frowned. "The necromancer? Is that a good thing or

a bad thing?" They had long ago dispensed with the formalities of title.

"My thoughts exactly!" Piran agreed, washing down his bread with ale. "Not that Mick ever listens to me."

"We've got a new alliance, and that frees Tormod to help with some of the other problems," Kestel added, giving Piran a poke in the ribs.

"Anyone notice I was gone?" Blaine asked, and began to work in earnest on his soup.

"Your absence is always keenly felt," Edward replied. "Mari is helping Dawe get the villages prospering again." Dawe Killick was one of Blaine's convict friends from Velant, and his black-smithing skills had been invaluable. He was also betrothed, with Blaine's blessing, to Blaine's younger sister, Mari.

"Judith is working with the servants and the farmwives to plan which crops to plant and how to preserve what's harvested," Edward continued. "She's hopeful that their efforts—now that the storms are gone and we've got a good growing season—will mean less hunger come winter." The last year had been harsh and hungry for those who survived the Great Fire, as unnatural storms, a backlash from the breakdown of magic, raked the countryside, and men were called away from farming to fight.

"That all sounds wonderful," Blaine replied. He, Kestel, and Piran had been gone for more than a month, taking the army where the need was greatest. Blaine was discovering that a warlord had no time to rest. They would leave again very soon, but for a few days at least, Blaine was intent on enjoying being back on safe, familiar ground. When he had been exiled to Velant, he had never expected to see Glenreith again. Now, he took nothing for granted.

"Several people are quite anxious to speak with you," Edward continued as they ate. "Mage Cosmin has asked numerous times when you were expected to return. I might be able to hold him off tomorrow until after you've had your breakfast," he added with an arched eyebrow, "but probably not much longer."

"That's fine," Blaine said. "Who else?"

"Lord Penhallow sent an urgent message that he and Sir Geir request to speak with you," Edward added. "I would imagine that Geir saw you coming, and has already gone to bring Penhallow."

Blaine exchanged a glance with the others. "Did they say what was so urgent? I sensed that there was something important through my bond with Penhallow. But that's all I got." Penhallow had saved Blaine's life by offering his blood, which also forged a *kruvgaldur* bond between them. From what Blaine could observe, that connection was not nearly as strong as the bond Connor shared with Penhallow and the Wraith Lord. Blaine could only pick up strong emotions or simple telepathic messages. He suspected Connor's bond both provided—and required—much more.

Edward shook his head. "No, he didn't. But he said that you must not leave Glenreith without speaking with Penhallow."

Kestel glanced at Blaine. "So no idea what that's about?"

Blaine sighed. "Nothing good, from the feelings I picked up. And if it's important for Penhallow to come himself, rather than just sending a message, and for him to pull Geir all the way from the Northern Plains, then something big is brewing."

"Pollard and Hennoch on the move again?" Piran asked, working his way through a second helping.

Blaine shrugged. "Probably, although I figured it would have taken them longer to lick their wounds before they could pose much of a threat. I guess we'll find out."

"There you are!" Dawe Killick said, sticking his head in the doorway. "I heard a rumor you were back!"

"Barely," Kestel replied. "Were you watching at the window with a spyglass?" she joked.

"Actually, I heard the dogs in the courtyard barking up a storm," Dawe said as he walked in to join them. He pulled out a chair and turned it around, straddling it. "So I thought I'd come down to check."

"Are they here?" Verran Danning glanced into the kitchen and grinned. Like Dawe, Verran was one of Blaine's prison friends from Velant, and for their three years as colonists, Blaine, Kestel, Piran, Dawe, and Verran had shared a homestead in the wilds of Edgeland. "Good. Don't start telling stories without me!" He was a thin man with sharp features and dark blond hair that stuck out at angles like a scarecrow. Before the war, he had been a sometime musician and ofttimes thief. Now, those skills paid off as McFadden's spymaster.

"Are the twins with you?" Zaryae was a step behind Verran. "Fill me in on the news!" Zaryae was Borya and Desya's kin, a talented seer. Dark black hair and dusky skin marked her as being from the western lands near the Lesser Kingdoms.

"Yes, we're back. No, the twins aren't with us. They chose to stay behind and help with translation, but they'll be here before too long," Kestel answered with a laugh. "And yes, we can give you all the news. Grab a seat and a beer."

To no one's surprise, Judith and Mari wandered in before they had gotten far with the story, greeting Blaine and the others with hugs and then settling in to hear their tales. The three travelers took turns telling about the battle, the dinner with Verner and the Solveigs, and then the dramatic alliance with the Plainsmen.

"You met Bayard himself?" Zaryae asked. "I *am* impressed. He's the stuff of legend out on the plains—bigger than life. I honestly thought he might just be a myth. Are you sure he's the real Bayard?"

Blaine shrugged. "Penhallow sent him, and I assume that he and the Wraith Lord would know. He was one of the Elder Council, before they disbanded."

"You do attract interesting company, Mick," Verran said, raising an eyebrow.

"Do you think they'll stand by their alliance?" Judith asked worriedly. "It seems so sudden to go from enemies to allies just like that."

"Yeah—it skips the whole disastrous war defeat first," Piran noted, finishing off his ale. "Actually, it's rather efficient."

"Yes, it is," Zaryae replied. "And that's why the Plainsmen do it that way. The nomads don't have vast numbers of people. Squander too many lives fighting, and there's no one to hunt food, protect the family, and father new children. Among themselves, they've devised ways to settle disagreements, smooth over bruised egos, and go on about their business without wasting a lot of lives."

"It's just that no one explained what was going on to the Solveigs—who aren't Plainsmen," Kestel finished. "So it escalated."

Zaryae nodded. "Exactly." She turned back to Judith. "So yes, I do think they'll abide by the agreement—especially with a leader like Bayard returned to oversee the arrangements." She shook her head. "He's practically a god to them."

"It'll take a while for Rinka to believe they've had a change of heart," Piran observed. "Maybe Bayard can work his godlike powers on her, too. She's not the trusting type."

Blaine leaned back in his chair, nursing the last of his ale. "It's a double win for us. Bleak Hollow can stop looking over its shoulder for attacks from the plains, and be on guard against whatever new attacks are coming. And Tormod is freed up to help us and Penhallow with the renegade *talishte*, while we figure out how to help Niklas with this new Nagok threat."

"Damn. Maybe when the twins get back, it's time for us to take the spy show back on the road. I never know anything that's going on since we stopped," Verran said. For several months before the last crucial battle, Verran, Desya, and Borya, along with several other handpicked men, posed as traveling performers and relayed essential information back to Blaine and Niklas.

"Be careful what you wish for," Kestel cautioned. "If this new general or warlord, Nagok, is as bad as Niklas thinks, we're heading for another big battle. There's rumor he may be a mage."

Blaine set his tankard down with a thud. "Maybe I'm a lousy warlord, but I'm sick to death of war. I'd really like to get on with building things. Every time there's a battle or a skirmish, something else gets burned down or wrecked, which is more for us to fix afterward."

Kestel squeezed his arm and gave him a peck on the cheek. "Actually, that makes you a good warlord," she said. "Good for the kingdom, that is."

Edward brought more tankards and a pitcher of ale to the table. Piran was the first to refill his tankard, though the ale brewed since the Cataclysm was a poor substitute for the quality brew to be had prior to the Great Fire.

"Mari and I are making headway with the villages," Judith reported, with a nod toward Blaine's sister, who sat next to Dawe, holding his hand. "They're anxious to have things back to normal—or as close to normal as we can come."

"In other words, they're tired of being hungry, losing their men to fighting, and having their livestock run off," Mari added. "So many men are either dead, off fighting, or too badly injured to fight, the women have had to figure out ways to do all the things they need to do—plus what the men did, too."

Judith nodded. "The villages are full of old men and little boys—sad, really."

"Niklas told me that a lot of the new recruits he's been getting are women," Blaine said. "They've lost their families, they have no marriage prospects, their homes and farms were destroyed, and they've had to toughen up to survive."

"Rinka told me they've seen the same thing," Kestel confirmed. "Young women coming out of the countryside, volunteering for their guards. If she thinks they're up to it, she takes them."

"While all that has been going on, we've been scavenging the deserted farms for seedlings, and taking clippings from the abandoned vineyards," Mari said excitedly. "And we've sent people to nurse the vineyards that might be salvageable."

"It's going to take time, several years at least," Judith said, "but we might actually have some drinkable wine again!" Since the Cataclysm, luxuries small and large had been in short supply. Good wine, ale, and distilled spirits had been hard to come by, and stock from before the Great Fire was gone. What passed in the interim was only barely drinkable, and far from ideal.

"I'll drink to that!" Piran said, raising his tankard, which was full once more.

"You'll drink to anything," Kestel said with a friendly poke in the ribs.

"We've patched up everything we can here at Glenreith," Dawe reported. "With the villagers working hard to get the crops in and tended, I've been helping out several days a week with the farriers and the blacksmiths." He sighed. "We lost a lot of experienced people to the war, so most of what I'm doing is teaching. My goal is to have a reasonably skilled person and a basic forge in each village by winter. Nothing fancy," he warned. "Just the essentials. Horseshoeing. Tools. Hinges. Barrel hoops. That would be a big improvement over what's out there now."

It was hard to imagine that just two years ago, Donderath was a thriving, sophisticated kingdom. Thinking about how much had been lost saddened Blaine beyond words. *We're not out of the woods yet,* he thought. *If men like Reese, Thrane, and Pollard have their way, Donderath will never be anything except their private fiefdom.*

They traded stories until the bell in the tower struck eleven times. "You've had a long day," Judith said, rising. "We need to let you rest." She gave Blaine a hug. "Glad to have you back safely," she said. "All of you."

Mari hugged Blaine as well. "It's always good to have you home, although you're never here long enough," she said. Blaine planted a kiss on the top of her head.

"Maybe someday," he sighed. "But not just yet. I'm counting on you to have some good wine for us when we do."

Mari laughed. "Make everyone stop fighting, and I'll personally stomp the grapes!"

Dawe clapped Blaine on the shoulder as he left with Verran and the others. "Get some rest," he said. "You've got too much on your plate. Enjoy being home for a little while." Edward followed them out, leaving Blaine, Kestel, and Piran and what remained of the pitcher of ale.

"It's really all hand in glove, isn't it?" Piran mused. "All the battles don't really matter if no one has food to eat, and the farmers can't farm if they've got armies overrunning their fields. It's like a dog chasing his tail—only the dogs have more fun." He took the last of his ale with a gulp, and then stared sadly at the bottom of his empty mug.

"Your guests have arrived," Edward said, returning to the doorway. "I've seated them in the parlor."

Blaine set his empty tankard aside. "Time to go find out just what's so important," he said, standing. "I have a funny feeling that it's not something I'm going to like."

Two *talishte* waited in Glenreith's sitting room, its most presentable area for company. The upholstered furnishings and wall hangings were the least shabby in the manor, and the best of what had not been sold off during the lean times.

Lanyon Penhallow looked to be in his thirties, but his eyes hinted at centuries. His dark hair was caught back in a neat queue that accentuated his angular, aristocratic features. Geir was a little shorter than Penhallow, and appeared a decade younger, with brown hair that fell loose to his shoulders.

"Welcome," Blaine said. "I trust your journey was uneventful?"

Penhallow nodded. "Fortunately so. Much more so than yours, I wager."

Blaine managed a wry half smile. "You could say that." Edward, always the proper host, had already brought a flagon of deer blood and goblets for their guests. "What brings you to Glenreith, so quickly and in the middle of the night?"

All except Penhallow found seats in the parlor's comfortable furnishings. Penhallow leaned against the mantle over the darkened fireplace. It was clear that he had a lot on his mind, and that worried Blaine. "Thrane has called the rogue Elders together— and they are summoning their broods," Penhallow said.

"How do you know?" Kestel asked.

Penhallow shrugged. "In part, because we have people watching Solsiden. But the proof lies in the sudden spate of killings and disappearances in the towns and villages all around Thrane's base. There are reasons *talishte* usually remain dispersed. Too many of us in a small area strains the food supply."

In other words, it goes hard on the local population of deer—and humans, Blaine thought.

"Why did he call them?" Piran asked.

"Thrane intends to wage war," Penhallow said. "It can mean nothing else."

"There's no other reason to gather so many *talishte* in one place," Geir added. He was one of Penhallow's most trusted warriors, and spent much of his time supporting Blaine as Penhallow's proxy. "Gathering that many *talishte* isn't sustainable for long. We're territorial, and groups that aren't part of the same brood tend to fight if they're in close quarters. Sooner or later, when it's that noticeable that *talishte* are preying on mortals, the mortals rise up and fight back."

Penhallow and the allied *talishte* found their sustenance from willing donors or animals and avoided killing mortals except in battle. Thrane and the rogue Elders saw mortals as inferiors to be used as they desired. If the two sides were to go to war against each other, that difference gave mortals like Blaine a deep personal interest in the outcome.

"Pollard and Hennoch were badly weakened in the last battle," Blaine said. "Surely they can't have gained enough strength in three months to pose a serious threat?"

"They've been recruiting," Penhallow said, beginning to pace. "The stragglers from Rostivan's and Lysander's armies, and any of Quintrel's mages who didn't die with him. What they can't recruit voluntarily, they conscript."

"Here we go again," Piran said with a sigh.

"Niklas has asked for additional troops," Blaine said. "He's running into problems on the northern border, bandits coming over the border from Meroven, and someone called 'Nagok,' who sounds like a warlord. We'll be heading up there in a day or two."

"Our spies think they're more than bandits," Penhallow

replied. "We suspect the 'bandits' are scouting and raiding parties, and they're carrying information—and supplies—back to a larger force."

"We're reasonably sure Thrane spent at least part of the time he's been missing in Meroven," Geir added.

"Meaning Thrane could be behind these raids?" Kestel asked, raising an eyebrow.

Penhallow nodded. "Not only behind the raids but causing trouble. I wouldn't put it past him to have been planning this offensive since the Cataclysm. It would be like him to have recruited *talishte* supporters, added to his brood, found mortal allies—maybe even equipped a large force waiting to strike. Thrane has always been a brilliant strategist."

Blaine felt a chill as the full import of Penhallow's comment hit him. "Thrane equips a Meroven-based force to come across the border and cause a disruption, drawing off our army, so that our resources are tied up and can't respond to whatever it is he's really planning?" He ran a hand back through his hair. "But what is it Thrane wants?"

Geir shrugged. "Control. The freedom to do whatever he wants, take whatever catches his eye, feed without constraint. There's always an undercurrent, a minority of *talishte*, who want to play god. That's one of the reasons we had the Elder Council, to keep those *talishte* in check."

"Some on the Elder Council sympathized with the predator way of thinking," Penhallow added. "But with the persecution under King Merrill's father and grandfather, they understood that giving in to lawlessness would have meant extermination."

"And without that threat, they're ready to flex some muscle," Kestel finished.

"Exactly," Geir replied.

"Some of the Elders sided with you," Blaine said evenly. "If all of you—and your broods—worked together, can you stop Thrane?"

Penhallow and Geir exchanged a glance. "We have a plan—but we need your help."

"Blaine's mortal," Kestel protested. "What can he do?"

"There's an artifact that we believe might be able to stop Thrane," Penhallow said. "Something called the Elgin Spike. It was crafted by mages long ago and used as a way to bring an end to the last *talishte* war."

"What does it do?" Piran asked.

"It was created to destroy not only a *talishte* but his entire bloodline, too," Penhallow replied. "Assuming that, after all the changes in magic, the Spike still works."

"That's a big assumption," Kestel pointed out. "You know how many magical items ended up tainted—and downright dangerous to the user—because of the problems with magic."

Penhallow nodded. "I know. I was around for a few of the more spectacular failures, if you recall. But if it does work, it could solve our Thrane and Reese problems in one blow."

"And if it doesn't?" Kestel asked.

Penhallow managed a wry smile. "Then we'll have to come up with a backup plan."

Piran let out a low whistle. "Damn. Got any magic swords lying around, just in case?"

Geir chuckled. "Not to my knowledge. But I can ask Dolan."

"So assuming the Spike works, what keeps *talishte* from wiping each other out?" Blaine asked.

"That's what made the Spike so dangerous," Geir said. "And why after that war ended, given the damage the Spike was capable of doing in the wrong hands, it had to be hidden."

"You've found it?" Kestel looked up hopefully.

Penhallow gave an enigmatic smile. "I hid it. Or to be precise, I instructed Arin Grimur to hide it for me."

Blaine, Piran, and Kestel exchanged a glance. "The man we met in Edgeland? But he said he had been exiled!" Kestel exclaimed.

"He could hardly go around announcing he was safeguarding a secret *talishte* weapon, now could he?" Piran said with a smirk.

"The Spike had caused too many problems, and it needed to disappear," Penhallow went on. "Grimur was weary of civilization, and was willing to be the Spike's protector. We fabricated the circumstances that led to his 'exile,' and no one seems to have guessed the truth in all these years."

Piran frowned. "If the Spike's been hidden all this time, how sure are you it will work? I assume Grimur didn't take it out and test it now and again. And how do you know Thrane hasn't figured out a way to protect himself from magic?"

Penhallow shrugged. "We won't know for certain until we try to use the Spike. Like any magical object, its power has limits. As for the other concern, I don't think Thrane could protect himself from the Spike unless he was a full mage, and a powerful one at that, which he isn't."

"We're going to need to go get the Spike—and Grimur," Geir said. "And we'd like to borrow a few people from your team to do it."

"Blaine can't run off to Edgeland in the middle of a war!" Kestel protested.

Penhallow shook his head. "No, he can't. But we do need someone who knows the people and the territory. Verran would be perfect."

"Verran's not a fighter," Blaine said.

"He doesn't have to be," Penhallow replied. "I'll be sending

Connor—and the Wraith Lord will go with him, which makes Connor a warrior with the Wraith Lord's skills. We'd also like to send Borya and Desya, since they're excellent fighters, and like Verran, they're ready to be reassigned."

"Who else?" Piran asked, crossing his arms over his chest.

"Zaryae," Geir replied. "Her foresight could be essential, especially on the trip out. Kierken is a mage. It's risky, but he might be able to use his magic when he possesses Connor. Grimur is also a mage. Nidhud will go as well, and along with Borya and Desya—and Connor with the Wraith Lord—they'll have plenty of fighters. Since Nidhud is a mage as well, that makes three full mages and a seer. Verran should be in his element—working the crowd, reconnecting with the people who knew all of you when you lived there, making sure the team gets a warm reception."

"We've secured the *Nomad* and a crew," Penhallow went on. "The same ship that brought you back from Edgeland."

"I agree with your choices," Blaine said carefully. Through the *kruvgaldur*, he could feel how important Penhallow thought this mission was, and weighed that as he responded. "They're good people with the right skills for the mission. And I can free them from anything they would have been doing for the fight here. But for a trip like that, you need to talk to them. I can't make the decision for them."

Penhallow nodded. "I plan to. But they're your people, and I wanted to fill you in first. You might have had them on assignment." He met Blaine's gaze. "After all, you're the most powerful warlord in Donderath, and the main commander of the war."

"Verran knew nearly everyone in Edgeland, and most of them liked him," Piran said. "That's something you couldn't have said for me."

"Another good reason why you're not an ambassador, Piran dear," Kestel joked.

"Can you trust the crew?" Blaine asked. Verran and the others were friends, as close as family. The trip to Edgeland was more than a month long, and no matter what the time of year, the seas were treacherous.

"Yes," Penhallow said without hesitation. "They're all men with seagoing experience who have a strong *kruvgaldur* bond to me or to our allied Elders. They're entirely trustworthy."

Blaine was still learning just what the *kruvgaldur* meant and how it worked for him. He knew his was not nearly as strong as Connor's, but no one had bothered to explain the details. "Is their bond strong enough to ensure their loyalty over such a great distance?"

Penhallow nodded. "It should. I chose only men who have a strong *kruvgaldur* bond."

"The *Nomad* was a big ship," Blaine said. "If you're going to Edgeland, we'll send supplies with you. We've heard nothing from the colony since we returned. It was hard enough to survive when there were regular supply ships from Donderath and the magic hadn't gone wild. I don't want to imagine how hard it's been for them, without supplies and without reliable magic."

Edgeland and the people Blaine and the others had left behind there were never far from his thoughts. He still thought of many of the people there as good friends, and prayed to Esthrane for their safety.

"What about on the return trip?" Kestel asked. "The *Nomad* holds four hundred passengers, in addition to the crew. Can Verran offer to bring back anyone willing to fight? We could use some fresh troops."

Penhallow nodded. "That can be arranged. I can also add some supplies from our provisions as well."

"Root vegetables, dried meat, tools, supplies the colonists would have had to rely on Donderath to provide like salt, dried plants that don't grow up there for making healing potions," Kestel rattled off. "All of those things would be more precious than gold. Anything we could send them would be much appreciated—and would make Verran a hero."

"That's what we're hoping for," Geir said. "There's no hiding a sailing ship coming into Skalgerston Bay, so let's make sure he gets a hero's welcome, does some good for the colonists, and has backup if he needs it from friends who are glad to see him."

"Do you want me to tell Verran and the others before I send them to Westbain, or do you want to do the honors?" Blaine asked.

Penhallow frowned. "I'd rather have as few people as possible know about the Elgin Spike until we have it safely in hand and use it against Thrane. Please tell them, and only them, just what they must know at the last possible moment. With luck, the Spike has slipped out of memory. By the time your people reach Westbain, we'll have the ship provisioned and ready to go. The fewer chances to compromise the mission, the better."

Blaine nodded. "Makes sense." He chuckled. "I don't envy you Connor's reaction. He didn't fancy Edgeland much—and he was only there for a month or so!"

"With all the weird artifacts we pulled out of the catacombs under Quillarth Castle, are you sure there aren't more things we can use against Thrane and Hennoch and the Meroven scum?" Piran asked. "I'm the last person to like relying on magic, but damn—if we can blow them up or burn them down from a distance with a little hocus-pocus, it saves a lot of lives."

That brought a smile to Penhallow. "Nidhud and the Knights of Esthrane have been working with all of the artifacts we recovered with that same goal in mind." He paused. "Although I suspect he might take exception to your wording."

"Edward said Cosmin is looking for me," Blaine replied with a sigh. "I figure he and his mages have either found something really useful or they've done a lot of damage and want to let me know it's all for naught." Since magic had been brought back under mortal control, the mages had a huge and dangerous task determining how the changes affected objects of power, and which pieces could still be safely used.

"I've got to admit that my mind is still back on Thrane and his rogue Elders," Kestel said. "Are they really so blind that they think they'll be able to slaughter mortals and people won't fight back?"

"Thrane and Reese plan to put Vedran Pollard on the throne as their puppet." Penhallow's matter-of-fact observation left them in stunned silence. The chill Blaine had felt grew deeper. Vedran Pollard was one of Ian McFadden's peers, and the bad blood between Pollard and Blaine's father had been legendary at court. To Blaine's mind, Pollard was Ian's equal for sheer spite and vindictiveness.

Piran spat out a string of curses. "Pollard? King?"

"I remember Vedran Pollard from court," Kestel said with disdain. "He was vain and cruel. Spending time with Reese and Thrane couldn't have improved him. He would be a disaster as a king."

"The only real alternative is for Blaine to be willing to accept the crown himself." Penhallow's voice was quiet, but it seemed to echo from the walls. For a moment, no one moved. Blaine caught his breath, thinking of a million reasons why the suggestion was preposterous.

"I've been thinking that for a while now," Piran said, without any hint of humor. "Who else?"

Blaine found his voice. "I never even cared about being a lord, let alone a warlord," he said. "King?"

Piran looked at Blaine with a sad smile. "In a way, the fact that you don't want it makes you the best person for the job, Mick."

"It's crossed my mind, since the last big battle," Kestel admitted. "The other warlords defer to you. You've earned the trust of the villagers and the people in Castle Reach. And Piran's right—who else could do it? Verner just wants to go home and farm his land. He's a decent general, but I don't think he's got the skills to be king."

"The people would never accept either of the Solveigs," Piran added. "Even if Rinka and Tormod were interested, and I don't get the feeling their ambitions run in that direction."

"Folville certainly isn't cut out to be king, and Voss isn't the type to want a crown," Kestel continued. "Who else is there? Niklas couldn't wait to leave Quillarth Castle when he was rebuilding it and get back out on the battlefield. The people won't accept a *talishte* king." She met Blaine's gaze. "Face it, Mick—it's got to be you. We've worked too hard, lost too many people fighting this war, to let it all fall apart when we win."

"King?" Blaine repeated, stunned. The idea would be laughable if he was not certain that they were entirely serious.

"When I go back to Westbain, I'll be gathering the allied Elders against Thrane," Penhallow said levelly. "They will want to know what is to become of Donderath, once Thrane and the Meroven threat are defeated. We're asking them and their broods to involve themselves in mortal affairs far more than *talishte* have done openly for centuries," Penhallow continued. "They could easily leave, and let the mortals sort it out for themselves, on their own." He looked dour. "I don't think you would find that a satisfactory outcome."

"And since you're asking them to stick their necks out, they have an interest in what happens after the fighting is over," Piran replied.

"Exactly," Penhallow agreed. "Of all the players since the Cataclysm, only Blaine could win the support of the allied Elders." He grimaced. "Of that, I'm quite sure."

"I would agree, from what I've seen," Geir said. "The allied Elders want to know that the next king of Donderath won't turn on the *talishte* and hunt us. You've won points with them by naming Nidhud and Penhallow as new Lords of the Blood. You promised Dolan that the Knights will have a seat at the table as the kingdom rebuilds. You're tied by the *kruvgaldur* to Penhallow. Connor—and the Wraith Lord—speak well of you." He gave a bittersweet smile. "There is no one else with credentials that compare."

Kestel laid a hand on Blaine's arm. "Could you really just walk away and let it all fall apart?" she asked quietly. "If you see another alternative, now's the time to say something."

Kestel knows there isn't anyone else, Blaine thought. *And she's right—we've fought so hard to put things back together after the Cataclysm, I can't just let it all fall to pieces again. That's what will happen without a strong king. So help me Charrot, I'd hand this off in a second if I could. But still, king?*

"Can I give the allied Elders assurance that you'll accept the crown, assuming we win the war?" Penhallow prompted, rousing Blaine from his thoughts.

Kestel gave his arm an encouraging squeeze, and Piran nodded soberly. "Yes," Blaine said, although his voice sounded distant and strange to him, as if it belonged to someone else. "I'll do it. You have my word—if we all live to see the end of this war."

CHAPTER
SIX

I N WESTBAIN'S TATTERED PARLOR, LANYON PEN-
hallow paced, hands clasped behind his back. "There's no
other way," he said.

"Surely, there are alternatives." Aldwin Carlisle, *talishte* lord
and formerly the Gold-masked member of the Elder Council,
frowned worriedly. "It seems . . . extreme."

The Wraith Lord was present only as a disembodied spirit,
but his outline was clear and recognizable. Kierken Vandholt
had existed for over one thousand years as man, mage, *talishte*,
and wraith. Connor could remember few circumstances when
the Wraith Lord looked so concerned.

"Thrane is a menace," the Wraith Lord said. "A powerful
menace. And with the assistance of some of the Elders—as well
as the sizable broods he and Reese and the others created—we
need to take drastic steps."

"I don't like it." Garrick Dalton, the Brown Elder, shook
his head. "The Elgin Spike was best forgotten, or better yet,
destroyed. We risk all our safety by bringing it to light."

"Thrane and Reese are already risking the safety of all *talishte*," Penhallow said sharply. "The situation in Donderath is

fluid. What happens now determines the fate of the kingdom for decades to come. If the mortals experience the full horror and devastation of a *talishte* war, something that has been half-forgotten as history or legend, we will see massive efforts to wipe out our kind. Thrane cannot win, but all of us can lose."

Bevin Connor, the only mortal in the room, listened in silence. He was assistant and liegeman to Lanyon Penhallow, bound by the *kruvgaldur* blood bond as well as by honor and an odd friendship. And as a powerful medium, he was the oft-times vessel for cloaking the Wraith Lord in a human body. That meant he was frequently privy to conversations and events about which other mortals remained blissfully, comfortably ignorant.

"Our numbers are hardly sufficient to do damage anywhere near the scale easily inflicted by mortal warfare," Carlisle argued.

"Mortals will forgive the excesses of other mortals," Penhallow replied. "They believe, rightfully or not, that armed equally, they could either hold their own or do the same. But they can never be armed equally to *talishte*. Open war between *talishte* will remind them that our kind can be true monsters. And they will, understandably, band together by the hundreds and thousands in daylight to destroy all of us."

"I gave up faith in magical objects' ability to change the world long ago," Carlisle said. "The Spike is a symbol, a short-cut to something we can do by other means." He paused. "You don't even know if it still works after the Cataclysm. For all we know, Thrane could be immune to its power, or it might be tainted—or inert."

The Wraith Lord's scowl deepened. "Perhaps. And we are developing alternatives in case the Spike fails. But the Elgin Spike has potent magic, and its use would solve our problem.

Other means would require vastly more effort, take much more time, and come at a far greater cost."

Connor watched the play of wills while trying to remain unnoticed. Although he had gained strength and other benefits from his *kruvgaldur* bond with Penhallow and his connection to the Wraith Lord, he was under no illusion that he was in any way in the company of equals. The last time he had seen Carlisle and Dalton, they had been masked and robed in the circle of the Elder Council, a group of the oldest and most powerful *talishte* who until recently held the power of destruction over all *talishte* in Donderath. He was, quite possibly, the only mortal to have witnessed the gathering and lived. And while before the Cataclysm, his role as aide to the late Lord Garnoc had brought him to court in the presence of kings and nobles, their power, and their potential for large-scale destruction, did not compare with the power of the *talishte* in this room.

"We have tried to solve the problem with more limited means," the Wraith Lord replied. Over the year of playing host body to the Wraith Lord's spirit, Connor had become highly attuned to the ancient *talishte*'s moods. Now, he realized how hard the Wraith Lord was trying to rein in his impatience and court the agreement of the recalcitrant former Elders.

"Penhallow and I testified to the Elders about the danger of Reese's desire for power. We committed our troops and our broods, as well as our own blades, to fight against Reese and his mercenaries," the Wraith Lord recounted.

"What of the Knights of Esthrane?" Malin Jarett asked. She was the only woman in the room, thin, beautiful, and imperious, and a former Elder who had hidden her features behind a Silver mask. As she spoke, she turned to look pointedly at General Dolan, who stood at rest just inside the doors to the parlor.

"My Knights have already played a sizable role in this

conflict," Dolan replied with a faint tone of disapproval. "More so than we have played in a mortal conflict for quite some time. At the behest of the Wraith Lord, we provided safe passage to Blaine McFadden from Valshoa, when he attempted to bind the magic there. The Knights fought in the Battle of Valshoa, on McFadden's side. We have just returned from playing an equally large role in the Battle of the Northern Plains, and in McFadden's successful re-anchoring of the magic at Mirdalur. Yet we are few in number. There are limits to our ability to directly change the course of events."

"It worries me that Thrane returns now, after being gone so long from Donderath." Dag Marlief had been the Elder known as Onyx. "We have only rumors about what he did in those decades, who sheltered him, what alliances he might have built."

Penhallow nodded. "Those questions worry me as well, and I fear we're about to discover those answers. I don't think we will like what we find out."

"Do you really believe that Thrane has built himself a secret army?" Jarett asked.

Penhallow turned to meet her blue eyes. "Thrane's never 'built' anything himself. But do I think it's likely that he has co-opted, conscripted, borrowed, or stolen an army by promising mountains of spoils? I would say that's in character—most likely with allies in Meroven, where we believe he spent much of his exile."

"I concur." The Wraith Lord's voice commanded attention, even though he was incorporeal. "Thrane has never played fair, even by *talishte* terms. He will do whatever it takes to win. And since he has announced himself in the game by his return, I think we need to take him seriously as a threat. Without Thrane, Reese had been defeated. Thrane's return changes everything."

"What would you have us do?" Dalton asked.

"Summon your broods," Penhallow replied. "Brace them for war. Rally them to the cause against Thrane, or compel those who will not rally to stand down and give no aid to Thrane's forces."

"You expect us to go to battle?" Carlisle replied, raising an eyebrow.

"I expect that the next major conflict will be a human battle masking a *talishte* civil war," the Wraith Lord rumbled. "The winner will decide the fate of the Ascendant Kingdoms for generations, perhaps centuries." He turned his gaze over the group in turn, and even the oldest of the Elders shrank back from his intensity.

"Don't fool yourself that neutrality is possible," the Wraith Lord warned. "Thrane will keep score, and he has shown himself to be particularly unforgiving. And don't believe that Thrane's vision of a kingdom where we rule openly and brutally is preferable, or even possible. Thrane's vision leads to a few, short years of carnage and madness, followed by extinction."

Something in the weight of the Wraith Lord's words gave Connor to suspect that over the course of a millennium, Kierken Vandholt had experienced those consequences. And although the Wraith Lord was quite good at hiding his thoughts away from Connor whenever he possessed Connor's body as his proxy, Connor had gleaned bits of memories, shadows of experiences that gave him glimmers of insight into Vandholt's history. Connor shivered. The purge Vandholt warned about was something he had survived personally, something he had seen destroy his brood and everything he cared about. Although the memory was a borrowed one, and incomplete, Connor felt its terror. The Wraith Lord was right. Devastation was imminent, and there was nothing that Connor could do about it.

"You think that Thrane can be defeated simply by besting him in a war?" Jarett asked incredulously. "Nothing short of the final death will dissuade him. Many powerful *talishte* have tried to pass that judgment. None have succeeded."

"That's why you want the Elgin Spike," Dalton said. "To make sure that Thrane and all his brood are destroyed, once and for all."

Penhallow crossed the room to where a large, yellowed map of Donderath and the rest of the Continent hung on the wall. Before the war, the combined crowns of the Continent had dared to call themselves the Ascendant Kingdoms, as if they had reached the pinnacle of achievement. Meroven and Donderath took up most of the land mass as the Greater Kingdoms. A handful of smaller states toward the south were the Lesser Kingdoms. On the other side of the Ecardine Sea were the Cross-Sea Kingdoms, once prosperous trading partners. No one had heard from those lands since the Cataclysm. To the far north lay Edgeland, a colony of convicts, and Velant Prison, now a ruin.

"Thrane and Pollard control Solsiden," Penhallow said, pointing to a small knife stabbed into a location to Westbain's north. "Hennoch's army has the surrounding territory, to the Meroven border. Our spies confirm that he's taken in survivors from the defeated lords, and any of Quintrel's mages who didn't burn.

"Voss has the territory south of Westbain, and the Wraith Lord's protections extend around Lundmyhre. McFadden's army and allies hold Castle Reach and Quillarth Castle," Penhallow said, indicating an arc to the west. "Birgen Verner's army holds from Mirdalur to the Riven Mountains, and the Solveigs have the western end of the kingdom, stretching as far as they care to exert control." He paused. "The Gray Elder,

Bayard, has gone to rally the Plainsmen, and with luck, ally them to Blaine McFadden and the Solveigs. That should free more troops to deal with the Meroven raiders."

"It would appear that McFadden and his allies already control Donderath," Carlisle observed.

"For now," Penhallow replied. "Bayard has gone to help put down uprisings among the Plainsmen. Blaine and his allies must now focus their troops on Thrane and the Meroven threat if they're to hold the kingdom." He paused. "If we're correct about Thrane's intent, he likely spent much of his time in Meroven maneuvering for a successful return. He may have built a network of supporters, outfitted an army, backed a warlord he thought likely to win. These northern raids are likely his doing, and we can't overlook the possibility that this new Meroven warlord, Nagok, may be Thrane's man."

"I suspect you're right," Dalton said. "It's doubtful that Thrane went to ground in a crypt for nearly a century. He would have found patrons in a city, enriched them, then enslaved them. That's his pattern."

Jarett nodded. "Wasn't that part of why he was exiled in the first place? Crimes not only against mortals but against *talishte* as well. And even then, he had supporters among the Elders, enough to make him outcast without destroying him."

"With Thrane in Meroven during his exile, then the possibility exists he may well have had a hand in bringing the war—and the Cataclysm—down on both kingdoms," the Wraith Lord replied. "It would be like him."

"What do our scouts tell us?" Dalton asked.

Penhallow turned away from the map and sat on the corner of a large, wooden desk. "Kierken and I sent scouts into Meroven after the Battle of the Northern Plains. They only just returned. They found Meroven in even worse condition than Donderath: burned, flooded, reeling from magic storms and unstable magic. When Blaine McFadden restored the magic, the effects reached at least as far as Meroven. That much we know."

"We assumed they lost their nobles and many of their mages, as we did," Jarett said. "Was that true?"

Penhallow nodded. "Yes. The king and the nobles are dead, manors and cities destroyed, power split among squabbling bandits and warlords. Mages on both sides targeted the leadership; the difference was that Meroven unwittingly destroyed the bond of magic when they destroyed the Lords of the Blood. But now, Meroven is rebuilding. Power is coalescing in the hands of a few successful military leaders. And magic works again for them as it does for us."

"Donderath was always the more prosperous of the two kingdoms," the Wraith Lord replied. "It's in Meroven's blood to look toward Donderath with resentment. They believe Donderath has more fertile land, a better harbor, and more plentiful herds. Whether or not that's true isn't the point. Meroven has always seen Donderath as a treasure to be plundered. And whoever does so successfully would win great standing, perhaps a crown."

"Which Thrane would be willing to promise, even if it wasn't in his power to bestow," Penhallow added drily.

"We have enough problems, without worrying about Meroven phantoms that may not come for a long while, if ever," Jarett said.

"Meroven is not a someday threat," Dolan replied. "Two of my Knights were among the scouts. Meroven has rallied troops not far from the border."

"Mobs are of little use without a leader," Carlisle observed. "They're easy to rally, and easy to crush."

Dolan shook his head. "Meroven has not been quiet this past year and a half. Factions there have battled for power, as they have here. Interestingly, the man who has emerged at the top was no one of consequence before the war, though he rose fast in its aftermath."

Dalton shrugged. "One could argue the same of Blaine McFadden."

"Many a man has risen to power from such beginnings," Penhallow chided. "Among mortals, and even more, among *talishte*. Birth is a temporary advantage. Will, cleverness, and ruthlessness matter much more in the long run."

"Our scouts have told us a leader has emerged in Meroven," Dolan continued. "A general who goes by the battle name of Nagok has already sent raiding parties across the Donderath border, as spies."

"Nagok," Carlisle mused. "In the Meroven language, that means 'night.'"

"Nagok appears to have the loyalty of his troops," Dolan continued. "More of interest is that he also appears to have the help of powerful *talishte*."

"Thrane and the rogue Elders?" Penhallow asked sharply.

"Maybe," Dolan replied. "We haven't identified where all of the Elders went after that last meeting. "Other than Bayard, and those of you gathered here."

"We've had reports of Red being seen at Solsiden," Dalton said. "And Aubergine was originally from Meroven, as I recall, so having him decide to slip across the border to fight for their side wouldn't surprise me."

"But you're right—we have no idea where Sapphire, Jade, and the others are, other than not here," Jarett said, curling her lip. "So it's entirely possible that some of the Elders who sided with Thrane have gone to Meroven to line up allies."

Connor remembered the masked figures in the standing stone circle. Thirteen Elders, before the council disbanded. Seven had supported Thrane, and that still left Saffron, Amber, and Emerald unaccounted for. Six, including the Wraith Lord, were allied with Penhallow. Onyx and his brood had the solemn responsibility of assuring that Pentreath Reese remained bound in the oubliette beneath his manor.

"What of the Meroven *talishte*?" Carlisle asked. "They weren't governed by our circle of Elders."

"Meroven had its own Elder Council," the Wraith Lord replied. "On occasion, there would be a formal meeting between the leaders, so we could communicate."

"We were never apprised of that," Carlisle bristled.

The Wraith Lord turned to him, unfazed. "You did not need to know."

"Was the Cataclysm a sufficient enough 'problem' to initiate communication?" Dalton asked, not attempting to hide the edge in his voice.

"Yes," the Wraith Lord replied. "But our summons has gone unanswered. We have heard nothing."

"So they either have no intention of working with us or they were destroyed or disbanded," Carlisle said.

"That was my conclusion," the Wraith Lord said. "We can't count on help from that side." *And we don't know whether Thrane played a role in breaking up their Circle, like he did here,* Connor thought.

"So we're on our own, against the renegades from the Elders and their broods, as well as Thrane, his brood, and the armies of Pollard and Nagok," Carlisle summarized.

Penhallow nodded. "Now you see why I believed circumstances warrant use of the Elgin Spike."

Jarett, Carlisle, and Dalton exchanged glances. They did not speak, but their expressions conveyed grudging acquiescence. "To use the Elgin Spike, one would have to know where to find it," Dalton said quietly.

Penhallow and the Wraith Lord nodded. "Yes," Penhallow replied.

"You know," Jarett confirmed.

Penhallow raised an eyebrow. "I hid it."

Carlisle reddened with anger. "And we were not told?"

"The Elders could not be trusted with the knowledge," the Wraith Lord rumbled. "As we have seen, the Elders were of divided loyalties, even back then."

"You go too far, Kierken," Dalton challenged.

"On the contrary. It's only now that we finally have the will to go far enough," the Wraith Lord replied. Something about his power shifted, becoming larger and more potent, filling the space with an uncomfortable fullness, although the translucent form never changed its size.

Dalton felt the shift, and inclined his head. "I meant no offense, my lord."

Interesting, Connor thought. *Even now, when the Circle of Elders has been disbanded, they still defer to him.* It was not the first time that Connor had felt a frisson of sheer terror when he realized the enormous power of the ancient spirit he allowed to fill his mind and possess his body.

"How will you reclaim it?" Jarett asked.

"I intend to send a trusted team," Penhallow replied. "Connor and the Wraith Lord will lead them. Nidhud from the Knights of Esthrane will also go with them. And Blaine McFadden has already sent several of his best people, ones with special skills, to accompany the group: a far-seer, one of the former convicts, and two warriors who have been changed by the wild magic of the storms."

Zaryae, Connor thought. *Along with Borya and Desya. But where are we going?*

"You choose not to accompany them?" Dalton asked, raising an eyebrow.

Penhallow shook his head. "I dare not leave Donderath, especially without the Wraith Lord present. Thrane is dangerous enough, even without other allies. We are the bulwark to hold him back until the others can return."

"Meaning he'll need more than your lip service," the Wraith Lord snapped. "He'll need you on the battlefield, along with your broods, ready to put steel to flesh to back up your fancy words."

"Where is the Elgin Spike?" Jarett asked.

Penhallow met his gaze. "Edgeland. Where it has been for more than a century. In the care of my servant, Arin Grimur."

"Edgeland!" Connor's voice rose. "You're sending me up to Edgeland?" The rest of the Elders had gone, leaving only Connor, Penhallow, and the Wraith Lord. Dawn was not far off, which would end the conversation. Connor had plenty of questions before then.

"Edgeland was the safest place I could reach," Penhallow replied with a shrug. He poured a goblet of deer blood from a decanter and swirled it before taking a sip. "A century ago, it was a true wasteland. Velant did not exist, and neither did Skalgerston Bay."

"I thought Arin Grimur was exiled," Connor challenged.

"It was a convenient lie," the Wraith Lord replied.

Connor had met Arin Grimur when fate and a drifting, damaged ship landed him in Edgeland right after the Great Fire. Theirs had been one of the few refugee ships to find a safe harbor, if one could call Skalgerston Bay 'safe.' It had been then that Connor had met Blaine McFadden and his friends and gotten mixed up with McFadden's efforts to restore the broken magic. Arin Grimur had saved their lives, more than once.

"Do Zaryae and the others know where we're going?" Connor asked. Making one round trip to Edgeland and surviving it was already pushing his luck. The idea of a second such trip frightened him to his marrow.

"Perhaps not yet. Blaine and I agreed that the fewer who know in advance, the better for our chances of success. I left it up to Blaine how much to share and when," Penhallow replied. He poured a glass of real whiskey, one of the few bottles that remained from before the Great Fire, and handed it to Connor. "Drink. You'll feel better."

Connor let the whiskey burn down his throat, savoring the rare luxury. He doubted the contents of the entire bottle would dull his dread of returning to Edgeland. "You're just going to spring it on them when they get here?"

Penhallow chuckled. "If necessary. More likely, Blaine will tell them before that. Verran is also being asked to go, to reestablish trade with Edgeland," he said. "I've already gathered provisions for your trip: weapons, clothing, supplies, and a ship. Blaine is making sure you take plenty of highly desirable and useful goods to share with the colonists."

Connor frowned. "It's a month's trip one-way," he said. "I doubt even magic could change that. What happens here, while we're gone?"

"I work with Voss and McFadden to hold back whatever Thrane unleashes against us," Penhallow replied matter-of-factly. "Which is why Kierken is accompanying you and I am not."

Another thought occurred to Connor, and he frowned. "Does the *kruvgaldur* reach to Edgeland?"

"The *kruvgaldur* reaches you where you are," the Wraith Lord replied. "Alive or dead. And you think distance matters?"

"The last time I was in Edgeland, the bond seemed weak," Connor challenged.

Penhallow raised an eyebrow. "Much has happened in the time since then. How many times have you needed my blood to heal? Each time you take my blood, it binds you more tightly and strengthens the *kruvgaldur*."

Connor had some experience of his own with the 'alive or dead' part, and it had been his *kruvgaldur* bond and Penhallow's blood that had brought him back again. The thought of returning to Edgeland was terrifying, but less so knowing he would be going with friends and with the lifeline of the *kruvgaldur*.

"When do we leave?" Connor asked. It was easier to just begin planning than to dwell on the dangers.

"Verran and the others should arrive in the next few candlemarks. We're preparing the ship to leave in the next day or so," Penhallow replied. "Given the time it will take to get to you Edgeland and back, I don't think we dare delay."

Maybe it's better not to spend too much time thinking about it, Connor thought. *Still, it takes some getting used to.*

Two candlemarks later, the doors to the parlor opened to welcome five travelers. They were dusty with the grit of the road, dressed to attract as little attention as possible. Connor rose to meet them, genuinely pleased to see his friends again.

"So this is where you spend your time when you're not getting knocked flat on your ass." Verran Danning hooked his thumbs in the waist of his trews and looked around.

Connor clapped him on the shoulder in greeting. "Just don't make off with what's left of the silverware, all right?" he bantered.

Verran made a face at him. "That takes all the fun out of it," he said with a wicked grin.

Zaryae moved up to greet Connor with a hug. "We're just glad to be here in one piece," she said, giving him a friendly squeeze before she released him. "We ran into bandits on the way here."

"She means that we had some fun," Borya said.

"Rather more than we expected," Desya seconded. The twins reminded Connor of ravens, with their dark hair and somewhat prominent noses.

Connor and Penhallow exchanged a glance. "Do we need to dispatch troops?" Connor asked.

Borya chuckled. "You can't kill them deader than they already are," he replied. "Desya and I considered it a warm-up."

"After all, it's been a couple of weeks since we've been in a good, death-defying battle," Desya drawled sarcastically. "We were starting to get soft."

Nidhud was the last to enter. He was a stocky man who was no taller than Connor but built heavier, like a bull. His dark eyes showed the shrewdness of centuries of battle. Nidhud was one of the Knights of Esthrane assigned to support Blaine McFadden. "Apologies for our delay," Nidhud said. "We were unavoidably detained on the road."

"He means that we had to stop to muck out the stables—in a manner of speaking," Borya supplied with a smirk.

"Come in and sit down," Penhallow said, welcoming them. "I've sent word for food to be brought. You've come a long way. Rest."

Connor resisted the urge to blurt out what was on his mind. *Might as well rest now, because we're being shipped off to the end of the world in a few days.* Instead, he took a sip of his whiskey, then poured glasses of whiskey or brandy for the newcomers, who found seats near the darkened fireplace. It was late summer in Donderath, dramatically warmer than Edgeland's 'mildest' season. Connor tried to still his apprehension and focus on the moment, where he was safe, comfortable, and still on dry land.

Servants brought plates of rabbit with stewed parsnips, onion, and radishes. Borya and Desya dug in with their usual gusto. Zaryae sipped tea and picked at her food, while Verran savored his whiskey before starting on the hearty meal. Nidhud was content with a goblet of blood.

"How are Blaine and Kestel?" Connor asked, anxious for news.

"Still besotted with newlywed bliss, when they're not fighting a war," Verran replied with his mouth full.

"They're both doing well," Zaryae replied with a reproving glance at Verran and the twins, a look that was openly and pointedly ignored. "There's been trouble on the Solveigs' border with raiders from the west. Blaine and the twins just got back from fighting out there."

"And the fight—was it successful?" Penhallow asked, sipping a goblet of deer blood as the others ate.

Borya nodded and swallowed before answering. "Thanks to Bayard. With luck, the alliance will hold."

Verran finished his food and leaned forward. "So, can we talk about why I'm here? I understand requesting the others. They're actually good in a fight. But me? I'm only an amateur spy compared with someone like Kestel."

"Your music could send the enemy screaming in pain," Desya needled.

"Or surrendering to end the torment," Borya added before Zaryae elbowed him, hard, in the ribs.

Verran took the teasing good-naturedly. "See what I mean?"

Nidhud's expression had grown solemn. "Except that you're one of Blaine's original companions," he said quietly. "One of the Velant prisoners and Edgeland colonists. And of the original group, the easiest to spare from present responsibilities."

"Yeah, expendable," Verran said with a sigh. "Can't send Blaine, he's busy being a warlord. Can't send Kestel or Piran, because they're watching his back. Dawe's about to get married, and he's a lousy fighter anyhow. At least I can throw rocks. Dawe's likely to get himself captured even if we leave him in Donderath," Verran said, looking first to Connor and then to Penhallow. "Please tell us why you're sending us back to that icy godsforsaken place. Blaine wouldn't say—only told me what he wanted me to do when we got there." His gaze locked with Connor's. "Come on, Connor. You've been there. No reason at all for a sane man to go back."

Connor sighed. "Yes, I've been there. But you're the real expert. You lived with the people. They know you and trust you."

"I understand why you would not want to return," Penhallow said quietly. "And if there were another way, I would not risk your lives. But there's a weapon secreted away on Edgeland that might be our only chance to defeat Thrane. I not only need to send a team I trust to retrieve it, but they need to know the people and the place for the best chance of success."

"You mean, in order to have a prayer of surviving the trip," Verran replied, arching an eyebrow.

Penhallow gave a dry chuckle. "Yes, if you want to put it that way."

"What is it that we're supposed to find and bring back?" Desya asked, all trace of humor gone. His golden eyes were completely serious. "What do you consider to be worth our lives?"

Penhallow nodded, as if he had expected the question. "You are certainly right to ask. And when I tell you, I believe you'll understand why the item is so dangerous—and so important—that it has been worth Arin Grimur's voluntary exile for decades."

"Grimur?" Verran said, frowning. "He was the *talishte*-mage who lived way out on the ice, the one who had Valtyr's notebook."

Penhallow nodded once more. "Yes. Arin is one of mine. And he has kept a very lonely vigil over one of the most dangerous weapons in the world."

"I thought Grimur was exiled for killing mortals, or something like that," Verran countered.

"What kind of story would you create if you wanted your person to be left alone?" Penhallow replied.

Verran thought about that and then nodded. "I guess so. But what could possibly be so bloody important?"

"The means to kill a specific *talishte* and his entire bloodline," Penhallow replied.

Everyone except Nidhud sat for a moment in stunned silence. Connor noticed that Nidhud winced at the description, but did not look surprised. Although Connor had heard the earlier debate between Penhallow and the former Elders, they had not bothered to describe the Elgin Spike's purpose. Now he could understand why.

"Pardon my asking, but why in Raka do *talishte* have such a weapon for other *talishte*?" Verran asked, eyes wide.

"We often speak of the threat to *talishte* posed by mortals," Penhallow said finally. "For an older, stronger *talishte*, it might take a mob of mortals to make a killing strike. But two *talishte* of equal strength can destroy one of us all alone."

"Like wolves, fighting for territory," Borya said.

Penhallow nodded. "Something like that. The only thing a top predator has to fear is another top predator." He grimaced, as if speaking of such things bothered him deeply. *It's hardly the kind of thing a* talishte *talks about with mortals,* Connor thought. *For a good reason.*

"Does it actually work? The Elgin Spike?" Zaryae asked.

"The Spike is made of obsidian, layered with powerful magic," Penhallow replied. "It was created by mages long ago and thought lost, but then the Spike was found and presented as a way to put down the last *talishte* war. It passed through many hands, with dire consequences, before the *talishte* discovered its hiding place. At that point, the Spike was secreted away from the king's vaults."

He paused for a moment, staring into the blood in his glass. "By this point the Knights of Esthrane had already vanished, the Wraith Lord was a legend not seen in many years, and mortals had turned against us. I thought that the Spike was too much of a temptation, and worked with my allies to make it disappear once more. I sent Arin, who is both *talishte* and a mage, to guard it, for however long required." He gave a sad smile. "Don't feel too bad for Arin's 'exile.' He's been quite happy in Edgeland."

"How's he going to feel about being bothered now?" Connor asked. "As I recall, the only way we met him was because we nearly died in a blast of magic and an avalanche."

Borya looked at him, grinning. "Really? That's a great story. And it sounds like something that would happen, especially if Piran was there."

"So you intend to use the Spike to destroy Thrane and Reese and all their progeny? Do you think it will still work? After magic was lost, a lot of artifacts either didn't work or turned dangerous," Connor asked quietly. The potential for destruction was breathtaking, and for one *talishte* to consider wielding such a weapon against others meant that Penhallow and the Wraith Lord saw Thrane as a truly dangerous enemy.

"We can only hope—it was made long, long ago. But we believe it's worth the risk. Thrane is raising armies, both mortal and *talishte*," Penhallow replied. "And if he wins, he'll put Pollard on Donderath's throne—and I wouldn't doubt that he's promised Nagok the throne in Meroven."

"So you think that Thrane and a bunch of really old, really powerful *talishte* with big families are going to start slaughtering mortals?" Verran asked. "That's scary."

"Actually," Nidhud interrupted, "you've got it a bit wrong. Thrane and his supporters won't begin with the mortals. They will come after any *talishte* that dares to oppose them, and once we have been destroyed, there will be no one of equal strength to stop them from doing whatever they would like to the mortals."

Verran drew in his breath. "Well. You just managed to make something that was already terrifying so much worse."

"The Wraith Lord will go with you," Penhallow said. "He and Nidhud, along with Grimur, can protect the Spike against most threats. Remember, they're mages as well as *talishte*."

You might have been talishte *in your own body, but I draw the line at gnawing on someone's neck for the cause,* Connor warned the Wraith Lord silently.

He heard Kierken Vandholt's deep laughter, as if from a distance. *I have demanded a great deal from you, Bevin, but I have no desire to have you 'gnaw' on necks. I believe, should the circumstances warrant, Nidhud and Grimur will be quite capable of that.*

"Blaine and I chose you because you had the best set of skills for the task," Penhallow said.

"And we could be spared without anybody missing us too much," Verran added.

"If we succeed, it could be the decisive strike of the conflict, ending the war before it truly begins," Nidhud said.

"How and when?" Borya asked.

"We've outfitted the *Nomad*, the merchant ship Connor and Blaine sailed back from Edgeland, for the journey," Penhallow said. "The *Nomad* is seaworthy and can take all of you and the provisions easily. I've already outfitted the ship for the voyage. We don't want to take the chance that Thrane and his followers might guess our intent."

"There is a threat, but it's not Thrane," Zaryae said. They turned to look at her, and Connor knew from her glazed expression and the soft, distant tone of her voice that she was seeing a possible future. "There is no time to wait. Enemies approach."

Just then, the doors to the study opened. Dolan stepped in. "We need to rethink waiting to launch," he said tersely. "Scouts have spotted ships on the horizon. Pirates are the best of the possibilities. If they close the harbor, you won't be going anywhere."

"Gather your things," Penhallow said. "You'll sail as soon as Voss can gather the crew."

CHAPTER
SEVEN

H OW COME WE JUST GET RID OF ONE PROBLEM, and ten more pop up in its place?" Niklas Theilsson muttered his question to the wind, not really expecting an answer. He sat astride his warhorse, looking out over the windswept Northern Plains. In the distance, the Riven Mountains jutted skyward.

"I could have done without coming back here, after the battle." Ayers, Niklas's second-in-command, put words to what Niklas had just found himself thinking.

" 'Never' would have been too soon," Niklas agreed. Not far from here, Niklas had commanded Blaine McFadden's army against the forces of Pentreath Reese and Vedran Pollard in the Battle of Valshoa. Now, months and many battles later, Reese was imprisoned and what remained of Pollard's troops had been sent running with their tails between their legs. For now. Niklas had learned the hard way that no enemy should be counted out until the body was in its grave. And perhaps, not even then.

"They're vermin, compared with what we've fought before." Ayers's voice cut through Niklas's thoughts.

Niklas shrugged ill-humoredly. "Vermin can be dangerous, if there are enough of them and they're cornered," he observed. "And there are other things we should be doing, rather than hunting down a bunch of bandits and marauders." The list of other priorities was long and exhausting: Rebuild Quillarth Castle and the city of Castle Reach. Reinforce the seawall by the main harbor in Castle Reach, and rebuild enough of the shipworks to set about repairing the seaworthy vessels that had not burned or sunk in the Cataclysm. Help the farmers and the millers and the brewers with their work so that neither the army nor the people would go hungry. Even with an army at his disposal, the tasks were endless.

"Makes you wonder how bad it is in Meroven, if they're coming over here to raid," Ayers remarked.

Niklas nodded. "And from what Rikard and the other mages have been able to scry, I'd say it's every bit as bad as it is here, maybe worse." Even here, in the sparsely populated plains, the devastation from the Cataclysm and the Great Fire was unmistakable. Farms, barns, and houses, even whole towns, abandoned and in disrepair. Manor houses, burned and left to rot. Those who survived the fire and wild-magic storms, the magicked beasts and the Madness, packed up what they could carry and gathered together in small settlements farther south.

"I thought Castle Reach had a long way to go," Ayers said, eyeing the dilapidated, lifeless village ahead of them. "And then we come out here, and I realize how much there is to do before Donderath comes close to being where it was before."

"One foot in front of the other," Niklas replied. "Just like when we marched back from the war. At least now, everything's not on fire." Niklas had led a group of weary, wounded, and soul-sick survivors across war-torn Donderath after the Cataclysm. Their journey had taken months, foraging for food, dodging storms and magicked beasts. The devastation had been fresh, then. Walled cities and small farms still smoldering from the Great Fire. Starving livestock, feral dogs, and desperate men seemingly around every corner.

"Aye," Ayers agreed. "We've come this far. Perhaps we can roundly trounce the marauders, send a few survivors home to warn off the others, and go back to what we were doing."

Niklas gave a deep sigh. "I doubt it will be that simple."

Ayers shot him a wicked grin. "Neither do I, but we can dream, can't we?"

Five hundred men had ridden north with Niklas and Ayers from Castle Reach, leaving the bulk of the army to protect the city. Now, Niklas rode at the fore of a small team riding along the foothills to drive back bandit gangs.

"If there are brigands holed up in there, they're mighty cool about it, with us sitting out here, sizing them up for the taking," Ayers observed with a nod toward the silent village a few hundred yards away.

Niklas snorted. "What choice do they have? It's too open to make a run for it, too far to the mountains to find cover. They'll wait us out, hoping we'll ride on."

"Do you think they're mages?" Ayers asked, eyeing the village suspiciously. If the bandits had claimed the village for their own, they had taken pains to hide their presence well. No telltale hoof marks or footprints marked the southern approach. The buildings, worse for the wear after a year exposed to the elements with no one to maintain them, were dark and silent. There was no motion except for the wind through the tall grass.

"Not according to Rikard. Unless they've got mages good enough to hide themselves from ours," Niklas replied.

By now, Niklas's men had circled the decrepit village. Even before the Cataclysm, the tiny hamlet of Irkenford had been little more than a crossroads trading town. The inn had burned in the Great Fire, along with the barns in the fields on the outskirts of the village. Two dozen sod houses with damaged thatched roofs circled a center green with a silent bell tower that had somehow escaped the flames and storms.

The village was small, but Niklas still had no desire to fight a battle through its narrow streets. Even against a smaller force, a street fight could go wrong in too many ways, especially when the enemy had time to set up defenses and claim the territory for their own.

"Let's bring the bastards to us," Niklas said grimly. "Do it."

Rikard raised his hands, closed his eyes for a moment in concentration, and then made a gesture in the direction of the lifeless village. A bell rang, clanging as if a madman swung from its ropes.

"Fire!" Niklas shouted.

Archers let loose a volley of flaming arrows. The arrows stuck in the roofs, catching quickly on the dry thatch and spreading on the wind. Smoke rose from the rapidly burning buildings as the bell clanged on.

"Look there!" Ayers shouted, pointing as a figure stumbled from one of the deserted houses, barely dodging another round of arrows that drove him back inside under the burning roof.

Niklas glanced toward Rikard. Thin, prim, and fussy, the mage had once been in service of a noble house. Now, he had gained an unwanted amount of experience in battle magic, and despite his preferences for the relative safety of a workshop, he had turned out to be quite good at creating havoc under pressure.

"At least twenty of them, with horses." Alsibeth had moved up close enough to where she could speak without shouting. Rikard had an arsenal of handy tricks he could do with his power. Alsibeth was a seer, frighteningly accurate, so her abilities were best utilized behind the lines of battle.

"Can you see what kind of weapons they've got?" Niklas asked, never taking his eyes from the burning village.

"Nothing unusual," she replied.

"Here they come!" Ayers shouted.

"Let's go get them!" Niklas shouted, standing in his stirrups as he led the charge.

Riders on horseback streamed from their hiding places, whooping and shouting fiercely. Mounted archers returned the bow-fire, sending arrows back toward Niklas's men even as his soldiers tightened their circle around the raiders, giving them nowhere to run.

"Fire!" Niklas ordered, and another round of arrows shot toward the marauders. Three of the men fell from their mounts, arrows protruding from their chests. Still the raiders rode on, caught between their burning hiding place and the incoming soldiers.

The marauders fired volley after volley, but Rikard made another gesture, and the arrows dropped from the air and landed harmless on the ground. The riders veered away, only to be shunted back again by the tight circle of soldiers, who bided their time, in no hurry to engage with swords when magic and arrows could harry their enemy at a distance.

"Behind you!" Rikard's shout warned Niklas an instant before an arrow zinged past his ear. He turned to see a dozen more Meroven raiders riding hard toward them from the rear, swords out and bows at the ready.

"Where in Raka did they come from?" Ayers growled.

"Somewhere we overlooked," Niklas muttered. "Listen up!" he shouted to his soldiers. "Every other man, turn to face the rear. We've got trouble! The rest of you, hold the line!" Riding like storm winds, a second wave of raiders thundered toward them from behind.

Meroven had been known before the Cataclysm for having some of the finest horses on the Continent, bloodlines coveted and prized by kings and nobles. That blood showed in the fast, sleek horses the marauders rode, horses that had seen enough of battle not to shy away from the clang of steel or the battle howls of their riders. *These aren't mere brigands,* Niklas thought, even before he first crossed swords with one of the wild raiders.

Twenty men rode at Niklas and his soldiers fearlessly, swords gleaming in the sun, disciplined in their attack. Half of Niklas's men turned to fight the enemy behind them, while the others fended off the raiders trapped between them and the burning village.

"Leave some of them alive!" Niklas shouted to his men as they rode hard after their attackers. "I want to find out what they know!"

"You won't be alive to ask us." One of the raiders rode straight for Niklas, veering off only when Niklas lowered his long sword and braced it like a lance. They circled again warily, and this time, Niklas took the offensive, swinging his sword hard enough to hear the snap of bone as the blade connected with the rider's arm, slashing through flesh. He swung again, and this time, his sword took the man's head from his shoulders, and the body toppled slowly from the horse, blood covering the corpse and its mount.

A second rider was after him by the time he had barely cleared his sword from the last man's body. The marauder looked to be barely out of his teens, but he rode as if he were born to the saddle, and he carried the sword in his hand with practiced ease.

This rider made no grand challenge of headlong attack.

Instead, he made a swipe with his blade at Niklas's horse, a strike Niklas only barely deflected before it gutted his mount. Grinning with his near victory, the marauder turned and came at Niklas again, looking for a weak point.

The raiders wore no uniform. As with Niklas's men, it was enough in these years after the Cataclysm to have clothes. Yet each wore a woven armband around his left arm, made of rope and fashioned with bits of stone and metal. Niklas had no idea whether it was a talisman or a symbol of the riders' group, but it marked them as a team, as did the black kerchiefs they wore loosely tied around their necks.

Before the raider could strike again, Niklas bellowed a cry and rode straight for him, and the sudden reversal of tactics threw the marauder off, just for a second. That was all the time Niklas needed to make his charge, swinging his blade to catch his opponent in the left shoulder, severing the arm with one blow. Grievously wounded, thrown off balance, the rider scarcely got his sword raised before Niklas cleaved him shoulder to hip.

The fight had turned. Niklas dared not look behind him, but more and more of the men who had held the perimeter against the raiders in the burning village now joined the skirmish against the new arrivals. Two of the raiders tried to turn tail and ride away, but Niklas's men easily rode them down. The marauders' numbers were waning, and Niklas saw only minor casualties among his own men.

"Remember, leave a few for me!" Niklas shouted. Dead or dying riders littered the ground. The tall, swaying grasses had been trampled down and sprayed with blood. Only two of the riders remained, and as Niklas watched, his men made short work of them, running one through and knocking the other from his mount with a deep gash to his thigh and a partly severed left arm.

"That's all of them." Rikard rode toward Niklas with Alsibeth close behind. Niklas turned toward the village, and saw nothing but smoke and corpses.

"How in Raka did we miss the second half of their men?" Ayers demanded, still flushed from the fight. He had a bloody gash on one arm, and was sprayed with enough blood that for a moment, Niklas feared Ayers had taken a serious wound before he realized his second was covered in the gore of his enemies.

"We didn't see them because they weren't here," Rikard replied matter-of-factly. "There was no one close. My guess is that they happened into us, perhaps scouting farther afield and returning to base."

Ayers thought about it for a moment, then gave a curt nod. "Could have happened like that, I suppose," he ventured.

"Geir said he'd join us after he took care of some business with Penhallow at Glenreith. I want him to read the survivors, see what we can learn," Niklas said.

"We'll find the least injured, see if we can patch them up long enough to live until nightfall," Ayers replied. "I'll take care of it."

Niklas looked to two other soldiers who were within hearing range. "You there. Gather up any horses you can find that the raiders left behind. Those are good mounts, and we're in need of some."

The soldiers headed off, and Niklas eyed the burning village. "Pity we can't get closer, see if there's anything we could learn from their camp." The flaming arrows had torched the thatched roofs of the closest buildings, but the fire had spread quickly in the dry summer heat, so that most of the structures were now ablaze.

"Every tactic is a trade-off," he sighed. "I can't complain. We would likely have lost more men if we'd had to fight them house to house."

"Any doubt about where they came from?" Ayers asked with a knowing glint in his eyes.

Niklas shook his head. "None at all. They fought like Meroven and they looked like Meroven. Gods above! I had hoped never to see one of those bloody bastards again in all my life."

"Let's get the prisoners situated, and get back," Niklas said. "I want to be in camp before nightfall, in case the raiders have more friends along the way."

Niklas watched as his men looted the dead and dying raiders for any weapons or supplies that might be useful. In a 'regular' war, such behavior was held in contempt. But the reality of Donderath's reduced circumstances had elevated scavenging to an art. *Make it do or do without,* Niklas thought with a sigh.

One of the raiders lay nearby, his chest still rising and falling as the man struggled for breath. A sword had taken him through the abdomen, and his entrails spilled out in a slick, stinking mass beside him. Niklas drew his sword and approached cautiously.

"Tell me what you know, and I'll give you a quick death," he offered.

The raider looked up at him, eyes shocky and unfocused. "What I know?"

"Why you're here. Who sent you? What you came for."

"Food," the man gasped. "Anything...we could carry. Not much left. Heard it wasn't...quite as bad here."

Niklas let out a short, bitter bark of a laugh. "You heard wrong," he replied. *Then again,* he thought, *he had no idea how bad things were on the Meroven side of the border.*

"Who sent you?"

"Captain..."

"You must have a commander, a warlord, someone in charge—"

"Nagok," the man gasped. His color was bad, pale and sweaty, lips faintly blue, eyes wide and white.

"Who is Nagok?" Niklas pressed, but this time, the man's lips worked like a fish out of water, and a rattling breath was the only answer he received. Honoring his word, Niklas brought his sword down like a stake through the heart. The man shuddered and went still.

"We've got five men who might live through the trip back," Ayers said, walking up and eyeing the scene as Niklas withdrew his bloody sword and wiped it on the dead man's cloak. "No guarantees. If we lose a couple of them, there will still be some left to interrogate. But Geir had better hurry. None of them are in good shape."

"Kill the rest of the wounded," Niklas ordered. He had long ago lost any compunction about killing in battle. But there was nothing to gain by leaving men to suffer or face predators in their dying hours. He could spare them that, at least.

"Aye, sir," Ayers said with a nod, and turned to shout the order.

Alsibeth came up beside Niklas so quietly that he startled and nearly drew his sword. "What do you make of it?" he asked her.

"I see...edges of a larger whole," she replied. "The hem of a garment. The point of a sword. Waves, as they break on the sand."

"What does that mean?" Niklas pressed.

"We don't see the whole, only the parts," Alsibeth replied, her voice dreamy and unnerving. "The tide is coming."

"Tide?" Niklas asked.

Alsibeth sighed and shook her head. "I can't tell you more, at least, not right now," she said, chagrined. "It's not like reading the answers from a book. More like stealing a glance at a tally with some parts smudged and other parts covered up ... hard to put the pieces together until you have more information, and then, it's sometimes too late."

That's a cheery thought. "So there's something bigger to come? Something bigger in the works?"

She shrugged. "I'm sorry. That's all I can see. But if I had to guess—and guessing can be dangerous when information is missing—I'd say that the riders are more than they appear. Spies maybe, or scouts. I don't know just yet."

Niklas nodded, reining in his frustration. "If you get any amazing insights in the middle of the night, wake me up and tell me, will you?"

Alsibeth managed a tired smile. "I will remember that, General."

The ride back to camp seemed longer than Niklas remembered it. A supper of trail rations awaited them, but he was too hungry to quibble about the menu.

"For once, you brought the troops back in reasonable condition," Ordel, the senior healer, said a few candlemarks later when he stopped by to provide a status report. "Patched up some gashes and cuts, a few bruises and scrapes, but on the whole, not too bad."

Niklas nodded, and waved him into his tent. Ordel stepped inside, and Niklas brought a bottle of amber liquid from a trunk at the end of his cot. The tent held only necessities, not even his folding table or campaign chair, which were back at the main base at Arengarte. He preferred having less to strike and set up when they were on the move, but the sparse amenities made him long for the few personal items he left behind.

Niklas sighed. The raiders almost certainly were going to be a more difficult problem than he had hoped. It might be quite a while before he saw his tattered 'luxuries' again. "Have a nip?"

Niklas asked, holding up the bottle. There wasn't enough whiskey in the world to take the edge off life in postwar Donderath, but it helped, a little.

Ordel nodded and took a swig. "They're getting better at distilling whatever goes into that stuff," he said with a nod. Wine had disappeared with the vineyards after the war. Ale depended on surplus grain, and last winter the devastation of the farm fields and the lack of men to work them made for hungry bellies and little left over. Then there was the 'whiskey' or 'brandy'—any drinkable concoction that could be distilled from whatever was on hand. Raw, potent, and sometimes dangerous, it would have to do until more stable times led to more reliable distilling.

Niklas shrugged. "It works. No one's gone blind or died, and that stuff gives such a nasty headache that it's sufficient warning to mind how much you drink."

"We managed to keep two of your five captives alive. The others were too far gone to save." He raised an eyebrow. "Do I need to tell you that my healers take a dim view of saving people just so they can be blood-read and then executed?"

Niklas sighed and looked away. "I take a dim view of it myself," he admitted. "Just not sure what alternatives we have. Bad enough if these raiders are just separate bandit gangs. They still require men and resources that could be used elsewhere, and our soldiers can be killed by bandits the same as by warlords."

"You're afraid there's more to it," Ordel replied. He wasn't a soldier, but he had lived among soldiers long enough to think like one.

Niklas took another slug from the flask, then carefully set it out of reach. "Yep. Alsibeth suspects so, too. And with raiders harrying the western side of the kingdom over by the Solveigs, it could take us a while to secure the borders."

"During which you're not fortifying Castle Reach and helping plant and harvest crops," Ordel supplied. Niklas nodded.

"Too many threats, not enough of us to go around. And you know that, sooner or later, Reese and Pollard are going to show up again," Niklas said.

Ordel looked over his shoulder at the dimming light just visible through the slit in the tent door. "It'll be dark soon."

Niklas nodded. "Geir knows how to find us." Left unsaid was just how tired he was of fighting, how weary he had become of killing. He did not have to put it into words, Ordel knew, and shared the feeling. Niklas listened as Ordel made his report. Just as he finished, Ayers rapped on the tent pole in lieu of a door and stuck his head inside. "We're past sundown," he said. "Geir's arrived."

Niklas and Ordel exchanged a look and got to their feet, following Ayers from the tent. Ayers had cleared a tent to give them a private space to interrogate the two bloodied men, who sat bound to poles in the ground.

"Good hunting today, I see," Geir said.

"Tolerably good," Niklas allowed. "Problem is, we've had repeated attacks by raiders coming across the Meroven border. This group we fought today was too professional to be brigands. What I'd really like to know is, are they scouts? And if so, who's the real enemy?"

Geir nodded. "And questioning in the usual manner revealed nothing?" Niklas knew that Geir disliked forcibly reading a captive's blood. He was willing to use his *talishte* abilities to aid their cause, but he had already made it clear that he was not a weapon to be wielded as they pleased.

"By the time we had the ability to ask questions, they were already in bad shape," Niklas said. "They fought hard, to their credit. But I need to know what I'm up against, if I'm to make the best decisions for Blaine on where the troops deploy."

"Then let's see what we can find out," Geir said. He walked toward the prisoner nearest him. The man appeared dazed, and Niklas wondered whether Ordel had dosed both prisoners with mild sedatives, something innocuous to *talishte*, to spare the men pain and fear.

"Do you know where you are?" Geir said quietly, bending down to one knee so that he could look the first captive in the eyes.

"Prisoner," the man mumbled. "Donderath."

"Very good." Geir's voice was languorous and comforting, and Niklas knew from having watched the process before that once Geir met the prisoner's eyes and used his *talishte* ability to compel cooperation, the prisoner would tell Geir anything he knew.

"Answer a few questions, and then you can rest," Geir said in a honeyed tone that made the man relax against his bonds, gaze fixed on Geir with a vacantly hopeful expression.

"Yes," the man slurred. "Questions."

"Why did you come to Donderath?"

The man sat slack-jawed for a moment, as if it took longer for him to retrieve the memories. "They said there would be food, weapons, cattle, women," he replied, his voice vague and dreamlike.

"Who said?"

"Commander."

Geir gave the prisoner a patient smile. "Were the cattle for you or for your commander?"

"Gather, for troops."

Niklas frowned. Geir, however, remained smiling at his compliant prisoner. "How many troops?"

"Lots."

Geir glanced toward Niklas, who nodded. When Geir turned back to the man, he met the prisoner's gaze. "You're going to rest now. Sleep soundly," he said with compulsion. "Feel no pain." The badly injured man slumped in his seat, eyes closed, fast asleep. Geir took his left wrist and lifted it, palm up, to his mouth. He made a clean bite, and drank slowly from the man's blood.

The other prisoner had been turned so that he could not see. "What's going on?" the second man cried out with as much energy as he had left. "What's he doing? Oh gods! What are you doing?"

After a few moments, Geir lifted his head and laid the man's wrist back on his lap. Not a fleck of blood remained on his lips. Niklas moved to speak, but Geir shook his head and moved around to where the second prisoner sat. "Sleep," he said quietly, and the worried prisoner relaxed, leaning forward in his bonds, head lolling. Once again, Geir drank from the man's wrist, stopping while the prisoner was still breathing, though both captives had paled, and the first man's lips were tinged with blue.

Finally, Geir stood up and turned to the others. "Both men are dying," he said quietly. "They bleed inside." He looked to Ordel. "I would consider it a personal favor if your healers can give them a deep sleep from which they do not wake."

Ordel nodded. "We can do that."

"Thank you."

Niklas had seen Geir fight in battle, watched him snatch enemy commanders from their horses and rip them limb from limb in the air to terrify their troops. Yet he also understood

Geir's distaste for killing, especially when the victims no longer posed a threat. As if he guessed Niklas's thoughts, Geir raised his head and looked at him.

"I've done much worse," Geir replied to the unspoken comment with a bitter smile. "But I prefer to choose from whom I feed, and to do so without killing when it can be avoided."

"I'm sorry for the circumstances," Niklas replied. "But it was the only way we'll find out what's really going on across the border."

Geir nodded. "And this time, it was for the best. I was able to read what the men had seen, even if they did not understand the import of what they witnessed. Their thoughts are focused on filling their bellies and bringing back cattle—or women—as spoils. But they are part of a much larger whole. Large enough to warrant being called an army."

"And their commander?" Niklas pressed.

Geir thought for a moment. "Their commander is not the real power. He reports to someone else, who also reports upward. A chain of command, to the warlord Nagok. The prisoner wasn't telling the whole truth about looking for spoils to carry home. Some of his missions have been spying, to uncover conditions on this side of the mountains and report back."

"So the raiders are carrying tales back to someone with a bigger army," Niklas summarized. "A warlord," Niklas added. "Damn."

"I'm afraid there's more," Geir added. "The prisoners have only seen the warlord at a distance. They are too unimportant to know more about his plans. But I saw the rally, where the men glimpsed their lord. He had *talishte* advisers."

CHAPTER EIGHT

"*TALISHTE* DID THIS—TO OTHER *TALISHTE*?" BLAINE asked, aghast at the destruction. He stood in the middle of an old cemetery that looked as if it had been the target of a massive lightning strike.

"What do you think?" Malin Jarett's voice was icy, and there was no missing the sarcasm.

"I think that whoever did this used magic," Blaine replied evenly, sensing the residue of power. "But that doesn't prove that they were—or weren't—*talishte*."

"Do you know of anyone with powerful mages who's out to kill *talishte* right now?" Jarett asked, clearly annoyed. "This is Thrane's doing—I'm certain of it. He and the rogue Elders are going after the broods of any *talishte* who refuses to align with him, or who aligns with Penhallow."

The graveyard held dozens of cairns and stone vaults. Most of those vaults lay broken and soot-streaked, their pieces scattered across the scorched ground. In places, individual graves and larger burial mounds had been dug into or blasted open.

"With the Great Fire, we lost the crypts that sheltered us beneath the manor houses," Jarett said. "Now we make do with what we can find, even if that means taking refuge in places like this, since tunnels and caves aren't always an option."

"I'm not sure how my army can protect your people from this," Blaine said, staring out across the devastated burying yard. "Not unless you plan to gather them in one place, which would increase your risk." He shook his head. "There are hundreds of graveyards across Donderath. We can't possibly station troops and mages at each one."

"I know that," Jarett snapped. "And believe me, asking for mortal help sticks in my craw. But my people have to take their day-rest somewhere, and while there's danger having a group in the same burying grounds, there's also a risk to going off alone."

"You believe Thrane is using mortals to attack during the day?" Blaine asked.

Jarett nodded. "I know he is. Cowardly, but true. He's saving his broods for real fighting, after he's done everything he can to reduce our numbers."

Blaine looked out across the countryside. Nature had already begun the work of repairing what was damaged by the Great Fire and the wild storms. Last year, when Blaine and his friends returned to Donderath, the land and its villages looked storm-torn, burned, and blasted. Now, at least some of the fields were green with crops, livestock with their young grazed in pastures, and villagers set about repairing the damage to their homes and barns. *If Thrane has his way, it will all be for naught,* Blaine thought.

"All right," Blaine replied. "If you can gather your broods into no more than half a dozen locations, we can guard them during the day." Jarett looked pleased, and moved to speak. "But," Blaine cut in, "in exchange, Niklas and I need more *talishte* fighters with the army, especially if Thrane is going to wipe out anyone who challenges his schemes. Today it's the Elders. But he'll come after us, too, since we're the only real mortal counterweight left."

"You want *talishte* soldiers to fight under mortal commanders?" Malin sounded like she had a bad taste in her mouth.

"You want mortals to defend your *talishte* broods against attackers, and possibly get caught up in a *talishte* civil war?" Blaine countered. "We're your only option. Traher Voss has his hands full keeping Castle Reach in check and patrolling the coast for pirates. The other mortal warlords are dead—or working for Thrane."

"All right," she said grudgingly.

"That's not all," Blaine replied. "You'll help us select twelve locations with suitable day crypts."

"But you said—"

Blaine held up a hand to forestall her protest. "We're only going to use a half a dozen at a time. Every night, different locations, identically guarded. The decoy locations will be just as diligently guarded, except that we'll be using real mages where the *talishte* are, and stand-ins at the other sites. Make it a shell game and bet that Thrane doesn't have enough mortals or mages to just attack them all, all at once. The more decoy sites we have, the better, but we can't afford to tie up too much of the army when there are Meroven raiders to fight."

Malin looked thoughtful. "It could work," she replied. "*Talishte* are notoriously difficult to organize. We don't like taking orders. But after the losses we've suffered," she said, with a gesture that took in the ruined burying yard around them, "I think they may listen to reason."

"Survival is a big incentive," Blaine said. "We can't protect *talishte* who choose not to stay with the group."

Malin nodded. "I'll propose it. I believe the other Elders will agree." She paused. "We'll need some additional soldiers to help us hunt and strike at Thrane's broods during daylight. You have Penhallow's word they will not be needlessly endangered."

"I'll hold him to it," Blaine said evenly. "My men aren't expendable."

Malin gave Blaine an appraising look. "We will honor Penhallow's promise. I can see why he speaks well of you." With that, Malin vanished into the darkness.

"Well, that was interesting," Captain Tonnerson observed drily as he and Blaine walked back to where they had left their horses and the other soldiers. Tonnerson was the commander Blaine intended to leave in charge of protecting cemeteries while he headed to the battle with Nagok. "Makes you wonder, when the big bad *talishte* Elders need help from the likes of us."

Blaine grimaced. "Not really any different, I guess, than kings and nobles needing protection from soldiers who came from the same villages as the people they wanted to be protected from."

Tonnerson was quiet for a while. "Want to bet Hennoch's soldiers are carrying out the attacks?" he said finally.

"I was thinking the same thing." Blaine smiled grimly. "Maybe he's just grateful not being sent to attack Mirdalur again."

Tonnerson guffawed. "Yeah, that didn't work out too well. How many times has it been now that he's been sent home with his tail between his legs? At least three."

Blaine nodded. "Don't underestimate him. We had superior forces—the Knights of Esthrane and the mages—and when he came after us at the Citadel, we had troops from the Solveigs and Verner, too." He swung up into his saddle. "Hennoch's gotten reinforcements, and new mages. Even Penhallow's a little worried about what Thrane's planning."

Tonnerson slid a sideways glance in Blaine's direction. "Worried? Or just duly concerned?"

Blaine hesitated, thinking about the conversation at Glenreith. "He and the Wraith Lord are taking the threat very seriously. I suspect he's had enough experience to know things can easily go wrong."

The next day, Blaine, a team of twenty soldiers, and a mage waited at a dilapidated graveyard not far from the ruins of a deserted old manor. This once-grand home had been deserted long before the Great Fire. Whether it had been abandoned because its owner's fortunes declined or because of some other personal tragedy, Blaine could not recall. Wherever the living had gone, they had left their dead behind in a sad, overgrown burying yard.

Blaine guarded a site where the *talishte* had actually gone to ground. Tonnerson watched over a decoy cemetery. The twelve burying yards Malin and the Elders had selected stretched from the Wraith Lord's manor at Lundmyhre to Westbain, where Penhallow headquartered his troops. Those locations were close enough to where Blaine and Niklas had camped their forces that the soldiers could be called back on short notice if there was an attack.

A noise made Blaine suddenly wary. He had hidden his men throughout the cemetery, behind cairns and bramble thickets, in the deep shadows around tall trees and alongside the crumbling stone vaults. Now, the sounds of hoofbeats heading their way was their signal to watch and wait, ready for a fight.

From where Blaine was hidden behind one of the larger cairns, he could glimpse the attackers' approach. Fifteen men on horseback were heading for the abandoned cemetery. They wore patches on the sleeves of their coats, marking them as Hennoch's soldiers, though what Blaine could see of their armor looked as if it had been pieced together from bits taken on the battlefield.

"This is the place," the leader said, gesturing for the others to stop. "Let's get to it. We've got three of these to hit today, and I want to make sure we're gone by late afternoon."

The men dismounted, leaving their horses loosely tethered near the road. They spread out, and Blaine was sure their first target would be the large cairn at the center of the graveyard. He waited until the enemy soldiers were well into the burying ground before he gave a clear, sharp whistle.

A curtain of crackling energy shot up from the tall grass, where Blaine's mage laid a circle to ward the tombs. In the next second, a sudden blast of wind hit with enough force to pick up half a dozen of the men and hurl them into the white-hot current. The raiders screamed as the flame consumed them, twisting and struggling against the power that held them helpless as their flesh sizzled and burned away until nothing but blackened bones remained.

The surviving soldiers cried out in alarm, searching for a way to strike back at their unseen enemy. Blaine's bowmen rose from the tall grass and let their arrows fly. Mage Aron's wardings permitted their spelled arrows to fly through the force-curtain, while repelling incoming missiles. So long as they remained within the warding, the raiders could not reach Blaine's soldiers or the cairns where their *talishte* patrons slept.

The enemy fighters who had not been swept into the energy-curtain turned and ran. One man stayed behind, his expression grim and determined. He raised his arm, palm out, and shouted a word of power as Blaine's archers targeted him, sending three arrows aimed for his heart. With a wave of his hand he batted the arrows out of the air, and in the next moment, a torrent of blue fire streaked toward Aron's force-curtain. For a few seconds, the blue fire vied against the white current, until the force-wall began to buckle, sparking and buzzing as the warding struggled to hold against the attack.

With a roar, the force-curtain fell, and the blue fire streaked past its boundary to hit a small cairn in a burst of fire. Flames engulfed the mound of stones, heating them white-hot, until the entire tomb exploded in a spray of splintered rocks. The attackers turned and gave a battle cry, charging toward the scorched line in the grass where the warding had been. In the same breath, more arrows flew, striking the mage in the shoulder and chest as his attention was diverted. Badly wounded but not yet dying, the mage snarled a curse and readied for another attack.

Aron reached up overhead, shouted a word of power, and brought both clenched fists down with all his strength. A heavy branch in a tall tree near the enemy mage came crashing down, knocking the wizard to the ground.

The mage struggled to one knee and brought his right hand palm down in a sweeping motion. Six of Blaine's men fell as if poleaxed, to lie motionless in the tall grass. Blaine ran at the mage, and as the outflow of power left the magic-user weakened, Blaine's sword whistled through the air, angled for the mage's throat. A strangled cry was all the wizard had time to make before the blade bit into his neck, but as the sword cut through flesh and bone, an arc of blue fire flashed from the mage's hand, though his aim went wide, deflected by Blaine's amulet. The mage's body swayed, blood fountaining down, and toppled forward, to lie facedown in the dirt.

Blaine turned, sword in hand, as more enemy fighters headed his way. His own soldiers surged forward to join him. The raiders eyed the oncoming line of soldiers and turned to flee, but while the mages had been battling, several of Blaine's men had slipped around behind, cutting the retreating fighters off from their horses.

Blaine swung his sword, venting his frustration on the raider, who found himself caught between two lines of attackers. Hennoch's soldier growled a curse, squaring off to fight since retreat was impossible. Blaine pressed forward with a series of strikes meant to set his opponent on the defensive, and the man returned the strikes with force and skill. It was a more even match than Blaine expected, and he recalculated his next move, relying on the flicker of magic that warned him a few breaths before his enemy struck. That instinct served him well as he dodged at the last second, barely missing a thrust meant to eviscerate him.

His opponent had been so sure of making a kill that he left himself open. Very much alive, Blaine seized the opportunity, delivering one pounding blow after another before he dove forward, slipping his blade between his attacker's ribs.

Blaine shoved the man hard, driving the sword hilt-deep into his chest, so that the fighter's quivering body hung suspended from the sword blade, his toes barely touching the ground. The raider gave one final spasm, stiffened with a groan, and then slumped forward, dead.

"That was the most suicidal thing I've seen someone do in a long time." Blaine turned to see Aron standing behind him, glowering. "You ran at a mage—a damn powerful mage—with a sword. Do you have a death wish?"

The battle was over. One empty cairn had taken a direct hit, but the rest of the burying yard was undamaged. Bodies littered the trampled grass, but Blaine was relieved to see that nearly all belonged to the enemy forces. Blaine sighed, and returned his attention to Aron. "No, I don't have a death wish. I have an amulet that deflects magic."

Aron moved closer, frowning suspiciously. "May I see it?"

Blaine removed the amulet on its leather strap from beneath his tunic. "Rikard and his mages created it," he said, holding the piece where Aron could get a good look.

Aron held out one hand, palm facing the talisman, and concentrated. He met Blaine's gaze and raised an eyebrow. "You got lucky this time," he snapped. "Amulets don't hold magic of that caliber forever, and I'm betting this isn't the first battle you've used it in. I wouldn't trust it against a powerful strike again."

Blaine let out a long breath. "Point taken," he conceded, tucking the charm back into his tunic. "And the next time, I want more archers. If we had taken their mage down with arrows, we could have saved ourselves a lot of problems. What about the men who got hit by whatever their mage did?"

Aron gave a lopsided smile. "Our men are in better shape than their men, I guarantee it." Together, he and Blaine walked over to where the six men had been felled by the enemy mage's magic. The men were just waking up, struggling for consciousness, but appeared otherwise unhurt.

"Are they damaged?" Blaine asked. Aron knelt next to the nearest man and examined the soldier, then shook his head.

"After I clipped their mage with that branch, he didn't have the strength to put a lot into his next move," Aron replied. "He knocked them out, that's all. Beyond some bruises, they'll be all right."

Blaine rose and headed toward where two soldiers regarded the charred remains of the enemy fighters who had been burned by Aron's protective warding. "Damn," Blaine said in an awestruck voice. Little was left of the men except for heaps of charred bones. "I'm glad he's on our side," he muttered.

"What do you want us to do with the rest of the bodies?" a soldier asked, with a nod toward the bodies that lay scattered around the empty cemetery.

"Leave them as a warning for the next ones Hennoch sends," Blaine replied. "Put them in a heap for the crows."

Three days later, Blaine returned to the main camp, leaving the cemeteries protected by his soldiers. The hectic preparations for battle did not quiet down until tenth bells. Blaine took his dinner in his tent. His campaign tent held few furnishings: a cot, a folding desk, a collapsible wooden chair, a trunk, and a small iron brazier, along with a stained carpet that covered the ground. It was enough to provide minimal comfort yet provide as small a burden as possible to move. He had barely finished eating when Niklas poked his head through the tent flap.

"Open for company? I brought whiskey," Niklas said, holding up a well-worn flask. Blaine waved him in, and Niklas found a seat on the floor on the other side of the small brazier that warmed a pot of tea and kept the night chill at bay. "Here—you look like you could use a slug," he said, removing the cap from the flask and passing it to Blaine.

Blaine knocked back a mouthful of the raw whiskey and handed the flask back. "Not bad," he said. "And I brought you another bottle from Glenreith."

"Much appreciated," Niklas replied, taking a swig himself. "Fortunately, things here were quiet while we were gone," he added, letting the rough liquor burn down his throat. "That's not going to last for long."

"At least that shell game at the cemeteries should protect the Elders and their broods and tie up Hennoch's soldiers for a while," Blaine said. "If the *talishte* really are intent on having a civil war, they're on their own. Not much we can do to help Penhallow—when *talishte* fight *talishte*, mortals are outclassed."

"I remember," Niklas replied drily. They had both been in enough battles to have seen just what *talishte* could do in a fight. Even a handful of *talishte* fighters deployed against strategic mortal targets could turn the outcome of a battle. Supernaturally strong and fast, and with some of them able to fly, *talishte* were formidable warriors. It was frightening to think about two *talishte* forces arrayed against each other, fighting at their full capacity. Few mortals who witnessed such a spectacle lived long enough to tell the tale.

"Don't worry—you'll have your hands full here," Niklas continued. "Between Hennoch staging strike-and-hide attacks on our flanks and the Meroven raiders, we're glad to have the additional soldiers."

Blaine filled Niklas in on the battle with the Plainsmen and the new alliance, as well as most of what Penhallow and the Wraith Lord had disclosed at Glenreith, everything except for the part about being king. Niklas passed the flask around again, and Blaine felt the whiskey's warmth relax muscles sore from the fight.

"We still don't know much about Nagok, the Meroven warlord," Niklas said. "He's still pretty much of a mystery. And I'm glad you brought more mages with you. We've been having a lot of wild-animal attacks—many more than usual."

Blaine raised an eyebrow. "You need a mage to take care of badgers and wolves?"

Niklas gave him a look. "Only when those badgers and wolves stop acting like wild animals and seem to be controlled—by someone."

"Controlled? Are you sure?"

Niklas nodded. "We are now. At first, we couldn't believe

that the animals might be acting with purpose—at least more purpose than scavenging our garbage or getting into the camp kitchen supplies. But the attacks are too frequent, and the animals are too aggressive."

"No one's provoking them? Baiting them?" Blaine asked. Niklas shook his head. "And your mages haven't figured out who's doing it?"

Niklas shook his head. "Not yet. And that's worrisome. The mages say controlling wild animals isn't easy. It's not something most magic-users can do, even if they're powerful, because it's hard to control more than one animal at a time, and almost impossible over any distance."

Blaine met his gaze. "So you think whoever's behind the attacks—Nagok or someone else—has a mage with a talent for beast calling?"

"Uh-huh," Niklas replied. "As if we needed more trouble than we already have, and a *talishte* war on top of everything."

For a few moments, they sat in silence. Finally, Niklas looked up. "Do you ever think about what's going to happen after the fighting stops?"

Blaine sighed. "I'm usually so busy trying to stay alive, I've got to admit I haven't made a lot of long-range plans." He smiled. "Except for marrying Kestel."

Niklas chuckled. "Kestel can help make sure you stick around for the long run. I'm surprised she isn't with you."

"She's coming to join us with Rinka Solveig and her troops," Blaine replied.

Niklas was quiet for a moment. "Back to the question. Assuming we live through all the fighting, what then?"

Blaine sighed and leaned back against his cot. "Go back to Glenreith, I guess. There's so much rebuilding to do, at the manor, the villages, Castle Reach. We've got a long way to go."

"What of Donderath?" Niklas asked. "Once we get rid of the rival warlords and the rogue *talishte*. What then? Divide up the Continent among the allies? How does that work—especially in a generation or two from now?"

Blaine shifted uncomfortably. "What are you getting at?"

Niklas gave Blaine a direct look. "Donderath needs a king, someone who honestly cares about rebuilding and who can be trusted not to loot what's left. Someone who can rally support if we're attacked. A leader." He paused. "Do I need to spell it out? None of the other warlords have everything that a good king needs—except for you." Niklas set his jaw as if he expected Blaine to push back, and looked surprised when his comment did not bring a quick denial.

"Penhallow and Geir made a special trip to Glenreith to try to convince me of the same thing," Blaine said with a sigh. "Kestel and Piran agreed with them."

"And are you convinced?"

Blaine looked away. "I never even cared about being Lord of Glenreith. I certainly didn't come back to Donderath to seize the throne."

"No one's saying that you did," Niklas replied. "In fact, it's pretty clear that you don't want it, which perversely means that you're probably the best person to give it to." He managed a wry smile. "None of the other warlords could rally enough support to take the crown without a fight—and possibly a civil war." He gestured toward the land beyond the walls of the tent. "Regular people aren't soldiers. They don't take orders. They have to be led. You could be a great king, Blaine."

Blaine looked back at his friend. "You've known me since we were kids—and you can still say that?"

"I'm not the only one," Niklas replied. "The men speak well of you, and more than once there's been speculation about a someday king." He met Blaine's gaze. "You always come up as the favorite."

Blaine sighed. "We've got a lot to survive before anyone should start measuring for a crown."

"I'll grant you that," Niklas agreed, taking one more swig from his flask and passing the last of the whiskey to Blaine. "But think about it this way. You've gone through more than anyone else to try to get Donderath back on its feet. Could you really just go back to Glenreith and let someone else run things, especially if it didn't go well?"

Blaine tossed back the whiskey. Niklas did not need a reply; he knew Blaine too well for that. *He's right, and so is Penhallow. I'd never be able to stand by and let someone wreck what we've worked so hard to build. But... king? That's going to take some getting used to.*

"Sleep on it. There's time to think things through—but don't rule it out, all right?"

"I won't—but until we're rid of raiders and rogue *talishte*, I've got bigger things to worry about."

Niklas left shortly afterward, called away to deal with a question from his night commander. Blaine blew out the lanterns and crawled into bed, but his dreams were dark, filled with vengeful spirits and old enemies held at bay by Carr's watchful ghost.

CHAPTER
NINE

"NOT EXACTLY WHAT IT USED TO BE, BUT MAYBE it'll be good enough," William Folville said with a nod, looking down at the section of stone wall that ranged from the embankment on the right side of Castle Reach harbor down toward the partially rebuilt city.

"It's a start." Traher Voss stood with his hands on his hips, staring at the harbor as if he were remembering how it had been before the Great Fire, when tall-masted ships of all kinds lay at berth in the waters at the docks and their crews went ashore to spend their hard-earned coin at taverns and brothels.

Many of those ships still lay at the bottom of the harbor where they sank when a green ribbon of fire burned the world. The ships that didn't sink took off for parts unknown.

Only a few had returned. One made it all the way to Edgeland and came back with a load of convict-colonists who wanted to return to their homeland. Another had sailed up and down the coastline, only to return home with a report of widespread destruction. Donderath was on its own.

"I guess it would be too much to hope that ships heading for Castle Reach might offer their assistance," Folville said with a sigh. He was just shy of thirty years old, a skinny man with sharp, rodent-like features, a mop of dark hair, and bad teeth.

Voss gave a derisive snort. "What do you think?" Traher Voss was a legend. He was in his middle years, stocky but not fat, broad-shouldered and bald-headed, with strong arms and hands calloused and widened by years wielding battle swords.

Mistrust came naturally to Folville. Before the Great Fire, he had led a band of thieves, pickpockets, and hustlers who called themselves the Curs. As the bastard son of a prosperous merchant and his trollop mistress, Folville had few illusions about life. His mother had taught him what she knew about surviving life on the streets, and when she died young of fever, he learned the rest of what he knew the hard way.

"Between the soldiers General Theilsson sent and the men you've provided, it shouldn't be more than a week before we get the wall finished," Folville said, changing the subject.

Voss's eyes narrowed as he looked out over the teams of men, women, and children working along the wall. Some carried stones, others chipped them with tools to make them lie flat, and the youngest ones walked up and down the line with buckets of water and sacks of bread. "How'd you get all those people to turn out?"

Folville shrugged. "I told them the truth." Fate had dealt him a strange hand, elevating him from the leader of one of Castle Reach's most successful hoodlum gangs to liegeman to warlord Blaine McFadden and defender of what remained of Castle Reach. It was an arrangement of necessity and mutual benefit.

"I know the city doesn't look like it used to," he said. The once-grand port had been burned, drowned, and battered by unnatural storms. *Gods, it's amazing that anything is left*, he thought. "But look at it up close, and you'll see how much work we've all done. Knocking down the buildings that couldn't be saved and taking what we could of the lumber and tiles, shoring up the damaged buildings, using what we could pick from the rubble to fix up the best of what's left."

A note of pride came into his voice. "So many people left the city and never came back that there's more than enough housing for the ones who stayed." Castle Reach had never been kind to its most desperate residents. He knew that from experience. "They own the city now," he said with a rare smile. "And they'll be damned if anyone is going to take it away from them."

He turned to see Voss giving him an appraising look. Folville ignored the glimmer of impatience he felt at being evaluated. Voss would not be the first to underestimate him, nor probably the last. "They earn food for time worked, and if they need something else—like a pair of shoes or a blanket—we'll do our best to find it for them for extra work." He shrugged. "Simple. Fair. There's so much that needs doing, even the children, elders, and cripples can work."

Voss gave a grudging smile. "McFadden picked a good liegeman," he replied, and chuckled at Folville's surprise. He clapped Folville on the shoulder, nearly knocking him off his feet. "You forget that I've been running a mercenary army for damn longer than I want to remember. Like herding wild dogs, or teaching wharf rats to march in a row. You're getting the work done. That's what matters."

For years, Voss had made his name and his fortune commanding private armies for Donderath's squabbling nobility, or lending out his sellswords to King Merrill if the army needed extra, expert soldiers for a special assignment. Yet Voss and his men had been curiously absent in the Meroven War, and Folville wondered if Voss's alliance with *talishte* lord Lanyon Penhallow had something to do with that.

Folville walked with Voss down the slope of the embankments toward the city. Much of the original wall that defended the port had been destroyed. In some places, the stones merely needed to be restacked. Other parts had been smashed, swept away in the high waves, or carted off by locals who needed them to shore up their own ruined foundations and cellars.

"How's the leg?" Folville asked one man, who nodded as he carried stones to fix a breach in the wall.

"Don't hurt me as much as it did. I can move it," he said, sticking out his leg and bending his knee a few times for show.

Folville grinned. "Good for you. Glad to hear it."

He moved down the line a few more feet, and a woman hailed Folville. "Cap'n! Thank you!"

"Glad to help, Daris," he said, continuing to walk. All the way down the line, people hailed him.

"You've managed to drive out the Red Blades and the Badgers?" Voss asked.

Folville nodded. "Cost some lives, I'll tell you that. Red Blades ran the Lower Nine for years, and they didn't much like giving it up," he added with a lopsided grin. The Blades and the Badgers had once been the rival hoodlum gangs to Folville's Curs.

"Badgers used to have the dockworkers and the seawall guards to back them up, and when they all went away and the trollops they ran couldn't make money 'cause there weren't any sailors in port, lots of the Badgers up and left, thinkin' there might be better times or at least more food elsewhere," he added.

"But you stayed."

Folville drew a deep breath. "Yep. The Curs aren't going anywhere. My folks saw what Lord McFadden did during that last big storm, how he got us warning before the blow, and saved folks himself. Ain't none of the highborns done that for us before."

Voss nodded. "Captain Hemmington and Captain Larson speak well of you and your organization."

Folville gave a sharp laugh. "That's funny, now. Never had guards say a nice thing about us before this. Usually, they were tryin' to run us out of wherever we were." He paused. "But those two, they're all right. For soldiers, I mean, regular ones, not mercs." He realized he was bungling it. "You know what I mean."

Voss chuckled. "Yeah. I think I do."

Folville looked down at the waterfront. A mix of soldiers and city dwellers labored there. A half-built wharf jutted from the shore. At the shoreline, men hauled rocks and mixed mortar to repair the seawall.

Voss's voice brought Folville out of his thoughts. "You rebuilt the lighthouse?" he asked, frowning as he stared at the tall wooden structure on the spit of land that jutted farthest out to sea. Before everything fell apart, the Castle Reach lighthouse had been the tallest and brightest on the Eastern Shore, marking the most prosperous port in the Ascendant Kingdoms. "Who do you think is going to see it? By all accounts, the rest of the Continent is hurting as bad as we are."

Folville grinned. "It's not to bring ships in. It's to keep ships out. There's no light in there. Lord McFadden helped us find some powerful far-seers," he added. "We have one up there day and night, scanning the water for ships. Just in case anyone decides to pay us a visit."

"And if they do?" Voss asked.

Folville's grin was tight. "We'll do our best to be ready for them," he said. "Every day, we send out men in boats to go up and down the coastline and watch for ships. Not to lead them in but to warn us before they come sailing into the harbor like they own the place. Between the mages and the boats, I figure it's the best early warning we're likely to get."

He raised an eyebrow. "And while we're doing everything we can, I sure would appreciate help from your men and General Theilsson's soldiers."

Folville gestured to the townspeople at work on the seawall. "There's more work to do than anyone could finish in a lifetime. And it's still a chore to feed everyone. We organized some teams to farm the land just outside the city walls. Same with the fishermen. We've got relays of men going out in small boats and bringing back what they can, but there are a lot of mouths to feed, and they're hungrier with all the work they're doing. I gotta say it hurt sending all that stuff on the *Nomad* when we got people in need here."

Voss nodded. "Aye. McFadden explained why we had to do it. I'm just glad we got her out of the harbor safely. And we've done our best to bring in whatever supplies we can to make up for what shipped out." He raised his face to the sea wind. "In the meantime, my men will be here, and so will the soldiers General Theilsson sent you. Defeats the purpose if we fight off the warlords inland and lose the harbor, don't you think?"

Folville relaxed, just a bit, and let out a long breath. "Glad to hear it. The townspeople want to help. They're afraid of outlanders coming in and taking what they've worked so hard to rebuild. But they're not soldiers. I can take the most promising ones and turn them into sentries and patrols, but if there's real fighting to be done, they'll be overwhelmed."

Voss clasped his hands behind his back as he walked. "Yes—and no. Never underestimate a cornered rat. No offense intended," he added with a wolfish smile. "Don't think of your people as soldiers. Think of them as street fighters. You know that word."

"By Esthrane's tits, the Curs are the best at street fighting," Folville said. "Never lost a battle on our home streets."

"And that was against an enemy that hailed from Castle Reach, and knew the territory," Voss replied. "Any outlander who comes into the city, either by land or sea, won't know these streets like you do. You're right: Ordinary citizens make lousy soldiers. But force an enemy to take a city house by house, and the game changes," he said, a predator's glint in his eyes.

"Regular folks get angry when someone comes into their streets and their houses," Voss said. "I've seen women beat men twice their size senseless with frying pans and children lead soldiers into ambushes or slit throats at night. People fight harder for what's theirs. Prepare your people for that, just in case, and no one can take Castle Reach from you." He paused. "And to make sure of it, you'll have soldiers to help as well."

"I hope you're right," Folville said as they left the embankment and headed down along the waterfront. "Because if Castle Reach falls, so does the inland, and Warlord McFadden's hopes for Donderath with it."

From here, Folville could see the shipworks, down by the unmistakable red roof of the Rooster and Pig Tavern. Once the pride of Donderath, the shipworks had built many of the kingdom's largest sailing ships, vessels that plied the seas bringing cargo back from the Cross-Sea Kingdoms and beyond, or taking prisoners north to Velant and returning with their holds full of crates of gemstones and barrels of salted herring.

The shipworks had collapsed in one of the last monstrous storms. Now, teams of men moved over the ruins like ants, clearing away rubble, cleaning debris out of the berths, rebuilding the scaffolding and docks so that someday soon, shipwrights could repair the large ships that had survived the storms, and build anew. *Someday, but not now,* Folville thought. Castle Reach was not yet ready for outsiders.

As they reached the walkway behind the seawall, a woman strode toward them. Betta was Folville's sometime lover and longtime second-in-command. She had dark hair cut chin-length, features that were too sharp to be conventionally pretty, and hard, blue-green eyes that never missed anything.

"Sentries just got back from the midday shift," she said, not bothering with greeting or preamble. "I think you're going to want to hear what they've got to say."

Folville glanced to Voss. "Care to join us?"

Voss nodded. "If there's something going on, my men will need to know about it."

"They're back at base," Betta said, then turned and walked away, certain that the men would follow. Folville could not help noticing the sway of her hips and the way her shoulders moved when she walked. *Damn, it's been too long.*

Betta led them past hundreds of soldiers and city dwellers working in teams on projects all along the waterfront. The late summer air smelled of salt spray and dead fish. Hearing the waves against the seawall was a comfort to Folville. Dangerous and fickle as the sea could be, the waves were constant, steady, and sure. He had fled from the worst of the storms, waited out the sheeting rain and the gusting winds, climbed to high ground to keep from being washed away in the floods. Still, there was nowhere else he would rather be than Castle Reach. It wasn't much, certainly no longer in its glory, but it was home.

'Base' was a solid stone building three stories high on Hougen Square, in the center of Castle Reach. "*This* is your headquarters?" Voss said with a hearty chuckle.

Folville could not resist a grin. "Yeah. It's not going to burn down or float away, and I figure if it survived the Cataclysm and all the magic storms, it can last a while longer."

"I like the way you think," Voss said, still chuckling. "Takes some nerve, boy, to call the king's tariff house your own."

Folville shrugged. "He's not using it, seeing as there is no king," he replied. "And if we get a king, I'll give it back." He raised an eyebrow. "Maybe."

All those years as an urchin in Castle Reach, Folville had crept through Hougen Square, mindful to stay out of sight of the king's guards around the tariff house. It had been grand and imposing, white marble gleaming in the sun, and the glimpse of its sumptuous interior when the doors opened was a reminder of King Merrill's power and wealth.

Now, the tariff house was scarred with soot and the high-water marks of several floods. Betta led them up the worn steps, and two of Folville's guards opened the heavy, carved oak doors for them. The regal furnishings, fine tapestries, and glittering crystal had long ago been looted or destroyed. Yet even without the trappings of monarchy, the grand old building had a shabby pride about it and a sense of strength and permanence that gave Folville a measure of comfort.

They followed Betta into a wood-paneled room furnished with a scarred desk, a battered chair, old crates, and scuffed barrels. No doubt an impressive large table and beautiful chairs would have graced the room before the Cataclysm, but those pieces were long gone, hauled away by those who could make use of them, or more likely, burned for firewood in the long, harsh winter.

Four men waited in the room, turning nervously as Folville and the others entered. The men ranged in age from their twenties into their middle years, all with the worn look of fishermen who had braved the worst that the sea had to offer. Their clothing was threadbare and they carried the smell of the sea on their skin and in their hair. Folville recognized the men, and noted with concern who was missing.

"We've gotten scouts back from the north coast and the south," Betta reported for Voss's benefit. "Two of the harbor scouts are back. We haven't heard from the other two, and they're now several candlemarks overdue."

Folville frowned. "We've had clear seas all day. They shouldn't have had any problem making it back."

Betta nodded. "Aye. It's reason for concern. But best you hear the tale they have to tell for yourself," she replied, and stepped back.

"All right, Thad, let's hear it," Folville said, crossing his arms over his chest.

Thad was a short man with hunched shoulders. He held his stained cap in his hands, nervously turning it. "I had the north coast this time out," Thad said. "Didn't see nothin' close by the city. But we went up the shoreline a piece, like we always do. Got to know some of the fishermen along the way, asked them to keep their eyes open for us, too."

Thad turned his cap in his fingers like a talisman. "We heard tell about strange boats at night, spotted off the shore. Small boats, couldn't have come from too far away. But they're not from here, leastwise no one admits to knowing who they are."

Voss shrugged. "Donderath's coast has always been a haven for smugglers," he said. "Have the villages reported thefts? Attacks?"

Thad shook his head. "No. But the men told me they'd seen places where it looked like a boat had been brought up on shore and taken out again, and someone used branches to smooth the sand and hide their tracks."

"Any chance some of the folks out on the Barrier Islands are still alive?" Folville asked. "They've always been partial to raiders and ne'er-do-wells."

"No one I know's cared enough to go look," Thad replied. "Could be them. But why?"

"And what's the point, unless they came to steal?" Voss mused. "Can't smuggle without a king's tariff to cheat."

"That's a good point," Folville said. "Anything else?"

Thad shook his head. "Nothing anyone can prove. Locals are saying that the ghost boats are back. Might be so, but I never worried much about ghosts myself. The living worry me more."

Folville knew the story of the ghost boats. The Donderath coast was known for its fishing. Thousands of men went out onto the water. Not all of them came back. Stories abounded of the ghost boats, fishing vessels that sank out on the ocean, unable to return their crew among the living, coming back as close as they dared to see the lights of home.

"Thank you," Folville said, and turned to the other men. "What have you seen?"

"Two of the fishing villages nearest Castle Reach to the south burned in the last several days," one of the men replied. "Everyone's gone. We went ashore, to see if there were survivors, but we didn't find anyone. No bodies, no livestock, no boats. Just the ashes, still warm."

"Any evidence of others making landfall?" Voss asked.

The men shook their heads. "Thing is, unless it was in the last few candlemarks since the tide turned, we wouldn't see anything," one of the other scouts said. He was a rawboned man with light-brown hair and hands scarred from hard work.

"If men were put ashore and then the boat went back to wherever it came from, the waves would take away the footprints mighty quick," he continued. "But that leaves the question, where would the boats be coming from, and why would they burn the villages?"

Folville and Voss exchanged a glance. "It's possible the Lesser Kingdoms sent sea raiders to scout the territory and bring back anything they could steal," Folville said. "But it's a long journey just to burn a few houses."

"Jak and Skot went into open waters," Betta said. "They came back. Hal and Eddard didn't."

"See anything out there?" Folville asked. Jak and Skot were among his most seasoned boatmen. Before the Great Fire, they had captained two of the large fishing boats that kept Castle Reach supplied with fresh daily catches. But the unpredictable weather and the strange magic of the Cataclysm changed the fishing grounds, and for most of the last year, fish had been in short supply.

"Well, on the good side, looks like the fish might be coming back again," Jak said. "Might have to do with the storms dying down. Or maybe it's the magic. We saw more fish in the last week than we've seen in months. If it keeps up, might be able to get my old fleet back together, start bringing in some real catches nice and regular," he said.

"He's right about the fish," Skot said. "But twice, on the horizon, I thought I saw the masts of ships. It was hard to tell, so far off in the distance. But I'd swear to the king that I saw ship masts, and then the next time the waves took us up again, they were gone."

"Thank you," Folville said. "Your news has been valuable. Stop by the guards downstairs and we'll make sure you get your pay."

Betta saw the men out and closed the door behind them. Folville sat down on one of the barrels as Voss settled his stocky frame onto an old crate. Betta crossed her arms across her chest and leaned against the wall.

"Well?" she asked. "What do you make of that?"

"Could be nothing," Voss said. "Hard to see much on the horizon in one of those small boats bobbing up and down."

"If it weren't Jak and Skot, I'd agree," Folville said. "But they've lived their whole lives out on that harbor. It worries me if they think they've seen ships that close."

"Maybe the ships want to trade," Betta said, although Folville knew she didn't believe it.

He gave a snort. "Trade what? We're just now getting to the point where nobody's starving. We don't have enough extra to trade, and what would we trade for? Gold's worthless. Maybe next year, we'll have whiskey and grain enough to trade for more food, or cloth or tools, but not now," Folville said.

"We never did find out how the Cataclysm affected the Cross-Sea Kingdoms," Voss said. "For a while, it was the least of our worries. And even if we'd thought of it, there weren't ships to spare. Long way to go only to find out they're in no better shape, and then not have provisions to come home again."

"Would it have hit them at all?" Folville asked. "After all, it was the Meroven mages and the Donderath mages getting caught up in the war that caused it."

Voss shrugged. "We know that losing magic here made the magic stop working on Edgeland, at the top of the world," he replied. "So there's a good chance the anchor for magic here could have been the anchor for magic in the Cross-Sea Kingdoms."

"Wouldn't be the kind of knowledge you'd want to get around," Betta said thoughtfully. "If you didn't have an anchor for the magic on your own continent, you might not want others to know that what they did to the magic could affect you."

"And if you had the only anchor for magic, you wouldn't want to make a target of yourself," Folville mused. "So you would keep the information as quiet as you could."

"I'd say that getting those walls back up just got more important than ever," Voss said. "I'll see if I can spare more men to help." He looked from Betta to Folville. "I don't think there's reason to panic people, but sooner or later, whether it's now or next year or whenever, the Cross-Sea Kingdoms or someone else is going to come calling. We want to make sure the harbor and the city are secure."

Folville nodded. "We'll step up the coast patrols, just in case, and I'll send men to the fishing villages to see what they know about the ghost boats and the burned houses. If we've got pirates out there, we don't want them getting it into their heads that they can do as they please."

Voss stood and stretched. "Gods above! I get stiff from sitting. Glad you shared the news with me. Don't see much more we can do than we're already doing, but it's good to know we're on top of things." With a nod to each of them, Voss headed for the door.

"I'll be in touch," he said. "You know how to reach me. And I'll talk to Penhallow, see if we can spare any *talishte* to help with the building. Might go faster if you had a crew that could work nights and move faster."

Folville repressed a shudder, but he nodded. "I'd take them if he'll send them, though I'll need to do some explaining to my men. Some of them are a bit jumpy about the biters." Betta looked away, her feelings clear in her face.

Voss left, and Folville turned to Betta. "You don't like the deal." They had been together long enough for him to read her movements, the way she held herself, the tilt of her head.

"I don't like biters." Years ago, when Folville had first met

Betta, there had been rage and bitterness behind that state-ment. Now, it was a simple, unequivocal statement of fact. Too much had happened in the years since then, too many horrors and far too many nightmares. Biters were just another monster in a long list.

"We could use the extra help. They're strong. We'll get more than double the work done. They not only work all night but they're faster than we are."

"They drink blood, Billy."

"We eat meat, but we don't eat people."

"It's not the same." Betta sighed and walked toward the window.

"Sure about that?" Folville countered gently. "We decide we don't eat people, so we don't. Penhallow's *talishte* don't attack his allies."

"That's not the same as not attacking anyone," Betta pointed out. "They still kill people, just not certain people."

Folville shrugged. "Yeah. So do we. It's complicated."

Betta did not reply, but she wrapped her arms around her-self, squeezing tightly. Folville let out a long breath. *We've all got our scars.*

"If invaders come, whether they're pirates or something else, they will kill to get what they want," Folville said quietly. "Pen-hallow's *talishte* are allies, not marauders."

Betta turned to look at him, rage and loss bright in her eyes. "*Talishte* killed my sister. You know that. How can you expect me to work with them?"

He met her gaze levelly. "The same way I work with Larson and Hemmington and the rest of Lord McFadden's soldiers. I choke down the anger and I take the help. And I remind myself, over and over again, that these aren't the soldiers that killed my family."

Betta swallowed hard, and let Folville put his arms around her. She rested her head on his chest. "We're survivors," she murmured.

He stroked her hair. Her arms encircled his waist. Strong arms, lean and muscular. Her body was just as thin and taut, made that way by years of living on the run, too many enemies, and too little food. "We've gotten to the top of the heap, Betta," he said.

"The garbage heap?"

He chuckled quietly. "Maybe. Castle Reach isn't exactly what it used to be. But we're not hiding in the shadows anymore. The Curs are running this city, not stealing food away from the wild dogs. We've got proper places to sleep and a decent chance no one's going to slit our throats during the night. By Raka! Look at us, living in the king's tariff house!"

"I know." Her voice was muffled. He knew Betta well enough that he did not take it as backing down. But once her blood settled, Betta was good at thinking things through, changing her mind if the evidence was good. "And you're right. We're vulnerable without the walls finished. If we've just gotten back on our feet, maybe other people have, too. And what are the odds they'd be friendly?"

They both knew the answer to that.

Betta gave him a squeeze and disentangled herself. "The city gardens are doing well," she said, and he knew that her abrupt change of topic meant she had come to a decision. She didn't like the biters coming, but she would find a way to live with it. He admired that in her. Practical.

"Enough to feed us for the winter?" he asked.

"Working on it," she replied. "If it's bare land inside the city or near the walls, we've got someone farming it. Guards helped me round up all the urchins we could find and give them to the wise women, so there are plenty of hands. Solved some other problems that way, too."

Betta and Folville had both been 'urchins' in their day. Even back then, before the Cataclysm, when Castle Reach was a wealthy city, life was short and miserable for an orphan on the streets. King Merrill's guards enjoyed hunting down the young thieves and pickpockets, the bread-stealers and coin-cagers. Easy prey. And when the city was full of the rich and powerful, the gap between the hungry and the overfed had been glaringly wide.

"Keep at it," Folville replied. "If we can keep people fed and sheltered, they won't go looking for new leaders. That goes extra for keeping them safe from attack. I kinda like this place. I want to keep it. Beats where we were before."

Betta shot him a wry grin. He was sure she remembered the cellars and rats, the lofts and bats, all too well. "Is that your idea of incentive?" she asked with a dry edge. "Don't worry. Even the slow ones understand food. And some of the old women planted some flax and rounded up the sheep that hadn't been eaten. With luck, we might have some linen and wool again before long. Better have, or we'll all be naked when these old rags fall apart."

Folville chuckled. "I don't know," he teased. "These are some of the best rags I've ever had." Clothing had been in short supply after the Great Fire except for what could be stolen from abandoned houses or looted from the dead. At the moment, Folville was wearing a pair of brocade breeches that were stained and threadbare in places, with a mismatched and equally stained doublet and a shirt that had seen better days. His shoes were good leather, although they did not match. Betta's outfit had been stolen from a dead guard, uniform trews and shirt and a too-large coat that still showed the sword cut and bloodstain that dispatched its original owner.

He leaned against the big, battered desk. It and a mismatched, stolen chair were Folville's seat of power, the place where he heard disputes between members of the Curs or the people under their protection, or where he met with allies like Voss.

Survive the end of the world, and you suddenly become more important, no matter what shape you're in, he thought. He had that in common with the scarred desk. *I'm the best of a bad lot. Nothing new about that.*

"Why does Voss want the shipyards up and running again?" Betta asked, taking a seat on the corner of the desk.

"We're a port. Sooner or later, we're going to need to go to sea again," Folville replied. "Donderath is rebuilding. Odds are, everyone else is too. One of these days, we'll go looking for them, or they'll come looking for us. If we're lucky, they'll want to trade. We'll be able to rebuild faster."

"And if we're not lucky, they'll come looking for us to take what we've got." Betta was quick on the uptake, and she didn't mince words. She was quiet for a moment, then turned to face him. "You're still thinking about meeting Simmons, down at the Rooster and Pig tonight?"

Folville nodded. "Don't see how I have a choice about it. He wants to parlay. I don't think anything will come of it, but until we can get the last of the Red Blades out of the city, a truce is better than open war."

"It's probably a trap. You know that?"

Folville shrugged. "It's as 'neutral' as territory gets. I'm not planning to go alone. I doubt Simmons will be alone, either. And I've already put in a word with Larson to have some extra soldiers in the area."

"I don't trust Simmons."

Folville's smile was cold. "Good. Neither do I. But he's still better than Raig and the Badgers."

"Does Voss know they haven't left, or did you spin him a tale?"

Gods, she knew him well. "I might have overstated our control," Folville allowed. "But it's mostly true. That big flood broke the Badgers' hold on the seawall, and they've never gotten their strength back." He smirked. "We feed our people better, and I'm not much for whipping folks."

"Maybe so, but Raig and his people are still holding their own on the northwest side," Betta said. "I was with the patrols there last week. There've been problems."

"And Simmons and the Blades still hold a corner of the Lower Nine," Folville admitted, naming a part of Castle Reach that had been seedy before the Cataclysm and had not improved since then. The Lower Nine, named for the farthest-flung blocks of the city, had been home to tanners and pig herders and a motley assortment of untrustworthy alchemists, cheap whores, and taverns rumored to poison their customers and steal their belongings.

"Sooner or later, we're going to have to take the territory from them," Betta said. "Although I never thought I'd see the day anyone would want to fight over that godsforsaken stretch."

Even among Castle Reach's down-and-out, there had been a pecking order. The denizens of the Lower Nine were at the bottom. Most of the Lower Nine had drowned or burned in the violent storms and the Great Fire, and along with it, many of the Red Blades gang. Folville and his people had fought them off block by bloody block afterward, keeping the Blades from taking a chunk of the ruined city. But the threat remained, another reason Folville was willing to do just about anything to stay in the goodwill of Niklas Theilsson and his guards, and Traher Voss with his mercenaries and 'friendly' *talishte*. By themselves, the Curs could not hope to hold the city, let alone rebuild. But with allies, the impossible became a lot more likely.

"Do you know how those lords with their manors got their bleedin' power?" Folville asked.

Betta chuckled. "I always imagined they stole it, like everyone else."

Folville shook his head. "Go back far enough, a couple hundred years or so, and it was because they did a favor for the king, or protected his ass in battle."

"There isn't a king anymore," Betta pointed out.

Folville met her gaze. "But there will be, sooner or later. The battles we've heard tell of, with McFadden and Theilsson and Penhallow and their allies, out on the Northern Plains and near the Riven Mountains? They're fighting off the other warlords for territory and power. For control of Donderath."

"And you're betting on Blaine McFadden," Betta said. "You think he'll be king?"

Folville shrugged. "Better him than the others, if there's to be a king. Maybe he'll settle for warlord, but sooner or later, someone will want the crown. He's already made me one of his Lords of the Blood. If we hold the city for him, if we do this right, I might get made a real lord, with land and a house. Imagine, Betta. We could do worse." His new ability to truthsense, gained in the ritual that restored the magic, had already been a valuable asset.

"And we will, if you've bet wrong," she warned. "We've thrown in our lot with McFadden, and everyone knows it. If he goes down, so do we—and there will be a line of enemies, his and ours, waiting to shove in the knife."

"You always know how to find the bright side in everything,"

Folville said with a sigh, but a note of affection colored his words.

"I have your back," Betta said. "And that includes telling you what you don't want to hear."

"So you're coming with me, to meet with Simmons?"

"Of course. Maybe things will go wrong, and I'll get to kick some Red Blades ass," she replied.

CHAPTER
TEN

THE ROOSTER AND PIG HAD SEEN BETTER DAYS. Before the Great Fire, the pub's garish red roof and bright-blue shutters had been visible from halfway out in the bay, and while the ships' captains had steered for the safe berths of the harbor, the soldiers steered to the Rooster and Pig for the best bitterbeer in Castle Reach and the least poxy whores.

The pub had taken a direct hit in the Cataclysm, leaving little but broken walls and smoldering ashes. One-Eyed Hank had staked his claim to the ruins, pressing his brothers, sons, and bastards into building the tavern back up again, cobbling together a roof and stealing enough shutters to get the place back in business. Word had it that Engraham, the old pub owner, had gone to Edgeland, so Hank had the place fair and square.

"Gimme ale." Folville bellied up to the bar. Hank gave him a nod, and his good eye blinked in acknowledgment. Hank was big as a bear, with a leather patch over his left eye and a wooden peg for his right leg. Anyone who might have thought that made Hank an easy target found out otherwise, the hard way.

"Haven't seen you in a while," Hank said as he poured ale into Folville's tankard.

Folville shrugged. "Been busy."

Hank chuckled. "Look at you. A legitimate businessman."

Folville gave a lopsided grin. "Don't go around saying things like that. I've got a reputation to maintain."

Indeed he did. Folville was well aware that the occupants of the Rooster and Pig were watching him as he entered. Glances shifted nervously between Folville at the bar and a big man who sat at a table in an empty corner of the room with two other men standing a few steps behind.

Folville took his tankard and headed to the table. Betta and Len, one of Folville's Cur bodyguards, stayed behind him. Patrons at several other tables took their drinks and left the tavern. Usually, Curs and Red Blades were only together for a fight. *Not this time,* Folville hoped.

"Simmons," Folville said in acknowledgment.

"Folville." Simmons glanced from Folville to Betta and Len with cold, dark eyes. "You're looking well fed." His words held an edge of resentment.

Folville shrugged. "Set aside your claim, disband the Red Blades, and swear allegiance to Lord McFadden and you get some of the spoils, too."

"That's what you came here to say?" Simmons growled.

Another shrug. "It's the truth." He took a sip of his ale. "So why did you want to meet, if nothing's going to change?"

"We've got a common enemy. The Badgers have been causing trouble."

Folville leaned back in his chair and took another sip of his beer. "Oh?" His scouts had given him reports of Badgers being active in the northern end of Castle Reach, but Folville was interested to see how much Simmons knew, and whether his information differed.

"There's a big stretch of nothing down the eastern side of the city, outside where the walls used to be," Simmons said. "You know, the burying yards and the burning ground."

Folville nodded. "Yeah, I know the place."

Simmons leaned forward. "Do you also know that the Badgers are moving into that space—or trying to?"

"How do you know?"

Simmons let out a coarse bark of a laugh. "Because my men have seen them, that's how I know!"

"What's in it for the Badgers?" Folville asked. "That's a wasteland."

"Huh. You would think that. Raig and the Badgers, they don't have shame. They've been looting the graves and digging through the cinders in the burn heaps, going through the garbage pits, to find things they can trade or use."

"Hard times are like that," Folville said, taking another swig of ale. "But what's that to you—or me?"

"He's gotten bolder. Been poking around our borders like he was looking to find out whether we'd stand up to him or not," Simmons replied. "We did—but it's been a while since Raig got that cocky. I don't like it."

Folville shrugged. "So, put him down." All three gangs had a long and bloody history with each other. Simmons and Folville had come to lead their gangs at about the same time, and remained in charge longer than usual. For that, Folville thanked the Cataclysm. With so much around them uncertain, a familiar leader was someone people could trust as the rest of the world burned. Raig, on the other hand, had taken his position by force just a few months ago. That made him an unknown, and forced Folville and Simmons into an uncomfortable truce.

"Not as easy as you make it sound," Simmons said, shifting in a chair that was too small for his bulk. "He's been recruiting from somewhere. The new Badgers aren't as dumb as they used to be. If I didn't know better, I'd say he was getting in guys who used to be soldiers."

"Oh, really?" Folville raised an eyebrow. "The only soldiers around Castle Reach should belong to Lord McFadden or his allies. And I just spoke with Traher Voss. The Badgers aren't getting men from him."

"Well, they look smarter and healthier than the dregs Raig usually gets," Simmons said. "And that's bad for business."

It certainly could be, Folville thought, *if the Badgers were connected to some other force out there.* "Any word on the street about whether he's got himself a patron?" Folville asked. His thoughts whirled, trying to come up with likely suspects.

Simmons shook his head. "No. But Raig's people don't talk about him to outsiders, at least not more than once."

"Why tell me?"

"Because if I know Raig, he'll get greedy if he's got a patron," Simmons replied. "Start looking to take more territory, especially if he's got new men and new weapons." He leaned forward. "And if someone's crazy enough to back Raig, that someone wants more than a beat-down third-rate city gang. Now that the city isn't on fire or under water, seems to me other people are going to want a piece of it."

Folville let out a long breath. "All right. I'll send some of my men to our far-east line to hold the territory. What are you going to do?"

Simmons downed his ale and wiped his mouth with his

sleeve. "Same. Just wanted you to know that I wasn't making a move on your boundaries."

"I'll see what I can find out about who Raig's been keeping company with," Folville added. "We could agree to share that information, if you're willing."

Simmons glared at him for a moment, then nodded. "Aye. Serves us both well to know who's really calling the shots. If I learn more, I'll tell you."

"I'm expecting our truce to hold," Folville said.

Simmons looked as if he had swallowed something that tasted bad, but after a moment, he gave a curt nod. "For now. We'd be fools to fight between ourselves when we've got a common enemy."

Maybe more than one, Folville thought. *Whoever holds Castle Reach holds the kingdom. We're sitting right at the eye of the storm.*

"Hey, Boss! Wake up! We've got trouble." Folville sat upright in the darkened room of the tariff house. Enough moonlight streamed through the cracked windows to let him recognize Teller, one of his lieutenants.

Folville's thin blanket fell aside. He was already dressed, an old habit from sleeping in cellars and doorways. His sword and knives were close at hand, as were his boots, which he began to pull on. "What's going on?"

"A couple of big ships just out of range of our mages and arrows, and some small boats already on their way in," Teller reported.

Folville cursed under his breath. "And of course, our defenses aren't ready yet. Damn!" He staggered as he shoved his foot into his boot, then belted on his scabbard. He and Teller banged on the doors of the rest of his inner circle, and one by one, Betta and the others came to the hallway, all traces of sleep gone from their faces, armed and ready.

"Kentel and Zost, head to the upper walls," Folville ordered. "Rouse anyone you can find. Get the archers up there, and roll a couple of the catapults into place. Some nice, heavy boulders can take out a mast or two, or sink one of those blackguards' ships." The two men nodded and took off at a run.

"Paketi and Mosser, get over to the mage tower. Wake up the mages on your way and see what they can do. Use the lanterns to signal the mages in the tower. See how much mayhem they can cause with the big ships, and if they can swamp the little ones, that's even better."

"Corwin, Rasserman, and Betta, come with me. We need to get down to the seawall and have a reception ready for any of those blighters who get into range."

"What do you want me to do?" Teller asked.

Folville clapped him on the shoulder. "Find Voss and make sure he knows what's going on. We can use the help. If he's got biters who can lend a hand, I'll take everything he's got."

"And then?"

"Keep doing what you're doing. Wake everyone up and get them to their stations. This is our city, dammit. No one's going to sail into our bay and take it from us."

The tariff house was two streets back from the new seawall. As Folville and Betta ran toward the waterfront, they heard the shouts of their people rousing the city to arms. Lanterns flickered to life in the windows. One of the bells that had survived the Great Fire began clanging and then another joined in, sounding the alarm.

"If they thought they were going to slip in with the dark, they've got a surprise coming," Folville said to Betta as they reached the wharf, where men, women, and children were already gathering, armed with whatever weapons were readily at hand.

Folville heard the *thwack* and *thud* of the catapults as they launched rocks into the harbor. Loud splashes followed minutes later, or the crack of wood and the raised voices of men cursing their luck. Torches burned along the half-built fortifications on either side of the harbor, and a waning moon cast a pale shadow across the water.

Archers and catapults forced the dozen small ships to stay toward the center of the harbor. As Folville and the others hurried to the edge of the half-rebuilt wharves, lanterns and torches lit up the night as the crazed bell ringers kept up their deafening clamor.

"I don't think they bargained for this," Betta said, looking out over the water.

"Surprised they're not turning tail. Hardly going to sneak in now," Folville observed. He strode into the thick of the action as men and women scurried up and down the harbor front, preparing for invasion.

"The wind's against them," Betta observed. "It's pushing them away from shore."

Folville narrowed his eyes. "Not exactly. It's pushing them toward the wrecks."

In the chaos of the Great Fire, every ship at berth in Castle Reach harbor had tried to head for the sea to escape the rippling green fire that fell from the sky and burned everything it touched. The earliest ships and the biggest ships had made it out of the harbor. Many of the others, overloaded and commandeered by panic-stricken city dwellers who knew little about navigation, ended up at the bottom of the bay. The last, hard year had too many life-or-death challenges to make dredging the bay a priority. And so the wrecks sat, an underwater abatis, their broken spars and keels a last line of defense.

Folville's gaze traveled up to the watchtower across the bay, where the mages were presumably hard at work. "When have you known the wind to blow out to sea like this?" he asked, lifting his face to the breeze.

"I didn't think mages could affect the weather anymore, after what happened before," Betta said.

Folville shrugged. "Maybe stirring up a breeze doesn't count. Or maybe that's all changed now that the magic's fixed for good. But feel that wind? It's pushing those rowboats right back to the ocean."

"That's it!" Folville shouted to the crowds along the seawall. "Let's show those bloody pirates that we're ready for them! Weapons out! Lanterns up. Let them see what's waiting for them!"

Folville and Betta stalked up and down the wharf front, rallying the onlookers to a show of defiance. Most had come to see what the ruckus was all about, but few went out at night in Castle Reach without a weapon, and so his call to arms was met by every type of tradesman's tool along with knives, staves, and more than a few lengths of rusted chain. Archers joined them, ready should any of the rowboats make it into range. The wind swept past them, gusting so hard Folville had to lean against it as it rushed out to sea.

Catapults on the embankments kept up a steady *clunk-splash*, sending missiles at the rowboats, which were now frantically attempting to row back out to sea. The wind buffeted them, making it difficult for them to steer, often putting the boats directly in range of the flying chunks of rocks and debris.

"I've counted at least four boats sunk so far," Betta observed.

Just then, a pillar of fire rose on the horizon. A moment later, Folville could see flames engulfing the tall masts and billowing sails of a large ship at the very edge of the harbor. Behind him, the crowd caught their breath in collective horror and took a few steps back.

"What in Raka was that?" Betta strained for a better look.

"Mages," Folville said, a note of glee in his voice. "By damn! They're doing it! They're holding the ships at bay!"

By now, the pirate attack had become a rout. Out of a dozen small boats headed for shore, Folville could see five still afloat. Bits of wood drifted on the choppy water. The flaming pirate ship would likely burn to the waterline. At this distance, Folville could not see whether the second ship had abandoned the boaters and sailed off, but he could not imagine the pirates choosing to get closer.

The catapult kept up its assault, and the wind shifted, just enough to bring the remaining rowboats into range. Over the howl of the wind, the crowd on the shore could hear the oarsmen's panicked screams, the crash of the catapult stones, and the crack of breaking wood.

And then, just as suddenly as it started, the wind stopped. Flames still lit the horizon. Waves lapped against the seawall, carrying broken bits of wood. Bodies floated on the dark surface of the water. The bells stopped clanging, and an eerie silence followed.

"We got them!" Folville shouted. Behind him, the crowd began to cheer, waving their weapons and shouting in celebration.

"It worked!" he said to Betta, staring out over the harbor with pride. "Even without the wall being finished, without the other defenses. They came at us and we drove them back!" For the first time in months, he felt a surge of hope. Perhaps all the plans he had made with McFadden's people were more than empty promises. If Castle Reach could hold its own against invaders, then the city might have a chance to make itself anew.

"Boss! Captain Folville!" A man's voice cut through the crowd's celebration, and Folville looked up to see Hoff, one of his lieutenants, fighting his way through the throng. Betta moved closer to Folville, and he was sure that she, too, had gotten a wary feeling from the urgency with which Hoff pushed through the people on the quayside.

"Boss, we got trouble," Hoff said. "The Badgers are attacking, and it looks like they've brought in pirates from the inlets up the coast."

"Damn." Folville gripped his sword in one hand and his long fighting knife in his other. It had taken more than a candlemark for him to gather his men from the center of the city, leaving some to watch the harbor while the rest headed for the eastern edge of the city and Badger territory. He dispatched his fighters in teams, just like in the old days, with instructions to hold off the Badgers and cheat them out of new territory, and gathered a dozen of his gang members to join in the fight.

"Hoff. Go find Captain Hemmington and Captain Larson. If the Badgers are bringing in outsiders, then this is more than a gang fight. I've already sent Teller to let Voss know what's going on. With a little luck, we don't have to go this alone."

Easier said than done, he thought as they approached the war zone. The eastern side of Castle Reach had never been prosperous, not even in the years before the Great Fire. It was a point of pride that Folville's gang had forced the Badgers into this godsforsaken corner, with the help of McFadden's soldiers.

Just slightly better than the Lower Nine, the East Side before the Cataclysm was home to cheap whorehouses, seedy inns, and disreputable taverns, and hardship had not improved it. Folville and Betta moved carefully, weapons in hand, through the darkened streets. The narrow alleys and shadowed ginnels stank of urine and fetid mud. None of the buildings had glass in their windows. In winter, boards covered the openings. Now, slats nailed over the holes let in air while keeping predators out.

"By Torven! Did you see the size of that rat?" Kendricks muttered.

"Trying not to look," Betta replied. "Thanks for that."

A half-grown boy emerged from the shadows as they approached. "Captain Folville? Munn sent me."

Folville looked the boy over. Wiry and dressed in dirty clothing that was patched and stained, he couldn't have been more than ten years old. The boy rolled his eyes. "I'm all there is. The rest of them are fighting. Badgers got here about two candlemarks ago. Munn said to wait for you, since you'd expect someone to represent him. Also said to ask you what in Raka took so long to get reinforcements. We're getting our asses kicked."

A few streets over, the clang of swords echoed from the buildings, along with the shouts and curses of fighters. Munn was the ward leader for this part of Castle Reach. So far, the invaders had been kept to the edge of the city, just inside the ruined wall, but without reinforcements, that would not last for long.

"What's your name?" Folville asked.

"Hugh, sir." A wicked knife was thrust through Hugh's rope belt, and a scar on his cheek told Folville that the boy was no stranger to the rough streets.

"Report."

Life on Castle Reach's streets had never been easy. Skirmishes between the Curs and the Badgers broke out every so often, flaring into blood and flames over a house or a street corner. Residents who stayed in the far edge of the city knew how to take care of themselves, a necessity because until the very recent help from McFadden's soldiers, no one official had previously been willing to lift a finger in their defense.

"We don't know how many Badgers managed to get past the wall," Hugh reported. "We're going after them, but it's slow going. The Young Pups are out in force," Hugh reported. "The Old Dogs rallied with the first attack. We're going house to house, looking for Badgers."

"Our teams got dice?" Folville asked.

Hugh nodded. "Yeah. Munn hands them out to every new fighter." Folville had organized the Curs into teams of six men, each with a single die and a set of six possible actions they had to memorize by heart. Depending on what the die rolled, they chose the corresponding action, guaranteeing random, unpredictable responses to attacks. It meant that neither Folville nor Munn needed to be in constant contact with the teams to get results.

"We broke out the weapons as soon as we knew the Badgers were serious," Hugh said. "Woke up the women and got them busy filling oil bombs. Everyone's armed."

"Street snares?"

Hugh nodded again. "First thing Munn did, and he sent the Pups to snare all the way back to Potter's Plaza."

Folville glanced around in the near dark, squinting as he scanned the buildings for snipers. Hugh chuckled.

"They're there," he assured. "Roofs and basements."

"Tell the others I'll make sure there's extra food and fresh clothes when this is over, if we drive back the Badgers."

"And good ale?" Hugh's eyes narrowed.

"And ale," Folville promised. "Now, get going, and make it fast!"

Folville moved forward. He had already sheathed his sword. It was too long a blade for the narrow alleyways of the Lower Ninth. In its place, he held a hunting knife in each hand. Knives worked much better at close quarters. He had been street fighting since he was younger than Hugh. This he knew how to do.

Attacks by the Badgers and the Red Blades had been happening for as long as the three gangs had existed, long before Folville's time. Before the Cataclysm, the wars between the gangs waged relentlessly, invisible to outsiders until they spilled into such violence that the king's troops grudgingly became involved, which was rare. No one else wanted the run-down sections of the city where the gangs fought for scarce resources, so outsiders left it to the residents to sort things out among themselves.

Folville had watched and learned. As a boy, Folville had been a scout like Hugh, learning the tunnels that ran beneath Castle Reach, a mapless warren prone to flooding at high tide and after sudden storms. As a teen, Folville had been in the teams that laid traps in the streets, set trip wires and garrote ropes, and threw burning pots of oil to set invaders on fire or light debris in a stone cul-de-sac. Later, he had been a decoy, offering himself as bait to lure angry rival gang members into dead-end streets or houses filled with hidden allies. He had plenty of scars to show for his time in the streets, but the experiences taught him as well as any military service.

Betta and the others moved cautiously in teams of two, alert for danger. Hugh and the Pups had already extinguished the street torches, so the dim glow of lanterns through slats and shutters were all that lit the way, along with the pale light of the waning moon. Folville's concentration was on the next few feet, the next doorway. He took nothing for granted. That caution had kept him alive this long. A rat squealed in the gutter, and Folville flinched. He let out a breath when he saw the creature scuttle away.

A streak of silver in the torchlight was his only warning. Folville felt the blade slice into the sleeve of his coat and skid down his vambrace. He blocked and slashed. One of his blades dug into his attacker's skin, and hot blood spattered his hand. In the half-light, Folville caught a glimpse of his attacker, a flat-nosed, broad-faced man twice his size.

The man was big and fast. The knife slashed again. Folville blocked the blade with one knife and struck with the other, scoring a cut on the man's forearm. Murder glinted in the man's eyes and he grunted in anger, coming at Folville with a series of powerful strikes that could have cut to the bone.

Out of the corner of his eye, Folville could see that Betta and the others had attackers of their own. Big Guy and his friends had slipped past the defenders, and now it was up to Folville's crew to keep them from moving farther into the city.

Feint, dodge, strike. Repeat. Fighting with a knife was faster than with a sword, rough and brutal. It had come easily to Folville when he was in his teens. Now, a decade older, he felt slow and sluggish.

Big Guy's blade sliced into Folville's shoulder just below his leather pauldron, and warm blood ran down his arm. Folville kicked hard, getting Big Guy in the knee, and while he was reeling, Folville went for the kill. He slashed his blade across the man's throat. Big Guy thrashed, and his huge fist caught Folville hard on the side of the head, knocking him backward, dazed. Blood sprayed as Big Guy's mouth worked, unable to draw breath. His eyes widened in shock in the instant before his body crashed down to the mud.

A battle yell echoed down the alleyway, and another man came at Folville. Still dazed from the blow to his head, Folville tried to get his bearings. He braced himself, knives raised to block the worst of the attack. The attacker ran toward him, shouting curses, closing the distance fast. Large knives glimmered in the man's hands, more formidable weapons than those Folville held.

Just as the man was nearly on him, a stout pole slammed end-first out of a nearby doorway, catching the attacker on the elbow with enough force that Folville heard bone crack. He saw his opening and went for it, landing a blow with his knife that slipped between the invader's ribs and into his heart as the old man in the doorway rocked back and forth, steadying himself on his staff, cackling in laughter.

"That's the way to do it! Get the bastards."

Folville came up in a crouch, only to see Betta finish off her attacker with a blade plunged hilt-deep into his belly, pulled up to the ribs like gutting a fish. She gave the dying man a kick and he fell backward, hands grasping for his bulging entrails. Emery and Droyan were holding their own with attackers, but before Folville could circle around, both had downed their opponents.

Folville turned to see the old man joined by several other residents. Old women and worn-looking younger women emerged, armed with staves of wood or heavy pots. Some held slingshots, common in the ginnels for hunting rats. Old men clutched staves, some with knives bound to their ends to form homemade pikes, along with battered scythes and stolen swords.

"Go on, lad. We'll hold the street," the old man with the staff assured him. "Ain't the first time, probably won't be the last. Send them all to Raka."

Folville grinned and gave the man a rakish salute. "You heard the man," he shouted to Betta and the others. "We've got Badgers to fight!"

They stopped long enough to bind up the worst of their wounds, then kept moving. Folville made it his business to know his territory. He had roamed these streets when he was one of the urchins like Hugh, picking up a coin or two for odd jobs, no questions asked, stealing when he couldn't, freezing and starving, running and hiding. As he rose in the ranks of the Curs, Folville had been in Munn's role, a quadrant leader, responsible for first a block of buildings, and then several blocks, with teams under his command. Even now, when Folville had gained leadership of the Curs through a mix of ruthlessness, luck, and street smarts, he made it his business to walk the streets he owned often, letting himself be seen, handing out food and clothing, bringing along healers with far more skill than the local hedge witches to treat the sick. That firsthand knowledge paid off under attack. Now, even in near darkness, Folville wound through the narrow streets, sure of his course.

Along the way, they could see evidence that Munn's men had done their work. Barrels and overturned carts blocked some roadways. Tangles of washing lines and fishing nets barricaded others. Snares of thin rope at ankle height in places could lame attackers, while loose rocks, dumped from conveniently waiting bins, covered streets with shifting, treacherous footing. The Curs were on their game.

The edge of the city had been dark when Folville and his team approached it, but now fires lit the night. *We can thank the Badgers for that,* he thought sarcastically. The Curs could move through these narrow, twisting streets with minimal light. They knew the tunnels and the 'mouse holes,' passages that opened from one tenement to the next through the walls of buildings so that defenders could run entire blocks without having to go outside. Rooftops, too, had their bridges and paths, if one knew where to look and had sufficient nerve and agility.

Warily, Folville and the others stuck close to the walls of the old buildings, hugging the shadows. Nearby, they heard shouts and the sounds of scuffling, and to their left, the pounding of running steps echoed in the darkness.

"This way," Folville said, gesturing for the others to follow. In a few turns, they reached the city's edge. Once a high stone wall had marked the borders of the King Merrill's palace city. Now what remained of that wall was blackened, blasted by the Great Fire. Vandals and storms in the year since the Conflagration had knocked down more of the old stones, leaving gaps in some places and mere rubble in others.

Cur archers were ducking behind the portions of the wall that remained, firing at the Badgers. Several of the city buildings rose two or three floors above the wall. Archers dodged back and forth at the empty windows, shooting down into Badger territory. Badger bowmen fired back. Rocks flew with deadly force, launched by slingshots or thrown with dangerous aim.

"We've held most of them back," Munn reported as Folville neared the Cur line.

"We met some of them on our way here, and took them out," Folville replied drily.

Munn nodded. "The Pups and the old ones will deal with the attackers that slip through, if we can hold more of them from getting in."

Folville took up a place on the ruined wall. Smoke roiled through the air, making it hard to breathe. The Badgers were lobbing bundles of oil-soaked rags that burned with heavy, dark smoke to make it more difficult to see. Torches and small bonfires dotted the night.

"There!" Betta shouted as shadows dodged in the smoke toward the city.

"On it!" Folville said, signaling his team. They ghosted after the invaders, knives ready.

Maybe to the Badgers the darkened buildings looked like easy pickings. Folville knew better. Doors would be barricaded, gates roped shut. Entrances held nasty surprises for the unwary. In these first blocks nearest the wall, make-do reinforcements had fortified the lower levels, reinforcing the walls and doors with whatever debris was handy. The Badgers would not take Cur territory without blood.

The first block of streets had no visible snares, giving attackers the belief that this ground would come easily. Folville knew that they were being herded, as surely as cattle to the slaughter. And when the Badgers figured out their mistake, it would be too late.

"Soon," Folville murmured. He had fought beside Betta and the others long enough that they knew each other's movements. The Badgers might have been trying for stealth, but to Folville's eye, they were clumsy and noisy, making it simple to follow them down the path the Curs had blazed for them.

That path led right to a dead end. Flanked by two buildings with the ginnels fenced closed, the street ended against the side of a third, hard-used tenement.

The Badgers slowed as they neared the end of the boxed-in street. It was the opportunity Folville was waiting for. On his silent signal, the Curs attacked. Betta slipped a knotted length of rope over the head of one of the Badgers and pulled hard, knocking him off balance as he struggled for breath. Folville lunged into the nearest Badger and shoved him hard against a nearby 'door.' The wooden panel gave way easily, opening onto a drop to the basement and jagged debris. They heard the Badger screaming all the way down, until the cries ended with a sudden, abrupt *thump*.

A second Badger came at Folville, knives ready. Folville blocked the slice meant to cut him open chest to gut, and thrust with one of his own knives. The Badger eluded him, only to dive toward Folger once more, and this time, his thrust scored a gash on Folville's upper arm. The Badger was bigger than Folville, but Folville was wiry, and he knew the area.

Above them in the wafting smoke and darkness was a pole sticking out from the wall, just over the doorway. Folville leaped straight up, grabbing on to the pole, and used his momentum to land a hard, solid kick right to the Badger's face. Bone smashed beneath his heel and blood flowed as the Badger let out a howl of anger and pain. Folville swung back before the Badger could get him in the legs with one of his blades, and took the opponent's momentary bloody haze to try to slide by, hoping for a clean strike at the man's back.

The Badger moved too quickly to let Folville pass. Blood flowed down the man's ruined face, and his eyes burned with fury. He had lost one of his knives when Folville kicked him, and he grabbed Folville with a meaty hand.

"Not so fast," he grated, words slurred from his rapidly swelling lip.

Folville took a fast, hard step toward the man, putting him off balance, and got in a kick to the man's groin, then brought the knife in his pinned arm down point-first into the Badger's arm.

The Badger went down hard, moaning in pain, and Folville got in the strike he had been waiting for, slipping his blade between the Badger's ribs from behind. The attacker gasped, then fell forward, splayed on the filthy street.

Betta had finished her first attacker, and was backing a second man against the wall. Just as the man took a step toward the gutter, Betta danced backward, out of the way of the hot water an obliging resident stood ready to pour from the upper window. The Curs expected the move and stayed out of the way, but boiling water poured over the Badger and he screamed as his skin began to blister and peel. He never saw Betta's blade going for his throat.

The darkened windows hid more Cur fighters. Rocks pelted the Badgers from every direction, hurled hard enough by slingshots and angry residents to open up bloody gashes. One rock struck a Badger on the temple with a wet crunch, lodging in the bone, and the man dropped to the ground, still. The remaining Badgers rallied with a bellow, rushing toward the Curs, who blocked the alley's only exit.

Rocks pounded the Badgers, hitting hard enough to break bone. Beaten, bruised, and bleeding, the attackers made their last rally.

Terror and rage filled the Badger's eyes as he came straight at Folville, intent on getting to freedom. Folville blocked him with his knives.

"Get out of my way!" the man shouted, brandishing a short, thick staff. Folville fell back a step and grabbed a barrel, hurling it at the Badger and knocking him to his back. Pritcher, one of Folville's team, drove his sword into the downed Badger's chest before the man could make a move to get back to his feet.

When Folville was sure his enemy was dead, he looked around to find only the Curs in the alley. Their supporters behind the darkened windows had melted into the shadows.

"Leave the bodies. We've got work to do," Folville ordered.

When they wound their way back toward the wall, Folville and Betta found the Curs shouting and whistling in celebration. The smoke was clearing, and while a few arrows and rocks still soared through the air toward the Badger side of the wall, no return fire answered.

"We drove them back—this time," Munn said, meeting Folville as he approached the wall. "They'll be back, I'm sure."

"Good work," Folville said, wiping away the sweat and blood that streaked down his sooty face with his sleeve. Munn and his fighters were bloodstained and dirty, too exhausted to join in the victory catcalls.

"It ain't over," Munn said. "I know because the Badgers had better weapons than they've ever had. By the Whore! Most of the time when they've tried to take ground, they've come at us with broken boards and rusty lengths of iron. This time, they had proper knives and swords, lots of them." He shook his head. "Someone's giving them weapons, and we'd better figure out who and why before they come back."

Folville stared out through the clearing smoke, past the wall and toward the dark horizon. "It's not the Red Blades. And there's no other gang in Castle Reach better equipped than the Curs."

Munn met his gaze. "Maybe you're not the only one to draw the backing of a lord who wants you to do his fighting for him, think of that? Don't need to be one of our enemies. It's enough that it's one of *his* enemies."

Folville had already considered that possibility. Holding Castle Reach against the Badgers and the Red Blades had not seemed like an impossible task when McFadden had offered soldiers and supplies for additional protection. Even rebuilding the city's defenses and its wharf had seemed a good bargain. Until now, the Curs had benefited from the alliance with food and weapons, hard-to-get supplies, and extra, trustworthy manpower. Now, the full price of allegiance started to become clear.

"I made an oath and I'll stick to it," Folville said. "As long as McFadden and his people keep their side of it. But before more Curs die, I'll find out who we're really fighting, and why they want this godsforsaken city."

"Better make it soon," Betta said. "Because I imagine they won't wait long to try again."

CHAPTER ELEVEN

"WHAT YOU'RE ASKING IS EASIER SAID THAN done." Mersed replied, shaking his head. The mage looked from Blaine to Kestel. "Very difficult, and dangerous."

"Especially since we don't want a repeat of what caused the Cataclysm in the first place," Cosmin, another of the Quillarth Castle mages, added.

Blaine, Kestel, and Piran sat in a small parlor within the partially rebuilt castle. The Great Fire had badly damaged the old fortress, and subsequent attacks and looting had left the castle far from its old grandeur. With the pirates pushed back for now, Blaine had sought out the mages to see what additional precautions could be taken to protect the port and enable the city to rebuild.

"That's the question," Blaine said, leaning back in his chair after they had finished dinner. "What can our mages do, with the way magic is now, that can protect the kingdom, or at least the harbor?"

"Oddly enough, probably the single biggest way to use magic to protect Castle Reach would be to crown a king," Viorel remarked. He was the third mage to join them, and together the three were the most senior and most powerful mages working with the artifacts and magical items that had been salvaged after the Cataclysm.

"What do you mean?" Kestel asked, purposely not looking in Blaine's direction as she leaned forward, anxious to hear Viorel's response.

"You know all about anchoring the magic and the Lords of the Blood," Mersed answered. "We're still trying to figure out how the magic that was finally brought under control is similar—or different—from what it was like before. What we do know is that prior to the Great Fire, when the battle mages all did their worst, Donderath received a level of magical protection through its king."

He hesitated, trying to find the right words. "Think of it like a sort of immunity. With a properly crowned king, the kingdom had a basic level of protection against minor magical threats. Not something as big as the Great Fire, but lesser attacks, the kind most likely to be launched by a single mage or a few mages working together."

"The kind of things we've been fighting off one at a time," Piran observed.

Cosmin nodded. "Exactly. When the Great Fire killed the king and the Lords of the Blood, it untethered magic from our control. That eliminated the magical 'immunity' as well, including any power that might have built up over the years through an unbroken line of succession."

"So we have to start all over again," Kestel supplied.

"Yes," Viorel said, nodding. "The first step was to re-anchor the magic correctly, which Lord McFadden did when he reestablished the bond and the Lords of the Blood."

"But we can't complete the rest of the protection without a properly crowned king," Cosmin said. "And kings, at the moment, are in short supply."

"What do you mean, 'properly crowned?'" Kestel asked.

Mersed looked as if he had been waiting for the question, and warmed to the subject with a scholar's zeal. "We're still piecing that answer together from the documents we've found. Needless to say, that kind of information was closely guarded. No one wanted enemies to find out the extent—or the limits—of their magical immunity."

"Makes sense," Piran said. "Kings usually have more than their fair share of enemies."

Cosmin nodded. "Exactly. And there would be additional incentive if, on top of the political ramifications, killing a king—especially ending a dynasty—left a kingdom open to magical attack."

"What we know so far," Viorel continued, "is that the coronation ceremony is key to conveying the magical immunity. Not unlike the ritual that anchored magic through the Lords of the Blood," he said with a nod toward Blaine.

Blaine repressed a shiver. Anchoring the magic had nearly killed him, and it had taken several near deadly attempts to get the ritual right. Mersed guessed his thoughts. "We intend to do our research thoroughly, m'lord, before we expose anyone to such magic, especially our future king. And that's the sticking point," he said. "The mages who presided over King Merrill's coronation are dead. If they understood the power conveyed in the ceremony, they aren't around to ask."

"We've found a few scrolls from mages who might have been part of the coronation of Merrill's ancestor who founded the dynasty," Cosmin added. "And there may be more down in the catacombs, but you've seen for yourself how dangerous it is to go exploring down there."

"Not my favorite place," Piran said adamantly. "Ghosts fighting old battles. Dead Knights of Esthrane that don't stay dead. Dark, spooky tunnels filled with things that try to kill you. I could do without going down there again."

"Agreed," Viorel replied with a nod. "But General Dolan, being one of the Knights of Esthrane, has had better luck than the rest of us retrieving artifacts and scrolls." Dolan, a *talishte*-mage, would be under the protection of the watchful spirits of the dead Knights of Esthrane buried in the catacombs. "In fact, we believe that the Knights are an important part of the ceremony—but we're not sure of the details yet."

"Interesting," Blaine remarked, "since the Knights would have been in exile for the last several coronations. If they were supposed to be part of the ritual and weren't, might that have affected the protection for the kingdom?"

"Perhaps," Mersed said. "I'll look into that."

"We've been working with the mages at Mirdalur and at the Citadel," Cosmin said. "I believe that with all of us working together—including the Knights—we'll figure this out. Of course, it's not much use without a king."

Blaine felt himself flush, and a nervous knot formed in his stomach. Piran and Kestel both gave him a telling look. Mersed's lips twitched into a knowing smile. "Your name has come up more than once as a preferred candidate, Lord McFadden," the mage said. "In fact, yours was the only name that has support from all factions."

"It's a bit premature, don't you think?" Blaine replied. "We're still under attack."

"Of course," Viorel said. "But when the day comes that the kingdom's borders are secure, this is a conversation that must continue."

Blaine sighed. "I know. And when that time comes, I'm willing to discuss it further. But right now, we've all got to live long enough to get to that point."

CHAPTER TWELVE

"THE SEA DOESN'T AGREE WITH YOU." ZARYAE came over to sit near Connor, who was clinging to his hammock and trying not to throw up.

"Not really," he managed to say without losing his meager supper. Rations had been much tighter on the panicked journey that set out the night of the Great Fire, but the nature of seafaring argued for lean portions. Given the state of his stomach, Connor wasn't certain whether that was good or bad.

"Chew on this." Zaryae reached into a pouch on her belt and withdrew a pinch of leaves, which she placed carefully in Connor's outstretched hand. "It will settle your stomach."

Connor did as she bade, and in a few minutes, his gut stopped clenching. "Thank you," he said, only now realizing that he was holding the ropes of his hammock in a white-knuckled grip. Gingerly, he flexed his hands, noting the rope marks pressed into his skin. "It was worse the last time."

Zaryae smiled. "I imagine so. Or rather, I'm glad that I can't really imagine it. You were very brave to climb onto a ship in the middle of the world catching fire."

Connor chuckled ruefully. "Actually, I wasn't brave at all.

I was frightened to death. My master, Lord Garnoc, had just been killed and so had the king. Garnoc gave me a mission I didn't understand, and all I could think about was how awful it would be to fail him if I died that night." He sighed. "I don't know what would have happened if I hadn't run into Engraham from the Rooster and Pig. He's the one who got us passage. He saved my life."

Their ship, the *Nomad*, was one of the few surviving large ships from before the Cataclysm. Most of its sister ships lay at the bottom of Castle Reach harbor or the bottom of the Ecardine Sea.

Their accommodations were purely functional. Nidhud had a coffin in a lightless interior room in the hold. The crew slept in shifts in another room strung with layers of hammocks, and the captain had his own cabin above deck. Connor and the others had a third room for their hammocks and supplies. That left the fourth compartment for supplies, including a dozen goats brought along to ensure that Nidhud had fresh blood. Blaine and Penhallow had rounded up whatever supplies could be spared to send with them for the colonists, trying to send as generous a bounty as possible. At a premium was anything that could not be made or grown in Edgeland, though since the Cataclysm, many such items were either in short supply or impossible to get. The stockpile of crates, barrels, and bins in the hold would guarantee a warm welcome once they got to Edgeland.

"Forty days," Connor moaned.

"Come on now," Borya said from where he and Desya were playing cards. "You can play cards and dice with us to pass the time. We'll keep you entertained."

Connor rolled his eyes. "That's almost as bad as playing with Piran. By the time we get to Edgeland, I'd probably have lost everything but a loincloth!"

Verran chuckled. "That's generous. Piran wouldn't have left you that." He had a pennywhistle and a few other small instruments in his sack, and as the others talked or gamed, Verran played quietly.

Connor looked over to Verran. "How are you about going back? I'm not thrilled, and I didn't go to Edgeland under the same conditions you did."

Verran laid his pennywhistle aside. "You'd be surprised how often I dream about that place," he said with a sigh. "Not all the dreams are bad. Mick and the rest of us made a pretty good go of it at the Homestead. We eked out some good times, from sheer stubbornness. But I can't say it was where I'd most like to go, if there was a choice."

"How do you think we'll be received, by the people you left behind?" Zaryae asked.

Verran crossed his arms and leaned back against the bulkhead. "Don't rightly know. I've asked myself the same question." He sighed. "I guess we'll know when we get there."

The next day was the fourth since the *Nomad* set out from Donderath, and thus far, the weather had been good. The days were sunny and it was hot on deck without shade. Borya and Desya enjoyed the sea air, and adapting to the rolling motion of the ship did not seem to pose them any challenge, with their natural acrobatic talent. On the other hand, Zaryae had to cajole Verran and Connor to go up on deck at least once a day.

"The fresh air is good for you," Zaryae said, bringing up the rear as she and the others climbed from the hold.

"I'm not having any trouble breathing down below," Connor grumbled.

"What I object to," Verran said, "is how the horizon goes all tippy when you're at sea. Not like a proper horizon should be, staying, well, horizontal. It goes up, it goes down, and then up again. Downright distressing."

"I try not to think about it," Connor said. "Best all the way around."

Zaryae gave an exasperated sigh. "You need to get out of the hold. People need sunlight."

"I've spent a lot of time lately in crypts. I've gotten used to the dark." In his mind, Connor could hear the Wraith Lord's distant chuckle. Connor was being difficult and he knew it. But although he had resigned himself to the trip, part of him was annoyed at being conscripted for the mission, and he was indulging a well-deserved—and totally useless—moment of pique.

Cheers and whistles rang out from the crew as they climbed onto the deck, but after a moment's confusion, Connor realized that the shouts were not directed at them. Borya and Desya were up in the rigging, putting on a fine show of climbing and acrobatic prowess. Even Captain Whitney watched, grinning his approval.

Since everyone else's attention was focused on the twins, Connor took the chance to get a good look at their captain. The ship's abrupt departure had allowed little time before this to interact with the crew, and Connor's group had stayed largely in their quarters, out of the way.

Sol Whitney was in his late thirties, with a weathered look that attested to long years spent out of doors. He had a wiry build with ropy muscles from the hard work of sailing a ship like the *Nomad*. Most of his pate was bald, and what remained of his dark hair was shaved close along the back. From what Connor had seen so far, the crew respected their captain, and Whitney acted with the calm assurance of someone who knew what he was doing. *I hope so,* Connor thought. *Since all our lives are in his hands.*

The wind was warm, and Connor raised his face to it and shut his eyes. It would probably take the entire voyage for him to get used to the continual rocking of the ship beneath his feet. *Just in time to sail back,* he thought.

"It's a fine day, m'lady. Glad to see you taking advantage of the chance to be up on deck," Captain Whitney said, and Connor opened his eyes to see the captain talking with Zaryae. She had dressed with practicality in mind. Her dark hair was caught back in a long braid that reached nearly to her waist. Today, she wore a plain work dress, though in her pack she had brought a heavy coat, tunic, and trews as well as sturdy boots for the hard trek inland on the ice once they reached Edgeland.

"Always good to see the sun," Zaryae replied. "What do your instruments tell you of the weather?"

Captain Whitney chuckled. "Perhaps I should ask you that question."

Zaryae smiled. "I wouldn't want to put your storm glass out of a job. And I daresay its insights occur more regularly than mine."

"Very well," Captain Whitney concurred. "I will take your word for that. But we're in luck: The readings look very good. That should mean clear sailing, at least for the next several days."

"I'd certainly appreciate that," Connor said, walking up beside Zaryae. Verran was standing where he could hold on to the railing, gripping the wood for dear life.

"Your friend isn't much of a sailor," Captain Whitney observed, with a nod toward Verran.

"I have to admit I share his sentiments," Connor admitted. "I'd much rather be on dry land."

"Those two certainly don't seem to mind," Whitney said, and glanced toward where the twins were tumbling down through the ropes to the applause of the sailors.

"I've never seen either of them mind being anywhere so long as there's something to climb," Zaryae said with a chuckle.

"They'll get plenty of exercise, then, between here and Edgeland. Might even let them help with the rigging if they're so inclined."

"I suspect they'd jump at the chance, and it would keep them from gambling away their buttons and coins," Zaryae replied with a smile.

Whitney laughed. "I'll see what I can do about that." He turned to Verran. "I heard you play when I was up on deck last night. You're quite good."

"Plenty of experience, playing in taverns for my supper," Verran replied.

"Ah. That explains it," Whitney said. "Well, if you're ever in the mood to play for an audience, I'm certain that my crew would enjoy some music with their dinner now and again."

"Happy to oblige," Verran replied, his gaze shifting everywhere but the constantly moving horizon.

"I have to admit that the idea of going to Edgeland on a few days' notice surprised me," Whitney said, watching as the crew went about their duties. "I'd made that trip a time or two before the Great Fire. Not the most pleasant sailing, up in the Northern Sea, especially toward the winter."

"Not too bad this time of year," Verran said. "The later it gets, once the Long Dark sets in, sailing gets tougher. Too much ice in the water."

Whitney regarded Verran at that, eyeing him as if reconsidering his original appraisal. "You sound like someone who knows."

Verran shrugged. "Live somewhere for six years, you learn how things work."

Connor could see the curiosity in Whitney's eyes, but the captain did not press for more information. "I've been up to Edgeland as well," Connor said, thinking to deflect Whitney's attention from Verran's past. "I was on one of the ships that sailed the night of the Great Fire."

"Which ship?" Whitney asked, his gaze turning sharply to Connor.

"The *Prowess*, under Captain Olaf," Connor replied.

Whitney's eyes narrowed. "The *Prowess* was lost at sea."

Connor nodded solemnly. "I know. I was on her when she went down."

Whitney raised an eyebrow. "So there were survivors?"

"A few," Connor said sadly. "Engraham from the Rooster and Pig made it. He and I were together. Some of the others made it as well. Captain Olaf didn't get to shore."

Whitney nodded. "I figured as much. Things were bad that night. Kind of amazing you made it out, given the circumstances."

There was something in Whitney's voice that made Connor look at him again. "How about you?"

Whitney looked away, toward the horizon. "I was out at sea," he replied. "On a cargo ship coming back from the Cross-Sea Kingdoms. We weren't sure we'd ever make it back—they'd set up a blockade due to the war between Meroven and Donderath—but I guess they wanted rid of us. The storms were terrible. Several ships were traveling together, and some of them foundered in the waves. Then the magic failed, and another of the ships sank because its owner had scrimped on repairs and used magic instead."

He sighed. "When we finally got back to Castle Reach,

we couldn't even sail into the harbor for all the sunken ships blocking the wharves. And the city itself…" His voice drifted off, but Connor knew the scene Whitney was reliving in his memories. It was the same that haunted Connor's dreams: Castle Reach, in flames.

Whitney shook himself out of it and turned toward Connor. "Lucky for you that you had the *Nomad*. How did you get her?"

"She was drifting in the current up near where the herring boats fished," Connor replied.

"The ship was deserted when the fishermen brought her in. So the colonists who wanted to come back had their chance." He rubbed his hands together, remembering the cold. "I didn't mind being able to leave."

Whitney chuckled. "Well, before long, you'll get to see it all again." He shook his head. "Lord Penhallow made it clear that my crew and I were to give your group our full assistance, no questions asked. So I'm not asking who you are and why we're bringing you up to the edge of the world and back. But the crew has been speculating, and the tales get taller with each retelling."

Whitney turned to meet Connor's gaze. "So if I were you, I'd keep your story about being on the *Prowess* and how you found the *Nomad* to yourself. Some of the men are plenty superstitious. Being aboard one ship that sank is bad enough. But sailing on a ghost ship, too? You don't need the crew muttering about curses. Understand?"

"I certainly do," Connor replied. Although the night was warm, he repressed a shiver. Out on the open sea, sailors were likely to be more afraid of a jinx than a *talishte* lord an ocean away. Stories about passengers believed to be unlucky always ended badly—for the passenger.

They took their dinner in their quarters, as they had since leaving Castle Reach, so they could speak freely. Although their rations were no different from those of the rest of the crew, Penhallow had spared them a few bottles of whiskey. One went to gain the favor of Captain Whitney, and the rest they kept for themselves, as Penhallow had provisioned the crew with ample casks of ale and grog.

"What do you make of the captain?" Verran asked, picking at his ration of dried meat and hard biscuits.

"Seems to know his business," Borya said. "Although I don't exactly know how it was Penhallow chose him for the trip."

"Whitney has a *kruvgaldur* bond to one of the other Elders." Nidhud's voice startled them, since his approach had been silent. He closed the door behind him, finding a seat on the floor.

"Well, that's interesting," Verran said. "I hadn't figured on that."

"Most of the crew are so marked, but not all," Nidhud replied. "Penhallow, of course, would have preferred the entire crew to be bonded, but time was of the essence."

"What about the others, the ones who don't have a *kruvgaldur* link?" Connor asked. "How can we know they're trustworthy?"

"The rest came from Traher Voss's mercenaries," Nidhud said. "Not a guarantee, but an endorsement. Voss runs a tight organization. His men are loyal, and skilled. Seems he had some experienced sailors who were game enough to get back on the water, they didn't care where they went."

"They'll care all right, once they get to Edgeland," Connor said with a shiver.

"Aw, come on, mate," Verran said. "It's not so bad in summer. Cooler than Donderath, but it's not like you're going to be stuck there for the rest of your life. It's practically balmy this time of year!"

Connor looked at Verran as if he had gone mad. "I was in Edgeland 'this time of year' last year. I nearly froze."

Verran gave an exaggerated sniff of mock disdain. "Then again, you and Mick were coddled nobles."

Connor rolled his eyes. "My father was such a minor baronet that his title wasn't good for much more than getting him invited to parties with free liquor and getting me taken on as Lord Garnoc's assistant." He knocked back his shot of whiskey at that. Garnoc's loss still hurt.

Verran turned to Zaryae with dramatic flair. "See that? First Mick keeps his most trusted companions in the dark about his title, and now we find out Connor's one of them, too. Next thing you and the twins will be telling me you're some kind of lowlands royalty."

Borya and Desya exchanged a glance and grinned wickedly. "Well, we don't like to brag," Borya said.

"But we've been meaning to bring this up," Desya said.

"Stop it, you two!" Zaryae said, laughing. She looked to Verran and shook her head, still chuckling. "Mind they don't feed you a line. Next thing you know, they'll have you addressing them as 'sir.'"

"And that would never do," Nidhud said drily. Connor and the others looked at Nidhud, trying to determine whether or not he was serious. His lips quirked, ever so slightly, at the corner, as much of a smile as Connor had ever seen from the Knight of Esthrane in the time he had known him.

Verran stretched and finished off his own shot of whiskey. "So once we get there, how do we find Grimur? He went off into the ice fields because he didn't want to be bothered by mortals. So we're just going to walk up to his cabin and knock?"

Nidhud shook his head. "No. The Wraith Lord is known to Grimur. That will be your surety. You have nothing to fear."

"Says the guy with the big, sharp teeth," Verran muttered.

Zaryae was watching Connor closely. "You're bothered by something," she said.

Connor shrugged, embarrassed. "It's nothing. Just ghosts."

"On the ship?" Desya asked.

Connor shook his head. "No. The ocean's full of them. So many ships over the years that went down in the deep places, and so many bodies that were never found or properly buried. They tug at me as we sail by, more in some places than others, wanting me to acknowledge them." *And in some cases, wanting to take me over,* he thought, but did not say the rest aloud.

"I can help you learn to shield," Zaryae offered. "You never had the benefit of being trained in your gift, did you?"

Connor sighed. "I didn't even realize I had a gift until I met the Wraith Lord. I mean, I knew I could see ghosts better than most people, but I really didn't think of that as a *gift*. And I certainly never thought I could allow ghosts to speak through me."

"Part of learning to use your gift is learning how to control it, instead of letting it control you," Zaryae said. "I was fortunate to have others in my caravan who had abilities similar to my foresight, who showed me how to keep it from taking over my mind." She touched his arm. "If you'd like, I can do the same for you."

Connor nodded. "I would be very grateful," he said. "The extra power I came away with as a Lord of the Blood was protection against being taken over against my will, but there's still a lot I don't know about my magic and how it works."

Zaryae smiled. "I would be glad to help—and we have the time on the journey." Abruptly, her gaze became distant, as if she had heard a voice from afar. Zaryae's eyes went wide, and she gasped. "We are all in very great danger. Death comes from the skies."

Before anyone could react, the ship made a sudden shift, throwing them all across the deck except for Nidhud. "What in Raka is going on?" Borya said, springing to his feet along with Desya and sprinting for the door.

"The captain was sure the weather was calm," Verran grumbled. He and Connor managed to grab on to hammocks, so they avoided sliding across the deck. Connor barely caught hold of Zaryae's arm as she tumbled, saving her from crashing into the opposite bulkhead. They had just reached their feet when the ship lurched again, throwing them off balance so that they clutched at the support posts to remain upright.

"Something's wrong," Connor said, and headed toward the door.

"If there's a problem, you're safest down here," Nidhud said.

"Depends on the problem," Connor retorted. "I fought my way out of the hold of a sinking ship once. I don't care to do it again." He pushed past Nidhud and climbed the ladder out of the hold.

The deck was a battlefield. "Stay under cover!" Borya shouted from somewhere in the shadows. Connor drew back just as something large and dark shrieked through the air as it dove at him, pulling up an instant before it would have rammed into the deck.

Desya slipped toward them, staying close to the railings for cover. "I'm going to fetch our bows. There's something out there, something big, and it's hunting." He dropped to the bottom of the ladder like a cat. An instant later, Nidhud appeared on deck.

"You decided to join us?" Connor asked.

Nidhud nodded. "If there's a fight, I may be useful."

Connor could hear Captain Whitney's voice shouting commands in the night. The deadly silhouette swooped again, and Connor strained to get a better look from where he crouched along the bulkhead. *Big, like a* gryp*, but not the right shape. Head's all wrong. Too much of a beak, skull's too narrow,* he thought.

Nidhud had brought his sword with him when he came on deck. "It's one of the monsters from the magic storms," he shouted. "A *hesper.*" Magic storms had plagued Donderath, a side effect of the Cataclysm. Monsters often appeared out of the storms, terrifying beings changed or summoned by the wild magic. Most of those creatures had been killed in Donderath by now, at least in the more populated areas. It had not occurred to Connor that some of those monsters might also have spawned from storms at sea.

"Can we fight it with fire, like we did the *gryps?*" Verran asked.

Zaryae turned to him. "You really want to use fire—on a ship in the middle of the ocean?"

Verran reconsidered. "Maybe not. But will anything else drive it off?"

Whitney's sailors were putting up a valiant effort. The seamen charged at the giant flying predator armed with cutlasses and belaying pins. Two of the sailors managed to get in several blows when the *hesper* dove at them, but despite the bone-cracking force of the strikes, the *hesper* used its strong wings to slap one of the sailors out of the way, and struck with its talons to grab the other before the man could react. Borya and Desya were in the rigging with their bows, but the darkness, the movement of the ship, and the swiftness of the predator made it difficult to land a killing shot.

Connor winced at the man's screams as he was carried aloft.

The cries were suddenly silenced as the *hesper* slashed at its prey and droplets of blood hit the deck below. In the light of the deck lanterns, Connor caught a better glimpse of their attacker. The monster was covered with dark, smooth feathers. Its skull was narrow and elongated, ending in a terrifyingly long, sharp bill. Powerful talons scratched across the deck, and the creature must have had keen predator's senses, given how easily it sought its prey in the dark.

The *hesper* carried its prey into the air. Its wings beat in lazy, powerful strokes that sent gusts of air across the ship's deck. As the crew and passengers watched in horror, the creature tossed the man into the air, stretched its bill open wide, and gulped him down, like a gull with a fish.

Zaryae had gone pale. "Sweet Charrot, not again," she murmured. Connor knew that Zaryae and the others had fought the *gryps* many times, and that Zaryae had lost a family member to the monsters.

Several of the men maneuvered a small ballista from beneath a tarpaulin. Aiming it was a challenge, as the *hesper*'s dives were steep and fast, and they dared not shoot at the creature when it was anywhere near their own masts or sails. That limited their ability, since the ballista's base could not swivel to track the airborne monster's moves. Some of the sailors ran belowdecks, to emerge with armfuls of heavy, rounded rocks and balls of plaited vines, ammunition for the ballista.

"Clear!" one of the ballista men shouted. With a thud, the small catapult sent a rock the size of a man's head into the air, aiming just ahead of the *hesper*'s path. The rock struck a glancing blow on the creature's side, and the monster shrieked angrily, circling to dive at the men manning the ballista. They dove for cover, and other sailors surged forward with spears and crossbows they had grabbed from a locker on deck.

"Pull!" the sailor holding the crossbow yelled. The powerful bolt nearly matched the speed of the *hesper*, lodging in its breast. Blood dripped from the wound, and the *hesper* faltered in the air, dropping several feet before gaining altitude again. The ballista crew lobbed another rock to catch the *hesper* while it was slowed, but once again, the creature managed to twist out of the way, so that the rock struck only a glancing blow against one of its taloned feet, snapping a claw in the process.

Enraged, the *hesper* dove at the deck, and one of its powerful, feathered wings swept the sailors aside before they could get off a shot. Archers from the rigging fired their arrows, but the tough feathers deflected most of the arrows like armor. One sailor came at the monster with a curse, swinging a grappling hook with all his might, intent on impaling the *hesper* with the hook's sharp tip. He landed a blow against the monster's side, only to be carried into the air as the creature beat its strong wings and lifted off from the deck. The sailor screamed as the creature carried him out over the dark, choppy waters and shook him and his hook loose, dropping them into the sea.

Some of the sailors pulled out slings and grabbed handfuls of small rocks from the pile of ammunition on the deck. Rocks pelted the *hesper*, and the creature shrieked and hissed, drawing back and out of range, but not yet willing to give up. The *hesper* flew slowly around the ship, looking for the safest angle from which to attack.

"Connor, I have an idea on how to defeat this thing. But you'll need to give yourself over to the Wraith Lord to make it work," Nidhud said, appearing so suddenly at Connor's elbow that he jumped.

The *hesper*'s talons put a long rip in one of the ship's sails. If the *Nomad* took more of that kind of damage, they could end up adrift in the middle of the ocean. That decided Connor. "Do it," he said, and opened himself to the Wraith Lord.

Kierken Vandholt had been many things over the last thousand years: soldier, mage, *talishte*, Elder. And for the last six hundred years, he had been a wraith, caught between life and death as a result of sacrifice, treachery, and the intervention of a goddess. Connor's gifts as a medium meant Vandholt could take possession of his body and mind, while leaving Connor's consciousness intact. They had forged a partnership of sorts, and as intrusive as the Wraith Lord's possession was, Connor knew he would have been dead many times over without it.

Connor felt the familiar frisson of power as the Wraith Lord's spirit slipped inside his body. By now, he had learned to withdraw to a corner of his mind where he was able to watch and influence as Vandholt moved his body with the deadly grace of a thousand-year-old *talishte*-mage.

You're planning to fight that thing? Connor asked the Wraith Lord.

Not physically, not if I can help it, he replied.

Then how?

Magic, the Wraith Lord replied.

You've never used me to do magic, Connor protested. *Will it even work with my body? I've got no magic talent at all except channeling spirits.*

The Wraith Lord chuckled. *How easily you dismiss your abilities! But yes, it will work. Magic is not a function of body, but of spirit.*

Connor stepped out of the shadows, with the Wraith Lord in control. He strode out onto deck amid the chaos. Captain Whitney had given the wheel to his second-in-command, and now Whitney was down on the main deck with the rest of his men, fighting off the *hesper* with their swords and lanterns.

"Go back below!" Whitney shouted when he saw Connor. "You're going to get yourself killed!"

The *hesper* shrieked and gyred, then it came at the deck with horrifying speed, its bill thrust forward, plunging like a falcon. From up on the rigging, Borya and Desya let fly well-aimed arrows. One of the arrows struck the *hesper* in its wing, and the other hit the creature's body forward of the wing joint. The *hesper* kept on flying as if it had not noticed the injuries. More arrows flew, and although several hit their mark, the *hesper* did not falter.

Nidhud had appeared beside Connor. "Let me take a crack at him." He raised both hands, muttered words of power under his breath, and pushed outward, as if shoving the creature away. Cold, furious power streamed from Nidhud's hands, glowing without burning, and it hit the *hesper* like the slap of a hand onto a fly. The *hesper* shrieked and fell, but caught itself just before plunging into the ocean, and let out a cry that sent chills down Connor's back.

"I think you made it mad," Connor observed.

The *hesper* swooped low, and wide, powerful wings downed sailors like bowling pins. This time, its talons raked across the lower deck, tearing up boards and leaving deep gashes in the wood. The *hesper* beat its wings and the sails rippled as the creature lifted away again, out of reach of the knives and belaying pins thrown at it. But before it could grab another sailor, the Wraith Lord and Nidhud stepped out to confront it.

"Together!" the Wraith Lord said through Connor, and Nidhud nodded. They raised their hands, and fixed their attention on the *hesper*. "Back!" The voice that shouted the command was Connor's, but the will belonged to the Wraith Lord. A surge of power filled Connor, unlike any he had ever felt before, rising from the center of his being and swelling until he thought he would burst from it. Energy tingled up and down his body, and as the Wraith Lord thrust out his right hand, palm open and outstretched toward the *hesper*, that power reached a crescendo and exploded in a blast of force.

The blast hit the *hesper* in its chest, driving it back across the deck although its talons scraped at the decking boards for purchase. With a crash, it slammed into the railing and fell, screaming, over the side.

The sailors and onlookers stood in stunned silence, and then a cheer went up from the seamen. *Not yet, lads,* the Wraith Lord murmured in Connor's mind, and his gaze never left the spot where the *hesper* had vanished into the sea.

An earsplitting shriek made the others jump. Beating its enormous wings hard enough that it sent spray up from the sea, the *hesper* lifted out of the ocean like a dark god, malevolent red eyes fixed directly on Connor.

"Everyone, take cover!" Captain Whitney shouted. The others ran, leaving Connor and Nidhud on the deck as the *hesper* hung on the wind above the waves just off the starboard side of the ship, eyeing them warily, trying to decide what to make of its upstart prey. "Get back!" Whitney warned.

As the *hesper* dove forward, the Wraith Lord did not hesitate. "Burn!" he shouted, and this time, fire streaked from Connor's outstretched hand. Flames engulfed the *hesper*, illuminating its fearsome outline clearly, showing its huge wings, sharp bill, and clawed feet in clear detail. Before its tumble into the sea, the creature's feathers might have gone up like tinder. Now, it was heat and not flames that the *hesper* felt. The monster shot up in the air to avoid the blast, but the Wraith Lord's *talishte* reflexes were just as quick.

Bright flame against the black night left trails of color in Connor's vision as the Wraith Lord kept the *hesper* in his blast.

The oil on the creature's feathers had kept them dry enough to ward off the initial firestorm, but as the Wraith Lord held steady with the flames, the feathers began to smoke. By now, the *hesper*'s beak was soot-streaked, and flesh peeled from its calloused legs. In a flash of light too bright to watch, the *hesper* burst into flames and its huge burning body fell out of the sky, twisting as it went. Its broad wings clipped the outer edge of one of the *Nomad*'s sails, and the sail burst into flame, like a beacon on the dark sea. Then with a loud splash, the *hesper* fell into the sea, causing a wave that rocked the ship and sending water high enough into the air that it crashed across the deck.

"Watch out!" voices shouted as the burning sail began to rain embers down onto everything below it. Sailors ran for buckets, but it would take far too long even for Borya and Desya to climb high enough into the rigging to douse the flames, assuming they could stand the heat. Even then, the water would be a fraction of what was needed to put out the fire.

Connor watched with a growing feeling of detachment, as if the world around him was receding down a long corridor. His body felt too heavy to move, and the thoughts that were his own were slow. His right palm was as sore as if he had touched a hot stove, and he felt as if he had just done a hard day's labor.

One more task, the Wraith Lord assured him. Connor felt the strange energy coalesce once more, humming through his body, gathering in his outstretched right arm with a tingling sense that rapidly became a pins-and-needles burn.

This time, the Wraith Lord directed Connor's arm toward the sea off the port side. The Wraith Lord mumbled words Connor did not catch, and made a scooping motion with his hand. A torrent of seawater poured down onto the burning sail from out of the sky. It doused the flames and put out the embers smoking on nearby sails. The unexpected deluge nearly threw

Desya and Borya from their perch, forcing them to cling to the rigging amid shouted curses. Sailors grabbed for something to hold on to as the water hit the deck with enough force to wash a man overboard.

The ship rocked with the hit, and then all was quiet. Blackened strips of cloth hung from the ruined sail, and the smell of burning hemp and oilcloth filled the air as charred bits of rope fluttered to the deck like dark snow.

"What in the name of the gods are you?" Captain Whitney said, staring at Connor with wide eyes.

"Tired," Connor slurred, and found that his legs would no longer support him.

Once again, I have pushed you too far, the Wraith Lord's voice sounded in his mind, but it was faint and far away. Then he heard nothing more except the *thud* of his body against the planking as he collapsed to the deck.

CHAPTER
THIRTEEN

CONNOR FLOATED IN A PLACE BETWEEN WORLDS. He remembered feeling fear, then exhilaration, and finally, overwhelming exhaustion.

Rest. You did well. The Wraith Lord's voice sounded in the darkness, a reassuring presence.

If you could do your magic through me, why wait until now? I can think of a couple dozen times it would have been quicker to just 'poof' the enemy out of existence. Exhausted as he was, Connor had enough energy left for a bit of righteous annoyance.

Do you remember the toll it took on you, just to allow me to use your body to fight with a sword?

That's not the kind of thing you forget. When the Wraith Lord had first begun to possess Connor, even a short battle had taxed Connor's strength to the breaking point. More than once in those early days, Connor had nearly died from hosting the Wraith Lord's greater power that burned through him like a candle held to a roaring fire. Permitting the Wraith Lord to fight through him in those dire situations had saved countless lives. Yet the injuries Connor sustained and the depletion of his own life force had forced Penhallow to take desperate measures to heal him. Those measures had bound Connor even more closely to Penhallow through the *kruvgaldur*, a bond that was telepathic and empathic. Over time, the depth of that bond had begun to make Connor stronger, more resilient, but at the cost of making him less and less mortal.

I dared not channel my magic through you, the Wraith Lord said. *Look at how just my essence taxed you sorely.*

That might be an understatement, Connor thought. *It damn near killed me.* Possessed by the Wraith Lord, Connor moved faster, struck harder, fought without fatigue, felt less pain—until his body could withstand the strain no more, and he collapsed.

You're only now strong enough to withstand such power, the Wraith Lord continued patiently. *And even so, only for short bursts.*

When you were…embodied…you could do more magic at one time? Connor's curiosity about the man Kierken Vandholt had been before he became the Wraith Lord won out even over his exhaustion.

Oh yes, the Wraith Lord replied. *I was an equal to any of the Knights of Esthrane, and perhaps even more skilled than some.*

So that's what it feels like to actually do magic? It had never occurred to Connor that he might experience the thrum of a mage's power through his own body, though he had occasionally wondered what it would be like to be able to harness that energy.

He had been in the presence of devastatingly strong magic more times than he cared to count, over the last year. First, the night of the Great Fire, and then at Valshoa and Mirdalur, when Blaine attempted to restore the magic. In between, in so many battles, Connor had seen what mages could do, and the sheer raw power of it, compared with his more subtle skill with spirits, had always awed and humbled him. And, to be honest, scared the shit out of him.

The Wraith Lord's laughter was a low rumble, like distant thunder. *For someone with so strong a gift as yours, your humility is amusing. You never cease to amaze me, Bevin Connor.*

Connor thought for a moment. *Could Nidhud have done what you—we—did?*

You saw his power, the Wraith Lord replied. *But talishtemages have a fundamental problem with fire magic. Even if they can cast it, the risk to themselves is so great most will not do so unless they intend it as a death strike. Mortals are much less flammable.*

They fell silent for a moment as Connor mulled over what he had seen in the battle.

Am I damaged from tonight's work? Did I die? Until that moment, it had not occurred to Connor that he and the Wraith Lord might be conversing in the Unseen Realm, the place between life and death where souls barred from the punishment of Raka or the rest of the Sea of Souls drifted for eternity, the wasteland of the afterlife, where Kierken Vandholt was condemned to wander.

You did not die, the Wraith Lord assured him. *But I erred in pushing you too far, though it was necessary to save the ship. We are still exploring the limits of your new strength, both through your bond to Penhallow and what you gained at Mirdalur, as a Lord of the Blood.*

Now that we know it's possible, can you call the magic up through me again?

The Wraith Lord chuckled. *Your spirit intrigues me, Connor. In one thought, you check to see if you are dead, and in the next, ask to channel the same power again.*

It's not meant to be funny, Connor replied peevishly. *I didn't know magic was even an option. Now that it is, even briefly, it might save me from getting sliced up in so many sword fights.*

I have no desire to damage so fine a host as yourself, the Wraith

Lord said with fond amusement. *You serve me well, as you do Penhallow. And like Penhallow, I have sworn to protect you as best I may. You are the pivotal person in this journey. If you don't survive, the journey fails and so may any attempt to use the Elgin Spike. So I will judge when and how we draw on my magic, and we will learn those limits together. Fair enough?*

More than fair, Connor acknowledged. *Now I think I'd like to sleep.*

"I was afraid we might not get you back." Zaryae's voice reached Connor through the last wisps of sleep.

He opened his eyes, finding himself in their quarters belowdecks. His hammock swung gently with the motion of the ship, and the light streaming in from the single porthole let him guess how much time had passed since the battle. "I'm here," he rasped.

Zaryae put a hand behind his head and helped him sit up enough to drink from a wineskin. "You had us worried."

"I thought everyone was used to this by now." Connor still felt weak and spent. His right hand was wrapped in strips of cloth.

"Not sure exactly what kept your hand from being burned to a cinder," Zaryae said, "but the skin is slightly blistered, so I made a salve and wrapped it."

"Thank you," Connor replied, dropping back against the hammock. "How is the ship?"

Zaryae sighed. "Worse for the wear, but not as bad as it would have been without your help. Borya and Desya are up on deck helping rig the spare sails Captain Whitney brought with us, thank the gods. Verran is lending a hand fetching and carrying, and helping spool the ropes."

"And I'm lying here, useless."

Zaryae chuckled. "You were plenty useful last night. And to tell the truth, I think it's probably for the best that you not make an appearance right away. From what I heard, the sailors are spooked about what happened."

"Which part? The monster or the mages?"

"Both," Zaryae said. She helped him sit once more, and spooned broth for him from a bowl of warm soup. "Whitney may be *kruvgaldur*-bound to one of the Elders, but I'm betting he's seen precious little magic, or at least, nothing of battle magic. Nidhud kept him away from you after the fighting was over, and made it clear that Whitney's oath to his *talishte* patron meant that Whitney had personally secured your safety with his own life."

Connor groaned. "I bet that went over well."

Zaryae lowered the empty bowl. "Whitney strikes me as a reasonable man. Anyone who's been at sea for a length of time has seen a lot of strange things. And I'm betting he had heard tales of such magic, whether he believed them or not. He'll come around."

"What about the crew? Do I have to fear being tossed overboard as a jinx?" Connor asked, feeling the warmth of the soup in his belly. Hosting the Wraith Lord took more than psychic strength and borrowed energy. That level of full body-and-spirit magic left Connor depleted as if he had fought a physical battle. With the heightened strength of the *kruvgaldur*, it might take only one or two days for Connor to get back on his strength, compared with the much longer recuperation he had required without the bond.

"I think you're more at risk of none of them wanting to come within twenty feet of you," Zaryae responded. "They were already leery of Nidhud, since he's *talishte*. But they don't know what to make of you." She chuckled. "If you'll forgive me saying so, you're far more powerful than you appear."

"That's the Wraith Lord, not me," Connor replied.

"Really? I've seen how you use your power," Zaryae differed. "You've done things with your abilities that didn't involve the Wraith Lord's magic or skill that turned the tide of battle. You don't fully comprehend just how powerful a gift you have."

"I know that it keeps nearly getting me killed," Connor grumbled.

"More to the point, it's saved you and your friends—and their cause—on more than one occasion," Zaryae pointed out. As she talked, she made a mixture of leaves and powders from her pouches, then moistened it with a few drops of water and made a small wad of it.

"Let this dissolve in your mouth. Don't chew it, but it won't hurt to swallow the juice. It will replenish your energy, and take away some of the pain."

"What about the ship?" Connor pressed.

Zaryae sighed. "Even with what you and Nidhud did, the *Nomad* took some damage. Broken railing, torn-up decking, and of course, the sails and rigging that were burned. It's going to cost us some time to fix what can be set right before we can move on, but Whitney believes we'll be under way soon. He's hoping he can repair the more serious damage in Edgeland, while they're waiting for us to do what we need to do."

"And in the meantime, we're sitting ducks."

Zaryae looked away. "Yes."

Connor frowned. "Talk to me. You've seen something, haven't you? We're in danger."

Zaryae fixed him with a matter-of-fact look. "Any ocean

voyage involves danger," she said. "Many things *could* happen, but that doesn't mean they *will* happen. Unfortunately, my foresight sees the possible, not merely the probable."

"What have you seen?"

Zaryae shivered and set aside the empty bowl, wrapping her arms around herself. "I see storms and darkness. I see danger in the dark water. I feel that death will brush close to us. And regardless of which possibilities come to pass, I fear that not all of those now on board will be among the living when we return to Donderath."

Connor sighed. "I'm not sure which is worse—me channeling the spirits of the dead, or you getting a glimpse of every possible thing that could go horribly wrong."

Zaryae managed a sad smile. "Our gifts, our magic, make us who we are. They're a tool, and a burden. No different than a sword that has to be wielded carefully so that it doesn't cut its owner as well as its foe."

Connor grimaced. "I can sheath my sword, and be done with it. No one's shown me yet how to sheath my 'gift.'"

"Unknown ship, closing fast!" the sailor on watch shouted from his perch high in the rigging.

Three days after the fight with the *hesper*, Connor had finally ventured onto the deck. The last few days had been sunny and still. This day was overcast, and the wind had picked up. Connor lifted his face to the sky, wondering if it would rain.

The weather had held long enough for the crew to rig the replacement sails and fix the worst of the damage to the ship. Connor had stayed in his quarters, recovering. Zaryae and Verran brought him food and supplied him with news. Borya and Desya remained with the crew, and their dexterity and fearlessness climbing the rigging won them the admiration of the sailors. Verran pitched in when he could, and kept the sailors entertained with music when there were no tasks for him to do.

Up by the ship's wheel, Connor could see Captain Whitney with his spyglass, scanning the horizon in the direction indicated by the scout. "How soon will you have the rigging finished?" he shouted down to the crew.

"A few more candlemarks, sir," Trad, Whitney's second-in-command, shouted back. "Bit more of a challenge in the wind, but we'll get them in place."

"We need to get moving right away," Zaryae said, staring at open water. "If that ship catches up, there's going to be trouble." She gathered her skirts and climbed the stairs, and Connor hurried behind her, though he was leery of coming face-to-face with Captain Whitney after what had happened.

"Captain!" Zaryae hailed Whitney. "That ship you've spotted. It's trouble. We need to keep it from catching up to us."

Whitney's gaze went from Zaryae to Connor. His eyes were suspicious, and Connor was sure he saw a glint of fear as well. "What's so important? We're not fully rigged yet."

Zaryae took a deep breath. "I see things, Captain. Things that haven't happened yet. And I know that if we close with that ship, there will be trouble."

Whitney raised his glass again. "Maybe. Maybe not. Here's the thing. The wind's picking up. My storm glass says we could be in for some bad weather. I'd hoped the men would have the rigging fixed before this, but there've been problems."

"Problems?" Connor asked.

Whitney's gaze narrowed as he looked at Connor. "One man died when the rope he used for support gave way under him. The replacement sail had a rip in it, so that took time to mend. The cordage was tangled, although my men swear it was stored properly. It's been one damned thing after another, which is why we're still sitting here when there's a storm brewing."

His eyes glinted angrily. "After the fight with that monster, I've now lost several good men and more are injured. We were running a slim crew to begin with, so that means fewer hands for more work. Now we might be in for another attack." He shook his head. "And we're only just into the voyage."

Zaryae shrugged. "My foresight isn't perfect, Captain. I could be wrong, but when my instinct is so strong, I've learned to trust it. Perhaps it's not the intent of the new ship to harm us. Maybe it's something about them drawing close that will cause a problem. All I've got is a warning. No details."

Whitney gave a harrumph and made a face that gave them to know exactly what he thought of vague predictions. "I'd thank you to keep your predictions between the three of us," he replied. "My men are still buzzing about what happened the other night." He turned to Connor. "If we get into a tight place with these newcomers, can you do something about it?"

"That would depend on what needs to be done," Connor replied.

"Can you magic up the rigging, fix it, and get us under way?"

Connor sighed. "Maybe there are mages who can, but I can't. I'm more use in a fight than anywhere else. My power comes and goes." That was technically true. *If he's jumpy about magic, I doubt he'd like the real explanation, that I've got to let a thousand-year-old* talishte-*mage possess my body in order to do anything he'd consider to be 'magic.'* "And Nidhud won't be able to help until after nightfall."

Whitney nodded. "All right, then. We're not entirely without defenses. Mister Trad—a word with you!"

Trad hurried across the deck and climbed the stairs to join them. "Sir?"

Trad and Whitney were a study in contrasts. Whitney was short and wiry, bald and hawk-faced, with a shrewd, intelligent look in his eyes. Trad was a head taller, broad-shouldered and brawny, with brown hair tied back in a tail and a scar that cut across his right cheek and eyebrow and a look that was street-smart, if not book-learned.

"We're vulnerable, and there's an unknown ship heading our way. Best to assume the worst. Make sure the weapons are in easy reach, and prepare for hostilities. But no one fires except on my order, or in response to their first strike. Clear?"

Trad gave a sharp nod. "Clear, sir." He headed back to the main deck, shouting orders to the riggers and calling out a few of the men on deck to follow him.

"It could be a merchant ship," Connor offered, although he feared Zaryae's premonition was correct.

Whitney gave a curt nod. "Maybe. But there's precious little of that, since the Cataclysm. Where would it be coming from, or going to? It's only been in the last month or two that small ships are making their way up Donderath's coast again, trading fish for crops. We're far away from the coast. So what are they doing way out here?"

"Could they be from the Cross-Sea Kingdoms?" Connor asked. "We never did find out what happened to them in the Cataclysm."

"Possible," Whitney allowed. "We're in the main shipping paths, or at least, what used to be the main routes before every-thing fell apart. More likely they're from a chain of islands off the northern end of the Continent. We've been sailing parallel to the coast, so while we're a good ways from Donderath, we're closer than you might think to the northeast reaches."

Connor had heard about those islands. They were known for only one thing. Pirates.

Whitney turned to Connor. "We're not defenseless, but we're at a disadvantage. Anything you can do to help would be mightily appreciated."

Connor swallowed hard. "I'll do what I can."

Out on deck, the sailors had split into two teams. One group remained hard at work on repairs, rigging the new sail. The other group prepared for attack. The ship's two ballistae were rolled out from beneath their tarpaulins, and sailors carried up boxes of stones and flammable balls of pitch-soaked rags with a stone core, wrapped in rope and vines. Others hauled out large rope nets and hung them from the rail to the rigging wherever they could do so without interfering with the repairs overhead.

Bowmen slung their crossbows across their backs along with quivers full of bolts, preferring them over the regular bows, given the strength of the wind. Spears stood at the ready in their racks around the masts, and marlin spikes were readily available, as were belaying pins. Every sailor carried a long knife or a sling, and some had both, along with pouches to hold their ammunition. Connor and his friends had their broadswords, as did Whitney and Trad, and some of the sailors had wicked-looking small axes that were shoved in their belts, close at hand.

From other lockers came a supply of bucklers and short swords, grappling hooks and caltrops. "Voss made sure that we were well provisioned," Whitney remarked drily. "He expected that you and your friends might attract the wrong type of attention."

Connor felt a surge of relief. The crew had fought well against the *hesper*, with no notice of an impending attack. He reminded himself that the sailors were drawn from Tra-her Voss's mercenaries, more than able to protect themselves. That meant the *Nomad* might be able to stave off any danger presented by the foreign ship without needing Connor's magic. He fervently hoped that would be the case.

I would advise reserving magic as a last resort, the Wraith Lord's voice sounded in Connor's mind. *Your strength is finite, and we have unknown dangers ahead of us in Edgeland.*

Thanks for reminding me of that, Connor replied, unable to keep the nervous edge out of his voice.

The mission on Edgeland may go smoothly, without peril, the Wraith Lord answered. *But I would not bet on it. Best to hold some defenses in reserve, until there is no choice.*

Just stay close, Connor warned. *This could go very bad, very fast.*

The Wraith Lord gave a low chuckle. *I am always close.*

Captain Whitney turned the wheel. Wind fluttered in the undamaged sails. "We can't move fast until the repairs are finished, but we can shift course a bit. If our newcomers have good intent, that should mean our paths don't intersect."

And if the other ship changes course to intercept, we'll know for certain they're up to no good, Connor thought.

"They're changing tack, sir!" Trad shouted. "Shadowing us!"

"Get ready for a fight, then, because they're going to catch us," Whitney yelled. "Keep those sons of bitches from boarding us."

As the other ship drew closer, Connor got a better look. Where their own ship, the *Nomad*, had seen use, it was as well maintained as circumstances permitted, not counting the recent damage. The hull was painted, the deck and railings stained, the sails were mostly undamaged and otherwise neatly patched, and the rigging was in good repair.

None of those things were true of the ship bearing down on them. Large tears in the sails were patched with black stitching, giving it a scarred and seedy appearance. The hull was painted a variety of mismatched colors, and the paint was peeling in places. The incoming ship's decking and railings were gray from the sun, and its rigging looked dangerously frayed. On the bow of the ship, painted in rough letters, was its name: *Lammergeier*.

"They're mad to go to sea in a bucket like that!" Connor exclaimed.

Zaryae had been watching so quietly that Connor had nearly forgotten that she was with them. "They aren't mad. They're desperate—and dangerous," she murmured. "I see…blood. It's not their habit to leave witnesses alive."

Whitney regarded her for a moment, then set his jaw. "Then we'd damned well better not let them get a foothold," he resolved.

Overhead, the sky had turned a steely gray. The wind had picked up enough that the men trying to repair the rigging were struggling to finish their work. And while the wind worked in favor of the *Lammergeier*'s crew, the *Nomad* was at a disadvantage, two sails short of fully rigged.

Whitney was already maneuvering the ship upwind. "If we're holding the weather gage on them, they can't easily ram us," he muttered. "Though we can dance around each other for a while."

Trad came to the bow of the *Nomad* holding a speaking trumpet. "Attention, *Lammergeier*! We wish to pass through these waters peacefully. Draw back, and we will not harm you. Engage us, and we will sink your ship to the bottom of the sea!"

Connor glanced at Whitney. The captain's eyes held a stubborn glint, and his lips were drawn back across his teeth in a determined grimace. *Perhaps there's a reason he is* kruvgaldur-*bond to one of the Elders,* Connor thought. *I may have underestimated him.*

The *Lammergeier* continued to bear down on the *Nomad*. As the pirate ship grew closer, Connor could see that it was outfitted with its own ballistae, and its crew was armed with grappling hooks and war axes, along with a ferocious assortment of pikes and swords.

"Cut them off!" Trad commanded.

Whitney steered the *Nomad* at the *Lammergeier* as Trad opened fire with the ballistae. The heavy rocks crashed down onto the deck of the *Lammergeier* and through the worn planking, sending the pirates scattering. As the pirates moved to return fire, Borya, Desya, and two other archers high in the rigging of the *Nomad* leveled their crossbows and fired at the men working the ballistae. The wind made it difficult to aim. Only one of the arrows found its mark, but it took a pirate through the shoulder, dropping him to the deck.

The pirates launched their own ballistae, and the *Nomad's* crew ran for cover. Two heavy, round rocks hit the deck with a thunderous *bang*, but although the *Nomad's* decking splintered, it did not give way.

Borya and Desya were used to shooting while standing astride galloping horses, so the motion of the ship did not faze them, though the wind was a challenge. They and the other bowmen fired again, and two of the quarrels reached their targets. But as Connor watched, he could see that what the *Lammergeier's* men were loading into the ballistae this time were not more heavy rocks but iron harpoons with long, trailing ropes.

"They mean to try boarding us!" Trad warned the crew. "Send them back to where they came from!"

The harpoons launched with a heavy *thud*, and their weight made them better able to fight the wind than the lighter quarrels. Both of the harpoons hit the side of the *Nomad*, but only one embedded itself into the ship's hull.

Whitney had a white-knuckled grip on the ship's wheel, maneuvering the crippled ship to keep its advantage upwind, as the *Lammergeier* tried to slip around it and gain the upper hand. On deck, Borya and Desya were still intent on picking off the ballistae men on the enemy vessel, while Trad's men kept up a consistent pounding from the ballistae. One daring sailor slung a buckler over his back and swung off the side of the *Nomad* with a battle-ax, slicing cleanly through the rope that attached to the harpoon before being quickly drawn over the side and out of harm's way by his mates.

The flicker of fire caught Connor's attention. Bowmen on the *Nomad*'s forecastle shot flaming crossbow bolts toward the *Lammergeier*, only to have the wind snuff out the flames and drop the charred quarrels into the sea. The ballista crew had better luck with their stone-weighted, rag-stuffed missiles, set aflame an instant before their release. One of the burning missiles hit the *Lammergeier*'s shrouds, catching the ropes on fire.

Two more crossbow bolts struck their targets, sending their victims tumbling over the side of the *Lammergeier* and into the water. A shot from the *Lammergeier* knocked one of the *Nomad*'s men from the rigging, and he fell screaming into the ocean. Both crews traded curses and obscenities, and as the ships maneuvered for position, it was clear that although the pirates did not expect an easy victory, they were unwilling to give up even in the face of well-armed resistance.

Connor eyed the clouds warily. Since the *Lammergeier*'s approach, the clouds had grown heavier and darker. Both boats were rocking harder now, and the horizon had grown nearly black, though it was candlemarks until sundown. Whitecaps rose in the waves, and the wind was growing steadily colder and stronger. The storm was coming up hard and fast, but neither ship seemed willing to run.

"They're crazy to force a fight in this weather," Connor said, his voice nearly lost in the wind.

"Don't underestimate what men will do when their pride is on the line," Zaryae replied. "Or when their backs are to the wall. By the looks of them, they may be desperate for anything they can steal."

"We'll all end up at the bottom if we don't get away soon," Connor said, gripping the railing tightly as the ship pitched on the waves.

Bodies floated on the sea between the ships, tossed by the waves, trapped between the two hulls. But as Connor watched, one of the corpses suddenly vanished beneath the water's surface.

"There!" Connor shouted. "Did you see that? Something snatched a body from the water!"

From the cry that went up on both ships, Connor realized he was not the only one to notice. The water between the two ships roiled, forcing them apart, and sailors began pointing and shouting from both of the warring vessels. A second body vanished, plucked from below and dragged into the depths.

"I don't know what that is, but we're getting out of here," Whitney muttered, turning the wheel to widen the gap between the two ships. The *Lammergeier* was already moving away, having lost its belly for a fight. *Or maybe, since we're in the pirates' home waters, they know better than we do what we've stirred up,* Connor thought.

A third corpse vanished into the waves, but this time, Connor caught a glimpse of an expanse of dark, slick skin that disappeared as quickly as it came. "There's a creature down there," he said, staring at the ocean, hoping it had just been a trick of the light.

Something slammed the hull of the *Nomad* hard enough to nearly knock Connor off his feet. "Was that the pirates?"

Whitney shook his head. "No. We got hit below the water-line, but we're nowhere near shore or rocks."

Whatever did that had to be big, Connor thought, fear rising in his throat. The water seemed to boil with the thrashing beneath the waves, and turbulence pushed the two ships farther apart. The *Lammergeier's* crew had already abandoned the fight and changed their tack, heading out to sea and southward.

Whitney attempted to maneuver the *Nomad* northward toward open waters. He signaled Trad, who shouted for the men to fill the sails. Thanks to the pirates, the two damaged sails had not been replaced, although the ship had taken no additional damage in the fight. Now, the lack of those sails might be the difference between outrunning what swam beneath the water and being eaten by a monster from the deep.

"There!" shouted one of the sailors on the main deck. Connor squinted to see better in the storm's gloom. A huge creature rose from the water. Its smooth skin was dark gray, and its snakelike body was as big around as a large hay wagon. Before it splashed beneath the waves once more, Connor got a glimpse of its head. The cylindrical body ended not in a head so much as in an open, gaping mouth with a strange protuberance that extended over the opening and dangled limply, like bait.

"*Tanoba!*" The cry went up from the crew, echoed one man after another. Some made the sign of the gods over themselves to ward off harm, while others raised their hands to the dark sky in supplication. A sick feeling twisted the pit of Connor's stomach.

"If that flying monster, the *hesper*, was left over from the wild storm magicked beasts," Connor said to Zaryae, "then so is the *tanoba*—"

She nodded. "It's an unnatural creature, like the *gryps* and the other monsters we've fought back in Donderath. And we both know just how dangerous those beasts can be."

"Look! It's going after the pirates!" One of the *Nomad*'s sailors pointed toward the ocean, where the huge, gray water serpent snaked after the unfortunate *Lammergeier*. The pirate crew saw the monster coming, and filled their sails in a desperate attempt to outrun the creature.

Connor watched in horrified fascination as the *tanoba* undulated through the waves. Once, he had seen a small snake swimming in a pond. It had amazed him that a thing without arms or legs could power through the water so effortlessly. Now, that wonder became utter terror.

The water rippled like the wake of a fast boat as the *tanoba* slipped through it, curving its powerful body to propel it through the waves. Just the portion of the *tanoba* visible above the water was frightening enough in size and strength, but Connor guessed that half or more of the sea serpent remained submerged. Someone had once told Connor that on land, snakes could slither as fast as most men could run. If so, then the *tanoba*'s speed had increased by the same factor as its size. The *tanoba* was closing the gap with the ill-fated *Lammergeier*, even as Captain Whitney sailed the *Nomad* away from the danger.

"Here," Whitney said, handing Connor his spyglass. "Watch if you want to. I've got a ship to steer."

Below on deck, Trad barked commands to the sailors, who were only too glad to comply. Repairs to the sails were put on hold as the crew worked to compensate for the missing canvas. Borya, Desya, and a few other sailors moved up and down the rigging like squirrels, sure-footed and quick.

"What do you see?" Zaryae had come up close behind Connor and stood by his right side.

"It's catching up to them," Connor reported. His gut tightened as he watched the *tanoba* close the distance to the

Lammergeier. The pirate crew, realizing they could not outrun the monster, had turned the ship to present the narrowest target possible. Ballistae hurled rocks that either bounced off the *tanoba*'s taut, gray skin or splashed harmlessly into the ocean.

The storm that had threatened throughout their battle now hit with full intensity. High in the dark clouds overhead, lightning flared, and far out to sea, brilliant white streaks touched down amid the waves. Wind lashed the water to whitecaps, sending spray high into the air, and thunder rumbled.

The wind was too strong for the pirates to use any flammable missiles. Slings were laughable against the muscular heft of the great sea worm. The crew of the *Lammergeier* tried to fend off the *tanoba* with their long, bladed pikes, but they could do little against its tough hide.

"Sweet Charrot," Connor said, his jaw tight with fear. Watching the *tanoba* strike was like something out of a minstrel's fantastic tale. The huge creature sank nearly out of sight beneath the water, and then with an explosive burst of speed, propelled itself straight up like a jumping dolphin.

"Torven and Esthrane keep my soul," Zaryae murmured, squinting to see better against the wind.

As they watched, the *tanoba*'s horrific size became clear. A creature easily twice as long as the *Lammergeier* burst from the surface of the sea and brought its writhing bulk down amidships. The mainmast fell like a tree to a woodsman, slapping hard against the water as it hit. The *tanoba*'s bulk and the force of its blow thrust the *Lammergeier* down into the sea, swamping its decks. The beleaguered ship rose on the next cresting wave, with the giant sea worm draped across its midsection. Then the *tanoba* began to thrash, its powerful, muscular form writhing against the deck of the rickety old ship. The foremast toppled next, then the mizzenmast, leaving the pirate ship dead in the water. The sea snake's movement rocked the ship violently, sending men screaming into the waves along with their puny pikes and useless ballistae.

The *tanoba* constricted its strong muscles, and its tail end whipped up out of the water on the opposite side of the ship, so that the monster's body wrapped itself around the hull. Connor caught his breath as the creature squeezed the ship so hard that its popping joints and breaking boards sounded like a thunderclap across the water. With slow, remorseless power, the *tanoba* rolled the ship onto its side.

The *Lammergeier*'s broken hull floated like a corpse for a few moments, then the monster gave another brutal squeeze, snapped the ship in half, and dragged it down into the depths.

Thunder boomed so close and loud that Connor jumped. Cold rain pelted them as the clouds opened and the storm caught up with them. So fixed on the lethal struggle between the *Lammergeier* and the *tanoba* had Connor been that he only now realized the new peril.

"What are you doing?" he asked as Whitney fought the wheel to force the ship to his chosen course.

"We can't outrun that thing, if it doesn't eat its fill of the pirates," Whitney said, tight-jawed. "The ship is already at a disadvantage for a fight without full sails. So I'm doing the only thing I can to keep that monster away from us."

"Steering into the storm," Zaryae breathed. "Gods preserve us."

CHAPTER FOURTEEN

——

ANG ON." WITH THAT, CAPTAIN WHITNEY
returned his full attention to steering the *Nomad* through
the waves.

Wind howled around them, and rigging slapped against the
masts as the wood creaked and groaned with the pressure of
the full sails. Rain slicked Connor's hair against his scalp, plas-
tering his clothing to his body. Zaryae's dress was soaked, and
she wrapped her arms around herself against the wind. Down
on the main deck, even Borya and Desya had abandoned their
posts high in the rigging, and they joined the deckhands, who
labored under the commands Trad screamed above the wind,
adjusting the sails so that the wind did not split them or cause
the ship to founder.

"If you see anything with that Sight of yours, I'd sure appreciate hearing about it," Whitney growled to Zaryae. "Get
below, both of you, before you catch your death."

Zaryae shook her head. "I'd be grateful for a canvas coat, but
I'd just as soon stay up here, if it's all the same to you. I have a
feeling you're going to need me."

Whitney's gaze slid to Zaryae with a mixture of skepticism and wariness. "You think so, huh?"

"I'd like to stay, too," Connor replied. "Although I'd appreciate something to keep the rain off me as well. Just in case there's anything I can do to help." *Magic.* Connor knew from the look in Whitney's eyes that the captain took his meaning right away.

"You might find some capes and hoods in the locker over there," he said, sparing a nod of his head to indicate a wooden box nearby. "If there are any to be had, that's where they'll be."

Connor worked his way carefully across the tilting, slippery deck, holding on tightly to some part of the ship the entire way. *After everything I've lived through, I've got no desire to be washed overboard.*

He returned with three worn capes and hoods, and steadied the wheel for Whitney while the captain put one on. Zaryae pulled hers over her head gratefully. Connor slipped into the cape and hood, though he was wet enough that rainwater ran down his back and legs beneath the coat.

"If you're going to stay with me, you'd best lash yourselves to the rail with that rope," Whitney directed. "Mind to use a slipknot, in case you want to move quickly."

The only reason for that would be if the ship was going down, Connor thought, in which case, it was a matter of drowning with the ship or later, afloat on the debris. *I've done that once. No desire to do it again. Do I have to nearly die every time I get on a boat?*

The *Nomad* plowed through the waves, though the sea had grown rough enough that the lower deck was awash with water. Waves slid beneath the rail, sluicing across the boards. Trad had sent all but the most essential crew belowdecks, and made sure that loose items and hatches were secured. Now, Connor knew, it was a matter of hunkering down to get through the storm as best they could.

Connor had managed to block out much of his first trip to Edgeland. *Or perhaps,* he thought, *the shock of so much lost all at once had been too much for his mind to grasp.* Now that he tried to remember, very little of those forty days at sea came to mind, save for the constant seasickness, the lead-cold fear, and the final, terrifying night when the *Prowess* went to the depths.

He did not recall the ghosts.

As Connor clung to the railing, soaked beneath his cape, chilled to the bone, faces began to form in the fog. He could not make out distinct features, but there was no mistaking the shapes and shadows that moved in the mist, the empty, person-shaped holes in the rain. Fish-belly-pale faces stared back at him with sightless eyes from the puddles on the deck. Cold fingers lightly touched his shoulders or trailed down his arms. In the howl of the wind, Connor heard the moaning of distant voices.

Those voices were growing closer.

At first, the murmuring was indistinct. Human, but unin-telligible, drowned out by the wind and the rain. Yet as the *Nomad* pushed on through the tempest, and the storm raged around them, both the voices and the images became much clearer.

Find us, the voices begged. *It's so dark and cold here.*

Bring us home, more spirits pleaded. *The tides leave us no rest.*

Give us your warmth. New voices, angry voices demanded their due.

Connor took a deep breath to calm himself, hardening his resolve to keep the spirits at bay. With his strengthened gift from being one of the Lords of the Blood, he had discovered that his power to see and hear ghosts was stronger than before, and those spirits could no longer easily force themselves upon him. That did not mean he could keep himself from hearing their incessant pleas or seeing their forms everywhere he turned. Maybe once his lessons with Zaryae were complete, he could shut the spirits out, but not yet.

So many of us. Hundreds. Thousands. Down in the dark. Don't you want to come to us? You can hear us. We'll tell you our tales.

Let us live again in you. Skin…blood…breath…warm. So warm. Our lives were cut short. Let us have yours….

Go away! Connor commanded silently. *I don't owe you anything. Your fate is your own. I can't save you, and my life belongs to me.*

You've got to sleep. We'll come to you in your dreams. Show you what it's like, down in the deep places where the fishes pick at your bones and the worms eat your eyes.

Leave me alone! I've done nothing to you, and I'll do nothing for you.

We could make a deal. We might even save your lives.

Connor hesitated. On one hand, he distrusted the ghosts. He could feel their hunger. Some of the spirits hung back, watching but saying nothing. From them, Connor felt resignation, regret, and hopelessness. A few challenged him, forcing their consciousness to the fore, vying for his attention and demanding what they wanted. Most were barely memories of their former selves, trapped between the mortal realm and the Sea of Souls, fading into shadows.

What kind of deal? Connor was certain any arrangement would be a fool's bargain. Then again, they were in the trackless sea, in a storm that even to his eyes was growing worse by the moment, with damaged sails, and still weeks to go before they reached their destination.

These waters are treacherous. That's why we're here, down in the dark. Our ships foundered. But we can guide you through.

What can you tell me that our captain doesn't know? Connor challenged.

There are mountains under the ocean, the voices replied. *They rise up from the deep, far below, where no light ever shines. But we see them, now. They cause the wicked currents that took our ships from us. They tore the keels from our ships and sent us to the bottom. The maps don't know them all. But we do. The dead know.*

And what would you ask in exchange? Connor said. *My life? My body? My soul?*

A breath, a bite of food, a drink of whiskey, warm blood... The voices drowned each other out as they vied for his attention.

Yet there is one of me, and thousands of you.

Without our help, you'll be joining us very soon. Very, very soon.

Angry and frightened, Connor pushed the ghosts away with what little mental shielding he could muster, and the howl of voices became a dull, distant roar. He came back to himself to find Zaryae watching him with concern.

"Connor?"

"I'm all right."

Zaryae's expression made it clear that she read the lie for what it was. "You've been staring into space with your lips moving for a quarter candlemark or more. What's going on?"

He met her gaze with an edge of desperation. "The ghosts of the ocean dead are fighting about who gets my warm body."

Zaryae caught her breath. "Sweet Esthrane. Can they... take it from you?"

Connor shook his head. "No—or at least, not easily. Not anymore. I've gotten stronger since the ritual at Mirdalur. And the Wraith Lord won't let that happen. What you've taught me helps, but we haven't gotten far yet. So I don't think the ghosts can take my body by force, but they could make it... uncomfortable."

"What will you do?" Zaryae asked.

For the moment, Connor left her question unanswered, and moved to speak to Captain Whitney. "Is there something special about the waters where we are?" he asked.

Whitney gave him a measured look, as if he had come to expect the unusual from Connor. "You mean besides most captains calling this stretch the 'Graveyard of Ships?'" he asked.

"Why do they call it that?"

Whitney frowned. "Bad current through here. In places, there are rocks high enough to scrape a ship's keel if you're lucky, and rip it out if you're not. Unlucky waters, that's for sure." He paused. "I wouldn't be here if it weren't for that monster and the storm. I bet that the current would be swift enough to keep that monster away from us, but it means we have to run the channel, around the rocks. Go to open water, and that thing might be waiting for us. It's a gamble either way."

"How good are your maps?" Connor asked. "Of the rocks below?"

Whitney frowned. "Why?"

Connor had no energy left for diplomacy. "Captain Whitney, I'm a spirit medium. I speak to ghosts, and they talk to me. And right now, there are several thousand restless spirits surrounding the *Nomad* waiting for their chance to welcome us to the ocean floor."

Whitney paled. "You're lying."

"I can let them talk to you, through me," Connor snapped, his patience grown thin with cold and fear. "But I don't think you'll like the conversation."

Whitney eyed him with a mixture of suspicion. Yet after what he had seen with Connor channeling the Wraith Lord's magic, Whitney could not wholly disbelieve. "Why tell me?"

"Because they've offered us a deal," Connor said. "They promise us safe passage through this place, past what they call an 'underwater mountain,' out of the current. They say your maps don't show everything, and that's how they ended up dead."

Grudging belief warred with fear in Whitney's eyes. "You're right about the maps," he said. "They're good enough, but not perfect. And the poor blighters who find out where they're wrong don't live to tell the tale."

"How sure are you that you can get us through the Grave-yard safely?" Connor asked. "The truth. The spirits ask a dear price."

"I've read the maps. Been through here once, and made it out. But that was in clear sailing," Whitney admitted. "Now, I can't get my bearings from the stars. In the big wide ocean, that doesn't usually matter. But here, being a little bit out of position can make a deadly difference."

"Would you listen, if one of the spirits guided me through?"

Whitney looked at him for a long moment before he replied. "How do you know these ghosts don't want us all dead? Maybe they're lying to you. Maybe they'll steer us right into the mountain, and we won't know better until we're just as dead as they are."

"Maybe," Connor admitted. "But I think I can assure that doesn't happen."

Whitney looked away, staring into the driving rain for long enough that Connor thought the captain was not going to answer him. "If you tell the crew I asked for your help, I'll keel-haul you, Penhallow be damned," Whitney threatened.

Given the interest the Wraith Lord had taken in him, Connor strongly doubted that Whitney would be able to make good on his threat. Still, he understood the captain's need to save face. "Zaryae and I will tell no one. You have our word on it."

"Then yes, I could use a guide," Whitney admitted grimly. "That is, if you want to make it to Edgeland as more than debris."

Connor nodded. "I'll make arrangements."

"Be quick about it. We're heading into the worst part," Whitney warned.

Zaryae laid a hand on Connor's forearm as he turned away from Whitney. "Bevin, talk to me. What are you planning to do?"

Connor met Zaryae's gaze. "What does your gift tell you?"

Zaryae closed her eyes and stood completely still for a few moments. "The danger comes from below," she said quietly, and shook her head sadly. "That could mean so many things. The *tanoba*. The current. The ghosts. The mountains below the water. Maybe something else entirely."

"If I can get information Captain Whitney doesn't have, information that could get us through the drowned mountains, isn't that worth the price? My . . . discomfort . . . for all our lives?"

Zaryae's gaze fixed him unwaveringly. "Discomfort? Or peril?" She paused. "What does the Wraith Lord think about this?" she asked, and looked vindicated when Connor winced. "You haven't asked him, have you?"

"There's not time."

"But there's time enough to nurse you back from the brink of death?" she demanded. "Do you have any idea what that's like for the rest of us?" For the first time, it occurred to Connor that Zaryae was close to his same age and, like him, struggling with a strong gift she could neither fully control nor understand. Seeing her standing there in a borrowed cape, soaked and shivering, he realized that he had never actually noticed how pretty she was, or that beneath her steel she was just as scared as he was.

"I'll be all right," he assured her, though he felt far from certain.

Zaryae's grip dug into his arm. "Swear to me, Bevin. Swear you aren't going to sacrifice yourself."

That's an easy answer, the Wraith Lord's voice sounded on Connor's mind. *I won't allow it.*

"Apparently not, according to the Wraith Lord." Much as he appreciated his undead patron's support and protection, it was exceedingly clear in some moments that he was not his own master.

Few men are, the Wraith Lord said, commenting on the thought. *Most who believe themselves to be are deceived.*

Can you guide us? Connor asked. *I would rather give myself over to you than to the cold dead from the bottom of the deep.*

Alas, no, the Wraith Lord said. *I could, perhaps, will myself to the floor of the ocean. But I would be a mere pilgrim, passing through a foreign land. I would have no special knowledge, no unique insight, perhaps not even the full impression of what I was seeing.* Connor imagined he could hear the Wraith Lord sigh in frustration. *Unfortunately, I cannot help you avoid your bargain if you seek a guide through the deep mountains. But I can ensure that your bargain is held to the letter, and keep your 'guide' from overstaying his welcome. I will not allow you to be taken, from me, or from yourself.*

What about Nidhud's magic? Can he do anything to help?

Sundown is many candlemarks hence, the Wraith Lord

replied. *The storm won't permit us to wait for him to rise. I fear you have no other alternative.*

Very well, Connor said, though what he contemplated made him cold to the marrow with utter, primal terror. He felt a surge of resentment, and shoved it down. *This is no different from choices made in every battle. Someone is in a position to shift the outcome of the battle. Always a choice between one versus many.*

Have a care not to value yourself too lightly, Bevin Connor, the Wraith Lord warned. *I know of no other medium on the Continent capable of doing what you have done, or able to withstand my spirit in battle, let alone to channel my magic. You are not replaceable. And I would answer to Lanyon Penhallow's full fury should I permit any permanent harm to come to you.*

Bring me back, Connor said, hoping his fear was not too evident in his thoughts. *I don't want to die.*

The Wraith Lord did not move to possess Connor, but Connor sensed him make himself apparent to the horde of ocean dead. *I am Kierken Vandholt, and Bevin Connor is my valued servant,* the Wraith Lord's voice spoke across the chasm between the living and the dead. At once, the cacophony of voices stilled, and Connor sensed the drowned spirits draw back in fear.

One spirit and one alone will be permitted to speak through him to guide this ship. Have a care that you do not misrepresent your abilities or intentions, the Wraith Lord warned. *If you cannot guide us safely through the mountain, if I sense your intentions are malicious toward Connor or toward this ship, or if you seek to harm him in any way or refuse to leave his consciousness when your task is complete, I will cast you out of his body, follow you into the places of the dead, rend your spirit into pieces, and drag you with me to the Unseen Realm, where you will wander for eternity.*

For the first time since the voices made contact with Connor, they all fell silent. *Those are the terms of the 'bargain,'* the Wraith Lord said. *And in exchange, during the time it takes to guide us by the shortest, safest route through the sea mountains, you will be a guest in his body. I am the final word on when your time is up. Defy me at your peril.* He paused. *Are there any among you who still desire to be our guide?*

Once again, silence stretched into the deep places of the ocean dead. The ghosts were silent for so long Connor wondered if their offer to guide was merely a ruse to possess him.

"If you're going to get a guide, now would be a good time," Whitney said tightly. "We're heading into the heart of the undersea mountains, the area they call 'Torven's Spine.'"

I can guide you. Connor peered into the rain and mist and saw the ghost of a man who looked to be in his third decade, with short dark hair and piercing dark eyes.

Who are you? Connor asked.

The spirit gave a rueful chuckle. *You mean, who was I? Remon was my name. I was the navigator aboard the* Wolf's Head, *a galleon from the Cross-Sea Kingdoms that went down in these waters many years ago.*

Pardon my directness, but if your own boat sank, why should we trust you? Connor questioned.

We didn't sink because of the mountains. We had 'run the ridge' and gotten through the shallow peaks. But there was a storm that night, much like the one tonight, and our foremast was struck by lightning. The mast damaged the hull when it fell, and the storm caused us to founder.

All right, Remon, Connor said after he sensed the Wraith Lord signal him to proceed. That meant Vandholt's spirit had made its own assessment of Remon and judged him worthy. *We're short on time.*

Connor took a deep breath, and gripped the ship's rail with both hands. He closed his eyes, shutting out the howling wind and the driving rain, the crash of the waves and the boom of the thunder. He could sense the Wraith Lord's presence beside him, and that of Remon. Connor forced his shoulders to relax, took in another breath, and let it out again, opening himself to their guide.

Remon. You may enter.

Remon's spirit hesitated, no longer self-assured. Then again, Connor had become used to being overtaken by the spirits of others. The chance to possess a living being and, for a time, experience his body as one's own was not common, and Remon might have needed a few seconds to figure out how to go about doing that.

Hurry, Connor urged. *We head deeper along Torven's Spine every second.*

Remon's ghost came at Connor in a rush, slipping through his skin. Connor jerked, stiffening at the abrupt possession, and he gasped as a long-dead man reveled in the half-forgotten senses of a living body.

Remember, you have a job to do, Connor cautioned.

Zaryae was watching him worriedly, but she did not touch him or move to block his path as Connor walked toward Whitney and the ship's wheel. For a moment or two, Remon's consciousness felt besotted with the onslaught of sight, touch, and sound. He nearly lost his footing, grabbing at the ship's rail as he struggled to adjust to control a flesh-and-blood body after such a long time.

"I'm...all right." The voice that came out of Connor's mouth had his tone but not his inflection, speaking the Common tongue with a Cross-Sea accent. "I am...Remon."

"Nice to meet you, Remon. Now get your ass over here and guide me through the sea mountains before we all end up at the bottom," Captain Whitney snapped.

Remon dragged himself along the rail, still fastened with a rope that gave him a few feet's distance to roam. Zaryae hung back but stayed close enough to intervene should help be needed.

Now that Remon had gathered his wits, he moved with the sure-footedness of a man used to living his life aboard ship. He glanced at the sails, assuring himself of their set.

"How exactly are you going to navigate?" Whitney challenged. "The clouds are so thick, we can't see stars or sun."

"By the movement of the water," Remon replied, "and the ghosts beneath the waves."

Whitney looked as if he had bitten into a sour apple, but he nodded. "All right. Steer me through."

Whitney stepped back, giving Connor the wheel. To Remon, the worn wood and tug of the weight against the wheel felt as natural as breathing. *All right, my brethren.* Remon spoke to the ghosts that filled the ether all around them. *Show me where we are.*

Remon looked out at the storm-tossed seas through Connor's eyes, and at the same time, Connor 'saw' the ocean in front of them through Remon's heightened awareness. Through Remon's ghostly perspective, the gray, wild waves became transparent as glass, and Connor could see down into the depths. Massive, black shapes jutted up from the sea floor, tall and jagged as the Riven Mountains, completely submerged except for a few places where the tallest peaks poked their highest tips nearly to the surface. Like the mountains Connor had seen on dry land, Torven's Spine was a series of ridges varying dramatically in height, with deep clefts between. The base of the undersea mountains was lost to sight in the darkness of the abyss.

Gradually, as Connor watched through Remon's consciousness, he saw more details emerge. It was as if he were on the ship, in his body, and simultaneously outside of the ship with preternatural senses, so that the heaving waves and crashing whitecaps became translucent to his sight and he was able to 'see' the ship moving to the right of a massive mountain ridge.

Remon's hands were sure and steady on the ship's wheel. Whitney's expression was a fraught mix of emotions, and Connor was certain it was painful for the captain to give over control of his ship to someone who was not even a member of his crew, let alone a man claiming to be guided by a ghostly navigator. It was a supreme act of will on the captain's part to refrain from taking back the wheel, and his fists clenched and released again and again as he fought his battle with himself.

I wish Whitney could see what I'm seeing through Remon's senses, Connor thought. *There's no way a purely human helmsman could get us through the mountain range in a storm like this.*

The ghosts of the depths moved with the *Nomad*, and Remon perceived them as a faintly glowing strand of light, tracing the perilous slopes and peaks of Torven's Spine, enabling Remon to guide the *Nomad* away from the deadly submerged rock.

The storm is making this difficult, Remon said. *This area is treacherous in good weather, but with the wind and the damaged sails, it's almost impossible to avoid moving side to side, and the clearance in a few passes is pretty tight.*

Watch out! Connor saw the peak so close off the starboard side that he might have easily poked it with a pike.

That's what I mean, Remon replied tightly. Whitney's hands were clenched white-knuckled, so tightly that Connor was certain the captain would have bloody nail prints in his palms. Rocks scraped against the hull, and Whitney's face went white.

"Steady," Remon said with a voice not exactly Connor's.

"The draft's deep enough here despite the tight fit. If we move to avoid scraping, we'll rip out the hull on the mountain ridge directly beneath."

Trad and the sailors on the deck below cried out in fear as the hull scraped again. Some prayed to Charrot for deliverance, while others pleaded with Torven to assure their souls safe passage, or begged Esthrane to spare their lives.

Remon's ghostly senses dispelled the darkness of the ocean depths, and with the help of the thousands of spirits from the Graveyard of Ships, the *Nomad* made careful headway through the treacherous passage.

"Halfway there," Remon said with Connor's voice. Zaryae moved to stand beside him, and reached up to touch his cheek with her fingers.

"You're burning up, when it's so cold I'm shivering," she said worriedly. "Connor, keep track of the time. If he burns up your body, you'll be no better off than the rest of the ghosts."

And if I save myself and sink the ship, we'll all join Remon and his friends—permanently, Connor thought.

He had grown accustomed, through the Wraith Lord's possessions, to gauging how well his body tolerated the presence of its ghostly guest. Through trial and error, and no doubt helped by the Wraith Lord's long existence and magic, he and Vandholt had reached an understanding of when Connor was approaching his mortal breaking point.

Remon had no such experience, nor did he have the Wraith Lord's magic to buffer the strain of the possession. And while the wind whipped around them and rain pelted them, Remon was reveling in the sensations even as Connor's body shuddered with cold and simultaneously burned from inside.

You're taking a toll on him, the Wraith Lord warned. *Don't dally.*

I don't dare move faster, unless you want to end up with a smashed hull, Remon shot back. *I've gotten us this far. Trust me to get us out. Then you can have your precious servant back.*

Through Remon's senses, Connor watched the *Nomad* make its slow progress through the perilous mountain passes. From what he could make out, thanks to their ghostly guides down below, the problem lay not in the main slopes and peaks of Torven's Spine but in some of the lesser outcroppings that jutted out to narrow the channel.

By now, Connor was feeling the strain of the possession. Though Remon handled the wheel with practiced confidence, Connor was growing light-headed. The combination of fever and chills sent his body into momentary spasms that were growing in duration and intensity, causing his teeth to chatter badly and his body to go rigid and tremble.

I can't contain you much longer, Connor said.

We're almost through.

Connor's grip on the ship's wheel was all that held him on his feet, though Remon guided the wheel with utter confidence. It was growing burdensome to breathe, and Connor was certain his blood was near the boiling point. His heartbeat thundered in his ears, and he was sure he could feel his blood coursing through his veins.

Beneath them, guided by the faint glow of a thousand drowned men's spirits, Connor could see ahead of them the end of Torven's Spine. The longer Remon remained in possession of his body, the more Connor felt a bond to those unfortunate spirits in the depths. At first, he could just make out the glowing trail they laid for Remon to follow. But now, as his union with Remon's spirit went on, he could hear their voices once again, not an angry howl like before but the low babble of a large crowd of people all talking at the same time. Part of him was intrigued by the conversation and longed to find out their secrets, but Connor resisted the pull, knowing that to join them would be death.

More things existed in the depths of the sea than Connor had dreamed possible. As his bond with Remon grew deeper, he caught glimpses of the abyss through the perceptions of the ghosts that guided Remon. Nightmare creatures wended their way among the spirits, things with lantern jaws and vicious teeth. Corpse-pale, shapeless monsters slithered through the cold currents, eyeless and alien. Stranger things swam in the silence of the deepest waters, down in the lightless bottom of the abyss. And while the ghosts paid the monsters no mind, Connor could not pull his gaze away, equal parts horror and fascination.

"Connor! You've got to come back to yourself. You've been possessed too long," Zaryae urged. She shook his arm, trying to get his attention. Remon was clear-eyed and alert, expertly steering the *Nomad* through the final section of the treacherous passage. Connor knew he was fading, and his tenuous hold on his own consciousness slipped in and out of control.

I will lend you my strength, but neither of us can sustain this forever, the Wraith Lord said. Connor felt the ancient spirit fortifying him, and across the miles, the *kruvgaldur* with Penhallow surged, giving Connor the strength to rally.

Just a temporary measure, Connor. We'll need to end your bond with the ghost as soon as the Nomad *clears the mountain pass.*

I can hang on that long, Connor replied, willing it to be so. He knew that without the Wraith Lord, and without the additional strength he had gained from the *kruvgaldur* and the ritual at Mirdalur, he would have already lost consciousness, or worse.

Not much longer, he repeated to himself. *Almost there. Not much longer...*

"Aha!" With a triumphant shout, Remon steered the *Nomad* through the final, narrow section of the mountains. Twice more, the rocky outcroppings passed so close beneath the waterline that those on deck could hear them scrape against the *Nomad*'s hull. The sky overhead remained dark with clouds, blotting out the sun, but the driving rain had stopped and the wind, mercifully, had stopped gusting. Most of the day had passed, and the shadows had grown long with the blue glow of twilight. The *Nomad* sailed onward, and Connor watched through Remon's heightened sight as the hull cleared the end of the glowing line and sailed into open water.

"We're through!" Remon cried out, and the men on deck echoed his triumphant shout. Connor gathered the last of his strength, ready to reclaim his body and collapse. But before he could gather his will to thank Remon for his help and demand that he depart, Connor glimpsed something large and dark in the waves ahead of them.

A *tanoba* was waiting for them.

CHAPTER
FIFTEEN

"DO I GET A KISS FROM THE BRIDE?" BLAINE MCFADDEN teased.

"For my big brother, sure." Mari stretched up on tiptoe to give Blaine a peck on the cheek. Blaine threw his arms around her and lifted her off her feet, and she laughed in a way he had not heard since they were children. He set her down gently and bent to kiss the top of her head, then clapped Dawe Killick on the shoulder.

"Welcome to the family—as if you weren't already part of it," Blaine said with a grin.

"Not something we really would have imagined a while back, huh?" Dawe said in a tone that reflected his happy surprise at the way events had unfolded.

"On the whole, I'd say we've done well for ourselves." Kestel Falke McFadden strode up to them. She embraced Mari and gave Dawe a joking punch in the shoulder. "Just to warn you—Dawe snores like a cow with a bad cold. I mean, at the Homestead, you could hear him all the way out in the barn," she added with a teasing grin.

Red-haired with green eyes, lithe and pretty, Kestel looked

radiant in her sapphire gown, a dress she had borrowed from Judith.

"Come and eat. There's plenty for everyone." Blaine's aunt, Judith McFadden Ainsworth, walked toward them, gesturing to the group to come to the table. She was in her fifth decade, and the hardships of the last seven years showed in her face, but sometimes when she smiled, it was possible to imagine what a beauty she had been in her youth. "Two weddings in one year! I never thought Glenreith would see such happy times again, siege and war be damned!"

Glenreith, the McFadden family manor house, showed the hard times of recent years. But tonight, the great hall was lit with candles and a bounty of food and summer flowers graced the large, worn table. Roasted lamb and braised suckling pig filled large platters, surrounded by bowls of freshly picked berries, chutney from last autumn's apples, breads, tarts, and pastries, fresh vegetables from the garden, and tankards of ale.

Robbe, Mari's son by her late first husband, sat in the wide window seat with a heaping plate of goodies.

"He's worked up a good appetite," Mari said, elbowing Dawe to look over toward where Robbe sat.

"He's a good worker," Dawe replied, taking some of the lamb and pig for his plate and adding some small potatoes and onions, as well as some of the pickled vegetables from the crocks. "I don't mind having him down at the forge with me at all. He's strong for his age, and he loves to pump the bellows."

"Robbe adores you," Mari said, giving Dawe's arm a squeeze. "And so do I."

Kestel slipped an arm around Blaine's waist. They hung back for a moment to let the others get seated. "I wish Verran and Zaryae and the twins could have been here," she said. "Connor, too." Hired musicians from the village played flute, lyre, and hand drum in one corner of the great room, but at Blaine and Kestel's wedding, Verran, Dawe, and the twins had offered their music as a wedding gift, much as they had played through many cold, dangerous nights to pass the time.

"I suspect that Verran, for one, would much rather be here than where he's headed," Blaine replied in a low voice that would not carry to the others, mindful of the need for secrecy.

"It's just the beginning of the Long Dark, so the weather's not too bad yet," Blaine went on. "And the trip gives us an opportunity to open up trade again with Edgeland. Plus, we can warn the colonists to be prepared for unwanted guests, in case anyone from the Cross-Sea Kingdoms shows up."

"I can't imagine that Connor is thrilled with the trip," Kestel said.

Blaine chuckled. "Poor fellow. No, I don't imagine he likes the idea at all. Who would, even in the best of circumstances? And don't forget, he barely made it to Edgeland alive, what with the Great Fire and then his ship breaking apart."

"On the other hand, he didn't make the trip in manacles," Kestel observed, raising an eyebrow.

"True," Blaine agreed, and they fell silent as they moved to join the others.

"Got three of you married off now!" Piran swaggered up, a full tankard of ale in his hand. "Not for me, thank you very much. I like being a free man. Too many whores, too little time."

"More likely, too little money," Kestel replied with a sniff. "Honestly, Piran, you need to find a woman who'll have you before you get old and wrinkly. Or you'll be pestering to stay in one of our extra guest rooms like a dotty uncle."

Piran laughed. "Nah. I just need a wench with bad eyesight. Besides, we all managed to live together at the Homestead, which was tiny compared with Glenreith. I could move into one of the rooms no one uses here and you'd never know I was even there."

"We'd know," Blaine observed wryly. "We'd see the servants hauling the kegs of ale up the back stairs."

Piran snapped his fingers, as if ruing the failure of his plan. "Damn. I'll have to work that out." He took a swig of his ale and wiped his mouth with his hand. He was wearing his best outfit, a brocade waistcoat over black trews and a white shirt, all of which had been looted from somewhere. Even so, Piran was never going to pass for 'respectable' company. And Blaine was fine with that.

"Are you still bending coins to amaze the trollops?" Kestel asked sweetly. Piran, another of Blaine's Velant allies and new Lords of the Blood, had gained extra strength from the ritual that had bound the magic.

Piran grinned. "Works every time," he said. "Or at least, every time I have a coin to spare. Ladies love a strong man."

"They mean how much you can lift, not how bad you smell," Kestel said with a grin, slapping Piran on the shoulder.

"Yes, well. They can't all marry up with a lord like you did," Piran bantered back. "Even if we didn't know he *was* a lord for six whole years, right, Mick?"

"He's never going to let you live that down," Kestel replied, rolling her eyes.

Blaine gave an exaggerated sigh. "Probably not. Then again, there are a lot of stories about Piran we don't have to stop talking about."

"You mean like the time he won the ale-and-herring contest by outeating and outdrinking everyone else in Ifrem's bar?" Kestel asked with a wicked grin.

Piran groaned. "I'd rather forget that time, thank you. Bloody herring."

"I see it didn't make you swear off ale," Kestel observed.

Piran frowned. "Wasn't the ale's fault. Nasty, awful herring." Piran and Blaine had both worked the dangerous, cold herring boats in Skalgerston Bay after they earned their Tickets of Leave. Neither one ever cared to see another herring again.

By this time, the minstrels had struck up a lively tune. Dawe and Mari were gesturing for the others to join them in a circle dance. The steps were familiar, as was the song. Even Robbe joined in. Blaine let himself dance without thinking about the steps, caught up in the happiness and energy of the moment. Just for an instant, if he shut his eyes, it could almost be as if none of the last seven years had ever happened, not the murder, the exile, or the many battles.

Kestel squeezed his hand, and Blaine opened his eyes once more. Her look gave him to know that she had guessed his thoughts. He gave her hand a squeeze in return. *No sane man would have asked for what befell me in the last few years,* Blaine thought, *but I've made good things from all of that. Friends. Kestel. Fixing the magic. Fixing up Glenreith. Trying to get Donderath back on its feet. I wouldn't have asked for the pain, but at least it hasn't been for naught.*

The tune switched, and Kestel led Blaine into another, faster dance, one that gave him no leeway to dwell on the past. He was certain she had arranged it that way. After several more spirited pieces, all of the dancers except Robbe drifted back to get more ale or just collapse into a chair.

"Do you think your aunt and Edward will ever make a handfasting?" Kestel asked quietly, her gaze going to where Judith stood beside Glenreith's longtime seneschal, no longer pretending to be employer and servant.

Blaine shrugged. "For all I know, they already have," he replied. "It would be like both of them to do it quietly, for their own satisfaction. After all, it's hardly as if the world outside cares." Once, such a pairing would have shocked Donderath's elites, and the social pressure to avoid scandal would have pushed Judith and Edward apart. But the years of hardship and the collapse of 'respectable' society left the survivors of the Cataclysm to make their way in an unfamiliar, and unfriendly, world. Whether the attraction between Judith and Edward had always been present, or whether it came late in life, Blaine had no idea. But after all the pain his aunt had suffered, he was glad that she had found happiness amid the ruins.

Blaine and Kestel nodded to the guard at the front doors of the manor as they walked arm in arm out into the sunshine. Soldiers guarded the manor's outer walls, and a protected corridor ran all the way from the front gates of Glenreith down to the permanent army camp over the hill at Arengarte, where Niklas Theilsson's father once owned a large farm and mill.

"Mersed and Cosmin said they strengthened the wardings right before we came back from Bleak Hollow," Blaine remarked. "I feel better knowing that at least one or two of the mages will be stationed here at Glenreith. They can move back and forth between here, Quillarth Castle, and Mirdalur as they need to, but it means the manor, the village, and the army camp have another line of defense."

"Now if they could just uncover an artifact that would make better beer!" Kestel laughed. "In all the centuries, wouldn't you have thought a mage somewhere would have come up with a bottomless vat of perfect ale, or the never-ending cask of wine?"

Blaine chuckled and turned his face up to the sun and closed his eyes, feeling the warmth. "You know, there were many times in Edgeland, I didn't think I'd ever be warm again," he said quietly.

Kestel drew in a deep breath of contentment and leaned

against him. "I know. I felt the same way myself. And I certainly never expected to make it back to Donderath."

"I wonder how Edgeland has changed," Blaine mused. "It's been a year and a half. So much has happened here. They might not have had all the wars and warlords we've dealt with here, but having the magic back, working and anchored, should have made things a little easier for them, I hope."

Velant Prison had been an unrelenting nightmare. Convicts who survived a few years in the prison and its merciless fields, laundries, and mines were granted Tickets of Leave, papers that let them become colonists instead of convicts and move from the prison into Edgeland's only town, Skalgerston Bay. The new colonists were granted a small amount of money and some land, enough for a garden to support themselves. Blaine, Piran, Dawe, Verran, and Kestel had pooled their money and land and built the Homestead, a small shared house and farm. Kestel had tended the livestock and farm while Blaine and Piran went out with the dangerous herring fleet. Verran played for money in the taverns, and Dawe took in smithy work. Some of the colonists ran businesses that served the sailors who brought supplies and new loads of convicts or learned a trade to get by, useful in a colony that often lacked essentials and received limited shipments from home.

"I sent a letter with Verran, just in case Engraham or Ifrem are still alive," Kestel said. "I tried to catch them up on the main news, although so much has happened, it would take a book to write it all down," she added. "Still, I asked them to send a letter with Verran in return, to tell us their news. There were some people I didn't mind leaving at the top of the world, but I'm surprised at how much I miss the ones I did like."

Blaine nodded. Velant killed the prisoners who posed a real

danger. The rest had been sent away for small crimes. "There wasn't much choice about depending on the people around you, whether you liked them or not," Blaine said.

Kestel chuckled. "I'll always remember the way the Spirit Lights looked in the sky, especially during the Ice Festival. They were beautiful. So was new snow—unless you had to go out in it. We certainly did the best with what we had."

"That's why I didn't jump at the idea of coming back, when we finally had the chance," Blaine said. "We'd built a good life there. It was hard, but less complicated than dealing with King Merrill's court and the nobles. We made it work. I had made my peace with it."

"You could have stayed," Kestel said quietly, taking his hand. "No one would have faulted you for not wanting to come back. We had no idea what shape Donderath would be in. After what happened to you, it's hardly as if you owed anyone."

Blaine shrugged. "I've often thought about that, wondered how things would have gone if I hadn't come back. Whether you and I would have finally gotten together," he said, tightening his grip on her hand. "Whether someone would have found another way to anchor the magic. Certainly, other warlords might have risen, to bring order to the mess. But then I wonder what would have become of Glenreith, and whether Carr might still be alive if I had stayed."

Kestel turned to meet his gaze. "Maybe things would have gone well in Edgeland. Or maybe with the magic broken, we all would have died. If you think it was important to restore the magic here in Donderath, remember how often a little bit of magic meant the difference between life and death up in Edgeland. The healers. Being able to make fire and light easily. So many things we relied on magic to do, or help with, because we had to do everything else the hard way." She shook her head. "For all you know, you might have saved the whole colony by coming back to fix the magic. And Grimur was quite sure that you were the only one who could do it."

Blaine shrugged uncomfortably. "Maybe. Although once upon a time, there had to be a very first Lord of the Blood, so it couldn't have always been inherited. But I'll grant you that coming back and putting the magic right would have made a big difference to the folks back in Edgeland." He sighed.

"We were always on the knife edge up there, but things were simple and clear," he continued. "Now, we're still on the knife edge, but nothing's simple or clear. Every time we defeat an enemy, like Quintrel and Rostivan and Lysander, we get a new crop, like the Western Raiders and the Northern Marauders."

"It's too bad Niklas couldn't have made it home for the wedding," Kestel said. "I know you miss him." Niklas and Blaine had been childhood friends, before Blaine was sent to Velant and Niklas went into the army to fight the Meroven War.

"He's doing what he does best, leading an army," Blaine said with a shrug. "But you're right, I would have liked to see him when we weren't talking strategy."

They walked on, up a small hill to where an oak tree stood on a rise overlooking the manor's farmlands and the valley below. Several stone squares set into the ground marked the family graves. One sat far apart from the others. Ian McFadden, rejected by his family in death. The rest were clustered together on the far side of the tree. Blaine stopped in front of the newest marker, over the grave of his brother, Carr.

"I wish Carr could have accepted Dawe and Mari together," he said in a voice just above a whisper. "They're so perfect for each other. He just couldn't get past being angry at me, for everything I cost him."

"We've been over this before," Kestel said patiently. "You saved him—and Mari—from that tyrant of a father. If it cost Carr his reputation and family fortune, well, look what happened to the rest of Donderath. It was just going to be a few years before everything went up in flames."

Blaine knelt by Carr's grave and said nothing for several moments. *I want to remember him the way he was before I left. When we were close. When he trusted me to do the right thing and take care of him. When he could stand the sight of me. And yet, at the end, he didn't betray me. That's something. I just wish it could have been different.*

"You know he's watching over you," Kestel said. "I mean, really *know*, not just hope like most people do. Tormod made that very clear. Carr is trying to make it up to you. Sometimes, people figure things out too late." She stood next to him with her hand on his shoulder.

"I know," Blaine said. "I just wish things had turned out differently." Finally, he stood. "Let's go in. There's a party to enjoy."

"Take the good times while you can," Kestel advised. "Because there's always something else sneaking up around the corner."

"You're a ray of sunshine," Blaine said with a mock glower.

Kestel shrugged. "I'm a realist."

"At least it's quiet for the moment," Blaine said. "Damn, but what I'd give just to sit around for an evening and play a few hands of cards!"

"Then do it tonight," Kestel urged. "Surely we can spare a few candlemarks. Just don't let Piran deal."

CHAPTER SIXTEEN

W E'RE MAKING PROGRESS, BUT THERE JUST aren't enough workers to do everything that has to be done," Dawe said as he, Blaine, and Kestel rode out toward the farm fields surrounding Glenreith. Four guards on horseback hung back far enough to allow them privacy for their conversation but remained near enough should trouble arise. A few days had passed since the wedding, and it was time to get back to work.

"The last few years have gone hard on everyone, but the villages and farms are especially short on young men to do the hardest work," Dawe continued. While Blaine and the others had gone to war, Dawe had remained at Glenreith, helping to fix up the manor and working with the farmers and residents to plant crops, brew ale, and begin the long process of repairing what war and the Cataclysm had destroyed.

"If the men didn't go off to the Meroven War, they ended up fighting for one warlord or another, or getting killed defending their land from bandits," Dawe went on. "A lot of people got killed in the Great Fire. Add it all together, and it's a real problem. The women are trying to pick up the pieces. Even the old people and the children are working in the fields, helping rebuild houses and barns and bridges, harvesting crops. But it's slow going," Dawe said. "Last winter, a lot of people went hungry, because the war destroyed the harvest. We're trying to keep that from happening again, but it's a tough job."

"We?" Kestel asked.

Dawe nodded. He brushed a lock of dark hair out of his eyes. "Edward and I have been meeting with anyone who would take the time to talk to us. We've gone looking for the guild masters, farmers, brewers, and millers who survived, and got them talking about what it would take to get things running again."

"And?" Blaine raised an eyebrow.

"Well, it's damn overwhelming, that's what it is," Dawe said. "You don't think about all the pieces that have to be in place just to have a village work or a farm function, but when those pieces aren't there, it all falls apart. So Edward and I meet every couple of weeks with a group from the surrounding villages. We send soldiers to help with rebuilding or plowing or fixing roads. Niklas put us in touch with Folville in Castle Reach, because they've had food shortages in the city and there's naught left to steal to make up for it."

"You're working with Folville? Since when?"

Dawe grinned. "You didn't think the rest of us were just sitting on our hands while you were off fighting, did you? Niklas ordered Captain Henderson to be our liaison right before your big battle on the Northern Plains. He has a group of residents, mostly older women, who gather the concerns and tell us what's going on in the city. Sooner or later—hopefully sooner—the countryside needs to start trading again with Castle Reach, as well as the other villages. But you can't have trade if the roads aren't safe and if there aren't any goods to sell."

"You've been busy," Kestel said. "I knew you were more than just a pretty face," she jibed.

Dawe laughed. "Don't discount the power of a pretty face. Judith and Mari meet with the women just as often as Edward and I meet with the men, figuring out where to get seeds, what crops to plant, how to get cloth production going again, how best to preserve what's harvested and get trade functioning so people can at least barter for what they need."

Blaine chuckled. "I'm impressed. How's it going?"

Dawe shrugged. "Slowly. And that's one of the problems. The seasons don't wait for people to sort out their problems. If we miss the opportunity to plant, it's gone for another year. When the Cataclysm destroyed barns, the livestock ran off. A lot of the cows and pigs and sheep and horses got killed by predators or stolen by armies—including yours," he said with a raised eyebrow. "We've been gathering up the ones we can find and breeding them, but that's a slow process. People ate their seed for the spring. Makes it hard to plant crops when there's precious little seed to be had. So the older women have been training the children on how to find plants that can be eaten, and how to gather seeds." He sighed. "There's far too much to be done, and not enough time to do it, but we're working hard."

"So this group we're riding to meet with, they're one of yours?" Blaine asked.

Dawe nodded. "Since you're at Glenreith for a little while at least, Edward and I figured it would be a good idea to let people see their lord—and maybe their future king—taking an interest."

"I am the most bedraggled lord anyone has ever seen," Blaine said. Like everyone in Donderath since the Great Fire, Blaine was dressed in worn, patched, and scavenged clothing that had seen far better days.

"You know, it's gotten so bad that most people strip the dead before burying them so the clothing can be reused," Dawe said.

Kestel's eyes widened. "Really? That happened in Velant, and on the battlefield, but I didn't expect regular people to do that sort of thing."

"Yeah," Dawe said. "Judith has led outings to find and bring back stray sheep, and she's organized the women into spinning and weaving groups. But sheep only grow wool so fast, and by now, every abandoned house has already been looted."

"Remind me to thank Aunt Judith for sparing us from becoming a kingdom of naked savages," Blaine said. "Funny how no one thinks of these things when they start a war."

"No one ever believes they're going to lose," Dawe replied. "Certainly not on the scale that actually happened."

"You'll be meeting with a fellow named Burnion," Dawe said. "He's been willing to work with us, and he seems to be able to get the others to cooperate, but lately I've been getting the sense that there's some friction going on behind the scenes," Dawe added.

"And the others?" Blaine asked.

Dawe shrugged. "Same mix of people you'd find anywhere," he said. "A handful willing to lead, some very hard workers, and the rest who do the least they can."

"Meaning there are some people who aren't completely on board with the changes?" Kestel prodded.

Dawe frowned. "I'm not sure. It might just be a family squabble."

"Thanks for the warning," Blaine said. "I'll tread lightly."

Both Blaine and Kestel wore thin chain-mail shirts beneath their traveling clothes. Kestel, as usual, had a variety of knives hidden in her clothing, close at hand. Blaine wore his sword and had both a long knife on his belt and a dagger in his boot. Dawe, who by his own admission was better at forging swords than using them, wore only a long knife and a shiv. Just in case,

Blaine wore the amulet the battle mages had made for him before the fight on the Northern Plains, one that caused dangerous magic to slide aside, deflected. Kestel's amulet, hidden beneath the neckline of her tunic, was a magical null, able to ground a blast of magic or temporarily dampen a mage's power in physical contact.

They rode to a village half a candlemark from Glenreith. Unlike in other parts of Donderath, the fences and barns were recently repaired, the fields were knee-high with crops instead of weeds, and the livestock looked healthy.

"All this is your doing?" Kestel said appreciatively, looking around at the change. "I remember riding through here last winter, on the way to battle. Everything was ruined and deserted."

Dawe's grin widened. "Yep. There are a few other villages doing well, and we've encouraged them to work together. It's a big improvement—and a huge amount of work."

The entire population of Penwich awaited them when they rode into the village. Fifteen gray-haired men and women stood at the fore. Behind them, townspeople of every age gathered, scrubbed clean and turned out looking their best, for the lord's approach. Children peered out of windows and climbed up balconies, and half a dozen ran shouting from the outskirts of the village when Blaine and his small group rode into sight.

Dawe and the others brought their horses to a halt in front of the group. Blaine's guards remained at a respectful distance.

An old man with a shock of unruly white hair stepped forward and made a deep bow. "Lord and Lady McFadden," he said. "Welcome to Penwich. We are honored by your visit. Lady Judith and Sir Dawe have told us much about you." He gave another low bow. "I am Burnion, senior speaker for Penwich."

Blaine inclined his head in response. "Greetings, Burnion,

and greetings, residents of Penwich." He hoped that Kestel was the only one able to tell how uncomfortable he was speaking as a lord to his subjects.

"We're honored that you've come to visit," Burnion said. "And if you will permit, we would like to show what we have accomplished."

Kestel smiled at the reference to 'Sir Dawe,' and Blaine was certain Dawe would take a ribbing for it in private, later.

"Sir Dawe has told me much about how hard you've worked," Blaine replied. "I would very much like to see the improvements you've made."

Burnion led them on a walk through the village and its fields, narrating the progress. Fields were planted, livestock grazed behind newly split fences, barns and homes showed recent patching. At each place they stopped, someone from the village presented Blaine with a gift: dried meat, a tanned hide, a wooden statue of Charrot made by a local wood-carver, a pair of iron tongs from the village forge. Dawe must have expected the tribute, because he had a basket at the ready and instructed one of the guards to carry the gifts after Blaine inspected them and praised their workmanship.

Blaine knew how to play his part. The villagers were struggling, and could ill afford the gifts, humble as they were. Yet the village needed its pride, and his acknowledgment validated what had been done, and would likely increase their cooperation. So he smiled and thanked them, and silently promised himself to make certain that Dawe received equivalent supplies to replace what was being given.

The women of the village were curious about Kestel, hanging back a few steps to watch her, speaking in hushed tones to each other. They were not used to seeing a woman in tunic and trews like a man, and her appearance—and her reputation—was likely to give the villagers something to talk about for a long time.

A woman with short gray hair came forward and made an awkward curtsy to Kestel. She looked to be in her middle years. Kestel bet she was one of the village 'wise women,' who presided over births and burials, weddings and ceremonies, often wielding significant but quiet power.

"My Lady Kestel," the woman said. "I am Merian, head of the weavers. I offer a gift for you, from the women of Penwich." In her arms was a neat bundle of wool cloth, which she presented proudly. "Made from the wool of our own sheep, dyed, spun, and woven here. May it keep you warm in the winter."

Kestel's smile was sincere. "Thank you," she said, accepting the gift and looking it over closely, remarking on the evenness of the dye and the careful weaving. The women beamed with pride. "Your work is very well done."

As Burnion led them around the village, most of the residents followed a short distance behind. A few villagers hung back. They said nothing and made no move to disrupt, yet they stood apart, and their expressions were skeptical, if not exactly unwelcoming. Blaine exchanged a glance with Dawe, who gave a nod of acknowledgment.

Burnion led them to the largest building in the town, an old barn that still showed signs of hardship. "I apologize that we have no finer place to receive you, but our people wanted to hear what you have to say, and this was the only building large enough."

"I welcome having them stay," Blaine replied. Villagers standing toward the back craned their necks for a better look at their lord and his new wife. None of these villagers were likely to have ever seen their lord, either Blaine or his father, except at a distance, and perhaps not even then. Blaine was also well aware that even in a village like Penwich, stories of his crime, exile, and role in restoring the magic were probably well known and oft repeated. Some might even have heard rumors of Kestel's exploits before her exile. *No wonder they're so anxious to have a look at their convict lord and his assassin-courtesan wife,* Blaine thought.

Dawe traded nods and smiles with a number of the villagers as they walked to the front. As Dawe looked over the group, he paused, just for a second, when his gaze fell on a man in his middle years sitting in the back of the room.

"What's the matter?" Blaine asked under his breath.

"Just spotted someone I've never seen before. That's odd. I thought by now I'd met everyone in Penwich."

Dawe took the chance to murmur a question to Burnion when they reached the front. "Says he's a hedge witch who showed up not long after my last visit. Made himself useful curing sick cows, and they let him stay."

"Something wrong with that?"

Dawe shook his head, but his expression was still thoughtful. "No, just surprised. We don't get a lot of strangers through here."

Two mismatched, carved wooden chairs sat in the middle of the barn floor behind a battered wooden worktable. Burnion escorted Blaine and Kestel to their seats.

Dawe stood to Blaine's right, and two of the guards took up places directly behind Blaine and Kestel, while the other guards stood at a discreet distance. Their presence was not missed by the villagers, who nudged each other and nodded toward the soldiers and their swords.

Burnion clapped his hands, and a line of women bearing food came from the shadows.

"Sir Dawe let it be known that we were not to do anything that might run us short, and that m'lord would be most displeased if that were to happen," Burnion said, glancing from Dawe to Blaine as if to confirm.

Blaine nodded. "Sir Dawe is correct. We would not have you go hungry just to honor us. You have made us very welcome already."

Burnion puffed with pride. "Thank you, m'lord. You are most gracious. But you have come a distance to meet with us, and we would not want to be poor hosts. So if you will permit, a humble offering to you and to Sir Dawe, from what has been raised so far this year. Our women will be honored if you would dine with us. And of course," he added, "we have provisions for your guards as well."

When Blaine nodded once more, the women began to set one dish after another on the table in front of Blaine and Kestel. A vegetable stew's thin broth tasted of herbs from kitchen gardens. Fresh-baked bread, still warm enough to melt butter, filled a basket. Village-brewed ale flowed to fill their tankards, and another basket of honey cakes finished the bounty.

Kestel lifted each dish in turn, inhaling their aromas with deep appreciation. Only Blaine and Dawe knew that she was using her well-honed senses as an assassin to check for poison. "These smell wonderful," she said, putting the small cakes back on the table as she finished. "Your cooks have presented a noble feast. We appreciate sharing your table."

I never got to see Kestel operate at court, Blaine thought. *And I know she didn't come from noble blood. But she plays her part as if she were born to it. I hope I do as well.*

As they ate, a small group of ragged children filed forward and shyly assembled into a line. On Burnion's nod, they sang a song popular before the Cataclysm. Blaine, Kestel, and Dawe clapped appreciatively when the children finished, and the blushing singers ran for the shelter of their parents' arms.

Next came a group of pretty young women carrying bundles of freshly cut flowers. Smiling and blushing, eyes downcast and self-conscious, the women heaped the flowers on the table and made a deep, practiced curtsy before backing away to join the crowd once more.

"I warned you," Dawe murmured to Blaine under his breath. Blaine felt himself growing impatient with the ritual, wishing they could get to the matter at hand. *Did King Merrill feel like this?* Blaine wondered. *Gods above, everywhere he went, people carried on with gifts and ceremony. How did he manage without grinding his teeth down to nothing?*

Finally, half a dozen musicians assembled with homemade flutes and drums to play several songs popular before Blaine's exile. The minstrels carried a tune well and played with enthusiasm. Blaine, Kestel, and Dawe clapped lavishly when they finished.

By this time, Blaine, Kestel, and Dawe had finished eating. Two men stepped up to move the table so that Blaine and Kestel sat facing the villagers, who had taken seats on the barn floor.

For most of a candlemark, Burnion, Merian, and Jocus, of the village elders, recounted the village's challenges and successes. Blaine heard them out, listening intently and asking questions. He had come prepared to pledge them what few additional resources he could spare, and while both men and material were scarce, Burnion and the others were grateful for the extra help.

So far, so good, Blaine thought. *Is that it?*

Burnion clapped his hands, and four men dragged two prisoners to the front.

Both of the bound men had been roughed up, with bloody noses, split lips, and eyes purpled and swollen.

"My lord," Burnion said, a tinge of shame in his voice. "I am sorry to have to bring this matter before you. But we have caught these two men destroying property in the village, a grave matter, given how hard we have worked to rebuild what was damaged."

"What did they do?" Blaine asked, studying the men. Something about the way they moved was not quite right. Both men fought against the ropes that secured their ankles and wrists. Their eyes were wide and unfocused, and their faces twisted in rage.

"We fought monsters," one of the men shouted, before Burnion could speak. "Monsters that came out of the ground, out of the trees. Monsters in the cattle, hiding there. Monsters hiding in the fields. We had to stop the monsters. Don't you see? They're all around."

"Monsters in the cows, monsters in people," the second man chimed in. "Have to stop the monsters."

Their tirade was cut short as the guards shoved rags in their mouths. Even gagged, they tried to shout through the cloth, struggling against their bonds.

"My lord," Burnion began. "Teron and Rav are sons of this village. They've never caused problems before. They were too young to fight in the war, so they stayed and helped the village during the Bad Year. Then a week ago, they took sick." Burnion shook his head. "We feared for their lives. They were fevered for three days, before the healer could break the sickness. They seemed to recover. Then last night, they lost their minds."

"What do you mean?" Blaine asked. "What did they do?"

"They slit the throats of four of my sheep," one villager man shouted from the audience.

"Killed my best calf," yelled another.

"Tried to set my shed on fire, after I'd only just built it," cried a third.

"Knocked down the fences around half of the east field," a woman put in. "My son saw them, but he couldn't catch them before they ran away."

"There were other damages done as well," Burnion said with a sigh. "They fought us when we tried to stop them. It took quite a fight to capture them. They were brought to me in the middle of the night, and we questioned them until dawn. But all they will say is that they were fighting monsters."

"Nothing wrong with my cow," the owner said from where he sat in the crowd.

"My sheep weren't no monsters, neither."

"What about my shed? And the fences?"

Blaine and Kestel exchanged a glance. *We've seen enough monsters ourselves. Could there be something to their stories?*

"Has anyone else seen monsters?" Blaine asked.

He looked out over the crowd to see heads shaking. "No, m'lord," Burnion replied somberly. "We remember the magic beasts. We feared they might have returned. But we found nothing. No footprints, no strange trails through the grass. We set a watch, but there's been no sign of any monsters at all."

"Remove the gag from that one," Blaine said, pointing to the prisoner who spoke first. "I would question him."

Warily, one of the village men removed Teron's gag. Blaine's own guards moved closer, hands on the pommels of their swords. Kestel shifted slightly in her chair, and Blaine was certain she had a weapon at the ready.

"Where are your monsters?" Blaine asked the prisoner.

"All around us," Teron said, his eyes rolling skyward as his head lolled in a circle. "You can't see them, but they're out there. They're tricky. They hide inside things, where they can't be found. But Rav and me have special eyes. We can see them even when they hide." The pupils of his eyes were wide.

"How long have you been able to see monsters?" Kestel asked, leaning forward to study the men more closely.

"Not long," Teron replied, shifting his attention to Kestel with the intense focus of a rabid dog. "Couldn't stand to see them for too long. It's Charrot's hand on us. We're his soldiers. Tells us where the monsters are."

"They're either drugged or magicked," Kestel murmured to Blaine. "I'd bet money on it."

"Could it be the gods speaking to them?" Burnion asked. "M'lord, are they speaking the truth about monsters we can't see, in our herds and hiding in the rocks and trees?"

Kestel stood up. "Let me examine them," she said. "I know something of these things."

"What are you doing?" Blaine murmured.

"Trust me," she said, and turned her full attention on the prisoner as she stepped down from the small stage.

She pointed to Teron. "Bring him to his feet." The two village guards grabbed Teron by the shoulders and dragged him to stand. Kestel moved close enough to look the young man in the eyes. As an assassin, Kestel was well versed in poisons and potions. Up close, she could smell Teron's breath and the odor of his skin, signs that he might have been drugged.

"Are there monsters in you, pretty lady?" Teron asked, watching Kestel with a smile that sent a chill down Blaine's back. "Let me see. I'm good at killing monsters."

Teron bucked against his captors, and lunged at Kestel. She blocked him with her left hand as her right moved up from her side, suddenly holding a dagger. But as her hand touched Teron, the man froze. His entire body went rigid, and his eyes focused on Kestel. In his gaze, Blaine saw terror and confusion.

"What's going on? Why am I tied up? Who are you?" Teron cried out. His eyes lost their too-wide, unfocused look, and the young man's gaze darted from one person to another, trying to make sense of his situation.

"Tell me about the monsters," Kestel ordered, keeping her hand on Teron's chest.

"Monsters? What—"

Rav tore free from his guard and slammed against Kestel, breaking her contact with Teron. Teron gave a strangled cry. His eyes rolled back and he collapsed to the floor. Blaine moved with Rav's guard to control the prisoner, who was twisting and kicking with all his might. Kestel knelt beside Teron.

"He's dead," she said, looking up at Burnion and the guards. "There's no reason—"

"Let me through. I might be able to help." The hedge witch scrambled out of the crowd and pushed his way toward the group huddled around the two prisoners. Teron's guards stepped back to let him closer. By now, Blaine and his guards had gotten Rav subdued and returned him to the control of the two village men who held him.

Kestel moved toward Rav and stretched out her hand to touch him, when suddenly Rav stiffened and screamed, then dropped motionless to the floor.

"They've been magicked," Kestel said loudly, and the crowd exclaimed in dismay.

Blaine saw the hedge witch shift his position, and dove out of the way as the man's hand came up, sending a blast of fire toward where Blaine had just been standing.

The blast missed Blaine, but caught one of his guards full in the chest. The guard screamed and dropped to the dirt floor of the barn, rolling back and forth to extinguish the flames.

The young men who had dragged Teron and Rav to the front

of the barn rushed the hedge witch. The false healer thrust his right hand out, palm open, and sent a streak of white, cold power toward the young men that hurled them a dozen feet through the air and sent them sprawling into the panicked crowd. The villagers screamed and rushed for the barn door, shoving and pushing to escape.

"Dawe! Get the others out of here!" Blaine shouted, fearing the crowd would trample each other in their rush. Dawe sprinted toward the back of the barn. Burnion shouted orders trying to get the crowd under control. Whatever the hedge witch—or mage, as Blaine suspected—was up to, Blaine wanted him to have as few targets as possible.

Blaine's second guard grabbed Kestel's chair and threw it at the hedge witch's head. The mage barely paid attention, moving his left arm in an arch that brought the chair crashing down to the floor well short of its target, then making a slashing motion that threw the guard against the wall as if he were a rag doll.

"How dare you!" Burnion shouted, shaking off the restraining hand of one of Blaine's guards and stepping toward the hedge witch. "Colter Hanne, we took you in. Welcomed you to the village. We needed a healer. You could have done well here. How dare you repay us like this?"

In response, Hanne snarled and pushed his right hand forward, sending a streak of fire toward Burnion. The older man dodged faster than Blaine would have thought possible, missing the worst of the blast, though the fire still caught Burnion on the left shoulder and he dropped to the floor, beating his hands against his burning clothing and crying out in surprise and fear.

"Why?" Blaine said, advancing on Hanne with his sword raised, trying to draw his attention from Burnion. Silver glinted as Kestel sent a dagger through the air toward Hanne's back. The blade stopped in midair and dropped to the ground as if it struck an invisible wall.

"Because you're here, m'lord," Hanne replied, emphasizing that last word sarcastically.

Burnion and one guard lay on the floor, burned and moaning. The guard thrown against the wall lay still, his head twisted at an unnatural angle. Two of Blaine's guards still stood by the doors, too far away to do more than keep onlookers out. The four men who had dragged Teron and Rav to the front had vanished along with the crowd. Dawe and Merian had gone to keep peace outside.

That left Blaine, Kestel, and one guard at the front of the room with Hanne. Blaine kept his sword raised, but did not try to move closer. Kestel was waiting for an opening. The guard stayed where he was, unwilling to charge Hanne's magic.

"Looks like we've got a standoff," Blaine said, giving Hanne a cold smile.

Hanne shook his head. "Is that how it appears? I'm just considering how best to kill you." Hanne's appearance had changed. He no longer stood hunched, and his limp had vanished. His face lost its look of gentle befuddlement, and he looked years younger. Intelligence and intent were clear in Hanne's eyes.

"You were one of Quintrel's mages," Kestel said, "in Valshoa. That's where I've seen you before." Hanne shifted to look at her. "One of his minor ones. No one important."

Blaine was certain the dig was intentional.

Hanne chuckled. "No, I wasn't one of the 'important' mages in Valshoa. But look! They're all gone and I'm still here."

"Quintrel's dead. He lost. Why keep fighting for his cause?" Kestel asked. She shifted her weight, and Hanne's hand moved defensively. Kestel held up both hands, palms up, in a placating gesture.

"Quintrel wasn't the only one who wanted McFadden dead," Hanne replied.

"You just wandered over here, hoping a village would take you in?" Blaine asked incredulously. "Seems like a thin plan."

Hanne seemed to enjoy the tension. "Does it matter? I'm here and so are you, and you're going to die."

"Not what I had planned for today, sorry," Blaine said, keeping a careful eye on Hanne's every move.

A moan sounded behind Blaine where Burnion lay. Merian appeared silhouetted in the barn door. Hanne's back was to the door, and Merian signaled for Blaine to stay quiet. She threw a large rock against one of the barn support pillars, and dove out of sight.

Hanne flinched toward the noise. Blaine and Kestel attacked at the same instant, closing in on Hanne from each side. Blaine came at Hanne with his sword, trusting the waning power in his amulet to deflect the worst of Hanne's magic. *At least now, there are fewer people to get hit if the magic 'slides' to the side,* Blaine thought.

Kestel had removed her amulet from around her neck and held it like a ligature between both hands as she threw herself at Hanne. She looped the leather strap around Hanne's neck like a garrote and pulled hard with a knee against the mage's back as Blaine struck with his blade.

The null amulet in Kestel's hands blanked out Hanne's magic. Hanne twisted and bucked, but Kestel was stronger than she looked.

"Careful," she warned, "won't take much to crush your throat now that your magic's not working."

Blaine brought his blade up under Hanne's throat. "Now we're going to find out exactly who sent you, and why." Blaine and the guard tied up Hanne while Kestel knotted the null amulet around the mage's throat.

She retrieved her throwing knife and gave Hanne a poke with it. "Wouldn't have minded putting this between your shoulders," she murmured in the captive mage's ear. "Still might, when we're through with you. Did you know Treven Lowrey? I cut him up good for trying to kill Blaine. And I didn't lose a wink of sleep over it, either."

Hanne paled and watched Kestel warily. She walked away, whistling a cheery tune, casually flipping her dagger and catching it by the handle. The guard dragged one of the chairs down from the platform and bound him to it with a length of rope.

Two soldiers from near the barn door sprinted toward Burnion and the downed guard. "Burnion's alive," one of the guards called out. "I've seen worse. A real healer could set it right. The other one is dead."

Merian strode up to them. "The villagers are safe. If your men can bring Burnion and your guard, we will take care of them."

Blaine nodded. "I'll send a healer from Glenreith to help."

"Very well," Merian replied. She looked to Hanne, and her gaze grew icy. "I want to know what this man has to say, after we took him in and gave him our trust." She withdrew a wicked-looking hunting knife from her skirts and, in a single movement, pressed the blade against Henne's throat. A thin stream of blood trickled down the blade where it cut gently into the skin above his larynx.

"You brought shame on Penwich," Merian hissed. "I'm betting you're behind those two poor lads who did the damage. Did you magic them? Tell me!"

Henne spat in her face. "I don't have to tell you anything."

Merian removed the blade from Henne's throat. The mage

gave a victorious chuckle. Merian wheeled, bringing the knife down alongside the mage's head, severing his ear.

"One way or the other, we intend to find out why you came here and did us harm," Merian growled. "I've heard it said Lord McFadden's *talishte* friends can read a man's blood, tell all his secrets when they drink from him. We can wait until dark and find out what they learn."

She raised the bloody knife to where Henne could see it. "Until then, I'll whittle on you. I doubt you'll do much magic without fingers," she mused. "And you won't need a tongue if the biters can read your blood. Or I could give you to Teron's father, and Rav's grandpap. They're the village butchers. Ever dress a deer?" she asked idly. "You cut from here," she said, pointing the tip of the knife to Hanne's sternum, "to here," she said, jabbing at his groin. "Guts fall out. Except, if you aren't dead to start with, that won't kill you right away. Maybe after a day or two, you'll be more talkative."

"I like her," Kestel whispered to Blaine.

Hanne had grown ghostly pale. He glanced toward Blaine, then back to Merian, realizing that no one was coming to his aid and his alternatives were growing increasingly bleak.

"A *talishte* can read your blood until the moment of death," Blaine said laconically. "It's still several candlemarks until dark. I could give you to the villagers and collect what's left of you at sundown."

Hanne swallowed, and blood dripped from the slice across his throat and his severed ear. "What do you want to know?" he asked sullenly.

"Why are you here?" Blaine asked.

Hanne gave him a baleful look. "To kill you."

"Why?"

"You killed Quintrel," Hanne snarled. "You and your army killed most of the other mages who were in Valshoa."

"Quintrel was out-of-his-head crazy," Kestel said. "And controlled by an evil *divi* spirit on top of that."

"Did someone send you?" Merian questioned. When Hanne did not answer, she raised the knife and moved toward his other ear.

"All right!" Hanne replied. "Yes. I was sent. I stayed alive because I was assigned to Hennoch's army. After the battle, Lord Pollard took any of Quintrel's mages who survived, and his biter friends turned any mages who had hidden in his territories." He glared at Blaine. "You're not the first to threaten to have a *talishte* read my blood."

"Why Penwich?" Merian asked, gesturing with the knife. Hanne blanched.

"Lord Pollard sent mages with healing and hedge-witch skills to the inns and villages in McFadden's lands," Hanne said. "Maybe even into Castle Reach. Said we should make ourselves useful, gain their trust, keep our ears open. If we had a chance to kill McFadden or any of his friends, we were to take it."

"But why Penwich?" Kestel repeated.

"We were invited," Hanne said with a malicious smile.

"Who dared invite you?" Merian demanded. "Tell us, or by the gods, you'll lose fingers until you do!"

Hanne swallowed hard. "One of Lord Pollard's spies met someone who didn't like the man in charge of Penwich. Thought he could do things better."

Merian's eyes had gone cold and hard. "Josse, that pig. Thought he'd take Burnion's place. He's a stupid, hateful man." She looked at Blaine, vengeance in her gaze. "Rest assured, m'lord, this man will be punished."

"We're going to have to alert our people," Kestel said. "Folville, too. They're going to have to find the mage-traitors."

Blaine shrugged. "Or, I can ask General Dolan to spare a few Knights of Esthrane for the job. Less chance that anyone gets hurt that way—except for the traitors."

"And the damage, you were sent to do that as well?" Merian's eyes were flinty.

Hanne gave a nasty smirk. "We were told to delay McFadden's progress in any way possible. Using those two fools to do it made that easy."

Merian dove forward before Blaine could stop her and sank the blade deep into Hanne's gut. "One of those 'fools' was my grandson," she snarled. "They were good boys, before you got a hold of them. And they'd still be alive if it weren't for you."

Hanne gasped in pain. Merian withdrew the blade, and wiped the blood on Hanne's pants. "Don't worry," she said matter-of-factly. "You'll still be alive by sundown, if the biters want your blood. But now my grandson and his friend are avenged."

Merian turned to Blaine and Kestel. "M'lord and m'lady. We are deeply sorry such things happened during your visit. Penwich will keep its bargain with you. Until Burnion heals, I will take his place. We will rebuild. And we will remember."

CHAPTER
SEVENTEEN

————

"N OW!" VEDRAN POLLARD SHOUTED AS HE raised his sword.

At Pollard's word, his army surged forward, screaming a war cry that echoed from the stone walls of Lepstow Castle, the domain of Dag Marlief, *talishte* Elder Onyx. Hundreds of soldiers stormed the gates as archers fired down from the high stone walls and guards hurled rocks down on the invaders.

Larska Hennoch was at the forefront, permitting Pollard himself to watch from a safe distance, just beyond the range of arrows. Pollard shifted in his saddle, but no matter how he moved, he could find no relief from the raw wound in his chest or the red, running sores that covered all of his skin except his face. Until Pentreath Reese was freed of his imprisonment, those wounds, mirror images of what Reese suffered from his torture, would remain. That was one of the prices to be paid for his *kruvgaldur* bond. *One of many,* Pollard thought.

Only Nilo knew that the wounds had grown so dire that it was impossible for Pollard to do more than skirmish. Pollard had defied his wounds to fight in the Battle of the Northern Plains, but even then, he had not been at the forefront of the fighting, and he no longer possessed the stamina to hold his own in an all-out fight.

Damn Reese! It would be bad enough to have to hang back because of age, or from an injury taken in battle. There's no shame in that, Pollard thought bitterly. *But I'm forced to be an onlooker when I could still make good use of my sword, because of wounds that aren't even my own. All because I'm bound to Reese, body and soul. And through him, to Thrane. All to win a throne!*

Pollard had no doubts that Reese knew exactly the price his many blood readings would impose on him, and how tightly Pollard would be bound by the intrusion. While Reese picked through Pollard's thoughts and memories at will, Pollard was denied a reciprocal arrangement. And because Reese was Thrane's get, and Thrane had insisted on his own blood readings, Pollard was bound not once but twice to masters who exacted a dear price for whatever favors they chose to bestow.

Nilo led the second wave of troops. As Hennoch's soldiers returned fire with the archers, Nilo's men readied a large, iron-bound battering ram and moved the siege machine into place in front of the castle's heavy gates.

The *thud* of the battering ram echoed from the castle walls and the nearby cliffs and shook the ground. The soldiers manning the machine sang in time to the pounding to synchronize their efforts. The low tones of the war song were almost lost with the crash of the huge metal-tipped log that smashed against the reinforced gates.

Out of archer range, small catapults slammed load after load over the wall. The shocks of hay and bundled cornstalks would spread their flammable cargo as soon as they hit.

"Mages, ready!" Pollard shouted. Half a dozen of his mortal mages moved to line up behind the soldiers on a ridge where they had an excellent view of the battleground.

"Fire!" Pollard commanded.

The mages each stood within a warded circle drawn into the dirt as they gathered their power. Balls of flame appeared over the wall, then dropped down into the dry grasses and stalks. Lepstow had no wooden roofs. Its *talishte* lord was too afraid of fire for that. Nor were there wooden walkways or outbuildings. Everything was made of stone or covered with tiles. But the bales of grass and stalks would burn fast and hot. *So will the soldiers,* Pollard thought. *And* talishte *burn like kindling.*

Let it burn, Pollard thought, watching as flames rose against the sky. Black smoke rose into the blue sky and from inside the castle walls, as panicked shouts and the *clang* of a fire bell made a descant to the steady rhythm of the battering ram.

As far as Pollard was concerned, Lepstow Castle could burn to the ground, and all its residents with it. What he sought was hidden well below the ground, deep in an oubliette far removed from flames or sunlight. Pentreath Reese lay staked and bound at the bottom of a deep pit. When the council had passed judgment, they had not thought it possible that a mortal army might breech their defenses. They were wrong.

Onyx had not factored Thrane into his plans. Nor had he accounted for purely mortal treachery. With the rest of the allied Elders' attention focused on helping McFadden win the Battle of the Northern Plains, it had been easy for one of Nilo's locals to infiltrate the mortals that supplied Lepstow Castle and gain their trust. Once the traitor was in place, it was just a matter of timing for him to slip poison into the castle cistern. All Pollard had to do was wait until the poison had time to take effect.

The poison was why Hennoch's assault was not met by defending mortal soldiers, and why the archers on the walls were few and their aim imperfect. They and all those within the walls were already dead men. Attacking in daylight meant that Onyx and any *talishte* allies were shadow-bound until sundown, unable to protect themselves.

The massive gates gave with a crash as the battering ram smashed and splintered the wood. A victory shout went up from the soldiers. By now, the grass and corn shocks were ablaze, and the archers on the walls had withdrawn, running for their lives.

Hennoch might be serving under duress, but he was an excellent commander, and his soldiers were disciplined and skilled. Hennoch himself led the first troops to enter the castle enclosure, as the mages scryed from a distance to ensure there were no reinforcements on their way.

When Nilo raised Pollard's colors above the battlements, Pollard and the mages led the rearguard troops down the slope to enter Lepstow Castle as victorious invaders. Pollard forced himself to hold his head high and move with his horse as if every shift and step were not excruciating. He knew his withdrawal from fighting was a matter of gossip among the troops. Nilo had told him as much. *Let them talk,* Pollard said, gritting his teeth against the pain. *Anything suffered is bearable, if one survives. I can suffer a lot to gain a crown.*

The smell of death was overpowering. Pollard gave a mirthless smile. *Apparently, the estimates of how long it would take the poison to work were conservative.*

Bodies were stacked against the inside of the castle walls. The courtyard smelled of rot and shit, and the warm summer days made the stench even worse. Flies buzzed everywhere, barely noticing the newly dead in preference for the bloated corpses on which they already feasted.

"The buildings are secured, m'lord," Nilo reported.

"Survivors?" Pollard asked, raising an eyebrow.

Nilo chuckled. "There won't be. Hennoch is seeing to that

now. Actually, it's more of a mercy to finish them off. They've seen the others dying. They know what awaits them."

"So the poison was effective," Pollard said, looking over the still bailey. Normally, a castle courtyard should have bustled with activity of servants carrying firewood or water from one building to another and children chasing chickens while stable boys exercised horses. The air should have smelled of roasting meat and baking bread, of horses and goats and cook fires, walls echoing with the voices of servants and the clatter of carts.

Instead, smoke hung in the air and the ground in the center of the bailey was scorched black. The bailey itself was eerily silent. Pollard's horse fidgeted, its nostrils twitching.

Hennoch's soldiers finished clearing the bailey, and proceeded to the keep. Lepstow Castle was old, perhaps even older than its lord. That meant that the next phase of the operation was more dangerous than storming the castle walls had been. Surviving a fight with mortals and arrows was relatively simple. Subduing an ancient, powerful *talishte* and his undead brood in order to get to his well-guarded prisoner was going to be much more difficult.

"Well?" Nilo joined Pollard, sidling his horse up alongside as Pollard supervised the troops' efforts to lock down the storage buildings, looting whatever could be easily carried as they went.

"Now we wait for sundown," Pollard replied. He was sure Nilo read his concern, though Pollard hid it from his expression.

"Have I mentioned that I don't like this part of the plan?" Nilo replied. "We're being offered up like lambs to the slaughter."

Pollard gave a sharp, short laugh. "Of course we are. I never thought anything else. Did you really expect Thrane to let us have a practice run at killing an ancient, powerful *talishte* and his brood?" Thrane was many things, but stupid was not among them. Pollard was certain the *talishte* lord was well aware that mortals could storm a *talishte* day crypt with fire and magic in daylight, besting even strong vampires at their weakest time of the day. He was equally certain that Thrane had no intention of giving him any ideas of attempting a coup against himself and his followers.

"So he expects us to wait here, like targets for the archer, as the sun goes down?" Nilo's eyes flickered with anger.

"Yes."

"To prove our loyalty?" Nilo demanded.

Pollard shrugged. "Partly. Thrane loves fealty. Mostly because he loves the idea of us squirming out here, watching the sun go down, knowing that there will be a gap between when Onyx and his followers awake and when Thrane and his brood can get here. And he will find it delicious that we are in fear of our lives for every second of it."

"Are you sure he'll show up?"

Pollard let out a long breath. "I am sure of nothing with Thrane. However, I've found self-interest to be a relatively reliable motivation, even for Thrane. He needs a mortal army, for exactly the kind of things we did today. So I doubt he'll allow Onyx to kill us." He paused. "At least, not all of us."

Nilo gave Pollard a murderous look, but said nothing.

"Go see to the mages," Pollard ordered. "They're our only real defense once it gets dark. Make sure they've got their wards in place and whatever other hocus they can muster up. I'll stay on the soldiers here to make certain we bottle up those *talishte* and keep them that way until Thrane gets here."

Nilo nodded. "I'm on it," he said, and spurred his horse to ride toward where the mages gathered near the keep.

Pollard turned his attention toward one of Nilo's commanders who oversaw searching and looting the bailey. "Captain Elsworth!" Pollard shouted. "A word with you."

Elsworth was a seasoned soldier in his early thirties, a veteran of many battles. He was spattered with mud and blood from the fight outside the gates, and seemed to be struggling to rein in a foul mood.

"M'lord?"

"Do you know what happens at sundown?" Pollard asked, making the painful effort to sit up in his saddle and look disdainfully at the captain.

"Yes, sir. The biters wake up."

Pollard nodded soberly. "Yes, they do. And what's to hold them in the keep rather than tearing out our throats?"

Elsworth swallowed hard. "Not much, sir, if you pardon my saying so."

Smart man, Pollard thought. "No, there isn't much," Pollard replied coolly. "The mages are sealing the keep, but there are probably tunnels all over this fortification and trapdoors in every building. And if you miss even one of those secret doors, there will be a bloodbath."

Elsworth nodded. "Aye, sir."

"*Talishte* are cunning," Pollard said sharply. "The doors may be well hidden. They could be halfway down a cistern, or under heavy crates. You'll have to seal the entrances with the materials we brought. Ash and rowan wood boards to close up doorways, covered with the mixture of buckthorn, dog roses, and juniper you have in the crocks. Make sure you have men watching every entrance you find, and that they have aspen and linden arrows. Choose your best archers: Nothing except a direct shot to the heart will kill these biters," Pollard instructed. *And for the oldest, even a stake in the heart won't be enough.* "Old *talishte* can withstand your arrows, so take off the head if it comes to that."

Elsworth swallowed again. *Surely he knows he's being sent on a suicide mission,* Pollard thought. But the captain straightened and gave a nod.

"It will be done, m'lord." Elsworth walked away with the manner of a man just sentenced to the gallows.

Silently, Pollard cursed Thrane and his brood, as well as Thrane's sadistic sense of humor. Yet if they could succeed at freeing Reese, and if Reese could be cured of his wounds, then Pollard stood a good chance that his own torment would end. *I inherited Reese's wounds through the* kruvgaldur, Pollard thought. *Let's hope I stand to inherit the healing as well.*

Tension rippled through the troops as the sun dipped lower in the sky. Hennoch and his soldiers encircled the keep. They had blocked the door with a removable barrier of ash and rowan, painted with the plant mixture the mages assured them would make it impossible for *talishte* to touch the wood.

Pollard could think of at least half a dozen ways such protections might be foiled, but it was the best alternative available. Thrane and his people, when they came, would need to make a quick entrance into the keep. Mortals could easily drag the barricades away from the doors, instead of having to rip out spikes driven into the stone. *If the mages are wrong about the* talishte *not being able to touch the wood-and-plant mixture, then it doesn't matter whether we lean the boards against the doorway or nail them tight. The* talishte *will pass through them like a knife through butter.*

Thrane had provided no help when Pollard had consulted him regarding how best to contain Onyx until the *talishte* reinforcements could appear. *"Figure it out,"* he said. *Of course he wasn't going to give me any suggestions of ways to keep a* talishte *bottled up. Doesn't want me to use it against him, even if the* kruvgaldur *would allow it,* Pollard fumed. *I bet he knows ways mortals have done it before. That's why the biters are so afraid.*

Rising up against Thrane and the rogue Elders was not a possibility, even with an army at his disposal. The *kruvgaldur* bond was too strong. Thrane would sense treachery long before Pollard could make good on his scheme, and given the nature of the bond, killing either Reese or Thrane might well destroy Pollard and Hennoch as well. *He's got us,* Pollard thought bitterly. *He knows it. And he has us out here, twisting in the wind, to make damn sure that we know it as well.* Thrane was powerful enough to keep his thoughts hidden from Pollard despite their bond. He seemed to enjoy keeping Pollard off guard and painfully aware of the one-way nature of their mental communication.

Just a breath after the sun disappeared beneath the horizon, Thrane appeared in the bailey. With him were twenty-five black-clad *talishte.* Pollard recognized some of them: Garin. Aslanov. Kiril. Sonders. Some, Pollard had never seen before. He wondered which of them might be among the renegade Elders. And then he wondered whether even together, they would be any match for Onyx and the obstacles that awaited them in the tunnels beneath Lepstow Castle.

"You're here." Thrane's voice thrummed with power and eagerness for the hunt.

"You ordered it so," Pollard replied, not bothering to look at Thrane as he addressed him.

"The poison worked?"

"You knew it would." Outright insolence or rebellion would not be tolerated, but Pollard reminded himself of who he was, or at least who he had been, by making at least a token effort at disdain from time to time.

Thrane's chuckle was cold and terrifying. "And did you wonder how I knew?" he asked in a dangerously smooth tone. "Of course you did. Best not to ask, of course. But here's something else you might want to know," he baited. "Those painted boards of yours wouldn't even slow down a *talishte* of Onyx's strength if he wanted to get out."

Pollard had suspected as much, although it was just as likely that Thrane was toying with him to get a reaction. He had already accepted the idea that he and the others faced down a nest of ancient *talishte* with nothing more than useless talismans. *Thrane could rip out my throat or drain my blood anytime he wants,* Pollard thought with the indifference that came with constant mortal fear. *If this is how he wants to squander my life, then that's what will happen.*

"You knew that, and let us believe otherwise." Pollard's voice was hard and flat.

Thrane grinned. "Mortals need their lucky amulets," he replied. "I'll admit that a newly turned *talishte* might find your barricades daunting, but not for long. But really, what harm did it cause? Your men felt they controlled the situation. It kept them busy, so they didn't have time to feel their fear. Not the first useless military gesture to pacify troops on the eve of battle."

Deep inside, in the part of his mind Pollard tried hard to hide away from the *kruvgaldur,* he seethed at Thrane's casual cruelty. *I am not expendable,* that hidden part of himself raged. It was the nugget of self that he hung on to, buried as deeply inside himself as he could hide it, in case someday, when he gained Donderath's crown, he might be his own master once again.

"What would you have us do now?" Pollard asked, maintaining an edge to his voice so it did not sound servile.

"Hold your ground," Thrane replied. "For however long it takes. I'm not surprised Onyx didn't attack. Once he comes out of his keep, he's vulnerable to mortal weapons. In there, in close quarters, he owns the darkness and the territory." He gave a terrifying grin. "Or at least, he believes he does."

With that, Thrane and the other *talishte* stalked toward the keep of Lepstow Castle.

Pollard and his army waited. No bell rang from the castle's tower, nor did the peal of bells from a nearby village tell the candlemark. It was difficult to gauge how long Thrane and his allies had been inside the keep, but by Pollard's rough estimation, several candlemarks passed.

Soldiers waited nervously in their ranks. The men were tired from the fight. They were hungry, too, since Hennoch and Nilo had made it painfully clear that the water and foodstuffs were poisoned. If any of the soldiers had doubted that before they broke down the gates, the stench of rotting corpses had made the point terrifyingly clear.

Nilo dispatched a handful of soldiers to move among the ranks, handing out dried meat and offering water from buckets drawn from barrels the army had brought with them. The scant rations would hardly constitute a meal, but they might stop soldiers from fainting of hunger.

Now and again, a shriek or screech would echo from somewhere in the complex. Then, silence. That the sounds seemed to come from everywhere and nowhere at once made them all the more terrifying. Most of these men had seen *talishte* in battle, at Valshoa, or on the Northern Plains, or at Mirdalur. These soldiers had witnessed comrades torn apart, heads ripped away, throats savaged. They had seen commanders snatched from their horses by an enemy that moved with inhuman speed and strength. Now, they stood nearly defenseless inside the keep—the lair—of one of the most powerful of the *talishte. No wonder they're terrified,* Pollard thought. *Any sane man would be.*

"Someone's coming!" The soldier who shouted the alert could not quite keep a quiver of fear from his voice.

Black-garbed men emerged from the keep's main door, waving, as had been prearranged, a blood-red kerchief as a signal. One of the *talishte* Pollard did not know came out first. *Of course, Thrane wouldn't risk leading the way in case one of the soldiers panicked and shot him full of arrows,* Pollard thought. Thrane followed, then two more *talishte* carrying what appeared to be a corpse in a shroud. Garin and the more senior *talishte* brought up the rear.

The undead fighters looked worse for the wear. Their clothing was shredded, torn nearly from their bodies. Deep bruises and oozing gashes might be gone by morning, but even at a distance, Pollard could see that the injuries were severe enough to have crippled or killed mortal fighters.

Hennoch's soldiers parted to let Thrane and his entourage pass. Nilo's command did the same. Pollard counted heads. Five of the twenty-five did not come back. Even Garin and Aslanov, two of the oldest *talishte,* were limping and bleeding. Thrane looked as if he had been in a tavern brawl. His usually immaculate clothing was covered with dirt and ichor, and from the amount of blood on one side of his head, it appeared that a handful of his carefully groomed hair had been yanked out by the roots. A sword slash across the chest gave disturbing glimpses of bone beneath the blood and tissue. Yet despite the injuries, Thrane strode up to Pollard with as much vigor as he had shown on his way in.

We both know something about making a good appearance in front of the troops. Never show weakness to an underling, Pollard thought. There was a degree of satisfaction in knowing that at least for an evening, Thrane might share in his suffering.

"We have him," Thrane announced as he approached Pollard. "Reese was not destroyed."

Pollard nodded. "Good to hear. What about Onyx?"

Thrane bared his bloodstained teeth. "Gone. Onyx and all his brood have been eliminated. There are no *talishte* left inside the keep."

"And your Elders?" Pollard asked, curious to see how they had fared.

Thrane shrugged. "Sapphire and Jade were destroyed, so were three of the others. The rest of those who came with me survived."

"How would you have us leave the castle grounds?" Pollard asked, keeping his voice neutral.

Thrane stared at the darkened, empty keep. "Burn everything. That will send a message to Penhallow and his traitor *talishte*. Tell your men not to dally. Once Penhallow realizes what we've done, there will be retaliation. When you return to Solsiden, come to the cellar. Reese will want a full report."

With that, Thrane walked briskly away for a few paces, then vanished in a blur of movement. His last comment sent a chill down Pollard's back.

"They get to Reese?" Nilo asked, approaching Pollard once he was certain Thrane was gone.

Pollard nodded. "Yes. And once again, we've been left in the lurch. Thrane wants our men to burn the place before we leave—knowing that Penhallow and the Knights of Esthrane might be on us any moment."

"While he and the other *talishte* are back at Solsiden by now," Nilo finished.

"Yes."

Nilo cursed creatively under his breath. "Well then, let's send all but half a dozen men back to camp, and see that we're well on our way before the others torch the castle." He met Pollard's gaze. "You know it's a symbolic gesture, setting it afire? I've been through most of the outbuildings and barns. Nothing's built with wood. I'd guess the keep is the same way. All a fire is going to do is call attention to us—the wrong sort of attention."

Pollard nodded. "Then rig it. Hold back one or two of the mages. Have the men set burning candles or oil lamps where there's anything that will burn. Get well clear, and have the mages tip them over. Or just wait for the candles to burn down and light the rest of it."

Nilo's reply was a slow grin. "I do like how you think. We can do that. And with luck, we'll be most of the way back before the flames go up."

"Don't trust to luck," Pollard advised, setting his heels to his horse. "It hasn't been on our side of late."

"Get out of the way, mortal." Marat Garin pushed past Vedran Pollard as he entered the small, dimly lit cellar room.

"Have a care," Pollard snapped. "I'm not your get."

"Watch what you say, or you could be."

"I doubt Reese would approve. He doesn't share well," Pollard replied. He stood against the wall in one of Solsiden's basement rooms as three *talishte* crowded around a still figure. The room had been prepared weeks before, changed from a storage area into a secure sickroom. Pollard held the only lantern, since he alone needed help to see in the dark. The room had a bed, washstand, and trunk. After centuries, Pentreath Reese's world had come down to this small space.

Pollard watched as the *talishte* carefully removed the cloth wrappings from the shrunken body on the bed. Before his capture and imprisonment, Pentreath Reese had been a tall man, powerful even without his *talishte* strength. Now, after months of starvation, imprisoned at the bottom of an oubliette, tortured with magical bonds, Reese looked like a shriveled corpse.

Thin skin pulled tightly over his skull. His eyes were sunken and closed. Blackened lips had drawn back, revealing his sharp teeth. The rest of him appeared to be mere bones beneath the rags that were left of his clothing. And in the center of his chest, a hole where Reese's foes had driven a thick wooden stake. *Talishte* as old as Reese could survive a stake to the heart, but it immobilized them while leaving consciousness intact. And so Reese had lain aware and unable to move, wrapped in rope made from plants that burned his skin, sprinkled with leaves that caused his skin to itch and blister, condemned to starve for fifty years as a punishment by the *talishte* Elders for his crimes.

And they say Hemming Lorens survived such a fate for more than seventy-five years, Pollard thought. *No wonder he went mad.*

"My lord requires food," Garin said, eyeing Pollard. "Bring it."

Pollard seethed at Garin's tone, but he kept his face impassive and leaned out of the room, barking an order to one of his *talishte* soldiers. "We've been gathering food for Reese since your plans were made," he replied impassively, turning back toward the others. "And if he requires more, it can easily be obtained."

Pollard stepped back as a *talishte* guard led a dazed young man into the room. He could see the hunger with which Garin and the others regarded the man, who had been captured only the night before on a lonely roadway not far from Solsiden. The captive should have been terrified out of his mind. Instead, he appeared drugged, or more likely, glamoured to make for easier feeding.

Garin pushed the man to his knees beside the bed and took

his wrist, feeling for a pulse and allowing the blood to throb beneath his fingers for a moment, as if savoring the smell of a delicious meal. The prisoner watched, utterly oblivious to the danger of his situation. Glamouring a victim was a generous act, a kindness unexpected of Thrane's brood, which enjoyed the terror and suffering as much as the blood itself.

Then again, Reese couldn't feed from a struggling donor, Pollard thought. *It's practicality, not kindness. That makes perfect sense. Once he's stronger, Reese will probably prefer his food wide awake and screaming.*

Long practice meant that Pollard could watch Reese sink his fangs deep into the man's arm and draw out the lifeblood without wincing. He had seen far worse on battlefields, and in the years he had been Reese's collaborator, he had watched Reese feed under far more horrific circumstances. Usually, Pollard felt only a profound sense of relief that this night, this time, it was not his blood being taken, not his life forfeit.

And thankfully, not Nilo or Eljas Hennoch, Pollard amended. Thrane considered all mortals to be interchangeable and expendable. Pollard knew better, and there were key people he would do everything in his power to protect, not for sentiment's sake, but because without them, his army could not function. Pollard had no illusions about how long his life would last if he ever ceased to be useful, either to Reese or to Thrane. *Whatever it takes to win a crown.*

A quiet moan escaped the captive's lips. Even in the lantern light, Pollard could see that the man had paled. Reese lacked the strength to tear into the artery, but his puckered lips closed around the wrist greedily, suckling the warm skin as the captive sagged against the bed frame. Pollard had seen *talishte* drain a man dry in minutes. Reese's weakness would likely prolong this death. Pollard felt nauseous.

Still, since Reese's release and the withdrawal of the stake that had pierced Reese's heart, the raw, agonizing sore on Pollard's chest had stopped its constant throbbing and begun to scab over. One of the *talishte* gentled Reese out of his filthy rags, while another soaked a cloth in the washbowl and began to wipe Reese's wrinkled, atrophied body from head to toe, cleansing away the poisonous powders used by his captors to torment him. Pollard could see the deep cuts where toxic ropes had cut into Reese's wrists and ankles. He knew the location of Reese's wounds well, since he bore their mirror image on his own body, a result of their *kruvgaldur* bond. *So do Garin and all of Reese's get,* Pollard thought. *But out of all the other mortals he's put in his thrall, I appear to be the only one bound so tightly that his wounds are mine. I'd feed him a thousand peasants to be rid of the damn itching and the constant pain.*

"Let me through." Thrane pushed through the doorway, and with a jerk of his head, dismissed all of the *talishte* except Garin, who was still holding the captive's wrist against Reese's mouth. Thrane gave a hiss of displeasure as he saw Reese, and let out a string of curses at the sight of his damaged blood-son.

"Has he spoken?" Thrane stared at Reese with a combination of concern and uneasiness.

Garin shook his head. "No. He's barely feeding. He's weak and not fully conscious. Give him time."

"We will hunt down the Elder Council for what they did to him," Thrane vowed. "We will destroy their broods, take their lands, seize their crypts. I want nothing of them to remain. Nothing."

"How will you do it?" Pollard's voice seemed loud in the underground chamber.

"What?" Thrane barely seemed to have heard him, his attention fixed on Reese.

"How will you punish Penhallow and the others?"

The question was not idle curiosity. Pollard knew Thrane's vanity. A plan clever enough to thwart the plans of the now-disbanded Elder Council would be a point of pride for Thrane, and boasting about it might improve his mood, raising the odds of survival for everyone. Pollard had learned long ago that any knowledge he could gain from his *talishte* allies stood him in good stead when it came to keeping what little autonomy he retained. For now, he needed Reese and Thrane in order to win the crown of Donderath for himself. But that would not always be so, and when that day came, he would seize his freedom.

Someday, he thought, before forcing his mind away from the possibilities. *Someday.*

"We will draw them out with attacks on the mortals they hold so dear," Thrane said. "Weaken their defenses by stretching them thin between our Meroven allies and the ambitions my agents have stoked in the Cross-Sea Kingdoms' mad king. When their armies are destroyed and their mortal allies scattered, we will destroy them and their broods." Anger transformed Thrane's features, bringing a flush of blood to his cheeks and lighting his eyes with a vengeful glint.

Pollard did not doubt that Thrane meant every word. *And we are all likely to go down in flames again because of it.*

CHAPTER EIGHTEEN

"WATCH YOUR HEADS!" NIKLAS THEILSSON shouted as a screeching black cloud descended on his soldiers. Thousands of frantically flapping wings stirred the air, their rhythm like a panicked heartbeat. Beaks drew blood and tore flesh, ripping hair from scalps. Talons raked faces and heads, and clawed at the horses' flanks. Sparrows, hawks, falcons, and warblers were bound together in a bloody truce, their rage fixed on the soldiers, who ducked and dove, beating them away with bleeding hands.

It started with a hawk, harrying the men in the front line, plunging again and again at the soldiers until they ran from its talons and beak. More birds joined the hawk, and by every law of nature, the hawk should have gone after the smaller birds. Instead, they joined ranks, chasing the soldiers. On more than one occasion, Niklas had run into a bird angry for having its nest threatened. Those birds had never pursued his men for long, nor summoned a flock of their fellows to launch a full-scale attack with no discernible purpose but to wound and destroy.

Niklas swung his sword, slashing through the body of a falcon, spraying him with blood as the wings fluttered uselessly and the bird fell from the sky. All around him, soldiers swung at an airborne enemy so fleet that they could scarcely land a blow. Blood streamed from Niklas's scalp and forehead where a kestrel dug its talons across his skin. Bloody gashes marked his horse's hindquarters, and his legs and arms were cut and punctured where he had been too slow to beat back an attack.

"What in Raka is going on?" Ayers shouted. His sword connected with a large hawk, big enough that the outstretched talons might have taken off his whole scalp had they connected, and he hurled the bleeding remains to the ground.

"Keep fighting!" Niklas yelled back. "We can't give up the ground we've gained!" All around his horse's hooves lay the bloodied, mangled bodies of more birds than Niklas could quickly count.

These birds shouldn't even be together, Niklas thought as he beat back the aerial attack. *If they're in sight of each other, they should be tearing each other to shreds—not ganging up on us. There has to be magic involved. Nothing about this is normal.*

He was covered with blood and feathers, scratched as if he had crawled through a tangle of hawthorn or nettles, and wary of the beaks and talons that aimed for his eyes. All around him, seasoned soldiers swore and cried out in pain from the frenetic onslaught. Horses panicked, throwing their riders. Vultures and hawks swarmed the downed men, tearing at their flesh despite flailing arms and kicking boots, while ignoring the still bodies of dead birds on which they could feast without danger.

The cries of the birds were deafening, and their wings raised a cloud of dust. The birds dove at the horses' heads, causing them to rear and bolt, forcing the riders to defend their mounts' eyes and faces at the cost of their own defense.

Then just as quickly as they came, the shrieking, razor-beaked cloud vanished, winging away as if at a signal only they could hear. And as the cacophony of shrieks and angry cries was silenced, Niklas heard the sound of hoofbeats.

"Stand ready!" he shouted, still blinded by the grit in his eyes and the dust cloud that kept him from seeing more than a few feet ahead. He reined in his balky, skittish mount to face the real threat, the army he could hear but not yet see bearing down on them.

Dark figures on horseback emerged from the billowing dust, a legion of men in armor whose metal helmets were worked to resemble the skulls of wild animals, twisted in nightmarish ways to be terrifying, monstrous predators. The bridles of their horses held sharp steel horns or antlers that extended in front of the horses' heads, and their mounts charged with heads lowered so that their steel blades were first to strike.

"Forward!" Niklas shouted as his line regrouped to meet the new assault. These new attackers were fresh to the fight, unlike Niklas's battered troops. They swept forward like a tide, scything their swords as their mounts ran forward with their deadly blades leveled. One of them ran his sword through a soldier as the armored horse tore through the throat of the soldier's mount. Niklas charged at the attackers, screaming a battle cry in sheer terror and frustration, rising in his stirrups to bring down his heavy sword with full killing power.

The grassland that had been empty just a candlemark ago was awash in blood and bird carcasses. Severed limbs and grievously wounded bodies littered the ground as the *clang* of swords rang out over the flat fields and the thunder of hoofbeats made the ground vibrate. Niklas choked down his own fear at the nightmarish spectacle of the black-clad warriors with their skeletal riders and murderous horses. The battlefield smelled of offal and sweat, and the dust churned up by the fight stuck in the eyes, noses, and mouths of the soldiers.

Down the line, Niklas heard the cries of his men and the shrieks of dying horses. He could not afford to take his attention from his adversary. Long-limbed and powerful, clad in black with a helmet that resembled a monstrous wolf, the enemy fighter wielded his heavy sword like a professional soldier, not a ragtag marauder.

Niklas swung, and the wolf-masked man blocked the swing, though its momentum was enough to make the swords in their hands vibrate painfully with the shock of the blow. "Who are you?" Niklas shouted. "Who do you serve?"

In response, he received only a feral snarl and a lunging, wordless attack. Despite his long years of soldiering and the horrors he had seen of war, Niklas felt a frozen lump of fear in his belly at an enemy that seemed utterly heedless of its own safety.

"I will not lose today!" Niklas yelled defiantly, mustering all of his rage as he swung hard. He had maneuvered to be at his attacker's side, in a place Niklas reckoned might be a blind spot. His blade sank deep into the rider's arm, and Niklas let out a triumphant shout.

"They bleed!" he shouted to his struggling soldiers. "They can die! Lay them out, boys! Knock them down!"

The rider turned on him with a snarl, the low, mad growl of a rabid dog. Emboldened, Niklas blocked and thrust, driving his blade into the neck of the rider's mount just behind where the hideous iron antlers were attached to the bridle. The horse shrieked and twisted, giving the rider no recourse but to focus on not being unseated. And in that moment, Niklas rushed forward, getting beneath the rider's guard and sinking his bloodied sword into the rider's side and out his belly. The rider fell backward as his dying horse bucked him free, sending the body to fall heavily to the ground.

To Niklas's right, Ayers brought his blade in a powerful slash that decapitated his opponent. The severed head, masked with the metal skull of a nightmarish panther, fell to the ground, knocking the head itself from the helmet.

"They're just men!" Ayers shouted. "Men can die!"

Terror turned to ugly rage as Niklas's soldiers took the offensive. The steel horns and antlers made a frontal attack too dangerous, so Niklas and his men quickly learned to approach the riders from the side, to look for each helmet's blind spot, and to strike at their opponents' mounts as much as at the soldiers themselves, something they usually avoided. The horses, too, were at a disadvantage. As frightening and deadly as the sharpened steel horns and antlers were, they changed the natural movement of the horses, weighed down their heads, and slowed their reactions. Niklas's soldiers rode forward screaming curses and obscenities, channeling their fury into the power of their strikes and the ferocity of their attack.

Dozens of Niklas's men lay bleeding and dying on the trampled field, but dozens of the enemy lay slain as well. That meant despite their terrifying appearance and the initial advantage of their mounts' helmets, the black-clad raiders were not immortal or untouchable, and Niklas's soldiers fought all the harder in retribution for the fear the enemy had forced on them.

It's turning, Niklas thought. *We're not losing anymore. We don't have to win—just force them to retreat. If we survive and can fall back to protected positions, I'm willing to claim it as a victory.*

The marauders, with their nightmare masks, had not counted on a foe that did not flee in terror. Niklas's soldiers screamed and howled, riding at the attackers with reckless bravado, wild-eyed and unwilling to yield. Seasoned as the black-clad riders were, Niklas's men had seen enough battle over the last few years to fear little that war had to offer. Once they had the measure of the enemy's weak point, Niklas's men exploited their knowledge, giving no quarter. After two bloody candlemarks of heated engagement, the riders drew back, then fled into Meroven territory.

"Let them go!" Niklas shouted. He was bleeding all over from scratches and punctures the birds had inflicted. His horse bore gashes and cuts as well, and he leaned forward to run a comforting hand down his mount's mane.

"Gather the wounded and the horses and fall back!" he ordered. Niklas gave a tired, bitter smile as he watched his troops go through the drill. Most remained on guard as others dismounted to find their wounded comrades, loot the bodies, and administer a death strike to any enemy soldier unlucky enough to be too badly injured to be captured and interrogated. This wasn't the stuff of legends. It was grimy, bloody work stinking of offal and piss, and looting the dead, once considered bad form, was now a routine of necessity.

How wealthy we were to leave a good blade on a corpse, or to allow usable gear to go to the grave, Niklas thought, remembering the beginning of the Meroven War, before the Great Fire and the Cataclysm, before the rules of existence changed forever.

Weary and wounded, Niklas's soldiers retreated to their fortified camp. Fresh soldiers came to attend to the wounded and guard the perimeter, as Ordel and the healers worked their way among the damaged and dying men, determining who to treat and who was already beyond saving.

"Thought you might want this, Captain." One of Niklas's men handed off a helmet he had taken from a black rider, before limping off to find a healer. *Doesn't matter what rank Blaine gives me, to the men who followed me home from the war, I'll always be 'captain,'* Niklas thought. Proud as he was of the responsibility Blaine had given him, he was proudest of earning the trust of his men as their 'captain' when the world around them went up in flames.

Niklas turned the helmet in his hands. It was well made, designed to be functional and to make a terrifying impression. The blacksmith who had crafted this helmet had envisioned an eagle, its features distorted to make it hideous and frightening. *First the bird attack, now men in scary animal-skull helmets. There's got to be a connection,* Niklas thought.

"Well, we lived through it." Ayers limped up to greet him. Dried blood matted his hair where the birds had clawed him, and fierce gashes marred his face, just missing his eyes. Crusted rivulets of blood darkened his eyebrows and streaked his cheeks. Niklas was sure he did not look any better.

"Yeah. Most of us. What in Raka was going on with the birds?" Niklas muttered. "There's got to be magic involved, and I want to know how to counter it!"

"I already took the liberty of calling the mages to your tent for a meeting," Ayers said with a tired grin. "They'll be there in half a candlemark, leaving enough time for us to eat first. I figured it was the best use of time, since the healers will be too busy with serious patients to worry about patching the likes of us up for a while." He paused. "And I was planning on bringing some whiskey, because I think we could sure use some after today."

Niklas nodded, certain Ayers could see the exhaustion in his face. "Were we able to take prisoners?"

"Got a couple. These troops looked tougher than some we've fought. I'm betting they won't talk except for the mages or the *talishte.*"

Niklas gave a shrug. "Fine by me. We have nothing to offer them. We can't afford to imprison them, and you're right— whoever the skull helmet folks are, they aren't going to be scared into changing sides." He sighed. "I hate this part of war."

At the moment, he ached from head to toe and he was starving and thirsty. Much as he wanted to sleep, experience had taught him the hard way that he would wake up feeling even worse if he did not see to his needs beforehand. He favored his leg where he had taken a gash, and his arms were tired and shaking from exertion. Finding out that the camp cook had already delivered food for them when they reached his tent was a bright spot in an otherwise horrific day.

"Here. You look like you need this even more than I do," Ayers said, pouring a few fingers of whiskey into Niklas's tankard, and then pouring a measure for himself. They ate in silence, so focused on the food and a chance to recover that they did not slow down for conversation. When they finished their meal and leaned back, Niklas could feel the whiskey taking the edge off his sore muscles and protesting joints.

"General Theilsson?" Dagur, one of the senior battle mages, called out, rapping on the tent post.

"Come in."

Niklas's field tent was sparsely furnished, just a brazier, cot, small trunk, and a wide, finished board he could use as a lap desk, as well as a worn rug that covered the ground. Chairs were an unnecessary luxury, as was a table. Niklas and Ayers sat on the floor, motioning for Dagur, Rikard, and their fellow mages to enter.

Dagur was thin and balding. Niklas figured the mage was in his fourth decade. In a worn pair of trews, stained shirt, and a threadbare woolen vest, Dagur looked more like a tavern keeper than a mage. With him were Rikard, Kulp, and Mevvin, younger mages who had distinguished themselves helping with the preparations to work an important ritual at Mirdalur several months earlier.

"Find a seat," Niklas invited, and Ayers passed the bottle

of whiskey to Dagur, who poured some into a tankard and knocked it back without comment, passing the bottle to his fellow mages.

Dagur was first to speak. "We really want to know what you saw out there, because there was some very strange, powerful magic going on. We did the best we could to interrupt it, but we knew we didn't cut it off entirely." He paused, taking in Niklas's bloodied appearance, and glanced over to Ayers, who looked no better. "Apparently, that wasn't good enough."

"That depends," Niklas replied, "on how bad it might have been without your help."

In response, Dagur passed him the bottle of whiskey. "You might want more of this," he said, raising an eyebrow. "Whoever these new raiders are, they've got a very powerful mage among them," he said, frowning as he eyed their wounds more carefully. "Those aren't all from sword fighting."

"Birds," Niklas replied. "A huge flock of them, all different kinds, attacking us like we were the first corn they'd seen after a long winter. They were fearless—and completely unnatural." The mages listened carefully as Niklas and Ayers recounted what they had seen.

"They were bewitched," Kulp said. He was a portly young man with a round belly and the stocky look of a brewer. Rumor had it that when he was not working magic, he made ale and mead. "I would imagine some of the frenzy you saw was the birds fighting the compulsion. That's why the attack broke off so quickly. Even a strong mage can't command so many beings for very long."

"Well, that's something, I guess," Niklas said. "Although they sure did enough damage in the time they had."

"We failed to cut off their mage completely," Mevvin added. "So we tried to punch holes in the magic or throw so much magic against him that he had to deflect some of his power to defend himself, which weakened his hold on the birds."

"Meaning that without your help, the attack could have lasted longer," Ayers summarized.

Dagur nodded. "Possibly. But not indefinitely—and that's the opportunity here. Every magic has limits. It might be limited by the skill or the strength of the caster, or by the ritual and objects it requires, or by the place or time, or by lots of other things. And anytime a single mage draws on his own power to use magic instead of tapping into the meridians, he—or she—runs a real danger of burning himself up, or draining himself dry."

"That's why battle mages work best in teams," Kulp said. "Some can defend while others take the offense."

"What kind of mage can summon birds like that?" Niklas asked.

Dagur sighed. "It can be done in a variety of ways, depending on the type of mage," he said. "Right now, with one encounter, we don't know that much about this mage's abilities. We don't know whether he's using an artifact with a very specific type of spell, or drawing on land and air magic, or something different entirely."

"How do we find that out?" Ayers leaned forward intently.

"Unfortunately, we're going to have to watch what he does next," Dagur replied. "We might get some inkling of what is going on from the captives, but they can only tell us what they observe, which may be highly unreliable. Let's see what else he throws at us, and that should give us a good idea."

"You weren't out there, in the middle of those birds," Niklas said with a glare. "We can't just watch and wait."

Dagur shook his head. "You misunderstand me, sir. I didn't mean we could do nothing. Based on what seemed to work—and not work—this time, we're already developing counter-magics, and ways to keep our scrying from being blocked so we can react faster, maybe even before the strike actually hits the soldiers."

"Anything you can give us helps," Niklas said earnestly. "I used to think birds were pretty. Now, I never want to see another one, and certainly not close up!" He paused. "Where does Nagok fit into this?"

Dagur shrugged. "Don't know. Right now, we've just got a name and wild talk from captives who never saw him. By Torven's horns! He might just be a legend."

"Or he might be real—real trouble," Ayers replied. "We've got to find out more about him and whether he's their commander—or the mage behind what we saw today. Or both."

"What do you make of this?" Niklas handed over the skull helmet they had brought back from the battlefield. Dagur handled it gingerly, studying it from all angles before passing it to the other mages to examine.

"The taint of magic clings to it," Dagur said. "Does it tell you anything?"

"I'm more concerned about how it looks than how it feels," Kulp said thoughtfully, holding the helmet so that it faced him straight on, as if it were a severed head. "Obviously, it was meant to inspire terror, and I'm betting it worked."

"Let's just say they made a dramatic entrance," Ayers remarked drily.

"It takes a lot of work to make a helmet like this," Kulp continued. "Far more than just a regular 'battle bucket.' And you fought a large number of men who all had these helmets, right?"

"No idea whether all the troops had them. We never got all

the way to the back ranks," Niklas observed. "But yes, the ones we fought, in at least the first third of their troops, all had helmets like that one."

"But they weren't identical," Ayers said, jumping in. "There were all kinds of creatures—large cats, wolves, dogs, birds, and all of them made strange and frightening."

Kulp lowered the helmet. "We need to consider the idea that the helmets may have a religious significance, or at least a superstitious one," he said. "All kinds of legends exist about ways men can take on the characteristics of animals during a fight. For an army to go to all the expense and trouble of these kinds of helmets, and for them to not be standardized, means that these beast shapes are very important to them."

"Do you think they're shape-shifters?" Ayers asked, trying to figure out where Kulp was going with his thoughts.

Kulp shook his head. "If they had been able to shift, surely they would have during the battle. They didn't, even when you drove them back." He sighed. "Maybe we can get something out of the prisoners to give us a better idea," he said. "It might just be symbolic. If we're lucky, that's all it is."

"And if we're not lucky?" Niklas asked, feeling a prickle on the back of his neck.

"Then we could be up against some of the nastier magics to tangle with," Dagur replied.

Another candlemark passed as Niklas, Ayers, and the mages discussed strategies and defense. Finally, a knock came at the tent pole. "Captain? We've got the prisoners ready to question, and Ordel says he can fix you both up now."

As the mages prepared for the first round of questioning, Niklas and Ayers trudged to the healers' tent. The tent smelled of liniment and poultices, healing tea and potions. A score of soldiers lay on pallets, bandaged and splinted, sleeping off the effects of the draughts and magic used to heal their injuries. Niklas did not need to go behind the tent to know that out there lay more young men side by side, covered with sheets until the night watch could bury them properly, the ones whose injuries were too severe for the healers to fix.

"Let's have a look at you." Ordel's manner was curt, which Niklas knew meant the healer was drained from his work and angry over the ones he could not save. Ordel gave Niklas and Ayers a cursory look from head to toe.

"Better than some I've had through here," he grunted. "Sit down. Better put something on those scratches so they don't go bad." Ordel shuffled over to a table and rummaged through the bags of powders and bottles of potions, then he grabbed a mortar and pestle and began to mix together the items he had chosen. One of his assistant healers came up to ask him a question, and Ordel barked the answer, sending the young healer away in a hurry.

The war is taking its toll, Niklas thought. Ordel had not seemed so abrupt, nor looked so haggard, before the last two battles. *Then again, he gets none of the triumphs and all of the failures.*

"Birds, huh." Ordel's voice was nearly a growl.

"Yeah," Niklas said as the healer spread a poultice on his wounds and used his magic to speed the healing on the deepest of the gashes. "Could have been worse. I didn't see any eagles."

"Humphf," Ordel grunted. "Wonder why not?"

"Actually I was rather glad—" Niklas cut off midsentence, and frowned. "You know, that's a good question. Why weren't there eagles? And owls and seagulls—"

"Don't tempt fate," Ayers replied. "It was bad enough without them."

Niklas shook his head. "You don't understand. There's

something to this. If Nagok, or whoever the mage was who called the birds, meant to do damage, why not bring in the biggest predators? Why even have the sparrows and warblers? Why not make it all hawks and falcons and why not bring in the big birds, like the eagles?"

"None of those around here," Ordel replied without looking up, although the question was not specifically addressed to him. "Have to go up into the mountains to find eagles. And any fool knows that hawks and such are territorial. Might only be a couple of them for a few miles around."

Niklas looked up and grinned. "That's it. Maybe this mage has limits," he said, feeling excitement despite his weariness. "I mean, why stop at birds? Why not call in foxes and wolves and feral dogs and bears, while he's at it?" He leaned forward like he was about to impart a secret. "Maybe he didn't because he can't," he said, eyes alight with the idea. "Maybe he's got to deal with what's nearby—and that's why he didn't bring in eagles and more hawks. Maybe his magic only reaches so far."

Ayers nodded. Ordel kept going about his business, treating their wounds and binding up the deep cuts. "All right," he said, willing to spin Niklas's theory out and see where it led. "Wouldn't be the first time we ran into magic that couldn't be everywhere. The closest we've ever seen to that was the Meroven mages who sent the Great Fire, Torven take their souls," he said. "And to do something on that scale, they had to work together."

"So maybe he's got a limited range," Niklas theorized. "And maybe that's why he only called birds and not every wild animal. Seems strange, doesn't it, if he wanted us dead that badly? Birds were bad, but bears would have been worse."

Ayers glared at him. "You are testing the gods," he said grimly. "The birds were bad enough."

"Hear me out," Niklas said, energized since the idea of their enemy's limits gave him hope. "You use your strongest weapon first, right? Who wants to fight longer than he has to? So if you've got catapults, you don't start with slingshots and work up. You bombard the shit out of them and try to flatten them into the sand first, and then maybe there isn't a 'later.'"

"I'm tired and my head hurts," Ayers replied grumpily. "You've lost me."

"If the mage could have sent something worse against us, he would have," Niklas said. "So maybe he has to use what's inside his range, and maybe he can only call one kind of thing at a time."

"How do you figure? There were all sorts of birds," Ayers argued.

Niklas made a dismissive gesture. "Yeah—but they were all birds."

"Maybe birds could get there faster," Ayers said.

"True," Niklas conceded. "So maybe he's got to work with what's at hand. He can't just 'poof' creatures into place from far away."

Ayers shrugged. "Thank Charrot for small favors."

"We know three things for sure," Niklas said as Ordel walked away and put down his mortar and pestle, and came back with a bottle of elixir and a cup. He poured a bit of the greenish liquid into the cup and thrust it into Niklas's hands.

"Drink," he ordered, interrupting the conversation. "Fascinating as this is, I have work to do."

Niklas glowered at him but obeyed, returning the cup so Ordel could refill it and pass it to Ayers. "Three things," he continued, ignoring Ordel. "First, that he called only birds—which may mean he can only use one type of animal at a time. Second, that the birds he called likely lived nearby, inside a certain range. And third, the attack stopped suddenly."

Ayers drank the elixir and made a face at the taste, shoving the cup back at Ordel. "Gah, that was awful," he said. "Trying to poison me after I survived the battle?" He returned his attention to Niklas. "So it stopped. So what?"

Niklas shrugged. "Maybe nothing. The attack could have been timed to put us off guard and damage us and then lifted when the soldiers were in place. Or," he suggested, "maybe their mage can't hold control of the animals for too long. Think about it—keeping all those minds focused, overcoming all that instinct to force them to act unnaturally. It's the same reason mages can't just take over entire armies like puppets. It takes too much magic."

"Captain?" one of the guards stuck his head into the tent. "The sun set. The *talishte* have risen. Kulp is looking for you."

"Go," Ordel said. "You're patched up—for now. Try to stay that way. Get out of my tent." The ghost of a smile softened his words.

"Trying out your theories about magic on me doesn't get you anywhere," Ayers said as they headed toward where the mages were holding the prisoners. "I'll grant you that it's an interesting idea. But you're going to have to try them out on Dagur and see what a real mage thinks."

"I intend to do exactly that, after we see what the prisoners have to say," Niklas replied.

CHAPTER
NINETEEN

THE MAGES HAD THE SECOND BIGGEST TENT, after the healers. Four mages and an apprentice slept and worked in the tent, and it was crowded with bedrolls and folding worktables, two trunks, and a brazier large enough to heat a small cauldron. Dried herbs and berries hung from the tent poles, and a ring of salt in a shallow trench surrounded the entire tent. Niklas saw a bundle of feathers on one table and shied away instinctively after the onslaught they had faced.

I don't think I'll be able to see a songbird for a long time without cringing, he thought.

Two men were seated on the floor, their arms, wrists, and ankles bound securely. They looked worse for the wear, with large bruises purpling from the injuries they had taken in the fight. Niklas knew that the healers would have done as little as possible to keep them alive for questioning. *No sense healing them completely if they're just going to hang,* Niklas thought, regretting the coldness of the decision even though he knew it was necessary.

The captives' skin was ashen, their breathing shallow. *They know they're dead men. Just waiting for the sword to fall.*

Geir was there, along with Ekkle, another of Penhallow's *talishte* on loan to Niklas. Both *talishte* looked grim, and Niklas knew that reading prisoners was one of the tasks Geir disliked most. "Thanks for being here."

Geir shrugged. "It's war. Perhaps I should worry if my dislike of this kind of thing ever lessens."

"Anything?" Niklas asked with a glance toward Rikard. He looked around. "I thought we had three prisoners?"

Rikard grimaced. "We did. That's how we found out that their mage placed a geas on the men so that if they were magicked, their hearts stop."

"Lovely," Niklas muttered. "Does that apply to *talishte*?"

Geir shook his head. "What we do isn't magic in the same sense. It's what we are. So the odds are good that I can read them." His glance told Niklas what he did not say aloud: *They're going to die anyway.*

Niklas looked to the two battered prisoners. He guessed they felt the effect of their wounds even if Ordel had blunted their pain. A wide bandage around the abdomen trussed up a belly wound on one of the prisoners, but it was likely to sour and go bad quickly, and even the healers could not always prevent that. The other man slumped in his chair as if all the fight had gone out of him, waiting for the end.

"We can make this easy or hard," Niklas said. "I have no desire to further your suffering. Tell us what you know of Nagok and his mages, of your army and its defenses, and you'll go quietly in your sleep."

"Never wanted to fight for that bloody freak in the first place," the man with the belly wound muttered, his Meroven accent thick. "I was just getting my farm working again, after the Burning Times and the Downfall," he said bitterly. "I even had a cow again. Got crops in the field. Wife's expecting a baby. Then the skull helmets came," he said, making the name a curse.

"You were conscripted?" Niklas asked.

The prisoner raised his face to meet Niklas's gaze with a baleful expression. "Kidnapped's the word for it. Hauled away like a criminal in front of my own wife, and her screaming and pleading. Thrown on a cart and locked in irons. What do I know of soldiering? Not much," he said with a bitter glance at the blood seeping through his bandage. He shifted in his seat and grimaced.

"Whole wagonful of us they had, and more like us," the prisoner said. "Fighting's been bad all year, what with the warlords fighting among themselves after the Burning destroyed everything. We could hardly get a crop planted without it being ridden over by one army or another. Then Nagok showed up."

"Where did he come from?" Niklas pressed. "Is that his real name? Where was he in the war?"

The prisoner shrugged. "Who knows? I'm just a farmer. But I can tell you what I've heard."

"He's *buer*, evil spirit," the other prisoner spoke up. "Bad seed."

"Tell me what you know about him," Niklas urged. "You owe him nothing. He stole your lives from you. Tell me, and we'll get your vengeance."

"Nagok was a prince," the second prisoner said, speaking the Common tongue with an equally strong Meroven accent.

"That's a lie," the first man argued. "The king and the princes died in the Burning Times."

"Maybe not all," the second man retorted. "How would we know?" He turned back to Niklas. "Nagok was sly. He was a bastard, so the crown wouldn't have gone to him, except for the Downfall. They say he poisoned his rivals, rallied what remained of the army, and crushed anyone who opposed him."

"Did he send the marauders, the ones who came over the border in the last few months?" Niklas asked.

"They were spies," the first man answered. "Sent to find out how bad off Donderath was after the Burning Times. People said only our magic failed, that Donderath prospered. We heard there was food here, and that things were as they used to be, that only Meroven suffered from the Downfall." His mouth twisted. "Those were just dreams."

"So the marauders were sent to size us up, steal what they could carry, and report back to Nagok?" Niklas pressed.

"Some were," the second prisoner replied. "Some were just bandits. If they didn't join him, and Nagok caught them, he killed them and hung their bodies in the trees as a warning."

"Is Nagok the only power in Meroven?" Ayers asked. "Are there other warlords?"

"There were." The first prisoner met Niklas's eyes, and Niklas glimpsed shadows of horrors in them. "His men went town by town, city by city. Just a few at first, more later. Anyone of account who survived the Burning Times they slaughtered. The men who fought back about being conscripted were burned alive with their families in their homes. He killed the other warlords and gave their soldiers the choice between allegiance and death."

"Son of a bitch," Niklas muttered.

"Indeed," Geir said.

"Is Nagok a mage?" Ayers asked.

"He styles himself such," the first prisoner replied. "Wears a headdress made of skulls and a breastplate made of bones. His walking stick is a leg bone, and his coat is made of men's skins. His familiar is a black wolf nearly big as a bear, and they say he rides it in the night and can travel without being seen."

"Is that what you've heard, or have you actually laid eyes on him?" Niklas asked.

"I've seen him," the second man replied. "And he looks just like that. Has a cloak made out of scalps—hair of all different colors, taken from his victims."

A thought occurred to Niklas. "Is he *talishte*? Is he a biter?"

The first prisoner cast a nervous glance at Geir and Ekkle. "No," he replied. "But they say his allies are—and that his master is a dark god returned from the dead who promised him he could rule all of the Continent."

"'A dark god returned from the dead,'" Geir repeated cynically. "Now, who might think of himself that way?"

Niklas cursed. "Oh, it just figures."

"Do you know the name of this 'dark god'?" Ayers asked.

"He is the Hemlock King," the second prisoner replied.

Geir swore. "That's Thrane, all right. Just how long ago did the Hemlock King return from the dead and make Nagok his chosen one?"

"I don't know," the second prisoner admitted.

"We never heard of him before this year," the first man said. "Doesn't mean much, since the likes of me don't know much of such things, but it wasn't like we'd heard of him in tales told to frighten children."

"Want to bet that Thrane's been the power behind Nagok's rise?" Geir said. "Sounds like his kind of plan. He's probably been preparing since the Great Fire, looking for a strongman to be his figurehead. He's been gone for seventy years, and now he saw his chance to come back and take it all."

"So is Nagok a mage or just a general?" Niklas asked.

"He acts like a hocus, and dresses like one," the second prisoner replied. "That's all I know."

"Who put the geas on you?" Dagur asked. "The curse that would kill you if I used magic on you?"

"Whenever they had rounded up a few dozen of us, they made us kneel, and Nagok and his 'priests' came out," the first man said. "First, he blessed us, telling us we would be unstoppable in battle. Then, he cursed us, so that no one could use us against him. That's all I know."

"How far can Nagok throw his magic?" Niklas asked.

The second man shrugged, but the first prisoner thought for a moment. "Don't rightly know," he said. "Except that our captain told us Nagok was lord of all he could see."

Ayers shrugged. "Might just be a turn of phrase."

Dagur looked thoughtful. "Or perhaps not," he countered. "Some magic is limited by the range of the senses—sight, smell, hearing. Especially for strong magic, a clear line of sight can be important."

"Does that mean if Nagok stands on a mountain, he controls everything beneath him?" Ayers asked with alarm.

Dagur shook his head. "No. And if he could manage to be taken up into the clouds, he wouldn't control the world," he added. "Usually, that means line of sight on flat ground, to the horizon."

"The birds that attacked us—was that Nagok's doing?" Niklas pressed, knowing that time was running out for the two men.

"Aye," the second prisoner replied. "He's a beast caller. That's how you know he's *buer*, an Evil One. He called down the birds on you, and they serve him."

"Does he call other animals?" Ayers asked.

The first prisoner nodded. "Wolves sometimes. Foxes. Wild dogs. Mountain cats. He can command them all."

"Horses?" Dagur asked, frowning. "Farm animals? Pet dogs?"

The second prisoner shook his head. "Don't think so. Never

saw him do it. He can spook them, but if he could have called your horses, why didn't he?"

"Well?" Niklas asked, turning to Dagur. "Why didn't he?"

Dagur chewed his lip as he thought. "Horses and livestock and pet dogs have a bond with us," he said. "They're intelligent, and they accept us as their herd or pack. That might protect us. I'll have to see what the manuscripts have to say about this."

"How long can Nagok keep his hold over the animals?" Niklas asked.

"Don't know how long he can keep it, but I ain't never seen him hold it for long," the first prisoner replied. "Maybe half a candlemark, or a little more. Not a full candlemark. Long enough to do some damage."

A frightening thought occurred to Niklas. "Can he call the magicked beasts? The *ranin* and the *mestids* and the *gryps*?"

The second prisoner shivered. "Aye. Monsters, they are. And he calls them to him, makes them do his bidding. He's *buer*, sure enough."

"Those helmets you were wearing," Ayers asked, "the ones that look like skulls. Why are they made that way?"

"Our captain said that Nagok's god told him the helmets would give us strength in battle and make our enemies fall down in fear before us," the first prisoner replied, his voice bitter. "Obviously that didn't work."

It was clear that both prisoners were fading fast. Just the effort of talking had taken a toll. "You've done a great service," Niklas said. "Now I will keep my promise."

Geir and Ekkle stepped forward and knelt so that they could look straight into the prisoners' gaze, capturing them with compulsion. "Sleep," Geir said. "Feel no pain. Your work is finished. Rest awaits." The two prisoners slumped to the ground, eyes fluttering closed, breathing shallow.

"They may have nothing more to tell us," Geir warned as he lifted the first prisoner's wrist. Ekkle positioned himself next to the second man. "But we'll see if there's more they know." He lifted the wrist to his mouth and carefully punctured the skin with his fangs, then fed until the prisoner took a last shuddering breath and fell still. A moment later, Ekkle finished his task.

Though Niklas had seen it done many times before, he could not avoid feeling a primal frisson of fear down his spine. *Like the time I came upon a wolf feeding on the body of a dead man,* Niklas thought. *Or seeing the crows pick out the eyes of the corpses on the battlefield. Tomorrow, it could be me.* And while he trusted Geir and the rest of Penhallow's brood with his life, deep inside, something old and primitive whispered that he was prey.

After a few moments, Geir raised his head. "What he told you was the truth as he knew it," he said. "I saw what he saw. Nagok's army is sizable. On the other hand, many of the fighters appear to be conscripts like this man. So Nagok has a lot of soldiers who can't fight well, but the sheer volume can be used to wear us down."

Niklas swore. "That's what Lysander did with the Tingur," he replied.

"A cynical—but arguably effective—strategy," Geir said with a shrug. "Something else of note. Although we've blamed the Meroven mages for the destruction of the Great Fire and the Cataclysm, from what this man has seen, I would say Meroven was damaged at least as badly, maybe worse. And the aftermath has been harsher for them," he added. "Having Blaine McFadden emerge as the unifying force has brought a much different outcome than having someone like Nagok triumph."

It was bad enough imagining what Donderath might have

been like had Blaine lost against the warlords he had fought, Niklas mused. None of those scenarios presented a kingdom in which Niklas wanted to live. By all accounts, Nagok sounded even worse than Donderath's most nightmarish prospects.

"What I saw was very similar," Ekkle said. "Conditions in Meroven are much worse, and that makes their people more desperate—and more willing to follow anyone who promises to improve their lot, no matter what they have to do to get that improvement." He paused, sifting through the thoughts and images he had read. "There appears to be a large *talishte* element in Meroven as well. The impressions are limited, just what the man glimpsed in Nagok's camp, but if they aren't all Thrane's get, then they appear to be of like mind and tactics—and at least one of them is a rogue Elder, I'm certain of it."

"Lovely," Niklas said drily. "Maybe we know now where Thrane spent the last seventy years."

Geir frowned, thinking. "I suspect that Thrane went farther than Meroven, if Penhallow and the Wraith Lord lost track of him. But he was always an opportunist. I wouldn't doubt that he saw the potential the situation in Meroven presented and positioned himself to reap the benefits."

"You're going to need to let Penhallow and the Wraith Lord know," Niklas said.

Geir nodded. "Penhallow will have an inkling through the *kruvgaldur*. And they are already considering ways to fight both Thrane and Reese."

"I thought Reese was locked up for fifty years," Niklas said, eyes widening.

"He was supposed to be," Geir replied. "Thrane managed to free him. The arrangement was designed to keep Reese from escaping on his own. It was never set up to withstand a siege by *talishte* rescuers."

"I hope Penhallow has a plan," Niklas said. "Because we're going to have our hands full with Nagok."

"He does," Geir replied.

"I'll have the mages consider how you might use limited range and limited control time to your advantage," Dagur offered. "Perhaps if we can find a way to clear the land of wildlife ahead of the troop movement, Nagok will have no animals to coerce," he mused. "It's a starting point, easier said than done, but that's the way with all strategic magic. Simple to come up with a great idea, hard to harness the power in a way to make it happen." He met Niklas's gaze and gave a curt nod. "We'll get right to work on it, and to finding ways to protect the camp as well."

Niklas looked down at the two dead prisoners. "I'll send soldiers to fetch the bodies. We'll bury them in the morning, as best we can. Gods above, I hate this part of soldiering."

"We need to let Blaine know what we're up against," Niklas said, turning to Geir. "See if he can move troops around to give us more men, if Nagok has an army of that size. And if Thrane's tied up in all this, then we'll be grateful for any support Penhallow can give us, because we can't fight crazy mages and mad *talishte* on our own."

Geir nodded. "I'll make sure both messages are received. Penhallow has been focused on the *talishte* impact of Thrane's return, and the dissolution of the Elder Council. I fear that both have grave implications for our kind, which are likely to spill over into the mortal world."

"Implications?" Niklas asked, sure that he did not want something else to worry about, but equally certain he could not ignore the threat.

"Thrane seems intent on causing as much damage as possible, in as many ways as possible," Geir replied. "Your attention is focused on Nagok, as it should be. Penhallow and the Wraith Lord are trying to stop a *talishte* civil war from happening."

"Because the Elder Council split?" Niklas asked.

"For centuries the Elder Council existed to keep such things from happening," Geir said. "Its purpose was to provide a court to settle disputes before they caused our kind to form factions. They knew that war among *talishte* was likely to cause large mortal casualties, and that would prompt a backlash that could be our downfall."

"So Thrane shows up, splits the council, and forces everyone's hand." Niklas rolled his eyes. "Wonderful. What does Thrane hope to gain, after everything's been burned to the ground?"

"Vengeance," Geir said with a shrug. "Against everyone who refused to acknowledge his 'greatness.' Satisfaction, in knowing that he had the power to wreak such devastation. Thrane is an old *talishte*. He remembers a time before mortals organized such large kingdoms, when they were scattered and vulnerable. Easier to hunt, fewer protections. I suspect he wants to turn back time, return the world to the way it used to be, the way he best understands it."

"As if I didn't have enough to worry about," Niklas replied. "Gods help us."

Geir's expression was somber. "I have found that the gods serve best when we take matters into our own hands."

Ayers clapped Niklas on the shoulder. "Come on," he said. "It's been a hard day. You need a little more whiskey and a good night's sleep. I can make sure you get one of those. Let's go."

Niklas had feared that sleep would be a long time coming, despite how exhausted he was. Yet he dropped off almost as soon as he lay down, only to wake with a start in his darkened tent to the fearsome howling of wolves close by.

"Shit," he muttered, lighting a lantern and dressing quickly, belting on his sword just in case. He walked out of his tent to find most of the camp stirring, soldiers turning out to see what was going on, armed and ready if the situation required a fight.

"Report!" Niklas snapped as he strode up to Dagur. Dagur was standing near the perimeter warding around the camp, staring into the dark plain beyond. The mage's hair was mussed as if he had not bothered to smooth it when he got out of bed, and he wore his cloak over a nightshirt and boots.

"Nagok has called wolves," Dagur replied, his attention focused out beyond the torches that lit the edge of camp. "There's a large pack out there, maybe twenty or thirty wolves."

"Big for a pack," Niklas remarked.

Dagur shrugged. "Not unheard of, especially when times are hard. Unusual, yes. But it makes me wonder if you weren't right about range. Wolves are territorial. Be interesting to see how many he can call. If it's more than thirty, then he's probably called more than one pack, which would mean the magic can reach a bigger area."

"Glad we could be your experiment," Niklas remarked acidly. "Will your wardings hold?"

Dagur shook his head. "The wardings around a camp like this are an alarm, not a wall. At best, we can weaken or delay a supernatural threat. The wolves are mortal, regardless of who or what controls them."

Just then, Niklas heard a commotion from the corral where the horses were kept. "What now?" he muttered, leaving Dagur and heading off at a run to see what the ruckus was about.

"Don't know what's gotten into them, sir," a soldier said as Niklas ran up. Wild-eyed horses kicked at the wooden fences, whinnying in fear and galloping around the enclosure, desperately looking for a way to escape. Soldiers climbed the fence into the enclosure, risking their lives to grab for bridles, trying to calm the more tractable horses.

Terrified by the howling and by the frenzied reactions of the other horses, the stallions bucked and nipped, kicking and rearing. Two soldiers went down beneath flailing hooves, barely pulled to safety by their comrades. Several soldiers dove back over the fence, unable to get close to the horses they were trying to calm.

"We're going to have to do something, or they'll either stampede or hurt themselves," Niklas observed.

"It's the wolves, sir. Spooked them good," the soldier replied.

Kulp ran up to join them. Like Dagur, he looked as if he had just rolled from his cot, shirt untucked, clothing likely plucked from the floor. "Dagur sent me to see what I could do."

"I thought you said Nagok couldn't magic the horses," Niklas demanded.

Kulp shook his head. "They haven't been magicked. They're reacting to the wolves—it's a normal reaction to an unnatural situation."

Kulp closed his eyes and held out his arms, palms out. For a few moments, he was silent, then he began a low chant under his breath. Gradually, the frightened whinnying quieted, and the wild galloping slowed, then stopped. After another few minutes, the horses were no longer frenzied but still shuddering and trembling in place, their gaze darting about, alert for danger.

Soldiers tentatively entered the enclosure, speaking calmly and carefully to the shivering horses, approaching them with whatever treats they could find in the feed sacks. One by one, they led the horses back to the far side of the corral.

Finally, Kulp stopped his chant. "Did it work?" he asked, shaking his head to clear his thoughts.

"They're not trying to break down the fence, if that's what you mean," Niklas replied. "How come you can magic them, when Nagok can't?"

Kulp smiled. "I didn't control them. I just blocked the sound of the wolves."

Niklas nodded in acknowledgment and headed back to his tent. The field camp was laid out on a grid with tents, stable, essential functions like blacksmiths and healers, cooking area, and latrines, surrounded by a stockade of wooden posts that could easily be erected in just a few candlemarks and struck just as easily when it was time to move out. Supply wagons, sledges, and movable war machines like catapults were also housed within the stockade. Two tall towers flanked the main gate, each one with at least one guard day and night.

A low growl stopped Niklas in his tracks. He was in one of the camp's 'streets,' the section of tents reserved for officers. Most of the men were still sleeping. The ones who had turned out to help with horses had been on night shift, and they were all at the stables. That meant the pathways around Niklas were deserted, lit only by moonlight and whatever dim torchlight spilled over from the torches on the main path.

Niklas drew his sword, and pulled a knife in his left hand. The growl came from behind him, though it was difficult to place. His heart was thudding, and he had broken out in a cold sweat.

An answering growl sounded off to Niklas's right. He crouched, watching and waiting. A full-grown male wolf lunged from the shadows, leaping into the air at chest level. Niklas swung his sword, burying the blade deep in the wolf's shoulder, biting into its neck and throat. Before the wolf dropped to the ground, Niklas sensed more than saw the second wolf attack. He threw himself out of the way, and the wolf's claws ripped open the shoulder of his jacket, slicing into the skin beneath. The wolf landed and turned quickly, head lowered and teeth bared.

Niklas stepped to the side, keeping both the downed wolf and its partner in view. His shoulder was bleeding, and he knew the injury would hamper his strength with his left hand. But in the few seconds he had to catch his breath, he sized up his opponent. The second wolf was a female, dark gray with yellow eyes, and it glowered at Niklas with a level of crazed intent he had only seen in a rabid dog.

"Get out of here!" he shouted, waving his arms and stomping. Without its partner to attack in tandem, there was an even chance the wolf might retreat. But the malice in the wolf's eyes was not natural, and the predator stood its ground. It made a deep-throated growl and then sprang, covering the dozen or more feet between them in a single bound, going for Niklas's throat.

Niklas brought his sword down with all his might, and at the same time, struck with his knife. The sword bit into the wolf's powerful shoulders, and the knife caught it in the chest, spilling hot blood over the rough fur. Teeth sharp as razors *snicked* just inches shy of his throat. The wolf lashed out, snapping for his arm, and Niklas dodged away as claws raked his thigh. The female wolf dropped to the ground, covered in blood, and collapsed in the dust. Taking no chances, Niklas did not turn away until he had beheaded both wolves.

By that time, he could hear howls echoing throughout the camp and the shouts of soldiers. "Everyone up! We're under attack!" he yelled, then staggered from the gash in his leg. "Wolves inside the fence! Swords ready!" he added. Soldiers turned out of their tents, running for their posts, swords in hand.

"I want all soldiers on the stockade! Archers, to your posts! I need slings and pikes! Move it, move it, *move* it!" Niklas shouted. He took stock of his injuries. The shoulder cuts were painful but not terribly deep. The gash in his thigh would need attention, but he could still move, thanks to years of practice struggling through battle injuries. Sheathing his knife, Niklas limped toward the main area of the camp.

He spotted two soldiers battling three wolves near the mess tent, and by the stable area four soldiers were keeping five more wolves from attacking the horses. Two archers and a soldier with a sling took aim from far enough away to be out of the wolves' lunging range. The night echoed with the howls and answering cries of the packs, the grumbling snarls, and the shouts of soldiers.

Yet as Niklas watched, the wolves now seemed less sure of themselves than the two that attacked him before. The soldiers held their ground, and the wolves, snarling and aggressive just moments earlier, appeared to be at a standoff. Soldiers outnumbered the wolves, but many times in the forest, especially in winter when game was scarce, Niklas and his men had fought off packs that refused to give up until they had lost at least half their members.

The wolves bared their teeth, but they were retreating, still watching the soldiers for any movement. Then as quickly as they came, they turned and ran as arrows and rocks pelted the ground around them. An arrow caught one of the wolves in the hindquarters and it fell back with a whimper, unable to run. One of the sling-men caught another wolf in the skull with a rock, and the animal dropped to the ground, dead. The rest ran on, vaulting the eight-foot-high fence as if it were a hedge.

"They're leaving," the guard on the tower shouted. "Wolves are leaving."

"Report!" Niklas shouted. He sheathed his sword and began to limp toward the small open area in the middle of the enclosure.

By now, all of his soldiers were at their posts. Several looked worse for the wear with deep cuts and gashes, shirts or pants ripped open and bloodied. Some of the soldiers were dragging the carcasses of the wolves toward the center of the camp.

"No men dead, sir," one of Niklas's lieutenants reported. "Several injuries—bites and cuts mostly. Looks like we killed about eight wolves, and at least twelve more got away."

"In the morning, take the bodies outside the stockade," Niklas ordered. "Double the guard and the patrols inside the fence for the rest of the night." As the soldier took off to do his bidding, Niklas limped toward the healers' tent. The large tent usually held the cots for the healers and room for half a dozen wounded, with a folding table for the medicines and potions the healers needed, plus bandages and other implements. As Niklas entered, he could see that two men sat on each cot, awaiting treatment.

"Half a candlemark," Ordel said over his shoulder as Niklas entered.

"What?"

"That's how long the attack lasted," Ordel replied. "Since I couldn't fight, I figured I'd do something useful while I waited for casualties. So I lit a notched candle when I first heard the alarm. And it was almost exactly at the half-candlemark point when the wolves ran away."

"Limits," Niklas said, intrigued enough by Ordel's finding to ignore his pain a while longer. "The limit of how long Nagok can compel beasts to do his bidding."

"Something like that," Ordel said. He grimaced as he took in Niklas's injuries. "Come in and have a seat before you fall down. I've got a full house, but we can squeeze you in," he added with a dry smile.

"There you are!" Kulp darted into the crowded tent. "General Theilsson!"

"Talk to me while Ordel patches me up," Niklas said, irritable from the pain and lack of sleep. "What were you able to find out?"

"We could sense the magic, but it was a distance away," Kulp replied.

"How far?" Niklas asked, swearing under his breath as Ordel began to tear away the ripped cloth of his shirt and pants to treat his wounds.

"The source of the magic was about half a mile distant," Kulp replied. "Give or take."

"How many wolves?"

"Wolves are damn hard to count in the dark, sir," Kulp answered. "Difficult not to count the same wolf twice. But the best I can figure, between thirty to fifty out there—mighty big for a normal pack."

Very big, Niklas thought. He and his men had faced wolves many times in their travels. Most of the time, the packs had fewer than ten wolves, and that was plenty to fight off, even for trained soldiers armed for battle. Fifty wolves, hunting as a pack, could do a lot of damage.

"Ordel figures the whole thing lasted about half a candlemark," Niklas said, then gritted his teeth as Ordel began to clean his wounds. The healer dripped an amber liquid into the gashes, and Niklas cursed, his body arching with the pain.

"Stings a bit," Ordel observed laconically. "But you don't know what's in those cuts. The potion will hold off pretty much everything, even lockjaw."

"Were the wolves rabid?" Niklas asked. After years of

soldiering, he no longer feared a quick, clean death. But he had once seen a man die of rabies, first frenzied and attacking everyone within range, then drooling and paralyzed, until the man suffocated as he could not draw breath. Niklas had no desire to die that way.

Kulp shook his head. "We're working with the healers to test the bodies before we take them outside the fence, but it doesn't look that way."

"I was there when the mage's control must have been wavering," Niklas said. Ordel covered his wounds with a poultice and then put his hand over them, using his healing magic to speed the wound's closing. After a moment, he withdrew his hands, revealing the gashes to be nearly healed. Still, he applied more poultice and wrapped the injuries in bandages.

"We've got very limited familiarity with beast calling," Kulp said. "But from what we know about control magic, we're making some projections. First—the control is limited because maintaining control requires the mage to keep his focus. He can't issue a command and go on about his business. He has to have the focus and the reserve of power to keep his will on the creature until the command is carried out."

"Which means the attack can't go on forever," Niklas replied, trying to take his mind off his injuries. "Since the mage is trapped in the magic until the command is carried out."

Kulp nodded. "Exactly. And that plays into the time-limit problem, which if you're right, seems to be about half a candle-mark. It's exceedingly difficult to maintain control of a high-level working for longer than that, even for an experienced mage."

"We need to get more information about Nagok and his army. If it's as big as the captives say, then we've got to get reinforcements," Niklas said, thinking aloud. "And it would help to know a lot more about his *talishte* connections."

"We'll have one of the mages scanning at all times, making note of when we can sense spikes and drop-offs in magic use." Kulp shrugged. "It's not perfect, but you might find a pattern that turns out to be important."

"Anything you get is more than we have now," Niklas said. "And if you and the other mages can figure out how to interrupt the beast-calling magic, that would help, too. Half a candlemark is forever when you're fighting wolves—or magicked monsters."

"We're working on it," Kulp replied.

"I'll send word to Blaine," Niklas said. "It will take time to send reinforcements, and I have the distinct feeling that time is running out."

CHAPTER TWENTY

WHITNEY TOOK BACK THE SHIP'S WHEEL FROM Connor at the sight of the giant sea serpent. Connor, still possessed by Remon's spirit, stumbled and would have fallen had Zaryae not gotten one shoulder under his arm and helped him to the rail.

Thank you for your help, the Wraith Lord said to Remon. *Now you must leave him.*

Wait! Connor said. *Remon—the* tanoba *is a creature of the deep. How do we fight it?*

Remon's spirit regarded Connor sadly. *I don't know,* he said. *It doesn't belong here. The wild-magic storms brought them, and they stayed.*

Them? Connor echoed with a note of panic. *There's more than one of those things?*

Remon nodded. *Not many but a few. They appeared when the magic was broken, out of the wild places. Other things, too. But the* tanoba *are the biggest.*

You haven't seen anyone fight them successfully? After all they had done to navigate the undersea mountains, Connor had no desire to be sent to the bottom by an oversized snake.

I don't wander the depths. I stay in the valleys of the mountains, Remon replied. *There are things in the deep places that are more dangerous—even to the dead—than the* tanoba. *I'm sorry I can't help you.*

Then leave him, the Wraith Lord commanded. *Because I can.*

In the time it had taken to maneuver through the sunken mountains, the moon had risen and the sun had set. As soon as the sun was below the horizon, Nidhud came up on deck.

"I'm sorry I could not be of help earlier," he said. "I knew of your danger, but I couldn't rise."

"We've got more trouble," Zaryae said, pointing out beyond the bow of the ship to where the *tanoba*'s head and forebody was just barely visible above the waves. "And Connor's nearly spent."

"I didn't get us through the mountain pass just to get ripped apart by a big swimming snake," Connor said, but even to his own ears, his voice sounded strained.

You are not strong enough for a battle, the Wraith Lord warned.

Then let's make it a skirmish they'll tell tales about in Raka, Connor said, gritting his teeth. "One big strike," he said aloud to Nidhud and Zaryae.

We will help you. The unexpected voice came from Remon. Connor could see the ghosts hovering around the ship.

Why? Connor asked suspiciously.

Because the monster feeds on the dead, Remon replied. *It has the power to destroy even spirits. We would be well rid of him, but we've had no way to do it. Help us as we helped you. And in return, the spirits of the deep will guide you safely to your destination and watch over you.*

Connor relayed what Remon offered. "It's a necrophage," Nidhud said. "All living creatures 'feed on death' after a fashion, since few get nourishment from the life force itself. But a necrophage gains its sustenance from the energy of death itself. That's why it poses a danger to the ghosts. It can actually eat them."

"Could it harm the Wraith Lord?" Zaryae asked.

Nidhud looked to Connor. "What does he say?"

Connor turned inward to Kierken Vandholt's spirit. *Can it?*

Doubtful, the Wraith Lord replied. *I am not merely dead. Not only am I* talishte—undead—*but I am now also a creature of the Unseen Realms. I imagine things exist that can do me damage, but I don't think the* tanoba's *magic is strong enough to destroy me.*

Then can we please get on with it? Connor knew the Wraith Lord could hear his exhaustion. *I can't do this much longer.* Connor felt himself growing weaker by the minute. Hosting the Wraith Lord was a strain in itself, without having also hosted Remon's spirit. The idea of once more channeling the Wraith Lord's magic made Connor fear for his life. Yet he knew in his heart that there was no alternative.

Was this how Blaine felt about trying to bring back the magic at Valshoa and Mirdalur? Connor thought. *Could he have been just as terrified? I never thought about it, but how could he not be afraid? This must only be a fraction of the power that he raised. I can't turn back now.*

Zaryae's eyes were closed, as if she listened to voices only she could hear. "If the beast feeds on death, then there is death aplenty in the sea," she said, coming back to herself and turning toward Nidhud. "Remove it from its feeding ground, and its power is limited."

"We're in the middle of the ocean!" Whitney snapped. "How are we supposed to do that?"

Nidhud stared out at the moonlit waves. Now and again, like a phantom, the *tanoba's* huge body slid through the waves.

Its thick gray form arched and curved above the waves, only to disappear once more beneath the surface. From time to time, its distorted head rose, clearly visible above the water.

Is it scenting us? Connor wondered. *Does it know we're here? It's faster than we are, and we've seen what it can do to a ship. We aren't going to be able to get past it on our own.* He returned his attention to Remon. *What do you propose?*

If the spirits work together, we can lead him on a chase, Remon replied. *That's how we usually get away from him. We'll draw his attention, then you use your magic to destroy him.*

You make it sound simple, the Wraith Lord said. *It is anything but.*

Got a better idea? Connor's patience and tact had been strained to the breaking point. *Because I'm all out of options.*

"I've only got one good blast in me before I'm down," Connor said tersely to Nidhud. "The ghosts have offered to distract the *tanoba* while we prepare to strike. Maybe Zaryae's foresight can provide some additional help. But we've got to do something now, before I collapse. And we're not going to get to Edgeland unless we get past that monster."

Nidhud nodded. "I agree. And I can only think of one way to do it. I will use my magic to lift the *tanoba* out of the water. Then you," he said with a nod to Connor, "or rather, the Wraith Lord, send a blast of fire. As we've seen in Donderath, fire is the only sure way to destroy the magic beasts."

"And if there are more of those things out there?" Zaryae said. "Few ships have sailed the open sea since the Cataclysm. We don't know what the magic storms brewed up since anyone has traveled this way."

Nidhud shrugged. "If this works, then we repeat the attack. If it doesn't, the point is moot." *Because we'll all be at the bottom of the ocean,* Connor thought.

"Do it," Connor said. "But let's get to it quickly, please."

Nidhud turned to Whitney. "We're going to need to get a bit closer," he said. "Not so close that the fire presents a danger to the ship, but my magic will be stronger the shorter the distance to its target."

Whitney looked at Nidhud incredulously. "You want me to steer toward that thing?"

Nidhud nodded. "Unless you have a better idea."

Whitney glowered and cursed under his breath. "No, I don't. You know I don't. First the sea mountains, now this. I'll do it, but I don't have to like it." With that, Whitney shouted orders to Trad on the lower deck. The sailors on watch were pointing at the *tanoba*'s silhouette in the moonlight. Whitney's second-in-command looked at the captain as if Whitney had lost his mind. Then he nodded and turned to the men, barking orders. To his credit, the men jumped to obey despite their fear.

"How far?" Whitney's voice was raspy with the wet weather, and there was no mistaking his foul mood.

"About one hundred feet or so should be good," Nidhud said.

"Oh, you're not asking much, are you?" Whitney grumbled. "Close enough for that monster to do to the *Nomad* what it did to the pirates."

"Hopefully not," Nidhud replied drily. "And we have resources they lacked." He turned to Connor. "Ask your friends to start keeping the creature busy so we can close the distance."

We're already in motion, Remon said. *Good luck.*

Connor was still leaning against Zaryae, who helped him back to the railing. "Thanks," he said, embarrassed at needing the assistance. "Does your Sight have a warning for us?"

Zaryae shook her head. "Only that there is danger, but I sense it no matter which course we pursue. I see no way to reach Edgeland without death."

"Whose death?"

Zaryae's gaze was sorrowful. "That remains to be seen."

Despite its damaged sails, the *Nomad* closed the distance quickly, and although Connor was in no hurry for the confrontation, he knew he could not channel the Wraith Lord for long. The sea had calmed after the storm, though the night wind was cool. Still, Connor felt feverish, and he knew it was the strain of the possession.

At the edges of his perception, Connor could see the faint flashes of light deep below the water as Remon and his ghostly companions led the *tanoba* astray, keeping it near the surface but distracted from the rapidly closing ship. *Can I see their light now because I allowed Remon to possess me?* Connor wondered. *Or because I have one foot in the grave myself?*

"We're almost there," Nidhud said, his voice taut. *Dare I think a Knight of Esthrane is afraid?* Connor wondered.

Nidhud is talishte, *but like all of us, he is still human,* the Wraith Lord said. *What has Penhallow told you about fear?*

I know what he's said, that even now after centuries, he still feels fear. But I think I'd feel less of it if I were immortal.

For yourself, perhaps, the Wraith Lord replied. *But only then do you realize how fragile mortals are. Have a care what you wish for, Bevin. The gods have ears.*

Connor grew silent, duly chastened. It was taking all of his energy to remain upright and conscious. Zaryae murmured instructions to Whitney, using her foresight to recommend the safest course to get the *Nomad* in position for their strike.

"Remon wants to know if you're ready," Connor said abruptly. "He doesn't know if they can keep the *tanoba* occupied much longer without casualties."

"Give him our thanks," Nidhud replied. "We'll take it from here."

"Ready?" Whitney brought the ship around so that Nidhud and Connor had a view of the *tanoba* unobstructed by the ship's masts or forecastle.

"Well?" Nidhud looked to Connor, who gave a curt nod.

"Do it," Connor said.

"Be ready. I can't hold that thing out of the water for more than a few seconds," Nidhud warned.

With that, Nidhud made a gathering gesture, and Connor felt power coalescing, building to a steady, deafening crescendo of light and sound. At the same time, Connor could feel the Wraith Lord calling magic to him and filling his spirit with power so that for a heady moment, power drove out all fear and pain, obliterating exhaustion and weakness.

Nidhud thrust out his right arm and made a grasping, scooping motion with his hand. As the dumbstruck sailors gawked and shouted on the lower deck, the *tanoba* rose from the water, held in Nidhud's invisible grip. Water sluiced off the monster's coils and the *tanoba* writhed, twisting and snapping its long, snakelike body from side to side to get free. For the first time, Connor truly understood the enormous size of the monster.

"Now!" Nidhud rasped, strain clear in his face and voice.

Now! Connor echoed.

The Wraith Lord's power surged through Connor like a lightning strike. Fire erupted from Connor's outstretched palm, a blistering torrent of flame hot enough that Zaryae stepped back and the air shimmered like the heat of summer. The sailors on the main deck cried out in fear from the spectacle of the suspended *tanoba* and the fiery burst.

The blast struck the monster, and flames fanned out along its gray, smooth hide. The beast gave an earsplitting shriek, twisting and bucking its muscular length against the force that held it away from its source of power. Nidhud's face was tight with concentration, and his whole body was rigid with the effort.

Flames bathed the *tanoba* with roaring heat, and the monster's slick hide began to char and blister, sending an oily, foul-smelling smoke into the air. Great strips of blackened skin peeled from the creature as Connor kept the flames focused on the *tanoba*, drawing from the Wraith Lord's presence and the *kruvgaldur* to remain on his feet. He remembered another mage who had perished sending a burst of flames from a damaged artifact. *At least if I finish this, the ship can get through to Edgeland,* Connor thought, willing himself to remain conscious.

The Wraith Lord's power flared, and the torrent of flame grew white-hot, so that the peeling flesh fell in cinders to the surface of the sea. The *tanoba* shrieked again, an alien, agonizing scream, and nearly twisted from Nidhud's hold.

"One more like that and I'll lose him," Nidhud warned through gritted teeth.

Sweat ran down Connor's face despite the brisk wind, and his entire being strained toward the direction of the firestorm. The muscles in his outstretched arm ached as if he held a heavy load. His shoulders and back seized and cramped, but he kept his attention focused on the blinding stream of fire.

The creature gave one final scream, coiling tightly as the flames burned through skin to muscle and viscera. And then, with a shudder, what remained of the *tanoba* collapsed limply against the invisible bonds that held it.

"Finish it," Nidhud instructed grimly. "We have no idea whether or not it can regenerate once it's back in the water."

Rarely had Connor seen one of the Knights of Esthrane show fatigue. Even more surprising was the sense he got of the Wraith Lord, of being stretched too thin. The Wraith Lord mustered his will, and one massive blast streaked from Connor's hand, incinerating what remained of the monster. The flames did not subside until fine black flakes scattered on the waves.

"I don't care what that thing was, it's not going to come back from that," Whitney murmured, and Connor could hear a mixture of awe and primal fear in the captain's voice. Below on deck, sailors cheered the victory and shouted praises to Charrot and his consorts.

"Let him go!" Zaryae urged as Connor sagged against the railing. His clothing was soaked with sweat and he was trembling uncontrollably. Connor fell to his knees retching and would have collapsed facedown on the boards if Zaryae had not grabbed his shoulders.

Well done, Bevin. This time, the Wraith Lord's voice seemed faint and far away. *But I fear I have pushed even your new strength to its breaking point.*

Connor heard a buzz of worried voices that grew more and more distant. He felt as if the fire had burned a trail through the core of his being, filling every vein and muscle with flames. It hurt to breathe, and he was so very tired. Every heartbeat drained what little strength remained. The world faded to black, so dark that even the stars did not shine. Then one by one, faint glowing lights pierced the darkness until they gathered like a fairy ring around Connor. He stared at the yellow pinpricks of lights, wondering how fireflies came to be so far out over the ocean. As he watched the flickering lights, at first smaller than a candle's flame, one of them stretched until a man's figure was clear. His skin was luminous, and the light appeared to glow from beneath his skin, shining with the warmth of a reading candle.

Remon stood within the circle, near Connor's feet. Connor found that he was lying on his back, but could not move. The pinpricks of light gradually expanded until a circle of glowing spirits stood encircling where he lay.

Am I dead? Connor asked. The thought held no terror, not if in death he could finally rest.

Nearly so. Remon's voice was sad. *We have come to stand vigil. Outside the circle, powerful forces are fighting.*

Monsters? Connor remembered enough of the battle to fear that more creatures like the *tanoba* might have appeared, and that his sacrifice might be in vain.

Perhaps. Mortals and immortals. They fight over your soul. Can you not feel it?

Connor tried to focus, but he was too exhausted to begin. *No. I can't feel anything outside the circle.*

Then rest, Remon said. *We will watch over you.*

And if the monsters come? Connor peered into the darkness beyond the glowing lights, but it was as impenetrable as a curtain.

Then we will honor your memory, Bevin Connor. Rest now, in peace.

CHAPTER
TWENTY-ONE

*M*ONSTERS HUNTED HIM IN THE DARKNESS. THE *toothy maw of the* tanoba *emerged out of the darkness, and the black emptiness of its mouth swallowed the horizon, engulfing him. He fell down the long shaft of the* tanoba's *throat, and as he fell, the scene changed, becoming the oubliette beneath Quillarth Castle, prison to an ancient, insane* talishte.

Connor landed on the pile of bones that had once been Hemming Lorens and saw the dry bones and yellowed rags of clothing crumble to dust beneath him. Everything tilted, and when his vision cleared, Connor was in the wet, stinking tunnels beneath the Rooster and Pig, running for his life through the darkness, chased by a huge black hound with long, sharp teeth.

He ran from the barghest, *feeling his lungs strain for air, slipping and falling and rising again in the slick, slime-covered tunnels far below the surface of Castle Reach. A glimmer of light caught his eye, and a door appeared at the end of the long, dark passageway. Connor hit the door with his full strength, slamming it open to find himself in Penhallow's well-appointed crypt, which was outfitted like a wealthy man's salon. Smoke was already curling around his legs from the passageway behind him. Once more, he was falling, bleeding, stumbling, and strong hands pulled him into another dark corridor, rocky and dank as the flames roared behind him . . .*

He roused to find himself confined to a pine box, buried alive, rocking in the water of an underground lake, hungry for air as the coffin banged and bumped on his journey through a subterranean river, scrabbling with his bleeding fingers against the wood. And then, the lid of the box opened, and overhead, green ribbons of fire twisted through the sky like a serpent, raining fire down on King Merrill's castle. Bells clanged, *insanely loud, and the green fire kept on falling as flames enveloped everything he knew . . .*

Connor awoke, or thought he did. He sat up in his bed, in the room at Quillarth Castle that was part of Lord Garnoc's suite when they went to court to serve King Merrill. His hands patted down across his chest, the familiar nightshirt, the comfortable bedding beneath him. In the distance, he heard the castle bell tower chime the second hour of the morning, and he slipped out of bed, sure that he had heard his master's call. The suite was the same as ever, with a writing desk, two comfortable upholstered chairs near the fire, and a small dining table, set for one. Lady Garnoc's silver-framed portrait awaited her husband's company. He crossed the sitting room and heard the call once more.

"Connor."

By the glow of the fireplace, he could see Lord Garnoc sitting in his reading chair. Garnoc was white-haired and bent with his seventy years, but his blue eyes were clear and incisive. "Where have you been, boy? I've been calling you."

"Apologies, m'lord," *Connor said.* "I didn't hear you. But I'm here now."

"You've been gone a long time." *Garnoc's voice was strong despite his years, just as Connor remembered it.*

"I've been away," Connor replied. Something about the scene wasn't quite right, but try as he might, Connor did not know what it was.

"I gave you a job. Did you do it?"

Now he remembered. A black disk with strange markings. A hidden map. And a trip through the night to visit a talishte lord. Connor extended his left arm. The sleeve of his nightshirt rode up to show the two faint white scars where the talishte had read his blood. "Yes, m'lord."

"Do you have a message for me? From Millicent?"

Lord Garnoc's beloved late wife, Millicent, had been a young woman when she sat for the painting, beautiful and full of life. Garnoc had never remarried, and he took a miniature of Millicent's portrait with him everywhere. "Well, speak up, Connor! You can hear her now. What did she tell you?"

"A dark message, m'lord. I fear to say it aloud."

Garnoc's gaze was straightforward, but there was kindness in his eyes as well. "Don't mince words. Tell me what she said."

"She said it won't be long now," Connor said with a catch in his voice. "That she'll see you soon."

Garnoc took a deep breath, then sighed and leaned back in his chair. "Ah. I expected as much. Very well. I've missed her so much." He peered at Connor with sudden intensity. "You're going to move on, too. Can't stay here. You don't belong here anymore, do you?"

"Where should I go?" Connor felt disoriented, lost and afraid. Leave the castle and Garnoc? They were all he knew. Yet that wasn't true. There had been other places, other masters, he was sure there had been, but those memories were just out of reach.

"Why, to the end of the world, m'boy. You've been there before." Garnoc's eyes narrowed, and he leaned forward urgently. "But listen here. This is important." His gaze seemed to transfix Connor.

"Stay away from Thrane. It will take everything you've got if you try to fight him, maybe too much. Mind now, and remember what I've told you."

Lord Garnoc's face was lit by the firelight, light and shadows flickering over his features, so that his eyes appeared sunken, his cheeks hollow, and as Connor watched in horror, Garnoc's skin stretched taut and his gray hair dulled. Garnoc's fine garments faded and decayed, until what remained in the chair was a weathered corpse in tattered rags.

Connor stumbled backward in terror, and something caught him behind the knees. He fell and kept on falling, but instead of the floor of his room at Quillarth Castle, everything around him was white and freezing cold. He could not tell down from up, left from right as he tumbled, and cold, wet snow filled his mouth and nose, threatening to suffocate him if he weren't crushed or frozen first. On and on he fell in a white wave of snow, until at last he came to a stop in the darkness of an icy tomb.

"Connor." The voice was familiar, but far away. "Connor." That voice again, closer now, joined by others this time. Small, glowing pinpricks of light, like distant stars, winked into life one at a time in the darkness, but their form was an unfamiliar constellation. Connor was used to the patterns of the stars he could see from Donderath, named for the shapes they formed of the high god Charrot, his consorts Torven and Esthrane, and the pantheon of lesser gods.

These dimly glowing lights formed a line leading off into the distance. "Follow the lights, Connor," a voice urged. "There's work to do."

Cold and alone, Connor took one halting step and then another, keeping his eyes on the lights. The glow dimmed as he passed each one, so that darkness stretched behind him. Going back was not an option. Gradually, Connor realized that it was growing lighter.

Full dark became dusk, and as the last few lights blinked out, Connor saw the first light of dawn above the horizon.

When he returned his attention to the path, Remon's ghost stood in front of him. "I promised I would see you safely on your journey," Remon told him. "You must return now. Remain safe, Connor." And with that, Remon's figure wavered and faded, lost in the rising sun.

Connor groaned and took a long breath. The first thing he noticed was the rocking of the ship, gently swinging him in his hammock. And in the next moment, it registered that his face was cold. The cold woke him, and his eyes opened. For a moment, he could not place where he was, and feared he was still dreaming. Then he realized that he was staring at the planks of the deck above him, still aboard the *Nomad.*

"Are you back? It's been long enough already." Connor turned his head to see Verran watching from a seat on the hammock across from him.

"How long has it been?"

"Four days," Verran replied. "Two days ago, Zaryae made us pour cold soup down your throat so you wouldn't starve to death. The rest of us took turns sitting with you, which for most of the time meant listening to you fidget and mumble while you thrashed around like a wild man."

Verran cleaned his fingernails with a small knife. "You know, I lived with Mick and Piran for three years at the Homestead, and every night was like a seat at the freak show when those two dreamed about Velant. I didn't bargain for a repeat performance."

"Neither did I," Connor croaked.

"Lie still," Verran cautioned. "I'll get in trouble with Zaryae if you fall out of your hammock. Borya and Desya got her to go up on deck and have a walk around. She's been sitting with you night and day."

Verran paused. "We've still got a ways to go before we get to Edgeland. The crew is testy. Then again, we've had pirates, monsters, and ghosts almost before we were out of sight of land. They're all glad you and Nidhud took care of the *tanoba*, but I don't think we're anyone's favorite cargo."

"But we're still alive," Connor pointed out. His mouth was dry and his muscles ached.

"That's true," Verran conceded. "Let's hope it stays that way. We're going to have enough problems once we get to Skalgerston Bay."

To Connor's relief, the rest of the voyage passed quietly. When the *Nomad* finally drew into Skalgerston Bay, he stood on deck with Zaryae and Verran, watching the port town come into view. Borya and Desya had spent most of the voyage up in the rigging helping the sailors, while Nidhud was down below in the hold, where he spent less and less time now that they were far enough north for the Long Dark to hide the sun.

"I really never planned to come back here," Verran murmured, his expression pensive.

"Has it changed?" Zaryae asked, scanning the row of low log buildings along the waterfront. It was much as Connor remembered it, although he would be the first to admit that after just surviving a shipwreck, his attention had not been fully on his surroundings.

"Not really," Verran said. He lifted his face to the wind. "There was never much. A marketplace for selling whatever the homesteaders could raise. A few taverns and brothels, but most of them were for the sailors who crewed the convict ships. Can't imagine that without the ships coming from home there'd be need for so many. A chandler and a cooper and a few other trades, the kinds of things the colonists need to get by. Looks like Ifrem and Engraham kept the Crooked House running," he said with a nod toward one of the buildings, a tavern near the wharfs.

"I mean, it's been a year," Verran continued. "Things don't change fast up here."

It was cold by Donderath standards, balmy for Edgeland. Out on the ice they would need the heavy coats and boots they had brought, but right now, Connor was comfortable with just his cloak.

"See that fort on the cliff?" Verran said, pointing to the silhouette of a ruined fortress on a forbidding bluff above the waves. The structure's stone walls were charred in places, and many of the rocks had been toppled or smashed. "That's Velant. That's where Mick and the rest of us spent three godsforsaken years of our lives." His voice carried a trace of bitterness, but it was not as hard-edged as Connor would have thought.

"Mick and Piran were at the front of the mob that broke Velant open the night magic died," Verran recounted. "They went in after Dawe." He glanced toward Connor. "Of course, that was before we found out Mick was a bleedin' *lord*." He was quiet for a moment, staring up at the ruined prison before he shook himself out of his thoughts.

"Now that we're here, do you have any idea how to get in touch with Grimur?" Verran asked Connor. "I'd just as soon not find him like we did the last time." Grimur had rescued them from an avalanche. Just thinking about it made Connor shiver.

"Nidhud said he could find him," Connor replied. "We can't do anything until after sundown anyhow."

Verran grinned. "I don't know about you, but I intend to see if Engraham's found a way to make as good bitterbeer at the Crooked House as he did when he ran the Rooster and Pig."

"We seem to have attracted attention," Zaryae observed. As the ship's masts came into view, people began to gather on the long-unused docks, eager for news. By the time the *Nomad* approached the wharves, a crowd was assembled. Just at the edge of the harbor, the *Nomad* dropped anchor.

"We'll wait for you here," Trad said from behind them.

Verran looked at the man as if he were mad. "What? You're expecting us to swim in?"

Trad shook his head. "We'll lower a rowboat for you. We don't know what the Cataclysm did to the depth of the berths, and we'd rather not run aground to find out. Can't imagine there've been any ships through here since the Great Fire."

"The *Nomad* got in and out of the bay just fine the last time," Connor said. "But we'll check and confirm the depths. We need to off-load the supplies." If other ships had also found their way to Edgeland, they had not remained in the bay, nor had they returned to Castle Reach.

"What about Nidhud?" Zaryae asked.

"He left word that he would see to his own way," Trad replied with a shrug. "I'm not going to argue with a biter."

Connor regarded Trad with suspicion. "How do we know you won't leave us here?"

Trad scowled at Connor. "Much as I might like that idea, Captain Whitney has given his word to Aldwin Carlisle to bring you back again safely, and he intends to keep his promise."

Not to mention the fact that his talishte *lord would know from the* kruvgaldur *if he didn't,* Connor thought.

"I wonder how Engraham and his mother got on at the Homestead," Verran mused. "We told them they could live there while we were gone, and if none of us came back to reclaim it in three years, it was theirs."

"Thinking of moving back?" Borya asked with a grin.

Verran fixed him with a glare. "Move back to the arctic, when I can sponge off Lord Mick in a right proper manor house and all, at a place that doesn't freeze my nuts off or stay dark half the year? And all I have to do to keep that soft position is risk my sorry ass on occasion and go out spying or sail to the bloody top of the world."

"Is that a no?" Desya asked.

Verran strained to see the faces of the crowd gathered on the wharves, and his bantering mood evaporated. "I'm not planning to move back," he murmured, "but I never thought that it would feel like home to come here again."

Throughout the final week of the voyage, Verran had grown more introspective, preferring to sit alone in a corner of their quarters playing his pennywhistle. Borya and Desya were seldom down below except to sleep, while Connor and Zaryae passed the time playing cards or telling tales, since Connor felt the crew's discomfort keenly whenever he did venture on deck. Still, it seemed that returning to Edgeland weighed heavily on the minstrel's mind.

"If Engraham's selling the bitterbeer he used to make at the Rooster and Pig, he's probably the richest man in Edgeland," Connor said. "Gods and Goddess! I haven't had a glass of bitterbeer since the Great Fire, and I thought that I never would again."

Verran mustered a pained smile and slapped Connor on the shoulder. "Then, my friend, you're in luck. You've just made the longest trek for a beer in history."

The crowd at the wharves had swelled to dozens by the time Trad let the rowboat down into the water, and their shouts when they saw that a boat was coming ashore brought more

colonists running. Connor and the others were still too far
away to make out individual faces, but from their stances he
could see that the townspeople were wary of newcomers.

"Let me do the talking," Verran said as they rowed to one of
the docks that was still standing.

"You didn't run out on any gambling debts that you forgot
to mention to us, did you, Verran, old buddy?" Borya asked,
and Connor heard an edge of nervousness in his voice.

"That would be Piran," Verran replied.

They rowed the boat close to the dock and threw the line
ashore. Connor saw the colonists craning their necks to get a
look at them. Verran made sure he was the first to step out of
the boat and onto the dock.

"Hello, everyone," Verran said in a big voice. "Did ya
miss me?"

"Oh, Sweet Esthrane, it's Verran Danning!" a woman said
loudly from the rear of the group. "Gods save us! Donderath's
started sending convicts again!"

Connor and the others could not resist a guffaw as Verran's
cheeks colored. "We are not convicts!" Verran said firmly.
"We're here on orders from Lord Blaine McFadden."

"You mean Mick McFadden?" a man yelled.

"He's a bleedin' warlord now, so watch your mouth," Verran snapped. "Anyhow, he sent us up here to take care of some
business. Hush-hush, very secret. Good to see all of you. Is the
Crooked House still open?"

"Aye, and the beer's better than when you were here," another man said, moving forward to clap Verran on the shoulder. "Welcome back. Staying long?"

Verran grinned. "Not too long—but I brought plenty of
supplies, and some news you're not going to believe!"

The crowd followed them to the Crooked House Tavern,

not far from the docks. On the way, Connor could see where fire and storms had scarred some of the log structures nearest the wharves. A few buildings looked disused, and he realized that without trade from the main kingdom and sailors making regular dockings, the town would need only the services they themselves could use and support.

As word spread, the colonists gathered around the travelers, shaking Verran's hand and slapping him on the shoulder or embracing him as if to assure themselves that he was real. Verran knew them all by name, though Connor quickly lost track in the press of strange faces. Zaryae slipped her arm through his to avoid being separated in the crush. Borya and Desya looked dazed and uncomfortable from all the attention, not in the least because their magic-changed eyes drew gasps and whispered comments.

Verran entered the Crooked House at the head of a parade of followers. Connor, Zaryae, and the twins stayed close behind, and the onlookers from the docks pressed inside after them, eager for news.

A man in his middle years with a bald head and a patch over one eye looked at Verran as if he were seeing a ghost. "By the stars! Verran Danning?"

"Hello, Ifrem! Still serving up Adger's rotgut, or have you moved up to a better grade of swill since I've been gone?"

A lanky man with brown hair came out of the back just then. "The mutton's done roasting if you—" he said, and stopped in his tracks, jaw open.

"Torven take my soul," Engraham gasped. "Verran." He looked to Connor, and his eyes widened further. "And Bevin Connor. How in the name of Esthrane—"

"It's a long story, one that I'll be glad to share over a pint or two of bitterbeer," Verran said with a wide grin. "And keep the beer coming. You won't believe what our very own Mick McFadden and the rest of my mates have been up to."

Gauging by the crowd that jammed into the Crooked House, their unexpected arrival was possibly the most interesting thing to happen in Edgeland since the Great Fire, Connor thought. Ifrem and Engraham, now co-owners of the pub, declared that Verran and his friends could have their drinks on the house, but the others had bloody better well pay their own tab. That settled, even the tavern owners strained to hear the stories in between filling a steady stream of empty tankards.

"Here's the good news!" Verran said as he climbed onto a chair so that everyone in the Crooked House could see him. "We brought a boat full of supplies—food, tools, seeds, and more. And we expect to be able to start up trade again between Donderath and Edgeland so you can send us more herring!" A cheer went up, giving Connor to suspect the colonists were well and truly tired of eating the briny fish themselves.

"What's the bad news?"

Verran let out a long breath. "That's a long story. And I'll tell you the whole thing in just a minute. But here's what's really important. We had to dodge pirates on the way out of Castle Reach, and we fought some off on the way here. They may be desperate enough to come to Edgeland. If they don't, it'll be someone else. So the harbor defenses need to be in place."

He paused. "And right now, there's a war for control of Donderath. Mick McFadden is a warlord now, and he's done a lot to pull the kingdom out of the ashes. But we're up against a big enemy. So if about four hundred of you want to go back to Donderath to fight, we've got room on the *Nomad* to take you, and Mick would be much obliged."

At that, the room erupted into a buzz of conversation, which did not subside until Borya let out an earsplitting whistle. Verran grinned. "And now, if someone would be kind enough to pass me a fresh bitterbeer, I'll start at the beginning and tell you a tale the likes of which you've never heard—and it's all true!"

If Connor had any doubts about Verran's newly enhanced magical talent to sway a crowd, he need not have worried, since Verran kept the crowd hanging on every word. Here and there, Verran looked to one of his companions to verify his assertions or to add a bit to the story, but it was clear that Verran was relishing being the center of attention with an audience for his performance.

"So Mick really was a lord?" a pudgy man at one of the tables said. "And he and Kestel got married? Well, whaddya know?"

"Anybody kill Piran Rose yet?" someone yelled from the back, and a number of people chuckled.

"Not yet," Verran responded, "although many have tried!"

"Tell him he still owes me two silvers!" the man replied. "With interest!"

"How about Dawe Killick? Didn't he go back with you, too?" a blond woman near the front asked.

"He was about to get married when we left Donderath—to Mick's younger sister," Verran said. "Dawe half runs Mick's manor house while Mick and Piran and Kestel are out fighting battles. Quite the country gentleman he's become!"

"What of Castle Reach?" Engraham asked, bringing them all a new round of drinks. "And the Rooster and Pig. Does it stand?"

Verran nodded. "It's still standing, but worse for the wear. And from what I've heard, Adger's rotgut beats what the new owner has been serving."

It took the better part of two candlemarks before Verran and Connor had answered the crowd's questions about the homeland they left behind. Connor had to admit that despite the hardship of brewing bitterbeer in an arctic outpost, Engraham's concoction tasted much more like what he had served before the Great Fire than anything Connor had drunk since then.

As the evening wore on, Verran had the chance to ask his own questions. Connor was certain that Verran had engineered the timing, since by now the crowd was drunk and in a fine mood. "What of Adger?" Verran asked. "And Fiella?" Connor searched his memory, recalling that Adger had been Bay-town's whiskey distiller, and Fiella was the head of the whores' guild.

"Adger's heart gave out on him last winter," one of the men near the bar replied. "Fiella and her girls are still making money, when there's any coin to be had."

"Peters and Mama Jean?" Verran questioned. "Wills Jothra and Annalise?" They were names Connor remembered his friends mentioning on more than one occasion, though he could not place them beyond recalling that they had been merchants.

"Wills Jothra married a girl whose daddy runs one of the herring boats," one person volunteered. "Peters and Mama Jean are no different from when you left. Annalise had a bad spell of fever during the last Long Dark, but she's better now."

"How was it here, when the magic came back?" Verran asked. "Did anything unusual happen?"

That was the crux of what Verran wanted to know, Connor thought. All the rest had been warming up the crowd. *He wants to see if there's anything strange going on, before we go out on the ice looking for a* talishte *mage who doesn't usually want to be found.*

"It got bad here, when the magic didn't work." All heads turned to Ifrem, who stood behind the bar, pausing from filling tankards. "Folks died. We might have gotten by better if there had still been ships from Donderath, but without them and with no magic…it was worse than usual."

Connor did not need to stretch his imagination to envision what had happened. Little flickers of small magic were used so frequently before the Cataclysm to mend structures, heal people and animals, preserve food, attract fish or game, patch boats, or do a hundred other useful things. After the Great Fire, Donderath had felt the hardship of having to relearn how to do those tasks without magic, and the toll had been great. He could only guess how much worse it was in Edgeland's brutal winter, without additional supplies, food, or medicine.

"Still haven't gotten rid of the damn magicked beasts that came with the storms," one of the women said. "Between the wild-magic storms and the run of bad weather we had this spring, it's a wonder any of us survived."

Connor and his friends knew the real reason the spring weather had been especially bad, and Verran shared that information with the colonists. Before the Meroven War, King Merrill's mages had used their magic to alter the weather, for battle and shipping and convenience. When control of magic faltered, nature seized the chance to readjust, and the shift was harsh. Castle Reach had lost many buildings to the high winds, storm surges, and huge waves. Connor did not want to imagine how much worse the storms could have been in Edgeland.

"Tell me about the beasts that came when the magic was wild," Verran said, and took another sip of his bitterbeer. He looked up at a taxidermied trophy above the fireplace. The mounted head was as large as a horse's, with a rack of antlers that were flat and knife-edge sharp. The lips were drawn back to reveal teeth as fierce as those of any lynx or wolf.

"We call those *capreols*," a stocky man in the back spoke up. "They look like that, and they eat meat. Run as fast as a horse, too, with those sharp teeth chomping right behind you. Take a man's head off in one bite, they can, if you're unlucky enough to get caught."

"You're joking, right?" Verran said. "I'm not drunk enough to believe that."

"Believe him," Engraham said. "I was in one of the hunting parties that went out to track down a *capreol* that had killed a farmer and some livestock not too far from your old homestead. We had quite a fight on our hands to bring it down, and even then, one of the men lost an arm."

"Nice place you brought us to, Verran," Borya said. "If the weather doesn't kill you, the wildlife will."

Verran silenced him with an impolite hand gesture. "Not much different from some of the things that chased us across Donderath, out of the wild-magic storms."

"Sounds like these things have even bigger teeth," Desya said. He pointed to another stuffed and mounted trophy, one that looked like a cross between a bear and a wolf.

"Those are *howlers*," a woman near the fireplace replied. "They hunt in packs like wolves, and they're smart, too. Made it hard to go out trapping on the far ice. I'll tell you, it's a load on your mind, between worrying about those things eating you, or having them eat what you trapped."

"At least you see the *howlers* coming. Most times, no one sees those damn *tunnelers* until it's too late," a bearded man spoke up from the other side of the bar. "About the size of a big dog they are, with bristly fur and very sharp teeth. They tunnel under the deep snow, and when the snow on top collapses, they rip their prey apart with their long claws." He shivered. "Saw a man die like that. Won't ever forget it."

"Have you had any luck at killing the monsters off since the wild magic went away?" Connor asked.

The hunter shrugged. "We do our best, but the ice goes on for a long way, and they've got plenty of places to hide. Usually, it's the hunters who get in a shot when they're out on their trap lines. Most of them go in groups now, because of the monsters. Sometimes one of those things comes in too close to the farms, and then we get up a posse and go after it."

"Don't know how the wild magic did it, but the monsters it gave us took to the snow like they were made for it," Engraham added.

"Not all of them," the woman who described the *howlers* said. "Don't you recall those fish things with all the teeth and tentacles that showed up during that really bad magic squall? Haven't found a one of them that wasn't frozen solid."

"Except for the one beyond the bay that got a herring boat," the bearded man corrected.

"Still, there's no telling where the wild magic got those things," the woman continued. "But the point is, they got dropped here, as if we needed something to make it even harder to survive."

The crowd showed no sign of being ready to move on as the night grew late. By the time Ifrem rang the bell for last call, it seemed to Connor that Verran had news about every colonist in Edgeland, and had promised to convey messages for at least a dozen to family back in Donderath.

"Remember!" Verran shouted as the group finally began to break up. "We can take four hundred home with us, but you've got to be willing to help us fight. If you're interested, Ifrem will take names," he said, volunteering the barkeeper, who glowered but did not disagree. Grudgingly, the crowd filed out as Ifrem shooed them to the door.

"I figured that was probably enough for your first night back," Ifrem said, locking the door behind the last patron. "If you need a place to stay, I've got the big room upstairs free."

Verran grinned. "Thanks, mate. I was hoping you'd have room for us. And we did bring lots of supplies with us, with orders from Mick to come home with a cask or two of bitter-beer. Figured that would work for money, since coin doesn't count for much these days." He patted his vest pocket. "Oh, and Kestel sent this," he said, retrieving a thick letter sealed with wax. "I guess she was afraid I'd leave out something important. She said to tell you that she wants me to bring a let-ter from you just like this back with me, catching her up on all the news about everyone."

Ifrem shrugged. "I'll see what I can come up with for Kes-tel," he said with a smile. "And I still take coin for beer, but like as not I also get paid in chickens and herring, plus some pota-toes and cabbage."

"At least you can make stew," Borya quipped. Zaryae elbowed him.

Verran leaned over the bar as Ifrem poured him another bit-terbeer. "I'll tell you two something I didn't tell the others," he said with a cagey grin. "Odds are good that—if we all survive the next big battle, our very own Mick McFadden is going to be the next king of Donderath."

"Mick, king?" Ifrem repeated, and let out a long, low whistle.

Engraham, on the other hand, did not seem completely sur-prised. "From what you've told us, he'd be the best choice," he said. "Everyone up here speaks well of him, and he's got a level head."

Ifrem nodded. "Aye, that's true enough. That's why he was on the Citizen's Council, once Prokief and the guards lost power. He had a clear head and a hard fist. That's what it takes."

Engraham cleared his throat. "By the way," he said, "save me a place on the ship. My mother passed to the Sea of Souls a few months ago. There's nothing holding me here now."

Verran nodded. "Done. And sorry to hear that."

Engraham shrugged. "Thanks to the Great Fire, and our ship ending up here, we had some time together, after all those lost years. It was more than I ever expected we'd have."

"Getting supply ships again and trading with the homeland would be a nice change," Ifrem said, changing the subject. "We could be a proper colony for once, instead of a dumping ground. We can always ship herring and rubies home, like we did before."

Verran shrugged. "Not sure there's much call for the rubies, since hardly anyone has two silvers to rub together, but the herring will be worth something. Folks have just started to get things fixed up. Everything's scarce still, but by spring, if all goes well, we'll have a lot more to trade."

"So now that the rest of them are gone," Ifrem said without looking up from where he stood wiping up the bar, "how about telling us why you're back?"

Connor and the others looked to Verran, who nodded. "Do you remember the map you gave Mick before we went to Donderath?"

"Uh-huh," Ifrem said. "Kinda figured that had something to do with it." He raised an eyebrow. "If you recall, I was a mage's assistant before I was exiled."

"That map turned out to be one of the most important pieces to help Mick bring back the magic," Verran said. "And now it turns out that something got hidden up here a long time ago that could stop a *talishte* civil war."

Ifrem gave Verran a calculating look. "So you're here to look for that *talishte* hermit, the one who helped you the last time."

"Anyone ever tell you you're a lot smarter than you look?" Verran said with a grin that tempered the sting of the comment. *It's like he never left, picking back up with everyone,* Connor thought. His dreams of Lord Garnoc made him wistful. *That's not something I can do. Except for Penhallow, everyone I had before the Great Fire is gone.*

"You know," Verran said, "Lord Arrington died the night of the Great Fire. Isn't he the one who hunted down the mage you worked for?"

Ifrem nodded. "Nice to hear that he finally got what was coming to him. And no, it doesn't change anything. I've rolled my dice. I'm staying here. Got nothing to go back to in Donderath, and from the sound of it, I'm safer in Edgeland."

"What about my father?" Engraham said, coming around the end of the bar. "Did all of the nobility die that night?"

"The king and all of the Lords of the Blood died except for Mick," Connor replied. "That was how the Meroven mages targeted their strike. They meant to take out the leaders, and they destroyed the magic at the same time. Lots of the minor nobility died, too, including your father, Lord Fordham. I'm sorry."

Engraham drew a long breath. "Well. Not like it makes that much of a difference, I guess. But I wanted to know."

"Alsibeth is alive," Connor said. "Working with Lord Penhallow now. Her foresight is even more powerful than before, since the magic returned. She saved my life a while back. We had a run-in with some monsters of our own." He tried not to shudder at the memory.

"Alsibeth always brought good business into the Rooster and Pig when she read fortunes," Engraham said with a smile. "And her customers actually paid for their drinks!" He paused. "When I go back, do you think I might be able to take over the Rooster and Pig again?"

Verran and the others laughed sharply, and Engraham looked taken aback until Verran explained. "A guy named One-Eye runs it now, and the beer's one step above horse piss," Verran said. "You show up with your recipe for bitterbeer, and I wouldn't be surprised if the residents of Castle Reach run that bum out of town."

They bade Ifrem and Engraham good night and made their way upstairs. The Crooked House had several rooms for overnight boarders upstairs. In bad weather, colonists who made the journey into Bay-town for supplies might choose not to brave a storm to return home, and decide to stay the night. Since the night was as warm and clear as it ever was in Edgeland, tonight the upstairs rooms were unoccupied. Still, for caution's sake, Connor and the others agreed they would prefer to sleep in the same room.

"Your friends are a hardy lot," Zaryae observed, lighting one of the lanterns. Borya knelt to build a fire in the room's fireplace to take the chill off as the night grew colder as Desya handed him wood and kindling from a nearby pile.

"Wouldn't have made it on the boat trip if they weren't," Verran replied. "Bad as our voyage up was, I can tell you that getting here on a convict ship was even worse."

"Packed like herring in a barrel on the last ship out of Castle Reach wasn't much fun, either," Connor added. He had felt edgy and restless all evening, and he knew that between the nightmares on the ship and the reality of being back in Skalg-erston Bay, the memories of the Great Fire loomed closer than they had in many months.

Zaryae laid a hand on his arm. "You've had a rough go of it," she said. "And it probably won't get better before we're back in Castle Reach. You should get some rest."

Just then, a knock came at the door. Connor and Verran reached for their swords. Borya and Desya took up positions on either side of the door, knives drawn, and Zaryae gripped a short sword, positioning herself just behind Borya. Verran went to open the door.

Nidhud stood in the doorway. "Glad to see you got settled in," he said, and entered as Verran welcomed him. "While you've been chatting, I was busy." As he moved through the doorway, Connor could see another man in the hallway.

"Hello, Verran, Connor. Can't say I expected to see you again." Arin Grimur, the exiled *talishte*-mage, entered the room, with a grin that showed the tips of his fangs. "We've got plans to make, if you're going out on the far ice tomorrow." He stood back to reveal a third man, someone Connor did not recognize, standing in the shadows of the hallway.

The stranger had a soldier's muscular build. His full brown beard and wild, curly hair gave him a wolfish look, and his dark eyes appraised the group warily. His shirt and pants were of the rough-spun cloth the colonists wove from their wool, dyed dark. When the man saw Verran, his eyes narrowed.

To Connor's surprise, Verran had grown red in the face. "What in Raka is *he* doing here?" Verran demanded.

"This is Kane," Grimur said.

"I know bloody well who he is," Verran snapped. "I saw his ugly face for three years in Velant, when he was one of the damn guards."

Borya and Desya hesitated, their knives still in hand, waiting for a signal. Connor looked from Verran's angry face to Kane's unreadable expression, and felt the tension grow. Zaryae stepped between Kane and Verran just when Connor thought the minstrel might take a swing at Kane.

"This venture will fail if Kane is not with us," she said, raising her head defiantly, daring Verran or Kane to challenge her. "Failure is certain without him."

"And can you tell me, if he comes along, are we sure to succeed?" Verran asked acidly.

Zaryae's gaze grew distant for a moment, and then she came back to herself again and shook her head. "Too many choices to say for certain, but the odds improve."

"Wonderful," Verran said with a glower directed at Kane, but he did not move to strike.

Nidhud gave a nod of thanks to Zaryae, and stepped forward. "Kane is a hunter—one of the best on Edgeland when it comes to the wild things that roam the far ice. Wolves and bears are the least of your worries."

"So we've heard," Borya said.

"As I recall, your buddy McFadden and the Colonist Council agreed to look the other way about who had been guards or prisoners as long as everyone got along and did his share," Kane said tersely. "Ask your friends the barkeepers. I don't bother anyone. I help out when farmers lose some sheep or goats to a bear or monster. I've even gone out on the herring boats when they were shorthanded. I belong here. Get over it."

Kane walked over to the fire and sat down cross-legged near the hearth. Verran positioned himself on the other side of the room, leaning against the wall where he could keep Kane in his sight.

"I thought you were going to get us where we needed to

go," Connor said, looking to Grimur. The *talishte*-mage was as Connor remembered him, dark hair in a queue, with fine features that despite his plain-spun clothing had an aristocratic silhouette to them.

"I will," Grimur said, moving away from the fireplace and toward the window, where he could see down to the empty street below. "But this is the Long Dark. You won't want to travel the ice by night without as much protection as you can get. It was never safe for mortals, but it's worse now since the wild magic left behind monsters we haven't killed yet."

"So Kane is extra muscle, is that it?" Connor asked. Verran had told them about the Long Dark, what the mages called 'polar twilight,' when the sky was not completely dark but no sun rose or set.

"That's the idea," Kane said, pointedly ignoring Verran. He was making an effort to appear relaxed, but Connor could see the tension in Kane's shoulders and the way he held himself. If he felt the need to strike, Kane would be on his feet and probably wrist-deep in someone's blood before anyone saw him move.

"How do you know you can trust him?" Verran asked. "He's already switched sides once."

Kane rose slowly and began to turn up the cuffs of his shirt. Borya, Desya, and Connor moved to put themselves between Kane and Verran. But to Connor's surprise, Kane stayed where he was. Instead, as his sleeves rose above his elbows, he held out both forearms. Small, white pairs of puncture scars dotted the skin between his wrist and his elbows.

"Kane has been my mortal servant since you departed," Grimur said. "I had grown tired of a completely solitary existence. He has eased my exile substantially, for which I am grateful. In exchange, he receives the benefits of the *kruvgaldur*."

He turned to Connor, knowing that Connor could meet his gaze without worrying about being glamoured. "Benefits you are quite familiar with, being bound to one *talishte* and serving a second as well."

Connor nodded, imagining that he felt the scars of Penhallow's bites prickle beneath his shirt. "True," he replied evenly.

"He is bound to me even more tightly than you are bound to your master," Grimur said. "He shares not just a *kruvgaldur* bond, but he is my mortal servant. I am certain of his loyalty."

"So?" Verran regarded Kane's bare arms with disinterest. "That means he can't turn on you. Doesn't mean the rest of us can trust him."

"Actually, it does," Connor said. While he did not know Kane, he did know about being a *talishte*'s mortal servant, and about the *kruvgaldur*. "At the lightest level of the *kruvgaldur*, it permits thoughts—and sometimes energy—to be shared. Like Blaine and Penhallow. My bond to Penhallow is even stronger, because he's brought me back from the edge of death a few times. That gives me a bond to him like what Grimur is describing," he added, feeling a little chagrined at speaking of the connection out loud.

"If Grimur orders Kane to protect us, Kane cannot disobey without Grimur knowing and without Grimur exerting some control over him, even from a distance," Connor continued. "And remember, Grimur was made by Penhallow. So in that sense, Kane is ultimately Penhallow's man." Kane rolled down his sleeves with an expression that dared the others to challenge him further. When they did not, he sat back down and returned his gaze to the fire.

"So here's what I don't understand," Borya said. "If you hid this Elgin Spike, why don't you just go get it and bring it back here? Why do we need to go out to the wilderness?"

Grimur looked at Borya with patient amusement. "Because we took precautions so that the stake would not be stolen or misused, even by me. Its hiding place is bound by powerful magic. Releasing the Spike requires the presence of an Elder, and two bound by direct *kruvgaldur* to Lanyon Penhallow."

"Direct?" Zaryae questioned.

"He means, by a bond created by Penhallow himself," Connor replied, sure of his answer although he did not know how he knew it.

Grimur chuckled. "A safeguard, so that I could not just make enough fledglings or servants to fulfill the requirement."

"Which is the other reason I had to come," Connor said, finally understanding Penhallow's insistence. "Because I can channel the Wraith Lord, which gives us an Elder, I satisfy both requirements, and if the Wraith Lord needed a physical body, he has one to use."

"Where are we going?" Borya had sheathed his knife, but he still looked skeptical about their new guide. "And how long will it take to get there?"

"There isn't a name for the place we're headed," Grimur replied. "And how long it will take depends on weather and what local wildlife we run into. Both have been unpredictable of late."

"What about supplies?" Desya's arms were folded across his chest.

"Anything you needed from the ship has been brought ashore," Nidhud said. "Grimur sensed through the *kruvgaldur* that Penhallow was sending someone, so he had most of the provisions ready to go. I helped him finish things up. We'll be able to get shelter at Grimur's cabin on the way up and back, and you'll have the means to make an overnight camp. He's already stored supplies along his trapline, so you'll have access to those as well as to the packs and equipment he's prepared for you."

"We've heard tales about the monsters on the far ice," Connor said, directing his comments to Kane. "I'm sure the *talishte* can hold their own. Can you?"

Kane met his gaze. His dark eyes were utterly cold. "Oh yeah," he replied. "The real question is, can you?"

CHAPTER TWENTY-TWO

"EVEN WHEN IT'S WARM HERE, IT'S BLOODY COLD."
Verran trudged through the snow, wrapping his scarf tighter against the wind. They had arranged for wagons to take them out past the homestead Verran used to share with Blaine and his friends, out to the beginning of the traplines. From here, Edgeland sprawled toward the horizon in stark, merciless arctic beauty.

Most people on Donderath would barely consider Skalgerston Bay, with its dozen or so shops and the few hundred homesteads that surrounded it, to be 'civilization,' Connor thought. But one look at the unforgiving wilderness that lay beyond the edge of the colony made the harbor town and its surroundings seem luxurious.

"I don't think I'm ever going to get used to walking with these things on my feet," Connor grumbled, stumbling yet again and barely keeping himself from tumbling into the snow. Grimur had obtained skis for each of them, together with long wooden poles to help them navigate the open spaces where the snow never melted.

"Really? I'm planning to take mine back to Donderath with

me." Borya grinned and pushed off with his poles, demonstrating once again the acrobatic ability that stood him in good stead whether performing or fighting. After the first couple of candlemarks, the twins were weaving in and out, gliding effortlessly down slopes and daring each other to try new feats.

Kane moved with the confidence of long practice, and Verran looked as if he had ventured on skis enough times that after a candlemark or so, the rhythm came back to him and he was skiing smoothly. Even Zaryae seemed to be able to transfer her gracefulness as a dancer to the new challenge, though she did not attempt any of the twins' more reckless exploits.

"Break a leg out here and I'm not carrying you back to camp!" Kane shouted as Borya and Desya whizzed past. The party lugged two sledges with their gear, in addition to the packs each person carried. Grimur had outfitted them well with food, firewood, equipment, warm clothing, and other essentials to help them survive several days and nights on their own in territory that was practically the definition of 'inhospitable.'

"It's harsh, but it's also beautiful," Zaryae observed.

"I guess so. I've been more focused on trying to stay alive than appreciating the landscape," Connor replied. For now, he and Kane hauled the sledges, although before long it would be time to return the task to Borya and Desya. Grimur and Nidhud had gone ahead to scout the trail for predators.

Connor looked out over the snow, squinting in the perpetual twilight. In the distance, he could see the silhouettes of the mountains that jutted from Edgeland's snowy plains. The colonists called them the Grief Mountains, and if they had another, official name, no one remembered. Sharp, high, and rocky, the crags jutted into the clouds. Unlike the mountains back on Donderath, no trees covered the slopes of these peaks, nor were there trees anywhere in sight since they had left the ring of forest that surrounded the coast. Icy snow formed an unbroken crust between them and the mountains. The ice crystals glittered in the moonlight, and drifted snow formed frozen waves as far as the eye could see.

"We've been in just as much danger back in Donderath," Zaryae said. "At least here, we get to be in danger in a new place."

Connor gave her a sidelong glance. "I think that's the strangest reasoning I've heard in a long time."

They trudged together in companionable silence for a while. Finally, Connor spoke. "Thank you again for patching me back together on the ship. And for helping me with my shielding. I've caused you a lot of extra problems."

Zaryae chuckled. "I learned about healing by patching up those cousins of mine," she said with a nod toward the twins, who were still experimenting with their skis. "It's unfortunate that you have so many opportunities for me to be of help."

Connor gave a rueful smile. "You have no idea how unlikely everything I've done in the last year has been. Most of the time, I can't believe most of the things that have happened to me."

"I don't know," she said, glancing out across the expanse of snow that shone blue in the moonlight. "When our troupe made that last crossing over the Western Plains, my foresight told me that we would see fire and ice. Even so, I could never have really expected all we've done since then."

"What will you do when it's all finally over?" Connor asked, finding it easier to fall into a regular rhythm moving across the snow when he did not think so hard about it. "The magic's finally fixed. The warlords can't fight over land forever. Sooner or later, they'll sort out who's in charge. Things will eventually settle down—I hope. What then?"

Zaryae shrugged. She reached up to tuck a wisp of dark hair

beneath her hat. "If you mean, do I have any special insight into my future, the answer is no. It's not like knowing in advance how a play or a story is going to end. And most of the time, what I see isn't really about me, or at least, not just me."

"You know, before the night of the Great Fire, I was about the least adventurous person you would have met," Connor said with a sigh. "I'd been apprenticed to Lord Garnoc from the time I was twelve, largely so my family didn't have to keep paying to feed, clothe, and educate me. Lord Garnoc was good to me," Connor recalled. "Even though I was just his assistant, I lived in Quillarth Castle whenever he went to court. I was in the same room with King Merrill more times than I can count. And the food was pretty good," he added with a laugh. "I never wished for more."

"And look at you," Zaryae replied. "You had a lot more to you than you ever suspected."

Connor gave a sharp bark of a laugh. "If I had heard someone tell a tale about adventures like the ones I've had, I'd have figured they were making them up."

"Circumstances have a way of showing us what we're made of," Zaryae said quietly. "We were supposed to play for Lord Corrender at his estate for a month or two, and then work our way back across the plains. I just assumed that was how life would always be, performing anywhere people would pay us, traveling from one place to another. Maybe combining with another troupe someday if Uncle Illarion had brokered a suitable husband for me or wives for the twins."

"Did you leave someone behind, when your troupe came east this last time?" Connor was surprised at how much he disliked the thought.

Zaryae shook her head. "No. I hadn't been in a hurry to make a match, and by now, I'd be considered a little too old."

Connor raised an eyebrow. "You're at least a few years younger than I am. That's hardly 'aged'!"

Zaryae shrugged. "Out in the Western Plains, things are different. Some of the girls marry not long after their moon days come on them. Most marry young. I wanted to learn more about my magic, and I liked traveling. Fortunately, Illarion didn't believe in forcing me to accept someone."

"I'm glad," Connor said, and immediately felt his cheeks flush. "I mean, if he had, I would never have met you. And then I'd probably be dead." He sighed. "I'm sorry. None of that came out the way I meant it to."

Zaryae laughed. "Don't worry. I think I know what you meant. And I'm glad I've met you too, Bevin, and not just because I've patched you up a few times." She paused. "It's only fair for me to ask you the same question. Did you leave anyone behind the night of the Great Fire?"

Connor shook his head. "No. Not that some of the girls at the castle weren't pretty. But I was at Lord Garnoc's beck and call all day and all night, and I didn't really have much time to myself." He sighed. "Truth be told, I wasn't much of a catch, since I had no inheritance or title, being the youngest son. I never really thought much about it, but I really would have had no prospects once Lord Garnoc passed on—and he was up in years. I imagine he would have made provision for me in his will. Perhaps I would have worked for one of the other lords. I'm not sure what would have become of me."

"Funny, isn't it? How you now serve two of the most power-ful men in Donderath, and count a warlord—perhaps the next king—as a friend?" Zaryae's eyes danced with good humor, sparkling with her continual surprise at the workings of the universe.

"I guess so," Connor admitted. "Though in the thick of

things, more than once, I would have given it all just to wake back up in my bed at the castle and find out it's all been a dream!"

Zaryae turned to comment, but before she could speak, the crust of snow cracked beneath her and she vanished beneath the surface with a sharp, frightened shout of alarm.

"Zaryae!" Connor shouted, managing to come to a halt and stop the sledge he pulled before they neared the lip of the hole. Kane heard his shout and poled over toward him, swearing all the while.

"*Tunnelers.* They're bad news."

From down in the passage beneath the snow, they heard a scream. "Get the twins!" Connor snapped. To the Wraith Lord, he added, *Help me, please.* And before Kane could object, Connor shrugged out of his pack, stepped out of the skis, and jumped into the hole after Zaryae.

Connor thrust his feet out against the tunnel walls to slow his descent. Once he was no longer in free fall, he jammed knives into the icy walls, one in each hand. With his back against one side of the tunnel and his feet against the other, he used the knives as pitons to aid his descent. He went as fast as he dared, knowing that every second of delay endangered Zaryae. *Then again, there's precious little maneuvering room in here,* he thought. *I'm not going to help her if I land on her.*

Zaryae screamed again, but the sound was muffled. This portion of the tunnel went almost straight down about fifteen feet, through layers of ice. He remembered the stories Blaine had told about the 'Hole' at Velant, an oubliette in the ice. The *tunneler* had created something similar, an effective way to trap prey.

Connor landed at the bottom with a soft *thump*. He had left his pack at the top, but he had a few emergency supplies in the pouches on his belt, including a candle, flint, and steel. In a moment, he had a flame flickering, and saw that from here, the tunnel went off at a right angle.

"Can you see anything?" Borya shouted down.

"Not yet," he called up, trying to keep his voice low. "Have a rope ready. I'm going after her."

The tunnel walls were covered with stiff black animal hair. The sides of the tunnel showed the claw marks of the beast that dug it, five long, deep scratches in a set. Here at the bottom, the odor was rank, a mix of animal musk, droppings, and entrails.

A high-pitched shriek sounded from ahead. Connor dropped to his hands and knees, trying to crawl while holding the candle in one hand. *Is there any way you can help?* he asked the Wraith Lord.

Not without draining you, which would be better saved for a fight, the Wraith Lord replied. *And in such close quarters, I'm not sure what skills I can bring to a struggle that you don't already possess.*

Resolute, Connor crawled along the fetid tunnel, wincing as the wax burned his fingers. He heard a roar not far in front of him, followed by Zaryae's scream. He heard scuffling just ahead, and realized that a dark shape was coming toward him in the close confines of the tunnel. Knife ready, he waited.

"Move!" The voice was Zaryae's, strained with tension, and she kicked back at him with her boot.

Not quite sure what to expect, Connor blew out the candle, dropped it into his pocket, and began shuffling out backward. The tunnel was a close fit, and the only way for there to be room for two where the shaft opened to the top was for Connor to prop himself against the two walls with his legs outstretched so that Zaryae could crawl out of the lower tunnel. She was covered with blood, but when he looked closer, he realized that little of it was her own. Zaryae gripped a bloody knife in her hand.

"It's wounded, not dead," she said. "He'll be after us. Let's get out of here."

"Climb!" Desya yelled. He and Borya held the rope they'd already dropped, while Zaryae went up it hand over hand with agility born of long training.

A low growl came from the tunnel and the scuttling of claws against hard ice. Just as the twins pulled Zaryae over the lip of the hole, the *tunneler* burst into the opening.

"Connor! Climb!" Zaryae pushed the rope over the edge for him to grab.

The *tunneler* was wounded. Blood matted its gray and black hair, and a deep gash ran across its neck and right front forepaw. But Connor doubted that its powerful hind legs were impaired, and its long, ratlike snout bristled with sharp teeth. From his awkward position wedged against the sides of the tunnel, he could not fling himself at the rope without dropping low enough for the *tunneler* to make mincemeat of his legs. Grappling with the *tunneler* in such close quarters did not look like a winning proposition, even with a wicked blade.

The *tunneler* snarled and launched itself at Connor. He scored a cut to the monster's face, and the beast dropped back with an angry squeal.

"Bring the rope over to this side," Connor yelled as he hitched himself up one step at a time, keeping a wary eye on the *tunneler* beneath him. It turned in circles, eyeing him hungrily, watching for an opening.

"I'm going to loop it under my arms," Connor shouted. "When I tell you, haul me up."

He leaned forward to slip the rope around his back and slid down the icy shaft several inches. The *tunneler* saw its chance and leaped, getting a claw into Connor's calf and opening up a gash. Connor cursed and jammed his knife straight down with both hands, slicing across the *tunneler*'s skull down to the bone.

The creature gave an earsplitting shriek that echoed in the icy shaft, but it fell back, splattering the ice with blood. Connor managed to wriggle upward, and got the rope behind him without falling again. The *tunneler* watched him with baleful black eyes, waiting. Connor made a second pass with the rope, and held on to the end with one hand.

"Pull!" he shouted.

Borya and Desya yanked the rope upward. The *tunneler* gave a scream of rage and leaped again, barely missing Connor's feet. But this time, the monster dug its claws into the ice, following Connor up the icy shaft.

If Zaryae hadn't wounded it, that thing would have me by now, Connor thought. The *tunneler* favored its wounded leg, but it scrabbled up the tunnel wall almost as fast as the twins were pulling.

"Pull harder!" Connor yelped, kicking at the monster with his boots. He landed a hard kick to the creature's bleeding skull with his heel, but the *tunneler* did not lose its grip, pausing only a moment before continuing its pursuit.

Desya and Borya hauled Connor over the lip of the tunnel and out onto the snow, pulling so hard they dragged him several feet across the snow when the tension in the rope finally eased. A few seconds later, the *tunneler* burst over the edge.

"Gotcha!" Kane brought his sword down just behind the monster's skull, severing its head. The creature shuddered, and its blood darkened the snow all around the hole in the ice.

Connor lay panting on the snow. Zaryae ran to him. "Are you crazy?" she snapped, fear and anger glinting in her eyes.

"Apparently, yes." Connor unwound the rope from around

himself as Borya coiled it back up and looped it over his shoulder.

Kane strode over. "What in Raka were you thinking?"

Connor tried to climb to his feet, and staggered with pain from the gash in his leg. Enough adrenaline was pumping through his system that he did not back down. "I was thinking that one of our team was down there with a monster," he challenged, taking a step toward Kane. "I was thinking that I was the closest one, and that meant it was up to me to help. I was thinking that there was no way I was going to leave Zaryae down there alone. Got a problem with that?"

Kane pulled back as if to throw a punch, and Connor steeled himself to take it.

But the blow never came. Kane stood for a second as if poleaxed, and then shook his head and glared murderously at Connor.

"Apparently I'm not supposed to knock some sense into you," he growled. "But you got lucky this time. I've seen *tunnelers* rip men apart. Next time, think before you go charging in." With that, he turned on his heel and strode off, leaving the others to scramble to keep him in sight. Borya and Desya shouldered into the harnesses for the sledges, and Zaryae looked worriedly at the blood dripping by Connor's heel.

"We'll have every wolf in Edgeland after us at that rate," she said with a sigh, pausing long enough to put a handful of healing leaves from her pouch against the raw wound and binding it with a strip of cloth.

"You were quite the hero back there," she said without looking up as she tied off the bandage.

"Seems like you already had it well in hand," Connor replied.

"Today I got lucky. Tomorrow, maybe not. If I hadn't managed to get in one good hit, it would have been very different."

Zaryae leaned forward and gave him a kiss on the cheek. "So thank you."

She dusted the snow off of her bloodied coat and stood. "Come on," she said with a jerk of her head in the direction the others had gone. "We'd better catch up."

Kane set a stiff pace, but after several candlemarks of trekking, they arrived at Grimur's small cabin. "We'll stay here tonight," Kane said. He opened the door and stood back so they could enter. "Grimur will be here shortly," he added.

The windowless, squat home had been built for one person, and although its occupant cared little about the cold, Connor noted that the cabin had a fireplace and that its log walls did a fair job of making the interior warm enough that they could sleep without worrying about freezing to death. A freshly killed deer hung in one corner, blood draining into a basin. Laid out on a table against one wall was a meal of dried meats, cheese, and bread, along with a bottle of whiskey and a bucket of water. After the danger and exertion of the day's trek, Connor thought food had never looked so good.

"So if this is his home, why isn't he here?" Verran asked, and bit into a piece of meat. "I figured he and Nidhud would be back by now."

"They wouldn't have gone out in high twilight," Kane replied. "They waited until it was dark. I imagine he wants to make sure we're as alone as we think we are," Kane replied, with an edge that suggested Grimur's whereabouts were none of Verran's business.

"He's *talishte*," Borya said, helping himself to some bread and cheese. "What does he have to worry about?"

Kane fixed him with a glare. "*Talishte* aren't invulnerable, just damn difficult to kill. It pays to keep your eyes open." He maneuvered around the rest of the group, which had found seats on the floor around the fire to eat. "He's probably check-ing for signs of wild animals—or magicked beasts, before we head out tomorrow."

Just then, the door opened. Grimur and Nidhud walked in. "Good to see that you've arrived," Grimur said. "I trust the first leg of your journey went well."

"We're still all alive," Connor replied. "That counts for something."

As the others ate, Connor and Zaryae recounted the fight with the *tunneler*. Grimur and Nidhud listened with concern. "You'll be less at risk in the terrain tomorrow," Grimur said. "Today you were crossing a large shelf of ice covered with packed snow. Perfect for *tunnelers*. Tomorrow, as you head toward the mountains, there's more rock than ice below the snow, so the *tunnelers* go elsewhere."

"Suits me fine," Kane said, hanging back against the far wall of the small cabin as if he were intent on not being a part of the group he guided. "Never have figured out a good way to see where those *tunnelers* have their holes. We were lucky to only hit one today."

"What about tomorrow?" Connor asked. "Where are we going, and what might be trying to kill us on our way?" His leg pained him, and after they ate, he hoped to have Zaryae apply her poultices and bind it more securely. Thanks to his bond with Penhallow, he would heal faster than usual, and he was better prepared to ignore the pain. Still, the next few days were likely to be grueling enough that he did not relish the idea of being hobbled, nor to have predators scenting his blood.

Nidhud chuckled. "Everything in Edgeland is designed to kill you. That's the nature of this place. But to your point, Arin and I were just scouting the first part of the route to your destination. It doesn't look like there have been any *capreols* in the area recently, though there are some old tracks."

"So those razor-antler things pass that way, just not in the last few days," Borya filled in. "How do we know they're not due to come by again?"

"We don't," Nidhud admitted. "Like the *tunnelers* and the *howlers*, the *capreols* don't belong on Edgeland. There isn't a way to predict their movements, because they haven't always been here. And since game is scarce, predators roam quite far in search of a meal. *Talishte* included," he added.

"I can attest to the scarcity of game," Grimur said. "I find that I must go farther and farther afield after deer than I needed to before the Great Fire and its wild magic brought the monsters to Edgeland. Yet one more reason I enlisted Kane's assistance. He can organize the Bay-town men into hunting groups to kill the monsters more easily than I can. It's in all our interests to keep them from depleting the food supply."

Connor could not help glancing over to the bowl of blood beneath the freshly slaughtered deer. He was all in favor of anything that kept predators well supplied with game meat, since the alternative would be the colonists themselves.

Outside, the wind had picked up. A howl in the distance was answered by another and then more, a sound that sent a chill down Connor's back. He had grown accustomed to wolves, though the creatures usually stayed well clear when he traveled with Penhallow, as if they knew they were not going to win a fight with a *talishte*. Something about these howls gave Connor to think that the creatures would not be so easily scared away.

"*Howlers*," Nidhud said, noting Connor's distracted expression. "Don't worry. They can scent *talishte*, and they won't usually pick a fight with one. I doubt they'll bother us tonight."

"Where, exactly, are we going?" Verran pressed. "I don't care if it has a name or not. I'm not a trusting sort, and I don't like wandering around a wilderness waiting to get eaten."

Grimur nodded, and went to a small desk against the wall. From a drawer, he withdrew a folded map of Edgeland. "There's nothing special about this map. Unlike the one Ifrem gave to McFadden, it's just a map of Edgeland, copied from one in the king's library at Quillarth Castle, and corrected over the last decades through my own wanderings."

He spread the map out on the desk, and the others crowded around. Connor could easily make out the location of Skalgerston Bay and Velant, and of Estendall, the volcano not far from the Edgeland coast. Over his years of 'exile' in Edgeland, Grimur had mapped the fjords and inlets of the Edgeland coastline as well as the lowlands and passes of the mountains closest to the colony. Grimur's map was far more detailed than anything Connor had seen before, including the map Penhallow had included with his own gear.

"The whole point of hiding the Elgin Spike was to keep it from being found," Grimur said drily. "I may have gone a bit further in that regard than Penhallow intended." He pointed to a spot on the map. "We are here. The Spike is here." His finger came down on a place in the foothills of the mountains, a distance Connor reckoned was at least another day's hike.

"Why there?" Borya asked.

"Because the hunters from Bay-town almost never go that far out on the ice," Kane replied. "Least they didn't before the magicked monsters started eating up the game. Before that, they could hunt and trap enough game close to the town to keep them within a one-day trek, and seeing how Edgeland's not the most welcoming place, no one saw the need to explore beyond that."

"Kane is correct," Grimur said. "But there were other reasons as well. Donderath has explored very little beyond what the kingdom needed for the prison and colony. But Donderath was not the first to come to these shores. Others have come and gone over the centuries, for many different reasons. Don't forget, Estendall is a place of power, which is why its eruptions have coincided with significant magical events. Nodes and meridians run beneath the land, as they did beneath Valshoa and Mirdalur. We're not the first to notice. I've had plenty of time to wander the mountains. And I found ruins from long ago, proof that other mages have come here over the centuries to work magic."

"So you stashed the Spike in the ruins of an old civilization in the mountains?" Connor said incredulously. "This sounds like Valshoa all over again."

Grimur chuckled. "I assure you, it is quite different. There is no lost city, just a forlorn old ritual chamber. It will seem very familiar, if you've been to Mirdalur or the Citadel of the Knights of Esthrane. It's a workspace for mages constructed to focus and contain power. I don't believe the mages who built it ever tried to live on Edgeland. I found no ruins to suggest that they did. Perhaps they considered Edgeland to be sacred, or merely too damn cold. We'll never know."

"Why there?" Zaryae asked.

"The Elgin Spike is a magical artifact," Grimur replied. "When I first brought it to Edgeland, I thought the Spike was safe with me here, since the cabin seemed so far from other people. Over the years, I started to look for a more secure hiding place, which led me into the mountains, and the ruins. They had not been used in a very long time, and the power beneath that spot seemed ideal to bind the Spike and keep it safe."

"What do we have to do to get it?" Connor asked. "Because we all nearly died at Valshoa and Mirdalur."

"Your part in this is simple. All that is required is for your blood to bear witness to the bond between you and Penhallow," Grimur replied. "The magic I worked allowed me to bind the Spike but not release the binding on my own."

"Where's the catch?" Desya asked, leaning in to peer at the map. "Traps to navigate? Time of the day or phase of the moon to access it? Special magical items needed?"

Grimur chuckled. "I kept it simple. All it requires is our presence—and the correct working of the counterspell."

"And without that?" Verran asked.

Grimur frowned. "Well. Let's just say things would go very badly."

CHAPTER
TWENTY-THREE

"DID YOU SEE THE SIZE OF THOSE *HOWLER* TRACKS?"
Borya said as he and Connor took their turn hauling one
of the sledges.

"I was trying not to think about it," Connor replied. Though
the creatures did not attack Grimur's cabin during the night,
their massive footprints—more bear than wolf—and the number of prints made it clear just how many of them had been
close by, and how big those beasts were.

"Desya and I have fought off wolves plenty of times, out in
the Western Plains," Borya said. "Can't say the same for bears."

"We're just lucky the magicked creatures can't spawn," Connor muttered. "At least this way, we've got a chance of killing
them all off someday." His calf hurt with every step, though
he refused to mention it. Zaryae had done all she could, and
Connor knew he was healing faster than normal. There was
nothing to gain by complaining, but that did not ease the pain.

"I'll be glad to be back in Donderath," Borya replied. "After
this, I don't think I'll complain that anything is cold again!"

"The last time I was here, the temperatures were dropping.

So it actually gets worse than this—a lot worse," Connor replied. Talking with Zaryae and the twins helped to pass the time as they trekked toward the mountains. Verran was reserved and snappish, still in a foul mood about Kane. Kane was consistently surly, which Connor guessed was his natural way of being. *Maybe that suits Grimur fine,* Connor thought. *Makes for less conversation.*

The Long Dark made it difficult to figure time, but from the position of the stars, Connor knew the day was far spent by the time they reached the foothills of the mountains. Kane led them with a tracker's instincts across the rough terrain. When the pass became too rough for the sledges, they shouldered the gear they would need for the night.

"I hope we're close," Desya said. "I don't fancy carrying this up the side of a mountain."

Despite Connor's fears that they might face a magically trapped obstacle course as they had in Valshoa, Grimur's description of the ritual space was accurate. A circle of standing stones much like those near Lundmyhre had been erected in a valley surrounded by large, sharp peaks. Once, the pillars and lintels must have all been upright, but weather and the earthquakes common when Estendall erupted had shaken some of the huge stones from their places and they lay toppled and broken. Most had remained in place, and even imperfect, the circle was imposing, and Connor felt a primal level of awe.

"Grimur says they called the place 'Erhenjal.'" Kane's voice was unexpected, and Connor startled, shaken from his thoughts. "He says he matched some of the runes carved into the stones with that diary he gave McFadden, the one by the old mage."

"Valtyr," Connor supplied. "The mage's name was Valtyr."

"Yeah," Kane said. "That one."

"Who made the circle?" Connor asked, drawn to move closer but wary of setting off any lingering protections.

"Don't know. Grimur says he doesn't know, either," Kane answered, looking up at the tops of the tall pillars. "But whoever they were, they knew how to build."

Kane turned to face Connor. "You see ghosts, right? See any around here?"

Connor had been on guard for any ghostly intruders as they neared the Grief Mountains. From the time they had set out from Grimur's cabin, Connor had sensed occasional flashes of presence, and guessed them to be hunters who had lost their way on the ice or fallen prey to wild animals. None of those spirits had made a move to communicate, and Connor was content to leave well enough alone.

From the time they entered the Grief Mountains, however, the sense of ghostly presence grew stronger. Connor had the clear impression that ghosts were watching their group as they entered the pass, willing them to leave. The ghosts did not attempt to stop their progress, but Connor found their baleful silence was unwelcoming. Whether or not they were malevolent still remained to be seen.

"You sense them." Zaryae had walked up beside Connor, and she laid a hand on his arm. Kane walked around the standing stones, perhaps checking for danger, or maybe as much in awe of them as Connor.

"Yes." It was a relief not to have to either hide or explain his abilities to Zaryae. Her acceptance of his gifts made Connor feel normal in a way no one had since before the Cataclysm.

"Friend or foe?"

Connor shook his head. "I don't know yet. Right now, they're trying to figure the same thing out about us."

"If no one actually lived here, why are there ghosts?" Zaryae asked.

"Good question," Connor replied. "If I could find out how they died, I might have a better idea of whether or not the standing stones are a danger."

"Grimur didn't think so," Zaryae replied.

"Grimur is a *talishte*-mage. There are a lot of things that wouldn't be a danger to him that could do us plenty of damage," Connor replied. "And there are predators that wouldn't even approach him that would pounce on us in a heartbeat."

"Can you make contact with the ghosts?"

Connor chewed on his lip as he thought. "I'm sure I can. But I don't know how or if the ghosts figure into the safeguards Grimur set up for the…item. I'd rather keep my distance unless they approach us, at least until Grimur is here to ask. I'd hate to blunder into setting off his protections."

"Have you had any visions?" Connor asked. The wind gusted through the pass. Zaryae shivered, and Connor moved closer to shield her, slipping his arm around her shoulder. She smiled appreciatively and leaned into him to escape the wind.

"I feel uneasy," Zaryae said, "and I'm not sure why. It's not the same as before Valshoa or Mirdalur. Then, I knew we were in for serious trouble. Here…" Her voice drifted off as she considered her words. "Here I have the feeling that the future is in flux, that things could go several different ways, some good and some bad." She shrugged and gave a weak smile. "Sorry. It's not a very precise gift sometimes."

"Just listen carefully to those voices you hear, in case anything changes," Connor said. "I hope Grimur's right and it's as simple as he made it sound. But I won't really believe that until we're safely back in Donderath."

They walked back toward where the others were already

setting up the tents Grimur had packed for them. Two canvas tents plus bedrolls would shelter them for the night. Verran was making a circle of small rocks for cooking and setting out some of the firewood. Borya rummaged through the packs for dried meat, cheese, and fruit and some hard bread, along with wineskins and water jugs. Borya arranged the sledges to block the entrance to the pass, making it easy for them to make a quick exit if need be, but presenting obstacles for any unexpected guests. Kane continued walking the perimeter, having put himself on first watch.

"We've still got a candlemark or so before Grimur and Nidhud join us," Borya said, craning his neck to see the sky for the mountains around them. Out beyond the pass, they heard distant howling. The two *talishte* had gone to scout the area, making sure they would be safe for the rest of the night.

"Let's hope they get here before those beasts do," Verran muttered, shaken by the howls.

Connor glanced over his shoulder, assuring himself that Kane was still out of earshot. "What's your grudge against Kane, other than that he was a guard at Velant?"

Verran glared at Connor as if he were daft. "Isn't that enough? You've heard Mick and Piran talk about what it was like in there. We got beaten, starved, frozen, worked like dogs, and worse. Kane wasn't the worst of the guards, I'll give him that. But he didn't do anything to stop bad stuff from happening, either."

With that, Verran walked away toward the mouth of the pass. "Stay where you can see us," Borya yelled after him.

"What do you make of him?" Desya asked with a jerk of his head toward where Kane was on the far side of the standing stones.

"If he didn't have a bond to Grimur, I'd be more inclined to worry," Connor replied. "But you saw what happened when he wanted to hit me. Grimur wouldn't allow it."

"Fine for you. What about the rest of us?" Borya asked.

"Penhallow wants us back safely. His intent carries through the bond. Kane can't harm us, or permit us to come to harm if he can avoid it without Penhallow and Grimur intervening," Connor said. "If he tries to betray us, Penhallow will know. And even though Kane is all the way up here, it wouldn't be good for him."

The *howlers'* cries echoed in the mountain pass, making it difficult to know where they were. *Close*, Connor thought. *Too close*. Much as he hated the thought of crossing the ice again and risking another encounter with the *tunnelers*, he had already decided that they could not return to Bay-town fast enough for him.

In the mountain pass, the perpetual twilight gave way to dark shadows. Connor and his friends lit the lanterns Grimur and Nidhud had packed for them and waited.

"Let's begin." Grimur's voice startled them. He and Nidhud stepped out of the darkness and into the glow of the lanterns. "This shouldn't take long." It seemed strange that no cloud of mist came when Grimur spoke. *No body heat, so no reason to see his breath in the cold*. And if the *talishte* did not need to speak, he did not have to breathe.

Kane joined the group, while Borya took his place on watch. Verran, Desya, and Zaryae hung back, curious onlookers without a role in the ritual. Nidhud, Grimur, Connor, and Kane walked into the center of the stone circle, and Grimur took a boline knife from his belt. Nidhud held a small wooden bowl. Once they were assembled inside the ring of standing stones, Grimur lifted his knife and began to walk widdershins in a circle between where the others stood and the stones themselves. As he walked, he murmured words Connor did not catch. Grimur was raising strong magic, setting a warding to contain the power he called—and perhaps, to avoid having the power be noticed by someone else.

The wards rose with a slight shimmer against the shadows. When Grimur finished, he walked back to where the others waited. Nidhud held out the wooden bowl. Kane was the first to push back his sleeve, baring his scarred left forearm. Grimur lifted the knife to each of the four quarters and murmured under his breath. Then he made a thin cut into Kane's arm, just enough to raise a line of blood and drip freely into the bowl.

Connor felt his heart thud as he extended his own arm and pulled back his sleeve. Grimur drew the sharp edge of the knife along the skin, and blood beaded up from the cut. Grimur added several drops of Connor's blood to the bowl, then thrust out his own bony arm and did the same. He flicked the knife blade over the mingled blood, adding his own to the mix, chanting.

Grimur held the bowl up to the night sky, turning to each of the quarters, then he lowered the bowl and walked to the center of the stone circle. Grimur dipped the knife into the blood and traced the blade in a circle on the thin dirt. He repeated the action three times, and then tilted the bowl, letting the crimson fluid drip into the center of the small circle.

"Once, I bid you open. Twice, I bid you open. Thrice, and it shall be done."

Connor blinked, and the ground in the center of the small circle had vanished. In its place was a shallow hole in the rocky ground. Grimur gave the blood bowl to Nidhud and reached into the hole, retrieving a cloth-wrapped bundle tied with strips of leather. He raised it carefully and passed it to Nidhud.

"You understand the power of the blade you hold," Grimur said gravely.

Nidhud nodded. "I will protect it with my existence, and see that it reaches Lanyon Penhallow safely," he promised.

"Now can we get out of here?" Kane asked, fidgeting. "I've got a feeling that something's about to go wrong."

Grimur nodded and began to walk the circle deasil, releasing the energy of the warding he had set. The iridescent shimmer blinked out, and they stood in the shadows once more.

Connor, the Wraith Lord said, *I can see beyond the mountain pass. There's a dangerous storm coming. You've got to get out of there.*

Before Connor could speak, Zaryae rushed up to the edge of the circle. "We're in danger," she warned. "There's a storm coming, a bad one. If it gets between us and Bay-town, we're not likely to make it back alive."

"I've just heard the same from the Wraith Lord," Connor said. "We're in trouble."

"True night is no time for mortals to be out on the ice," Grimur argued. "We could lose you to the *howlers* or *capreols*— or to the *tunnelers*—as easily as to a storm."

"We have three mages," Nidhud said, looking to Grimur and to Connor as the Wraith Lord's proxy. "And we're all fighters. Beasts can be defeated, but storms are more powerful than most magic. I agree with the Wraith Lord. We have no choice but to head back now."

"Can I say that trying to outrun a storm is a really bad idea?" Kane objected. "It's suicide."

"Your shelter was not designed to withstand a full storm," Grimur replied. "And if a storm brings feet of fresh snow with it, you'll find it much harder to hike back."

"We spent the day walking," Kane argued. "Now you want us to turn around and hike another day?"

"You don't have provisions to be stranded here," Grimur countered. "The nearest of my caches is still a two-candlemark walk from here, in good weather. And while you would have difficulty navigating in a storm, the magicked beasts have no such problem. You would be easy prey."

Kane looked from Grimur to Nidhud, then to Connor and Zaryae. He threw his arms up and rolled his eyes. "All right. Since you're not going to listen, let's strike camp and get going. Bay-town isn't getting any closer."

Zaryae went to talk to the twins while Connor walked back to where Verran was standing. "I heard," Verran said before Connor could tell him about the change in plans. "And for once, I actually agree with Kane. I think it's suicide." He frowned. "The only problem is, staying here is even worse."

They packed up the tents and provisions quickly, although Connor could not help a wistful sigh as they loaded the equipment back on the sledges. He could have used a night's sleep, especially when he already ached from the day's trek. He saw the same weariness in the others' faces, along with a reflection of the fear that he felt in the pit of his stomach.

"If we shift the provisions around, perhaps one or two people could rest on the sledges for a bit, while the others pull," Zaryae suggested. "We might not drop in our tracks as quickly."

"Grimur and I can help," Nidhud offered. "That will relieve you of some of the burden."

Reluctantly, they left the relative shelter of the mountain pass and headed back across the ice. Grimur and Nidhud took the first turn pulling the sledges, and where it would take two of the others to pull each of the sledges with the extra weight of a person on it, the two *talishte* barely seemed slowed by the load. The twilight glow cast the snow in an eerie blue, making everything around them seem unreal. Connor and Zaryae, by virtue of their injuries, were the first to rest on the sledges. Although Connor doubted that he would be able to sleep as the sledges ground across the ice, he found himself waking from deep slumber two candlemarks later.

"Verran and Desya are going to rest next," Borya said as he exchanged places with Nidhud to help pull the sledge. Kane shouldered into the other harness, while Nidhud went to scout the path ahead.

Although it had been less than a day since they had passed this way, their tracks were already obliterated by the constant wind. No new snow had fallen yet, and what remained from previous storms had become crystalized with ice. The wind picked up the frozen snow and swept it across the ice, stinging and sharp when it hit skin. The temperature had grown much colder. Connor and the others were glad for their heavy boots and coats, hats, scarves, and mittens.

Nidhud returned half a candlemark later. "We're being shadowed by a pack of *howlers*," he reported. "Probably the ones that caught your scent on the way in."

"I thought you said the *howlers* weren't likely to bother us if *talishte* were with us?" Verran questioned.

Nidhud raised an eyebrow. "And they haven't—at least, not yet. They're merely following us, for now. Most of the time, *howlers* won't attack *talishte*. But if they're hungry and game is scarce, or they believe their pack is up to the challenge, then they may test their strength."

Though his muscles still ached and he would gladly have slept much longer, the few candlemarks of sleep helped more than Connor expected. *Don't tarry,* the Wraith Lord warned him. *The weather is moving in quickly, faster than I originally expected. You may not make it back to Grimur's cabin before it strikes, but the less time you spend in the storm, the better your chances.*

We can't move any faster, Connor grumbled. *Nidhud and Grimur could, but the rest of us could never keep up, even if we abandoned the sledges. We'll have to do the best we can.*

By Connor's calculations, they should have about five more candlemarks to go before they would reach Grimur's cabin. The faster they could cover ground, the better their odds against any predator stalking them.

Snow began to fall, and the wind grew stronger. The group kept on trudging as Kane and Borya took their turn to rest. On the horizon, Connor could make out slouching silhouettes that moved in parallel to them. *Howlers,* waiting for a chance to strike.

"We're almost to where the deep snows give the *tunnelers* room to maneuver," Grimur warned. "Once we get there, we'll need to spread out more so we put less pressure on the top snow. That way, there's less chance of someone breaking through into the *tunnelers'* holes."

Connor glanced back to the horizon. The *howlers* were gone. A warning prickled at the back of his neck.

"Danger!" Zaryae cried. Dark shapes seemed to appear out of the snow itself as the *howlers* ran toward them from all directions, a dozen strong.

"Kane! Borya! We're under attack!" Zaryae shouted as she drew her short sword, a hunting knife clutched in her left hand. Connor and the others readied their swords, while Nidhud and Grimur chose a direction to face off with the charging beasts.

Help me! Connor summoned the Wraith Lord. *Whether I fight with my sword or with your magic, I'm starting out tired and injured. I can't protect them on my own.*

Nidhud swept his right arm in a powerful arc, and two of the *howlers* went reeling, slammed by an invisible force. Grimur pushed forward with both palms out, sending two more of the beasts tumbling head over tail. Verran had a sling and a pouch of rocks, and a wicked knife hung at his belt. He sent his missiles singing through the cold air with deadly aim. One of his rocks struck a *howler* between the eyes, and the beast dropped to the ground, unconscious if not dead. Kane's sword held off a thickly built gray-and-brown *howler* that sprang with a deep, guttural growl.

Borya and Desya echoed the howls of the predators as they slashed at the beasts with their blades, managing to stay out of range of the huge, powerful paws and wickedly sharp claws. Zaryae positioned herself to watch Connor's back. A dark-gray male came slinking toward Connor, sizing up its prey. One ear was notched from old fights, lips parted over large, sharp teeth.

The now-familiar tingle of magic surged through Connor as the Wraith Lord possessed him. Something alerted the *howler* to the change, because its eyes narrowed and it slowed its advance. Connor did not wait for it to spring. The Wraith Lord's spirit swept away his exhaustion and dampened the pain, making him faster and stronger. With a roar of his own, Connor rushed toward the *howler*, moving with the deadly confidence of a warrior who had seen a thousand years of battle.

A second *howler* headed for Connor, only to stop in its tracks as a ball of packed, hard snow smashed across its forehead. Zaryae grinned in triumph, and the *howler* reoriented itself warily, giving Grimur the chance to send the monster reeling with a blast of magic. Zaryae made another ice ball, and this time, her target was the *howler* attacking Borya. Her aim held true, smacking the creature on the side of the head over one ear.

Its hesitation was enough to give Borya the opening he needed to dive forward and sink his blade into the beast's side.

Connor knew that while Zaryae could defend herself at close quarters with a knife, swordplay was not her strength. Her well-aimed ice balls were not as lethal as Verran's sling and rocks, but as she danced back and forth, emerging to throw and then dodging behind the fighters again, she kept the creatures distracted, and harried them enough to give Connor and the others an advantage.

"Are you crazy?" Kane shouted at Zaryae. The *howler* took a swipe with its huge paw and missed Kane by inches, a strike that would have torn out his midsection, but Kane twisted at the last minute and brought his sword down hard, severing the *howler*'s head.

The Wraith Lord's full focus was on the *howler* that stalked Connor. Whatever the *howler* made of the change that had come over Connor, the creature was not willing to give up without a fight. Behind him, Connor heard the shouts of Borya, Desya, and Kane as they fought the *howlers*, and the *hum* and *thwack* of rocks hitting their targets with deadly accuracy as Verran wielded his sling and Zaryae lobbed ice balls. Nidhud and Grimur were keeping half the pack occupied, forcing them back with magic that threw the creatures across the ice time and again. Undaunted, the monsters always returned.

It was a test of wills, Connor thought, to see which one of them could get close enough to strike. He had to get in close to land a blow with his sword, but that put him in reach of the *howler*'s massive paw and its curved, strong claws. He moved in swiftly, getting in a strike that bloodied the *howler*'s front shoulder but did not sever the limb. The *howler* roared in anger and pain and sprang, and Connor felt the swish of a paw barely miss him, while the claws opened a gash on the sleeve of his coat.

Not for the first time, Connor rued the fact that although he was faster and stronger than without the Wraith Lord's help, possession did not grant him full *talishte* abilities. Against mortal opponents, the edge he gained was enough. But the *howlers* were creatures of the wild-magic storms, unnatural beasts endowed with more than their share of lethal abilities.

Connor saw an opportunity and took it, diving toward the *howler* to slide his sword between its ribs. The beast wheeled, striking a glancing blow that caught Connor on the shoulder and sent him sprawling. The *howler* gave a mighty shake and Connor's sword went flying, only to skitter away on the icy crust of snow. The beast's claws had raked his left shoulder, opening up his coat and skin. Blood ran down his arm, and the injury combined with the force of his landing slowed Connor's reactions. He saw the *howler* crouch, then leap, claws outstretched, fangs bared.

A rush of power filled him, and before he could fully register his reaction, Connor's right hand came up and fire erupted from his palm. The blast struck the *howler* square in the chest, engulfing it in flames and sending it flying through the air, hard enough to crash through the skin of ice on top of the snow when it landed. The beast screamed, its thick fur on fire, writhing as it tried to free itself. The air was full of the stench of burned hair and flesh.

"What in Raka are you?" Kane swore, registering what had happened despite his own desperate fight.

"Angry." Connor rose to his feet, still full of the Wraith Lord's power. He strode toward the *howlers* Kane and Verran fought. One of the beasts was dead, its skull cracked open by Verran's rocks, lying in a pool of blood in the snow. Another was dazed, shaking its head after a glancing hit. Kane danced in and out of range of a third *howler*, and both he and the creature looked the worse for the wear. Kane's shoulder was bloodied, and he had a gash on one thigh. The *howler* had a deep, bloody slit in its side, so that the flesh hung away revealing its ribs. Another strike had cost it an ear and part of the skin on its face. Still the *howler* was not going to give up easily.

"Move!" Connor yelled. The streak of fire he sent barely missed Kane, and struck the injured *howler* with its full force, enveloping its body in flames. The creature screamed, but the fire was hot enough to peel the skin from the bones, and within seconds, the *howler* collapsed dead in a charred heap.

Glancing around, Connor could see that half the pack was down, dead, or wounded too badly to get up again. That left six *howlers* still fighting. Nidhud had stopped trying to throw the *howlers*, and instead used his magic to grasp the huge animals in an invisible grip, then twist or bend them to snap the spine. Grimur's magic crafted an invisible claw of his own that could tear out the beast's throat or crush its skull. That left four.

Borya and Desya, to their credit, had taken down two of the creatures with just their sword skill and quick reflexes. The snow around them was trampled and bloody as they fought two of the remaining monsters. Borya looked as if he were actually enjoying the match, while Desya was favoring his left leg, and Connor could see that Desya's pants were dark with blood.

Connor could feel the effects of channeling the Wraith Lord. He was waning and he knew it. Though he had sustained the magic much longer aboard the ship, he was not fully recovered enough to withstand another outpouring of equal energy. *I might have one more blast in me before I land on my face in the snow,* Connor warned. *Let's make it count.*

Before he could determine a target, a new shadow rose out of the semidarkness behind them. This figure was much larger than the *howlers*, a massive form that stood as tall as a draft horse but even more thickly set, and from its head sprang a rack of antlers easily as wide across as a man's height. The four remaining *howlers* abandoned their fight and ran for the shadows.

The new creature moved as fast as a horse at full gallop, straight at Zaryae. Before Connor could get a clear view of what was happening, Kane ran into the path of the monster, shoving Zaryae out of the way. The beast ducked its head and rammed into Kane with the full force of its flat, broad antlers, edged as sharp as any sword. The antlers caught Kane in the belly and cut him in two, scooping his upper body into the air and tossing it aside as the lower half sank into the bloody ground.

"Kane! Zaryae!" Connor took a step, but Zaryae was between him and what he guessed must be a *capreol*, so sending a fiery blast was out of the question until he could get a clear shot.

Grimur was the first to move, and he jumped into the air, waving his hands frantically over his head. "Hey! Hey! Over here!" he shouted. The *capreol* snorted and pawed its front hooves. Grimur took off with a blur of *talishte* speed, charging the *capreol* with an answering bellow. The huge, horned creature snorted and stamped its forelegs, answering the challenge. At the last moment, Grimur veered off at an angle with the *capreol* in pursuit.

"Has he gone mad?" Verran said with disbelief.

"Everyone! Follow but stay back!" Nidhud shouted. Connor mustered his remaining strength and headed after Grimur at a distance.

Connor's boot crunched down through an inch of snow and he froze. *Grimur said we were close to the end of the rock shelf. That means the deep snow, and tunnelers. And Grimur's heading right out into it with the* capreol *behind him.*

"Stop there!" Grimur shouted as Nidhud ventured closer. The *capreol* galloped across the hardened snow at its full speed.

Grimur's movements looked more like skating, and Connor realized that the *talishte* was using his speed to reduce the weight he placed on the snow, in case the *tunnelers* had hollowed it out beneath him.

"Connor! Fire—now!" Trusting that Grimur could get out of the way, the Wraith Lord's power rose once more within Connor and he thrust out his arm, releasing a torrent of fire that hit the *capreol* broadside in its huge torso. Grimur's silhouette was barely visible through the flames, but suddenly the crust of snow crumbled beneath where he and the monster had been standing. The break sounded like thunder, and a huge sinkhole spread across the ice, sending a cloud of snow and ice crystals into the air. The *capreol* bellowed, and dropped into the sinkhole, its hooves scrabbling to find solid ground. Grimur vanished.

"Grimur!" Connor shouted. He took a step toward the sinkhole.

"Don't move!" Nidhud shouted. "The whole crust could go. Back up—slowly."

Before Connor could argue, he saw something rising amid the snowcloud. Grimur's head and shoulders came into view, and then the rest of the *talishte*, hovering in the air. Grimur set himself down on the ice a safe distance from the sinkhole, unharmed.

From deep in the *tunnelers'* ice shaft came a horrible, screeching sound. It was quickly drowned out by the vicious growls of dozens of *tunnelers*, attacking their helpless prey. The sound made the blood drain from Connor's face as he pictured the carnage in the close confines of the ice tunnels. The rest of the group was waiting restlessly for them to return. Unsure of how much the others could see, Connor gave a terse recap.

"What do we do about Kane?" Borya asked, nodding toward where the fighter's remains lay.

"I will see to him." Grimur's expression was somber. He collected Kane's savaged body and carried the pieces a short distance, paying no attention to the blood that dripped in a steady rivulet down his arms. When he had reached a suitable place, he set down Kane's body and then used his magic to scrape out a deep trench for a grave. He made another gesture, and the icy snow fell back into place, covering the body, and then added a thrust of power to harden the ice in place. For a moment, Grimur stood over the grave, head bowed.

"If the land between here and Grimur's cabin is lousy with *tunnelers*, and the crust is broken, how do we get back without ending up like that monster with the antlers?" Verran hissed, keeping his voice low.

"We move carefully, spread out to minimize the weight on the ice's surface," Nidhud replied. "And hope that luck is with us."

Connor had already come to the conclusion that neither day nor night were safe anywhere on Edgeland's far ice, even with the help of two powerful *talishte*, but he kept his opinion to himself. Grimur wiped his hands in the snow to remove the worst of the blood and then headed back to join them.

"Stay about six feet apart," Grimur warned them. "We want to avoid putting too much weight on the ice, but if we get a true blizzard, we don't want to be separated. Nidhud will go first, and use his magic to sense the *tunnelers* beneath the surface. Connor should go second, so that any information the Wraith Lord shares with him can affect our path. I'll bring up the rear, in case we're attacked again."

The wind was blowing harder now, and snow fell at a steady

pace. "Let's get moving," Grimur said brusquely. "We've still got candlemarks to go, and the storm is closing in quickly."

The next two candlemarks seemed like an eternity as they traced a meandering line across the ice to avoid the *tunneler's* traps. "I can't see the whole ice field at one time," Nidhud muttered to Connor at the forefront of the party. "Just a few feet in front of us. So while I'd love to go faster, we can't without ending up like the *capreol*."

Borya and Desya hauled the sledges. Verran kept his slingshot handy, though his supply of stones was running low. Zaryae had made half a dozen ice balls, which she kept at the ready by turning up the edge of her long coat like a sling. The Grief Mountains behind them were completely hidden in the snow squalls of the storm.

Crusted snow slowed their steps, and the indirect course sapped their energy. Despite his heavy coat, Connor was cold to the bone. Every muscle ached, and he was utterly weary. Only the knowledge that death would come quickly should he stop to rest kept him on his feet. Ice clung to the scarf covering his face as his breath condensed and froze, and his hands and feet were numb. Zaryae had begun to stumble, and she accepted Connor's arm without protest. Nidhud and Grimur had shouldered the sledges, since it was all the others could do to keep on moving. After another candlemark, they reached firm ground once more.

"Unload the sledges," Grimur said. "We can safely leave the supplies here," Grimur said. "I can come back for them tomorrow. We're not far now from my cabin. Get on the sledges and Nidhud and I can drag you the rest of the way."

Connor, Zaryae, and Verran collapsed onto one of the sledges while Borya and Desya swallowed their pride and accepted seats on the other. Connor was sure the two *talishte* were also exhausted, but he had seen enough *talishte* strength firsthand to accept that Grimur and Nidhud were still in less danger from the elements than the mortals in the group.

"Come on," he said, jostling Zaryae. "Stay awake. We're almost back to the cabin."

"So tired," she said, her voice quiet and slurred.

"If it weren't so damn cold, I'd threaten to sing," Verran said. "But Connor's right—none of us dares fall asleep."

Connor and Verran huddled close to Zaryae, trying to shield her from the wind and share what little body heat they had. Zaryae's head lolled on Connor's shoulder, and he kept up a murmured running conversation, urging her to remain conscious. The sledge sank through the inches of new powder and ground over the icy, granulated snow beneath. Wind howled across the wide-open, frigid landscape and large flakes fell like a white curtain from the clouds overhead. Dimly, Connor was aware that Penhallow and the Wraith Lord gave him a mental nudge whenever the cold and exhaustion threatened to overwhelm him.

"We're here." Grimur shook Verran awake.

"We need to get Zaryae inside and warm," Connor said. "I haven't been able to rouse her for a little while now."

Grimur and Nidhud lit the lanterns. Connor carried Zaryae to the cabin and laid her down on the bed. Though Grimur himself had no need of blankets, the cabin was obviously outfitted for the comfort and safety of occasional mortal guests. "Come on, Zaryae," Connor coaxed, though his hands were shaking so much it was difficult to unfasten her heavy coat and pull off her boots. Connor's hands and feet felt numb and leaden, and his face tingled painfully as circulation returned.

"Wake up," he urged. "Please. Wake up." Zaryae's skin was pale and cold to the touch. She murmured groggily, but

Connor was unsure whether that meant she had heard him. He stripped off her sodden gloves and scarf, and wiped away the snow from her fur hat. Then he and Borya bundled her in blankets while Desya got a fire going.

"Once that fire gets going, we can move her closer," Verran said. "But don't try to warm her too quickly. That doesn't go well." He made a face. "Believe me, I know more about frostbite and ice sickness than I ever wanted to learn."

"You don't look so good, either," Borya commented archly, taking in Connor's condition. "I don't pretend to know how you channel that ghost lord, but you look ready to drop."

"I'll be all right," Connor protested, too worried about Zaryae to focus on his own discomfort.

"All of us are ready to drop," Verran argued. "We'll take turns sitting up with her. Once the rest of us warm up, we can bundle together under the blankets and use our body heat to break the chill, but we have to have heat ourselves before we can share it."

Grimur went back outside and returned with a cauldron of something that had frozen solid in the snow. "Venison stew. I figured you'd want something warm, but it will take a bit to thaw. In the meantime, there're dried meats and provisions on the table."

Verran filled a kettle with snow and placed it on the hearth to boil, and a second pot of snow farther back from the flames to melt for drinking water. Then he joined the others, who were dividing up the dried meat, cheese, and herring, plus thick slices of bread. "For someone who doesn't eat, you put on a good dinner," Verran remarked.

"I find it useful to be prepared," Grimur remarked. "Now that your needs are met, Nidhud and I must hunt. Today has been...taxing...and tomorrow comes soon." With that, he and Nidhud headed out of the cabin and back into the snow.

"Let's just hope there's some game dumb enough to be out in a storm," Verran remarked. "I don't fancy being a snack."

Connor felt light-headed with exhaustion and hunger, glad to take his portion of the food and sit down on the floor beside Zaryae's bed. "Once the stew warms up, we should try to get some of the broth into her," he said. "She's chilled through."

"After all that, I sure hope the fancy knife turns out to be worth it," Verran said.

"If it's as powerful as Penhallow believes, it could remove Thrane as a threat—and Reese and his followers, too," Connor replied. He turned his attention inward to the Wraith Lord. *Testing the Spike is obviously out of the question, but is there a way to make sure its magic still works, and didn't get corrupted by the Cataclysm?* Connor had firsthand experience with artifacts that had become dangerously changed when the Cataclysm changed the magic. He had no desire to add to those nightmares.

There's no good way to 'test' the Spike, the Wraith Lord answered. *For obvious reasons. First, it would be a wanton disregard for life, in addition to the fact that it would surely tip our hand to Thrane. And as you know, magical objects don't have unlimited uses. It would be a pity to test it and use it up before the real battle.*

What if it doesn't work?

Penhallow and Dolan and I have come up with secondary plans. But all of them are more difficult, more dangerous, and certain to cost more lives, Vandholt replied. *Let's hope that the Spike retains its power, for at least one more use.*

Borya lifted an eyebrow. "Penhallow must trust you quite a bit. Did it ever occur to you that Thrane isn't the only one the knife could be turned against?"

The thought had crossed Connor's mind, and he had understood why Grimur handed off the knife to Nidhud. *By now you should know, it is not a lack of trust, Bevin,* the Wraith Lord's voice supplied in his mind. *Nidhud is better able to guard the knife on the trip home. But he could not have obtained it without you. You've done well.*

I'm too tired to care about Thrane or Reese or the wars back in Donderath, Connor replied silently. *Right now, I just want Zaryae to wake up, and I want to fall asleep. After everything that's happened, surely that's not too much to ask?* He did not expect an answer, and despite his best efforts, resigned himself to sleep.

CHAPTER
TWENTY-FOUR

WHEN DID THEY SHOW UP?" BLAINE MCFADDEN handed off his reins to a groomsman as Kestel swung down from her horse to join him. It was late in the day, and they and their contingent of guards had ridden hard to make the journey from Glenreith at Dillon's urgent summons.

"Three days ago, m'lord," Dillon said. "Folville sent us word directly as soon as the messenger arrived. That's why we had a *talishte* take the message to you at Glenreith. We knew it would take time for you to get here." Before the Great Fire, Dillon had been the assistant to the Exchequer. After the Cataclysm, with the king and the seneschal dead, Dillon had stepped up to do his best overseeing the efforts to repair and refurnish what remained of the castle. The strain of his responsibilities showed in Dillon's pinched features, and his hair had thinned dramatically in the past year with the stress. Still, there was a grim set to his jaw that indicated he intended to see his charge through, no matter what.

"How do we know they're ambassadors—and not spies?" Blaine asked as he and Kestel followed Dillon up the castle steps. Piran and a dozen soldiers followed at a respectful distance.

"Of course they're spies," Kestel chided. "That's what ambassadors are. The rest is just ceremonial."

"Which is why we gave them the best quarters to be had in the castle, and then kept them confined there, 'for their own safety,'" Dillon replied with a sly smile. "I've tried to balance according them due respect and not showing them anything so nice that it might suggest Donderath is a plum to be plucked."

Thank the gods Kestel and Dillon know how to play this game, Blaine thought. *If they can coach me through the formalities, I won't complain about being the figurehead.*

"Are you certain they came from the Cross-Sea Kingdoms, like they claim?" Blaine asked.

Dillon met his gaze. "We're certain of nothing, m'lord. A messenger showed up under a white flag in a rowboat four days ago. He claimed to be from the Cross-Sea Kingdoms, and said that the ambassador and his entourage wished to come ashore to meet with our 'king.' Captain Folville sent a messenger to me, and I dispatched a *talishte* to you."

"Excellent job," Blaine said. "Now what do we do?"

"I've plied them with the best whiskey we have available," Dillon replied. "Rummaged up the wherewithal to cook them dinners I'm not ashamed to serve, though of course, nothing close to what would have been protocol...before."

Blaine shrugged. "No point in making comparisons. Those days are gone for good."

"And I've sent them musicians and entertainers every night," Dillon continued. "I also made certain that the servants who attend them know to report on anything they hear, but answer questions in the vaguest possible answers."

"Good, good," Kestel said. "Does the suite where you've put them have listening holes?"

Dillon gave her a crafty smile. "Of course."

"The rooms have listening holes?" Blaine asked, feeling as if he had somehow missed an essential part of the conversation.

Kestel chuckled. "Sure. How do you think the king knows so much? Ears everywhere—especially when there are foreigners around."

Dillon grinned. "They haven't said much, which tells me that they know the game. From what they *have* said, I gather that their trip across the ocean was relatively peaceful, and that we're having better weather than where they're from."

"Is there any way to confirm that they are indeed from the Cross-Sea Kingdoms, and not just pirates?" Blaine asked.

Dillon and Kestel thought for a moment, then shrugged. "In the old days, a visit like this would have been arranged months in advance," Kestel said. "Letters and gifts would have gone back and forth. Our ambassador would have known their ambassadors, and had a good idea who the servants and minor functionaries were, too. Anyone out of place would have stood out. Nothing would have been a surprise or left to chance. But now..."

"It's the first ship from elsewhere we've seen since the Cataclysm, with the exception of those pirates Folville and his men fought back a few weeks ago," Dillon replied. "None of our ambassadors survived the Great Fire, and if it was this bad where the delegation came from, that might be true for them as well. So there's no one who can verify or gainsay."

"Handy if you're trying to fool people," Blaine pointed out.

Dillon nodded. "Agreed. But just as inconvenient if you're who you say you are, with no way to prove your credentials."

"Have any of our people seen their ship?" Kestel asked as they accompanied Dillon down the corridors of the castle. Before the Great Fire, Quillarth Castle had been much larger, and it had been decorated to reflect King Merrill's wealth and power. Empty hooks along the stone walls showed where tapestries once hung. Bookshelves and alcoves were bare. Paintings and sculptures were absent, too. Most of the treasures burned or were destroyed on the night of the Cataclysm or were looted by Reese and Pollard in the aftermath. What few remained had been carefully secured in the castle's cellars, safeguarded until a less tumultuous time came upon the kingdom.

"No. Folville said he'd see what information his men could gather, and tell us what they find out," Dillon replied. "For all we know, it's the same pirates changed into fancy clothes, but just as eager to plunder."

"Here we are," Dillon said, leading Blaine and Kestel to a doorway. "This will be your room. There are empty rooms on both sides and across the hallway for your guards." He sighed apologetically. "You know what it's like here, so you know not to expect this to function like the castle it was. But we can offer the basics. There's food enough, and servants to fetch your wash water and draw a bath. And what passes for brandy is in the decanters."

"You've done well," Blaine said. "Thank you."

Dillon opened the door to the room and led them inside. "Here's your room, m'lord—and m'lady," he added. "Not as fancy as it once was, but there's furniture and linens, which are in short supply these days."

Blaine had occasionally accompanied his father to court when he was younger. In those days, he had been so awestruck at the possibility of glimpsing King Merrill or his queen that Blaine remembered few other details besides the glittering mirrors and impressively large coaches.

The mirrors were gone now, shattered or in storage. So were the paintings and many of the fine furnishings. The carpets that remained were threadbare and soot-stained. But the four-poster bed looked relatively unscathed, and its linens, while worn, were finer than anything they had at Glenreith.

"I've taken the liberty of procuring some clothing for both of you," Dillon said, clearing his throat. "I hope you don't mind, but I thought it might help to dress the part."

"We're grateful," Kestel said, grinning. "I can't tell you how long it's been since I've had a new frock." That she had spent most of the last six months dressed for battle went unsaid.

"The clothing is hardly new, but it's the best we could find. I hope it fits you."

"We can make do," Blaine replied. "Thank you. You've gone to a great deal of work to present Donderath in its best light."

"I've set out uniforms for your bodyguards as well," Dillon replied, though his cheeks colored at the praise. "Not exactly regulation for the king's guards, but close enough to represent us well."

Kestel looked to Blaine. "You know there'll be no living with Piran after this."

Blaine looked from Kestel to Dillon. "I've spent more time at Quillarth Castle after the Great Fire than I ever did before the Cataclysm. My memories of court were from when I was just a boy. The only negotiating I've done since then has been with warlords and *talishte*." He shook his head. "I'm going to need some quick instruction if our guests are to take me seriously."

Dillon chuckled. "I suspected that you might not feel as much at ease as Lady McFadden, so I've taken the liberty of going in the opposite direction. We've let our guests know that you are Donderath's dominant warlord, Lord of the Blood, and victor of countless battles, triumphant over mages and magic beasts." He raised an eyebrow. "It's not far off from the truth," he added. "If you'll excuse my being blunt, we painted you as a brutal power to be reckoned with."

"A little intimidation won't hurt, especially if they're really here to see if we're an easy conquest," Blaine replied.

"Exactly."

"Piran will never let you live this down," Kestel said, chuckling. "And he's going to love every minute of it."

"What's the plan now that we're here?" Blaine asked.

Dillon indicated a nearby washbasin, and a waiting bathtub and towels. "I'll send someone up to see to your bath and help you get ready. I shall present the delegation to you at dinner in the great room, after which there will be brandy and cakes in the small parlor. Your servants at dinner will be guards in disguise. My people will handle all of the food and drink with care, so there will be no opportunity for tampering."

"You just need to look stern and dangerous," Kestel said to Blaine with a grin. "I'll worm their secrets out of them. Oh, I haven't had a good game like this in a long time!"

Blaine chuckled despite the circumstances, then turned back to Dillon. "If you haven't already tried to send a *talishte* to take a look at the 'Cross-Sea' ship, see if you can get one out there tonight. I'd like to know a little more about what we're dealing with, and we don't have time to wait for Folville to report in."

Dillon nodded. "Done, m'lord. And I've taken the liberty of also having two of the mages you stationed at the castle with my servants tonight. They won't announce their true purpose, but they will scry to ensure we aren't about to be attacked during dinner, or have magic used against us by one of your guests."

He paused. "Mage Rikard will join you for dinner. Normally there would be a tableful of noble guests, but we're short on nobles these days, so we'll settle for just matching your numbers to theirs, four to four. Rikard served in noble houses before the war, so he should handle himself well, and if things do go wrong, he'll be one of your first lines of defense."

Blaine sighed. "I had heard it said that social occasions are just concealed warfare, but by the time all of this is done, I think it would have just been easier to fight it out and be done with it."

Kestel nodded. "Fights actually take less time than a full royal dinner party did back in the day when the entire court was present."

Dillon winced. "I wasn't involved with such things back then, but it was impossible not to overhear Seneschal Lynge when he was beside himself readying one detail or another. And it went on for months!"

"Let's impress them with how dangerous we are and send them on their way," Blaine said. "I've still got the Meroven raiders to deal with."

"Ah, but at least here, we get a hot bath!" Kestel said with a satisfied sigh. "And I, for one, intend to take full advantage of the opportunity."

Two candlemarks later, Blaine and Kestel had finished their baths and dressed for their dinner with the ambassadors. Blaine adjusted his collar and swallowed. "The next time I complain about my armor, remind me of how many layers of clothing it takes to dress for a court dinner."

Kestel pirouetted in front of the mirror. "Go ahead. Complain. You don't have nearly as many layers as I do, or skirts to manage." She admired her reflection for a moment. "Personally, I always enjoyed dressing for court. Except back then, I had a lot more jewelry." Even without gold or gems, Kestel looked striking. Her hair was wound into a style popular before the Great Fire, and the servants had managed to find her rouge and powder, along with some kohl for her eyes.

"You look beautiful," Blaine said. "Maybe when all the fighting is over, you'll have more opportunity to dress like this if you want."

"You mean, instead of being up to my elbows in blood on a battlefield?" Kestel replied. "That would be a nice change. But not all the time. Between Edgeland and the battles, I've gotten used to work dresses or trews. Much more comfortable!"

Their banter helped to ease Blaine's nervousness. *I never cared about taking back my title, let alone impersonating—or actually being—the king,* he thought. *But there's no one else to do it. And the other warlords and I can hardly meet with the delegation by committee. I won't pass for a born-and-bred king, but perhaps I can do better than outright barbarian.*

"I don't like it that I can't wear my sword," Blaine complained.

Kestel rolled her eyes. "No one is wearing a sword. Protocol." She gave a crafty grin. "On the other hand, everyone will likely have knives, a dirk or two, maybe a shiv hidden in the boot and a garrote in a pocket. At least, I do."

"I've got a dirk up my sleeve and a knife beneath my coat, and you saw me put the shiv in my boot," Blaine said. "I suppose Piran will be armed to the teeth as well."

"Count on it," Kestel replied. "And we've both got our amulets, even if their power is waning. If the 'ambassadors' turn out to be something else, we've got some protection against direct magic. Your talent of sensing magic should help in that regard, too."

Dillon and his servants had outdone themselves. Quillarth Castle's great room was still imposing, even without the huge tapestries and life-sized paintings that once graced its walls. Dillon had assembled a respectable collection of furnishings to provide a formal dinner seating. Vases of fresh flowers served as centerpieces atop the best linens that had survived the Cataclysm. Once, the huge great-room table could have seated fifty guests for a formal state dinner, resplendent with silver and crystal. Now, a much smaller table was set with damaged finery for tonight's event.

Dillon had managed to assemble dishes, utensils, and glassware for the occasion. The pieces did not match, but they made a respectable presentation nonetheless. Though the evening was pleasantly warm outside, the castle always held a chill with its thick stone walls, and so a fire blazed in one of the three large fireplaces. The great room's huge iron candelabrum had been pillaged soon after the Great Fire for its metal, but Dillon had assembled enough candles and lanterns to cast a pleasant glow, and the long late-summer evening meant additional light through the tall, narrow windows, many of which were still, rather surprisingly, intact.

Blaine and Kestel entered together, after a uniformed page sounded a trumpet to herald their arrival. Piran followed them, dressed in a brocade frock coat over velvet trews. Behind Piran were Rikard and the rest of their guards, wearing King Merrill's livery. Blaine's breath caught in his throat as he saw that a huge Donderath flag hung where one of the tapestries had been, directly behind the seats at the center of the table where Blaine, Kestel, and Piran were to sit.

The Cross-Sea ambassadors rose to their feet at the sound of the trumpet, and made courteous bows as Blaine and the others entered. "M'lord," Dillon said in his most sonorous voice. "May I present our esteemed guests. Ambassador Heldin, of the Cross-Sea Kingdoms."

Heldin was a stocky man in his fourth decade with a closely trimmed head of dark hair sprinkled with gray. He made a bow. "Your Lordship," Heldin acknowledged. "It is an honor."

He looks like the real thing, Blaine thought from the way Heldin stood. Kestel gave Blaine a nearly imperceptible nod, signifying that she too thought Heldin could be a real ambassador. *Interesting.*

"Assistant Ambassador Jacoben," Dillon announced. To Heldin's left was a tall, spare man with the look of an archer. Jacoben's hands were covered with small, healed scars, and as he straightened from his bow and his hair shifted over his forehead, Blaine glimpsed another scar near his hairline.

Either he has seen battle or being an ambassador is a very dangerous business where they come from, Blaine thought.

"Secretary to the Ambassador Iston." Short and wiry, Iston looked to Blaine as if he had more muscle than an ambassador's secretary should possess.

"And Undersecretary Vishal," Dillon said. Vishal was muscular and compact, with sharp features and dark, cold eyes.

Servants dressed in mended finery brought out hearty game meats and roasted root vegetables in succulent gravy as well as fresh greens and berries. Though not the endless number of courses for a true royal banquet, Dillon and his kitchen staff put on a good show worthy of the castle. They had even managed to secure a few bottles of wine.

"Our compliments to your staff, Your Lordship," Heldin said. "This is a most gracious meal, even more remarkable given our regrettably short notice."

"We're honored by your visit, Your Excellency." Blaine regarded the ambassador with the cool reserve Kestel had instructed him to project. If anything seemed amiss to his visitor, the stranger was self-possessed enough not to let it show.

"Your kingdom appears to be rebounding from the recent unpleasantness." Heldin had the aura of smooth civility Blaine remembered seeing in lifelong courtiers. Such skills were, he knew, a necessity to keep one's position—and perhaps one's head—in the political currents of court. *I'm badly out of practice with my court manners,* Blaine thought. *And I had very little practice to begin with.*

"Things are certainly on the mend," Kestel replied. "We've had scant news from abroad. Did the…unpleasantness… affect the Cross-Sea Kingdoms?"

A shadow crossed Heldin's face, but he recovered with a breath. "Regrettably, yes, m'lady. Fire fell from the sky, destroying much of the capital city and damaging the palace. King Ronfi and the crown prince died in the Devastation, as we refer to that awful night," Heldin said. "As did many, many people."

"As you can see, the Great Fire also touched Quillarth Castle," Blaine said. "King Merrill died that night, and Castle Reach burned."

"I'm curious, m'lord," Jacoben said. "Were there any other… more unusual…effects of the Devastation here in Donderath?"

Kestel gave him a puzzled look. "What kind of unusual effects?" she asked, utterly believable in her apparent confusion.

It was clear Jacoben did not want to speak openly. "Weather fluctuations, tidal changes, maybe even a disruption of magic?" he prompted.

"The weather is just now beginning to return to normal," Blaine replied. "We had some severe storms with very bad winds, high waves." He took another sip of wine. "But in the last few months, conditions are becoming more stable."

Heldin nodded. "We, too, have seen more severe weather since the Devastation. And as you've said, those changes appear to be tapering off." He weighed his next words carefully. "Did you observe any effect on your people?"

It was clear that Heldin was fishing for information without wanting to tip his hand. Blaine enjoyed watching Kestel handle the situation, putting her natural charisma and beauty to work for her as well as her seduction magic, which marriage and wartime gave her scant opportunity to use. "The weather was so extreme, I've heard that our poor farmers had some difficulty planting and harvesting their crops," Kestel replied. "Too much rain, turned cold too early, that sort of thing. And you?"

"Much the same, m'lady," Vishal replied. Heldin did not look at the undersecretary, but he shifted slightly in his seat, as if uncomfortable. "Our mages reported that the magic fluctuated much like the weather. I can't help wondering, did Donderath experience that as well?"

Interesting, Blaine thought. *Heldin is supposed to be in charge, but he actually seems scared of Vishal.*

"I wouldn't know about the mages," Kestel said with a beautiful smile. She shifted, showing the cleavage of her gown to its best advantage. It was a move guaranteed to ensure that she had their guests' full attention. "But some of the workers of small magic—healers, musicians, and all—had difficulty for a little while. Then it all came back again, as if it never left." She gave a shrug that further enhanced her allure. "So it's as it should be."

Blaine watched the faces of their guests as Kestel spoke. Heldin was paying close attention, though he seemed willing to permit Vishal to take the lead. Iston's attention was on everything except the conversation as his gaze roamed around the great room, or he examined Piran and Rikard closely, as if wondering about their purpose. He tried to make his interest in Blaine and Kestel appear casual, but Blaine bet Iston was mentally recording every detail. Jacoben was on edge. More than once, his gaze drifted to the doors, or up to the waning light that spilled through the long windows. Underneath it all, Blaine sensed a subtle, probing magic.

Vishal turned to Blaine. "We had heard that magic became inaccessible in Donderath, and came back again. Is that true?"

"Is that what happened in the Cross-Sea Kingdoms?" Blaine returned the question with a question. Maybe over the course of the rest of the evening their guests would prove themselves to be trustworthy, but so far, Blaine had a niggling sense that something was not quite right.

Iston looked uncomfortable, while Heldin chafed to take the lead once more in the conversation. Heldin slid a sidelong glance at Iston and cleared his throat. "My lord, we did not mean to appear to press you for information. But we have had no word at all from Donderath since the Devastation, where once our kingdoms shared strong trade. It has taken us this long to assemble a ship to see for ourselves what occurred here. So we are, understandably, eager for news."

Blaine sat back in his chair as the servants cleared the dishes for the first course. "The Great Fire caused a lot of damage, in Castle Reach and beyond. Any ships able to leave port that night fled filled with refugees bound for anywhere they could go. Surely some of those ships reached the Cross-Sea Kingdoms?"

Jacoben shook his head. "I regret to tell you, Lord McFadden, but they did not. Otherwise, we would have had a better idea of what had transpired here."

Kestel bumped Blaine's ankle under the table. He knew what her signal meant. *He's lying.*

"I'm sorry to hear that, Assistant Ambassador," Blaine replied. "We had held out hope that those Donderan subjects would be able to come home, now that all is well."

"And your people have been able to recover so quickly from such a disaster," Vishal remarked. "Remarkable."

Blaine fought to keep his expression neutral, disliking Vishal's tone, as if he were sizing up an object to be acquired. Piran, who had never claimed to have the tact for diplomacy, looked openly angry. Rikard was watching Iston closely. Blaine noted that Rikard had laid his right hand palm down on the table, and was absently tracing lines and circles on the table linens. Blaine's ability to sense magic told him that both Rikard and one of the newcomers were engaging in a subtle battle of magical wills.

"We did not make the journey from mere curiosity, Lord McFadden," Heldin said. "We came seeking trade. We can offer you grain and iron ore, as well as woolens. Those are just the goods we've brought with us. If we reach an agreement, any goods we produce in surplus may be agreed upon."

"We have herring and rubies," Blaine said, his voice utterly serious. Piran coughed and needed a drink from his goblet to recover. "Unfortunately, the war with Meroven and the Great Fire reduced our crop yield last year. We have enough for our people, and our next harvest promises to be very good, but we have no surplus to trade right now."

Listen to us posture and lie, trying not to admit weakness, Blaine thought. *Heldin seems to be a professional. I'm betting he's a real ambassador. The others are no more diplomats than Piran is, and probably only present as muscle. The question is, why are the 'ambassadors' really here?*

Conversation ceased with the second course. Blaine noticed that Rikard continued to trace figures on the tablecloth almost continually, and felt the tug and push of competing magics. *Wardings?* Blaine wondered. *Or some other kind of magic?*

Dillon's servers brought out baked herbed fish, caught fresh from the bay, as well as a stew of mussels and onions. As the food was served, Kestel turned her brilliant smile on Vishal. "So tell me, Undersecretary, who rules the Cross-Sea Kingdoms now?

Vishal looked as if he had swallowed a clam shell. That was obviously not a topic he wanted to pursue. "With the king and the prince dead, the crown passed to Edelton, the king's brother," he replied.

"Edelton Turnfoot?" Kestel asked, and Iston choked. "Don't I recall some hint of controversy about the prince's... deformity?"

Jacoben could not have looked sourer if his wine had gone bad. "We do not speak of such things these days, m'lady," he said. "Out of respect."

He means, out of fear, Blaine decided, noting the nervous glance Iston shot toward Heldin.

"You know, I met King Ronfi and Edelton Turnfoot... I mean, Prince Edelton... once at King Merrill's court," Kestel continued as if she were just chatting with an acquaintance. "The king seemed nice, and he and King Merrill shared quite a few jokes on that occasion." She took a drink of wine, intentionally appearing to drink more than she actually swallowed. "The prince, on the other hand, was... shall we say, less than a gentleman."

Her eyes widened as she leaned forward, once again using her bosom to intentional effect. "He made indecent proposals to Lord Correnders daughter, and ordered a groomsman whipped for not feeding his horse from a silver platter!"

"M'lady," Heldin said beseechingly. "We are your guests, and representatives of the king. I beg of you, do not place us in an uncomfortable position."

Seems like Vishal and the new king don't have much of a sense of humor, Blaine thought. *And if Edelton was passed over for the crown and got it by default, he's probably got some old grudges to settle.*

Vishal picked at the fish on his plate. "The circumstances

have required changes for all of us," he said. "I was acquainted with your father, Lord McFadden. Before his untimely death." He did not look up, but the barb was unmistakable. "And now, after time in the north, here you are, the king-emergent." His smile was patently false, and it did not reach his eyes. "Quite a tale there, I would guess."

"A very bloody one," Piran said. Everyone turned to look at him. Piran had leaned back in his chair, with a deceptively casual attitude Blaine knew meant Piran was ready for a fight.

"Last year, there was a very powerful mage and three warlords who wanted a piece of Donderath," Piran said, recounting his story as if it were nothing of consequence. "They're all dead now. Lord McFadden's allies are strong and their armies victorious. It has been a very good year." Piran fixed Vishal with a smile that was the equivalent of a thrown gauntlet. Heldin looked alarmed. Iston seemed distracted, as if he had heard none of the exchange. Jacoben glanced from Heldin to Vishal as he was looking for a cue on how to react.

"You know, usually I tell people that Piran exaggerates," Kestel said with a big smile as the servants cleared the plates once more. "But not this time. Actually, I'd say he has been modest, especially about his part in it all."

Kestel fixed Vishal with a look that the undersecretary would have been a fool to misinterpret. "Piran had earned himself quite a reputation with King Merrill's army before the Great Fire. So had Niklas Theilsson, Lord McFadden's other general. Add an alliance with the most powerful *talishte* in the kingdom and the mercenary Traher Voss and it creates an unstoppable force." As pleasant as her tone was, the warning was clear. From Vishal's reaction, at least a few of the names were known to him.

"We're quite interested in reestablishing trade with the

Cross-Sea Kingdoms," Blaine said, hoping to lessen the tension. "Tell me, are your people trading in coin these days, or barter?"

"Coin is never refused," Heldin said. "But we are open to barter, if the items are of use to us." Once again, Blaine's impression was that Heldin was the most honest of the bunch. Whatever hold over him Vishal had, it was clear that the 'undersecretary' held the real power. The two appeared to have conflicting agendas, with Vishal seeking information and a potential weakness to exploit, while Heldin had a genuine interest in acquiring goods needed in his kingdom.

"I'm curious," Blaine said as the servants brought the next course. "What have you heard from Vellanaj and Tarrant in the Lesser Kingdoms?"

Rikard reached for his wineglass, and Blaine noticed that the mage fluttered his fingers oddly as they closed around the stem. Blaine could sense the push and pull of probing magics, advancing and retreating in a silent test of wills. Iston regarded Rikard with a thinly veiled glare. The warring magic continued, the invisible equivalent of Rikard tugging the power one way and Iston pulling it back in his direction.

"The destruction there was nearly complete," Heldin replied, earning himself a pointed glance from Vishal. "There's nothing to be gained by hiding it," he chided his companion. "It's the truth. The waterfront was still a row of burned-out buildings. It looked deserted, except for some wretched stragglers," he said. "We didn't try to land. There appeared to be no point."

Blaine nodded, appreciating the candor. "We've had some problems with raiders from the Western Plains," he replied, reciprocating the truthfulness. "We've struck a solid alliance with them, and the Plainsmen are now part of Donderath's fighting force."

"What do you know about pirates?" Kestel asked, as if the idea had just popped into her head. Jacoben's gaze slid to the side. Iston's expression went blank, and Heldin looked as if he would have liked to be elsewhere. Only Vishal met her gaze, unfazed.

"I'm not sure I take your meaning, m'lady," Vishal replied. "We encountered no problems on our journey to Donderath."

"That's certainly good to hear," Kestel replied with a smile. "I was wondering if you'd had a problem back home, with pirates attacking your coast."

"Has that been an issue here?" Jacoben asked.

"Desperate times tend to embolden thieves of all sort," Blaine replied. "There have been a few incidents, quickly put down. We were just wondering if the same sort of thing was happening to your kingdom."

Dillon's servers brought out the third and fourth courses, a hot clear broth with vegetables and roasted game hens. Blaine was sure the eight chickens now on the serving platter had been running around the palace grounds earlier that day. The hens were stuffed with diced apples and dried fruits in a bread mixture, a sumptuous presentation of otherwise modest ingredients. Once again, he made a mental note to commend Dillon on his ingenuity.

"King Edelton has very little patience for miscreants," Heldin replied. "His measures are sterner than those of the late king, whom Edelton has said was too generous in his clemency."

Translation: Edelton is heavy-handed, maybe despotic, and no one had better get out of line, Blaine thought.

"What of Edgeland?" Vishal asked as if he had not been paying particular attention. "Donderath had a prison and a colony in the far north. What's become of them since the Great Fire? I assume you have connections there still." Another barb, and a reminder that the 'diplomats' knew of Blaine's convict past. *Do they also know about Kestel's reputation as a spy and assassin, and Piran's somewhat legendary military exploits?* Blaine wondered.

"Velant no longer functions as a prison," Blaine replied, declining to add how he knew. "It closed right after the Great Fire. Edgeland is still a colony of Donderath, and Donderath still lays claim to Edgeland and its waters." *Let's just put that out there on the table,* Blaine thought. *Because I'm sure it's what Vishal is really asking.*

"I might have assumed the former convicts would have relished a chance to come home," Heldin said. "Since King Merrill is dead."

"They didn't want to come back," Piran replied with the same calculated offhandedness. "Some people just like the cold." He shrugged. "Actually, without Velant, Edgeland isn't so bad. The colonists have made their peace with it, and the colony is self-sufficient. And very Donderan," he added pointedly.

"Do you expect to restore trade with Edgeland?" Jacoben asked. "I wouldn't think rubies have the same demand as they did when there was a nobility and a court."

Fishing for information again, Blaine thought. "We promised the colonists that we would protect them and do everything we could to help them. Those are our friends up there. I mean to make good on that promise, and I take a personal interest in their welfare." He met Vishal's gaze directly, making his point clear.

"We might be interested in establishing a trade route to Edgeland, when everything is more settled," Heldin said. "With the permission of the Donderan government, of course," he added. "As my colleague noted, rubies are not as highly regarded these days as herring might be, since the Devastation affected our fishing waters."

Hmm, Blaine thought. *That's one effect I hadn't heard about causing a problem for our folks. I'll have to make sure Folville asks the fishermen what they're finding.* "That's certainly a possibility," he replied. "And Edgeland is always interested in trade when it involves tools, seed, food that will keep, livestock— that sort of thing. We'll be sending more ships of our own in that direction once the surplus is available."

They had finished their course, and Dillon cleared his throat at an appropriate lull in the conversation. "There is hot *fet* and desserts in the parlor," he announced, "as well as brandy. This way, please."

Blaine gave Kestel his arm and they led the way, with Piran and Rikard behind them. The four diplomats filed after them, Heldin in the lead, and Iston brought up the rear, followed by two more of Blaine's guards. Blaine recognized mages Nemus and Leiv among the servants. Blaine led them into the castle parlor, a room where King Merrill would have hosted smaller gatherings, where the scale was less grand and more intimate.

A small fire burned in the fireplace to take away the chill. Quillarth Castle always seemed cold, as did Glenreith, thanks to the thick stone walls and drafty windows. Dillon and his staff must have gathered all of the best remaining furniture for the parlor, along with paintings, vases, and small statues. Carpets graced the floor, with only a few scorch marks to attest to what they had survived. The two guards remained outside as the doors to the parlor closed.

"You're fortunate that so many of your treasures survived your Great Fire," Heldin said, looking around at the well-appointed room. "Our main palace was almost completely destroyed."

A table of desserts was laid out for them, and once again, Dillon had risen above constraints to provide a spread that looked more lavish than its humble components. Tarts made from the last of the winter apples and dried currants sat next to a warm bread pudding, brandied pears, and syllabub. A decanter of brandy with goblets was set out on a side table, and pots of *fet* and hot wassail steamed on the hearth.

"Our compliments to your cook," Jacoben said, eyeing the treats. "Your hospitality has made it possible to almost forget that the entire unpleasantness ever occurred."

On rare occasions, Blaine was able to indulge a moment's fantasy like that, a fleeting self-delusion that all was as it should be, as it had been. Those momentary fantasies were bittersweet, cherished nonetheless. Jacoben's comment, together with the hunger in his eyes, once again made Blaine wonder whether the Cataclysm had fallen even harder on the Cross-Sea Kingdoms than on Donderath.

The desserts were as delicious as they looked, and when everyone had eaten their fill and had a glass of brandy or a cup of wassail or *fet*, Blaine led them to the couches near the banked fire. The velvet and brocade upholstered furniture was worn but still serviceable, giving the room the feel of inherited heirlooms rather than scavenged finery.

"I'm not sure whether such things drew your attention in the old days," Heldin said, "but the Cross-Sea Kingdoms had an embassy in Castle Reach for many, many years under King Merrill and his forbears. Regrettably, there has been no communication from our embassy since the Great Fire, and as we confirmed when our ship landed, the building was destroyed, the ambassadors presumed dead."

Heldin leaned forward. "With your permission, we would like to reestablish an embassy in Castle Reach," he said, meeting Blaine's gaze. "It would be a first step toward reopening trade. We might even be able to assist with the supply of specialized tradesmen and artisans as Donderath rebuilds, should you find some skills to be in short supply."

Blaine weighed the request carefully. On one hand, it was inevitable that the nearby kingdoms would want to open their embassies once more, if for no other purpose than to serve as a haven for their spies. Trade, when there was surplus to spare, would go a long way toward improving Donderath's lot, and there were nonessentials that nearly everyone in Donderath enjoyed that had become unavailable since the Cataclysm, luxuries that would be pleasant to have once more.

Yet Castle Reach was far from safe or even fully secure. Despite Folville's support, Blaine's army was stretched thin. And though Niklas and Folville had been developing their network of informants, Kestel had told him that it was still much less useful than the spies King Merrill had in his heyday. Which meant there were an insufficient number of observers to make certain that the ambassadors were not causing trouble.

"I appreciate your offer," Blaine said. "But we're not recovered to the point where I could assure the safety of your diplomats," he said. "I wouldn't want us to reopen relations, only to see them harmed by an unfortunate incident."

"May I be frank?" Heldin said. Blaine nodded. "King Edelton is not a patient man. We came at his behest, with the intent that we reopen diplomatic ties and that one Cross-Sea Kingdoms ambassador and his staff—that's me—would remain here in an official capacity."

"And you hesitate to return without accomplishing your mission?" Kestel asked. Heldin looked uncomfortable, but nodded.

"The new king does not tolerate failure," Heldin replied. "I fear that, if we were to return under those conditions, our careers would be at an end."

Careers? Blaine thought. *Or lives?*

Jacoben watched closely to see how Blaine would respond. Vishal's attention was on Heldin, his brows slightly furrowed as if he was not entirely happy with the direction of the conversation. Iston seemed to be daydreaming, with a faraway look in his eyes. Rikard also had a slightly unfocused glaze. Blaine's sense that magic was in play grew stronger.

I'd bet money that Rikard and Iston are having some kind of subtle duel. What's at stake? Is Iston trying to influence me? Plant intentions? Rummage through my thoughts? The deflection amulet was probably causing Iston heartburn, if he meant to use magic to sway Blaine. As if she was on the same line of thinking, Kestel rose to pour herself another cup of wassail and returned to sit near Iston with a smile.

"I see your cup is empty," she said in her best hostess manner. "May I get more for you?"

Iston came out of his daydream with a jolt, and Blaine wondered if Kestel's null-magic charm had interrupted Iston with unpleasant suddenness. Rikard's lips turned up in a slight smile, as if he had won a point. "No thank you, m'lady," Iston managed, somewhat distractedly. "I'm fine." Satisfied, Rikard crossed his arms and leaned back. Kestel remained where she was, sipping her wassail and returning her attention to the conversation.

"We wouldn't be expecting an impressive building," Heldin added. "Anything with a good roof will do. It just needs to be habitable, or nearly so. We understand how things have been. This would be a beginning, a place to start. As conditions improve, quarters can always be upgraded."

"And we are empowered to open trade immediately," Vishal said. "As a gesture of goodwill, we've brought several crates of goods to offer, as well as the gifts your steward was kind enough to present for us." He nodded toward a table on the other side of the parlor, where several unusual items sat on display.

"If we may, perhaps now is a good time to offer the goodwill tokens we have brought," Jacoben supplied.

Blaine and Kestel hung back, letting Rikard move ahead of them. Blaine doubted that the gifts were set apart like they were by accident. Dillon had seen the dangers of magical objects firsthand; he was unlikely to take chances. Blaine resisted a smile when he noticed a thin line of salt that encircled the sitting area but did not include the table of gifts, protecting those within the circle. His own heightened abilities warned him that the items had been touched by dangerous magic.

"How beautiful," Kestel said, making sure to stand well inside the salt circle. Four items sat on the table. A lacquered and lavishly decorated small chest was the kind of piece often seen in royal homes before the Cataclysm, done in a style of art Blaine recognized as being unique to the Cross-Sea Kingdoms. Next to it was a silver vase of excellent craftsmanship, and beside that was a delicate lace tablecloth. The fourth gift was a large sapphire in a silver necklace setting. All of the gifts were of enormous value, and each represented items for which the Cross-Sea Kingdoms were renowned. Despite the beauty of the offerings, none of Blaine's party made a move toward the table.

"M'lord McFadden," Heldin said. "I would like to present each of you with the gift especially chosen for you." He moved toward the table, but Rikard blocked his path.

"I'm afraid I can't allow that," Rikard said with a polite but firm smile. The other two mages disguised as servants moved up to stand beside him.

Heldin bristled. "And why not?" he demanded.

Rikard was unruffled by the ambassador's indignation. "At

least one—maybe more—of the items has been tainted by dark magic. It would be unsafe to handle them."

"Now see here," Jacoben retorted. "We carried those items personally. They've never been out of our sight. It's not possible for someone to have tampered with them without our knowing it."

Rikard ignored Jacoben and looked directly at Iston. "Unless one of your people did the tampering, with or without your knowledge," he said evenly.

"Lord McFadden, I must protest!" Vishal said angrily. "This is an affront to the ambassador and to the Cross-Sea Kingdoms."

Rikard took the bluster in stride. "I don't think you're surprised," he replied. "Since throughout dinner and afterward, I've had to counterspell the magical attacks by your mage," he said, pointedly looking at Iston.

Vishal had been standing slightly behind Kestel. He had a piece of thin cord pulled tight around her throat before Blaine or Piran could move toward him. Iston lobbed a strike of pure blue-white energy that crackled like fire from his outstretched hand, aimed for Rikard's chest. Jacoben faced Blaine and Piran with a wicked-looking knife that had appeared in his hand. Heldin bleated out a choked cry and dropped to the floor, covering his head with his hands.

"We tried to do this peacefully, but you leave us no choice," Vishal said. "The Cross-Sea Kingdoms intends to lay claim to these lands, and we'll do it with or without your assistance."

Everything happened at once.

Kestel drove her elbow back into Vishal's gut as she brought her hard-soled shoe down with force on his instep. At the same time, she grabbed his wrist with one hand and used momentum to simultaneously pull his hand free of her throat while throwing him over her back as she suddenly bent over and leaned forward. Vishal went rolling onto the floor, only to find Kestel astride him with a knife against his windpipe, drawing a thin line of blood.

Rikard countered the energy strike with something that looked like the ripples in a pool, hanging in midair. The rippled air absorbed the strike, then vanished as Rikard made a grasping motion with his upturned palm, violently closing his fingers into a fist. Iston grabbed for his groin with a cry of pain as his knees buckled and he fell to the floor. Rikard brought both hands together as if around an invisible neck, and Iston gasped for air, his eyes wide, and stopped struggling.

Jacoben lunged at Blaine. Blaine blocked with his own knife, drawn from inside his frock coat, and Piran dove forward, sinking his blade deep into Jacoben's chest. The assistant ambassador's mouth opened and closed mutely as he sank to his knees, clutching his chest, and fell forward.

"I had nothing to do with it, I swear!" Heldin yelped from where he was curled into a ball on the floor. "This was all Vishal's doing! Please don't kill me!"

"Guards!" Blaine shouted, and the doors swung open as four soldiers ran into the room, quickly followed by several more dressed as serving staff.

"They attacked," Blaine said. "One of them's dead. That one is a mage," he said, pointing at Iston.

"I'll handle him," Rikard said, walking over to the moaning man and making a gesture over his head. Iston suddenly went limp and his eyes rolled back in his head. "He won't wake up until I wake him," Rikard said. "Still, a good idea to bind him, strip him, sprinkle him with salt, and gag him."

"Do it," Blaine ordered as two guards stepped up warily to take Iston away.

"I'd better go with them," Rikard said. "Just in case. I've put a warding over the tainted gifts, and I'll send a couple of my mages back to collect them. In the meantime, Nemus and Leiv will stand watch over them. Don't touch them, and you should be fine." Blaine nodded his assent.

"I guess you'll want me to wait before I kill him," Kestel said pleasantly, still pinning Vishal to the floor with her knife against his throat. The cord Vishal had tried to use to strangle Kestel hung loose around her neck.

"I'd like to interrogate him first," Blaine said. "Then we can decide how he dies."

Kestel gave an exaggerated sigh. "Very well," she said, moving out of the way as two more guards came up to bind Vishal and drag him to his feet. "But if I've got a bruise on my throat, I'll be most put out."

"What about him?" Piran asked, pointing to where Heldin remained kneeling with his face against the floor, hands clasped behind his neck.

"Please don't kill me! I didn't want to do it. They made me do it," Heldin begged.

"Search him for weapons, tie him up, and sit him down on the couch," Blaine said to Piran. "And we'll start our conversation over."

Guards removed Jacoben's body as servants brought rags to mop up the blood. "Sorry about the carpet," Piran muttered. One guard carried Iston's limp form while two more dragged Vishal to his feet. The undersecretary fought them, his eyes murderous.

"There will be consequences for this," Vishal threatened. "We would have made a deal with you. Now, we'll destroy you."

"Get in line, mate," Piran snapped. "You're not the only one who wants to fight us for the kingdom. You're not even the scariest one."

When their three attackers, the guards, and Rikard were gone, two soldiers shut the door but remained inside, along with the mages. Blaine and the others returned to their remaining prisoner. Piran poured himself a drink of brandy and offered one to the others. Kestel accepted; Blaine declined.

"Now," Blaine said, sitting down on the couch opposite Heldin. "Let's have the real story about who you are and why you're here."

Heldin looked terrified, but he took a couple of deep breaths and color came back to his face. "My name is Aton Heldin, and I am—was—a real ambassador," he said, his voice a bit breathier and higher pitched than before. "I survived the Devastation because I happened to be on a hunting trip out in the forest when the fire fell. When I returned, the palace, the nobles' manors, and the ambassadors' offices had been destroyed—as well as most of the city. The king was dead, and after some battles between a few of the king's heirs, Edelton Turnfoot won the crown," Heldin continued. "He is a brute," he added. "There was good reason he was passed over in the succession. The man is a monster, but he's good at taking what he wants. His supporters seized the castle and there's no one strong enough to challenge him."

"Why are you here?" Blaine asked, meeting his gaze.

"The Cross-Sea Kingdoms are on the brink of collapse," Heldin replied. "Famine. Terrible storms. A *talishte* uprising that slaughtered hundreds. So many are dead from the Devastation and the famine that crops aren't getting planted. What didn't burn has been sacked and looted. It's coming apart at the seams."

Heldin paused. "We were also at war with Meroven, before the Devastation," he continued. "There has been bad blood between our kingdoms for a long time, and while we fought over different issues than what drove Donderath's conflict with Meroven, in the end, the outcome was the same. The Devastation just finished off a long, debilitating war that drained our coffers and siphoned off our young men. The truth is, due to the war and King Ronfi's penchant for spending, the kingdom was already nearly bankrupt before the Devastation. We have had to deal with reduced circumstances for some time now," Heldin admitted.

More of Thrane's meddling? Blaine wondered. *Especially if there was a* talishte *uprising involved there as well. Perhaps we've underestimated Thrane's ambitions.*

"Edelton sent us out to see if the Lesser Kingdoms and Donderath were better off," Heldin finished.

"So you could steal what we had?" Piran accused.

Heldin nodded. "Sorry to say, but yes," he said. "Edelton forced me to come. Threatened to kill me if I didn't cooperate. I was supposed to be the respectable one to put a good face on everything. Vishal was there to keep me in line."

"Vishal wasn't a novice at this kind of thing, was he?" Kestel said, glowering as she rubbed her throat with one hand.

Heldin shook his head. "Before the war, Vishal was head of the king's secret police. He wasn't a man to cross. Nasty temper, seemed to actually enjoy killing people." He winced when he looked at the growing bruise on Kestel's neck. "My apologies, m'lady. It did my heart good to see you give it back to him." Kestel's reply was a satisfied smile.

"What was Iston doing, the magic Rikard blocked?" Blaine asked.

Heldin looked abashed. "That was Vishal's way, using mages

to manipulate people or force them to do his bidding. Iston was one of his men, from the secret police. He was likely trying to use his magic to plant suggestions in your minds, make you want to agree to our terms, tell us what we wanted to know." He sighed. "He's good at that kind of thing, very dangerous."

Once again, Blaine was glad for the deflection amulet he wore, and Kestel's null-magic amulet. "And Jacoben?" he pressed.

"Jacoben was the younger son of a noble who went to sea with the navy and ended up with pirates," Heldin admitted, a flush coming to his cheeks as if he were utterly embarrassed by the company in which he found himself. "He was here at the behest of the ship's captain, to find out Donderath's weaknesses."

"So you're part of the pirate attack," Kestel guessed.

Heldin nodded. "Yes, m'lady. Reluctantly on my part, but true. We were sent to steal first and then show up as ambassadors and offer to protect you from those pirates. We really expected to find anarchy, so it surprised us when you fought off our first ships."

"First ships?" Kestel repeated with alarm, exchanging a glance with Blaine.

Heldin sighed. "Aye, m'lady. We came ashore to find out whether the opposition we met with the first raid was just lucky, or whether there was a larger force behind them. There are more ships, awaiting a signal from Jacoben and Iston. If we made the signal at the appointed time, they would hold off and allow us room to maneuver. But if we missed the signal, they would know something went wrong, and attack." He looked up at Blaine and met his gaze. "We've missed our signal time. The ships will be closing on your port very soon."

"Can you countermand them?" Blaine asked.

Heldin shook his head. "No. Jacoben was the only one with

the code, though he needed Iston's magic to send it. They never really trusted me. I'm really just along for show." He took a deep breath, and continued.

"I will cooperate fully with anything you want, tell you answers to whatever you ask," Heldin said. "Just please, give me asylum. I hate King Edelton. I'm not a brave man, but I'll do anything I can to bring him down, or at least, thwart his plans to hurt Donderath."

"How about those gifts," Piran said with a jerk of his head toward the warded table.

Heldin sighed. "They were all tainted, one way or the other. The lacquer box contains a *dubav*, an evil spirit that will do the bidding of a powerful mage. Iston's used them before to harry an enemy."

"Like a *divi*?" Kestel asked, remembering what it had taken to destroy Vigus Quintrel and the entity that had possessed him.

Heldin's eyes widened. "You know of such things?" He paled. "A *dubav* is nothing to trifle with, but it's a troublesome spirit, not a killer."

"And the other 'gifts'?" Piran asked.

"The lace was woven with magic spells worked into the warp and woof. I don't know what the particular spells were for that piece, but it would be like Vishal to sow discord, bring ill health, that sort of thing."

"The vase?" Blaine questioned.

"Most likely a piece that would let the giver listen to what was said nearby, through magic," Heldin said. "Such items are very common in the Cross-Sea Kingdoms. It's how King Edelton and his spies know everything that goes on."

"And I'm guessing the gem is cursed?" Kestel said, peering at the items while making sure to stay well back of the wardings.

"Yes, m'lady. Another of Iston's specialties. I don't know what the curse would do, but he usually prefers something subtle, like causing terrible headaches, or making the wearer discontent with everything."

"Lovely," Kestel said sarcastically. "The more you tell us, the less inclined I am to allow the Cross-Sea Kingdoms anywhere near Donderath."

"What about the pirates?" Blaine asked. "There's already been an attack on Castle Reach. What now?"

Heldin looked contrite. "I am so sorry. But it's already too late. We were sent to either bring you—the leaders—under our control or kill you. Without Jacobsen's signal, the other ships will arrive to do battle. In the end, it would be the same— warships coming to conquer—just a matter of timing. Five warships, armed with mages and catapults, each with an army in its hold." He shook his head. "You can't win."

Blaine's eyes narrowed. "Watch us." He exchanged a glance with Kestel, and then looked back to Heldin. "You know you can't go back," he said. "And from what you've told us, there's not much for you to miss. Help us defeat the invaders, prove that you've renounced King Edelton, and you can earn your freedom."

Heldin lifted his head. "I supplied information. I did not join in the fight against you. That should count for something."

"You were willing for your companions to curse us or kill us," Blaine countered. "I could argue you changed sides to save your life. If you want sanctuary here, perhaps even a role as an ambassador again, then you need to throw in your lot with us wholeheartedly. Burn your bridges to them, and you're welcome here."

Kestel smiled brightly. "Cross us, and you're just another spy to execute," she added.

Heldin swallowed hard. "I understand," he replied. "And I cannot go back, so I must make my way here. I will give you all the information I have about the ships and their weapons. But I know very little. Vishal is the one who knows the details, and he will never betray the king." He looked defeated. "I know this about Vishal," he continued. "There is a geas on him. If magic is used to read his mind, the geas will rip his mind to shreds."

Blaine nodded. "I'll let Rikard know." His mouth was a hard line. "Let's see if his geas can protect him against a *talishte*."

Before Heldin could respond, the doors to the parlor opened. "My lord," Dillon said. "Word from Captain Folville. Enemy ships have been spotted."

"Is Voss involved?" Blaine asked.

"Folville said that Voss's first squad was in position, and word was sent for reinforcements," Dillon reported.

"Good," Blaine said. He looked to Dillon. "Lock the ambassador in a room with barred windows. Keep a guard in the room so he can't signal the ships. If he causes any problems, have one of the *talishte* glamour him. Other than that, make him as comfortable as an honored guest."

"Yes, sir," Dillon replied.

He turned to Heldin. "If you've got any other insights, anything at all that might help us win, this is where you start to prove your change of allegiance."

"I understand," Heldin said.

Blaine passed along the warning for Rikard about Vishal to Dillon. "He'll need to be *talishte*-read," Blaine said. "He won't cooperate willingly, and we can't take what he knows by magic. Iston likely has the same geas. Do the same for him as well."

"And when they have been read?"

Blaine met Dillon's gaze. "Heldin says he has changed sides.

I believe him, but we'll have one of the *talishte* read him just to be sure. Hang the others. They can't be trusted. We don't have the food to waste on prisoners, and it's likely more merciful than what they'd get from their own king."

"As you wish, m'lord," Dillon replied. "Pity we didn't find out before we wasted good provisions on them."

"Think of it as a last meal," Piran said, his anger clear in his voice. "And now, it's time to teach those lads in the ships how to swim."

CHAPTER
TWENTY-FIVE

——————

"I HADN'T PLANNED ON BATTLE," BLAINE MUT-
tered as he fastened his cuirass and buckled on his sword. In
the time that had passed since the unfortunate ambassador and
his party had been hauled off for questioning, Quillarth Castle
had armed itself for war. Guards shucked off the costume of
servants and dressed for the fight. Pikes, crossbows, battle-axes,
and swords appeared, and the lower levels of the castle were
barricaded against attack.

"It seemed too easy to just have dinner with a couple of
ambassadors," Kestel replied. She had changed from her gown
into tunic and trews with a cuirass of her own, along with vambraces and a sword, as well as a wicked knife and a collection of
small dirks in a bandolier she wore like a sash across her chest.

"Actually, after what Vishal pulled, I'm in the mood to
knock some heads together," Piran said, suiting up in similar
attire and strapping on an impressive collection of weapons.
"Pity Rikard won't be joining us."

"With luck, he should find any other traps they laid and dispose of any cursed items. And thanks to the *talishte*, we got

some useful information out of the prisoners, so we're as prepared as we can be," Blaine replied.

In the distance, Blaine could hear the muted *thud* of catapults as the ships in the harbor lobbed ballast rocks at the wharf and dockside, and the men in the shoreline fortifications answered with missiles of their own.

"Part of Front Street is burning," Kestel reported from where she watched from the window. "But so is one of the ships." Her voice was sad, filled with the same weariness of war Blaine felt in his marrow.

"Before we go rushing down to Castle Reach, I'd like to get a bird's-eye view," Piran said. "Folville's at street level, and so is Voss. We might spot a weakness from up here that they can't."

"The tallest towers were destroyed in the Great Fire," Kestel said. "But if we can get up into what's left of the third floor, we're high enough up to see a long way."

"Get Dillon," Blaine said to the soldier by the door. "We need him. Fast."

A few moments later, Dillon appeared in the doorway. "M'lord?"

"You know the safest routes through the damaged parts of the castle," Blaine said. "We need to get to the highest vantage point so we can see what's going on in the harbor."

"All right," Dillon said. "Follow me." He took a lantern and led them down a hallway, then through corridors that smelled of dust and disuse. Since so much of Quillarth Castle had been destroyed in the Cataclysm, Blaine sometimes forgot just how large the building had been in its prime. Since then, Dillon and others had labored to restore what remained of the castle to usability, and Niklas's troops had worked to rebuild the castle's defenses. Yet now, heading down a dark, abandoned corridor still bearing the scorch marks of the

Great Fire, Blaine was reminded pointedly of how much had been lost.

Dillon stopped at a locked door. "It gets dangerous beyond this point," he said, going through a ring of keys on his belt. "That's why we keep the doors to this section locked. At least here, there's a solid floor remaining. Other places, the doors just open into thin air."

He jangled the keys, found the one he wanted, and turned it in the iron lock. "Watch your step," he cautioned. "There's still a lot of rubble, the walls have been damaged, and there are some pretty big holes in the outer walls where you could fall through to the courtyard."

Dillon shouldered the door open and lifted his lantern. Up ahead in the darkness, Blaine heard rats squeaking. As he and the others stepped through the doorway, Blaine understood Dillon's warning. Chunks of stone and plaster littered the corridor. Great sooty streaks marked the stonework, and some of the walls leaned dangerously. Portions of the ceiling were missing. In some places, the holes overhead exposed rooms in the floor above, but in other areas, the gaps opened up to the night sky.

"This way," Dillon said, gesturing for them to follow. He picked his way over the fallen stone with the surefootedness of a mountain goat as Blaine and the others did their best to keep up.

After a few more turns, they came to what had once been a corner room. Most of the walls remained, except for the corner itself, which had been smashed away. Dillon ventured through the rubble until he got to about three feet from where the walls and floor dropped off to nothing.

"I wouldn't go closer to the edge than this, m'lord," he advised. "This old building's been through a lot, and the damage in this wing was pretty bad, as you see. I don't trust the edge not to give way or to drop something on your head from up above."

"I don't think we'll have to go any closer," Blaine said. "This does the job."

Spread out below them was the city of Castle Reach and the harbor. Torches illuminated the towers on either side and dotted the water's edge to the wharfs, where the torches became a solid line.

The sound of battle reached them, even at this distance. Shouts and screams, the shrieks of women, the thunder of rocks hurled against stone walls. Five foreign ships sat at the entrance to the harbor, giving the royal city a thorough pounding. Two of the ships faced the wharf, their catapults trained on the quayside, bringing down the front walls of the nearest buildings and making it dangerous for Folville's troops to mass along the waterfront.

Three more of the ships faced the embankments on either side of the harbor, answering catapult volleys with deadly fire. One of those ships was partly afire. Both sides would be using archers, Blaine knew, though they were too far away to see them or to hear the *zing* of arrows. Small boats maneuvered around the warships, attempts by the invaders to land their own soldiers, and by the city's defenders to attack the ships at the waterline.

"If those ships get to the seawall, we don't have the men on the ground to defeat them," Blaine said. "Not if they have as many troops as Heldin said they did."

"He could be lying," Piran said. "He's lied about everything else."

"I'm sure they brought some level of troops, and he couldn't lie to the *talishte*—but he could have been misinformed," Kestel said. "Even if Heldin has the total wrong, it won't take a huge force to overrun the city, and Voss can't get reinforcements into place that quickly. Folville's fighters are a relatively small group, and Captain Larson's garrison is less than fifty men. It would be a slaughter."

"Donderath's navy is at the bottom of the sea," Blaine said, looking at the harbor in frustration. "I wouldn't put it past Folville or Voss to have small boats going out in the dark to strike at the waterline, but it's a suicide mission."

"You can bet both sides have mages as well," Piran muttered. "The catapults and archers have a limited reach. If the ships' catapults manage to cripple ours, there's no way to keep them from sailing right into the harbor."

"Actually, there is."

Everyone turned to look at Dillon. "It's something King Merrill built not long before the Great Fire," Dillon said. "We were fortunate enough not to need it, and most people have likely forgotten about it, since it was never used."

"What kind of defense?" Blaine asked.

Dillon swallowed hard, as if his throat had gone dry. *Poor guy was an Exchequer's assistant,* Blaine thought. *Now he's the castle seneschal with a dungeon full of spies and a bay full of pirates. No wonder he looks like he would like to be anywhere but here.* Yet despite everything, Dillon's expression showed his resolve.

"It's a giant chain, m'lord, a boom," Dillon said. "And a net of metal cords. Goes from one side of the harbor to the other, and when it's not needed, it lies at the bottom, below the depth of the keels. King Merrill's engineers designed the chain and net to be raised by a capstan set into the castle side of the harbor."

"Where's the capstan?" Piran asked, peering out at the battle in the harbor below.

"Along the harbor cliffs, there's a plain-looking stone building," Dillon explained. "I probably shouldn't even know it's there, but I handled the payment to the builders and the blacksmiths who forged the chains. Went down to inspect it myself, since it's bad business to pay without verifying that the work's done right."

"So you've seen it?" Kestel pressed. "You know it actually exists?"

Dillon nodded. "But I only visited the once, to make certain construction was complete."

"Do you know if it works?" Blaine asked. "You said it was never used, but did they at least test it?"

Again, Dillon bobbed his head. "I made them raise it, so I could see for myself," he replied. "It took four men—the capstan is quite large, and the chain and net are understandably heavy. It's not a fast process, but the mechanism worked well." He paused. "I haven't been down there since the Great Fire. The stone building is above the high-water mark on the cliffs, but sheltered enough that it might have escaped the Cataclysm. As for the chain and the net, there's no telling whether they've rusted solid after all this time. But if you could get it to work—"

"We could trap the ships where the catapults and archers can do their worst, and force them to use small boats if they try to land their soldiers," Blaine finished, feeling a surge of hope.

"Don't you think Folville would have used this mechanical marvel, if it still existed?" Piran asked.

Dillon shook his head. "The project was kept very quiet," he replied. "Most of the harbor work was done at night, with ships blocking the view from the wharf. I was told to say nothing about it, other than to Seneschal Lynge and the men directly involved," he added. "King Merrill felt the defense would be most effective if it was not anticipated, and he didn't want the spies at court to send word to their home kingdoms."

"Can you get us there?" Blaine asked. "If we could take a couple of guards with us and we could raise the chain and net, then Folville and Voss can pound the stuffing out of the enemy ships, and burn them to the waterline."

Dillon looked scared to death, but he raised his chin and met Blaine's gaze. "I can lead you down there, and I've got the key to get you in." Dillon had no desire to go looking for adventure, but Blaine knew from experience that the man would finish a task once he was resolved to do it.

"The sooner we can get down there, the sooner we might be able to turn this fight," Blaine said. "Let's go."

Soldiers opened the huge gates of Quillarth Castle's walls for the small group to ride through, and closed the gates behind them with a resounding *thud*. Smoke hung in the air from the burning ship and buildings, from the torches and the flaming missiles hurled by harborside and ship-based catapult crews. Four soldiers accompanied them, as well as Dillon, who rode in the front, leading the way.

Their hoofbeats clattered in the night as they rode as fast as they dared down the empty streets. Between the late hour and the danger of invasion, anyone still awake was wisely indoors. Dillon led them to the outskirts of the city, then stopped near the edge of the cliffs.

"We can't take the horses down the path," Dillon said, dismounting. "We need to tether them here and go the rest of the way on foot."

They were several hundred feet closer to the wharves than the catapult towers, but even so, the sound of large war machines' constant bombardment was like rolling thunder, echoing from the cliffs. One of the enemy ships was fully ablaze, and between its fire and the moonlight, there was enough light to pick their way down the steep path without needing lanterns, sparing them worry about attracting attention.

The ground underfoot was rocky, and shifting pebbles made footing treacherous. They made their way down cautiously, holding on to the rocks on the cliffside, acutely aware of the sheer drop on the other side. This close to the battle, the smoke was thick, drifting through the air like low clouds.

"There," Dillon hissed, pointing toward a nondescript, squat stone building that sat carved into the rocky cliff. It was high tide, and the waves lapped not far below them.

"Get us in," Blaine murmured. Dillon found a concealed path that led to the building, a rocky goat trail nearly hidden by scrub bushes that looked as if no one had passed that way in a very long time. They had to move carefully, flattened against the cliff one person at a time, but soon they were all gathered on the outcropping that held the mechanical building.

"We're going to need light," Dillon said, withdrawing a small glass lantern with shutters, which he lit, as the others stood between him and the edge of the outcropping, blocking anyone's view of the building. Dillon withdrew a heavy iron key and turned it, but the door stuck closed.

"Let me throw some weight behind that," Piran offered, ramming the door with his shoulder. It grudgingly gave way, and a dark opening yawned before them, its stale air heavy with mildew.

"Let's see if this marvel still works," Blaine murmured as Dillon led them into the building. The windowless square room was barren except for a huge capstan in the middle. Dillon hung the lantern on a hook as one of the soldiers pushed the door closed behind them.

"Well, there it is," Dillon said. "At least we know it survived the Cataclysm."

"What do we need to know to operate this?" Piran asked, walking in a circle around the capstan. "Any traps? Release levers? Magic wards?"

Dillon shook his head. "No—at least, none that were on the plans I saw during the project."

"I doubt that anyone bothered to set magic wards around something like this," Kestel said. "And if they did, after the Cataclysm, any wards that might have been set would have been broken when the magic failed."

Piran had completed his examination. "I don't see anything that looks like a trap or a lock. It looks like the rest of the siege machines I've seen—big, brawny, blunt tools without a lot of finesse." He grinned. "Kind of like me, come to think of it."

"Let's start trying to move that capstan," Blaine said. "If it hasn't been used since before the Great Fire, it might not move even for oxen."

"Was that directed at me?" Piran asked with a straight face.

"Kestel—better watch the path, just in case. It's probably going to take all of us to even budge this thing."

The men put their shoulders to the wheel, even Dillon, as Kestel took up watch at the door. Dillon had said the mechanism required four men. All seven of them managed to find a place along the capstan's spokes, pushing with all their might.

"Nothing," Piran said disgustedly.

"This time, let's pull," Dillon suggested. They adjusted their stance, and lent their weight to the effort, pulling for all they were worth. The mechanism creaked, gave a few inches, and stuck fast.

"If we had flat ground and a little more room to maneuver, I'd hook up a horse to it, just to get it going," Blaine mused.

"We're not going to get a horse down that trail, and mules are in short supply," Piran replied.

"It moved that time," Dillon said. "Maybe we can jostle it loose."

They got into place once more, working the capstan forward and back until the mechanism gave another rattling groan and began to move, making them work for every inch.

"Danger!" Kestel shouted, and the next thing Blaine knew, there was a flurry of motion at the door to the mechanical room.

"Keep it going!" Blaine ordered. "Piran, and you," he said, pointing at one of the guards, "with me!"

Blaine, Piran, and the guard ran toward the fight. Kestel already had one man down, but more were on their way. Unwilling to be trapped inside the mechanical room, and wanting to give Dillon and the others cover so they could raise the boom, Blaine and Piran ran through the door with a bloodcurdling war bellow, with the guard following hard on their heels.

Three more enemy soldiers were heading their way, and Blaine glimpsed more climbing the rocky path. It was clear from the soldiers' surprise that they had not expected to come under attack, but they launched themselves into the fray without hesitation. Eight soldiers struggled up the trail from the foot of the cliff, and Blaine bet that one rowboat had made it to shore from the invading ships.

Eight against eight should have been an even fight, except that Dillon was no swordsman, and four of Blaine's men were inside the mechanical building forcing the balky capstan to raise its burden. Then again, with one attacker already down, that made it seven to four. Shoulder to shoulder with Kestel and Piran, Blaine did not give the odds another thought.

"You shouldn't have come here," Blaine grunted as he swung his sword at a rangy soldier with enough force to sever a limb. "Go back and leave us alone."

"Too late for that," the soldier replied, blocking Blaine's swing and answering with a forceful press of his own that made Blaine step back to remain clear of the man's blade.

Blaine felt his battle magic awaken, giving him a few seconds' prescience to warn him of his attacker's next move before motion signaled the blow, increasing his reflexes just a bit more than a well-trained mortal. He moved slightly ahead of the next swing, brought his sword up to block, and tore back and down with the knife in his left hand, opening a deep, bloody tear across his opponent's ribs and belly. Warm blood splattered his face and arms as the soldier gasped and dropped to his knees. Blaine's sword swung again, and the headless corpse *thudded* to the rocky ground.

"I warned you," he muttered to the dead man.

Piran was holding off two attackers, and by the look of it, he was getting the chance to work off his frustrations with the ambassador's delegation. Piran's sword training came from the Donderath army, but his fighting techniques were learned in the alleys of Castle Reach. His opponents were competent with their blades, but it was clear they had little experience with combat that did not follow formal rules. Piran was not much of a believer in rules of any kind.

Piran dove, skewering one attacker in the nuts. He swung at the second opponent while the soldier was distracted as his comrade fell to his knees, howling in pain and shock, hands gripping his groin. Too late, the second soldier saw the sword coming for him. He blocked badly, and Piran's blade knocked his sword away, slipping between the man's ribs.

Piran walked toward his first opponent, who was rolling back and forth in a bloody pool, sobbing with pain. He raised his sword to dispatch the man as Blaine looked up.

"Leave one of them alive!" Blaine yelled. "I've got questions for them."

Blaine's new opponent took his eyes off Blaine for a fatal few seconds to glance at his downed companion. Blaine swung hard, getting under the soldier's guard, opening his belly with one savage slice.

"You're not the one," Blaine said as the man grabbed at his spilling entrails with a gasp of pain and shock. Blaine's second swing took the man's head from his shoulders.

From the mechanical building, Blaine heard the steady *clanking* of gears and the grunts of the men pushing the balky capstan. It was impossible to see whether their efforts were paying off, since the water beneath them was black in the darkness. Blaine hoped that Dillon was correct about the boom and its functionality. He had no desire to retake Castle Reach street by street from a foreign invasion force.

The area outside the mechanical house was narrow and covered with gravel, but the four defenders managed to block the doorway. The guardsman and his attacker circled one another, looking for an opening. The Cross-Sea soldier swung, and Blaine's guard evaded the strike, taking advantage of the soldier's overreach to sink his blade into the man's thigh. Hobbled, the soldier swung badly, and the guard's sword *thunked* into his shoulder, severing the man's sword arm. Soaked with blood, screaming in mortal fear, the soldier collapsed to the ground, waiting for the deathblow as the guard stepped forward and thrust his sword into the soldier's heart.

Two of the soldiers approached Kestel, and one had the bad luck to snicker when he realized she was not a man. "I've got better ways to spend time with you, pretty lady," he said.

"I don't." Kestel came at him in a flurry of motion that forced him back into his companion. Before her hapless opponent realized he was in trouble, she had scored a deep gash on his right shoulder and a wicked cut across his ribs.

"Hellcat," the second soldier snarled, moving to box Kestel in. She hardly took her eyes off her first opponent, flicking her wrist with the accuracy of deadly practice. The soldier had taken two more steps from sheer momentum before he realized he was a dead man, with a knife hilt-deep in his chest. He drew a hideous, gurgling breath and toppled like a felled tree.

"Do you have a live one?" Kestel yelled to Blaine, eyeing her prey with malicious amusement. The soldier had lost all his former arrogance, and by the smell of it, had soiled himself in the bargain.

Piran walked over to the man he had skewered in the balls. The wounded soldier howled as Piran towed him with his boot. "Yeah, if he doesn't bleed out before we get him back to the castle. Damn, and I thought scalp wounds were bad!"

"Want a spare?"

Blaine eyed the man Piran had wounded. Piran was busy tying the man's wrists together and giving the captive one of his fallen comrade's wadded up shirts to press against the wound. "Don't think so."

"Please!" the last soldier begged. "I outrank that man. I know things—I can tell you more plans than he can. And if you don't stab me, I won't bleed to death before you can ask me all your questions. I can be very helpful!"

"Oh, all right," Kestel said. "Drop your sword." The terrified man complied. Kestel kicked the sword out of reach. "Hey, Piran, how about tying this one up, too." She kept her sword point against the terrified soldier's jugular until Piran had securely tied the man's wrists and hobbled his ankles.

"You didn't tie your prisoner's ankles," Kestel pointed out.

Piran raised an eyebrow. "I damn well made sure he isn't going to run away from us. We'll be lucky if we don't have to carry him."

Blaine walked up to where the defeated prisoner knelt. "How many were on your ship?" he asked.

"Three hundred," the man replied tonelessly. "Same for the other ships. Mostly conscripts. Things are bad at home. Not enough food, not enough work. The king rounds up men and carts them off, then gives them uniforms and sends them to war with all the neighboring kingdoms. I guess he figures most of us won't come back."

"What was the battle plan?" Piran asked.

The prisoner gave a bitter laugh. "Plan? Survive the voyage, hope to Raka you had more food than we did, and steal anything we could send home."

"Were you sent to occupy Donderath?" Blaine asked, and Kestel nudged the man with her sword's point when he hesitated.

"Yes, if it was worth it," the man admitted. "Meaning—if you had food and weren't living in burned-out ruins. Looks like you did better than we did, so yes—if those ships land, they're going to do their damnedest to take what you've got."

"How does your king hope to control a conquered nation an ocean away?" Kestel asked. "Fifteen hundred soldiers could overrun the city, but our armies are much larger. You couldn't hold on to it for long."

The prisoner sighed. "We hadn't counted on you having armies," he said. "I doubt it occurred to the king that you weren't at least as bad off as we are. He probably thought we'd sail in here without any trouble, march around and intimidate the locals, and start shipping anything useful back home."

"Surprise," Piran drawled. "We've already chewed up and swallowed much scarier enemies. I'd almost feel bad for you, except that you were planning to loot the city we just got cleaned up."

"Tell me about your mages," Blaine said. "How many? How strong? What kind of magic?"

He had not thought it possible, but the man looked even more scared at the mention of magic than he had before. "I stay away from the hocuses," he said, almost stammering. "Nothing but trouble."

"Answer the question," Kestel prodded.

The captive swallowed hard. He was trembling with fear, and Blaine felt a stab of pity, since he was obviously not cut out for soldiering. "There's a hocus on each ship, I heard the sailors say. They don't like that one little bit." He took a deep breath. "Never saw the one on our ship do much of anything, tell you the truth. But I've heard all kind of tales."

His words tumbled out, and perhaps he thought that the better his answers, the more likely he was to remain alive. "They say our hocus can call down lightning, and throw fire from his fingers," he said in a rush. "One of my mates said he heard the hocus can kill a man just by looking at him, and set a fire with a thought."

Assuming he's right, that's hedge-witch-level magic, nothing like Quintrel's people, or battle mages like Rikard, Blaine thought. *Maybe their powerful mages were killed in the Great Fire.*

"Lord McFadden!" Dillon emerged from the mechanical house sweat-soaked but grinning in triumph. "The boom worked! We're all sure to be sore and bruised, but from what we can tell, the mechanism worked!"

"Hey, Mick!" Piran called. He had walked toward the edge of the path, looking down over the harbor. "I think he's right. Take a look."

Kestel and the guard remained with the bound soldier and his injured companion as Blaine walked over to join Piran. In the time that had passed since they had looked out on the bay the last time, the tide of battle appeared to have turned in Folville's favor.

"Ships are stopped," Piran noted. "You can bet they'd have driven right up the middle if they could."

The ship that had been on fire was burned to the waterline, just a smoldering wreck. A second ship was burning, its sails alight, forecastle aflame. Blaine could see soldiers jumping from the doomed ship, flailing in the dark water. The catapults from the embankment still *thudded* as they sent rocks and debris raining down on the ships that were now stranded in the harbor they had intended to attack. Caught between the boom in front and the wreckage of the two burning ships behind, the other three ships lacked the wind and the maneuvering room to get clear.

Dark shapes moved across the clouds, diving at the remaining ships. Men screamed and ran for cover as *talishte* attackers snatched sailors from the decks and dropped them into the deep water of the bay. Two *talishte* swooped down on one of the ships, pushing the portable catapult through the railing and into the sea. The other catapult was smashed to bits on the wrecked deck of the burning ship.

Without their war machines, the ships were sitting targets as the catapults up above lobbed volley after volley. Some of the large stones hit the water, sending up violent splashes that rocked the ships, scattering or crushing the men who were swimming desperately for shore. Other stones crashed onto the decks of the ships, shattering masts, shredding sails, and smashing through the hulls.

A flotilla of small fishing boats sat in a solid line on the harbor side of the chain barricade. Archers took shots at the landing boats filled with soldiers.

As Blaine watched, something burst up from beneath one of

the landing boats, lifting it out of the water and capsizing it, sending its occupants into the water. More *talishte*, Blaine bet, though from the terrified screams that rose from the bay, he was certain the enemy soldiers imagined even more frightening foes.

All along the waterfront, angry citizens stood shoulder to shoulder. Blaine spotted Traher Voss's battle flag, meaning reinforcements had arrived. "Voss is there," he said, pointing to the flags. "Folville will be all right. Voss's men will make short work of the survivors."

As he spoke, a volley of flaming arrows sailed toward the stranded ships, lodging in their sails and rigging. Wave after wave of burning arrows rained down on the luckless invaders, until the bay blazed with firelight.

"Poor dumb bastards," Piran said, shaking his head. "Then again, all the better for us. Voss and Folville are making short work of them."

"Which means they aren't going to need us to hurry down there," Blaine said, knowing Piran could hear the note of relief in his voice. "Frankly, I'd rather see what the *talishte* read from our ambassadors, and what they can find out from these two," he said with a backward glance.

"Biters?" The prisoner's eyes widened with fear. "Oh, gods. Don't feed me to the biters! I've helped you. Told you everything. Sweet Torven and Esthrane! Don't let them feed on me!"

"Can't help you with that," Piran said as Dillon and the other guards emerged from the mechanical building. "See, we need to know everything, and there's one way to find it out. But since you've been helpful, as you say, we can put in a word for them to make it quick."

The soldier collapsed, sobbing into his hands. "Get him on his feet," Blaine said to the guards. "Someone's going to have to carry the other one. Let's get them back to the castle, see what they can tell us. We're done here." He turned to Dillon and the guards. "What you did in there changed the course of the battle. Thank you."

Kestel gave her prisoner over to the guards and came to join him. They were all splattered with blood, though fortunately little of it was their own. Kestel peered down into the firelit harbor and watched for a moment in silence. "In an awful way, it's actually rather pretty from up here, with the fire reflecting on the water," she mused. "I don't imagine it's pretty at all down there."

"No," Blaine agreed. "And it's going to leave a mess in the harbor, after we'd only gotten part of it dredged." He sighed. "But it's better to stop them there than burn the city to drive them out."

Kestel nodded. "Think they'll try again?"

Blaine shrugged. "If the Cross-Sea king is as crazy as Heldin said, maybe. Then again, it should send a stern message when none of his ships return and his troops are never heard from again. It could take months for them to notice. He might even have more ships headed this way, for all we know."

"They won't be landing at Castle Reach," Kestel said.

"No," Blaine agreed. "But you know as well as I do that the coast is full of inlets. After the 'pirates' attacked, Folville and Voss set up patrols along the coastline, but it's an impossible task."

"Still, the farther away they have to land their men, the harder it is to mount a surprise attack," Piran ventured. "That weighs in our favor."

"Two men, stay with the capstan," Blaine ordered as they readied for the trip back up the cliff. "I'll have fresh soldiers sent to relieve you as soon as we reach the castle. In the meantime, stay sharp. If one boat of enemy fighters could make it to shore, there could be another. Until those boats are sunk and the men aboard them drowned, they're still a threat."

"Aye, m'lord," the ranking guard replied. "We'll watch carefully. No one will get by."

"The boom and net will stay up until we lower them," Dillon said. "Indefinitely, if we want. I'm still quite pleased that they worked after all this time!"

"I'm glad I didn't realize that you thought there was a good chance they wouldn't, when we were making our way down that goat path," Piran replied with a glare.

Dillon shrugged. "Nothing ventured, nothing gained, as they say. I figured it was worth the risk, if it worked."

"If there were still such things as medals, I'd give you one," Blaine said. "Look down there," he added, pointing to the harbor. "Your boom and net saved a lot of lives. We'd have never known about it without you."

Dillon looked utterly embarrassed. "Just doing my duty, m'lord. The gods smiled on us tonight."

The soldiers went up the narrow path first, followed by Dillon, Blaine, Kestel, and Piran. To Blaine's relief, their horses were where they had left them, fidgeting with the smoke and noise that rose from the bay. The two prisoners were slung over the rumps of the soldiers' horses like sacks of grain for the ride back to the castle.

Clouds of smoke gusted across the road, dimming the stars. After surviving two attacks in one day, Blaine was hoping he could look forward to a hot bath and a glass of whiskey, but experience cautioned him not to count on such rare luxuries until they were achieved.

The soldiers at the castle gate stopped them only briefly, opening the way for them to ride on to the castle. Dillon swung down from his horse, barking orders to the castle staff as soon as his feet touched the ground. Six more guards were sent down to the mechanical building, and they were heading toward the gate before Blaine had even handed off his horse to a groomsman.

"Take the prisoners to Rikard," Blaine ordered the soldiers who came to meet them. "Have him question them like the others."

"Very well, sir," the ranking soldier replied. "And afterward?"

Blaine sighed. "Hang them with the two ambassadors," he said wearily. "Make sure the *talishte* read them before that. We need every bit of knowledge we can pry out of them."

"Yes, m'lord." With that, the castle guard took the two prisoners and headed toward Quillarth Castle.

Blaine turned to one of the other nearby soldiers. "Go find Captain Larson or Captain Hemmington," he ordered. "Get me a status update on what's going on in Castle Reach with Folville and Voss. If they need more soldiers to hold the waterfront, we need to know."

"Yes sir," the soldier said, taking off for the stables to get a horse for the ride into town.

Blaine, Kestel, and Piran made their way up to the parlor. In the time they had been gone, all signs of the fight with the false ambassadors had been removed, and a reasonable attempt had been made to remove the bloodstain from the carpet. Piran poured a glass of whiskey for each of them, and collapsed into a chair by the fireplace with a dramatic groan.

"What a day!" He tossed back his whiskey.

Blaine sipped his whiskey, but he could not manage to match Piran's exuberance. He drifted to the window, looking out through the cracked glass toward the glowing wreckage in the Castle Reach harbor. After a few moments, Kestel joined him.

Kestel touched Blaine's arm. "You don't have a choice about it, hanging the Cross-Sea spies or those soldiers," she said quietly, guessing that his mood went deeper than mere exhaustion. "We don't have the extra food to keep them prisoner, and they can't go free." She paused. "Heldin might be useful. I don't think his heart was really ever fully in the attack. I think he can be brought along." Kestel shrugged. "And if not, you can always kill him later."

Blaine nodded. "I know. But knowing doesn't make it easier. I tell myself that as long as this sort of thing keeps me up at night, I must not be a monster. If it ever stops bothering me... I'll have one more thing to worry about."

A knock came at the door before Kestel could answer. "M'lord," Dillon's assistant, Coban, said from the doorway. "I apologize for the interruption. I know it's been a long day. But there's a messenger from General Theilsson, and he says his message is most urgent."

Blaine and Kestel shared a 'what now?' glance. Blaine nodded. "Very well. Send him in."

Disheveled and dirty, looking as if he had come straight from the battlefield, Geir walked into the room. "Niklas and Penhallow send their greetings," he said with a tired smile.

"I will be back with a flagon of deer blood," Coban promised without being asked, and headed for the kitchen.

Geir looked utterly spent. Kestel embraced him in greeting. "Sit down. Rest," Blaine said. "You look like you've had a rougher day than we have, and ours is one for the legends."

Geir nodded and sank into one of the seats. "I came in from the north, but I could see a battle in the harbor. What's going on?"

Blaine and Kestel took turns filling Geir in, first about the false ambassadors and their treachery and then about the invasion force and the fight at the mechanical house. "You're right," Geir said. "You've had quite a day."

Coban entered with the deer blood and a goblet. Geir poured himself a glass, drank it slowly, and leaned back. "That's better," he said tiredly. "Thank you."

"Things must be pretty bad for Niklas to send you in such a rush," Blaine said. "What's happening? Is he still fighting the marauders in the north?"

Geir nodded. "And it's not getting any better. The marauders aren't robber gangs like we originally thought. Those were the strike teams, sent to spy and loot. What's coming across the border now qualifies as an army. It's organized and I'd bet that a lot of the fighters are former Meroven soldiers."

"Damn," Blaine said. "I bet Niklas feels right at home, fighting them all over again."

Geir raised an eyebrow. "Actually, he described it in much more colorful language, but that was the gist of what he said."

"What does he need? Rinka Solveig and her army are on their way to join up with him, and we'll be going back there, too, once this is resolved," Blaine said. "When I get a report back from the harbor, I'll know whether Folville and Voss have the situation down there in hand. So I can shift some of the men we assigned to the west and bring them to help Niklas, but it will take time to move them."

Geir nodded. "The reinforcements would be appreciated," he replied. "Niklas and his army are holding their own, but they won't be able to hold off Nagok forever without additional help—and Voss's men are busy."

"This means we're going to be riding north, doesn't it?" Piran said from where he slouched in his chair. "I knew it was too much to expect that we could have a day or two without killing someone or nearly being assassinated."

"Technically, only Blaine can be assassinated," Kestel corrected with a wicked gleam in her eye. "The likes of you just gets regular-old murdered."

Geir glanced at Blaine, who despite everything, had a shadow of a smile at the banter. "Are they always like this?"

Blaine shrugged. "Usually, they're worse." He sighed. "Yes, it means we're going to have to go north. We can't afford to be overrun from any direction." He looked back to Geir. "What of Penhallow and Connor? We haven't had word in quite a while. Do you know if the voyage to Edgeland was successful?" His bond through the *kruvgaldur* was still new enough that Blaine had little practice interpreting the impressions he received.

"They've reached Edgeland," Geir reported. "From what Penhallow has been able to read from the *kruvgaldur*, Connor and the others obtained the artifact—with some danger involved—and are on their way back."

"We're never going to hear the end of this from Verran." Piran sighed. "Might as well expect a whole new set of songs about snow." He looked over to Blaine. "Maybe he'll bring back some fresh herring for you."

"Forget the herring. I want news!" Kestel said, excitement glinting in her eyes. "He'd better come back with gossip about everyone we knew. Engraham and Ifrem and all the others— I want to know what they've been doing, how they are, what happened when the magic came back. Dammit! It's been too long."

"Dear Kestel, much as I miss our friends, it could never be too long to be gone from that accursed place," Piran replied. Kestel made a face at him when Piran was not looking.

"They were actually worse, cooped up together all winter during the Long Dark in Edgeland," Blaine said to Geir. "It's how they handle stress."

Piran raised his nearly empty glass of whiskey. "*This* is how I handle stress," he said, rising to pour himself a refill. "Annoying Kestel is what I do for fun."

"I consider annoying Piran to be an art," Kestel said with a straight face. "And that makes me a virtuoso."

Blaine chuckled, knowing that their friendly sniping was their way of dealing with the idea of heading into yet another series of battles. "Do you see any end in sight to all of this?" he asked Geir, taking a swallow of his own whiskey. He recounted what they had learned from Heldin about the Cross-Sea Kingdoms' involvement in the Meroven War and their *talishte* uprising.

Geir drained his goblet and poured more from the flagon. "Unfortunately, I don't think we'll see an end soon. Thrane is a danger to be reckoned with, especially with the rogue Elders on his side, and we're certain he's had a hand in Nagok's rise to power. And perhaps, given what you've shared, meddled beyond our shores. That's a very disturbing thought."

"But Penhallow has some of the Elders siding with him as well," Kestel said, growing serious once more. "Doesn't that balance things?"

Geir gave an eloquent shrug. "Balance, yes. But neither side can settle for balance. The only thing either side can accept is the utter destruction of the enemy. And right now, anything could tip the scales one way or the other."

CHAPTER
TWENTY-SIX

D O YOU THINK THEY WERE REALLY AMBASSADORS?"
Betta asked.

Folville gave her a look. "What do you think?"

Betta chuckled. "Does it give you a hint that I already activated the Wharf Rats?"

The 'Wharf Rats' was the name Folville had bestowed on the orphans and urchins who made their homes wherever they could take shelter near the harbor. Years ago, Folville and Betta had been among them, on their own from a young age, eking out a living and stealing what they needed. Folville knew that any attempt to rescue or organize them would be like herding feral cats, so he mobilized them, gave them a name and a mission, and paid them in food, clothing, and shelter. In response, they gave him their unwavering loyalty. Those who showed promise became full-fledged Curs when they were older.

"Good. Learn anything from them?"

Betta leaned back against one of the building's wood-paneled walls and crossed her arms over her chest. "Plenty. Tresta shadowed them all the way up to the castle gates. Heard one of the men giving the others orders about what and what not to say, warning them what would happen to them if they failed," she said. "The Rat who reported it said they sounded more like high-wayman than highborns."

Folville nodded. "Then the lighthouse seers were right. They're scouts for an attack." The rebuilt lighthouse at the entrance to the harbor no longer held a massive mirrored fire to attract ships and lead them in. Castle Reach wanted no outsiders, at least, not until the city was restored and its defenses were at full measure.

Betta nodded. "Afraid so. The seers believe that the one ship we see is just a decoy. They foresee other ships, war ships with soldiers."

"We need to get Voss involved. We can't hold the town on our own, not even with Larson and Hemmington's help," Folville said.

"Sent a runner a candlemark ago," Betta said with a smirk.

Folville took her in his arms and kissed her. "You're so smart, you should have been a man," he said jokingly.

With a snort, Betta kneed him gently in the crotch, just enough to make her point. "All of the brains, no breakable balls."

"Truce!" Folville said with a laugh. "You're fine the way you are!"

"What are you going to do?" Betta asked, sobering.

Folville sighed and stepped back. "Fight. It's what we do."

"Do you think it's the pirates, in different clothes?"

Folville cursed. "Of course. They're coming at us, trying to see where we're weak."

Betta began to pace. "They sent the pirates, and we killed them. They sent more pirates up the coast. We found them and killed them. So it worries me that they've tried again."

"Maybe they didn't expect us to actually be organized," Folville said thoughtfully, leaning against the battered desk. "They might have thought they'd find a wasteland—maybe even that we deserted Castle Reach. It might have thrown them that we could stop them from just walking in and taking what they wanted."

"Then why even try the ambassador angle?"

Folville shrugged. "They found out we were more organized than they expected, and decided to play along. Think about it. If the Great Fire actually hit everywhere, who has ambassadors? And who's sending out delegations? It's a charade."

"You know, if you're wrong, we've probably just started a war."

Folville shrugged. "Not worried about it. From what we've seen of the pirates, they're as poor as we are. Armies are expensive. Sending them across a sea is even more expensive. And for what? If we're lucky, they'll get a good look at us and go home and tell everyone else we're not worth the trip. Let us rebuild in peace."

Folville, Betta, and four dozen of the Curs assembled on Castle Reach's wharf front, peering out to sea.

"That can't be good." Folville shaded his eyes to see the four sailing ships on the horizon.

"Do ambassadors come with their own fleet?" Betta asked.

Folville's expression was answer enough. "Not unless they mean to conquer," he replied. "Everyone! To your stations!"

The Curs had gone from being a well-organized street gang to being a reasonably well-trained extension of Blaine McFadden's army. More importantly, the Curs, like the Wharf Rats, knew every squalid inch of Castle Reach, its gutters and sewers, the fetid tunnels and forgotten attics, and the long-abandoned cellars. They could move through the war-damaged city like ghosts, hidden and unseen, traveling forgotten old tunnels and squeezing through ginnels outlanders could never find.

"I see you've already mobilized your people." Traher Voss strode up, hands on his hips, a man who was used to being in charge and being obeyed. Folville lifted his head and mustered his best bravado.

"They're in place," Folville said. "No one is getting past the waterfront without going through them."

Voss nodded. "Good. Very good. I've got men up and down the coast, with most of them on that side of the harbor," he added with a nod toward the shipworks end of the bay, the easiest beach for landing. "Considering it's nothing but cliffs on the other side," he added, glancing toward the sheer bluffs that rose from the sea on the left.

"What about the catapults?" Folville asked.

At that moment, he heard a loud, distant *thunk* and then, minutes later, something large and solid flew into the harbor ahead of the lead ship, sending up a huge spray of water. A few moments later, a second missile and then a third followed. The incoming ships drifted to a halt.

"Right now, my men up there are supposed to keep those ships from landing," Voss replied. "If there's a hint of an aggressive move, if landing boats deploy or archers show themselves, the catapults start aiming for those masts and decks. Signal us if you see something—you're closer to the action."

Folville smiled. "We're thinking along the same lines," he said. "Do you have *talishte*?"

Voss nodded. "Not much good until nightfall, but after the sun goes down, they'll be here. What are you going to do? This is your city."

"Yes, it is." Much as Folville had decried the city's excesses and exclusions before the Cataclysm, or bemoaned its hardship and hunger afterward, he could not imagine being anywhere else. "And those bastards are not going to set foot in it."

"We've got boats," Betta said, her face flush with excitement, eager for a good fight. "We can tie them together and barricade the harbor."

Voss shook his head. "Those sailing ships will go right over you," he said.

Folville gave him a sidelong look. "When we dredged the harbor, we only dredged the outer section," he said with a crafty smile. "Not the wharves. We meant to get back to it, but you know how it goes..."

Voss raised an eyebrow. "So there are still sunken ships down there?"

Folville nodded. "Oh yeah. Out to where the bottom drops off to really deep water, the harbor floor is lousy with the ships that sank the night of the Great Fire," he replied. "We were going to clear the harbor in stages. But then there were the floods and the bad weather this spring, and it didn't happen."

"Can you lure them in?" Voss asked. "Put your ships just inside where the wrecks are. You're almost daring the pirates to come after you, and scuttle themselves in the process."

Folville grinned. "I like that. And we'll have plenty of archers too, just in case. Plus I've sent the Wharf Rats up to help with the catapults. They'll lug rocks and debris so there'll be no shortage of heavy things to throw at them."

"Now, that's a proper Castle Reach welcome," Voss chuckled. "Keep a sharp eye out. They'll probably send some small boats in once it gets dark. That's what I'd do. Shoot them on sight."

"With pleasure," Folville replied.

Candlemarks later, Castle Reach harbor was under siege. Much as he hated boats, Folville saw no other course except to lead the insolent flotilla that waited in a line across the bay, staring up at the huge hulls of five enemy sailing ships.

"Hold steady, lads," Folville yelled above the wind. They had positioned themselves, as Voss suggested, just inside the undersea ridge of sunken ships that blocked clear entry to the wharves. If the Cross-Sea ships insisted on sailing for the docks, they would rip out their hulls on the ships' graveyard beneath the waterline. Yet if they were to get that close, dozens—or hundreds—of men would swim for shore. Folville had no desire to fight them.

"Watch out! They've got catapults of their own!" one of the boatmen yelled.

The shipboard catapults were smaller and lighter than the massive war machines on the embankments, but they could still fire rocks heavy enough to kill a man or sink a small boat.

"Scatter!" Folville shouted. "You're harder to hit if you're moving, and we're almost too close for them to hit."

He eyed the ships angrily. They were likely catapulting ballast stones, which would be plentiful. He watched the trajectory as stones sailed over the small boats, smacking into the seawall and the wharf front. The line of defenders ran for cover, then pulled back out of range.

"Looks like Voss's men have the catapults ready," Folville warned his boatmates. "Get ready for some waves," he said as he waved the torch back and forth.

Moments later, he heard the *thud* of a catapult and the whistle of something large flying through the air. A crash followed as the large rock smashed into the deck of the sailing ship nearest the cliffside.

A few seconds later, the *clunk* came again, and a ship on the other side of the harbor lost a mast as the men in the boats with Folville cheered and hooted. A burning orb sailed through the air next, hitting the sails on the damaged boat and setting canvas and rigging alight. Even from a distance, Folville could hear the panicked shouts of sailors as they raced to contain the damage. Bits of flaming sailcloth fell like fiery rain onto the decks, and still the catapults kept up their bombardment, alternating fire and stone.

"That's how it's done!" Folville cheered, raising a fist to the sky in defiant triumph.

"Go back where ye came from!" one of the men in the next boat shouted.

"Watch out!" The cry went up too late, and before the sound died on the air, there was a *crunch* and screams as one of the rocks crashed through the bottom of a small boat, tossing its occupants into the water.

Moments later, a large rock fired from the embankment catapults sheared part of the prow off the nearest ship, sending sailors screaming as the figurehead and bowsprit tore away and fell into the harbor. Folville and his companions hung on to the sides of the boat, staying low as the waves rocked them.

In the boat next to Folville's, a man cried out and clutched his chest, tumbling overboard with an arrow protruding from his ribs.

"By Torven! Retreat!" Folville shouted, and the cry echoed up and down the line. Arrows *zinged* through the air around them like angry bees. He heard more shouts and cries of pain as the rowers put their backs into their strokes, retreating toward the shoreline and out of bow range. Folville felt a sting. He looked down to see a slice through his shirt that was red with blood and realized he had nearly taken an arrow.

"Now what?" one of the men said.

Folville looked up at the sun. "We let the catapults hold them off, and wait until dark. We can maneuver more then, and be harder for them to shoot."

"I've got an idea," Folville shouted to the boats on either side of him. "I'm heading to shore, but I'll be back. The rest of you, hold the line. Their arrows can't reach you here." The message was repeated down the line, and Folville fidgeted until the boat made it back to the waterfront.

"How is it?" Zeke was a Cur and one of Folville's lieutenants.

"Not good," Folville replied with a curse as he waded ashore and helped to pull the boat up behind him. "They've got archers and small catapults. We had to fall back, and I hate doing that."

"Looks like the big slings on the embankment made a few hits," Zeke said with a nod toward Voss's catapults.

"Yeah, but if the ships move in too close, it'll be harder for the catapults to hit them," Folville said.

"They can't get in past the wrecks, can they?" Zeke asked.

Folville shrugged grumpily. "Wouldn't think so, unless they're willing to scuttle themselves, but I'm not a sailor." He began to stride toward the far end of the docks. "Come on!"

"Where are you going?" Zeke asked, running to catch up.

"I've got an idea, for after it's dark," Folville replied. "I'm not about to let Voss's men get all the credit for saving our city."

The harbor-crane building hunkered beside what had been the deepest berth in Castle Reach's harbor. The roof had burned during the Great Fire, and storms had pounded the stone building during the Cataclysm, but it had been built well, and it withstood the assault.

"What are you looking for?" Zeke asked, following Folville as he picked his way across the debris that littered the crane-building floor.

"Those," Folville said, pointing to two large wheels next to a huge capstan and a large windlass. The treadwheels once powered the harbor crane, so that four men at a time, two in each wheel, could supply the energy to the giant crane and unload the heaviest boxes from the cargo ships that had once crowded the bay. The treadwheels could also power a windlass, enabling the harbormaster to draw in a heavy barge or a disabled ship.

"What are we unloading?" Zeke asked, looking utterly confused.

"If this works, we're going to 'unload' some of those pirates—right into the sea," Folville said, determination tightening his voice. He sighed as he looked around the crane house. No one had needed the huge machine since the Great Fire, and it sat rigged as it had been on Castle Reach's last day before the Cataclysm.

"Go get three sturdy men and the largest harpoons you can find. They're with the rest of the weapons, in the main camp," Folville ordered. "Two or three harpoons if you can find them. And as much thick rope as you can carry." He put his hands on his hips. "They want to sail into our harbor? We'll just extend some forceful hospitality."

Zeke took off, and for the next candlemark, Folville worked with the heavy crane rope. He was glad that the windlass was already wound, and managed to get it connected to the treadwheels. "No idea whether that rope is rotten or not," he muttered to himself, though the rough hemp seemed solid enough as he handled it, and the upper floor of the building had shielded the rope and the mechanism from the weather once part of the roof was gone.

"Got them!" Zeke announced as he returned. Three of the biggest Curs accompanied him, men who actually made Zeke, with his thick neck and powerful arms, look average by comparison. They carried wicked-looking harpoons with sharp steel points, and coils of heavy rope.

"Good, good," Folville said. "Bring everything over here. We've got work to do."

*   *   *

Two candlemarks later, Folville's bastardized machine was ready, and he left Zeke in charge with orders while he returned to the flotilla. Torches lit the waterfront and dotted the shore on either side of the bay, the better to ensure that enemy landing boats did not come ashore in the dark. Voss's men kept up their bombardment from the embankment, interspersing the debris they hurled with weighted, flaming balls that quickly set one of the invading ships aflame.

The enemy ships were in the middle of the harbor. They had not moved forward far enough to be scuttled on the wrecks, and positioned in the center of the harbor, they were a difficult shot for the catapults, whose missiles hit only once out of every third shot.

"You are completely crazy," Betta said as Folville gathered two of the small boats and their crews together.

"So they say," Folville replied. "And the rope may break. The windlass might fall apart. On the other hand, it's our fastest way to wreck one of their ships—maybe more."

The nearest ship, the *Gull,* was the likely target, and to Folville's glee, it was also the smallest of the five. Flaming missiles from the embankment catapults had already reduced its sails to soot-streaked rags, meaning it could not use the wind to pull against the towrope. The ship had a relatively small catapult, and Folville and his accomplices took a zigzag course to avoid the rocks that crashed into the water, staying well into the shadows of the ship and out of the moonlight to avoid being targeted.

"Throw it!" Folville ordered. A brawny man with the practiced aim of a whaler hefted the harpoon confidently and heaved it with his full might at the hull of the Cross-Sea ship, lodging not far above the waterline.

"Get us out of here," Folville hissed, and the oarsmen began to move them silently back toward the flotilla behind the tangle of wrecks on the harbor floor, carefully letting out the rope that was attached to the harpoon. Once they were safely out of archer range, Folville lit a small torch and held it up, the signal to Zeke and the men in the crane building.

The harbor windlass gave a mighty groan as the old gears creaked into motion. As Folville watched, the heavy rope gradually grew taut, rising to the surface and then above it as the windlass created an inexorable pull.

"Fall back!" Folville shouted, and the flotilla withdrew to a safe distance, as the rope strained against its burden.

"Either it's going to tear a hole in that hull, or we're going to drag that ship right into the wrecks," one of Folville's companions muttered.

"That's the idea," he replied.

The catapults on the embankment thundered again, and this time, one of their large rocks smashed down through the decks of an enemy ship, toppling a mast and raising screams and cries of alarm from the sailors on deck. Folville's crews cheered and hooted, yelling insults and catcalling.

In response, the *Gull*'s shipboard catapults sent another volley toward the flotilla, falling short and raising a large splash as the rocks hit the water. Folville grinned as the shouted taunts from his crews grew bawdier.

"It's working!" The shout brought Folville's attention back to the winch line. Folville grinned as he watched the tight line strain. Caught like an injured whale, the *Gull* was being slowly pulled toward shore—and to the man-made shoals of wrecked hulls and broken masts beneath the water.

"Stay out of their range!" he shouted to warn the others, though the archers aboard the *Gull* appeared too distracted by their ship's mysterious trajectory to take careful aim. Even at a distance, Folville could hear the *Gull*'s captain shouting orders, trying to regain control of his panicked crew.

With a hideous crash, the *Gull*'s keel collided with the ships' graveyard beneath the waters. Dragged on by the harbor windlass, the doomed ship continued forward, shuddering as sunken debris tore at its hull. The *Gull* was clearly being towed, all pretense of sailing under its own power dispelled. From what Folville could see, the crew was making every effort to stop the forward motion, even as the ship suddenly came to an abrupt halt, with a jerk that toppled men out of the rigging.

The harbor winch did not care that the *Gull* had become hopelessly snagged on the broken ships beneath the waves. The heavy rope stayed taut, continuing to pull. Folville heard a cracking like ice after the winter thaw, then a thunderous *boom*, and the rope went suddenly slack, pulling with it a chunk of broken planking. The *Gull* listed, taking on water fast through the hole in its hull.

Another cheer went up from Folville's crew, but there was little time to celebrate. "Look! They're dropping boats!" one of the men down the line yelled. Folville squinted, trying to see in the darkness. Behind them, torches lit the waterfront and Castle Reach residents waited with whatever weapons they could find to 'greet' the attackers. Out on the water, with their backs to the torchlight, it was dark, lit only by moon and stars.

The second closest ship, its sails afire, was indeed lowering launch craft into the water.

"No one gets past!" Folville shouted. His belly was a hard knot. "Don't let those bastards get to shore!"

As Folville turned, he thought he saw a glimmer of light halfway up the cliffs on the right-hand side of the harbor. When he looked again, the light was gone, and he shook his head, wondering whether his eyes had played a trick on him. "Row them down!" Folville shouted as his oarsmen began to row in earnest toward the incoming small ships. "Capsize them! Use your oars. They won't take our city from us!"

Folville had often heard it said that most sailors could not swim. He wondered if it were true. Every fisherman he had known could swim, and he bet that was true of the men and women in the flotilla. "Send them to the fishes!" he shouted, and his oarsmen put on a burst of speed, coming at one of the incoming small boats amidships, ramming it with their metal-plated prow.

The soldiers in the enemy boats had swords. Folville's men had oars, which were twice as long. Folville grabbed one of the oars, swatting a blade out of a startled soldier's hand and then shoving him hard in the chest, knocking him into the dark water and bringing the oar down with a *crunch* on the man's head when he surfaced.

Folville's boat rocked dangerously, splashing him with spray, but he could not resist a triumphant cry as he brought the edge of the oar down on another enemy soldier's skull, splitting it like a ripe melon. Most of the soldiers tried to duck or flatten themselves to avoid the blows. A few dove overboard, only to be clubbed as they bobbed to the surface. Some tried to grab the oars away from their attackers, only to be shoved backward, out of the boat and into the water.

"That's the way!" one of Folville's men cheered, and soon up and down the harbor, the flotilla boats took after the incoming landing craft, capsizing the invaders, beating at their crews with heavy oars or getting in well-placed bowshots from close range.

"What's that?" As Folville's boat drew back from the over-turned, empty craft they had just fought, Folville could hear the distant *clank* of heavy chains. Corpses floated on the surface all around them, and the light from the burning ships cast the entire scene in nightmare shades of fire and shadow.

"Can't tell," a man from the nearest boat called back. "But look! Something's up there, and it's coming after the sailors!" he said, pointing to the dark sky.

Folville looked up, still puzzling over the *clanking* noise, and saw shadow figures diving through the air, silhouetted against the burning sails. One of the figures snatched up a screaming sailor from the deck of the ship and carried him aloft like a giant bird of prey. To the shouts and screams of the men on deck, the figure held out their shipmate with one outstretched hand. He reached out with the other hand and tore the head from the man's shoulders, sending a bloody shower onto the deck before he casually tossed the headless corpse among the sailor's screaming comrades.

The boat rocked violently beneath Folville's feet, and he heard a ghastly, shuddering breath, then one sodden arm swung over the side and a wild-eyed, half-drowned enemy sailor tried to haul himself in.

His weight made the boat lurch to one side, throwing one of Folville's men into the water. Folville butted the pole end of his oar into the enemy sailor's forehead, knocking him backward but not unconscious. The man flailed and kicked, grabbing on to Folville's crewman, who was desperately trying to get back to his shipmates.

The two men were too far away for Folville and the others to intervene, and there was no way to pull their mate into the boat without dragging the panicked enemy sailor as well. The two men fought like mad dogs, with Folville's man tearing at his attacker's hair, clothing, and skin, trying to free himself, even as the sailor clung with panic borne of imminent death. A wave swamped the two men, and then another, and when the water fell again, they were gone.

"Sweet Charrot!" The cry made Folville turn to see one of Voss's *talishte* hovering in the air just above the surface of the choppy waves. Several of the men in his boat shrank away in horror, but Folville grinned.

"Damn, I wish I could fly!" Folville said. It did not escape his notice that the *talishte* was bloodied to the elbows, and that his dark clothing was wet with blood.

"I'm to tell you that someone has raised the boom chain from the cliffs," the *talishte* said. "And the metal net beneath it. The ships are trapped in the harbor. Voss expects more men by sunrise." With that, he vanished, moving too quickly for Folville to see where he had gone.

"Over here!" Folville had barely processed the *talishte*'s news before he heard Betta shouting for him. He turned to see pairs of the small fishing boats, so common in Castle Reach's harbor, sitting in a line from one side of the bay to the other.

"Pull your men back," Betta shouted. "We're stretching fishing nets across the water. No one's going to swim through them! And that big thing the king built last year, over on the cliffs? It's a sea net. Damned thing actually works. The ships can't go anywhere, and Voss's men are pounding them to the waterline."

"So I heard," Folville said. "Everyone! Head for shore. The fishermen will take it from here!"

Cheering and singing, shouting insults at the stranded enemy ships, Folville and his flotilla rowed for shore. When they reached the wharves, he saw that Zeke and the men from the harbor crane had already strung up the chunk of broken hull, still attached to the harpoon and rope, as if it were a prize catch. Shouts and cheers greeted the returning boatmen, as women and children ran up and down the dockside, looking for returning loved ones.

Folville glanced down the line of boats. At least thirty such craft had gone out with him. Only nineteen returned. Those who did not find their family members among the survivors fell to their knees, keening in sorrow. A few bedraggled men and women who had fallen overboard and managed to swim back to shore were bundled in cloaks near the bonfires that dotted the beach. Folville knew that they were the lucky ones, and that the arrows and catapults had claimed the rest.

"Your crazy idea actually worked!" Zeke exulted, bounding up to slap Folville on the shoulder.

"I felt like a donkey in a gristmill," one of the other men who had walked the treadwheel said, "but damn, it worked!"

"Good work," Folville said, clapping Zeke on the back. "If the trading ships ever come back, you've got a job!"

Folville walked down the crowded harbor front. A small group of mourners were gathered at the edge of the dock, praying to Torven, master of the Sea of Souls, for the safe passage of their loved ones to the eternal resting place. Others paced the water's edge, shouting for friends and family who had not returned with the others, refusing to give up hope that they might yet wash up unharmed or float back with the debris that had already begun to choke the berths. A few pious souls sang praises to Charrot, Esthrane, and Torven around a small bonfire. Most were gathered in groups of two or three, gesturing toward the ships in the harbor, and recounting what they had seen.

Amid the chaos, his attention strayed to the spectacle of eight men in unfamiliar uniforms who were bound and kneeling, jeered and prodded by the crowd. "Where did they come from?" Folville asked as Dakker, another of the Curs, hurried past.

"They managed to get one of their boats to shore, on the far edge of the docks," Dakker replied. "Barely landed before we nabbed them."

Folville walked up to the prisoners. "What was your plan?" he asked. When no one spoke, he clucked his tongue. "Hardly worth it to keep a secret now, don't you think? Your fleet has burned and sunk. You're the only ones who made it to shore. At least dazzle us with your brilliant plan, so we're all duly impressed."

The men regarded Folville balefully, but one of them lifted his head with defiance. "They told us the harbor would be undefended, and if they found otherwise or if the negotiations were successful, they'd send us a signal," he said bitterly. "They said we could just sail in and take what we wanted, that you were all either dead or had run away long ago. This was supposed to be an easy run."

Folville shook his head. "Someone gave you very bad information," he replied. "Are there more ships coming?"

The speaker shrugged. "Maybe. Not for a while. I'd heard they were going to wait to see what we brought back."

"Going to be a long wait," Folville replied. "You know how this has to end."

The speaker gave a short nod. "Since we've failed miserably, can you at least make it quick?"

Folville felt a stab of pity. He knew little of war personally, but his entire life had been a fight. *Can't win all the time. Just have to hope the times you lose aren't fatal. These fellows got the short straw.*

"What do you want done with them?" Zeke asked.

Folville looked out across the harbor. Smoke hung heavy in the air. Two of the ships were burning, one nearly down to the waterline. From what he could see at a distance, the catapults had broken the masts on a third, and scuttled a fourth. The last ship, hemmed in between the wrecks and the boom chain, had no hope of escape. The fishermen's blockade with its nets stretching across the bay remained in place, ensuring that no boats or swimmers from the enemy ships would get through. If there had been soldiers in the holds of the other ships, they were lost to the sea now. The battle for Castle Reach Harbor was over except for the mopping up.

"Hang them off the arm of the crane," Folville replied. "We've got too damn many corpses in the harbor already."

CHAPTER
TWENTY-SEVEN

——

"YOU SURVIVED." PENTREATH REESE'S VOICE WAS a raw whisper, but for the first time since he had been rescued from the oubliette beneath Onyx's manor, he was conscious and lucid.

"In a manner of speaking," Pollard replied. "Your suffering was visited on me every moment of the day since your capture. And I endured it without the benefit of being *talishte*."

Reese gave a gravelly chuckle, a sound that made Pollard think of a corpse expelling the last breath in its lungs. "Good," he wheezed. "Very good."

Pollard shoved down the white-hot anger and kept his face carefully neutral. "You're gaining strength," he observed.

"Liar," Reese shot back. "I am a shadow of myself. It will take time," he added, and despite the frailty of Reese's voice, Pollard could hear steel beneath it.

"You wished to see me?" Pollard prompted, having found that efficiency provided an excellent protective screen to reduce the amount of time he spent in the company of his master, and helped him to keep revulsion out of his reaction.

"Yes." Reese spoke slowly and sibilantly, drawing the word

out like a snake's warning hiss. "I must have richer food if I am to heal. I require you to find it for me."

Pollard frowned. "We've brought you nearly one hundred mortals," he said. "Almost all sturdy young men and women, very few old or sick."

"Not good enough," Reese snapped.

"What do you require?" Pollard replied in the bland voice courtiers used to mask annoyance. *I'll be damned if I'll add 'm'lord,' no matter what he thinks he's entitled to,* Pollard thought.

"Bring me ones full of life," Reese demanded. "Pregnant women. Women at their moontime. Girl-children just at the cusp of maidenhood. Young men who have not lain with a woman. Bring them to me. Their blood is rich."

Pollard thought he was long past disgust for his master, only to find that Reese had exceeded his low expectations once again. "Of course," he said. "But such requirements may take a bit more time."

"Get them!" Reese's voice was a harsh rattle, and his emaciated frame shook with the effort of his shout. Even in his current condition, Pollard knew Reese could snap him like a twig.

Pollard inclined his head in acknowledgment. "Shall we continue to bring you less perfect food as well? The patrols have rounded up another twenty captives."

"I will make do...until you supply me," Reese growled. "Send them to me. I hunger."

"As you wish," Pollard replied, with just enough edge to his voice to let Reese understand that Pollard was more than servant. *At least, that's what I tell myself,* Pollard thought. On the other hand, he could count himself lucky that for the moment, both Garin and Thrane were not present. *I should be thankful for small favors.*

He left Reese's underground convalescent chambers restraining his urge to run. Nilo was waiting for him outside the front door, and they walked down the front steps in silence, not speaking until they were in the remnants of what had once been Solsiden's formal gardens. Nilo listened silently as Pollard recounted Reese's demands. Pollard could see Nilo's temper rising as he spoke. "He has no idea how difficult that will be," Nilo fumed.

Pollard made a dismissive gesture. "He doesn't care."

"Bad enough to have talk about people disappearing, even though we've tried to take travelers and strangers, people who wouldn't be missed," Nilo ranted. "But this—it's likely to bring an uprising."

Pollard shrugged. "Marat Garin and his ilk would probably welcome an excuse," he said. "They've gotten overconfident."

Nilo scowled. "They've forgotten that if enough mortals rise up, even they are not invulnerable."

"They'll care when the peasants head our way with torches and pitchforks," Nilo muttered. "Or at least, head your way— I'll be with the army and have to save their sorry undead asses."

"I would have thought that immortality might make one more careful, more aware of consequences," Pollard said. "But apparently not. Or maybe, death doesn't change how people were before they died." Though the sympathetic wounds he shared with Reese had begun to heal since his master's release, the price was not only Reese's constant presence but being overrun with the broods of Garin and the rogue Elders, as well as their toadying mortal servants and sycophantic hangers-on. *No different, perhaps, than those who cling to the hem of any petty despot or strongman,* Pollard thought, *but infuriating, nonetheless.*

Thrane, Garin, and the other Elders needed sustenance as

well and had decided that drinking the blood of cows or deer was beneath them. They, at least, fed more circumspectly most of the time. Part of the second floor had been given over to their 'herd' of donors, captive humans whom Thrane and his fellow *talishte* fed from as they pleased. This arrangement meant the people of the herd lived somewhat longer, and a favorite might last for several days, perhaps a week or two, but it was always the same in the end.

I'm running out of room to bury the bodies, Pollard thought. *And there are too many to burn. Thrane and Reese are going to bring the mob down on our heads with their arrogance. As if I needed something else to worry about.*

"I don't get the impression that Reese was ever the cautious sort," Nilo observed. "So...any ideas on how to do this and keep from leaving a trail back here?"

Pollard sighed. "Go a day's journey or so away from here. Spread the word that one of Esthrane's priestesses will be blessing children and youths and women with child. Set up a tent down the road and out of sight of the village. Grab them as they come in."

Nilo raised an eyebrow. "You're a cold son of a bitch," he said.

"Always have been," Pollard replied with a shrug. "I've found that it works." He paused. "Oh, and one more thing. Send a whore to Eljas Hennoch. Make it clear to her that if he doesn't sleep with her, we'll kill her. That should inspire her. Post watchers at the peepholes in his room—shouldn't be difficult given the subject. Make sure it happens."

"You're removing his eligibility?" Nilo asked with a sly smile.

"Larska Hennoch is useful to me," Pollard replied. "And to Reese and Thrane, regardless of whether or not they consider most mortals to be interchangeable. He will be most helpful if his son remains alive."

"What from Thrane?" Nilo asked. "Now that Reese is free, what's his plan? Sooner or later Penhallow and the other Elders will retaliate. We need to be ready."

"Thrane has been gone since the night after Reese was freed," Pollard replied acidly. "I suspect he's gone back to talk to his Meroven puppet."

"Nagok?"

Pollard nodded. "Thrane's quite taken with Nagok. He's bound him with the *kruvgaldur*. And it was Thrane who helped Nagok rise to power, after the Devastation in Meroven," he replied. "He worries me."

"You sense a threat?"

Pollard shrugged ill-temperedly. "There is always threat when there's a new favorite," he said. "Nagok is quite probably insane. And he is powerful. We need to remain visible—and valuable."

Nilo nodded, and Pollard knew he understood what was not said. Just like at court, where nobles constantly maneuvered to gain and keep the favor of the king, Thrane kept his vassals off balance and insecure, so that each would continually look for ways to outdo his competition. At court, a noble who fell from favor might miss invitations to hunt with the king or attend a ball. Those who fell from favor with Reese and Thrane stood a much higher risk of becoming food. *I have played this game too long and at too high a price to finish without the crown of Donderath,* Pollard thought. *It's all for naught if Thrane grows too fond of Nagok. Let him rule Meroven. Donderath is rightly mine.*

"You have a plan?" Nilo asked.

"Forming one," Pollard said. "And we require the full cooperation of Hennoch to make it work. Nagok will see us as rivals or as expendable. We must give Thrane a reason to value us, so that we don't lose his favor."

"And?"

"We have two opportunities," Pollard continued as they walked. The grounds were no longer carefully planted and the shrubbery maze had not been groomed since the Great Fire. Here and there, portions had burned down to the roots, and the wild storms and winds had uprooted other sections. Instead of manicured forms, the bushes grew shaggy and wild. Yet the ruined maze was one of Pollard's favorite places, one of the few areas he could go and feel some distance between himself and his masters.

"Theilsson's portion of McFadden's army has ventured north," he said. "They're far from reinforcements, and our scouts say his encounters with Nagok have not gone well. It will be a while before McFadden can reach him with more troops. If we could break Theilsson while he's vulnerable, it might even deliver McFadden into our hands, if McFadden were to show up and find the other half of his army has been destroyed."

"That would certainly be to our credit," Nilo chuckled. "It would eliminate the only other real competition for control of Donderath—or its throne. And the other chance?"

"Voss's men have gone south to Castle Reach," Pollard replied. "To fight the Cross-Sea threat. From things Thrane has said, I suspect he had a hand in that, too. Their assault leaves fewer men to guard Westbain or Rodestead House. While McFadden would be the prize, attacking Penhallow's territories would strike a blow at Thrane's enemies, for which he would note our value."

"I'll take my army to fight Theilsson," Nilo said. "Hennoch's troops are better suited to strike-and-flee attacks at Castle Reach from inland."

"I'll take soldiers to attack Rodestead House," Pollard added. "Westbain, too, if the opportunity presents itself. Voss has soldiers at Rodestead, and Penhallow's still using Westbain as his base. An attack should distract him, pull off some of his people." Pollard and Nilo both knew the truth: that Pollard was not yet recovered enough to do more than skirmish. His wounds healed far slower than Reese's. Though it was possible to heal and strengthen through the *kruvgaldur*, Reese was more inclined to tap Pollard's energy to restore his own faltering reserves, just as he was more likely to use the bond to spy on Pollard's movements than to feed his servant any information.

Nilo nodded. "Sounds good."

Pollard gave a grunt. "Send mages with both armies," Pollard said. "As many as you can pry loose. I'll take some with me, too. You'll need them. Theilsson travels with battle mages— he'd be a fool not to if he's going up against Nagok. And it's reasonable to expect that there are mages in residence at Mirdalur, whether they're working on artifacts or merely holding the territory for McFadden. Those mages could be diverted to the front lines within a day."

"Doesn't sound like it will be a quick win," Nilo observed.

"Would you rather go up against the Wraith Lord at Lundmyhre?" Pollard asked, raising an eyebrow archly.

"Point taken," Nilo replied.

Pollard knew that Nilo was aware of Pollard's near obsession with the Wraith Lord and his mortal servant, Bevin Connor. Connor was the only other person whom Pollard had ever known to be bound by more than a superficial *kruvgaldur* link to an ancient, powerful *talishte*. The differences in their situations had not escaped his notice, increasing his bitterness about how Reese chose to use the hold he had over Pollard, and how Thrane exploited that bond for his own purposes.

"What do you make of the Cross-Sea pirates?" Nilo asked, bringing him out of his thoughts.

Pollard shrugged. "Not much, given that our scouts have said little. If Thrane's really involved, then they're more of a threat to McFadden and his allies than to us. All the same, it wouldn't hurt to get a few more of our men into Folville's territory, so that we get better information."

Nilo snorted. "Folville keeps his inner circle small. They're people he's known for a long time, and they're insanely loyal. Newcomers don't get close to him. That's been the problem—every time we send men to Castle Reach, they disappear."

"Send better men." Pollard was silent for a moment. "Eliminating Folville would be a noteworthy accomplishment," Pollard mused. "He's canny and shrewd, but still an easier target than Voss. McFadden depends on him and his street gang to help hold the city. Folville's whole operation depends on him—kill him, and they're just a bunch of riffraff. I doubt any of his lieutenants could rally them."

"Do you really think we could occupy Castle Reach? McFadden's got a sizable number of soldiers at Quillarth Castle," Nilo countered.

Pollard shrugged. "Occupying it isn't the goal. Leaving it burning and in chaos would be a plum. McFadden would have to conquer it all over again from Folville's rival gangs, with the Cross-Sea raiders chomping on his heels. He'd have to divide his troops, and his focus." He gave a cold smile. "Light enough fires, and he can't put all of them out."

"It's a good plan," Nilo said. "But first, you and Hennoch have to survive your meeting with Nagok."

Pollard nodded. "Thrane, no doubt, wants both sides to properly intimidate each other. And spy on each other, so he can see which one of us provides the more sensational betrayal of the other. It's his idea of a game." He and Hennoch had been commanded by Thrane to meet with Nagok. It would require several days' journey from where Pollard was based at Solsiden to Nagok's camp farther north, at the Meroven border. In Pollard's estimation, it was like leaving the viper's lair to venture into the bear's den. "I guess it's time to meet the monster," Pollard muttered.

Nagok had claimed a corridor of land at the Meroven border for his incursions, an area within the lands defended by Pollard's troops, which Pollard considered to belong to Donderath. Nagok's men also streamed through the mountain passes of the western ridges of the Riven Mountains, stretching down into Donderath like the grasping fingers of a reaching hand. *And that is exactly what Nagok is, a clutching, grabbing hand with very long fingers indeed,* Pollard thought. *I'll be damned if he'll enlarge Meroven at Donderath's expense. I haven't worked this hard to gain the crown of a shrunken kingdom. As far as I'm concerned, that's my land he's taking. And I intend to get it back from him, one way or another.*

"Are you sure he's not setting you and Hennoch up to be eliminated?"

The thought had occurred to Pollard. "I'm sure of nothing. But if that's his plan, I have no intention of cooperating."

CHAPTER
TWENTY-EIGHT

NAGOK HAD PITCHED HIS FORWARD CAMP JUST inside the Donderath border, an assertive claim to the lands of Meroven's perennial adversary. The stockade was sturdy, made of wooden posts carved into a point at the top, painted black. Ropes tied with human skulls and bones hung down from the fence, a terrifying warning to all who approached. Towering wooden totems of animals stood on either side of the gate, carved with the snarling faces of predators ready to strike. Wolves, eagles, panthers, and bears, badgers, and hawks were all depicted as their prey might see them, just before the fatal strike. Beaks wide, maws open, teeth bared, and claws unsheathed, the creatures had been carved with uncanny realism, enough to make Pollard shudder as he passed.

Perched on platforms above the fence like gargoyles were a few terrifying additions that had not been among the animals in the totems. A life-sized carving of a beetle-like creature squatted with its insect eyes trained on the gate, and Pollard recognized it as a *mestid*, one of the magicked beasts brought by the wild-magic storms. Next to it was something that looked like a huge crab, big as a large dog, a *ranin*. And beside the *ranin* was a nightmarish winged creature with fierce talons and a sword-sharp beak, something Pollard knew from bitter experience was a *gryp*. All of the monstrous creatures glared down at those who dared ride through the gates, looming sentinels and reminders of Nagok's power.

Even the wooden gates bore large carved pictures that hung down over the boards, testifying to Nagok's power as a beast caller. In one of the scenes, it showed a cowled and cloaked man on a rise, arms outstretched, and from his feet raced snarling beasts—real and imaginary—toward a common enemy. In the second scene, the triumphant predator beasts carried home bodies and severed limbs to gift their master, while the land around them lay piled high with corpses.

Nagok likes to make a strong first impression, Pollard thought cynically. *Is he mad, or just very clever?*

The interior of the stockade was as theatrical as its exterior. Guards walked along the perimeter, each with a steel helmet forged in the shape of a menacing animal head. The soldiers were clad in black, wearing cloaks trimmed in wolf fur. Around their necks hung bone talismans, some with the skulls of raptors, others with the long, sharp teeth of predatory animals.

In the center of the camp was a semicircle of carved wooden heads on steel spikes, but as Pollard neared the heads, he realized they were the scowling faces of watchful gods, not trophies of vanquished foes. A small fire burned in the middle of the semicircle, and Pollard saw that offerings had been laid beneath each of the heads, and that the animals depicted matched those in the totems by the gates.

Are they gods? Pollard wondered, eyeing the fire-lit carvings. *Or are we to think Nagok is a god?*

Nagok's campaign tent was large and black, with red flags

streaming in the wind. It hunkered on the hill like a hungry beast, an association Pollard was certain was completely intentional. As with the outer gates, ropes tied with skulls and bones both human and animal were festooned from the tent poles. Pelts from wolves, foxes, panthers, and other predators hung from the sides of the tent, tufted with feathers from eagles, hawks, and owls, kestrels, and falcons. A garland of teeth and talons hung over the tent flap, and all who entered were obliged to bend beneath it to enter.

They say this Nagok is a beast caller, that he can force wild animals to do his bidding, Pollard thought. *Yet he decorates with their skins and skulls. I doubt he treats his human allies with more loyalty. What stinking shit pile has Thrane gotten us into?*

Two guards stood outside the entrance to the tent, each holding the chains that restrained large, snarling, muscular dogs that snapped their teeth as Pollard and Hennoch approached.

"Lord Thrane sent us," Pollard said to the guard on his left, a tall man with a powerful build who wore a wolf-skin cape and a metal helmet in the shape of a wolf skull. "We're here at Nagok's request."

The guard said nothing, but nodded his assent. Then he and his companion each took a step back so that the vicious dogs no longer blocked the entrance. Still, they did not retreat farther than absolutely necessary, making it a test of wills for Pollard and Hennoch to pass between the lunging, growling guard dogs that fell short of their legs and cloaks by scant inches.

Pollard had expected a strategy meeting with a general. He found himself in the receiving tent of a self-styled king, or perhaps the shrine of a dark god. There were no tables set with maps with which to plan campaigns and discuss the movement of troops. Instead, torches lit the far end of the rectangular tent, one on either side of a raised, throne-like chair of heavy, carved wood. One arm of the chair was carved in the likeness of a bear, its mouth wide open and teeth bared. The other arm of the chair was a carving of a dire wolf, a creature long gone from Donderath but present in its legends and nightmares.

"Come closer. You're expected." The voice was deep and resonant, and Pollard had the feeling he had somehow ended up in an elaborately produced stage play. Guards in their steel-skull helmets stood in a silent line against the shadowed walls of the tent. Pelts and hides covered the floor. The air smelled of musk and incense. And at the far end, on his carved 'throne,' sat Nagok.

Though Pollard took care to keep his hand well away from his sword, his mind calculated how long it would take him to draw his weapon as he and Hennoch walked toward Nagok. *It wouldn't matter*, Pollard thought. *Even if we could defend ourselves against him—which we probably couldn't—the guards would be on us in a trice, and they'd loose the dogs, for good measure.* Not for the first time, he wondered if he and Hennoch had been sent for Nagok to dispose of, a gift from their fickle *talishte* master and his maker. *Then again, it's like Thrane to play both ends against each other. He'll use us as his spies, and read our blood when we return. We're his tools. I know that, but does Nagok?*

"So you are Vedran Pollard and Larska Hennoch. Interesting." Nagok did not elaborate, but Pollard suspected that whatever about them Nagok found of note was likely not positive.

Pollard studied Nagok, sizing up this new competitor. He guessed Nagok was in his early thirties, broad-shouldered and average height, with long, dark hair that fell loose to his shoulders. Muscled arms showed beneath his skin cape over a coat that appeared to be made of patched-together human scalps. Nagok wore a breastplate made from human arm bones lashed together with leather strands. Next to his throne sat his steel skull helmet, more menacing than anything Pollard had glimpsed among the guards.

Nagok's features were not handsome, but determination showed in the set of his jaw and the glint of his eyes. A scar cut across his nose and cheek, and the nose was misshapen, broken more than once. Despite all that, an undeniable aura of charisma and power radiated from Nagok, and it was clear from his expression that he was well aware of the effect he had on those around him.

Magic? Pollard wondered. *Or just the natural charm of a potions seller?*

"Thrane speaks of you," Nagok said, lounging in his throne, making it clear he had no intention of rising to greet them. "Some good. Some not."

"I've heard the same of you," Pollard replied without inflection. *I know his kind,* Pollard thought. *Young and cocky, sure old dogs like us have nothing to offer. It always comes as such a surprise when the 'old dogs' whip their asses.*

"Your reputations precede you," Nagok said lazily. "And rumors of your ambitions."

"As with you." *And so we dance,* Pollard thought. *A game of what is said and what is implied.* "It's been a while since I've been to Meroven. I've heard the Devastation went harder on Meroven than the Cataclysm hit Donderath."

"True," Nagok replied. "But I've restored order, and consolidated power. Meroven is under control." He smirked. "You can hardly say the same of Donderath."

Pollard shrugged. "Less damage from the Cataclysm left more contenders to power. We've eliminated all but one of the threats." *Two, if I count Nagok—which I do.* "We have enemies to fight. Tell us why we've come, and let's get down to it. Our troops are waiting for us."

Nagok rose languorously, like one of the great predatory cats. He moved gracefully, light on his feet like an acrobat or a well-trained swordsman. Yet as he walked closer, Pollard got the answer to the question he most wondered. *He's breathing. He's mortal.*

"Thrane's attention has been with his blood-son, as is proper," Nagok said. "He is my patron, and master, as he is yours," he added. "And since we are his trusted commanders, he asked me to impart the plan to destroy Blaine McFadden and his armies."

Do tell, Pollard thought. *This should be interesting. And it raises a question: Has Thrane bound Nagok as his human servant? Likely. While technically, I belong to Reese, and through him to Thrane. Is there a way to turn that to my advantage?*

"First of all, speak nothing of the details to the *talishte* at Solsiden," Nagok warned. "Thrane does not trust any that are not his brood or that of Reese. He does not believe that all of the rogue Elders truly support our ascendancy."

Of course they don't. They're not going to step aside and let Thrane grab all the spoils. Just because they opposed Penhallow and the Wraith Lord doesn't mean they're loyal to Thrane. Talishte are, first and always, loyal to themselves, Pollard thought.

"If he doubts their loyalty, I'm surprised they still exist," Pollard replied.

Nagok's smile was chilling. "Thrane conserves his resources," he said. "While the *talishte* lords may not be united in wanting to see Thrane ascendant, they are of one mind to wish to see Penhallow fall. It will require their broods to make that happen, and to Thrane's mind, destroying Penhallow and crippling the Wraith Lord is worth the alliance.

"In fact, that's why your master sent you," Nagok said in a confidential tone. "Because there's a large battle commencing, and he wanted you well away from Solsiden."

"What about my men?" Pollard demanded, worried that Nilo and his troops were going to be caught up in one of Thrane's schemes. *Just like Thrane to tell Nagok something he 'neglected' to tell me, to give Nagok the upper hand.*

"Don't worry—there's no place for mortals when *talishte* war among themselves," Nagok replied. "Thrane has no need of your army in this." He leaned forward. "Would you like to see what's happening? What your master knew but did not deign to tell you?" The hint of a smile touched the edges of his thin lips.

Pollard hesitated. Nagok did not share information without a price. He felt as if he were in one of the old creation myths, offered a dark secret by a darker god. It was no revelation that Thrane and his *talishte* kept their own counsel, particularly on matters relating to their own kind. Pollard had long ago acknowledged that he was brought into situations only when Thrane or Reese decided he could be useful. That limited knowledge might hinder Pollard's ability to strategize with the big view in mind did not seem to be of concern to them.

Still, the chance was too good to pass up. "How is it you can show this to me?" Pollard asked, curious but cautious. *Once you've shown curiosity, you've taken the bait. And he knows it.*

Nagok smiled, and Pollard felt a shiver go down his spine. "Follow me." He sauntered over to a rectangular object draped with black cloth, and pulled the covering away. Beneath it was a mirror, but one unlike anything Pollard had seen gracing the walls of manors or palaces.

The surface was not silver, and it did not reflect the scene in front of it. Instead, it was glossy obsidian, yet as Pollard stared into the mirror, the gleaming surface shifted like oil on water, with patterns that swirled and moved of their own accord. Pollard had no magic of his own, but he had been around strong magic enough to know its signature, and to understand that the prickling feeling on the back of his neck and the hair that rose on his arms was a primal warning that he was in the presence of power.

"Not much to see right now, is there?" Nagok said offhandedly. He went to a side table and selected a glass ball about the size of a large apple. Nagok lifted the ball with one hand, spoke a few murmured words, and passed his other hand over the orb. The glass ball sprang to life with an inner glow, and just as suddenly, the image of the inside of Nagok's tent appeared in the dark reflective surface of his mirror.

"Quite handy, don't you think?" he asked rhetorically, turning in a slow circle so that the ball took in all of the tent. *It was disconcerting,* Pollard thought, *to see his own image looking back at him from something that was not a reflection.*

Pollard forced himself to look unimpressed and gave a dismissive shrug. "What good does that do us? Thrane isn't fighting his battle here."

Nagok's thin-lipped smile let Pollard know that the beast caller understood the game being played. "No, he isn't," Nagok conceded. "But I know where he is fighting—not far from here, actually." From the end of the same table that held the glass balls, he took a thick leather glove and falconer's arm sheath and fitted them on with the ease of long practice.

Nagok strode out of the tent and into the night. He raised his face to the dark sky, gave a chilling call that sounded more animal than human, and looked expectantly up at the stars.

For a moment, there was silence. Then a great dark shape winged toward them, and a raptor's cry filled the air. An eagle descended to alight on his outstretched left arm, folding its broad, mighty wings around it. Nagok spoke in low tones to the bird, which regarded him without fear, a pet of sorts.

As frightening as Nagok's display of power was, Pollard could not ignore the awe of seeing such a magnificent creature at close range. "Beautiful, isn't she?" Nagok said, his voice betraying both pride of possession and the knowledge that the possession was envied. "Did you think I only call wild beasts to my service?"

Nagok held up the glass ball, and spoke again to the eagle. The creature gave a shrill cry, then lifted up from its perch on Nagok's arm. The mage tossed the glass ball into the air and the eagle seized it in its powerful talons, then winged into the night sky.

"Have you ever wished to fly?" Nagok asked. He beckoned for them to follow him. "You've had a journey, and in a moment, we'll eat and you'll tell me of your wars. But first, I offer you this," Nagok said, gesturing toward the obsidian mirror.

Pollard stared at the mirror, transfixed. The world spread out in miniature, bathed in moonlight. He recognized landmarks—a river, a road, a manor—but they were small compared with the wide horizon that stretched as far as the eye could see. Hennoch caught his breath, and Pollard only barely managed to dampen his wonder into an expression of ennui. *Is that how the world looks to birds? How small our monuments seem, from that perspective.*

Nagok whispered to the mirror, and the eagle flew lower. Pollard recognized the setting. He and Hennoch had ridden near the place just a candlemark earlier. The buildings and landscape grew magnitudes larger, and Pollard could make out figures moving so rapidly that he at first mistook them for shadows. It was a long-abandoned mining town, and the empty mines were ideal crypts for *talishte*. Judging from the fight under way, it appeared that their resting place had been discovered.

Pollard leaned forward to see better. The eagle made slow circles, gliding on a thermal, so that the scene took them toward and then away from the fight. At this distance, it was impossible to make out whose side the fighters were on. Still, there was no missing the terrifying brutality of the actions. One group of *talishte* were raiding the crypts of another.

"The creatures are my eyes and ears," Nagok said. "I ask what they have seen, and they tell me. I command them to watch for me, and they comply."

Secretly, Pollard was certain that Nagok's power had less range and more limits than the beast caller suggested, but he said nothing. *Maybe that's Thrane's real reason for sending us here. To find a weakness that he can exploit. Interesting. I'm sure Hennoch and I are being used. The question is, by whom? Or if by both, where does the greatest advantage lie to my interests?*

The battle continued, both sides evenly matched in speed and ferocity. Pollard had seen *talishte* fight in the Battle of Valshoa and in skirmishes at Mirdalur, but that had been a handful of undead fighters against a largely mortal army. Individually, the *talishte* had the advantage, yet their numbers were small enough that they could not hope to prevail against so large a force. In those battles, the *talishte* had adapted their tactics to yield the greatest number of casualties and inspire the most fear.

Now, Pollard glimpsed what *talishte* fighters could really do, untrammeled by a mortal army. He watched in horrified fascination. It reminded him of the conflicts he had seen between wild beasts. Once, while riding across a barren area of northern Donderath, he had seen two male wolves fighting over a female. The wolves had been equally matched in brawn and determination, and they had fought with utter abandon. By the end of the conflict, the wolves had battled with such ferocity that one lay dead and the other was too badly wounded to claim his mate.

Perhaps I should heed the lesson of that fight, Pollard thought, suppressing a grim smile. *The two dominant males destroyed each other, and the prize was no doubt claimed by a less powerful male who won by surviving.*

"Whose *talishte* are fighting?" Pollard asked.

"Sapphire's brood," Nagok replied. "Along with Amber's get. They found a nest of Penhallow's loyalists." *That confirms the whereabouts of those two missing rogue Elders,* Pollard thought. *As Nilo and I suspected. But are they with Nagok as advisers or spies? Or to make sure he remains under Thrane's control?*

What an interesting show he's putting on for us, Pollard thought cynically, observing with the vigilance that had kept him alive thus far. *He demonstrates his power and his ability to place us under surveillance without needing to threaten us personally. But I wonder: Is the lesson intended for us, or for Thrane?*

"If you know where the fight is, could you not send your creatures to help?" Hennoch asked. "A few wolves might turn the battle, and we're not far from the fighting. They might reach there in minutes."

Nagok did not appear interested in the suggestion. "I don't think my *talishte* allies will need the help. Indeed, they might take offense. I suspect that by the time my wolves could reach them, the battle will be over. See? Our side is already taking the upper hand."

From what Pollard could see, one side was gaining the advantage. But before the battle was resolved, the eagle suddenly gyred away, rising into the night sky and presumably returning to his master.

"What happened?" Hennoch asked, staring at the obsidian mirror in confusion. "The fight wasn't over yet!"

Nagok gave a shrug. "Not finished, but decided," he said as if the matter were of no account. "Eagles are intelligent birds. He may have feared he was discovered."

Something about Nagok's blithe response struck Pollard as false. *Perhaps the eagle feared discovery,* Pollard thought. *A talishte able to fly might have been able to damage the bird. But none of the talishte were in the air. The fight was on the ground, and the eagle was high enough overhead to be of no interest to them. What if the eagle had reached its limit of compulsion?* Pollard wondered. *What if our beast caller can't keep his creatures under permanent control?*

He hid the shadow of a smile. *Nagok has limits. The eagle was gone for somewhere between half a candlemark and a candlemark. So maybe that's how long he can maintain his hold over a creature. Hennoch was right—sending in wolves or other hostile creatures might have turned the battle sooner, with fewer casualties for his allies. So that raises another couple of questions. Did he refrain from doing so in order to weaken his allies as well as his enemies? Or can he only control one type of creature at a time? And the fighting was close to his location. I wonder how far his range extends?*

For the first time since they had set out from Solsiden, Pollard felt hopeful. *Nagok is powerful, but not a god. And if Thrane's talishte allies spend their forces battling Penhallow's allies, it reduces the total number of powerful undead. Advantage—ours.*

"Your eagle is a formidable ally," Pollard said as they followed Nagok outside again. The huge bird of prey gave a shrill cry and flapped down, dropping the glass ball into Nagok's hand before coming to rest on his vambrace. Nagok handed off the orb to Pollard, and reached into a small pouch on his belt, giving a treat of dried meat to the eagle before launching it on its way.

Pollard took the opportunity to examine the glass ball. In his hands, it was unremarkable. No glow hinted at latent magic, and no hidden power tingled at his touch. It was deadweight.

"Can you supply the ability to scry like that to our army?" Hennoch asked, eyeing the glass ball acquisitively. Such an advantage was something commanders could only dream of, unless they had *talishte* spies who could take to the air, and that was limited to nighttime spying only.

Nagok gave a condescending smile and reclaimed the glass ball from Pollard. "Unfortunately not," he said, though his tone suggested he thought it was anything but unfortunate. "The birds won't listen to a common mage, and it requires particular talent to also activate the orb and the scrying mirror."

Translated message: I'm far more powerful than your mages, who can't hold a candle to what I can do. Interesting detail— want to bet Nagok can only control one bird at a time, for a short period and a limited distance, and he's only got one special mirror? Limits, again. Pollard stepped back half a pace, using the distance to better observe Nagok. Nagok moved with swaggering grace, every word and action designed to exert dominance and impress them with his power.

I've seen men of real power, from King Merrill to the Wraith Lord, Pollard thought. *They couldn't care less what others think of them, and they aren't constantly posturing. Nagok is young and quite taken with himself. That's likely to make him overreach. He's using Thrane, and Thrane is using him. Both of them are using me. That's fine for now. Donderath needs a king. And once Blaine McFadden is out of the picture, I'm still the only real option. I can be patient for a crown.*

"We've come a long way to meet with you," Pollard said as they returned to the tent. In the short time that they had been out of the tent, a repast of mutton and roasted vegetables had been set out for them, as well as tankards of ale and a bottle of brandy. "And while we appreciate your generous welcome, we will need to leave early on the morrow. Tell us of your plans, and we will share ours," Pollard continued. "So that we can rid Donderath of both Penhallow and McFadden."

"Of course," Nagok replied. "But first, we dine."

Under the best of circumstances, Pollard found formal dinners tedious. Now, he found his patience strained, and he wished they could get down to the business at hand. Nagok had no intention of rushing through the meal, and as they ate, he regaled them with stories of his victories in Meroven. Pollard had no doubt the litany of successes was well rehearsed for effect, and he strained to listen for insights Nagok might not have intended to reveal.

Nilo and I were right about Thrane's meddling with the Meroven talishte *and their equivalent of the Elder Council,* Pollard thought. *And while he claims to have defeated the other Meroven warlords, it sounds like the kingdom was in such bad shape, there wasn't much opposition. At least, nothing that compares to what we've had to fight to get this far. Easy victories lead to pride. Pride's led to many a downfall. Maybe Nagok isn't quite as invincible as he believes.*

When they finished eating and servants had cleared away the dishes, Nagok unrolled a map of Donderath on the table and anchored it open. "We have drawn Theilsson's army to the north," he replied. "And while Theilsson has fought well, we've not yet brought our full might against him. He has already taken many casualties, and his men are tired. I would suspect that he has sent word to McFadden for reinforcements—perhaps even led by McFadden himself," Nagok said, barely hiding a smile of satisfaction with his own cleverness.

"I need you to make sure McFadden's allies don't come to his aid," Nagok said, sparing a glance to Pollard and Hennoch. "As I've been told, it was Traher Voss's troops that turned the balance of the Battle of Valshoa. He must be kept busy elsewhere."

"We have been fortunate to have the Cross-Sea pirate attacks focus Voss's men on the Castle Reach harbor," Pollard said. "Those attacks have kept both Voss and Folville busy at home, unable to be relocated."

"We can't count on the Cross-Sea forces to continue their assault," Nagok said. "I have asked Thrane to dispatch your men to attack Castle Reach, Westbain, and Rodestead House to keep those forces bottled up."

Pollard carefully avoided a smile. *Exactly as we hoped*, he thought. "A wise strategy," he said, with a warning glance at Hennoch to give no indication that they had already planned to do just that. *Let Nagok bear the brunt of the fighting. His army can take the casualties for a change, and preserve my men for when I need them. Fine with me if he stays up here in the northernmost corner. I'll thank him not to further damage the kingdom I plan to rule.*

"Pressure must be kept on Penhallow's fortifications, especially during the day when he's at his weakest," Nagok said. "Thrane's allies will continue to strike at his brood and the get of his Elder supporters. Your men must whittle away at his human troops, reducing their numbers, destroying their morale. They're no doubt bound by *kruvgaldur*, so I don't expect wholesale defection. But your attacks can kill as many as possible, and pen them up so they can't turn the tide of our battle with McFadden."

"What of McFadden's other allies?" Pollard asked. "Tormod Solveig the necromancer and his bloodthirsty sister. Birgen Verner and his troops. Have you factored them into your plans?"

Nagok made a dismissive gesture. "Verner is of no concern to us. The man has no ambition, and is unlikely to bestir his troops so long as he sees no immediate threat to himself. As for the Solveigs, they're far from here, busy with their own concerns from the west. I don't see them storming across the kingdom to come to McFadden's defense."

Personally, Pollard was unwilling to write off the other warlords so easily. *Nagok considers nothing but their self-interest because self-interest is all that motivates him. I suspect the Solveigs and Verner are more like McFadden, damnably obliged to keep the letter of their agreements. Nagok might have a care to consider just how well Thrane will keep his promises, especially if he's counting on being gifted with the crown of Meroven. I know to watch my back, and I'm not counting on Thrane's largesse to get the prize I want. Neither Nagok nor Thrane care whether Donderath burns, so long as they control it. I would prefer not to rule a kingdom of corpses. In that, perhaps, McFadden and I have some sentiment in common.*

"Hennoch's troops are already near Castle Reach," Pollard replied. "Once we return, I'll send them on to harry the city. I will personally make sure that Westbain and Rodestead House remain under siege." He paused, intending for his silence to be taken for thought, when he had already known his question long before.

"Can you spare any of your beasts?" Pollard asked, as if the answer was of no importance. "Could any of your lesser mages travel with our troops and command packs of wolves or panthers? We would gain a formidable advantage."

"My mages, regrettably, have so many responsibilities with my troops that they cannot be spared," Nagok replied. "It's unfortunate, but it can't be helped."

"Ah. It was worth asking," Pollard said with a shrug. *So his beasts have the same constraints as his birds. He's the only one who can control them. An advantage—and a liability.*

"When will you make your assault on McFadden's troops?" Hennoch said. While Pollard had been watching the interaction as intelligence gathering, sizing up Nagok as a future opponent, Hennoch had grown increasingly impatient with talk and panoply. For all his faults, Hennoch was a straightforward man who preferred action to politics. If he had his way, Hennoch no doubt would have preferred to ride back to Solsiden with his orders that very night.

"Within a fortnight," Nagok replied. "I'll have the rest of my forces in place by then. Right now, the positions of our adversaries work in our favor. We must strike before the circumstances change."

With luck, Nagok, Thrane, and McFadden will destroy each other, and the kingdom will go not to the most powerful or the cleverest but to the one most invested in remaining alive the longest. I intend to be the last man standing.

CHAPTER
TWENTY-NINE

W AS IT WORTH IT?" CONNOR WATCHED PENHALLOW
unwrap the Elgin Spike from its shrouding. He noted
that Penhallow was careful not to touch the artifact. The
Wraith Lord's translucent form stood nearby, observing with
interest. Arin Grimur, who had returned with them from Edgeland, hung back, watching. Tormod Solveig had joined them as
well, journeying to Westbain with a portion of his troops while
Rinka took the rest of the army north to join Niklas and Blaine
against Nagok.

"It gives us a chance we wouldn't otherwise have," Penhallow said. "And that's something important." He turned toward
Grimur. "Thank you, Arin, for what it's cost you to keep this
safe all these years."

Grimur shrugged. "The solitude did me good. And I didn't
mind the snow. I'll be happy to not have the White Nights, but
I might go back for the Long Dark. My cabin's locked up tight,
waiting for me."

Connor shivered just thinking about it. *Two visits to Edgeland in one lifetime are too many,* he thought. "I hate to say it,
but getting the artifact might have been the easy part in all

this," Connor observed. "How is someone going to get close enough to Thrane to use it?"

"I'll admit that's a difficulty," Penhallow said. "We expected Thrane to attack the allied Elders. So far, he's used proxies to do it, without putting himself at risk."

"That's not surprising, given that it's Thrane, but it does make our job harder," the Wraith Lord replied.

"Do you have a plan?" Grimur asked.

"We're working on it," Penhallow replied. "There are... variables."

"Best we figure out something soon," the Wraith Lord warned. "Too many mortals are disappearing—presumably to provide food for Reese to recover—and we'll be facing a mob with torches if we don't bring an end to it quickly."

Outside, a thunderstorm raged, driving rain against the windows, wind howling through the shutters. "What's the next step?" Connor asked.

"Nidhud has gone back to brief Dolan and the rest of the Knights of Esthrane on Thrane's latest moves, and what we know about Nagok," Penhallow replied. "We're certain Nagok is one of Thrane's puppets. I expect Nidhud to return tomorrow night with Dolan and an updated battle plan."

"Is Nagok as fearsome as his reputation?" Connor asked.

Grimur shrugged. "He's a beast caller. That's a rare magic. I haven't seen a powerful beast caller in over a century."

"Longer than that," the Wraith Lord said, frowning as he thought. "And powerful—but not invincible. In some ways, I would argue that when mages are especially powerful in one area, they are more limited in others."

"I agree." Grimur nodded. "A beast caller's real strength is surprise. Calling down a pack of wolves or a flock of birds and forcing them to attack creates panic. In some ways, it's more unsettling for nature to turn on an army than for them to face ghosts or even animated corpses."

"How can we turn his limits against him?" Connor asked. "And are there ways we can make his strengths of less impact?"

"I believe that's where I come in," Tormod Solveig said. "The question is, how can I use my necromancy against Thrane and Reese without causing problems for our allied *talishte*?"

"It can be done," Grimur said. "Your power as a necromancer only affects our kind during daylight. So you—and Connor— could make the first strike against the mortal soldiers and at least some of Thrane's brood before dark."

"After dark, once the *talishte* awaken, I can offer other magic as well as my sword, but I agree that I'm best used before dark," Tormod replied.

"Mages always face a threefold limit," Grimur replied. "Range, duration, and intensity. So Nagok is not invincible."

"I've got watchers with Niklas Theilsson's troops," Penhallow said. "We should be getting a report from them in a day or so. If we watch for patterns in how Nagok uses his power in battle, we'll know his limitations."

"Nagok is not our immediate problem," the Wraith Lord said. "It's Thrane we need to worry about. He's never been reticent about making fledglings, and he's had a long existence in which to make them. The rogue Elders also tended to have larger broods, with fewer compunctions about turning—or killing—mortals. That puts us at something of a disadvantage."

"Perhaps," Penhallow said. "On the other hand, I've fought some of their brood, and they did not make wise choices on those they turned. Loyalty only counts for so much. Intelligence, initiative, creativity—that's what turns the tide in a battle."

"We've got to protect our people," the Wraith Lord said.

"That last attack of Thrane's cost us a dozen *talishte*. The allied Elders are concerned."

"So how do we stop Thrane?" Connor asked.

"We get him to overextend himself," the Wraith Lord replied. "That's one of the things that led to his downfall, long ago."

"How do we get him to do that? Surely his defeat taught him not to repeat the same mistake," Tormod said.

Penhallow's smile was sad. "*Talishte* were once human, Tormod. How often do mortals make the same mistake again and again?"

"I had hoped that learning might come with a long existence," Connor replied.

"Sadly, not as often as you might expect," Grimur said. "Thrane is as grandiose as ever, and as willing to allow others to die for his grand schemes. Witness his current path. Donderath is a blank canvas. There is plenty of room for him to carve out a territory for himself, rule it as a lord. If he dealt humanely with the mortals, he would be left alone. But of course, he wants to rule it all."

"Rule a wasteland, after the fighting is done," Connor muttered. "But how can you even get close to him? He's surrounded by his brood, and Reese's brood."

"We take the battle to him," the Wraith Lord said with a predatory smile.

The next evening, Westbain's great hall was crowded with *talishte*. Nidhud and Dolan, as well as several of the other Knights of Esthrane, stood at the end of the long table along with Penhallow. While the Wraith Lord could make himself seen and heard for a limited time without Connor's help, to address the gathering of allied Elders, he had asked to use Connor's body for greater physical presence.

For once, Connor did not mind. *I'd rather be possessed by an ancient* talishte-*mage in a room of* talishte *than be a mere mortal. Sheep among wolves and all that.*

If you are a sheep, then it is a sheep with fangs, claws, and a remarkable survival instinct, the Wraith Lord replied silently, drifting off into a baritone chuckle. *You are hardly a 'mere' mortal.*

All of the allied Elders with the exception of Bayard were there. Aldwin Carlisle, Garrick Dalton, and Marin Jarett stood together near one wall holding half-empty goblets of deer blood, watching Nidhud and Dolan skeptically. Dag Marlief—Onyx—had been destroyed in the attack that freed Reese.

"Our plan to destroy Thrane involves using ourselves as bait," General Dolan said. Tonight both he and Nidhud wore the full regalia of the Knights of Esthrane, and Connor was certain it was to evoke the memory both of the Knights' legendary prowess as warriors and their uncanny level of success, a reputation that had once led mortal kings to banish them as a threat.

"Thrane is certain of his superiority. And if we allow him to choose the time and place of his strikes, he has the upper hand," Dolan continued. "He has amassed an army, and he's itching to use it. So we'll be his targets, one way or the other. But if we present opportunities that appear too good to pass up yet are carefully managed to provide us the advantage, then we'll either decimate his troops or sour his allies."

"Why should he go after us more than once?" Carlisle asked, swirling the blood in his goblet. "Surely after the first loss, he'll realize that the game is rigged against him."

Dolan nodded. "That's why the opportunities must be offered close together, so that he must choose 'and' and not 'or' without time to evaluate between. They must appear logical, and we must appear to take reasonable precautions. And we must move in utter secrecy." He paused. "I believe we have traitors among the broods."

A babble of voices strenuously objected. Dolan raised his hand for silence, and acknowledged Garrick Dalton. "Our broods are bound to us by the *kruvgaldur*," Dalton protested. "How can there be traitors?"

"The *kruvgaldur* is strongest with the get you made directly and the mortals whom you have bound most deeply," the Wraith Lord replied through Connor. "It remains strong between maker and fledge, but each generation weakens the strength of the bond back to you. Past the third generation, it is unreliable as a means of forewarning, and limited as a means of control, best mostly for surveillance. That is even truer for the bond between you and the human servants of your get."

"The *kruvgaldur* is strongest for urgent needs, life-or-death warnings," Dolan replied. "But we have all heard of progeny that found ways to destroy their makers. For disloyalty, the *kruvgaldur* is a lazy bond. It must be actively monitored—preferably by reading the blood—in order to fully know the intent of one's get. How many of you read your broods individually on a regular basis? How many have ever read the get of your get? Their servants?"

Reluctantly, the former Elders shook their heads. "That is why we insisted that tonight's meeting be among our inner circle," the Wraith Lord said.

"You have your human servant," Jarett said petulantly.

The Wraith Lord fixed him with a glare. "And I am

inhabiting his mind and his body. Can you do the same?" Annoyed, the *talishte* looked away.

"We will arm you," the Wraith Lord continued. "Each of you will be given a destination. We fully expect you to be attacked, either on the route or when you reach where you're going. You and your direct get will know of the ruse—and you must blood-read them to ensure their loyalty," the Wraith Lord said.

"Half of your brood will go with you, half will remain with the loyal get," Dolan continued. "Those who go are the bait. Those who remain will be the strike force. I will leave it to you to decide which half you personally wish to be in, but Thrane's men should see a mix of Elders staying and going."

"And the traitor? What about finding him?" Carlisle asked with a set of the jaw that told Connor he meant to deal permanently with that problem.

"You are to do nothing to find the traitor, or even acknowledge outside this room that there is a traitor," Dolan said. "If we do anything at this point to root out the disloyal ones, Thrane will know and our ruse won't work. We'll know soon enough who the untrustworthy ones are. And when they show themselves, you may deal with them as you see fit."

"All well and good that we draw off the rogue Elders and their broods," Dalton said. "But what of Thrane?"

Nidhud nodded. "A small team will go after Thrane and Reese. We've chosen *talishte* with the skills we believe can defeat him. He'll have minimal mortal support to use against us here, at Rodestead House and at Mirdalur."

"I've dispatched Geir to warn Niklas Theilsson and Blaine McFadden, along with Traher Voss," Dolan said. "Pollard and Hennoch will find quite a few *talishte* from our broods waiting, along with Penhallow's soldiers and several mages. It won't be the rout he expects, and in the meantime, Theilsson and McFadden will bring their army against Nagok, while Pollard and Hennoch are engaged a few days' ride distant."

"Nagok also has *talishte* at his disposal," Jarrett pointed out.

"Nagok is Thrane's man," Penhallow said. "The *talishte* that support him are Thrane's get, except for Aubergine. Destroy Thrane, and we destroy their only reason to be loyal to Nagok."

I notice you're not mentioning the Elgin Spike, Connor observed silently.

No, we're not. We're not going to remind them of it. The less said, the better, the Wraith Lord replied in his mind. *Also why Grimur is keeping to his rooms, since his presence would be a reminder.*

"Your plan is full of uncertainties," Carlisle said. "It's risky."

Dolan nodded. "All battle plans are," he acknowledged. "But we believe that a concerted, multifront strike against Thrane's allies and Thrane and Reese themselves will prevail." He paused and looked around the room at the *talishte* assembled there. Once again, Connor was very aware of being the lone mortal in a room full of ancient predators.

"I cannot emphasize how important it is that this initial strike be successful," Dolan said. "Right now, Thrane is arrogant. He's sure that we're too disorganized to rise against him, and that his plans are too clever for us to comprehend. He doesn't know the full scope of the resources at our command. If we attempt this strike and fail, Thrane won't present such an easy target again. We may lose our chance to win, and the cost will be dear indeed."

The next two candlemarks were spent hammering out the details, as the former Elders asked a seemingly endless series of questions, some pertinent, some not. Dolan, Nidhud,

Penhallow, and the Wraith Lord answered with more patience than Connor could muster, doing their best to win over the headstrong Elders and gain their full cooperation.

"I've taken the liberty of placing a geas upon everyone in this room," the Wraith Lord said, and there was an audible rustling as all those present turned to stare at Connor. "For all our safety, I have insisted that what has been discussed here not be mentioned to any but the intended partners."

"You have no right—" Jarett said, a flush coming to her face.

"He has every right," Carlisle said. "Kierken is correct. We all stand to lose everything if someone among us speaks of our plans too widely. And while I would like to believe that all of my former Elder Council fellows understand discretion, I fear that too often in the past, we have learned of council business shared indelicately."

Everyone in the room avoided looking at Dalton. The *talishte* had gone rigid and particularly pale, and Connor wondered if this was an old matter and a sore subject. *Dalton knows why I've done such a thing*, the Wraith Lord commented to Connor. *And while neither he nor the others like it, they understand the consequences.*

"We'll see if Thrane takes your bait," Jarett said. "If not, then it's time we took matters into our own hands." One by one, the Elders filed out, disappearing into the night.

Thank you for your service, the Wraith Lord said. *I will depart.* And with that, Connor shuddered and felt Kierken Vandholt's spirit leave him.

Connor sagged against the table. He took a deep breath and straightened. "When you form your strike force to go against Thrane, I'm going with you."

"Absolutely not," Penhallow and the Wraith Lord said in unison.

Connor raised an eyebrow. "It makes no sense to leave me behind. Without me, you lack the full power of a mage and a fighter, as well as the physical prowess of a *talishte* who is older than Thrane."

"Even with me in possession, you are not full *talishte* in strength or immortality," the Wraith Lord said. "You are not quite as fast, nor can you fly."

"Neither can you," Connor observed.

"I don't want to lose you," Penhallow said. "You're too valuable an asset to me. Thrane would see you as a weak point, use you against us."

"Factor that into the plan," Connor said, raising his chin defiantly. "He knows the Wraith Lord can possess me, but he was dismissive of it back at Lundmyhre. He hasn't seen us fight together, and I bet he doesn't know that the Wraith Lord's magic is enhanced when he's got a body to use."

"I cannot sanction this," the Wraith Lord said.

"Yet he has a very good point," Dolan remarked. The Wraith Lord's spirit turned to glower at the Knight of Esthrane, and Penhallow's expression made it clear that Dolan's remark was unwelcome. "With his help, we nearly have Kierken Vandholt at his full power," Dolan continued. "It's likely to take all of us, at full strength, to defeat Thrane and the rogue Elders, not to mention Nagok. I fear that in this, there is no real choice if you wish to win."

"Connor, there will be many *talishte* that don't survive these battles," Penhallow said. "It is very likely that you could be injured too badly for us to heal you. You don't have to do this."

"I've come this far," Connor said. "I've seen what the Wraith Lord can do through me. And if Thrane and Nagok win, I have to live with the consequences, in a Donderath I don't want to see exist. I have a great deal at stake as Bevin Connor, aside from *talishte* and spirits and Elders. This is my kingdom, too. And if I were not in Lord Penhallow's service, I would be fighting with Blaine McFadden's army." He crossed his arms, as if daring them to disagree.

The Wraith Lord chuckled. "I have the distinct impression, Lanyon, that if he could, he might run off and enlist, just to make his point." His tone was a mixture of respect and fond indulgence. "Once again, you never cease to amaze me, Bevin."

Penhallow looked as if he would have let out a long sigh, had he needed to breathe. "I fear he has a good point, and it is well taken. Very well. But," he said, his tone growing stern, "I do not consider you to be expendable. Kierken will do his best to protect you, but I also expect that you will take good care, under orders of your master, to come back alive and in one piece."

Connor inclined his head in acknowledgment. "Agreed, m'lords. And I am most definitely intending to come back from this." Unbidden, the warning he had received from Garnoc in his delirium echoed in his mind, and he forced it away. *I've always known this could cost me my life. At least if it does, I'll have done something that mattered.* He felt a mixture of excitement and nervous nausea. "Now, what about that plan?"

Connor found Zaryae sitting on the garden terrace when he left the strategy meeting. "I'm late," he said. "I was afraid you wouldn't wait."

Zaryae smiled and took his hand. "I figured you would find me one way or another when you were done. Westbain's not that large."

Connor sat down next to Zaryae on the stone bench and she

rested her head on his shoulder. Their friendship had become more than that on the long journey back from Edgeland, and Connor was grateful for her company. *It means a lot that we both understand how it is to live with a magical gift that can be more of a curse. I can't imagine trying to explain it to someone who hadn't experienced magic of their own.*

"Are the plans set?" she asked.

Connor nodded. "As much as plans ever are." He looked out onto the moonlit gardens. Before the Meroven War, Westbain had belonged to Vedran Pollard. Penhallow had seized it, partly in retribution for Pollard's men having burned Penhallow's day crypt. Though Westbain had not suffered as much damage as the manors belonging to Lords of the Blood, the Great Fire and the Conflagration had gone hard on the old home and its lands.

The gardens were overgrown, burned in places, while in other spots, large trees and bushes had been torn up by the roots. Still, with a little imagination Connor could envision what it must have looked like in its prime. A ruined fountain stood empty in the center of what were once sculptured hedges. Gravel pathways led down toward banks that had been filled with flowers and now overflowed with weeds. At the far end was a weathered pergola that had somehow escaped the fire.

"Verran and the twins are packing to return to Glenreith— or to wherever Blaine's army is now," Zaryae said, looking down into the old gardens.

"Aren't you going with them?" Connor asked, pulled out of his thoughts by her unexpected comment.

Zaryae shook her head. "I'm staying here. I want to help with the fight against Thrane. And I want to be with you."

Connor squeezed her hand. "I want you near, but I want you safe even more," he said.

She drew back and turned to look at him. "And where would

I be safe? Glenreith? Maybe, but my foresight would be no use to the fight. Castle Reach? Mirdalur? Doubtful. Camping with Blaine's army would be even more dangerous." She paused. "There isn't anywhere 'safe' where I can be of use. So I might as well be here."

Connor bent down and kissed the top of her head. "There is a plan. I wish I could tell you more, but I can't, and to be honest, it's safer for you this way. Does your Sight tell you anything?" Connor asked.

Zaryae shook her head. "Not yet. It's often silent when I want most to know something," she added ruefully. She looked at him thoughtfully. "You're planning to go with them, aren't you?"

Connor sighed. "Yes. Penhallow argued against it, but even he had to see the wisdom of it. My gut tells me that it is important that I be there."

"You're still not *talishte*, even with the Wraith Lord's help," Zaryae warned. "And if you're hurt too badly, Penhallow may have no choice except to turn you."

"I know," he said, putting his arm around her shoulder. "But they're all risking their existence as well. And it won't be worth living if Thrane and Nagok win and Vedran Pollard gains the throne. And if Nagok takes the throne of Meroven, how long before he decides to finish what he started and add Donderath to his empire? Thrane wouldn't stop Nagok—he looks at everyone in Donderath as nothing more than food. If Blaine and Penhallow and their allies can't win this, who else will try to stand against Thrane and Nagok? Maybe no one—at least, not in our lifetime."

Zaryae sighed and snuggled next to him. "Enough of war. It will come soon enough. Tell me another story about how it was before the war. I never saw Castle Reach before it burned."

For the two months they had been stuck aboard ship going to Edgeland and coming back, Connor and Zaryae had entertained each other with stories. Connor had already shared the unexpected adventure on the night of the Great Fire that sent him to Edgeland the first time and ended up with him in Penhallow's service. Zaryae had recounted what had happened to the performing troupe she and the twins had traveled with from the Great Fire to when they met up with Blaine at Rikker's Ferry.

Now that the big tales had been told, what remained were everyday stories, reminiscences about a world that was forever gone. And while Connor would not have considered those memories to be particularly noteworthy before the Cataclysm, they had become more precious among the ruins. Zaryae listened as Connor told a story about one of the war councils he had attended as Garnoc's assistant. It struck Connor as he spoke that although all the people in his tale had been powerful and well-known before the Great Fire, he was the only one who had survived.

"Tell me a story I haven't heard before," Connor said when he finished his tale. "Something to take my mind off war."

Zaryae chuckled. "I told you all my good stories on the ship."

"Then tell me a bad story," he said with a smile. She grew pensive and turned away.

"I didn't mean it that way," Connor cajoled. *How can I hold my own with ancient* talishte *and muddle it so awfully with a woman?*

Not so difficult to fix, the Wraith Lord's voice sounded in his mind. *Get her talking. Find out what's bothering her. Show her that you care no matter what she tells you.*

I'm getting romantic advice from a thousand-year-old ghost?

Don't discount the value of experience! the Wraith Lord said with a chuckle. *And now I'll leave you two to yourselves. She's a good one, Connor. Don't mess this up.*

And with that, the Wraith Lord left him. Connor felt so totally out of his depth that he almost called Vandholt back. Then he drew a deep breath and laid a hand gently on Zaryae's shoulder.

"I'm interested in any story you want to tell me," Connor said. "Good or bad. I love you, Zaryae. Your stories are important to me."

For a moment, he thought she would walk away, but then she moved to face him. "I guess you'll hear it sooner or later, from the twins." She hesitated again, then plunged ahead.

"We had to leave the Lesser Kingdoms and our tribe because of me," she said finally. "My Gift. It was before I knew as much about how to use my ability. I was so young," she added, shaking her head at the memory.

"My foresight came on me with my moon days," she said with a blush. "At first, I would just blurt things out, things that I saw. People thought I was crazy. Then, when my predictions came true, they thought I was a witch. They were afraid. So were my parents."

"They didn't value what you could do?" Connor asked, taking her hand as he listened.

"They were scared of me," she said quietly. "The gift of foresight isn't unknown among my people. Some who have it become very powerful, tribal leaders, advisers to the king. But it's not something you learn, or practice. One day it's not there, and then next day—all of a sudden you're 'prophesying.'" She looked down at her hands. "It changed me in their eyes. I wasn't their daughter anymore."

Connor felt himself go cold with anger. "What did they do?"

"They sent me away," Zaryae said without looking up. "To live with my uncle."

"Illarion?" Connor asked. Zaryae nodded. Connor had met Illarion before the Battle of Valshoa. He had lost his life on the perilous journey into a hidden, guarded mountain pass.

"He was my mother's brother. And he took me in, no questions asked, even though he had children of his own. Borya and Desya were his grandsons. Kata was his niece."

She paused. "The four of us grew up like siblings. Sometimes, I could pretend that there had never been anything else, that they were my real family and I was their sister."

"But something changed to make you go wandering," Connor said.

Zaryae sighed. "Illarion taught me how to guide my gift, how to keep from blurting things out. For a while, that worked. And then I saw something so powerful I couldn't help it. I foresaw the death of the wealthiest man in the city. It was a murder. I tried to warn him, but I was too late—and the magistrate thought I had something to do with it."

She tightened her grip on his hands and looked at him with a fierce expression. "Illarion gave up everything for me, and so did my cousins. He assaulted the sheriff to free me, and we took off with just a couple of horses, a wagon, and all the goats and chickens we could carry, plus what he and the twins had been able to throw together on a moment's notice."

Zaryae was quiet for a moment, remembering. "We fled into the Western Plains. After a while, they stopped chasing us. But it was done. None of us could ever go back. Illarion had the idea to create a traveling performance group. The twins were excellent riders from herding the flocks. Kata had an amazing singing voice, and the two of us could dance."

She blushed. "We were young enough and pretty enough that it didn't really matter how well we danced, men would throw coins," she admitted. "The twins learned to do some fancy acrobatic tricks. Illarion was our master of ceremonies, and back then, he could sing and play instruments as well. After a while, I learned to control my gift enough to be able to tell fortunes without saying too much."

"You survived," Connor said. "You made a way for yourself."

Zaryae shrugged. "It was hard. Sometimes food was scarce if coin was lacking. We traded for some things and stole when we had to, or begged." Her jaw set. "Illarion never let us down. He always found a way. He kept us together, and alive."

Zaryae stared off at the dark garden for a moment. "We weren't the only ones who left the Lesser Kingdoms," she said quietly. "There were others, outcast for a variety of reasons. If they had a talent and they weren't a danger, Illarion let them travel with us so long as they could provide for themselves. After a while, we traveled between the outposts in the Western Plains, holding our own little show. People would come from all around to see us. Word spread even to Donderath."

"That's how you came to play for Lord Corrender, right before the Great Fire," Connor prompted.

Zaryae nodded. "We played at some of the small border towns, and then were invited to hold a show at the lesser cities. Somewhere in those backwater places, a person who knew Lord Corrender heard of us, and I guess he thought it would be great fun to have us perform for him. That's how we were camped close enough to be in the path of the Great Fire," she said, her voice going quiet.

"When it was over, Illarion, Borya, Desya, Kata, and I were the only ones who survived," she added. "Borya and Desya— you know what happened to their eyes. Kata was so terrified by what she saw that night she never spoke again. My gift blasted wide open. Illarion lost his ability to play and sing, and the fire nearly killed him," she said.

"And so you went back to wandering the Western Plains after the Cataclysm, playing for small towns, begging for coins," Connor finished the story. "And that's how you were in Rikker's Ferry when Blaine found you."

"Yes, and no," she said. "We went to Rikker's Ferry because it was a null spot, a place where magic didn't work. We were trying to hide from the magic storms. We had run from them so often. We were tired," she said. "I had a vision that a man would come to that town who needed us, and a warning for him. We had nearly given up by the time Blaine came." She smiled. "But I knew he was the one for the vision as soon as I saw him in the audience."

Connor slipped his arm around her, and this time she leaned against him. "Thank you," he said. "Thank you for trusting me with your story."

"Not as exciting as the stories you've shared about the adventures you've had with the Wraith Lord," she said.

"Not nearly as funny as the stories you told me about chasing goats and chickens through rainstorms and performing your way out of a scrape with raiders," Connor countered with a smile.

They were quiet for a while, looking out at the moon and the garden. Finally, Zaryae spoke. "What will you do, when it's finally over?" she asked. "When the war ends. What will there be for you?"

Connor stared at the ruined hedgerow. "I haven't really had much time to think about it," he said. "It's been rather slam-bang since the night of the Great Fire." He let out a long breath. "I was Lord Garnoc's man. He's gone now. And for as long as I live, I'll be Lord Penhallow's man—and the Wraith

Lord's—because of the *kruvgaldur*. While I'm a Lord of the Blood, I don't really know what that means for my future..." His thoughts spun, and he struggled to pull them together. "I've been so busy just surviving moment to moment, I haven't really thought about 'after.' There wasn't a reason to worry about it, before now," he added, and gave her a squeeze. Zaryae smiled, and Connor held her close for a few moments.

"Assuming Penhallow survives, I suspect I could have a position with him for as long as I want it—for life, even," Connor said. *And thanks to the* kruvgaldur, *my life will be longer than usual, if I live through the war.* "Blaine's made it clear I'm welcome at Glenreith as well, and I'm grateful. But I think my place is here, or at Rodestead House, with Penhallow and the Wraith Lord."

He turned to her. "I have to admit, both he and the Wraith Lord have grown on me, too." He grinned. "Don't tell them—it would go to their heads. But sadly, I'm not sure it matters. The odds are pretty high that I won't come back from this one."

Zaryae regarded him in silence for a moment, and sighed. "Bevin, my gift is silent on this. I wish I could tell you otherwise. Please promise me that you'll do whatever you can to come back?"

"I'll do my very best," Connor replied.

Zaryae leaned forward and kissed him, long and lingering. She chuckled at the look of surprise on his face before he collected his wits and returned the kiss. When they finally pulled back, he was certain that he must look poleaxed with surprise.

"I know we don't have any guarantees," Zaryae murmured. "But we do have tonight to be together."

"Zaryae...are you sure?"

"Bevin Connor, I have never been more sure of anything in my life," Zaryae said as she stood. The moonlight shimmered on her skin as Zaryae let her dress drop to the ground. She reached forward, taking Connor by the hand and pulling him with her.

He moved to say something, and Zaryae put a finger to his lips. "I love you, Bevin. Nothing that happens is going to change that. I don't know what's going to happen tomorrow, but we can make this night our own. Please, give me that." He nodded, overwhelmed with emotion, and then words were no longer necessary.

CHAPTER
THIRTY

"I SAW WHAT REESE LEFT BEHIND WHEN WE LIBER-
ated Westbain," Connor said to Tormod Solveig as they
regarded Solsiden. "I don't want to think about what we're
going to find with Thrane in charge."

Connor and Tormod rode at the fore of a contingent of the
Solveig army, hundreds of men strong. It was just after noon,
and the sun was high in the sky, meaning that even a *talishte*
of Thrane's age and power should be drowsy and besotted, if
he was awake at all. It was their best chance to clear away the
mortal protectors and use Tormod's magic without jeopardiz-
ing their *talishte* allies.

"You're sure that your magic can coexist with the Wraith
Lord possessing me?" Connor asked. "He's still *talishte*."

Tormod chuckled. "In his case, the lack of his own physical body
makes the difference. The Wraith Lord is a *talishte* spirit. During
the day, I have power over *talishte* because they become corpses.
He doesn't become a corpse because he doesn't have a body of his
own. And remember—once the sun sets, my magic has no hold
on the *talishte* because they're animated by the Dark Gift. At that
point, I'm no more than a swordsman for your cause."

"I've bumped up against a mage's limits before," Connor replied. "That's always where things go wrong."

"Let's hope that's not the case today," Tormod replied. He turned to his soldiers. "Archers—in position!"

Solsiden's defenders had a double line of archers on the wall walkway, partially hidden behind the crenellations. Tormod's bowmen also formed a double line, protected by their long shields and their helmets, as the rest of the soldiers hung back out of bow range.

"Fire!" Tormod shouted. Bowstrings twanged, as a hail of arrows sang through the air. Some of the arrows struck the guards near the gate, and despite their armor, they felled two of the soldiers while the others scrambled to adjust their shields. Thrane's archers returned fire, and soon the ground around Tormod's bowmen bristled with arrows, while more of the missiles bounced off the long shields that protected the soldiers' bodies. With each volley, Tormod's archers moved a few steps closer.

Connor and the other soldiers closed ranks around Tormod, protecting him as he sent his magic toward Solsiden, reaching out to the dead and undead within its walls. Connor's magic as a medium jangled at the brush of Tormod's power, similar yet very different. Tormod's eyes were shut in concentration, and he lifted his hands, palms up, gathering and directing his power.

Connor stared nervously at the manor. Tormod's power slipped past the walls and heavy gate, bypassing the archers and the soldiers inside the stronghold, seeping deep beneath the ground into the day crypts of Thrane's *talishte*. For several moments, nothing seemed to happen. And then, shouts sounded inside the walls, followed by screams.

"Look!" one of the soldiers cried out, pointing as plumes of dark smoke began to rise from inside the walled courtyard. First a few, then more and more plumes rose until the air over Solsiden was dark with the smoke, and the air smelled like a funeral pyre. The archers on the wall kept up their defense, but their aim became erratic as more cries and shouts rose from within. As the chaos distracted the wall's defenders, Tormod's archers more often found their targets, dropping so many of the enemy bowmen that only a handful remained to protect the gate.

Another shriek rent the air, and abruptly the archers on the wall turned toward the inside of the courtyard, firing at an unseen enemy that suddenly claimed their full attention. Whatever was happening inside drew a panicked reaction from those within the walls. Connor shifted in his saddle, increasingly uncomfortable with the power that tingled across his skin, and sidestepped his horse to move a little farther away, disturbed by the effect Tormod's necromancy was having on him. *I'm alive, but I'm fighting the urge to run away*, Connor thought. *I'm so jittery I can barely stand it. No wonder talishte don't like necromancers, even if the magic isn't directed against them.*

What you feel is a faint shadow of how a necromancer's power feels to a talishte, the Wraith Lord said. *He has no power over my spirit, but when I possessed a body, I met more than one necromancer, and each time, barely survived the encounter.*

Throughout it all, Tormod's expression was taut with concentration. He gave a twist of one hand, a push of his other hand, and suddenly, the gates of Solsiden opened. Standing in the doorway were dozens of rotting, animated corpses, some bristling with arrows.

"Expect there to be armed mortals inside!" Tormod shouted to his troops. "Charge!" His soldiers surged forward. Tormod was fearsome in his black armor, riding at the fore of a tide of soldiers who descended on their enemy wailing and shrieking, a move calculated to strike terror into the enemy soldiers.

Connor, possessed by the Wraith Lord's spirit, rode with the vanguard. Connor felt his own mortal fear mix with the heady exultation of the Wraith Lord's love of the fight. As always when the Wraith Lord took command of his body, Connor marveled at the grace and expertise that was not his own, the moves of an expert warrior honed over a millennium of existence. Connor's own abilities as a soldier were much improved, but he knew he could not hope to mimic the Wraith Lord's skill, even if he had several centuries to practice.

Before the Cataclysm, Solsiden had belonged to Lord Arvo. Parts of the manor had been destroyed in the Great Fire, and Connor could see where its protective wall had been rebuilt in places. Two towers stood on either side of the massive wood-and-iron door that barred the entrance. Connor had wondered whether Thrane's mortal soldiers would surrender, anxious for the opportunity to break from their oppressive *talishte* lords. But the soldiers' fear of their *talishte* masters outweighed everything else, even when an army of the dead rose from their graves.

The walking corpses parted at Tormod's command, allowing his soldiers to ride into the enclosed courtyard, where it looked as if a battle had already been fought. Much of the hard-packed ground was scorched and blackened, covered with piles of ash that drifted in the breeze. The courtyard smelled of putrid meat and decay. The dead men formed ranks between Tormod's army and the frightened soldiers who defended Solsiden's manor house.

Connor could not stomach more than a glance at the dead men Tormod had called from their graves. These were not *talishte*, but the hastily buried victims of Reese's hunger and Thrane's excesses. Bloated and decomposing, skin blackened and sloughing off, they were the stuff of nightmares. Long fingernails protruded from shriveled, bony fingers. Empty, sunken eye sockets stared everywhere and nowhere, while the skin of the lips had pulled back to reveal the teeth in horrifying rictus. Some of the bodies were more recent dead, their death wounds still visible as bloody puncture marks on their arms and necks. Several of the corpses had their throats slit, as if Thrane and his brood were in such a hurry for the blood that they could not be patient enough to merely bite their victims.

Despite the horrors, Thrane's soldiers rallied, in between where the corpses stood at slack attention and the manor house itself. Ashen and wide-eyed with terror, they remained at their posts, weapons ready though Tormod's better armed forces outnumbered them.

"Throw down your weapons and surrender," Tormod ordered. "Surrender now, and we won't kill you."

"We can't let you pass!" A young officer stood on the front steps of the manor, sword in hand, terrified but resolute. "Leave us. You have no business here."

Tormod spoke a word of power and the walking corpses moved forward faster than Connor would have believed possible. They climbed the steps after their quarry, advancing without fear. The soldiers cried out in terror, setting about themselves with their swords, but the dead vanguard never slowed, even as swords slashed away limbs and blades opened gashes in decomposing flesh. Relentlessly, the corpse army crushed the soldiers beneath their feet or against the walls, pressing forward until the manor house defenders were destroyed.

Before Tormod had the chance to move toward the house, more soldiers streamed from the barracks in the rear of the courtyard. With a glance to assure himself that the corpses had been successful, Tormod turned to face the new foe. Several dozen soldiers attacked on foot, rallying with a battle cry.

Tormod Solveig rode at the helm of his army like an avenging god, setting about himself with his sword and clearing a bloody path for his men to follow. Connor gave himself over to the Wraith Lord's skill as Kierken Vandholt's spirit animated his body. Together, Connor and Tormod led the way to the gates, leaving a wake of corpses behind them, bloodying themselves, shoulders to thighs, in the spattered gore of their enemies. Thrane's soldiers fought well, but either Tormod's magic had badly unnerved them or they realized there was no escape. The battle was fierce but short, and in the end, the courtyard lay littered with fresh bodies, and the hard-packed dirt ran with blood.

"What of the *talishte*?" Connor asked. "How about Thrane?"

Tormod nodded toward the ashes that now covered the ground in the courtyard. "My magic called the lesser *talishte* to their deaths in the sun," he said. "Two dozen are dead. They were of middling power, neither Elders nor new fledges. I suspect Thrane sent the rest after the allied Elders."

"And Thrane?"

Tormod shook his head. "I can't sense Thrane or any powerful *talishte*. But I do sense strong magic blocking my power, a place deep beneath Solsiden that I can't reach." He shrugged. "It would be like Thrane to ward a stronghold. He had a fear of necromancers, and he sent assassins against me more than once, although Rinka and I overcame them fairly easily." The hard glint in Tormod's eyes made Connor sure that it had been anything but 'easy.'

"Find the mortal servants and take them prisoner," Tormod shouted to his soldiers. "Offer them the chance to surrender, but if they fight you, kill them. I want the boy, Eljas Hennoch, taken alive."

Connor, guided by the Wraith Lord, led one section of the troops into the manor house's upper floors, while Tormod rallied another third to descend into the cellars. The rest of the soldiers remained in the courtyard, on guard should more of Thrane's men appear from a hidden redoubt.

Connor suspected that the servants had watched the courtyard battle from the windows, because they offered no resistance, sinking to their knees with their hands raised in surrender at the sight of the soldiers. Connor led the way going door to door, weapons ready, finding only a few dozen terrified servants, who prostrated themselves and begged for their lives.

"Round them up," Connor ordered. "Collect them all in one or two rooms. Check them for weapons. Don't let anyone out until Commander Solveig or I give the order." He left a dozen soldiers to round up the servants on the first floor, and took the rest up the wide stairway to the second floor.

The second floor was in worse shape, with the damage from the Cataclysm rendering one wing uninhabitable. Most of the rooms were empty, although a few frightened servants, cowering in alcoves, threw themselves on the soldiers' mercy. One soldier remained guarding a door at the end of the hallway. When he saw the well-armed invaders heading his way, he threw down his sword and raised his hands in surrender.

"Where's Eljas Hennoch?" Connor demanded, though he was quite sure he could guess.

"In there," the soldier replied, kneeling as the soldiers grew closer. "Please don't kill me! I didn't hurt him. I don't know anything!"

"Take his weapons and tie his hands," Connor ordered with a glance toward two of his men. "We'll let General Solveig decide what to do with him." He looked at the captured soldier. "Give me your keys to the door."

"Please don't take my keys!" the man begged. "Lord Thrane promised to do terrible things if I fail my duty. Please, kill me and then take the keys."

Connor looked at the frightened man with pity. "We've come to kill Lord Thrane," he said. "Now, give me the keys."

Sobbing with terror, the soldier removed the keys from his belt and tossed them on the floor at Connor's feet. "Take him away," Connor ordered, and the remaining soldiers closed around him as Connor turned toward the locked door.

"Stand back!" he shouted through the door. "We mean you no harm. Stand away from the door." Connor turned the key in the lock and opened the door, sword at the ready.

"Did my father send you?" A young man stood against the far wall of the room. Bars covered the windows, though the rest of the room was the comfortable bedroom of a middling nobleman. A stack of books lay on a writing table, along with a lyre and a pennywhistle.

"Eljas Hennoch?" Connor asked. The prisoner carefully kept both hands in view and made no move toward the soldiers, giving them no opportunity to mistake his motives.

"I'm Eljas," the young man replied. Although he was pale and slender, he appeared to be clean and adequately fed.

"We serve Lord Penhallow, allied with Lord McFadden," Connor said. "Our forces have come to destroy Thrane and his get. We bear you no ill will. If you'll come peaceably, we'll get you to safety."

Eljas did not move. "Is my father dead?"

The young man had a quiet courage that impressed Connor, and maintained his dignity despite his reduced status. "I don't know," Connor answered honestly. "His troops are at Castle Reach, and I have no word of how the battle goes."

Eljas inclined his head. "Thank you," he said quietly. He glanced toward the window, noting the afternoon light, which was far spent. "You'll want to be gone before sunset," he observed.

Despite Eljas's self-possession, Connor saw fear and resignation in the young man's eyes. "Have Thrane or Reese bound you to them? Read your blood?" he asked.

Eljas shook his head. "No, though they've threatened time and again." Moving slowly, so as not to cause alarm, he carefully pushed up both sleeves and held his unmarked forearms out for inspection, then drew open the neck of his shirt to show the smooth, unscarred skin of his neck.

Connor nodded, relieved. *There's no telling what the Spike will do to those tightly bound by the* kruvgaldur *to Thrane and his get. At least Eljas is spared that much.*

"Bind his wrists as a precaution," Connor ordered the soldiers, "until one of our *talishte* can assure us that he's not bound to Thrane. He's to be treated cordially unless he causes trouble," he added with a warning glance toward Eljas. "Place him with the servants until I call for him."

Eljas made a shallow bow. "Thank you, sir," he said, and dared to meet Connor's gaze. "My father had no love of Lord Thrane and no interest in his schemes. I was his surety. He was a pawn in this as surely as I was. I doubt that will spare his life, but it needed to be said."

Connor nodded. "Understood, though I can make no promises or guarantees."

"Then I trust you all the more for your honesty," Eljas replied, holding out his wrists to be bound. Two soldiers led him away, and Connor watched him go before turning back to the remaining soldiers.

"Let's clear what's left of the upstairs, and then get back to the courtyard. There's work to do," Connor ordered.

Several candlemarks later, Connor and Tormod waited in the darkness with Penhallow, Dolan, Grimur, three of the Knights of Esthrane, and a dozen *talishte* soldiers, as well as Elek, a scout. "Looks like Thrane's Elders took the bait," Elek reported. "We did what you said—told our extended broods that the allied Elders were moving half their get to a new safe house. The rest stayed behind and waited. The traitor got word to Thrane, because his *talishte* hit us right where you figured they would."

"Is the fight still on?" Penhallow asked.

Elek nodded. "Unequally matched, to my eye. With Onyx destroyed, there are only three Elders left with us, now that Gray went to handle the Plainsmen and the Wraith Lord is with you." Even with Sapphire and Jade destroyed, that left five of the rogue Elders who sided with Thrane.

"And are all of the rogue Elders in the fight?" Connor asked the question, but it was the Wraith Lord who sought the answer.

"Our scouts have confirmed that Aubergine is here," Elek replied. "He and his brood left Meroven last night." He smirked. "That's how we found the traitor in Carlisle's extended brood. He had a lover among Aubergine's get. Carlisle has disposed of him."

Penhallow nodded. "The Knights of Esthrane and the 'loyal' get—they struck from the rear as planned?"

"Yes," Elek said. "But the battle is fierce. I wouldn't like to wager money on the outcome."

Just your existence, Connor thought.

Such is ever the case, the Wraith Lord responded silently. *As you well know by now.*

"I came to tell you that we've spotted Amber, Emerald, and Saffron fighting our Elders with their broods," Elek reported. "With luck, that means only Red remains with Thrane tonight."

"One Elder and a *talishte* of Thrane's age will be challenging enough," Penhallow replied, "since Thrane is sure to have Reese's men as well. Maybe Reese himself, if he's healed sufficiently." Pentreath Reese might not have been old enough or powerful enough to have been one of the Elders, but he was still strong enough to pose a significant threat.

"None of the *talishte* I destroyed were of any significant age," Tormod said, and if it made him nervous to be a necromancer among ancient *talishte* warriors, he did not show it. "That tells me Thrane and Reese, along with their favorites and your rogue Elder, are likely in his hidden room."

Elek nodded. "I'd say so." He glanced at the small team headed for Solsiden. "I wish you good hunting," he said, though he sounded skeptical.

"You also," Penhallow replied. With that, Elek disappeared into the night, headed back to the fight.

"It changes nothing," the Wraith Lord said.

"True, but confirmation is always helpful," Dolan concurred. "Although I have never fully trusted scouts' reports." He gave a grim smile. "I know from experience how easily appearances can be staged to mislead."

"Agreed," Grimur replied. "Is McFadden in position to take advantage of the shift if we win?"

"Blaine had a thorough briefing ahead of time," Penhallow said. "He was part of the planning process, and he had tactics in place to capitalize on any opportunities we create for him. This is really a two-pronged attack in the same battle: us against the *talishte,* and Blaine against the mortals."

Talishte *warriors, a necromancer—and me,* Connor thought. *I must be out of my mind.*

And us, the Wraith Lord corrected, emphasizing the plural. *Don't forget—most of our group are mages as well. Neither Thrane nor Reese have magic. We are a formidable enemy.*

We have no idea how many talishte *Thrane and Reese can field against us,* Connor fretted.

You've heard the reports, the Wraith Lord replied. *Thrane seems to have spread himself thin. He's overconfident. That's exactly where we want him—and why we must win on our first try. If he becomes wary, he'll be much more difficult to destroy.*

Connor had his own opinions about how to define an 'easy' kill and he was sure the night's work was not what he had in mind, but he held his tongue. No doubt the Wraith Lord was privy to his thoughts. *None of us believe this will be easy, Bevin,* the Wraith Lord said. *Only that it may be less difficult. It's a slight distinction, but an important one nonetheless.*

Securing Solsiden had been the first step. Penhallow had brought a dozen of his most trusted *talishte* fighters with them, men of whose loyalty he was certain, and three of the Knights of Esthrane came under Dolan's command.

Mortals think talishte *are invincible,* Connor thought. *Here I am, surrounded by some of the oldest, most powerful* talishte, *and I wish that were true.*

Beneath Solsiden were cellars, dungeons, and catacombs, and according to Grimur, therein lay a weakness—and the route to find Thrane.

"I knew Lord Arvo, at King Merrill's court," Connor mused as they followed Grimur. Before the Cataclysm, Solsiden had been Lord Arvo's manor. "He was on the War Council. I'm sure he took no notice of me. He and my former master, Lord Garnoc, frequently disagreed."

"Arvo was a pompous ass," Penhallow replied. "He was part of the anti-*talishte* faction of lords, and put pressure on Merrill to keep us banned from court." Connor suspected that Pollard knew that, and may have found a perverse satisfaction claiming Arvo's family manor for his *talishte* lords.

"This is the place." Arin Grimur had led them out into the middle of a deserted pasture. Tall grasses, as high as Connor's thighs, bent in waves in the summer wind.

"Are you certain?" Dolan asked, peering around them in the darkness. Penhallow and Dolan had specifically chosen the dark of the moon to make their move, and out here, far from the manor or the welcoming lights of a village, the darkness enveloped them.

"I'm certain." Grimur nodded determinedly. "The last Lord Arvo might have disliked *talishte*, but the man who was lord a century ago had *talishte* protectors and retainers. Back then, he used the passages beneath the manor for day crypts, and the *talishte* had a way in and out that led here, so that they could leave to feed without using the formal entrances and exits."

"Don't you think Pollard or Reese would have bricked a passageway like that up, if it didn't collapse in the Cataclysm?" Connor asked.

Grimur shook his head. "They didn't find it. I made sure of that before I led us here. The passage exists—and it leads into the cellars. Where we come out, exactly, I'm not certain, but there's a door and it works. I didn't dare go farther. The entrance is just damn difficult to see in the dark—which was the whole point of putting it out here." He looked from Penhallow to Dolan. "I'm sure this is the redoubt Tormod sensed."

Tormod nodded. "I can feel the magic from here," he said. "Whoever layered the protections did well. It's very strong. And the wardings were specifically charged against necromancy." He gave a wan smile. "But other magic will be just as deadly."

Dolan turned to Connor. "Here," he said, passing an object wrapped in tattered canvas to Connor, who knew even before he touched it that he held the Elgin Spike. "We believe that the Wraith Lord will be the best one to use this," he said gravely. "The rest of us will fight to create the opportunity for you to do what must be done."

The entire mission rests on me, Connor thought, feeling sick to his stomach, but he nodded bravely.

On us, *Bevin,* the Wraith Lord reminded him. *You are not alone in this.*

In a few moments, Grimur located the entrance, a hidden, sloping hole that led beneath the meadow and deep into the hillside. Penhallow stationed two of his men to secure the entrance behind them, and headed belowground. The others navigated the dark, cramped passageways easily, but Connor stumbled and bumped against the rough rock walls.

Give control to me, Bevin, the Wraith Lord said. *I can see what you cannot.* With a sigh, Connor allowed the Wraith Lord's presence to come to the fore, as it did in battle, while his own consciousness retreated to watch from a distance.

Gradually, Connor's eyes adjusted. Trusting the Wraith Lord to guide him, they moved steadily through the twisting passageway, which appeared to be partly natural and partly dug by hand. No one spoke.

Thrane and Reese have to know through the kruvgaldur *that their get have been destroyed,* Connor thought. *Surely they felt the necromancy, even if their wardings protected them. They're going to be ready for us, and very, very angry.*

Grimur had been in Solsiden years ago, long before it was damaged in the Great Fire. He had drawn the floor plan as he remembered it, providing a map of the rooms most likely to be where Thrane and his entourage could be found.

Before long, the cold, damp passageway ended at an old wooden door. An iron lock secured the entrance. Tormod stopped a distance from the doorway. "We've reached the wardings."

In other words, it's too late to turn back now.

Dolan took the lead with Connor, Tormod, and Grimur right behind. Two of the *talishte* fighters were next, then Penhallow and the rest of the fighters. Dolan gave a warning nod. Connor tensed, ready to react.

Cold, brilliant light flared, blindingly bright as the mages concentrated their power against the wardings. Connor retreated to the far corner of his mind, giving himself completely over to the Wraith Lord. Words in languages Connor did not know drifted through his consciousness. Fearsome power tingled through his veins and found expression in the magic the Wraith Lord loosed against Thrane's defenses. Penhallow and the other *talishte* backed up, away from the rippling force that pounded at the shielding. Though Connor did not pretend to understand the arcane energies being harnessed, he could feel the texture of the magic shift, ebbing and flowing, changing direction, probing for weakness. *They're not just trying to batter the warding down by force,* he thought. *They're adjusting the magic, switching approaches, changing tactics.*

The wardings yielded with a silent explosion of light and brilliant colors, and while there was no sound, the magic reverberated in Connor's mind with enough force to make him reel. Thrane's magical protections fell, and the battle was on.

A dozen *talishte* fighters came at them before the last glow of magic had faded from the air. Feral and snarling, Thrane's *talishte* defenders launched themselves at full force against the invaders, while Thrane and Reese themselves were nowhere to be seen.

For as often as the Wraith Lord had taken control of his body during battle, it always amazed Connor that he could move with the silent assurance of one of the *talishte*, and fight nearly with their speed if not their strength. While Tormod was neither *talishte* himself nor possessed by a *talishte* spirit, he used his magic to enhance his fighting speed, making it an almost even fight against undead attackers. Connor noted that Tormod, more than the *talishte*-mages, relied on his magic to increase the damage of his blows or repel an attack. Gauging from the number of enemy fighters that fell to Tormod's blade, his strategy was effective.

The Wraith Lord moved forward steadily, with a preternatural confidence Connor himself did not fully feel. *After a thousand years, I've learned that I've already faced most dangers there are to face,* the Wraith Lord assured him silently. *There isn't as much left to fear.*

I'm a good bit shy of that age, Connor retorted. *And I find the world filled with new and horrifying things nearly every day.*

The tunnel opened into a set of rooms likely dug as an emergency shelter, repurposed by the *talishte* into a redoubt of day crypts. Now, it was a crowded battleground, made all the more dangerous by the cramped conditions. The battle was joined; there was nowhere for either side to run, no chance for withdrawal. Connor felt his stomach clench with fear. He was painfully aware of the magical artifact he carried beneath his jacket, and the fact that he—and the Wraith Lord—were the key to the success of the night's work, and the war itself.

Strike Thrane through the heart with the Elgin Spike, and all his get crumble to dust along with him. It sounds easy when you say it. Not so simple to do.

Thrane's *talishte* fought like men with nothing to lose, and perhaps their fear of their maker outweighed any survival instinct they possessed. *Not new fledges, but not his eldest get by any means,* the Wraith Lord judged as he cut his way through the attackers. *So either Thrane has his best fighters still with him or he's sent all his senior brood to fight the allied Elders. Either way, they'll be dust by the time we're done.*

Connor desperately hoped the Wraith Lord's optimism proved true, but he could not help hearing the echoes of the more ominous warnings from Garnoc and Zaryae. *Perhaps they will all prove true in some way I can't yet grasp,* Connor thought. *No matter what, all I can do is hold on, and pray to Esthrane that we make it to dawn.*

Black ichor splattered their armor and trickled down the walls as they cut their way through Thrane's defenders. *Talishte* corpses crumbled into dust as the fighters struck them down, but the frenzy of battle sent the particles flying, coating them all with the ashes of the dead. The defenders were no match for the skill and magic of Penhallow's invaders. When the last of the *talishte* guards fell, the double doors at the end of the hallway stood undefended. Two of Penhallow's *talishte* fell back to hold the entranceway, while the others advanced.

With a burst of speed, Dolan, Penhallow, and Grimur led the attack. Dolan's magic blasted the wooden doors open, splintering them and propelling wooden shards across the room. Grimur followed with a torrent of fire that caught two of the *talishte* unprepared. A dark-haired man with the look of a pickpocket and a slender man with close-set eyes screamed and flailed as the flames took to them like dry kindling. Their skin drew tight and peeled away, then bones charred, and in seconds, the two *talishte* were nothing more than bits of charred scraps.

Thrane and Reese were fast enough to get out of the path of the fire, moving in a blur of motion. A thin blond man stepped to the fore and thrust out his right hand, sending an answering sweep of flame billowing toward the attackers. Dolan, Tormod, and Grimur barely raised protective shields in time. The Wraith Lord grabbed Penhallow and pulled him into the protective field that deflected the flames inches in front of Connor's face. Behind them, the other *talishte* scrambled out of the way of the blast as the Knights stepped forward to block the fire with their wardings. It was too crowded for the rest of Penhallow's fighters to move into the room, so they secured the doorway, making certain no one could enter or leave.

The instant the fire stopped, Dolan and Grimur countered, focusing their magic on the blond mage. Dolan struck with a brilliant shaft of yellow light lancing toward the mage, while Grimur made a slashing motion with his hands, meaning to take the man off his feet.

Thrane did not wait to see how the mage battle fared. He struck with a feral cry, going for Penhallow as Reese ran for Connor. Two more *talishte*, a stocky man with a fighter's build and a fine-featured, dark-haired woman, launched themselves at Tormod and the two Knights behind Connor.

Just behind where the two *talishte* had been incinerated, heavy tapestries burned, flames lapping against the thick stone walls. Smoke filled the air and stung Connor's eyes.

Sonders and Marat Garin are the two who caught fire, the Wraith Lord told Connor as he parried Reese's brutal sword swing. *Vasily Aslanov is the mage—the Red Elder. The other two are Kiril and Elise.*

If Reese expected Connor to be the easy kill, he was sorely

disappointed. The Wraith Lord moved with the skill and practice of a millennium, comfortable in his borrowed body. Reese's blows were powerful and artless, hoping to win by battering his opponent into submission. The Wraith Lord struck with equal power, knocking aside Reese's blade and going on the offensive.

Penhallow and Thrane circled each other warily, swords ready, looking for a weakness to exploit. Thrane moved first, feinting to the left and then thrusting to center, intent on running Penhallow through. Penhallow anticipated the move and met Thrane's sword with a parry that might well have broken a mortal's arm.

Behind them, Kiril and Elise battled Tormod and two of the Knights, and from what Connor glimpsed, while they were well matched in battle skill, Tormod and the Knights held an advantage with magic. Dolan and Grimur remained locked in a battle of magic with Aslanov, and while to Connor's eye it appeared that the three men were trading nothing more than grunts and angry expressions, the movements of their hands and the tingle of energy that flowed around them suggested that strong magic was expended and contained in a deadly, silent contest of wills.

Reese swung again, but the Wraith Lord met the blow with enough power that he rocked Reese back on his heels. Kierken Vandholt's spirit inhabited Connor's form with a larger-than-life vitality and a lust for battle that was wholly alien to Connor's own deliberate personality. Dangerous as it was for both the Wraith Lord and Connor to share a body, even in the direst of circumstances, Connor could not escape the feeling that the Wraith Lord savored every moment of embodiment, every wince of pain and surge of victory. Connor, on the other hand, had grown used to the feeling of clinging to the reins of a bolting stallion, catching glimpses of wonder amidst terror.

The fire spread from the tapestries to a wooden bookshelf. *We don't have too long before the whole room goes up, or the air runs out. How many times have I nearly been burned or buried alive?* Connor thought.

The action around him kept him from pondering the question. Kiril had gained the upper hand against one of the Knights, though both men were bleeding from deep gashes that would have killed a mortal, and Tormod's left shoulder was bloodied. Blood streaked Elise's face and stained her shirt. She appeared to be losing her battle, though an expression of grim determination suggested that she would not yield easily.

With a cry of victory, Aslanov made a ripping motion with his hands, and the air around him flared with streaks of white-hot energy. Dolan stumbled back, already working a counter-spell. Wild-eyed and teeth bared, Aslanov went for the kill. A bolt of raw power surged from Aslanov's right hand, catching Grimur full in the chest as the Edgeland mage formulated his own counterspell. The killing magic rushed into Grimur through a gaping wound in his chest, so that his body glowed from inside, a fearsome light that set his bones in silhouette against his skin, as if he had been filled by the sun itself. Light burst from Grimur's eyes and mouth, tore loose from his fingertips, and held him for a few seconds lifted off the floor, transfixed.

In the next instant, Dolan loosed his magic with a howl of anger, stirring a maelstrom around Aslanov, a contained vortex that swept up the dagger-sharp splinters from the ruined doors and hurled them at gale force into Aslanov's body like lethal quills. Grimur's corpse fell to the floor, then withered and collapsed into dust. Enraged, Dolan's shouts grew louder and faster, defying Aslanov's attempts to break free. Aslanov was bleeding from dozens of wounds all over his body. One long shard buried itself deep into Aslanov's left eye, while another tore into his throat, opening an artery. Dolan tightened the circumference of the vortex to just slightly more than the width of Aslanov's shoulders.

The whirling shards tore at Aslanov from every direction, opening long gashes in his flesh, ripping at his scalp and clothing, embedding themselves like hundreds of shivs in his body. With one final, triumphant shout, Dolan wrested his right hand in a half circle, and a long, thin shard impaled itself in Aslanov's heart.

The rogue Elder's body stiffened and jerked as dark blood spilled from the mortal wound. Aslanov's eyes went wide with the certainty that the last death was upon him. The vortex vanished, wooden bits falling to the floor with a clatter. Aslanov's body bucked again, fighting the inevitable. Then his gaze fixed on Dolan and he gasped a single word. Dolan fell as if pole-axed, immobile, and Aslanov began to crumble like a charred rod, until nothing but dust remained.

Elise screamed and fell to one knee as her assailant's blade slashed down through her shoulder, severing her right arm. Tormod lunged forward, slipping his blade between her ribs to take her through the heart. In the same instant, Kiril swung a mighty blow, slicing through his opponent's neck. As the body fell to one side, Kiril ducked and picked up the bloody head, throwing it with *talishte* strength to catch Tormod squarely between the shoulders. With a roar, the other two Knights of Esthrane rounded on Kiril, crossing swords so quickly and with so much power it sounded like the peal of bells.

Mortal fear drew Connor's full focus back to his quarry. Reese and Thrane fought with the fury of mad dogs. Though Connor had gained endurance, hosting the Wraith Lord's spirit for a prolonged fight at *talishte* intensity was rapidly draining his energy. Drawing on his *kruvgaldur* bond with Penhallow would do him no good, since Penhallow was locked in desperate combat.

We can't come this far, just to fail!

We haven't failed yet, the Wraith Lord answered in a grim voice. Connor and Penhallow were fighting back to back as the flames leapt from bookcase to sofa, and from there to other old tapestries.

Thanks to the Wraith Lord's skill, Connor was relatively undamaged, though he had taken gashes on his left forearm and his right thigh. Reese had taken a dozen wounds as well, and his shirt and pants were sodden with blood. Penhallow looked worse, as did Thrane. Both were bleeding from gashes deep enough to expose bone. A slice across Penhallow's cheek had almost taken his eye, covering his face and neck with blood. Thrane had lost an ear, and a gash laid bare his ribs.

A look passed between Penhallow and the Wraith Lord, something Connor did not understand but Kierken Vandholt grasped immediately. "Kierken, do you remember?" Penhallow said.

"Yes." No sooner had the Wraith Lord spoken than he and Penhallow pivoted. Caught by surprise, Reese was unprepared for Penhallow's sudden attack, a flurry of lethal sword blows that forced Reese away from Thrane, requiring Reese's full attention to avoid being cut to ribbons.

The Wraith Lord dove forward, Elgin Spike in one hand, sword in the other. He knocked Thrane's sword arm wide, giving him the opening he needed to sink the Spike deep into Thrane's heart.

Connor gasped as fire lanced across his belly. A bloodied dagger was clutched in Thrane's left fist, and a vengeful grin spread across Thrane's face.

The Elgin Spike flared, blindingly bright, and Thrane howled in agony, eyes wide and staring, mouth open in an anguished cry. His skin sloughed from his body like a snake shedding its old coils, revealing naked muscle. Sinew and ligaments twisted free from bone, snapping loose like frayed cables. All the while, Thrane's eyes bulged and his skinless face contorted in agony.

Finally, stripped of skin and muscle, Thrane was a living skeleton, and then with a final burst, the Elgin Spike shattered his rib cage, splintering bone. The shards of what had been Thrane caught fire, burning with unholy light, leaving only ashes to flutter to the ground, along with the spike.

Reese screamed, a high-pitched wail of terror as the curse of the Elgin Spike spread to all of Thrane's get. Like his maker, Reese trembled and jerked convulsively as his body unwound to its basic components, his eyes open and aware, mouth twisted in a scream. And then, like Thrane before him, Reese's bones shattered, burning to cinders.

Solsiden was suddenly silent as the victors stared in stunned horror at their vanquished foes. Connor groaned, dropping his sword, and sank to his knees, both hands clutching his bloodied belly. "Thrane—all his get—destroyed?" Connor gasped.

Penhallow's eyes widened. "Kierken! What have you done?" He rushed to catch Connor as Connor sagged to the ground in a spreading pool of blood. "Dolan, Tormod! Help me!"

Strong hands grasped Connor's shoulders and laid him on his back. Penhallow's face was all that Connor could see, and fear was clear in his eyes. "Hang on, Bevin," Penhallow urged. Dolan staggered to his feet and stumbled to where Penhallow knelt next to Connor. Even with the Wraith Lord possessing his body and Tormod's necromancy clinging to his spirit, Connor's breath came in short, sharp breaths bright with pain.

"Kierken, Tormod! Don't you dare let go of him!" Penhallow muttered.

Dolan fell to his knees beside Connor and pried Connor's hands away from his ruined belly. "Sweet Esthrane," he murmured.

"Save him!" Penhallow ordered.

"Not that easy—"

Stay with me, Bevin. It would be most inconvenient to lose you now, the Wraith Lord's voice sounded with compulsion, though even he sounded worried.

Dolan was chanting, while Tormod recited words of power under his breath that encircled Connor's soul with glowing, golden bands of light. Penhallow offered his bloodied wrist pressed against Connor's mouth, starting a trickle of cold dark blood down Connor's throat. Garnoc's warning echoed in his mind. The room seemed distant, the conversations far removed. Zaryae's voice sounded in his mind.

Don't let the darkness take you, Bevin Connor, she urged. Connor wanted with all his heart to reply, but his body seemed far beyond his control.

I'm sorry, Connor thought as light and sound slipped away. *I've done all that I can do.*

CHAPTER THIRTY-ONE

CAN'T THEY TAKE A HINT?" PIRAN GRUMBLED. "How many times do we have to whip Hennoch's ass before he stops trying to invade our territory?"

"Apparently more times than we've already done," Traher Voss replied.

"You're thinking like a defender, not a thief," Folville added with a raised eyebrow, testimony to how often he had been on the other side of the equation. "If the prize is rich enough, a determined raider isn't going to be easily turned away."

"More to the point, if you have Thrane as your lord, self-preservation means picking the possible win over the certain loss," Piran muttered.

The small group was gathered in a stout stone building near the city wall that Folville had appropriated for his base for the battle on this side of the city. Betta and Captain Hemmington were there, as well as Captain Larson. Voss and Piran left guards outside the room and around the building, just in case. Bogdan, Voss's senior mage, was also in attendance, as was Doru, the representative for the soldiers who had returned from Edgeland. Most of those soldiers had gone with Blaine

McFadden toward the northern battles to join Niklas Theils-son, and a quarter of the new force had remained in Castle Reach to help rebuild and ward off attackers.

"How many?" Voss always struck Folville as a man who had places to be and things to do, someone who preferred conversation pared back to the fewest number of words possible.

"About two thousand men," the scout replied.

"That's more than they sent the last time," Folville replied, shaking his head. "Good thing we sent the Cross-Sea pirates to the bottom of the ocean. I've got no desire to try to protect the harbor while we're also trying to keep an invading army from burning the city!"

"It won't go well for any of us if Hennoch makes it through that wall, so we'd best make plans to ensure it doesn't happen," Voss said in a clipped tone. "I've got one thousand men deployed between the coast and Quillarth Castle. They've got to help defend the city and the castle—and keep Hennoch from reaching the coast and trying to come around by water. So they'll be a help, but they won't all be in position to hold the city wall." He grimaced. "The rest of my men are at Rodestead House helping hold Penhallow's territory, too far away to recall on short notice."

"Understood," Folville replied. "Have they finished the chain-and-net barriers?"

Voss nodded. "Aye. All you asked for, and a few more besides." He paused. "We've got archers on the wall, and my troops are thickest where the wall is weakest. We've still got some *talishte* from Penhallow. Not a lot, but half a dozen or so. They'll help us fight from sunset to sunrise."

"Good," Folville said. "Captains?"

Hemmington and Larson exchanged a glance in acknowledgment, and Hemmington spoke. "We've got two hundred men from Blaine McFadden's army," he said, "and one hundred more off the boat from Edgeland, plus a few hundred that are protecting Quillarth Castle. I've assigned our archers to the wall as well, and we've got some mages who can help play havoc with their troops—or keep their mages from playing havoc with us."

"What about the Badgers and the Red Blades?" Folville asked. "They've been quiet. Not that I'm complaining, but it makes me suspicious, and I really don't want to be attacked from behind by enemies inside the city." *Look at me,* Folville thought. *I've gone legitimate, and I'm out of touch with what's happening on the street.*

"The Curs have the city-proper staked out for our territory," Betta replied with pride, though one glance told Folville she had been thinking the same thing. "We pushed them back into the garrison by Quillarth Castle, and the Blades helped force the Badgers outside the walls. For now, the truce is holding."

Folville swore. "So they aren't close enough to backstab us, but they might join up with Hennoch's troops. Lovely."

Betta shrugged. "It's the best of a bad situation," she said.

"How do we know they aren't already working with Hennoch?" Voss asked. "You can bet Hennoch sent spies before he dispatched an army, and they would have gone right to anyone who's got a bone to pick with McFadden's surrogate, and promise the moon in exchange for help."

"We don't," Piran replied with a sigh. "In fact, we should assume that's the case."

"I'll check in with my spies," Betta said. "They're always watching for outsiders approaching the Blades and the Badgers," Betta said. "The other gangs are too tight-knit for us to have spies on the inside, but I do have some informants among the mothers, sisters, and girlfriends who don't approve of the things their men are doing, and they pass me some information from time to time. I'll see what we can find out."

Folville stared at Betta. "Really? Is that something we need to worry about with the Curs, our own families selling us out?"

Betta grinned. "Of course not," she said. "Because we've got people constantly finding out who needs food, or clothing, or a hedge witch to doctor someone. They need it, the Curs make it happen. And we discourage stupid fights, which keeps their men in one piece. If someone has been kissing up to one of the other gangs, I'll find out about it. Our spies know where their bread is buttered."

Folville turned to Bogdan. "What about the mages?"

Bogdan nodded in acknowledgment. "We've been busy," he said. "Still working with the mages up at the castle and a couple of the Knights of Esthrane, trying to figure out if any of the artifacts they've got from before the Great Fire may be of use. They could only spare two mages from the castle, me and Anders, but we brought a couple of magic items that should help us ruin Hennoch's day," he said with a wicked grin.

"Anything else?" Folville asked.

"Anders and I have been spending a lot of our time in the towers scrying—which is how the scouts knew where and when to look for the invasion force," Bogdan answered. "We'll 'see' them coming before anyone else will, if you know what I mean."

"Any luck with some real defensive magic?" Piran asked. "Something useful, like blowing people up and knocking people down?"

Bogdan raised an eyebrow. "We've got a few tricks up our sleeves."

Folville glanced around the room at his allies, who each gave him a nod as he made eye contact. "Then we all know our parts," he said finally. "Let's go—and Charrot keep our souls."

The others filed out, and even Betta left with a kiss blown in Folville's direction. *Keeping Castle Reach on a war footing had taken a toll,* Folville thought, closing his eyes and letting out a deep breath. *He and Betta had not had time together in—too long,* he thought.

He felt far older than the year it had been since the Great Fire fell. *A year, and I go from running a gang to running the city, and I'm no richer to show for it. It's a lousy bargain.*

Two days later, Hennoch's troops arrived.

"The nets are up," Betta reported to Folville as they waited behind the Northern Gate.

"We'll see when they realize it," Folville replied. "Time to get to work." He turned and yelled for his men to get into position.

Folville shaded his eyes and looked out from the Northern Gate tower. Hennoch's army marched toward the city, rank after rank of soldiers, most of them well armored. Hoofbeats and bootsteps thundered between the city walls and the rolling hills beyond.

"Here comes trouble," Folville muttered.

Before the Great Fire and the Cataclysm, the Castle Reach wall had never been breached. Tall and thick, it had been built hundreds of years ago, and reinforced by every king of Donderath, including Merrill. Two city gates granted access, with heavy iron-and-wood doors, iron portcullises, towers, and archers' slits. The imposing walls and impassable defenses had served the city well, but fire, wild magic, and vicious storms had taken their toll. Several of the towers had fallen, and the wall had collapsed in two places. Hemmington and Voss had assigned soldiers to the effort to rebuild the wall, but the project was only partially complete.

To the west, the wall enclosed the approach to Quillarth Castle, ending at the Castle's walls and the high cliffs. To the north, the wall ran the length of the Old City, curving to run east of the shipworks and the Rooster and Pig and ending along the rocky harbor precipice. The harbor itself was the fourth wall, reinforced thanks to the measures taken to thwart the Cross-Sea Kingdoms' invasion.

Piran and Hemmington commanded several hundred soldiers at the westernmost breach and the castle gate, while Folville and Larson held the Northern Gate. Voss and a contingent of his troops staked out the breach on the eastern section of the wall. Betta and the Curs patrolled the city and the harbor, to make sure that Hennoch had not managed to sneak a strike force inside the city walls.

"Getting through Squattertown is going to slow them down," a soldier next to Folville observed.

"That's the idea," Folville replied, but he felt his stomach clench nervously as the army approached.

Before the Great Fire, Castle Reach had been a hub for commerce, drawing people from all over the kingdom who hoped to make their fortunes. When the land inside the walls filled to capacity, newcomers erected a sprawling ring of wooden buildings, what those within the main city dubbed 'Squattertown.' Much of Squattertown burned in the Great Fire, and since then the ruins stood deserted. But in the last two days, Folville and the Curs had found a use for the wreckage.

Folville leaned against the stone sill of the archer slit as he peered out, watching the progress of Hennoch's troops. As Folville and his allies had guessed, Hennoch had no intention of letting Squattertown slow down his march. They pressed forward, going around the ruined buildings and broken walls, relentlessly fixed on their goal. The soldiers in the front lines wore helmets and carried large shields, making it difficult to target them with arrows. Behind the lines of marching men, there was no missing the war machines Hennoch had brought with him—catapults, trebuchets, and a battering ram, the instruments of a siege. Hennoch was determined to win.

Yet Squattertown was already working in the defenders' favor. Hennoch's soldiers were forced to go around the tumble-down houses and sheds, splitting up their solid line. The narrow streets and low overhangs made it difficult for the soldiers to keep their shields in front of them.

Folville drummed his fingers nervously as the army marched closer. "I thought your people set traps," Larson said, coming over to watch the army's advance.

"Wait for it," Folville muttered.

Halfway into Squattertown, the ruins began to fight back. Fishing nets appeared from everywhere at once: springing up to block streets, falling from overhangs to tangle soldiers in their knots, and suddenly hoisting unwary soldiers high off the ground. Castle Reach had been a busy fishing port, and old, abandoned nets were plentiful. The nets might have been too torn or damaged to catch fish, but they had no difficulty ensnaring soldiers, who cursed and fought to free themselves.

"Now!" Larson shouted. The catapults on either side of the Northern Gate began firing. Rocks at first, then flaming bundles. The front line of Hennoch's army took the brunt of the attack, unable to easily turn in the confines of Squattertown's narrow streets, hemmed in behind by their own companions and tangled in netting.

The *thud* of Folville's catapults echoed from the hills. Hennoch's war machines were still too far away to hit the city wall, but his soldiers were well within range of Castle Reach's defenses. Two flaming missiles, one fired from each side, hit the trapped soldiers, setting them ablaze. There was nothing their comrades could do to help, since the fishing nets made it impossible to move quickly or to pull the burning men free. Squattertown's ruins burned like kindling, with the help of casks of oil and heaps of pig fat Folville's men had strategically planted in the buildings they targeted with their fiery bundles.

Archers waited behind crenellations the length of the wall, hoarding their arrows for attackers that came into range. Men with slings crouched at the ready, armed with heaps of rocks and bits of metal. Behind the wall, defiant residents prepared for attack with buckets to fight fires and weapons should the attackers get through the wall. More archers waited at the uppermost windows, and at street level, men and women with slings and homemade pikes mustered to defend what was theirs.

All the while, the city's catapults kept up a steady, pounding beat. The catapults kept Hennoch's soldiers scrambling, smashing unlucky soldiers with heavy rubble or burning more of the ruins with chunks of wood soaked in oil and set aflame. Hennoch's soldiers spread out, picking their way through the trapped streets of Squattertown. Angered by the nets and fire, they pushed onward, moving a few more blocks closer to the wall.

"Go!" Folville shouted to Bogdan and Anders, who awaited his word. Beneath the dirt of the Squattertown roads lay rickety boards covering dozens of hastily dug pits deep enough to swallow one or more soldiers. The boards sustained the weight of the attackers only with the help of magic, and with a word, Bogdan and Anders withdrew their power. All along the front line of Hennoch's advance, soldiers suddenly dropped out of sight, trapped in holes too deep to easily escape.

Farther down the wall, Folville could hear Voss and Piran shouting commands to their catapult crews, keeping up the nonstop bombardment. "Now!" Piran's voice rang out. The *twang* of crossbows added a counterpoint to the beat of the catapults as flaming quarrels targeted the soldiers who struggled forward toward their objective. Archers let loose their arrows, picking off the mounted officers first.

"Do it!" Folville ordered. Bogdan and Anders moved forward again, raised their hands palms outward toward the attackers, and began a low chant. As the afternoon sun set the abandoned Squattertown in long shadows, nightmarish creatures, barely glimpsed and then gone once more, darted just at the edge of the skittish soldiers' vision.

"What in Raka is that?" Frightened cries rose from the advancing soldiers, who were trapped between catapult barrage from the front and the fire behind them.

"There's something out there!" Soldiers shouted warnings as the hideous creatures remained just out of their line of sight. Folville chuckled, knowing that Bogdan and Anders were casting a powerful illusion intended to add to the panic.

"Hold your position!" a voice rang out. Folville peered through the slit to locate the commander. Hennoch rode a large black horse, and he sat near the front line, just beyond the range of the archers. He eyed the wall like a prize he was determined to win.

Shadow creatures streamed from doorways and windows as the mages gave a final push to their illusion. Men cursed and shouted as tendrils snaked around arms and legs, hideous maws filled with jagged teeth snapped just shy of skin and bone, and monstrous creatures attacked at full speed. Soldiers scattered, and some of the men in their panic fell into the hidden pits or staggered back toward the burning buildings.

"That's all we can do for now," Bogdan said as he and Anders dropped their illusion. Both mages looked worn by the effort.

"That's fine," Larson said, intently watching the enemy's advance. "You put a scare into them. They won't be quite so cocky now."

Folville kept an eye on the war machines at the rear of Hennoch's army. Getting them into position would be difficult with the traps Folville's men had set, but should Hennoch's men be able to do so, the advantage of the battle could change quickly.

"We need to take out those bloody machines," he said as his own catapults kept hammering the invading forces. Much of Squattertown's remaining buildings were in flames, burning hot with the flammable materials Folville's men had packed into the ruins. Sections of Hennoch's army were cut off from each other by blocks of flaming buildings or cross streets intentionally blocked with rubble and netting. Squattertown was a death trap, intended to be the graveyard of any army foolhardy enough to try to move through it to reach the city.

The afternoon waned, and Hennoch kept up his relentless advance, sometimes gaining only a block or two before having to fall back, then moving forward once more. It was difficult to accurately estimate how many of his troops remained, but to Folville's eye, he would have guessed that at least a third of Hennoch's soldiers were dead or too wounded to fight.

"Why isn't he giving up?" Larson mused. The catapults and archers on the city walls kept up a relentless assault, mowing down every line of soldiers that ventured within range. Chunks of oil-soaked wood, jugs of oil rigged with cloth fuses, and loads of pig fat made perfect flaming missiles for the catapults to launch into the midst of the invaders. Spattered with oil or melted, burning fat, men shrieked and ran as the flesh burned from their bodies. Still, Hennoch's soldiers pressed forward.

Precisely at dusk, the first attack came from the air. "Weapons ready!" Folville shouted, raising his crossbow as a dark shape dove at him from above, teeth bared and clawed hands outstretched.

"By Charrot—they're godsdamned biters!" one of the soldiers yelped, barely retaining the presence of mind to squeeze off a shot from his crossbow as the creature came at him with supernatural speed.

"Fire!" Folville yelled, loosing a shot that caught another *talishte* in the shoulder, too high to take him through the heart. The attacker swung, and his fist landed a blow that broke Folville's left arm as it threw him ten feet through the air to land in a tumble against the tower wall. At least twenty enemy *talishte* stormed the wall, getting inside the city's defenses as the attacking army had not been able to do.

With a groan, Folville dragged himself to his feet, cursing at the pain from his damaged arm. He gripped his sword with his right hand and ran into the fray with a mad battle cry, as the *talishte* ran at the line of tower defenders, bowling them down.

Two of Folville's men battled *talishte* attackers, and they were getting the worst of it, from what Folville could see. He ran at his opponent just as one of the two fighters managed to land a blow with his knife, stabbing deep into the *talishte*'s arm, and the second man struck with his sword, opening a gash on the *talishte*'s thigh.

The *talishte* roared with pain and anger, striking a blow that sent one of the men tumbling with the sickening *snap* of breaking bones. Folville cleared the distance between them as the *talishte* remained intent on the second man, who continued to battle for his life despite the odds. The *talishte* lashed out, getting a hold of the second man by the shoulder and casually tightening his grip to break both collarbone and shoulder. Folville launched himself at the *talishte* from behind, sinking his sword deep between the attacker's ribs, into his heart. The *talishte* arched, letting out a deafening shriek of anger and pain, then his body began to tremble, teeth chattering and limbs twitching spasmodically, until his form collapsed into ash.

More of the dark shapes filled the air, and by their shouts, Folville knew that some of Penhallow's *talishte* had risen to defend the city. He glimpsed *talishte* battling in midair over the flames of Squattertown, darting in and out of the clouds of smoke that rose from the burning wreckage. Some of Penhallow's *talishte* had taken jugs of oil with wicks, lighting the crude bombs and then dropping them onto Hennoch's catapults and war machines, setting the equipment afire.

"Careful with your arrows," Folville shouted. "Some of those are on our side!"

Breathing hard with terror and exertion, Folville ignored the pain in his left arm, running toward another *talishte* soldier who was barely pinned down by four of Folville's men. Dark shapes in the sky made Folville fear that Hennoch had sent yet more biters to fight, but these *talishte* barely touched down before they dove into the fight, taking on their undead adversaries in a blur.

"Traitor!" one of the enemy *talishte* snarled as Penhallow's man clotheslined him with enough force to have torn the head from a mortal.

"Scum!" the allied *talishte* returned, ducking a deadly punch and raking his opponent with the dagger clenched in his left fist.

Penhallow's men were outnumbered by three, but the sight of reinforcements heartened the city's defenders. The *talishte* attackers did not back down, and for every strike the mortals managed to land, it seemed the *talishte* got in two, bloodying their attackers and hurling them out of the way. That only served to enrage Folville's soldiers, who ran at the *talishte* invaders without thought for their own safety, fighting with a maddened zeal that took the enemy fighters by surprise.

Folville joined the fight, shouting obscenities. He landed a slash to one of the enemy *talishte*'s leg that cut to the bone. Larson pulled a crossbow at point-blank range, quarrel loaded and ready, and worked the trigger before the *talishte* realized the threat. The arrow caught the enemy *talishte* in the chest, and a second later, Folville's sword swung through the neck, severing the spine. The head and body had turned to ash before they hit the ground, and a cheer went up from the mob.

Up and down the wall, Folville's men and Larson's soldiers battled enemy *talishte* as, in the sky overhead, two well-matched forces struggled for control. Neither the city defenders nor the attackers dared use their arrows to turn the advantage, since it was impossible in the gloom to tell which side the combatants served. The burning wreckage of Squattertown lit the night, casting the battle in firelight shades of red and orange.

Cold, strong hands seized Folville, dragging him over the edge of the wall. Larson grabbed for him, managing to seize him by the ankles. Four men threw their weight into it, holding on to Larson to pull against the *talishte* until Folville feared he would be pulled apart.

Farther down the wall, Folville saw a *talishte* grab one of the defenders and hurl him over the side. Folville struggled, but the *talishte*'s grip was unbreakable, and tight enough that Folville was certain his wrist would break.

Just as Larson and the others were losing their struggle against the *talishte*'s superior strength, the enemy biter stiffened and arched, then gave a howl of agonized terror. As Folville watched in horror, the hand that gripped his wrist blackened and shriveled, first to the brittle skin of a mummified corpse and then to bone. For one awful moment, the *talishte* maintained his grip, turning a fleshless, screaming skull toward Folville only inches from his face. And then, in the next instant, the *talishte* crumbled into dust.

With the *talishte*'s grip suddenly broken, Larsen and the other soldiers stumbled backward, dragging Folville with them, until they crashed against the tower.

"What in Torven's name happened?" Folville gasped.

"Look!" Larson said, pointing. A pitched aerial battle had raged just moments before; now suddenly the sky was full of ashes as Hennoch's *talishte* shriveled to corpses, then imploded into ash.

"It's not affecting our *talishte*!" Folville watched as Penhallow's brood remained hanging in midair, apparently as stunned as the mortals were.

Folville glimpsed Hennoch suddenly clutch his arm and pitch forward, nearly falling from his horse. A few moments later, Hennoch slowly righted himself, holding his left arm against his chest as if it were wounded. He reached into a pouch near his saddle and withdrew a white cloth that, to Folville's utter astonishment, Hennoch began to wave as he rose to stand in his stirrups.

"Lay down your weapons!" Hennoch shouted to his soldiers. "City of Castle Reach!" Hennoch yelled up to the defenders on the wall. "We surrender!"

CHAPTER
THIRTY-TWO

T HE WOLF'S HOWL MADE BLAINE'S BLOOD RUN COLD. His horse, well trained for battle, hesitated, wary on an inborn level to heed the warning. "Damn Nagok!" Blaine muttered.

Thirty large wolves stared down a group of mounted soldiers, emboldened beyond nature and reason.

"Can you turn them away?" Blaine yelled to Mage Rikard, who rode close to Blaine and Kestel.

Rikard shook his head. "Not when they're bewitched like this," he said.

The wolves snarled and advanced, teeth bared, heads lowered for attack. "Ride!" Blaine shouted, rallying his troops.

Blaine rode toward the wolves, bow at the ready. His arrow grazed the shoulder of a large wolf. Kestel's aim with a dagger was true, taking down a wolf with a blade to the neck. Two of Blaine's soldiers gave chase to another wolf, while two more paired up against a fourth.

Dirt blasted into the air, surprising a charging wolf and bringing it to a sudden, skidding halt. A second explosion of dirt stopped another wolf in its tracks. It growled warily at the small hole left behind in the ground. All over the battlefield, dirt flew into the faces of the charging wolves, forcing them to change their course, slow their attack, and separate from their pack.

One glance revealed the source. Rikard and his fellow mage, Kulp, remained on the sidelines, but they held their hands outstretched toward the fighting, and every time one of the mages clenched his fist, another shower of dirt blasted from the ground, spooking the maddened wolves.

"Ride them down!" Blaine shouted, reining in his horse and going after the nearest wolf. Dirt sprayed up as several hits in succession made a line that cut off the wolves at every turn. Rattled by the explosions, the wolves shied away, giving Blaine and the soldiers an advantage.

Blaine swung his sword, beheading one wolf as another came bounding forward. His horse reared, kicking with enough force to smash in the head of the lead wolf. Kestel threw another dagger, hitting a third wolf in the hindquarters. Dirt sprayed into the air all around them, and Blaine realized the mages were making sure the wolves could not run in straight lines to attack, slowing their approach and giving the bowmen an advantage.

Blaine sheathed his sword and grabbed the crossbow from his back. It thudded as he sent a quarrel into the nearest wolf, stopping him in his tracks. His next shot went wide as one of the explosions kicked dirt into the air just as Blaine's quarrel flew toward its target. Kestel dropped that wolf with a well-thrown knife.

Across the battlefield, one of Birgen Verner's captains marshaled a phalanx of archers against ten more wolves. Blaine's soldiers battled another six wolves, which left seven of the bewitched creatures prowling the battlefield.

In the distance, Niklas's contingent of soldiers fought the human invaders, with help from Rinka Solveig and her troops. Rinka's blood-red armor, sculpted to have the appearance of a dragon, was easy to spot, as if she dared her enemies to focus on her as their target.

Sweat and grime ran down Blaine's face and soaked his shirt. They had been fighting hard since daybreak, and he was hungry and bone weary. The battlefield was an abattoir, covered in the bodies of the wild beasts Nagok had manipulated with his magic. Blaine was weary of killing, numb from the horrors of the battlefield, but there was much left to do. Donderath would not be secure until Nagok was defeated, and both armies knew the fate of the war hung in the balance.

And in the back of his mind, Blaine wondered how the strike against Thrane would go for Penhallow and Connor. Though he had been part of the planning and had endorsed the attack, he was well aware of the danger. Taking out Thrane could turn the course of the battle, but it was likely to come at a high price. *Is this what it's like to be king?* Blaine wondered. *The constant choice between life and death? Why would any sane man fight to gain such a burden?*

Fresh troops from the former convicts of Edgeland brought new energy into the ranks of Blaine's army. After fending for themselves in the arctic wastes and surviving Velant's harsh discipline, the returned colonists knew how to fight and how to hunt, whether or not they had been soldiers before their exile. Three hundred had come north to fight alongside Blaine and Niklas, while one hundred had stayed in Castle Reach to help protect the harbor and the castle. The new soldiers fought like madmen, seeing for the first time what damage the Great Fire had brought to their homeland.

"Over there!" Kestel cried, pointing toward three wolves

stalking them from behind, while four more closed in from the side.

Blaine wheeled his horse, readying his bow once more. The wolves were fast and tough, with razor-sharp teeth. Blaine let fly an arrow, and this time he hit his mark, striking the wolf just behind the shoulder and dropping it to the ground.

A second wolf circled Blaine, running for the horse and not the rider. Blaine pulled back hard on the reins, and his horse reared, kicking with its strong, iron-shod front hooves. The first kick struck a glancing blow, knocking the wolf from its feet. The wolf scrambled to its feet for another charge, and the horse's hooves flew once more, smashing in the front of the wolf's skull.

Kestel's hand moved, sure and fast, and steel glinted as it flew toward its quarry, lodging in the eye of a maddened wolf that stopped in its tracks and toppled to the dirt.

A deep growl cut through the night. A huge gray wolf, nearly the size of a dire wolf, fixed the soldiers in its baleful glare, head lowered, bounding toward them. Blaine and Kestel held their ground.

The other soldiers backed away, clearing a large area. Blaine rode to one side, while Kestel rode to the other. Their horses shied and whinnied in alarm, and Blaine fought to keep his spooked mount under control. The wolf was massive, muscles rippling beneath the fur as it ran. It focused on Blaine and headed for him, taking a swipe with one huge paw that Blaine and his horse barely avoided.

"Hey! Over here!" Kestel shouted, trying to draw off the wolf. For the moment, the wolf was fixed on Blaine, and it lunged into the air with a deep growl, swatting at Blaine with its broad, powerful paw and its long, deadly claws.

Blaine's horse shrieked in panic. The wolf's teeth *snicked* shut inches from Blaine's arm, and the paw raked his thigh with a glancing blow as he wheeled his horse at the last moment to avoid the full weight of the wolf slamming into his mount. Blaine aimed his crossbow, and the force of the quarrel at close range threw the wolf backward several feet, to lie dead on the pockmarked ground.

Kestel took up her bow, and her arrow struck one of the wolves in the hindquarters. The beast howled and dropped back as blood matted its thick, dark fur. Another wolf growled, circling Kestel, a throaty, primal sound that made the hair on the back of Blaine's neck stand up. Kestel's arrow hit the wolf in the chest as two more closed on her and the rest stalked Blaine and his horse.

Four soldiers rode toward them, shifting the odds away from the wolves. Blaine was grateful for the help, though Kestel looked as if she was enjoying the challenge.

Another wolf advanced on Kestel. The maddened creature growled, shaking its head and shoulders to look even more frightening. Blaine readied his bow, as did Kestel, unwilling to allow the wolf to get close enough to strike again.

The wolf snarled, ready to leap. Just as it was about to spring, it sat down heavily, with a glazed look on its face. It shook its head, sniffed at the air, turned, and loped away in the opposite direction. Across the battlefield, the remaining wolves broke off their attack as abruptly as they had started it, running for the foothills.

"Let them go!" Blaine shouted to his soldiers.

Rikard rode forward to meet him as Kestel joined. "Nagok's compulsion runs deep," Rikard said. "That's the first time I've tried to distract the animals, and Kulp did his best to throw illusions to frighten them—bears, fire, that kind of thing." He chuckled. "Fortunately, Kulp's magic was invisible to our own troops."

"The explosions helped," Kestel said, slinging her bow over her shoulder. "Seemed to rattle their focus." In the distance, Blaine heard shouting, evidence that the battle was heading their way.

Rikard nodded. "Glad we could help. Animal minds are quite alien, by the way. Nagok's gift is a remarkable—and rare—type of magic. I wish he had been willing to do something constructive with it." Rikard shrugged. "Still—I had the feeling, there for a moment, that Nagok was fighting us for control. I think the entire attack ended earlier than it was meant to."

"So by pushing back and distracting the wolves, you may have weakened Nagok?" Kestel asked, intrigued.

"Not weakened permanently, but tired him out, so that he had to quit sooner," Rikard replied. "Unfortunately, there's no way to know for certain."

Kulp looked down at Blaine's leg, which was bleeding. "We need to get that bound," he said. "It sounds like there's more fighting coming this way."

Blaine let Kulp call for a battlefield healer to speed the healing in his leg and bind it up with cloth as Rikard went to talk to the other commanders. The healer had barely finished his work and headed back behind the lines when the thunder of hoofbeats and the roar of the fight pushed toward them. Across the valley, Blaine glimpsed the half of his army led by Niklas. To the right, Rinka Solveig and her troops, along with several hundred Plainsmen. Birgen Verner and his soldiers flanked the Meroven troops, so that the allied warlords trapped Nagok's forces between them.

"We need to be out there," Blaine grated, swinging back up to his saddle.

"Did you get any more out of Geir about what's pulling the Elders away from the fight?" Kestel asked. The need for utter secrecy had required Blaine to keep the plans from everyone, even Kestel.

Blaine nodded. "Penhallow and the Wraith Lord are attacking Thrane's stronghold, with Tormod's help." He shrugged at her glare. "I swore to Penhallow I wouldn't say anything to anyone. It wasn't that he thought someone would tell. He was afraid it could be read from someone's mind. So that ensures Nagok won't have the rogue Elders' help—and perhaps be without most of their broods, too," he added, certain that later on, Kestel would have something to say about being excluded.

"You think the one they call Aubergine will actually leave Nagok in the middle of a battle?" Kestel asked.

Blaine shrugged. "Penhallow seemed to think so—I wouldn't doubt that *talishte* politics trump other agreements."

"So we lose 'our' Elders to the showdown, too?" Kestel surmised. Aldwin Carlisle, Garrick Dalton, and Malin Jarett were as difficult and demanding as any mortal aristocrats, but their help holding off Nagok's army had reduced the toll of mortal lives and kept a balance of force against Nagok's *talishte* fighters.

"That's the plan," Blaine replied. "Let's just hope whatever's going on plays out in our favor."

"Does your bond to Penhallow tell you how it's going?"

Blaine shook his head. "Just a vague impression of danger and battle. I don't think it's settled yet." The images he received were often incomplete and jumbled. *If this is what seers have to interpret, I don't envy them their job.*

Kestel leveled a look at him. "We're going to talk about this later."

"I rather suspected that would be the case."

The next wave of attackers were soldiers, and as deadly with their swords and axes as the wolves had been. Blaine's soldiers and the fighters under Niklas's command swept back and forth together across the flatlands, gaining ground, falling back, and surging forward again. The corpses of men and horses fell alongside the bloodied remains of the wild animals, amid the trampled high grass.

Through it all, Blaine spotted Aron, Dagur, Kulp, Rikard, and Mevvin moving around the edges of the battle, using their magic to slow the enemy's advance or distracting Nagok's troops with blasts of fire and sudden explosions. He looked up, and saw a large eagle turning in wide, slow circles above the battlefield. In the next heartbeat, he felt a frisson of power as subtle magic slipped over him and his troops. Not hostile, but odd. Blaine thought he caught glimpses of strange shadows overhead, but he was too consumed with the battle to think too long about it.

Half a candlemark later, during a lull in the fighting, Blaine motioned Dagur over. "What's going on?" he asked. "I thought I saw something strange overhead, between us and the clouds."

Dagur nodded. "Illusions. That eagle belongs to Nagok, and he's using it to scry for him. So we gave him something to look at of our own making that should mislead him about how the battle is actually going." He glanced skyward, assuring himself the eagle was gone. "We've also been using our magic to drive the wild animals as far away as we can. With luck, that will put at least some of them—and hopefully the biggest predators—beyond Nagok's reach."

"If he can only control one type of beast at a time, then

when he's commanding the eagle, he can't send other creatures against us," Blaine replied. "At least that's something."

Nagok's troops fought with such frenzy that Blaine wondered if the mages had been wrong about whether or not an entire army could be bewitched. The Meroven soldiers gave no quarter and asked for none, wielding broadswords and war axes without remorse. Some of the men looked old enough and fought well enough to have been part of the Meroven War. Others fought with the fury of men who dared not return if not victorious.

"We've got your back, Mick!" Sergei, one of the new fighters from Edgeland, shouted as he and a dozen others battled their way near where Blaine and Kestel were fighting.

"Glad to hear it!" Blaine shouted back, never taking his eyes from the Meroven fighter attacking him. The outlander fought with manic intensity, striking blow after blow that had little plan or skill but were dangerous in their sheer ferocity. *What has Nagok threatened them with if they fail?* Blaine wondered as the Meroven soldiers pressed forward. Death seemed to be the least of their concerns, and honor was unlikely to be motivating their mad advance.

The press of soldiers was too thick to use a bow, and so Blaine and Kestel set about with their swords, a long blade in one hand and a short sword in the other. Both were bloodied to the elbow and thigh, less with their own blood than that of their adversaries. The day was warm, and flies buzzed in black, shifting clouds over the battlefield, reveling in the feast of shit and dead meat.

"We've got to gain ground before Nagok can send his beasts on the offense again," Blaine yelled to Kestel. "If he's weakened, now's the time to strike!"

Apparently the same thing had occurred to Niklas, who

was galloping toward Blaine. Niklas was spattered with blood, and his uniform was cut and torn. His lip was split, and his bruised knuckles made it clear that he had recently fought hand-to-hand. "We've got to make a push," Niklas said, reining in his horse as he approached. "Every time Nagok uses his beasts, he wears down our forces."

"Agreed," Blaine said, eyeing the shifting Meroven line. "And he should be weakest after he's spent himself to control the beasts. Tonight may be our best chance if most of the *talishte* are otherwise occupied. Bayard should be joining us after dark, so we can split the Plainsmen from Rinka Solveig's soldiers if we need two different strike forces."

Niklas nodded. "We've set Nagok back on his heels with the reinforcements. I'm sure he thought he was just going up against me and my troops, and he got a lot more than he bargained for. But we need the mages to help us keep his soldiers off balance. They've been doing a good job catching things on fire and setting other traps and distractions. It helps."

Despite the additional troops from Edgeland and nearly all of Blaine's full army, the Meroven attackers presented a fearsome enemy. The outlanders fought like dark spirits from the Unseen Realms, tireless and pitiless. Blaine's army was weary but resolute, determined to break the Meroven threat.

The last push had regained precious ground. But as the sun set, Blaine felt a shiver of foreboding. Torches lit the open plains, and the moon was dark. Niklas and Blaine shouted the order to charge forward, and the ranks of foot soldiers and men on horseback surged toward the Meroven army. Two armies met with a clash of swords and shields, and the sound of the battle rolled down the valley like thunder.

Nagok rode at the center of his army astride a huge black

warhorse at least nineteen hands high. Beside him loped a large black wolf, easily keeping pace with the horse. Nagok's steel helmet was forged to look like the skeletal head of a giant wolf. A breastplate of yellowed bones covered chain mail. Several dozen of Nagok's fighters wore similar steel skull helmets. Those soldiers wore dark armor, and the champrons of their mounts had razor-sharp steel horns or antlers.

Blaine rode full tilt into the fray as the field became an open melee. Kestel was an excellent swordswoman, but for this strike, she rode with a bow and quivers full of arrows, riding at full speed so that the enemy soldiers were obliged to get out of her way or be ridden down, veering unpredictably to avoid being blocked in or cut down, sending arrow after arrow with deadly aim. Blaine's gift of battle forcsight served him well, helping him dodge at the last minute or rein in his horse mere breaths before a strike might have had his head.

Rikard, Dagur, and the rest of the mages had not yet made their move, but Blaine could feel power rising all around them on the darkened battlefield. It prickled at his senses, like a coming storm, intangible but very real. Another magic vied against the first, and Blaine guessed that his mages and Nagok's mages were locked in their own arcane struggle. He was weary in every bone and sinew, bloodied and bleeding, but he was certain that before this night was through, their fate would be decided.

By morning, either he or Nagok would be dead.

More creatures bore down on them, monstrous beings with skeletal heads and elongated bodies. It took Blaine a moment to realize that what he saw were men riding standing up on their saddles, dressed in fearsome costumes with totem-like heads resembling the skulls of monsters, their horses similarly armored to inspire terror.

"They're just men!" Blaine shouted to give courage to his soldiers. "They bleed like anyone else!"

A hideous keening cry echoed across the plains. Creatures coiled and slithered, charged and flew toward them, the stuff of nightmares and hallucinations. The monsters were opaque, shadows that glided rather than ran and disappeared when they turned, like a paper shown on edge. Soldiers struck at the creatures with their swords, but the blades went right through without doing harm.

"They're illusions!" Dagur shouted, though his voice was lost above the chaos. Verner's soldiers held their line, and the hideous creatures washed over them and past them without doing any damage. Dagur and the other mages took up positions behind the front line of the battle, trying to disrupt the powerful, overwhelming illusions cast by Nagok's magic-users.

"Hold your positions!" Verner shouted. "They can't hurt you!"

Blaine raised his sword for the charge, and felt a wave of magic hit him like the incoming tide. The force was invisible, but potent, sweeping men from their saddles and knocking horses off their feet. Blaine felt as if he were drowning as the air was sucked from his lungs and his head grew light. He clung to the reins and used his knees to grip his mount to hold his seat. He was dimly aware of a sudden flare from the amulet inside his tunic—the one Rikard and his mages had made to deflect the worst of a magic strike—that warned him it was nearly spent.

The amulet flared once more and went dull as a force too strong to fight tore Blaine from his saddle and hurled him to the ground.

Kestel ran from the fray and helped Blaine to his feet. Nothing was broken, but every inch of him was sore, and he was winded from the fall. "My amulet won't do me any good now," he said. The cloud of nightmare creatures billowed toward them like a looming storm.

Kestel threw her arms around him as the storm clouds hit, and her null amulet shone brightly, driving back the darkness, carving out a circle of space around them through which the monsters could not pass. The illusions seemed real, and the *snick* of sharp teeth sounded so close behind Blaine that he flinched, but the amulet's light held, giving Blaine and Kestel the ability to see that the monsters were nothing but cleverly shaped shadows.

"We've got to do something!" Blaine said, but Kestel clung to him fiercely.

"Do what? You're not a mage. Neither am I. The monsters might not be real, but the power behind them is!"

They stood at the center of the maelstrom, as the wind that bore the nightmare beasts howled around them. The air grew freezing cold, and it smelled of blood and death. The light of Kestel's null amulet was fading. Though the creatures were only illusion, it was an overwhelming hallucination, and it left Blaine and his allies open to attack.

A figure took shape amid the storm of magic that raged all around them, glowing and insubstantial. Carr McFadden's ghost stood sentinel, holding gleaming, spectral swords in both hands, protecting Blaine and Kestel as the shadow monsters swarmed around them.

Night had fallen, and amid the dangerous illusions of Nagok's shadow army, the *talishte* fought in no-man's-land. The mortal fighters had fled, save for Blaine and Kestel, and the blood-soaked ground belonged to the dead and the undead. A dozen *talishte* of Penhallow's get battled at least as many or more from the rogue Elders' broods, and they, too, seemed to know that this night would decide their fate.

The *talishte* battled like warriors of legend, moving at impossible speeds, meting out and taking blows that would have snapped mortal spines and crushed mortal skulls. Geir's blade slashed down along his opponent's ribs, opening his chest to the bone, only to have the injury begin to heal as soon as the sword was removed. A broadsword skewered one of Penhallow's get through the abdomen, but the injured *talishte* freed himself by moving backward at blinding speed, then brought his own sword across his opponent's belly so that the entrails bulged from the raw wound, until it closed minutes later. Overhead, airborn *talishte* tumbled and dove like eagles fighting to the death, showering the ground with cold blood and bits of dead flesh.

Whether the two sides were so evenly matched that neither could gain the upper hand, or whether the stalemate was enabling long-overdue vengeance to play out, Blaine did not know, but the undead fighters battled with a primal savagery that made the wolves' attack seem elegant by comparison. Blaine glimpsed Geir rising like a bloodied god, hair lank and matted, his clothing ragged and spattered with gore, a damaged warrior bent on utter devastation.

The ranks of the *talishte* had thinned, each side losing some of their fighters, when they rose to meet each other for a final reckoning. Two ranks of immortals, fighting in midair, finishing a centuries-old feud.

Geir's fighters charged. Before they could strike at their opponents, Thrane's *talishte* screamed and began to writhe, hung against the black night sky. The enemy *talishte* went still, then their bodies crumbled, spreading the dust of their ancient flesh and bones across the empty, bloody battlefield, until the last of their remains vanished on the wind.

"What in Raka just happened?" Kestel breathed, still holding Blaine tightly within the fading protection of the null amulet.

"Penhallow and Connor won," Blaine replied, sensing a rush of relief and triumph through the *kruvgaldur*, tempered with loss and fear. "The Elgin Spike worked. But I'm afraid it's come at a steep cost." Blaine concentrated, trying to make sense of the jumbled, distant impressions he received through the *kruvgaldur*. At that instant, the last faint light of Kestel's null amulet blinked out. Carr's ghost turned slowly, gave Blaine a lopsided, sad smile and an ironic salute, and winked out of sight.

The mortal army had fallen back, leaving an empty swath of devastation where the two *talishte* forces had clashed. "Come on!" Blaine said, grabbing Kestel's wrist and heading toward where he had last seen Nagok astride his warhorse. Niklas and a small group of soldiers fell in behind them as Geir and the surviving *talishte* swept on ahead.

Nagok was unmistakable astride his massive black warhorse. His huge black wolf stayed at his side, snarling and snapping at the advancing soldiers. The wolf sprang at one of the *talishte* soldiers, and the undead fighter caught the heavy animal easily. The *talishte* held the wolf at arm's length by its throat, unfazed by its fangs and claws, then with a casual, violent shake of his wrist that broke the wolf's neck, the *talishte* hurled the man-sized creature at three of Nagok's soldiers, knocking them to the ground.

Nagok shouted for his predator protectors as Blaine's *talishte* fighters bore down on him, but Rikard and the mages had driven the creatures out of range. A cadre of loyal supporters surrounded Nagok, but the *talishte* set on them with fury, ripping Nagok's protectors limb from limb. The terrified warhorse reared, throwing Nagok from his saddle.

"Geir! Call them off!" Blaine shouted. "I've got to finish this!"

Geir shouted a command and the *talishte* drew back, forming a corridor to where Nagok struggled to regain his feet. The skeletal helmet had been ripped from his head, leaving deep, bloody gashes along his scalp and face. The rest of his armor looked as if it had been punctured by war axes or pikes, and deep cuts, spaced as wide as the fingers of a hand, clawed across the armor covering his torso and legs. Blaine wondered how much Thrane's destruction damaged Nagok, and whether he could use that to his advantage in the fight.

Blaine advanced, sword drawn. "Pick up your weapon," Blaine shouted to Nagok. "You wanted to loot Donderath to enrich your own kingdom. Your master intended to give Donderath's throne to Pollard. What did he promise you? The crown of Meroven?" Blaine's smile was bitter. "Did you really believe he would keep his word, even if you won?" He shook his head. "We will not allow that. Now face me, and die in fair battle, or the *talishte* will finish what they started."

For the first time, Blaine got a good look at his mortal enemy. Nagok's breastplate of human bones had been shattered. The long dark hair that framed his face was matted with blood and sweat. He might have been a few years older than Blaine, but the cold reckoning in Nagok's dark eyes was bitter and reptilian.

Nagok gave a guttural growl and lunged. He brought his sword down two-handed in a brutal strike that forced Blaine back a pace and shook him to the bone. Blaine struck back with a war cry, drawing on his pain and rage and fear to deliver three pounding strikes.

Eyes blazing with sheer hatred, Nagok stalked toward Blaine, watching him like a starving wolf, looking for weakness.

Without his magic, cut off from his predators, his *talishte* allies, and his mages, Nagok was left with nothing but his sword skill. He was a few inches shorter than Blaine but stockier, and what he lacked in reach he made up for in power. Blaine was fast, with longer arms that gave him an advantage. As they circled, with the fate of a kingdom in the balance, Blaine called on the stubborn will that had enabled him to survive Velant and Edgeland's brutal cold.

"You're defeated," Blaine grated, his throat dry and raw from the fight. "Donderath is not for Meroven to plunder."

"You think I'll be the last you see of Meroven?" Nagok rasped. "You're wrong. There will be others. You'll never be rid of us." He rallied, running toward Blaine with a mad howl, swinging his sword with all his might in powerful, killing blows.

Blaine let the fury and terror of the day fill him, let it find release in the strong, scything strikes of his broadsword, meeting Nagok's swings with fierce determination. Their swords rang loud against each other, steel scraping against steel. Nagok lunged again, and Blaine blocked the blow, pushing Nagok's blade out of the way and sinking his short sword between Nagok's ribs.

Nagok opened his mouth to speak, but blood bubbled from his lips. He fixed Blaine with a killing glare, and as he sank to his knees, Blaine swung his sword again, severing Nagok's head from his shoulders as his body tumbled to the side.

The allied armies and the *talishte* cheered, while Nagok's troops knelt in surrender.

Kestel and Niklas hurried to Blaine's side. "You did it!" Kestel said with a tired grin. Her face was streaked with blood and dirt, and her clothing was ripped and bloodied. Deep scratches marred her cuirass and vambraces. Niklas also looked worse for the wear, spattered with gore and grime. Blaine imagined he looked at least as bad himself.

"We're not done yet," Blaine said, tearing his gaze away from Nagok's headless corpse. "Pollard and Hennoch are still out there, and they won't rest until this is finished—one way or the other."

Geir joined them, moving swiftly and silently as only *talishte* could. "Congratulations," he said, inclining his head in acknowledgment.

"Penhallow's strike was successful?" Blaine asked.

Geir nodded, and his wan smile was enigmatic. "Under the right circumstances, with the right tool in the right hands," he replied. "Penhallow and the Wraith Lord—and Connor—have been busy tonight."

"The other Elders?" Niklas asked.

"Those made by Thrane or his get are destroyed," Geir replied. "The remaining Elders battled among themselves tonight, drawing Thrane's allies into an ambush." He glanced at Blaine. "What I can read through the *kruvgaldur* suggests victory for our side, but the price was dear."

Blaine nodded. "That was my impression as well. I had hoped you might have gleaned more details."

Geir shook his head. "Unless Penhallow intends to convey an explicit message, I receive impressions, images, bits and pieces, just like you do. I suspect he's been too busy to attempt to contact us with more than that. We'll know the specifics soon enough."

"Tomorrow, you can take troops to go deal with Pollard at Rodestead House, and I'll send men to handle Hennoch," Niklas said, laying a hand on Blaine's shoulder. "After we get this locked down tonight. Rikard and Aron are making sure there's no funny stuff from the Meroven mages, while Dagur and Kulp and Mevvin are setting wardings and traps around the camp perimeter so we won't be disturbed."

Blaine started to turn away, but Niklas tightened his grasp for a moment, and Blaine looked back at him. "Rest tonight, and take plenty of soldiers with you. No one expects you to be a god. You've already proven that you'll be quite a king."

CHAPTER
THIRTY-THREE

THE AFTERMATH OF THE BATTLE STRETCHED into the predawn hours. Blaine and Kestel finally relented and got some sleep after Niklas and Geir insisted they rest before taking on Pollard. The remaining candlemarks passed far too quickly, and in the morning, Ayers, Niklas's second-in-command, was already waiting with fresh horses and a squad of fifty men.

"No telling what you'll run into," Ayers said, handing off the reins. "About a third of our troops are still in the field chasing down deserters, so the last sighting the *talishte* had of Pollard put him at Rodestead House." He paused. "One piece of news you'll find interesting. A *talishte* messenger came for Geir after you and Kestel finally went to get some rest. Hennoch won't be a problem. Once Thrane's *talishte* were destroyed, Hennoch surrendered to Folville and Piran outside Castle Reach."

"Now, that's interesting," Blaine remarked. "So Geir is sure that all of Thrane's get were destroyed?" It was what they had hoped from the Elgin Spike, but Blaine had experienced enough unwanted surprises from old magical objects that he welcomed confirmation.

Ayers nodded. "He's being pretty damn cagey about the whole thing, but yes—he's sure. And I guess if there's a way to destroy that many *talishte* at one time, I can understand not wanting the method to be widely known."

Blaine frowned. "Pollard and Hennoch served Reese and Thrane. I can't imagine that they weren't marked with the *kruvgaldur*. Was Hennoch harmed when Thrane's *talishte* were destroyed?"

Ayers shrugged. "Geir said Hennoch was weakened by the strike, but was expected to recover. Pollard served Reese longer and was also bound to Thrane, so you may find Pollard was more badly damaged when you catch up to him."

Someday, Blaine vowed he would ask Penhallow more about the *kruvgaldur*. *If I'm to be king, I need to know exactly how beholden I am,* he thought. "Pollard would be dangerous even if he were dead and cremated," Blaine remarked. "What about Nilo Jansen—his second-in-command?"

Ayers brightened. "That's where we had a bit of luck. Turns out Jansen had brought some of Pollard's troops up to fight for Nagok. Our men and Geir's *talishte* made mincemeat out of his soldiers. Our men caught Jansen slinking away on foot and deserting what remained of his army," he added with disdain.

"Interrogate him, and then hang him," Blaine ordered. "He's caused enough trouble already."

Ayers nodded. "General Theilsson has the hanging tree ready. The mages have already had a go at him. Didn't get much out of him that we didn't already know. But the *talishte* haven't had their chance at him yet." By now, he had walked with Blaine and Kestel to where their horses and the soldiers waited.

Ayers gave a wan smile as Blaine swung up to the saddle. "Charrot go with you," he said. "Maybe soon, we can put all this fighting behind us," he added as Blaine and the others turned and rode away.

It took three days of riding for Blaine and the others to reach Rodestead House. The fire-scarred manor belonged to Penhallow and had been badly damaged in the Great Fire. Voss had been overseeing the rebuilding, and had left a contingent of soldiers at Rodestead House when he took the bulk of his army south to Castle Reach.

Blaine had no idea what to expect. For all he knew, the fighting could have ended in the days it took to ride from the northern battlefield. But when he and the others arrived, they found the battle still raging, with two small, equally matched forces dug in and fighting to the finish.

Bodies covered acres of ground: men, horses, and beasts. Carrion birds picked at the remains, and misty wisps drifted here and there, ghosts powerful enough to make themselves seen without the help of a mage. Vultures and crows tore at the bodies, and there would be enough to gorge on for days, given the battle's toll. Here and there, a few soldiers moved among the dead, looting the bodies and administering the deathblow to those still lingering.

"Looks like our side has been giving as good as it's gotten," Kestel observed. She looked as tired as Blaine felt, but she flashed him a courageous grin like a blood-splattered warrior queen. Before long, Blaine heard the clatter and shouts of battle, and as they crested a rise, saw two forces still hard at war.

Voss's soldiers fought against a decidedly smaller army that had been pushed back to defend a copse-lined rocky hillside, the attacking army's last redoubt.

Pollard won't give up so long as he breathes, Blaine thought. *He's wanted the crown too badly for too long.*

Blaine and his soldiers rode down toward the battle, only to be intercepted by a line of rearguard defenders.

"Halt! Identify yourselves!" the young officer shouted.

Blaine reined in his horse and signaled for his soldiers to come to a stop. "Lord Blaine McFadden and troops, come to help you finish this up so we can all go home."

"Lord and Lady McFadden," the officer acknowledged. "Glad to have your help."

Reinforcements gave new vigor to the fighters as a cheer went up in greeting. Blaine and Kestel fought their way toward the front lines as Blaine tried to find Pollard amid the combatants.

"He's not on the field," Blaine muttered to Kestel. "I'd know him if I saw him, and he's not here."

"Do you think he's ducked out on them?" Kestel asked, wiping her blade clean on a dead man's cloak.

Blaine shook his head. "There's nowhere for him to go." His gaze settled on a small stone structure nearly hidden among the trees in the section most vigorously defended by Pollard's troops. "I think he's badly wounded, and they're hiding him."

"Take the copse!" Blaine shouted, pointing toward the small stand of trees. "We want what's in that building!"

Blaine and Kestel rode into the battle, swinging their swords with renewed vigor. His troops followed him, and Voss's soldiers sent up a cheer, heartened at the reinforcements. A young captain appeared to be the ranking enemy officer, and as Blaine and Kestel rode toward him, the captain dealt a deathblow to his opponent, and wheeled his horse to face his new challengers. His mouth twisted into an ugly snarl as he recognized Blaine.

"Throw down your weapon," Blaine shouted. "Nagok has lost. Jansen is dead, and Hennoch has surrendered. Thrane and his get have all been destroyed. You cannot win."

The captain's expression was contemptuous. "We will not yield! I'll see you in Raka!" the captain screamed, charging toward Blaine, his sword leveled like a lance. Blaine jerked his reins, managing to get out of the way of the killing strike, but the sword took his horse in the neck, spraying them with warm crimson blood. Blaine leapt from his dying horse, landing in a squat as the captain rode for him again, but before Blaine could strike, Kestel neatly removed the captain's head from his shoulders.

Pollard's troops seemed to sense that their final hour was at hand, because they fought like madmen, intent on dying with valor if they could no longer win the war. He was certain that they knew death awaited them, whether they fought or surrendered. Blaine's soldiers were happy to oblige, and spurred on by the knowledge that the battle was nearly won, they attacked Pollard's troops with abandon.

Shouts, curses, and battle cries rose in a deafening cacophony, along with the *clang* of steel. The final assault was a blood-drenched free-for-all, and then, as the last of Pollard's men collapsed from their wounds, the battlefield was eerily silent. It was all over within a candlemark.

"Cover us!" Blaine ordered the soldiers closest to him. "I'm going in," he said, jerking his head toward the windowless stone building at the center of the copse.

"I'm going with you," Kestel said, a sword in one hand and a dagger in the other.

Blaine approached the small building carefully, wary of traps or magic, but with the soldiers dead, nothing blocked his way. Now that he was closer, he could see that only three of the four walls were still standing, and part of the roof was gone. That left enough light inside for him to see the building's sole inhabitant, a gaunt man in bloodied armor sitting on the ground and leaning against a wall.

Blaine barely recognized Vedran Pollard. Pollard's skin was ashen, and his eyes looked shadowed and sunken. Still, his gaze burned with hatred when he recognized who had found his hiding place. Blaine did not venture closer, certain that Pollard, no matter how badly injured, would not be unarmed.

"If you want the crown of Donderath, you'll have to fight for it, boy," Pollard grated. "Then again, you're twice the murderer your old man ever was."

Blaine knew Pollard was baiting him, trying to push him into an attack. Far too much was at stake to make that kind of error, though Blaine struggled to rein in his anger. "You can't win. Thrane and Reese have been destroyed, and Reese bound you tightly enough to take you with him."

Pollard gave a cold laugh. "Sure I can win. I can kill you, just like I drove that worthless cur of a brother of yours to slit his own wrists. With you dead, I still win."

Pollard moved to hurl a dagger. Just as he was about to strike, a glowing form took shape between Blaine and Pollard. The ghost was unmistakably Carr McFadden, and for a moment, the steel of his blade looked almost solid, real, and deadly. Carr's ghost passed right through Vedran Pollard, lingering just a second as he overlapped the man who murdered him, so that Pollard's eyes widened in fear and his entire body trembled.

Now, Blaine!

Whether he heard Carr's voice or imagined it, Blaine charged forward, and his sword took Pollard in the heart. Pollard's body crumpled beneath the death strike, but his gaze remained unrepentant until the light vanished from his eyes. "It's a better death than you deserved," Blaine muttered, withdrawing his bloodied sword.

For a moment, the battlefield was eerily silent. After the din of battle, the silence was jarring. Blaine stared down at Pollard's bloodied corpse. *It's finally over,* he thought, looking from his bloodied blade to the body at his feet.

Carr's ghost took shape one last time, standing next to Pollard. Now that his death was avenged, the ghost no longer manifested with its wounds, and Carr gave Blaine a rakish, bittersweet smile, then raised a hand in farewell, and vanished.

"Carr's gone," Blaine said as Kestel came to stand beside him. "His ghost was just here. We got our vengeance together." His throat was tight, and he stared at the empty space where Carr's ghost had been until he was sure that his brother's spirit was not going to reappear.

Behind him, the soldiers were cheering wildly, shouting his name over and over, and celebrating the unexpected good fortune of being alive. Blaine heard little of it, his attention still focused on the empty space where Carr had been.

"He made it up to you," Kestel said quietly, slipping an arm around his waist. "And he's at peace. The war is over. Now we can rebuild."

He leaned down to kiss her, heedless of the blood and dirt and sweat, as the fury of the fight turned to utter amazement that he had survived. "It's not quite over yet," he murmured. "There's still one thing left to do."

CHAPTER
THIRTY-FOUR

I WARNED YOU. LORD GARNOC'S VOICE WAS A familiar, safe haven in the darkness. *You've gotten mixed up in things that are too big for you. Now, there's a price to be paid.*

For a moment, Garnoc's image was as clear as if the old man stood next to Connor. He saw concern and regret in Garnoc's eyes and something else—pity. *Garnoc was a good master to me,* Connor thought. *Why does he look so sad?*

Ghosts surrounded Connor. Pale revenants hovered around him, pressing against his skin, desperate for what little body heat Connor still retained. They pushed against his fragile shielding, shattering his defenses. Connor could neither block their wailing voices nor shut out their spectral images. He remembered that the protection of the Wraith Lord and his new gift as a Lord of the Blood meant the ghosts could not take him by force, but it did not stop the spirits from attacking him, trying to weaken his protections.

"Depart!" A man's voice sounded with authority, and while Connor did not recognize the speaker, the ghosts scattered as an invisible wave of power rolled out from the dark silhouette at the edges of Connor's perception. The magic swept the ghostly attackers away like an ocean wave, leaving Connor blissfully, blessedly alone except for his protector.

"I will keep them from bothering you," the man said, and Connor knew it must be Tormod Solveig. "Rest. You have nothing to fear from them," Solveig added. Darkness and silence washed over Connor, blotting out everything else.

"Has anything changed?" A different voice, nearby. Penhallow's voice, and Connor's new master sounded worried.

"He's restless," Zaryae replied, very close. "He moans in his sleep, and I can't tell whether he's in pain or trying to say something."

"We made a bargain with the gods to keep him," Penhallow said. "I don't know whether he'll thank us for it or not."

Wake up, Connor. This time, it was Kierken Vandholt's voice, sounding inside Connor's mind. *Your body is healed enough to sustain you. It's time to come back.*

Connor groaned and opened his eyes. He stared up at an unfamiliar ceiling, painted with a faded scene of clouds and gods. A real bed, not an army cot, supported him, with good sheets and a woolen blanket. Despite the blanket, Connor felt cold to the marrow, and he shivered.

A warm hand clasped his. "You're safe, Bevin." Connor slowly turned his head and saw Zaryae sitting in a chair next to his bed. Her eyes were red-rimmed, and it looked as if she had not slept in days. Wisps of dark hair struggled from her usually immaculate braid.

"How long?" he rasped, his voice dry. Zaryae helped him sit up enough to drink, and pressed a cup of water against his parched lips.

"The battle was four days ago." Penhallow moved into Connor's sight, standing behind Zaryae. "What do you remember?"

Connor settled back into his pillow and struggled to think.

"I remember the battle against Thrane," he said slowly. "We freed the boy," he added.

"Eljas Hennoch," Penhallow supplied. "He's been through a lot, but he'll heal. His father surrendered at Castle Reach."

"There were so many prisoners in the dungeon," Connor murmured. He guessed that they were still at Solsiden, where they had fought their battle against Thrane and Reese. "What about them?"

"Pollard was supplying 'food' for Reese, to heal him," Penhallow replied wearily. "Reese's damage was substantial. We think Thrane grew bold and stopped worrying about retaliation, and just began gathering mortals and bringing them here for his brood to drain."

"Sweet Esthrane," Connor said. He was quiet for a moment, thinking. "Thrane's dead?" It was difficult to know what was real and what had been his imagination. The dreams had been so real, he doubted that he could tell vision from truth.

"Thrane was destroyed, along with Reese and all their get, everywhere," Penhallow confirmed. "You helped us turn the course of the war. Losing his *talishte* support damaged Nagok, and Blaine's army and their allies defeated him. Pollard was routed without his *talishte*, and Hennoch surrendered as soon as he saw Reese's get disintegrate."

Relief and the satisfaction of completion washed over Connor. "So it's over?" he asked.

"The fighting's done," Penhallow replied. "There's a lot of cleanup to do before everything's really settled."

Connor turned back to look at Zaryae, and something he saw in her eyes told him that Penhallow had not given him a complete answer. "What else?" he asked. "I heard you say something about a 'bargain.' What did you mean?"

His right hand went to his abdomen, where he remembered

being badly wounded. Mortally wounded, perhaps. He had believed it was his time to die as he had fallen to the ground, covered in blood, cut open like a gutted fish. And yet, as his hand felt beneath his nightshirt, the skin was unbroken, only a thin, smooth scar. A shiver went down Connor's spine. "Did you turn me?"

Zaryae's grip tightened on his hand. Her skin felt so warm, and Connor felt so cold. *Am I* talishte? *Is this what it feels like to be undead?*

"We didn't turn you." Kierken Vandholt's spirit took shape beside Penhallow, appearing nearly solid. "And we didn't let you die. But there was a cost for bringing you back."

Connor swallowed hard. "Tell me," he said, mustering his courage. He looked to Zaryae, but she bowed her head so that he could not see her tears, and she clasped his hand in both of hers.

"I bargained with Esthrane for your soul." The Wraith Lord regarded Connor with a mixture of emotions in his expression.

"You bargained with a goddess—for me?" Connor repeated incredulously.

"It was the only way to save you without making you *talishte*," Penhallow said.

"What does that mean?" Connor asked, feeling completely out of his depth. He had not spent a lot of time thinking about the high god Charrot and his consorts, Torven and Esthrane. Though he had made the ritual offerings over the years, attended the celebrations and ceremonies on holy days, it had all seemed remote from everyday life. He did not disbelieve in the gods; but he had never dwelled on the thought of their reality. Suddenly, that distinction now seemed urgent.

"When I exchanged my soul to save my king, centuries ago, Esthrane granted my prayer, but doing so meant that I wander the Unseen Realms, instead of finding my rest in the Sea of Souls," Kierken Vandholt replied. "And thus, I became the Wraith Lord, not doomed to Raka but unable to cross into a final rest."

"You bargained the same for me?" Connor's voice barely rose above a whisper.

"It was the only way," Vandholt said sadly. "We had only three choices: Turn you, lose you, or this."

"You didn't want to become *talishte*," Penhallow said. "We respected your wishes. But we didn't think you wanted to die, if there was another option." He looked to Zaryae, who had raised her head, though she was crying silently.

"What does it mean for me, while I live?" Connor asked, torn between relief that he had survived and terror of the unknown. He wracked his brain to remember all that the Wraith Lord had said about the Unseen Realms, and much that he recalled was fearsome, a place between life and death filled with fallen immortals, of which Kierken Vandholt might be the least dangerous.

"It does not change your *kruvgaldur* bond to Penhallow or your connection to me," Vandholt replied. "Penhallow's blood was still necessary to heal you, though with help from the mages—and Esthrane. You retain the benefits of that bond—a longer-than-mortal lifespan, greater resilience, and our ability to communicate with you. And you retain the extra gift you received as a Lord of the Blood, your enhanced defenses against hostile spirits," the Wraith Lord added. "In fact, those abilities will be strengthened because of this. But you have been touched by the goddess. She granted our prayers to save you. And every blessing comes with a price."

Vandholt hesitated. "While you live, you are also now the servant of Esthrane, as I am. She is a fair but stern mistress."

"So I'm still mortal," Connor said, reasoning it out. "A little stronger than before. But I'll die eventually, and when I do—"

"Your soul will wander the Unseen Realms, as mine does, and you will continue to serve Esthrane," Vandholt replied. "For eternity, or until she releases you."

Connor took a deep breath, trying to process what he was hearing. "What happens to *talishte* when they meet the final death?" he asked, leveling his gaze at Penhallow.

"Being turned doesn't change our souls," Penhallow replied. "At least, I don't believe it does. The topic has been debated. We still fear Raka and hope for the Sea of Souls. Some believe that the blood required by the Dark Gift dooms us, but I believe we can redeem ourselves by the actions we choose."

"So *talishte* don't go to the Unseen Realms?"

Vandholt's apparition nodded. "No. That I can say with certainty. Where they go I can only state as a matter of belief. In that, I agree with Lanyon."

"If I were turned, would it change the bargain?" Connor asked, his thoughts reeling.

"It would extend your existence, forestall the reckoning," the Wraith Lord replied. "But it would not change the terms. If you were destroyed as a *talishte*, you would likely become a wraith for the duration of your service. A bargain with a goddess cannot be unmade."

"Thank you for saving me," Connor said finally. "I didn't want to die." He met Zaryae's gaze with what he hoped was a brave face. "As for the rest, it's a lot to think about. But I guess I've got time to figure it out."

Penhallow left a few minutes later, and the Wraith Lord's ghost dissipated, leaving Connor and Zaryae alone. Connor no longer felt bold enough to look at Zaryae, and after all he had been through, the question of what this change would mean to her loomed large. *There wouldn't be a discussion at all if they had let me die,* he thought. *So I guess a slim chance is better than no chance. Still, I'm broken, marred. She could do better.*

"This doesn't change a thing, Bevin," Zaryae said as if she had read his thoughts.

"It changes *me*," Connor said, his voice catching. "How can it not change the way you see me?"

"They told me that you died," Zaryae said fiercely. "I mourned you. The *talishte* who saw you fall told me what happened. And if the goddess was listening, then she didn't just heed the Wraith Lord's prayer, she heeded mine as well, because I begged her to save you if there was any way at all to bring you back to me," she continued, gripping his hand tightly. "Even as *talishte*."

He turned back to look at her. Zaryae had stopped crying, and he saw the same determination in her eyes that he had glimpsed when they had been in battle together. "How can you say that?" he asked incredulously.

"Because having you be undead and with me would still have been better than losing you," she replied with certainty. "I'm sorry, Bevin. Maybe I was selfish to want to keep you here. I know that saving you came at a high price. But so did losing you." She lifted their twined fingers to her lips and kissed them. "I love you, Bevin. That hasn't changed at all."

"What a mess." A week had passed since Connor had awoken, and the damage from the battles was far from being cleaned up. He held hands with Zaryae as they walked together, partly from affection and partly because he had not fully regained his strength.

Solsiden itself was largely undamaged from the fight, except for the courtyard, which bore scars of the violence. Yet in the dungeons below, the sight that unfolded made Connor despair of ever being able to undo the damage of Thrane's brief hold on power.

The dungeons were packed with badly wounded prisoners, some drained nearly to the brink of death. Most appeared to be barely clinging to life, filthy, emaciated, and delirious.

"What will become of them?" Connor asked Penhallow after he and Zaryae emerged, shaken, from the prison area.

"For now, we've kept them glamoured, as a mercy," Penhallow replied. Even he appeared worn and weary. "We'll save the ones who can be healed, and the healers will lessen the misery of those who can't."

"What of their memories?" Zaryae asked. It was a potent question. Return the survivors to their villages with the memories of their abuse intact, and the horrors were likely to spark retaliation against all *talishte*, punishing the liberators since those who committed the atrocities were already destroyed. Remove the memories, and the prisoners returned less than whole.

"The healers can blur the worst of the memories," Penhallow replied. He raised a hand to forestall argument. "I know that it's a judgment call, a bit of playing god. But if their memories strip them of their reason, where's the benefit in healing them?"

"Even blurred, there will be evidence about what happened here," Connor said. "And reprisals."

Penhallow nodded. "Which is what Kierken and I counseled from the start, when we argued against Thrane and Reese. *Talishte* cannot rule by force." He paused. "That's why we are forming a new Elder Council."

"But you lost so many of the eldest *talishte*," Connor replied. "Who will take their places?"

Penhallow gave a bitter chuckle. "Since I am now, by attrition, one of the oldest surviving *talishte*, I will be one of the new Elders. Kierken will return, of course. Dolan has agreed as well, meaning that the Knights of Esthrane will have a voice, as they should have had all along. Carlisle, Dalton, and Jarett survived the battle with the rogue Elders and have agreed to resume their responsibilities. Perhaps, in time, we will add others, but it's enough for now. We will be fewer than the old council, but *talishte* are fewer as well." He shook his head. "Thrane and Reese, with their grab for power, managed to do what King Merrill and his ancestors could not—cut the number of *talishte* nearly by half."

"Will you rebuild your broods?" Zaryae asked. Connor's thoughts went immediately to the wretches in the cells below.

"Not from the prisoners," Penhallow replied decisively. "That's for certain. But yes, over time, cautiously and carefully, we will gather new fledges to our broods. It's a necessity for us to survive, as you have seen. Some threats cannot be met by mortal servants alone." Chief among those threats, Connor knew, was the danger posed by other *talishte* as well as mortal vengeance.

"What about Tormod Solveig?" Connor had nearly forgotten Solveig's presence, until he glimpsed the black-clad necromancer in the torch-lit courtyard. Solveig's back was turned to them, but a blue-white glow surrounded him, and Connor's magic as a medium told him that Solveig was in the midst of hundreds of ghosts.

"He calls it 'sifting the dead,'" Penhallow replied. "Once Tormod regained his strength after the battle, and after he interrupted the attacks on you while you recovered, he set about dealing with the ghosts Thrane and Reese left behind." He grimaced. "As you can imagine, the number is substantial."

"What can he do for them?" Connor asked. Despite the horror of the ghosts' attack, Connor was curious about Tormod's necromancy and how their magic differed.

"For those who want to move on, Tormod can ease their passage to the Sea of Souls," Penhallow replied. "And for those who want to remain, Tormod says he can help them be 'unstuck' from this place so that they can go home, or at least go elsewhere."

"Thrane wanted to kill Tormod because of his necromancy," Connor said quietly. "Will the new Elders try to hurt him? After all, he helped us win," Connor added defensively.

Penhallow shook his head. "Kierken and I have already made Tormod's safety a condition of admission to the council," he replied. "So long as he doesn't use his magic against lawful *talishte*, we won't harm him."

A *talishte* guard appeared in a blur of motion beside Penhallow. "My lord," the guard said, "There's a mob heading for the gates. Mortals, with weapons. What are your orders?"

"Hold the gates, but avoid killing anyone if you can," Penhallow answered. "There's been enough death."

The guard bowed in acknowledgment. "As you wish, m'lord."

Zaryae turned to Penhallow. "It serves no purpose to allow the mob to destroy you and your *talishte*, when you saved them."

"I don't intend to let them destroy us," Penhallow said, sounding wearier than Connor could recall. "But they'll just come back with a bigger mob if we drive them away with force." He gave a wan, bitter smile. "Trust me on this, Bevin. I've seen it too many times before."

"I believe I can help." Tormod Solveig had joined them while Penhallow was speaking. "If you can turn them away without starting another battle, it would be a step toward putting all this behind us," Penhallow said. "Do what you can."

Penhallow went to see to the situation at the wall, in an effort to make sure his orders were carried out. Connor and Zaryae climbed the tower, where they could see and hear what was happening below.

A mob of at least a hundred angry men gathered outside the battered gates to Solsiden. They carried scythes, hoes, staves, and torches, raising their weapons threateningly and shouting for the gates to be opened and their captured loved ones to be returned to them.

"We have destroyed Lord Reese and Lord Thrane," Tormod Solveig said, standing in the center of the wall walkway. "Lord Pollard is also dead. Their troops have been routed. They will not trouble your villages anymore."

"We want our people back!" shouted a man at the front of the crowd. The others yelled their support.

"Our healers are with the captives now," Tormod answered them. "We will return them to you when they are able to travel."

"Liar!" the leader of the mob shouted. "The biters won't let them go. Death to biters!" The crowd took up the chant.

Connor stared down at the angry mob in horror. "I don't want to have done all this, just to burn because of a crowd gone mad," he said. But he knew that he lacked the strength to fight. Just climbing the stairs to the tower had winded him.

The mob surged toward the gates, pounding against the heavy wood-and-iron doors, but their makeshift weapons had little effect against walls meant to withstand a siege. Yet while the mob outside might not be able to break into Solsiden, if their numbers grew and they camped around the outskirts, they could cut off supplies and make peaceable rebuilding impossible.

"Give us our people back," the leader shouted. "Or we will be avenged."

"You can't win," Tormod replied. "These *talishte* are not your enemy. They destroyed the ones who harmed your people. Give us a truce, and we will return your people to you."

"Don't believe him! He's working for the biters!" Again the crowd rushed the gates, hammering against them in a vain attempt to get inside.

Connor knew the attack could be easily repulsed by Penhallow's troops, and that even mortals could have turned back the assault with archers and boiling water poured through the murder holes.

"They can't win," Connor said to Zaryae. "And if we use force against them, it's all the harder to ever make peace so that the allied *talishte* aren't in danger."

"Look!" Zaryae said, pointing. Ghostly shapes began to take form outside the castle walls, between the gate and the attackers. The mob gasped and fell back, weapons ready, expecting a trick. Instead, more glowing ghosts manifested, appearing nearly solid.

"These are your dead," Tormod shouted down to the crowd. "We have destroyed their murderers. I can return their spirits to you, to stay among you or move on as they see fit. We will return the living to you in a few days. But there must be a truce. No good can come of more fighting. The enemy who harmed your people is dead."

The ghosts moved forward, one by one, toward the crowd. Some of the mob reacted with sobs or cries of anguish as a loved one was recognized and a death confirmed. Others responded with shouts and curses, striking at the revenants with staves and scythes as if to prove they were a deception. A few took trembling steps toward the apparitions, to assure themselves that they were indeed the ghosts of their loved ones.

"No truce!" the man at the fore shouted, and a few in the mob behind him took up the cry. The appearance of the ghosts seemed to have shaken the others, since some of the mob stepped back from the edges of the group, while others murmured among themselves. "Death to biters!" The mob rushed forward again, only to find that they could not pass the line of ethereal protectors.

"Your dead do not desire more bloodshed," Tormod shouted. From where Connor and Zaryae stood, Connor could see the toll the magic was taking. Tormod was sweating despite the cool night, his face flushed with the effort of will, his whole body trembling with the outpouring of power.

"The ghosts may want to hold off the mob, but Tormod can't feed them the power to do it forever," Zaryae murmured, holding tight to Connor's arm.

The sound of hoofbeats made Connor worry that the villagers at the gates were about to get reinforcements. "Penhallow might not have a choice about needing to defend the manor," Connor said. "Not if the villagers bring enough of a crowd against us." He waited nervously as the riders drew closer, and realized he was holding his breath as the newcomers appeared at the edges of the torchlight.

"Stand down!"

The voice came not from Tormod Solveig but from behind the mob. Men on horseback rode into the circle of light cast by the torches. Blaine McFadden emerged at the head of a group of soldiers who more than matched the size of the mob.

"There will be no reprisals," Blaine ordered. "We will help your villages rebuild and help you bury your dead. My soldiers will keep the peace. The men who harmed you have been destroyed. I have no desire for more fighting, but if you will not stand down, you will bear the consequences."

For a moment, Connor feared that the hotheaded leader might charge, despite the fact that his mob was obviously at a serious disadvantage against a well-armored and heavily armed contingent of soldiers. The more practical-minded among the crowd began to disperse, disappearing into the darkness. Then with a muttered curse, the leader threw down his stave, and the others lowered their weapons.

"Go home," Blaine shouted as the soldiers parted ranks to line both sides of the road leading from the manor. "The war is over. It's time to rebuild."

Cowed by the reinforcements, the mob broke up, but from the muttering and surly looks it was clear that many were unconvinced. Only when the last of the villagers was gone did Blaine ride up toward the gates, waiting for the big doors to open.

By the time Connor and Zaryae made it to the bottom of the tower stairs, Blaine and his troops were inside the walls, and the gate was shut once more. Penhallow and Tormod came out to greet him, and Blaine swung down from his horse. "Trouble with the villagers?" he asked with a jerk of his head toward the walls.

"I can't blame them for being angry, after what Pollard and Thrane did to their people," Penhallow acknowledged. "But the damage can't be undone."

"I feared worse," Blaine replied as his men dismounted and saw to their horses, unloading the supplies they had brought. "I intended to be here sooner, but several times along the way from Castle Reach, we saw groups of mortals attacking crypts and cairns during the daylight, and had to stop to run them off." He shook his head. "No telling whether or not there were *talishte* in the crypts, but the intent was clear."

Blaine turned to Connor and Zaryae and managed a tired smile. "It's good to see both of you alive and well," he said.

Connor slipped an arm around Zaryae's shoulders, and she leaned into him. "We're all right—now," he replied.

"Thank you," Penhallow said. Blaine fell in step between Penhallow and Tormod as they walked back into Solsiden, with Connor and Zaryae behind them. He led them into a small, sparsely appointed salon. On their way, Penhallow spoke to one of his *talishte* guards, who went to find food and drink for their guest.

"We brought provisions," Blaine went on. "Not a lot, but all we could bring with us given the situation. I thought that fresh supplies would be a help."

"The pantry was pretty empty," Zaryae admitted "Thank you." Thrane had obviously worried more about feeding his *talishte* brood than he had their mortal captives or servants."

When they had settled into chairs, Blaine recounted the final battle with Nagok, as well as his last fight with Pollard. "Niklas and Bayard should have the situation well in hand," he said, "especially with the extra help from Rinka and Verner."

"I'm relieved to hear Rinka is well," Tormod replied. "And I'm certain she will want to know that, remarkably, I have survived without her at my elbow." His tired grin softened the words, and Connor guessed that Rinka Solveig's protective streak sometimes proved a bit much for her brother, well-intentioned as it might be.

"What of the twins?" Zaryae asked. "Are they all right?"

Blaine nodded. "The last I saw them, they were putting a

fright into Nagok's troops, riding with the Plainsmen," he added with a chuckle. "I think their new assignment suits them."

Two *talishte* guards brought a tray of hot tea, bread, and some cheese and sausage, as well as a flagon of deer blood for Penhallow. Penhallow sipped from his goblet in silence for a few moments as the others ate. "Geir told me much of what you reported," he said finally, "though it's always interesting to hear another view of a battle. So Nagok is vanquished?"

Blaine nodded. "And the rogue Elders? There was no trace of the one you called Aubergine among Nagok's *talishte*, at least, not that we saw."

"He was with Thrane," Connor replied. "Dolan recognized him. Aubergine is dead."

"All of the rogue Elders were destroyed," Penhallow added. "Several were Thrane's get, so they died when he died. The Elgin Spike retained its power."

"What happens to the Spike now?" Blaine asked. "Will you use it to make sure the *talishte* control their broods now that the war is over?"

Penhallow hesitated, and Connor knew that the question touched on a delicate subject. "We are reinstating a new Elder Council of the most powerful among us who are committed to living peaceably among mortals." He gave a knowing smile. "The Spike will be returned to Edgeland in a new hiding place. Nidhud is willing to serve as its guardian, at least for a while." He raised an eyebrow. "Of course, there is no need to broadcast among *talishte* that the Spike is once again 'lost,'" he added.

Blaine chuckled at the implication. "Let them wonder?" he said, drinking his tea and savoring its warmth. "As good a tactic as any, I guess. And one that supports your authority among your own people while minimizing the threat that the Spike might be misused."

Penhallow gave a nod of acknowledgment. "Indeed."

Connor turned to Blaine. "What about Hennoch?" he asked. "We freed his son." Eljas Hennoch was surprisingly well recovered, considering his treatment. "Eljas has been asking about his father's fate."

Blaine let out a deep breath. "Hennoch surrendered to Piran as soon as it was clear that Thrane's *talishte* were destroyed," he said. "We knew he only fought for Pollard to save his son's life. So I gave Hennoch a choice, for himself and his soldiers—death, or exile to Edgeland."

Connor chuckled. "In a way, he's getting off easy, since there's no more Velant."

Blaine nodded. "And there won't be, ever again, if I have any say in the matter. But the colony is going to need new workers once trade opens back up again, and new defenders, in case we haven't seen the last of the Cross-Sea Kingdoms. My sense is that Hennoch is a man of integrity who found himself in a bad situation. I think he and his men could be a good addition to Edgeland."

"So I take it he agreed to exile?" Zaryae asked.

"He really didn't need to think about it long, given the alternative," Blaine replied wryly. "I assume Eljas will want to accompany his father, unless he has family here to rejoin." *Exiling Hennoch and his men was a smart move,* Connor thought. It made Blaine look fair, even magnanimous, while avoiding slaughter.

"Will Edgeland remain a place of exile?" Zaryae questioned.

"I hope that the need for exile is rare," Blaine answered. "Still, I'd rather have the option to spare a life rather than keep people like Hennoch in prison or be forced to hang them. So the situation may still arise, now and again, but I hope that Edgeland can become more of a true colony, self-sustaining

612 • GAIL Z. MARTIN

and with most residents able to travel back and forth to Donderath if they choose."

Already thinking like a king, Connor thought. "So the war is truly over," he said. After everything that had happened, it seemed impossible to believe the fighting was finally done.

Blaine nodded. "Yes. And now the hard part starts—rebuilding."

CHAPTER
THIRTY-FIVE

I CAN'T BELIEVE WE'RE BACK IN THESE BLOODY catacombs," Piran grumbled. Deep beneath Quillarth Castle, the necropolis held the catafalques and crypts of the dead kings of Donderath as well as those of nobles, vaunted generals, and the founder of the Knights of Esthrane. Blaine and the others had been down in the catacombs before, each time fraught with danger, since the dead here did not remain quiet.

"The mages and Dolan say it's where we need to do the formal investiture, in order to restore a level of 'magical immunity' to the kingdom," Blaine replied, making a face at the term. "Whatever that means. But they're sure that the ancient coronation ritual has to be done a certain way, and I don't want to find out what happens if it gets done wrong." Piran grimaced, and Blaine was sure he was remembering how working the ritual to re-anchor the magic had nearly killed them when it was not performed correctly.

"But we get a party afterward, right?" Piran asked, trying to cover his own nervousness. "Food, drink, pretty girls?"

Kestel elbowed him. "Food and drink, yes. But I've already warned the pretty girls. Sorry."

They bantered in hushed voices, out of respect for the occasion and because the catacombs seemed by their nature to require whispers. All of the new Lords of the Blood were present. Dolan conferred with Cosmin, Viorel, and Rikard on the magic to be worked, while Seneschal Dillon fussed over the crown. Later, for the public ceremony, Judith McFadden and Mari, Zaryae and Desya, Rinka Solveig and Geir would join them, but for now, only those who were part of the ritual braved the dangers of the castle's catacombs.

Blaine tugged at his collar. Dillon had managed to have suitable clothing reworked from what he had been able to beg, borrow, and scavenge, since fine brocades, velvets, and silks could not yet be made anew. From what Blaine had seen in the mirror that morning, Dillon had outdone himself, putting together an outfit truly worthy of a king. Dillon had also found a suitable gown for Kestel, one that played up her red hair and coloring, complementing her figure, and making her look every inch a queen. Piran and Niklas wore uniforms befitting their role as generals, and even Folville showed up dressed suitably for his new position as the Lord Mayor of Castle Reach.

"Everything is ready," Dolan said. Dolan and Nidhud both wore the gray cloaks and surcoats that marked them as members of the Knights of Esthrane. They and the rest of the Knights would have a prominent and visible role in the public coronation ceremony and in the government that Blaine would forge as Donderath's new king.

Blaine tamped down his nervousness, and Kestel gave his arm a reassuring squeeze. Then Blaine followed Dolan to the center of the large, circular plaza in the catacombs, the hub from which many corridors branched off into the darkness of the huge necropolis. Dagur, Rikard, and the other mages had set two warded circles that were nearly complete, leaving an opening like a door to admit the participants. Blaine looked solemn as he stepped into the smaller, inside warding, and Dagur completed the circle around him. In the outer circle, the twelve Lords of the Blood took their places: Penhallow, Connor and the Wraith Lord, Nidhud, Borya, Tormod Solveig, Birgen Verner, William Folville, Traher Voss, Piran, Verran, Dawe, and Niklas. Each of them, like Blaine, wore the obsidian disk that had been part of the ritual to restore the magic. Kestel and Dillon stood outside the circles, watching intently. The mages—Dolan, Dagur, Rikard, Cosmin, and Viorel, along with several assistants—had already prepared the chamber with candles and incense, as well as a number of unusual artifacts Blaine did not remember having seen before.

Then there was the crown itself, which was older than the state crown Blaine had glimpsed on the occasions when he had seen King Merrill in his finery. It was a plain crown made of steel, beautifully wrought and embellished with studding instead of gems, quite a contrast to the more elaborate crown Blaine would wear for his public coronation. The crown sat on a pedestal inside the second ring, nestled on a faded velvet cushion. Next to it, lying atop a satin pouch, was a torque made from twisted strands of precious metal. Beside the torque lay a single golden earring set with a blood-red ruby.

Torches in sconces lit the round room, and Blaine could not avoid glancing down the darkened corridors, worried that they would overstay their welcome. The catacombs beneath Quillarth Castle were often overrun by the spirits of the dead, and their never-ending battles could prove deadly for mortals unlucky enough to be caught up in the action.

Dolan finished the outer warding, and the mages stood outside that circle of power, making a third ring with their bodies. Assistant mages stood behind the more powerful magic-users, holding hand drums and bells, chimes and small cymbals. At Dolan's signal, the drummers and bell ringers began to play, singing a low, repetitive chant that echoed in the shadowed vaults and catacombs.

Blaine shivered. There was magic in that chant, and every beat of the drums and shimmer of the bells raised its power. The inner circle, previously invisible, began to glow, like dust particles in a beam of sunlight. The outer circle became a coruscating curtain, glinting with multicolored, iridescent light.

Unlike in the ritual to restore magic, Blaine had no labyrinth to walk, no invocation to make. Dillon and the mages had been vague about what would happen next, and Blaine was still not sure whether that was because they wanted him to react to the events without prejudice or because they truly did not know. He suspected the latter, which only added to his nervousness.

The chanting continued, and the power rose, filling the chamber. Gradually, misty figures joined the outer circle. Many of the ghosts were dressed in clothing or armor that marked them as the dead of centuries past. Some, he recognized. Lynge, the martyred seneschal, and Geddy, his assistant. Torsten Almstedt, the founder of the Knights of Esthrane. King Merrill, Merrill's father and grandfather, and kings from long ago, whom Blaine recognized from their portraits and tapestries.

How is anyone going to cross the wardings to convey the crown, if that's what this is all about? Blaine wondered. Then three ghostly figures stepped forward, and he realized that the wardings would pose no barrier at all to them.

Torsten Almstedt's ghost grew more solid as he moved toward Blaine, empowered by the magic and by the energy of the catacombs themselves. He crossed the first warding effortlessly, moved past the Lords of the Blood, and lifted the torque. The second warding slowed him only for a second, and then he stood directly in front of Blaine, his gaze solemn.

"Blaine McFadden. You are not of royal blood, yet today, a new dynasty begins in you. Do you swear to protect this kingdom and its people with your life, your blood, and if need be, with your soul? Think before you answer," the ghost warned. "What is done cannot be undone."

"I swear."

Almstedt placed the torque around Blaine's neck. The metal was cold, but Almstedt's ghostly touch was even colder, and Blaine tried not to shudder. "The yoke of King Dacen, the first of Donderath's warrior kings," Almstedt intoned. "Wear it always, so long as you are king, as a symbol of the burden you have undertaken to keep this kingdom from harm." With that, Almstedt stepped back and made a shallow bow, then vanished from beside Blaine, only to reappear outside the second warding once more.

King Merrill's ghost was the next to move through the wardings, and he lifted not the crown but the earring. The living eyed the specter with regard, and bowed as he passed by. Merrill was a generation older than Blaine, and Blaine's late father had earned the king's gratitude in wars long past. But Merrill had also known Ian McFadden's dark side, which was why he had exiled Blaine for Ian's murder instead of having him executed. Now, Merrill's melancholy gaze fixed Blaine in a piercing stare.

"This gem has been part of the legacy of Donderath's rulers since time before memory," Merrill's said, his voice clear but filtered, as if coming from a great distance. "You will wear this for as long as you live, and it will bond with your blood. That bond creates a shield against most dark magic." He sighed. "As you well know, it cannot protect against everything. But this relic will protect you, and the kingdom, against many potent threats."

With that, Merrill reached up to Blaine's right ear. His hands felt as solid as those of a living man, though cold as a corpse. With a sudden push, Blaine felt the sharp stud of the earring pierce his lobe, allowing a few drops of warm blood to trickle down his neck. The earring warmed rapidly, as if its ruby took sustenance from his blood.

"Keep this kingdom well," Merrill charged, stepping back and regarding Blaine solemnly. "The spirits of the dead will be watching." As with Almstedt, Merrill's ghost made a shallow bow and vanished, only to appear on the outer ring of onlookers.

The third ghost was Kierken Vandholt. Here in the catacombs, he did not need Connor's body to make himself seen, a commanding man with a powerful physical presence, even as a specter. Vandholt lifted the steel crown in his large, broad hands. He was the most ancient spirit of the three, a millennium old; mage, *talishte,* and warrior. The mortals parted to allow him to pass, but Vandholt's gaze never wavered from Blaine.

"The Vottomer crown is the oldest surviving crown of Donderath kings," Vandholt said. "It is a warrior's crown, simple and strong like armor. It is even older than I am, and this crown remembers its past. Wear it knowing that the eyes of all those who came before you are watching. Take counsel from the living, but understand that with the three relics you have received, you may also seek wisdom from the dead. They are your safe passage to these chambers. Do not disappoint." With that, Vandholt lifted the crown, and Blaine knelt, inclining his head. The Wraith Lord set the steel crown on Blaine's head, and Blaine felt a tingle of power pass through his body.

"Rise, King Blaine of Donderath," Vandholt said solemnly. "Restore your kingdom and its people."

Vandholt made a low bow, and the other onlookers, including the Lords of the Blood and the mages, even Kestel, went down on one knee in fealty. Blaine stared out at them, completely at a loss, overwhelmed by what he had just heard and seen.

"Rise," he croaked. "We have work to do."

The chanting and drumming shifted, and as they had built energy before the ritual, now the slower cadence dissipated the magic that had been called. Dolan and Dagur released the wardings, and the shimmering power vanished. One by one, the ghostly audience drifted away.

The Lords of the Blood crowded around Blaine. "Congratulations, King Mick," Piran said with a grin. "I guess this means I have to let you win at cards, now that you're royal and all."

Verran and Dawe clapped Blaine on the shoulder, then their eyes widened as they realized they had touched the monarch without permission. "We made it through Velant together," Blaine reassured them with a self-conscious smile. "I'm not going to stand on ceremony now."

Kestel stepped up to join him, and gave a deep curtsy before he pulled her to her feet and kissed her. "This changes nothing between us," he whispered fiercely. "Nothing."

As Blaine accepted the well-wishes and congratulations from his friends and allies, the ritual seemed like a half-remembered dream, important but difficult to believe. Connor seemed to guess his thoughts.

"It really happened," Connor said. "Down here, magic is stronger—you may have noticed," he added with the knowing raise of an eyebrow. "The Wraith Lord could make himself present without me, although I've gotten used to him by now." He managed a wan grin. "That really was King Merrill. He

even nodded to me as he passed by, as if he remembered me
from when I served Lord Garnoc!"

Dagur and Rikard pushed through the crowd, with Dillon
a step behind. "You'll have plenty of time to celebrate later,"
Rikard said, steering Blaine by the elbow. "Thanks to the
ghosts and the artifacts, that should be sufficient to reinstate
the general protection against hostile magic," he said. "And
technically, you're king. But," he warned, "until the people
see you crowned, you aren't king in their eyes, and that's what
really invests you with the power."

"What he means is, we've got another stop before the big
banquet," Dagur said. "And people are waiting."

Blaine had insisted that the coronation be held after dark, so
that the *talishte* could attend. He had sworn to Penhallow and
to Dolan that their people would be full citizens of Donderath,
and Blaine was resolved to start out as he meant to go on.

Quillarth Castle was far from its former glory, but Dillon
and his helpers had worked a small wonder readying it for the
coronation. Banners and pennants, reworked from badly damaged tapestries, linens, and even carpets, added a festive air.
Torches and bonfires lit the bailey and the courtyard, and inside
the castle, lanterns at every window made the damaged castle
look more like its old self than at any time since the Great Fire.
A new bell tower had been erected, wood instead of stone like
the one that fell in the Cataclysm, and a salvaged bell had been
readied to peal glad tidings once the new king was crowned.

Flags flew from the parapets and the gates, and while Dillon
had confided that they had been made from dyed bedsheets, by
torchlight they looked regal. *Bed-linen flags and pieced-together
banners, remade finery and salvaged relics. What will it take to
bring back the kingdom that we lost?* Blaine wondered. *And if*

*that kingdom can't ever be again, what must I do to create some-
thing just as good, maybe even—someday—better?*

The task set for him was daunting, and Blaine dared not
think on it too long. Only the knowledge that he also could
not walk away and entrust Donderath's fate to chance gave him
the courage to step forward when the trumpets blared, and he
looked out on a sea of hopeful, skeptical faces challenging him
to make them believe.

"We are gathered to crown a new king of Donderath!" Dillon proclaimed. For the moment, he guarded the coronation
crown, rescued from its hiding place beneath the castle. Unlike
the steel crown, this was the formal crown of the kings of Donderath. He held up the crown, and the crowd cheered.

The ceremony was being held on the broad landing in front
of the main doors to Quillarth Castle, a place visible to all
those assembled in the courtyard. Blaine stood at the top of
the stairs in the center with Kestel at his side. The Lords of the
Blood stood on either side of him, mortal and *talishte*, living
and undead, mages and those without magic, a show of solidar-
ity. Judith, Edward, and Mari stood behind Blaine, dressed in
their own reclaimed finery for the occasion, along with Zaryae
and Desya, all of whom he considered to be his family.

The Knights of Esthrane stood at attention on one side of
the broad main walkway, while Dagur, Rikard, and the mages
faced them on the other side, looking scholarly and wise in
robes salvaged from the ruins of the University. Next to the
Knights were more of Blaine's generals and allies. In a section
of special guests, Rinka Solveig stood with the surviving allied
Elders. The crowd grew quiet as the trumpets sounded again.

"Tonight, Blaine McFadden, Lord of Glenreith, Warlord of
all Donderath, will become your new king," Dillon announced.

Another cheer went up from the onlookers, echoing from the high stone walls.

King Merrill had received his crown from the elder members of his family, recognition of the continuation of the royal bloodline. Blaine and his advisers had debated how the crown should be bestowed, finally agreeing to the only workable arrangement. At the sound of the trumpet, all twelve Lords of the Blood stepped forward as Blaine knelt among them. Gathered around him in a half circle so that Blaine was never hidden from the crowd's view, the Lords of the Blood all held the crown, placing it on Blaine's head together. They paused for a moment, letting their hands rest on his head in blessing, conveying their silent prayers and hopes for the monarchy.

Then, as the trumpets sounded once again, Blaine rose to his feet and lifted his head, gazing out over his people, who had now become his subjects. "All hail King Blaine!" Dillon shouted, and the crowd echoed the phrase in a roar.

"All hail King Blaine! All hail King Blaine!"

With that, Blaine waved in acknowledgment, and as Kestel moved up beside him, he stood and received the cheers of his well-wishers. Musicians took up their instruments, beginning with a regal fanfare and quickly moving to popular dance tunes. Before the night was through, Blaine was certain that they would be playing tavern favorites, and figured Verran might even sneak out to be among them. Dillon had planned an evening of celebration, with food carts and bonfires, performers and parades, accompanied by plenty of music and free ale.

"You know, most of the people out there will decide whether or not they like me as king by how good a party we throw for them tonight," Blaine said to Kestel as they moved inside the castle for the official coronation dinner.

"Then it's a good thing I worked with Dillon to plan the festivities," Kestel said with a grin. "Judith and Zaryae lent a hand, too." She winked at him. "Don't worry—by the time they sober up tomorrow, they'll be singing your praises for a long time to come."

Blaine doubted it would be that easy, but he smiled and nodded, still not quite believing the turns of fortune that had brought him to this moment. More trumpeters welcomed them to the great hall, which had been restored, if not exactly to its former glory, to a reasonable approximation suitable for such a grand occasion. Tapestries and paintings that had been hidden away since the Cataclysm now hung in their former places, while new pennants and banners had been made to fill the spaces left by those pieces damaged irreparably in the war. Candles and lanterns of all shapes, sizes, and materials formed a glittering strand down the center of the long table, banked by fresh flowers and fragrant branches. The fine place settings of King Merrill's time had long ago been looted, but enough mismatched pewter trenches had been gathered to serve everyone.

"I think all the ceremonies have made me hungry," Blaine joked, savoring the aroma of roasted venison and onions.

"Then you're in luck," Kestel chuckled. "I happen to know that the menu tonight really will be fit for a king."

For the first time since his return to Donderath, no one was trying to kill him. Blaine found that thought as satisfying as the platters of food Dillon and the castle staff had prepared. The feast was a testimony to Donderath's recovery, and to a successful planting and harvest. Succulent venison with root vegetables, crusty bread, and passable ale made for an excellent meal, along with an impressive variety of desserts. Plenty of deer blood meant a bounty for the *talishte* guests as well. Blaine and Kestel sat at the center of the long table. Judith, Edward,

Dawe, and Mari were on Blaine's right, while Borya, Desya, and Zaryae were to Kestel's left. Connor was next to Zaryae, and after the meal, Blaine's first official action as king would be to perform a handfasting. Piran, Verran, Niklas, Penhallow, and Geir were directly across from Blaine and Kestel, along with Engraham from the Rooster and Pig. The rest of Blaine's allies—the mages, the Elders, and the Knights of Esthrane— all joined in the feasting.

"Do you think we'll ever have this group together again?" Kestel asked, leaning her head on Blaine's shoulder.

He took a sip of his ale, and shrugged. "Who knows? Rinka and Tormod—and Birgen—will head back to their lands in a few days, to rebuild. Gods know, we need that. Voss says he'll sign a contract with me to have his people handling security for Castle Reach, the port, and the seacoast within twenty miles. And with Folville as the Lord Mayor of Castle Reach, and Voss's men rebuilding the shipworks, we might just have a port and sea trade again."

"I'm quite taken with heading up the castle and royal forces," Piran said with a grin. "But I hope you're not going to make us wear those wretched uniforms Merrill's castle guard wore."

"Oh no," Kestel laughed. "Merrill's colors were gold and purple. Blaine was leaning more toward orange and red, with a hat to match." The look on Piran's face was worth it, right before the queen nearly laughed hard enough to choke.

"We'll talk," Blaine said with a raised eyebrow. "I hate orange."

"I think it'll be a while before we hear anything more from Meroven," Niklas said, finishing off his venison. "At least, I hope so. But we'll have the borders patrolled. And I intend to have troops in place for the harvest, so we can do our damnedest not to have another hungry winter."

Judith and Edward had made a private handfasting while Blaine was off at war. They looked at each other with real affection, and Blaine was happy that in all the loss and hardship, they had found each other. Mari and Dawe would add a sibling for Robbe in the fall, and since Blaine's new home would be Quillarth Castle, he had officially bestowed the title of Lord of Glenreith on Dawe. Only Carr was missing. It helped to know that he had gone to the Sea of Souls in peace, and the extra time they had been afforded together with Carr's ghostly presence helped to ease the pain, but Glenreith would never be the same without Carr.

"Have you decided where the two of you will go, after the wedding?" Kestel asked Zaryae and Connor, as if she suspected the melancholy direction Blaine's thoughts had taken.

They exchanged a glance, giving Blaine to guess that the answer was not entirely settled. "To Solsiden and Westbain, most likely," Zaryae replied. "To help Penhallow and the Wraith Lord with the cleanup."

Penhallow cleared his throat. "I just want to go on record, along with Kierken, that we intend to rebuild Westbain for the newlyweds, as our wedding gift to them." He gave a rare smile. "Only fitting, after all that they've braved on our behalf."

Connor and Dawe were not the only ones to be gaining lands and titles. Piran, Verran, Niklas, Borya, and Desya had all been granted noble titles and vacant manors, as befitted Lords of the Blood. The Knights of Esthrane had already begun rebuilding their Citadel, and Dolan had confirmed the rumor that he intended to restore Mirdalur as a working manor. Dagur, Rikard, and the mages were committed to restoring the University at Castle Reach to its former glory, and maybe even other sites, like the Lyceum at Tobar.

"I wanted to thank you for bringing Bayard to Bleak

Hollow," Rinka Solveig said. "Together with the twins," she added with a nod toward Borya and Desya, "I think we can open trade routes up before winter to the Lesser Kingdoms and the null villages. If the harvest is as good as we expect, we should have plenty to sell, and as I recall, a few of those villages brewed some fine mead and lager," she added with the pleased expression of someone who expected to turn a handy profit.

"Let us know if you'll be trading iron goods and ale," Dawe said. "Now that the villages around Glenreith have gotten their feet under them again, the forges are turning out good, sturdy tools and bridles, and by next summer, we're expecting to see a better grade of ale and whiskey from our brewery and distillery."

"I'm waiting for the wine you promised me," Kestel said with a raised eyebrow. "I haven't had a decent glass since before Velant, and I'm long overdue!"

"Speaking of which," Piran said, "Voss told me he thinks we'll have three new seagoing ships ready by the time the ice breaks up in Skalgerston Bay. We can reopen the Edgeland trade when the White Nights are back, and you know what that means."

Kestel, Piran, and Verran all looked at Blaine. "Herring!" they said in unison.

Blaine glanced up at Dillon, who was, as an excellent seneschal, standing right behind him. "Make a note, please," he said. "You can add herring to all the castle menus to improve trade with Edgeland. But there's to be none on my plate. Ever."

"Noted, Your Majesty," Dillon replied, with just a hint of laughter in his voice.

Blaine smiled, listening to the buzz of conversation, warmed by good food and drink and the knowledge that at least for now, they and the kingdom were safe. Blaine glanced over to see Kestel watching him, and he guessed that she was thinking along the same lines. He stood, and the conversation quieted.

"A toast," Blaine said, lifting his glass with his left hand while he took Kestel's hand in his right. "To a new beginning—for Donderath, and for us. May the gods grant us and this kingdom peace, prosperity, and safety, and the wisdom to never forget the price it required to obtain them."

Tomorrow, official business would require the attention of Donderath's new king. But tonight, Blaine was surrounded by family, friends, and allies in quiet celebration, more than he ever expected, and all that he needed.

ACKNOWLEDGMENTS

Thank you, readers! Because you read, I write. Whether you're just discovering my books or whether you have been with me from the start, I deeply appreciate each and every one of you.

Many thanks also to my agent, Ethan Ellenberg, and his team. I appreciate everything you do.

Lots of gratitude and appreciation for my editor, Susan Barnes, and the whole Orbit crew, including Laura Fitzgerald, Ellen Wright, Anna Jackson, Lindsey Hall, Gemma Conley-Smith, and all the other folks who work hard to make my books a reality.

Conventions are the heart of the sci-fi/fantasy community, where readers and authors meet. Thank you to Arisia, Illogicon, Ad-Astra, Mysticon, Awesomecon, Capclave, Lunacon, Chattacon, Libertycon, Ravencon, Balticon, ConCarolinas, ConGregate, Dragon*Con, Origins Gaming Convention, Atomacon, Philcon, World Fantasy, Contraflow, Confluence, and the Arizona and Carolinas Renaissance Festivals, who always make me feel at home and who have welcomed me as a guest author— as well as the new conventions I have yet to experience. I am very grateful for the opportunity to be part of convention programming, meet wonderful people, and give back to a community I truly appreciate.

Thank you to my Thrifty Author Publishing Success Network Meetup group, an awesome group of writers. We have so much fun and have all come so far.

Many thanks also to my author, artist, musician, performer, and reader convention friends and Renaissance Festival regulars, who help me survive life on the road; to the fantastic bookstore owners and managers, who carry on a valiant fight on the front lines of this crazy publishing industry; and to my social media friends and followers, who are always up for some online mayhem.

And most of all, thanks to my husband, Larry Martin, who plays a huge part in bringing all the books and short stories to life. He's my best first editor, brainstorming accomplice, proofreader extraordinaire, and now official coauthor of our new Steampunk series, *Iron & Blood: A Jake Desmet Adventure.* The books wouldn't happen without him, and I'm grateful for all his help and support. Thanks also to my children, who are usually patient with the demands of the writing life, and for my dogs, Kipp and Flynn, who are experts at dispelling writer's block. It takes a village to write a book, and I am grateful to each and every one of you!

extras

about the author

Gail Z. Martin is the author of the new epic fantasy novel *Shadow and Flame* (Orbit Books, 2016), which is the fourth and final book in the Ascendant Kingdoms Saga; *Iron and Blood*: *A Jake Desmet Adventure*, a new Steampunk series (Solaris Books) coauthored with Larry N. Martin, and *Vendetta: A Deadly Curiosities Novel* in her urban fantasy series set in Charleston, South Carolina (Solaris Books). She is also the author of *Ice Forged*, *Reign of Ash*, and *War of Shadows* in the Ascendant Kingdoms Saga, the Chronicles of the Necromancer series (*The Summoner*, *The Blood King*, *Dark Haven*, *Dark Lady's Chosen*) from Solaris Books, and the Fallen Kings Cycle (*The Sworn*, *The Dread*) from Orbit Books, plus the novel *Deadly Curiosities*. Gail writes several series of ebook short stories: *The Jonmarc Vahanian Adventures* and the *Deadly Curiosities Adventures,* and with Larry N. Martin, the Steampunk *Storm & Fury Adventures.*

Gail's work will appear in several new anthologies in 2016. An all-new Blaine McFadden adventure, *No Reprieve*, takes place during the Velant Prison years and is posted on Orbit Short Fiction. Watch for Blaine and his friends to return in more short stories and novellas set in Velant and on Edgeland. Gail's stories have been featured in anthologies including *Heroes, With Great Power*, *Athena's Daughters*, *The Big Bad 2*, *Dance*

Like a Monkey, *Realms of Imagination*, and the British Fantasy Society's *Unexpected Journeys,* plus an illustrated story in *Icarus: A Graphic Novel*. Other US/UK anthologies include *Magic: the Esoteric and Arcane* (Solaris), *The Bitten Word*, *Rum & Runestones*, *Spells & Swashbucklers*, and *The Mammoth Book of Ghost Stories by Women*.

Stories Gail coauthored with Larry N. Martin have recently been featured in anthologies including *Clockwork Universe Steampunk vs. Aliens*, *Alien Artifacts*, *The Weird Wild West*, *The Side of Good*, *Space*, and *Contact Light*.

Find her on the web at AscendantKingdoms.com, on Twitter @GailZMartin, on Facebook.com/WinterKingdoms, at *Disquieting Visions* blog, and GhostInTheMachinePodcast.com. She leads frequent conversations at goodreads.com/GailZMartin, participates on Reddit/Fantasy as GailZMartin, and posts free excerpts of her work and the occasional free novella on Wattpad at wattpad.com/GailZMartin.

Find out more about Gail Z. Martin and other Orbit authors by registering for the free monthly newsletter at www.orbitbooks.net.

if you enjoyed

SHADOW AND FLAME

look out for

BLACK WOLVES

by

Kate Elliott

1

The whole business stank of rotting fish.

From his position braced high in the branches of a sprawling lancewood tree that overlooked an unremarkable trail cutting through forested hills, Kellas felt the familiar warning itch between his shoulder blades. Something about this ambush wasn't going to go right, and yet he had a job to do and a secret to hide and no choice except to stick it out to the end. If those cursed smugglers didn't show up, he'd be no closer to the truth than he had been a month ago when he'd joined this company of Black Wolves on the hunt for a traitor in their ranks.

A breeze blew into his face off the nearest height but he smelled nothing except the dense scent of vegetation and the memory of rain. Birds had long ago resumed their chatter and song, no longer disturbed by the presence of six men.

The soldiers had set up an ambush point at dawn. They'd been slipped information that stolen goods would be smuggled down this specific trail under the guard of a demon and its armed confederates. The subcadre commander, Denni, had picked this spot because of the sprawling canopy of the lancewood tree and a flat patch of ground where they'd been able to dig a pit. By now it was midafternoon.

Kellas's vantage in the tree allowed him to study his companions hidden in the surrounding undergrowth. He was certain one of the other five was the disloyal Wolf leaking information to the very outlaws they were meant to capture.

Which one?

Crouched on a branch below Kellas, Ezan breathed noisily. On the stream side of the path, Oyard and Battas shifted around, brush rustling loud enough to almost drown out the gurgle of the distant stream. They were all so cursed loud.

Maybe they were all in on it.

On the mountain side, Aikar whispered to Denni. Idiot. Didn't he know how voices carried on a still day? Maybe he hoped his words would carry a warning on the breeze. Kellas wanted to signal Aikar to be silent, but Denni was senior of this subcadre and thus in charge. Any initiative Kellas took might give away his cover of pretending to be a lowly tailman new to the Wolves.

As if the restlessness of the others made him doubt their careful preparations, Denni tugged experimentally on the pit rope where it stretched across the path under cover of artfully layered ground litter. They hoped to trap a demon on one of the stakes set in the pit and cut off its skin. It was a good plan, if it worked.

A new sound teased at the edge of Kellas's hearing, a slapping that he identified as the thud of feet falling on dry leaves and dusty earth. A moment later a voice floated on the air.

"Sure, the king claims he's sending in his best troops to protect us, but then we're the ones who have to feed and house them above what we already pay in taxes."

Two men strode into view. Both carried hunting spears.

"He's like a baker selling bread for what seems like a good price, only then you discover he's been mixing sawdust in with the flour all along."

"Would the pair of you keep your mouths shut?" said a woman who was not yet quite visible beyond a bend in the path, although movement flashed through the dusty leaves. "You'll warn off the pigs before we have a chance to strike."

As Kellas tried to estimate heads and bodies in an oncoming group that he still couldn't really see through the leaves, a glimmer of pale cloth caught his eye.

The hells!

The most infamous demon of all wore a white cloak. Was she guiding the smugglers in person? He had accomplished a lot of things in the last eight years but he'd never tangled directly with a cloaked demon and its perilous magic. A racing clamor of excitement disturbed his concentration but he calmed it with slow, measured breaths.

The two spearmen in the front passed over the pit without noticing the give in the ground and headed under the wide canopy of the lancewood tree.

And there she was! Wearing a white cloak and armed with a bow and quiver, the demon strode into view and turned to signal to someone unseen behind her. Right on target, Battas and Oyard each loosed an arrow from their hiding place. Both arrows struck her in the chest just as a gaggle of fourteen youths carrying bows and spears appeared on the trail. They had the gawky eagerness of children out on a thrilling expedition, sacks slung over their backs. The ones in front stopped short as the demon choked out a warning. Their stunned, horrified expressions were so heart-breaking that a kick of fury made Kellas tremble even as he held his position in the tree.

The demon was using adolescents to cover its tracks, exactly the kind of cold calculation that made cloaked demons the most dangerous creatures in the Hundred, the true threat to the peaceful rule of the king.

A second woman appeared at the rear of the band. She was also wearing a white cloak.

With a shock Kellas realized both women wore the braided headbands and ritual white capes common to acolytes of the Lady of Beasts, who was both hunter and healer.

Neither of these women was a demon. They were priestesses dedicated to the goddess, leading a cursed practice hunt for training their youth.

He shouted, "Halt! Halt where you are! Denni, pull the trap now before the kids fall in!"

He grabbed for a rope he had strung from a higher branch of the lancewood, vaulted off the branch, and swung down, gauging distance and depth as he tucked up his legs. He planted the two men with a foot in each chest. The impact slammed him to a halt as they went down. He flipped in the air as he released the rope, and landed on his feet behind them.

Denni snapped up the rope to release the trap. The ground gave way to reveal the pit and its deadly stakes. As the children cried out in confusion, the injured woman staggered like a drunk, then slipped into the pit. She screamed as a stake impaled her.

One of the men Kellas had knocked over scrambled up, jabbing at him with his spear as he hissed out hoarse words. "Cursed cowards! Pissing dogs! You promised us no one would get hurt!"

A pair of arrows—Aikar's reds—slammed into the man's back and he toppled forward.

The wounded priestess was still bellowing, voice ripped raw by pain.

"Run! Run!" shouted the woman at the rear, and the children scattered uphill.

Denni shouted: "Round them all up! They're all under arrest!"

The other spearman rolled up to his feet and jabbed at Kellas's back. Kellas sidestepped with a spin and in the same motion drew the sword from his back. The man thrust again. Kellas slapped away the haft, cut in, and struck with the pommel under the man's chin. The man staggered back, then cut the point of the spear toward Kellas's head. Kellas ducked under the haft and again stepped inside, striking the man in the throat with the hilt of his sword. With a grunt, the man sagged into him, toppling him back. Kellas let the weight carry him down and rolled sideways out from under as the spearman collapsed to the ground.

Turning, Kellas saw Battas, Oyard, Aikar, and Ezan racing up the path after the children.

He cut a length off the swinging rope and tied the prisoner's feet and hands. Denni slid carefully down into the pit to the woman thrashing below. He stabbed her through the eye; a mercy, seeing how a stake had pierced her raggedly through the belly, a wound no one could heal. Then Denni grasped the cloth of her cloak in his hand and looked up with a shake of his head.

"It's just ordinary wool, not a demon's skin," he said to Kellas.

The hunter shot by Aikar clawed at the dirt, hacking out an incomprehensible word before going limp. Kellas made himself watch as the man's life drained away. Some demons could also see a person's spirit rise out of the dying. Kellas saw nothing except red blood, withered leaves, and gathering flies.

The other four tromped back into view, herding the frightened children, with the second woman trussed so tightly she could barely keep up as Aikar prodded her along. One youth was missing.

"Heya, Kel!" shouted Ezan. "You can't follow orders and help us capture these? What are you doing? Standing around looking pretty?"

"What kind of heartless people march their children into harm's way?" said Denni, which was exactly the question Kellas wanted to ask. Of all the awful things he had seen in his eight years in the king's service, adults abusing their own children or callously using them as bait and bargaining chips disgusted him the most.

Young Oyard scratched his smooth chin as he pursed his lips thoughtfully. He did not look much older than the youths they had just captured. "Someone passed us bad information."

"Throw all your bags to the ground," said Kellas curtly, and of course the youths obeyed, too terrified to do otherwise. They were only carrying a few days' stock of humble food: flat bread, cold rice wrapped in nai leaves, and sour balls of cheese.

"What, you hungry again?" Ezan asked jokingly in his usual ass-witted way, ignoring the dead woman and the crying children as if their grief and pain were of no more interest than the trees.

Kellas sniffed at the pungent, salty goat cheese. "Neh. Just checking to make sure they're not smuggling valuable goods. I think the real smugglers are somewhere else. They purposefully sent this training group along this path guessing it was a good place for us to set up an ambush and figuring the king's soldiers would not attack two priestesses and their pupils."

Ezan laughed mockingly. "Whsst! Where did a small-time criminal like you get so smart?"

Kellas grinned, pretending sheepishness as he decided on a

plausible lie that would deflect any suspicion that he knew more than he ought. "Eh, you've caught me out, me and my shameful ways. I got arrested for smuggling, me and a bunch of lads. We used to round up neighborhood children and have them carry the goods while the militia was searching us instead. It worked for a while until one of the kids got hurt and we got beaten up by the neighbors and turned in by them for endangering their little ones."

As he spoke he watched the eyes of the surviving man and .woman, hoping they might betray their comrade with a glance, but they kept their gazes fixed to the ground. Both had the stunned look of people who haven't yet made sense of what has just transpired. He had to wonder if they were actually ignorant and had been used as unsuspecting bait. Yet when Denni slapped them, asking what they knew about the smugglers and if they were part of a decoy plan, they stubbornly said nothing.

"I can make them talk," Ezan boasted.

"Shut up, Ez," said Denni. "Let's go."

His words broke the surviving priestess's silence. "What about our dead?"

Denni gave her a glare that made her cower. "We leave them. Chief Jagi will decide what's to be done and whether he'll allow your people to come back and fetch them."

The youths began to cry again, and several, weeping copiously, wrapped the dead priestess in her cloak and arranged her hands on her chest in the traditional custom observed for the dead.

They made an uneasy group as they hiked out of the steep upper valley with the sobbing youths and the two uncommunicative adults. In his capacity as tailman, the newest and supposedly least experienced and thus most expendable member of the cadre, Kellas took the rear guard. He was sure they were being watched and there was in fact still one youth unaccounted for, but he heard nothing and saw no one except, once, a crow perched on a fallen log in a clearing. Its black eyes were trained on them with the inhuman intelligence native to crows. When he swung around and took aim with his bow, it took wing and vanished over the treetops.

He grinned briefly. He'd never have skewered it, as some men might who took pleasure in the killing rather than in the challenge. He allowed himself three breaths to savor the empty path, the fragrant air, and the peaceful forest. A pillar of sunlight cut down through an opening a fallen tree had made in the forest cover. Its lustrous brilliance illuminated a patch of the vivid flowers known as sunbright that had grasped this chance to bloom. Their simple beauty staggered him, like the kiss of an ineffable joy.

A branch snapped, but when he looked that way he saw nothing moving among the trees. As the noise of the others faded, he left behind the sunlight and the flowers to follow them.

After a while they passed a pair of upcountry farms ringed by stockades that protected against deer rather than armed marauders. Their commanding officer, Chief Jagi, waited with his command staff just beyond the village where the path forked in three directions. He took their report, then delegated a different subcadre to fetch the two bodies and haul them down to the crossroads at the market town of Sharra Crossing where the two dead people would be strung up as a warning to others not to break the king's law and trouble the king's peace.

"You think they are in league with the smugglers, Chief?" Denni asked.

Like all of the officers in charge of companies of Black Wolves, Jagi was Qin, a foreign soldier who had arrived in the Hundred sixteen years ago together with the man who had brought peace to the land. In his month with this company Kellas had not heard

Chief Jagi raise his voice, not once. But beneath his pleasant voice and mild temper ran the steel of a man who got what he wanted by never slacking. He turned his gaze on the prisoners, who went as still as rabbits sensing the shadow of a hawk.

"As it happens, I just received word that this morning, while we were up here setting our ambush, the king's portion of hides and sinew being stored in a warehouse near Elegant Falls went missing. Someone stole the tithe set aside for the king while we waited for smugglers who never came. Those who participate in a decoy are part of the conspiracy and thus are criminals. Unless you are willing to speak and convince me otherwise I must assume this supposed hunting party was part of the plot, which therefore means the two who died today are guilty of crimes against the king. According to the law, the bodies of criminals shall be displayed after execution as an example to those who might think to follow them."

Kellas could not help but put in, "The local folk won't like seeing one of their holy women hung from a post until her flesh rots away and her bones fall to the earth like so much rubbish. They'll see it as disrespect."

"Then they shouldn't have used holy women and innocent children as pawns in their game, should they? String the corpses up according to the law." Chief Jagi ignored the stony stare of the surviving holy woman and the outraged gasp of the other spearman as he turned to Denni. "Escort the prisoners to the fort. The two adults shall be taken before the assizes, and judgment passed. Assign a steward to find the parents of the children. Tell the steward the parents must pay a fine to get them back. Afterward you and your subcadre can take liberty until your regular duty tomorrow."

They marched the prisoners to the fort and turned them over to the sentinel-guards—regular soldiers under the command of a Hundred-born captain, not Black Wolves under the command of a Qin chief—who were in charge of the cages. Instead of lying down to rest, they washed thoroughly in the tubs while the soldiers who had been stuck in the fort surrounded the washing planks to find out what happened.

"Told you there'd be nothing up in the hills," said one fellow who was engaged in an ongoing duel with Ezan. "But we got some news. Besides the stolen hides, a farmer up by Elegant Falls saw a ghost woman out walking in the night."

"Same as the other?" demanded Ezan. "Cloaked in a pale demon's skin?"

"Think you'll get a chance to kill a demon, Ez?" Denni laughed as he rinsed off his sweaty, sodden hair. "For fifteen years Wolves have been chasing the last four cloaked demons, and never took one down. Heya, lads, what say we go down to that thrice-rotted inn and drink what passes for decent rice wine here in this cold-cursed valley?"

Chief Jagi rarely offered spoken praise to the Wolves under his command, but he had other ways of showing that their performance had met with his approval. So Kellas swaggered out with the others—swaggering was necessary—and they put on their cold-weather cloaks and hurried down the main road to the village of Feather Vale. It was a thirsty walk with dusk sinking down over them.

Chief Jagi had made an arrangement with an inn on the outskirts of the village. His men could take their liberty there as long as they did not fight with the locals and broke nothing, and his steward paid up the bill at the end of each week. The place was nothing special: It had a long porch where folk stowed their sandals and boots before going inside. The inn's single room was floored with old rice-straw mats and made comfortable with low tables and threadbare pillows for seating. Here in the hills it

actually got cold at night in the season of Shiver Sky, so the room
was cunningly fitted with small, lidded iron pots that had vents
and a grated bottom with a plate beneath to catch ash; in these,
charcoal burned to warm a man's legs.

Aikar hadn't bothered to wear a cloak. None of the locals
gathered for an evening's drink were wearing cloaks, either; it
wasn't cold to those accustomed to upcountry weather. The two
women who worked in the tavern carried plain wooden trays and
poured rice wine into crudely glazed cups, farmers' ware. The
smoke from the warming stoves stung Kellas's eyes. Images from
the skirmish in the forest flashed in his mind: A fern spattered
with blood. Aikar shooting the man who had spoken. The missing
youth. The way the spark of life vanished from once-living flesh.
How did it leave? Where did it go?

For a region plagued with smuggling and theft, the folk here-
abouts were cursed casual about their security, not even building
proper stockades or posting a guard at an inn that had a supply of
liquor in the back room. He closed his eyes to listen.

The locals at the table behind them were speaking in low
voices. "...bad enough to have Wolves hunting in our woods. If
they hear about Broken Ridge, they'll never leave."

Broken Ridge. That was better. Now he just needed to figure
out what and where Broken Ridge was.

The rice wine had been heated to cure the cloying sweetness of a
third-quality brew, and its drowsy flavor went to his head as the day
and night he'd been awake caught up with him. He had the knack
of dozing lightly, alert to any change in those around him. He could
nod out, wake instantly to murmur a pointless comment—"Is that
so, Ez? Did you really do that?"—and fade out again.

The locals discussed an upcoming wedding. The door tapped
shut once, twice, a third time. A man vomited. Water splashed
over the porch outside, rinsing away the mess.

Was that a horn's cry, far in the distance?

He stiffened to full wakefulness, but it had only been a sound chasing through his dream. Often a random sound or sight prompted a reminder of an earlier assignment. A year ago, after he had eliminated the hieros of a Devourer's temple in the town of Seven for plotting sedition against the king, horn calls had chased him for days as he had been pursued by an angry band of locals.

"So the wind came up, and mind you, when the wind comes up, it makes the water that much more dangerous." Ezan was telling the story of a canoe chase across the Bay of Messalia, him in one canoe and a fugitive in another. Ez had a southern way of talking—his vowels twisted wrong and half of his *b*'s turned to soft *v*'s—and a braggart's way of making more of the story than was likely there. But he sure as the hells was impressing the others, who were more drunk than they ought to be with black night to be traversed between here and the fort.

"After ten mey out on the water they were getting tired, I'll tell you." Ezan mimed men panting and blowing as their arms and backs fatigued with the stroke of paddles. "Then we came around the cliffs of Sorry Island right into the swells of the open ocean. Cursed if their steersman didn't lose his nerve and then his paddle. Their canoe flipped right over. Dumped them all into the ocean. Five were smashed onto the rocks before we could come up to the swamped boat. But the gods were with us, for the man we were chasing we fished right out of the water and hauled back to Sandy Port to stand at the assizes for his crimes."

"Hu! Ten mey out and ten mey back, and you never stopped for a rest or a drink? Paddling all that time?" asked Oyard with a snort of disbelief. Although the youngest Wolf in Third Company, he was always the quickest to question whatever everyone else assumed was true.

"What? You don't believe me?" demanded Ezan. He drained

his cup of rice wine and thumped it down on the table, daring the others to match him.

Kellas glanced around the tavern. It was very late, and the rest of the locals had gone home, but the two women who ran the inn had not yet worked up the courage to ask the soldiers to leave.

"No one of you can match that feat, can you?" Ezan went on. "A sad day when they had to let your broken swords into the Black Wolves. Haven't you done a single impressive thing beyond surviving training? Chief Jagi's the kindest officer you'll ever serve under, I promise you."

The other men considered this question so seriously that Ezan's jutting chin relaxed as he contemplated his victory in the boasting stakes.

"I grew up in the hills," said Aikar.

"What, like around here?" Kellas asked in the tone of a sloppy drunk.

Aikar hunched up his shoulders. "Anyway, I never saw the ocean until I went to Nessumara for training."

Denni, Battas, and Oyard were plains-bred farm boys who had never done a cursed exciting thing before they'd joined the king's army and then made the cut that elevated them out of the regular ranks into the king's elite soldiers, the demon-hunting, bandit-killing, ruthlessly effective Black Wolves.

"I'll drink to such a hells impressive tale, Ez," said Kellas. "I reckon you grew up there on the shore, neh? Got used to paddling such long distances."

"That I did. It's what everyone does, go out to fishing spots, to the breaker islands to gather shellfish and birds' nests." Ezan was the kind who grew more pleasant the more he felt he had one up on you. "No reason any of you should have spent time on the water. How about you, Kel?"

Kellas had once paddled and swum across half the Bay of

Messalia in the dead of night to infiltrate a reeve hall, where he had stolen a pouch of dispatches while his compatriot had murdered the hall's crippled marshal. Then they had swum and paddled back, no one the wiser. But he shook his head just as if he did not know that the distance from Sandy Port to Sorry Island was three mey, not ten.

"I'm just a city boy from Toskala, Ez. You know me. Kicked around awhile, got arrested, was given the choice of joining the army or a work gang. Picked the army, got chosen to run with the Wolves, and they sent me here to serve as a tailman in Chief Jagi's company."

"Aren't you thirty?" asked Oyard, who was eighteen. "That's old to be a tailman."

"He didn't lie about his age to join up like you did, Oyard," said Denni with a laugh.

"I'm a slow learner," allowed Kellas with a lazy smile that attracted the notice of the younger of the women. She came over, ignoring the other men in favor of offering a friendly look to Kellas.

"Are you hoping for one more drink, lads?"

"No cause to keep you up later than you're accustomed to, verea," he said as the others protested that they wanted another drink. "We're the last ones here."

"If you're willing to spend your chief's coin on one more drink, I'll bring it," she said. "I'll say this. Those Qin outlanders are so honest that a merchant could leave his entire chest of leya with any one of them and not have to count the coins when he got it back."

She gave another smile to Kellas and walked back to the counter.

"What is it with you and women?" Denni muttered. "You're not that good-looking."

"I show a little courtesy." For once he was unable to keep a ribbon of contempt out of his tone. "Which you lads would think well on, rather than keeping these two women up all night for your own selfish pleasure."

"Tell me you aren't eyeing the younger one and thinking of keeping her up all night for *your* own selfish pleasure," Ezan said with a coarse laugh.

"I can't take what's not offered."

Cursed if that didn't start all but Oyard in on stories of women they had loved and lost, or temple hierodules who had taken their fancy and milked them dry. There were few things more tedious than arrogant young men bragging about sex, as he knew perfectly well. But there was an edge to their boasting that made him uneasy.

The woman came back with a warmed vase as Ezan was speaking.

"...and then she said, 'No, ver, I don't think I've a mind to,' and I said, 'We've come too far for me to hear no, don't you think, lass?' and so I..."

The woman's expression shaded from tired good humor to scarcely hidden disgust just as Ezan glanced up to see it. Kellas jarred the table with his legs.

"Aui!" The table's edge kicked into Ezan's gut.

"I'm going outside to piss," Kellas said, too loudly, and he made a show of staggering to the door.

As he'd hoped, the others followed, remembering their full bladders. Once they were outside, the stars and the rising half-moon made them consider the lateness of the night and the distance back to the fort, not to mention the rumors of a demon. They set off at a brisk march. He glanced back to see the younger woman standing on the porch of the inn watching them go. He knew that look. If he could slip away, he'd find a welcome.

But the people who served in the secret auxiliary of the Black Wolves—the silent wolves—lived by three rules, the third of which was: No dalliance when you're working. Never. Self-control before all else. It was drilled into them: self-control and the ability to endure pain.

She pinched out the lamp's burning wick and slid the door shut behind her. The men soon left behind the inn and village, Kellas sticking to the back to keep one eye on the man he was by now almost certain was the traitor.

Perhaps whipped into competition by Ezan's story, Denni began telling the tale of how he had earned his subcadre command in a long-running campaign against outlaws in the Soha Hills. Afterward the well-to-do landowners who had suffered most under the outlaws' depredations had set out a three days' feast. The rice wine flowed freely, the lovers were eager, the music ran like a mountain stream, as it said in the tale. Best of all, their company had gotten a commendation from King Anjihosh himself, who had ridden out with his officers and his son to meet with the local council.

"I will say this," said Denni, "Prince Atani has a shine to his face. The king is an impressive man, truly, but the gods themselves have touched the boy, for he has that look about him. A thoughtful gaze more like that of a full-grown man than a lad just sixteen."

"Never saw the king's son myself," Kellas lied. "Looks like his sire, does he?"

Not much, the others agreed, except maybe about the eyes and hair. Maybe he resembled his mother, but since no one had ever seen her face in public, her being a Sirni outlander with her bizarre outlander custom of remaining behind the palace walls, it was impossible to say. But they all agreed the king's son possessed an essence of special strength and brightness.

"What is it the Sirniakans say of their god?" Denni said. "The Shining One? Like that."

Ezan waved a hand dismissively. "Those southerners can keep their Beltak god on the other side of the mountains. No call for an outlander god to come traveling here."

"I wouldn't say so, not where Chief Jagi can hear you," said Denni.

"Aui! He's not Sirni. He's Qin. None of the Qin worship that shining god, do they? It's those hidden palace women with their peculiar ways who brought Beltak to the Hundred. I've never heard Chief Jagi say one thing about gods, except setting flowers on a rock dedicated to the Merciful One one time, and then because he was with his wife. She is a proper Hundred woman and cursed pretty even for being a few years older than our elderly Kel here, if I may say so."

"I wouldn't, and especially not where the chief can hear you," said Denni.

Having to pretend to be something so his own comrades would not suspect he was spying on them was getting cursed tangled. He changed the subject. "When I was a lad we never called Hasibal the Merciful One. Hasibal is the Formless One. I don't know where this Merciful name came from. Do any of you?"

Naturally Ezan had an opinion. "It comes from the south of the Hundred, from Olo'osson and Mar—"

A horn's cry split the quiet. Three blats, a long blast, three blats, a long blast, three blats. As one, they shifted to a run. Soon after they heard hooves and saw a gleam of lamplight off to their right. Riders were moving through the countryside.

"The hells!" cried Aikar, stopping dead in his tracks.

"A demon!" shouted Ezan. "Eihi! When I'm off duty! My chance for glory, spoiled!"

Abruptly Ezan cut off the road to tear madly across a recently harvested field. Kellas hesitated for only one breath, then raced after him. Crop stubble scraped his calves and crunched under his boots. His eyes had adjusted. He measured the shadows that marked the irregularities of ground and thus kept to his feet when Ezan stumbled and crashed to his knees in a shallow ditch.

A flutter of movement crossed before them like the pale wings of a bird trying desperately to get off the ground with an injured wing. A face flashed into view: a woman, running.

A cloak flowed and rippled around her. The fabric bore a disturbingly bone-white sheen.

With a grunt of effort, Ezan lunged up from his knees and grabbed for her ankle. His fingers grasped the hem of the long cloak. Blue sparks sizzled along the fabric as it wrapped over Ezan's face. He screamed in agony and pitched forward.

She staggered, dropped to a knee to steady herself, and looked up directly at Kellas.

The hells!

Her gaze devoured him, for that was the particular sorcery of cloaked demons. It was the same as being clouted over the head with a hammer and then having knives driven in through your eyes to leak your thoughts into the air.

Her voice was cool and clear. "You are one of the king's silent wolves. Let me see what you know."

So easily she tore through his mind to discover his secrets: the modest wine seller's shop in Toskala where silent wolves like him went to get their orders; the face of the nameless man who had given him his orders for this assignment; Esisha, who had been his partner in several missions and died two years ago; a safe house on the Gold Rose Canal in Nessumara where he had slept for three days in hiding after sinking a ship laden with a cargo bound for Salya...

As if Salya were a beacon and he a moth drawn to the light,

his thoughts eddied and trawled him down into a memory from eight years ago. His pride recalled the admiring glance of a beautiful woman on the crowded streets of Salya's busy port. His skin remembered the salty embrace of the warm waters of the Bay of Messalia as he swam to Bronze Hall on his first serious mission. He would never forget the hot pleasurable rush of triumph he'd felt when he pulled himself over the gunnel and into the waiting canoe with the dispatch pouch wrapped in oilcloth tied to his back, although he doubted he would recognize the beautiful woman now if he passed her on the road.

At last he managed to blink, the effort a stab of pain in his head. The king's Wolves were honed for exactly such an encounter, trained to fight demons. With the blink he ripped his gaze away from hers. To keep free of the power of her magic, he forced his gaze to follow the swells and eddies made by the demon's skin, which looked like a cloak. Beneath she was wearing leather trousers and a vest, both garments splashed with mud. She had a body made strong through honest work. She might have been any ordinary woman who had just finished a hard day's labor in a rice paddy somewhere in the Hundred where there was still water in the rice fields at this time of year. That was the glamor with which demons dazzled their prey before they ate out their hearts and stole all their secrets: They made you believe they were just like you.

He drew his sword. The others were calling out, having lost sight of him and Ezan. The troop trotted past some distance away, lanterns swinging.

Sweat broke freely on his brow as the breeze carried away the memories that had seemed so vivid moments before. "Begging your pardon, verea, but I have to kill you."

He thrust the short blade into her gut. It sank hard and swiftly right into the core of her flesh. She grabbed his arms and tugged him closer until they were face-to-face. The cloak whipped across his hair, lighting sparks of pain along his head that made him reel. For all that she had a sword in her belly, she was the one holding him up.

Her eyes were dark with the grip of pain. Yet she mocked him. "Very polite, I am sure, ver. You were well brought up by your mother and aunties. But you will not kill me this night. You have already told me what I need to know. And you'll find nothing at Broken Ridge because we've already cleared out the rice that was being stored there."

She shoved him back with more strength than any human could possibly muster. His sword was dragged out of her flesh. She slammed him across the chest with the palm of her hand. The blow lifted him off his feet, and he hit full on his back and lay there, stunned, as a vast cloud of wings filled his vision. Ez was still whimpering on the ground beside him, face and hands blistered with a fierce burn, but even so the young soldier was trying to roll over to stand.

Kellas climbed laboriously to his feet, dizzy and stumbling, but it was already too late. The demon mounted a winged horse and flew off into the night.

Hooves pounded. Men shouted. The lights swayed drunkenly. Soldiers approached.

With a curse Ezan threw up on Kellas's boots.

The noise of his retching brought Denni, Battas, and Oyard racing up. After them came the mounted troops with lanterns bobbing and swaying. They converged as Ezan, doubled over, heaved out more bile. Kel took a step out of its way. As Chief Jagi himself arrived, Ezan straightened up with a grimace of pain that hurt to see.

"This cursed hells-ridden limp noodle had the demon within his grasp after I took these cursed burns stopping her in her tracks. But she got away from him. Ass!"

Chief Jagi glanced at Ezan, then at Kellas. Like all the outlander Qin soldiers who had ridden into the Hundred in the company of King Anjihosh, he rarely showed emotion. A narrowed gaze was brutal enough. Disappoint your Qin chief, and he'd simply deem you useless to him and cast you out of the Black Wolves.

"Which way did she run?" Jagi asked.

"She flew off on a horse," said Kel, his head aching. Lantern light glittered on the blood and spew that streaked his sword. "I got my blade in her gut. It didn't make a cursed bit of difference."

"Stupid fuckwit," said Ezan, and then he fainted from the pain, thank the gods.

Chief Jagi signaled. The troop broke into four groups and spread out to cover the ground all around, but they all knew they would find no trace of the creature.

"You kept your wits about you," said the chief to Kellas when they two were standing alone.

"I still failed."

"Next time you'll kill one. But you know the rules. Any man who speaks to a demon must return to Toskala to give full particulars to the king. Anything else you want to tell me?"

"Yes. The traitor is Aikar."

2

"And was the traitor Aikar?" asked King Anjihosh.

"Yes, Your Highness."

"How did you come to single him out?"

"He lied about being local to the area. I knew it from the way he spoke, the way he was easy with the local customs, and how he never got cold when we were all shivering. During the ambush he shot the man who started talking, and did it so quickly I guessed he was trying to shut him up before he revealed anything. In the confusion when Ezan and I encountered the demon, Aikar fled, which sealed it. It turned out that when Chief Jagi emptied most of the fort to chase that demon, two others flew into the fort and released the prisoners."

"So the demon you confronted was another decoy. Did Aikar get away?"

"No. I was able to track him down and turn him over to Chief Jagi before I left Asharat to come here to give you my report."

"What did Chief Jagi do with him?"

"Jagi executed him and hung his body at the crossroads."

"Very good."

The king stood with a sword sheathed at his belt and a knife held lightly in his right hand as if he hadn't decided whom to use it on yet. No one who looked at this commanding middle-aged man would doubt he had spent his life as a soldier, even if he now spent most of his time as a wise administrator of the Hundred, a land he had saved from disorder and conflict.

His gaze shifted briefly past Kellas's face to the garden that surrounded the open pavilion in which the two men met. Walls surrounded the garden, beyond which lay the various wings and courtyards and buildings of the palace complex. Always cautious and alert, Anjihosh valued his security. From where he was seated, Kellas could see two reeves and their giant eagles circling above the palace; there were at least four on palace watch during the day. On the ground, the king's personal guards were all Qin soldiers. Kellas had counted seven such guards stationed in and around the pavilion and garden. An eighth stood directly behind Kellas, who sat cross-legged on a pillow in front of the king. Given that Kellas had been required to relinquish his weapons and be strip-searched before entering the palace, he recognized the arrangement for the soldier's tactic it was. Armed and standing, Anjihosh had an advantage over a seated, unarmed person, especially when his guards were armed as well.

The king addressed the clerk seated at a low table, who had recorded Kellas's report. "The village councils in the Asharat Valley will be dissolved and replaced with a military governor. Taxes will be tripled. The councils and a normal rate of taxation will be restored once the smuggling and theft are halted and those responsible turned over by the locals to the assizes. That is all. You are dismissed."

When Kellas made to rise, the king indicated the clerk, so Kellas sank back down and waited as the clerk gathered up his implements, stowed them in a box, and departed. Anjihosh waited as well. The king was not a pacer. He had the ability to stand with utter, focused stillness, as if all the pacing were going on in his mind, out of sight to all except demons.

"So, Tailman Kellas, here you are," said the king with a quirk of the lips whose flash of humor startled Kellas. "Ironic that you had to assume the lowest rank for this particular mission, considering that in the last eight years you have become my most efficient and productive silent wolf. I think a promotion is in order."

That Kellas managed not to grin ecstatically or clench his hands to fists in triumph, much less leap up in excitement, was testament to the hardened discipline of his training. He inclined his chin slightly to acknowledge the praise and blinked about five times to bleed off the surge of adrenaline.

"Now that one cloaked demon can identify you, we must assume they all can. I will have to put you on different duty for a while."

"Yes, Your Highness." The flutter in his belly gradually eased as the king sheathed his knife and drew his captain's whip, tapping it thoughtfully against a thigh.

"I wonder what task you would be best suited for..." His intense gaze could not rip into people's minds to expose their memories, but it seemed to Kellas that the king had such a canny understanding of the men under his command that he fathomed all the depths of Kellas's heart and self regardless. "Not a desk job certainly, given my memory of our first meeting? Do you recall it?"

Aui!

Of course he remembered the rash argument eight years ago in a tavern with his equally bored and pathless friends, when he had boasted he could and would climb the promontory called Law Rock even though it was both impossible *and* against the law. He remembered his reckless disregard as he started up the cliff face where no one, not even the city militia, dared follow. Three times during the climb he had really believed he was about to lose his grip and plunge to a bloody death, but he hadn't. When he had dragged himself over onto the top of the towering rock plateau that overlooked the city of Toskala, soldiers had surrounded him with bristling spears. For a moment he had thought they meant to force him back over the edge to his death. Instead they had marched him to a stone cell. He'd been too exhausted to resist when a sad-faced ordinand had shaved his head for execution. They had swept up the hair, tossed him a clean linen kilt and vest, and marched him out onto the wide plateau of Law Rock as it began to wake beneath the lifting veil of night. The memory had burned into his head so vividly he could taste and feel and smell it all over again.

Air smoky with an oily residue threads up from lamps that illuminate their path. The stern profiles of the soldiers and the gleaming hilts of swords flank him. Wind teases along the stubble of his scalp, all that remains of his much-admired hair. Soon his spirit will be shorn from him in much the same way as his hair was.

He thinks they are leading him to the assizes court for a dawn execution but instead they halt before an ironbound gate set into a whitewashed wall. A pair of soldiers with the foreign features of the outlander Qin take him down a corridor without windows, alcoves, or identifying markers.

The corridor offers no escape route, not even for a young man as strong and agile as he has just proven himself to be. The foreign-born Qin soldiers, although married into the Hundred and living with wives and children just like anyone, have the most fearsome of reputations: It is said they are utterly fair and completely ruthless.

They reach a bronze-plated door and cross a threshold into a simply furnished room whose ceiling is tented with draped fabric. A latticework wall screens one side of the chamber. Morning sunlight stripes gold over rugs piled four deep.

A man sits cross-legged on a brocade pillow watching two children intent on a game involving a large marble square striped in pink and white stone, three bone dice, and a cadre of miniature animals carved to exquisite perfection out of ivory. Kellas does not recognize the specifics of the game they play, but the children's expressions have a charm that can coax a smile even from a condemned man. The older is a handsome boy of about eight years whose smile lights his face like fire. The girl, a little younger, has piercingly intelligent eyes and a robust laugh. She is winning, but the boy finds the turn of play funny rather than upsetting.

"The horse! I knew it would be the horse!" he chortles as she pushes a carved horse from a white stripe onto a pink stripe and crows to mark her victory.

The seated man marks Kellas's entrance before returning his attention to the children at play. The two soldiers halt Kellas beside the door.

"Who is that, Papa?" asks the girl, looking up. "Is that the man who climbed Law Rock? Grandmother says you have to kill him because he broke the law and defied you. Mama says he should live for being bold."

"He is already dead," says the man. He opens a small chest and collects the ivory figures, placing them into tiny silk-lined compartments carved to fit each piece's contours.

The boy's eyes widen as he stares at Kellas. "Is he a ghost? But he can't be a ghost because people can't see ghosts. Only demons can see ghosts."

"Who told you that?" The man's cool voice has a pleasant timbre, but its tone makes Kellas shudder.

"Thinwit," says the girl disdainfully to the boy. "You promised not to tell." She turns an acute and fearless gaze on the man. "It isn't fair if you get mad at someone else because Atani talks too much!"

Trembling, the boy rises to stand as stiff as a spear. "I don't want to tell you, Papa."

"Was it your mother the queen?" says the man, too evenly.

"I will not speak."

The girl leaps to her feet. "Stupid!"

"Dannarah. Sit down." The man does not raise his voice.

She sits.

"Atani, sit down."

The boy plops down as if strings holding him up have been sliced through.

"Enough." The man does not sound angry, merely thoughtful. "Of course any words that pass between you and your mother remain private between you. A son remains loyal to his mother above all things, Atani."

"What about a daughter?" asks the girl.

"Daughters love their mother, but daughters leave."

"I'll never leave! I don't want to leave you, Papa. You won't make me, will you? Not like Mama's brothers made her travel far away from her home."

"She traveled far away from her home in order to marry me. Had she not done so, you would not be here. So what are we to make of that?"

"You won't yell at her, will you, Papa?" asks the boy worriedly. He is really quite uncannily good-looking. His plea makes his features brighten with compassion.

"I never yell at her, Atani. Surely you know that."

"You never yell," agrees the girl. "But sometimes you don't talk to her for days and days and days, and then she cries."

In a shocked tone, the boy murmurs, "Dannarah!"

Kellas sucks in a sharp breath, waiting for the man to slap the girl for her impertinence, but the man merely closes the chest's lid and fits the clasp to its hook. The Qin soldiers seem to be observing the fabric strung from the ceiling. How they manage to keep their faces devoid of emotion he cannot comprehend. For himself, adrenaline has pumped exhaustion out of his flesh. He wants to crawl out of his skin.

But what would be the point? He is already dead.